T0316966

De l'atelier au laboratoire

Recherche et innovation
dans l'industrie électrique
XIXe-XXe siècles

From Workshop to Laboratory

Research and Innovation
in Electric Industry
19-20th Centuries

P.I.E. Peter Lang

Bruxelles · Bern · Berlin · Frankfurt am Main · New York · Oxford · Wien

Yves Bouvier, Robert Fox, Pascal Griset & Anna Guagnini
(dir./eds.)

De l'atelier au laboratoire

Recherche et innovation dans l'industrie électrique

XIXe-XXe siècles

From Workshop to Laboratory

Research and Innovation in Electric Industry

19-20th Centuries

« Histoire de l'énergie » / "History of Energy"
n° 1

Avec le soutien du ministère de l'Enseignement supérieur et de la Recherche / DRRT Alsace, du conseil régional d'Alsace, du conseil général du Haut-Rhin, du CRHI (UMR 8138 IRICE).

Conseil Général

Toute représentation ou reproduction intégrale ou partielle faite par quelque procédé que ce soit, sans le consentement de l'éditeur ou de ses ayants droit, est illicite / No part of this book may be reproduced in any form, by print, photocopy, microfilm or any other means, without prior written permission from the publisher. Tous droits réservés / All rights reserved.

© P.I.E. PETER LANG S.A.
Éditions scientifiques internationales
Bruxelles / Brussels, 2011
1 avenue Maurice, B-1050 Bruxelles, Belgique
www.peterlang.com; info@peterlang.com

ISSN 2033-7469
ISBN 978-90-5201-656-6
D/2011/5678/18

Ouvrage imprimé en Allemagne / Printed in Germany

Library of Congress Cataloging-in-Publication Data
De l'atelier au laboratoire : recherche et innovation dans l'industrie électrique, XIXe-XXe siècles = Between workshop and laboratory : research and innovation in the electrical industry / Yves Bouvier ... [et al.]. p. cm. -- (Collection "Histoire de l'énergie" ; no 1) Includes bibliographical references. ISBN 978-90-5201-656-6
    1. Electrical engineering--Research--History. 2. Electric industries.
    3. Electrical engineers--Biography. 4. Research teams--History.
    I. Bouvier, Yves, 1975- II. Title: Between workshop and laboratory.
    TK15.D43 2010   621.309'034--dc22   2010048489

CIP also available from the British Library.

« Die Deutsche Nationalbibliothek » répertorie cette publication dans la « Deutsche Nationalbibliografie » ; les données bibliographiques détaillées sont disponibles sur le site http://dnb.de. / "Die Deutsche Nationalbibliothek" lists this publication in the "Deutsche Nationalbibliografie"; detailed bibliographic data is available on the Internet at <http://dnb.de>.

Table des matières / Table of Contents

From Workshop to Laboratory

Research and Innovation in Electric Industry 19-20th Centuries

Introductory Remarks

Robert FOX

The aim of the Mulhouse conference was to explore ways of enlarging our conception of the nature and sites of industrially related research in electricity. In proposing this focus, the organizers did not underestimate the importance of sophisticated, well equipped in-house laboratories as sources of success: from the time such laboratories emerged as common accoutrements of well founded companies in the early twentieth century, they have had an ever more central (and now well studied) role both in fundamental innovation and in pursuit of equally important if less eye-catching goals such as economy, safety, and efficiency in the day-to-day processes of industry. Hence there was certainly no intention that such laboratories and their academically trained staff should be ignored. Speakers were simply invited to range widely. In particular, they were asked to extend their brief to include forms of research and settings for such research that lay outside the walls of the conventional laboratory. Research, in other words, was to be conceived as being as much an affair of workshops and sites of production as it was of laboratories[1].

By the time we gathered in Mulhouse in December 2005, such goals were not new. We were already able to draw on a secondary literature that offered some answers and posed key questions. In 1991, for example, W. Bernard Carlson had advanced his conception of craft knowledge as a crucial element in the achievements of Elihu Thomson at General Electric in the late nineteenth century[2]. At GE, as Carlson

---

[1] In this pairing of workshops and sites, I draw on the terminology and general thrust of Robert Fox and Anna Guagnini, *Laboratories, workshops, and sites. Concepts and practices of research in industrial Europe, 1800-1914*, Berkeley (CA), Office of the History of Science and Technology, University of California, 1999.

[2] W. Bernard Carlson, *Innovation as a social process. Elihu Thomson and the rise of General Electric 1870-1900*, Cambridge, Cambridge University Press, 1991.

described it, Thomson's achievement, like that of many inventors, rested upon a mixture and constant interplay of craft knowledge and scientific knowledge. A few years later Wolfgang König developed his notion of 'industry-based-science'. In a book and classic article, he opened perspectives on forms of science that drew their problems, research strategies, and techniques from the industrial rather than the academic world, the world of doing rather than the world of knowing[3]. König's analysis, focussed on the German electrical industry in the late nineteenth and early twentieth centuries, encouraged us to analyse the interaction between science and industry as complex, multi-faceted, and reciprocal rather than as a straightforward passage of ideas and knowledge from the scientific laboratory to a quite separate world of industrial practice.

Long before Carlson and König wrote, of course, historians had become used to complexity. But engagements with complexity have often served to engender as many historiographical loose ends as they have helped to tie. The most pertinent of the loose ends for the Mulhouse conference was the very category of research. As the organizers felt, the shifting boundaries of what has constituted research since the industrial revolution of the eighteenth century call for fundamental re-examination in ways that transcend present-day conceptions of the activity. Think, for example, of the largely unsung pioneers who installed France's first hydroelectric power-stations in the Alps or the Pyrenees towards the end of the nineteenth century. It is hard to see the activity in which these pioneers were engaged as anything but research. A telling case was that of Aristide Bergès, outstanding among the French innovators of his day in hydroelectricity. The essence of Bergès's achievement in the valley of the Isère was his mastery of steadily greater falls of water over a period of three decades or more. His path to that achievement was distinguished by a capacity to respond, and to do so creatively, to a succession of technological challenges of the type that Thomas Parke Hughes has analysed as 'critical problems', the problems that guide and focus the efforts of inventive minds and generate innovation.

Two comments on the problems that early hydroelectricity faced are in order here. One is that the problems were usually mechanical, linked to the difficulty of manipulating water at ever-increasing pressures. Hence most of the problems required for their solution the practical skills of a mechanical engineer (which Bergès possessed in abundance)

---

[3]   Wolfgang König, *Technikwissenschaften. Die Entstehung der Elektrotechnik aus Industrie und Wissenschaft zwischen 1880 und 1914*, Chur, Fakultas, 1995 and "Science-based Industry or industry-based science? Electrical engineering in Germany before World War I", *Technology and culture*, No. 37, 1996, p. 70-101.

rather than an advanced background in physics, mathematics, or electrical engineering (the elements of which Bergès possessed, though without their being the main weapons in his intellectual armoury). The second comment is that, in the pioneering phases of hydroelectricity, laboratory-based research was of little value. What mattered were full-scale experiments, conducted on the installation itself. Such on-site investigations were informed first and foremost by practical know-how rather than theoretical knowledge. For the participants in the conference, however, they were not to be confused with simple rule-of-thumb tinkering and, to return to my initial point, certainly not to be excluded from the category of research.

The broad conception of research that the organizers of the conference had in view made it necessary to broach other, related questions. In particular, what were we to say about location? Any rethinking of the category of research inevitably entailed a parallel rethinking of the term 'laboratory'. It seemed to follow that the places where Bergès and other pioneers of hydroelectricity conducted their trials should be regarded as laboratories for the historian's purposes. It is easy, too easy, to see such places as having little to do with the scientifically sophisticated laboratories that have grown up over the last eighty years. The reality is that their history cannot be seen as separate from that of laboratory-based research. The two forms of research, in fact, are inextricably related and have to be studied accordingly.

One consideration here is that the well endowed laboratories of, say, the 1930s, with a focus on innovation and the quest for fundamentally new products or methods of production, emerged from far simpler facilities, often from installations whose primary purpose was the relatively routine work of quality-control and testing. The point emerges strongly from Muriel Le Roux's account of the evolving provision for research in the Pechiney company[4]. As Le Roux shows, important early work on aluminium was performed at Pechiney in the nineteenth century with none of the materially and intellectually advanced tools that would have been regarded as normal a few decades later. Le Roux's term of 'proto-recherche' to describe what was being done fits the bill perfectly, evoking the sense of change while retaining the activity as something we can and should properly define as research.

Another study that reinforces the point is Nicole Chézeau's *De la forge au laboratoire*[5]. A central theme of this book is the continuity

---

[4] Muriel Le Roux, *L'Entreprise et la recherche. Un siècle de recherche industrielle à Pechiney*, Paris, Éditions Rive droite, Institut pour l'histoire de l'industrie, 1998.

[5] Nicole Chézeau, *De la forge au laboratoire. Naissance de la métallurgie physique (1860-1914)*, Rennes, Presses universitaires de Rennes, 2004.

between the advanced techniques and theories of twentieth-century metallurgy and their roots in the European and American workshops and production lines of iron and steel manufacturers in the nineteenth century. Chézeau resists the temptation to see this world of workshops and production as distinct from the one in which Henry Chatelier, Floris Osmond, and others refashioned metallurgy after 1900, introducing the now familiar battery of microscopes, bench-based chemical techniques, and phase diagrams. Instead, she demonstrates that the world of Le Chatelier and Osmond not only had roots in the less 'scientific' workshop tradition but also remained close to it. The emergence of metallurgy as a 'big' science emphatically did not entail the either the disappearance or the irrelevance of the practices of the workshop and the factory-floor. The boundaries between the two realms were shifting, and porous to a degree that makes the very notion of boundaries a potentially misleading one.

With such considerations in view, the Mulhouse conference set itself a fluid but clear agenda, and it pursued the agenda through studies of which the contributions to this volume and a recent special issue of *Annales historiques de l'électricité*[6] are the revised versions. As these introductory remarks have indicated, the emphasis was on the need to rethink some of the most fundamental categories we use, as historians, in our analysis of the relations between science, technology, and industry. That led in turn to an engagement with change and a recognition of the difficulty of retaining firm definitions when we try to apply these to different periods, locations, and industries. The historiographical challenge was formidable, and the participants in the conference were only too conscious of what remains to be done if we are to achieve the goal of a truly integrated account of the many faces of research in the field of electrical technology since the mid-nineteenth century. Case-studies in themselves cannot be the complete answer. But when such studies reflect ideals of inclusivenss and breadth of perspective of the kind that speakers set themselves in Mulhouse, they not only add to our stock of knowledge of a subject with immense potential for further enquiry; they also, and more importantly, suggest directions that future work might take. Those at least were the purposes of the conference, as they also are of this volume.

---

[6]   "Recherche et innovation dans l'industrie électrique", published as *Annales historiques de l'électricté*, No. 5, 2007.

The Competitive Advantages of the Inventor's Workshop

Lessons from the Career of Nikola Tesla, 1885-1905

W. Bernard CARLSON[1]

Department of Science, Technology, and Society University of Virginia

Much of the literature on the rise of the electrical and electronics industries assumes that the development of these industries was highly dependent on scientific theory and that innovation ultimately had to be done by scientists working in the laboratories of large-scale corporations[2]. Yet despite the best efforts of financiers and managers to use science and technology to create barriers to entry in these industries (and thus protect their huge investments), a central feature of both industries has been the fact that individual inventors and small firms have always been able to penetrate these fields and introduce radical technologies[3]. From the invention of the telephone by Alexander Graham Bell in the 1870s to the development of television by Philo T. Farnsworth in the 1930s to Steve Jobs and Steve Wozniak and Apple Computer in the 1970s, individuals have consistently broken into the electrical and electronics industries with new technology that has reordered the business landscape. How is it that individual inventors are able to do this? What resources do they mobilize and what strategies do they follow to gain an advantage over the corporate giants?

[1] Acknowledgements: This paper was prepared while I was a Fellow at the Lemelson Center for the Study of Invention and Innovation at the National Museum of American History. My overall research on Tesla has been supported by a major grant from the Alfred P. Sloan Foundation. Wc4p@virginia.edu.

[2] W. B. Carlson, "Toward a Non-linear History of the Linear Model of R&D: Examples from American Industry, 1870-1970" in T. Davila, M. J. Epstein, R. Shelton (eds.), *The Creative Enterprise*, 3 vols., Westport, Praeger, 2007, t. 1, p. 43-76.

[3] Ruth Schwartz Cowan develops this theme in her chapter on communications technologies in *A Social History of American Technology*, New York, Oxford University Press, 1997, p. 289 and p. 298-299.

To think about these questions, I will describe the laboratories or workshops used by Nikola Tesla. Tesla is best known for inventing a practical alternating current (AC) motor, but he also worked on an ambitious scheme to transmit electric power wirelessly. In this paper, I will suggest that, by working in a small laboratory, Tesla gained a competitive advantage over rivals such as Thomas Edison or Elihu Thomson and that he was able to think about more radical technologies than the engineers at General Electric or Westinghouse. In particular, I believe that in his small operations Tesla succeeded when his business partners were able to help him focus on developing patents that could be sold or licensed. Moreover, in his laboratory, Tesla did not have to worry about either contributing to scientific theory or solving manufacturing problems; instead, he could concentrate on developing apparatus that fully captured new phenomena, whether it be a rotating magnetic field or electromagnetic resonance. And finally, Tesla skillfully used his laboratory as a stage for dramatically introducing his inventions to investors and reporters.

Heroic Inventors and Patent Strategy

Before plunging into the details of Tesla's laboratories in New York, we need first to understand something about his business model – that is, how he expected to make money from his electrical inventions. It is easy to imagine invention to be a cost-free activity in that great ideas are supposed to come to individuals while they play or experiment in their garages or attics. In reality, invention can be a costly and time-consuming activity requiring special equipment, numerous test models, and the help of skilled technicians. To cover these costs, inventors and their patrons need to convert an invention into a business proposition as quickly as possible, and it is for this reason that inventors secure patents on their ideas.

In late nineteenth-century America, once inventors had patents, they could pursue one of three basic strategies for making money from them[4]:

- First, they could use the patents to create their own new business to *manufacture or use* their inventions. Because patents prevented others from manufacturing the product or using the process, the inventor earned a profit from his monopoly position. An example

---

[4] In the twentieth century, of course, inventors and managers have devised other patent strategies. For instance, R&D labs often patent new technology in order to use the patents as bargaining chips in negotiating with other companies. Similarly, individual inventors such as Jerome Lemelson, followed an infringement litigation strategy; after securing patents, he sued firms who were infringing or illegally using the technology covered in his patents. Lemelson won a number of large court settlements while other firms also chose to settle out of court and pay him royalties.

of this strategy is how George Eastman used his patented system of roll film to build up Eastman Kodak beginning in the 1880s[5];

- Second, inventors could grant *licenses* to an established manufacturer. Under the license, the manufacturer might be required to pay inventors royalties for each item manufactured. For instance, after securing a patent for a "road engine" in 1895, George B. Selden collected from automakers a fee of $ 15 for each automobile manufactured in the United States. Selden was eventually defeated in court in 1911 by Henry Ford[6]; and

- Third, they could *sell* their patents outright to another entrepreneur or business enterprise. The inventor would realize an immediate profit and would avoid the risks of having to manufacture and market his invention. Elmer Sperry, for example, developed an electrolytic process for white lead in 1904 that he sold outright to the Hooker Electrochemical Company[7].

For the most part, historians of technology have assumed that inventors followed the first strategy, largely because that strategy led to creation of long-enduring firms such as General Electric or Eastman Kodak. However, for the average nineteenth-century inventor, this strategy was highly risky, capital-intensive, and likely to pay off only over the long run. Moreover, it required that the inventor master the intricacies of manufacturing and marketing, and many inventors lacked these business skills. I suspect that some inventors only decided to set up businesses for manufacturing or using their inventions after they had exhausted the possibilities for selling or licensing their patents. For instance, Bell and his backers initially tried to sell the telephone patent to Western Union in 1876, and it was only after Western Union declined to buy it that they set up the American Bell Telephone Company and began building exchanges[8].

Given the risks associated with manufacturing, many nineteenth-century inventors preferred to either sell or license their patents. During the 1870s, Munn & Company, the patent agency affiliated with *Scientific American*, urged its inventor clients to pursue the licensing strate-

5   R. V. Jenkins, *Images and Enterprise Technology and the American Photographic Industry, 1839 to 1925*, Baltimore, Johns Hopkins University Press, 1975.

6   W. Greenleaf, *Monopoly on wheels; Henry Ford and the Selden Automobile Patent*, Detroit, Wayne State University Press, 1961.

7   T. P. Hughes, *Elmer Sperry: Inventor and Engineer*, Baltimore, Johns Hopkins University Press, 1971, p. 91-93.

8   W. B. Carlson, "The Telephone as Political Instrument: Gardiner Hubbard and the Formation of the Middle Class in America, 1875-1880" in M. T. Allen, G. Hecht (eds.), *Technologies of Power Essays in Honor of Thomas Parke Hughes and Agatha Chipley Hughes*, Cambridge, MIT Press, 2001, p. 25-56.

gy[9]. In particular, licensing was seen as being highly profitable since one could grant a large number of licenses to different firms or for use in different territories. With his incandescent lighting system, Edison and the Edison Electric Light Company made a handsome profit by granting licenses to central station companies in dozens of cities. As a strategy, though, licensing had a downside in that the inventor had to be ever vigilant against competitors infringing his patents, lest the licenses lose their monopoly power. By not aggressively defending its patents in the mid-1880s, the Edison Electric Light Company inadvertently allowed several competitors to spring up, and one of those competitors, the Thomson-Houston Electric Company, eventually took over the Edison Company to form General Electric in 1892[10].

It was within this context that Tesla and his backers crafted their business model for invention. As Tesla came up with new electrical inventions, he would seek to patent them. His backers provided the money necessary to cover laboratory expenses and patent fees. However, to earn a profit on their investment, his backers sought to sell or license his patents to either established manufacturers or other investors who planned to set up new companies. Hence, the name of the game for Tesla and his backers was not manufacturing his inventions but rather selling or licensing them.

Significantly, the strategy of selling or licensing patents poses its own challenges for the inventor and his backers. One has to know people in the industry who might be looking for new technology, then one has to generate interest and excitement in the patents that are for sale, and finally one has to negotiate favorable terms. These negotiations involve much bargaining since the seller (*i.e.*, the inventor) asks the highest possible price in order to recover the costs of invention while the buyer seeks to minimize his risk (how much will it cost to convert the invention to a product? will the product sell?) by keeping the price low. At the same time, the inventor also has to keep in mind that he may not have the only patents for sale and that too high an asking price may send the buyer to other inventors. Hence, to get the best possible price and not drive away the buyer, the inventor and his backers may use all sorts of arguments to persuade the buyer that the invention in question is the best possible version and offers the greatest potential. For the inventor

---

[9] *The Scientific American Reference Book*, New York, Munn & Co., 1877, p. 47-50.

[10] H. C. Passer, *The Electrical Manufacturers, 1875-1900: A Study in Competition, Entrepreneurship, Technical Change, and Economic Growth*, Cambridge, Harvard University Press, 1953, p. 151-164.

and his backers, then, the art of persuasion is often the best hedge in the risky business of selling or licensing patents[11].

Having suggested that Tesla's business model was to sell or license his patents, let's examine how this strategy played out in two episodes in his career: the AC motor (1885-1890) and wireless power (1890-1905).

Tesla and the AC Motor

Tesla was born in 1856 to a Serbian family living in the military frontier district of the Austro-Hungarian Empire, in what is today Croatia. Tesla's father was a Serbian Orthodox priest who hoped his son would follow in his footsteps. As a teenager, Nikola was stirred by a faith in science and he instead pursued engineering at the Joanneum Polytechnic School in Graz, Austria. There he eagerly attended the lectures in physics given by Professor Jacob Poeschl.

It was during Poeschl's lectures in 1876-1877, that Tesla became interested in his first and most important invention, an AC motor. While watching his professor trying to control the sparking caused by a commutator on a direct current (DC) motor, Tesla suggested that it might be possible to design a motor without a commutator. Annoyed by Tesla's impudence, Poeschl lectured on the impossibility of creating such a motor, concluding "Mr. Tesla may accomplish great things, but he certainly never will do this"[12]. Poeschl intended that his remarks should curb Tesla's flights of fancy but they instead stoked the fires of his ambition. As he pursued his studies in Graz and then Prague, Tesla puzzled about how to make a spark-free motor. Rather than build an actual motor, Tesla preferred to picture motors in his mind and imagine them running[13].

In 1882, Tesla went to Budapest, hoping to work for friends of his family, Tivadar and Ferenc Puskás. An ambitious promoter, Tivadar had traveled to America and convinced Thomas Edison to give him the right to introduce Edison's inventions in continental Europe[14]. In Budapest,

[11] W. B. Carlson, "Nikola Tesla and the Tools of Persuasion: Rethinking the Role of Agency in the History of Technology", annual conference of the Society for the History of Technology, Minneapolis, november 2005.

[12] N. Tesla (hereafter NT), "My Inventions", *Electrical Experimenter*, May-October 1919; reprinted as *My Inventions: The Autobiography of Nikola Tesla*, ed. B. Johnston, Williston, Vt., Hart Brothers, 1994, p. 57. Hereafter cited as NT, *Autobiography* with page numbers from 1994 edition.

[13] NT, *Autobiography, op. cit.*, p. 59.

[14] For biographical information on Tivadar Puskas, see http://www.budpocketguide. com/TouristInfo/famous/Famous_Hungarians10.asp (viewed 14 December 2004). I am grateful to Keith Nier for calling this source to my attention.

brother Ferenc was planning a telephone exchange using Edison's improved telephone. Unfortunately, Ferenc was unable to give Tesla a job at once, and while waiting, Tesla became seriously depressed. Convinced he was going to die, Tesla only recovered with the help of a new friend, Anthony Szigeti. To help Tesla regain his strength, Szigeti encouraged Tesla to walk each evening in the City Park[15].

It was during one of these walks with Szigeti that Tesla hit upon the perfect idea for his motor. Admiring the sunset, Tesla began reciting lines from Goethe's epic poem, "Faust", when suddenly he envisioned the idea of using a rotating magnetic field in his motor[16]. Up to this time, inventors had designed DC motors in which the magnetic field of the stator was kept constant and the magnetic field in the rotor was changed by means of a commutator. Tesla's insight was to reverse standard practice: rather than changing the magnetic poles in the rotor, why not change the magnetic field in the stator? This would eliminate the need for the sparking commutator. Tesla saw that if the magnetic field in the stator rotated, it would induce an opposing electric field in the rotor, thus causing the rotor to turn. Tesla surmised that the rotating magnetic field could be created using AC instead of DC, but at the time he did not know how to accomplish this.

Over the next five years, Tesla struggled to acquire the practical knowledge needed to realize his motor. After helping the Puskás brothers build their telephone exchange in Budapest, Tesla joined Tividar in Paris where they both went to work for the Edison Company installing incandescent lighting systems[17]. In 1884, Tesla was transferred to the Edison Machine Works in New York[18]. There, Tesla had little personal contact with Edison and was assigned the task of designing an arc

---

15   It is significant to note that Szigeti is never mentioned by name in Tesla's 1919 autobiography, although he is mentioned in N. Tesla, "An Autobiographical Sketch", *Scientific American*, 5 June 1915, p. 537 and p. 576-577. Tesla and Szigeti became quite close, and Szigeti worked with Tesla in Paris, Strasbourg and New York. Around 1890, Szigeti left Tesla, and his departure deeply upset Tesla. See Nikola Tesla testimony in *Complaint's Record on Final Hearing, Volume 1-Testimony, Westinghouse vs. Mutual Life Insurance Co. and H. C. Mandeville* [1903]. Item N. Tesla, *Motor Testimony*, Nikola Tesla Museum, Belgrade, Yugoslavia, p. 235-236 and p. 321-324. Hereafter cited as NT, *Motor Testimony*.

16   NT, *Autobiography, op. cit.*, p. 60-61.

17   NT, *Motor Testimony, op. cit.*, p. 186.

18   NT, *Motor Testimony, op. cit.*, p. 186. As Seifer (p. 30-31) points out in his biography, there is no documentary evidence that Charles Batchelor wrote a letter introducing Tesla to Edison by saying "I know two great men and you are one of them; the other is this young man". See M. J. Seifer, *Wizard: The Life and Times of Nikola Tesla*, New York, Birch Lane Press, 1996. O'Neill mentions this letter of introduction, but provides no reference or source. See J. J. O'Neill, *Prodigal Genius: The Life of Nikola Tesla*, New York, Ives Washburn, 1944, p. 60.

lighting system. When the Edison Company decided not to pay him a bonus for his design, Tesla quit in disgust[19].

Tesla was quickly hired by Benjamin A. Vail and Robert Lane from Rahway, New Jersey. These two promoters encouraged Tesla to patent his arc lighting system, and Tesla dutifully assigned his patents to them, assuming that they were going to manufacture equipment and compete with Edison. Vail and Lane, however, decided that the real opportunity lay in operating an electrical utility. Consequently, once Tesla had his arc lighting system running in Rahway, his backers fired him and reorganized themselves as the Union County Electric Light and Manufacturing Company[20]. Abandoned by his patrons, Tesla was forced to work as a ditch-digger[21].

In the midst of hardship, Tesla mustered the energy needed to file a patent application for a thermo-magnetic motor in March 1886. Although his idea for a motor powered by heating and cooling magnets proved unworkable, Tesla told his foreman at his ditch-digging job about his invention, and the foreman introduced him to Charles F. Peck. Peck had made a fortune on Wall Street by organizing the Mutual Union Telegraph Company in the early 1880s as a competitive threat to Western Union and then forcing the robber baron Jay Gould to buy Mutual Union in order to protect his holdings in Western Union[22]. Intrigued by the thermo-magnetic motor, Peck offered to underwrite Tesla's efforts at invention. Because he was not a technical expert, Peck invited Alfred S. Brown, a superintendent at Western Union, to join him in supporting Tesla.

To permit Tesla to get started on perfecting his inventions, Peck and Brown rented a laboratory for him in lower Manhattan in the fall of 1886. They agreed to share any profits arising from Tesla's inventions, with Tesla receiving a third, Peck and Brown splitting a third, and a third to be reinvested to develop future inventions. Peck and Brown covered all expenses related to securing patents and paid Tesla a month-

[19] NT, *Motor Testimony, op. cit.*, p. 193. In his autobiography (p. 72), Tesla said nothing about working on the arc lighting system and instead explained that he quit when he was not paid $ 50,000 he thought he had been promised for redesigning the dynamos.

[20] Entry for Tesla Electric Light and Mfg. Co., New Jersey, Vol. 53, p. 159, R. G. Dun & Co. Collection, Baker Business Library, Harvard University. Hereafter cited as "Tesla Co., R. G. Dun & Co. Collection".

[21] O'Neill, *Prodigal Genius, op. cit.*, p. 65 and Nikola Telsa to Institute of Immigrant Welfare, 12 May 1938 in J. T. Ratzlaff (comp.), *Tesla Said*, Millbrae, California, Tesla Book Co., 1984, p. 280.

[22] J. D. Reid, *The Telegraph in America and Morse Memorial*, 2 ed., New York, John Polhemus, 1886, p. 601-605.

ly salary of $ 250. In April 1887, Tesla, Peck, and Brown formed the Tesla Electric Company. And in May, Szigeti came to New York in order to work as Tesla's assistant[23].

Tesla's first laboratory was located at 89 Liberty Street in New York's financial district. The laboratory was just around the corner from the offices of Mutual Union at 120 Broadway. On the ground floor was the Globe Stationery & Printing Company, and Tesla occupied a 15 by 25 foot room at the back of the second floor. The lab was strictly utilitarian, furnished only with a workbench, stove, and a dynamo manufactured by Edward Weston. To provide power for the dynamo, Peck and Brown made a rental agreement with the printing company. Because Globe used its steam engine to run the presses during the day, the company could only provide power at night to Tesla. As a result, Tesla got into the habit of working on his inventions at night[24].

At Liberty Street, Tesla devoted himself to perfecting the thermomagnetic motor, but when it failed to materialize, Peck encouraged him to take up the AC motor. Building on his vision in Budapest, Tesla now began experimenting with using several alternating currents in his motor. In doing so, Tesla was a maverick since most electrical experimenters at the time used only one alternating current in their systems. In September 1887, Tesla discovered that he could produce a rotating magnetic field by using two separate alternating currents fed to pairs of coils on opposing sides of the stator[25]. In modern engineering parlance,

---

[23] NT, *Motor Testimony, op. cit.*, p. 196. See also Anthony Szigeti, 1889 deposition in *Nikola Tesla: Lectures, Patents, Articles*, Belgrade, Nikola Tesla Museum, 1956, p. A-398.

[24] The address for Mutual Union is from New York City, Vol. 391, p. 2625, R. G. Dun & Co. Collection, Baker Library, Harvard Business School, Boston. See also William B. Nellis testimony in NT, *Motor Testimony, op. cit.*, p. 122-123 and p. 132.

[25] The discerning technical reader and Tesla admirer may be quite rightly wondering why I attribute the discovery of having the currents out of phase to 1887, not 1882. Previous biographers have assumed that if Tesla said in his autobiography that he understood everything about his AC motor in the Eureka moment in the park, then he must have known everything, including the importance of using several currents out of phase. After carefully studying Tesla's statements in his autobiography and in patent testimony and investigating what was known about AC in the early 1880s, I have come to the conclusion that it would have been exceptional for him to be thinking about AC in terms of phase in 1882. The topic was simply not widely discussed in textbooks available circa 1882. Moreover, if he had known about the importance of using two alternating currents out of phase, why did he not experiment with such currents with his motor in Strasburg in 1883? Instead, I think the most sensible way to establish when Tesla had this insight is to pay attention to when he first started using out of phase currents in his experiments and that was in the summer and early fall of 1887.

we would say that the two currents are 90° out of phase with each other, and Tesla's motor would be said to be running on two-phase current. Elated, Tesla and his patent attorney Parker Page filed in the fall of 1887 a series of patents broadly covering AC motors using the principle of a rotating magnetic field. In these patents, Tesla introduced the idea that multi-phase (or as he said polyphase) AC could be used to effectively transmit power over long distances.

For Tesla, the concept of using two separate alternating currents to produce a rotating magnetic field was a grand idea; it was simple, it was elegant, and it satisfied his aesthetic sensibility. At the same time, this grand idea bothered Tesla's backer Brown. In order to deliver two separate alternating currents to Tesla's motor, it was necessary to run four wires from the generator to the motor. Since the AC systems then being introduced by the Westinghouse and Thomson-Houston companies employed only two wires, Brown recognized that Tesla's motor was not very practical since it would require more copper wiring than the competition. Brown challenged Tesla to design an AC motor that could run on two wires. Within a few weeks Tesla presented Brown with a variety of designs for what Tesla called split-phase motors. In these motors, Tesla split the single incoming current into two branches; by placing an induction coil in one branch and a resistor in the other, Tesla created two out-of-phase currents that could then run the motor. In addition, he also split the current using capacitors and transformers in novel circuits[26].

Tesla worried that his attorney Page would file patent applications only for the practical split-phase motors and neglect the applications covering the grand principle of a rotating magnetic field. Consequently, Tesla neglected to tell Page about his split-phase designs for six months. It was only at the last minute that Page got Tesla to disclose the two-wire designs so that patents could be filed for both the broad principle and the specific applications[27]. This delay in filing weakened Tesla's long-term patent position and forced Tesla to engage in years of infringement litigation. Enthralled by the perfect idea of a rotating magnetic field, Tesla inadvertently compromised his legal and financial position.

As it became clear that Tesla had come up with a promising AC motor, his patrons began to think about how to promote it. For Peck and Brown the name of the game was not to manufacture Tesla's motor but rather to sell the patents to the highest bidder. In the late 1880s,

---

[26] NT, *Motor Testimony, op. cit.*, p. 160, p. 173-174, p. 210, and p. 329.

[27] NT, *Motor Testimony, op. cit.*, p. 164-166, p. 175, p. 208, p. 308-310, p. 416-417, p. 420, and p. 423.

electric lighting companies were considering shifting from DC to AC since AC could be transmitted over greater distances and thus reach more customers. However, to offset the costs of building larger AC networks, utilities had to move to round-the-clock operations. Utilities had to complement the nighttime lighting load with a daytime load of providing power to electric motors in factories and streetcars. Hence, circa 1887-1888, there was a lively discussion in electrical circles about the need for a practical AC motor[28].

Peck and Brown injected Tesla's AC motor into this discussion by promoting Tesla's inventions energetically but carefully. The right people – the entrepreneurs running electrical manufacturing companies – had to learn about his inventions in the right way, scientifically and objectively. In the 1880s, dozens of inventors were turning out hundreds of electrical patents, many of which were of little value. For instance, the Thomson-Houston Company was inundated with offers of patents from inventors, including one for a dubious product called "electric water"[29]. Peck and Brown therefore had to chart a course whereby they could capture the attention of electrical manufacturers and convince them of the commercial potential of Tesla's patents.

In framing their promotional efforts, Peck and Brown had to overcome Tesla's obscurity. Since he had arrived in America in 1884, Tesla had kept to himself and he had not joined any of the newly formed electrical organizations such as the American Institute of Electrical Engineers, the National Electrical Light Association, or the Electrical Club of New York[30]. Aside from the several electricians he had met working in the middle ranks of the Edison organization, Tesla knew few people in the electrical engineering community. Not knowing anything about Tesla, the electrical fraternity might well wonder how a young man of thirty-two from an unknown part of Eastern Europe could have developed such a promising AC motor. Was it everything he claimed it was?

---

[28] In January 1887, *Electrical World* observed "The system of distribution by means of secondary generators [i.e., transformers] has at last obtained a foot-hold in this country, where if all the promises which are made for it are substantiated, it will not require long to establish itself in public favor". See J. Wetzler, "The Electrical Progress of the Year", *Electrical World*, t. 9, 1 January 1887, p. 2-3. A year later, Wetzler wrote "The prominent feature of the year in electric lighting is the number of systems of distribution by means of induction transformers which have been brought out or elaborated. Prominent among these are the Westinghouse system". See "The Electrical Progress of the Year 1887", *Electrical World*, t. 11, 14 January 1888, p. 18-19.

[29] W. B. Carlson, *Innovation as a Social Process: Elihu Thomson and the Rise of General Electric, 1870-1900*, New York, Cambridge University Press, 1991, p. 244 and p. 265.

[30] NT, *Motor Testimony, op. cit.*, p. 256.

To get the right "buzz" going about Tesla's motors, Peck and Brown sought the endorsement of an expert, Professor William Anthony. Educated at Brown University and Yale's Sheffield Scientific School, Anthony had been Professor of Physics at Cornell University from 1872 to 1887. While at Cornell, he had built dynamos and established the first electrical engineering program in the United States. Wishing to perfect his own electrical inventions, Anthony left Cornell in 1887 to become the electrician (chief engineer) at the Mather Electric Company in Manchester, Connecticut. Possessing both academic credentials and commercial experience, Anthony must have seemed ideal to Peck and Brown for evaluating Tesla's motors[31].

In March 1888, Peck and Brown sent Tesla to visit Professor Anthony in Manchester. Tesla prepared two special motors for Anthony to test. Significantly, both were polyphase designs and not split-phase machines since Peck and Brown were worried about revealing too much of what Tesla had accomplished[32]. The tests went well, and Anthony found that Tesla's AC motors were as efficient as the DC motors currently available. Impressed with Tesla's inventions, Anthony wrote to Dugald C. Jackson, who was teaching electrical engineering at the University of Wisconsin:

I [have] seen a system of alternating current motors in N.Y. that promised great things. I was called as an expert and was shown the machines under the pledge of secrecy as applications were still in the Patent Office. I have seen such an armature weighing 12 pounds running at 3,000 [rpm], when one of the (ac) circuits was suddenly reversed, reverse its rotation so suddenly that I could hardly see what did it. In all this you understand there is no commutator. The armatures have no connection with anything outside. [...] It was a wonderful result to me. Of course, it means two separate circuits from [the] generator and is not applicable to existing systems. But in the form of motor I first described, there is absolutely nothing like a commutator, the two (ac) chasing each other round the field do it all. There is nothing to wear except the two bearings...[33]

Peck and Brown followed up Anthony's evaluation by contacting the technical press. Knowing that the polyphase patents would issue on 1 May 1888, they invited editors from the electrical weeklies to visit the laboratory. In the closing weeks of April 1888, Tesla demonstrated his

---

[31] "Electrical World Portraits-XI. Prof. W. A. Anthony", *Electrical World*, t. 15, p. 70 and NT, *Motor Testimony*, p. 214.

[32] One wonders, too, if Peck and Brown wanted Anthony to give them an outside opinion so that they could evaluate Tesla's claims that the polyphase motors were more promising than the split-phase designs.

[33] W. A. Anthony to D. C. Jackson, 11 March 1888, quoted in K. M. Swezey, "Nikola Tesla", *Science*, t. 127, 16 May 1958, p. 1147-1159 on p. 1149.

polyphase motor to Charles Price of the *Electrical Review* and Thomas Commerford Martin of *Electrical World*. Both Price and Martin were favorably impressed, and Price ran a story about Tesla's motors just after the patents were issued[34].

The centerpiece of the promotional campaign was Tesla's lecture to the American Institute of Electrical Engineers (AIEE) in May 1888. Tesla titled his AIEE lecture "A New System of Alternate Current Motors and Transformers". While his title was modest, he immediately made bold claims for polyphase AC:

> I now have the pleasure of bringing to your notice [...] a novel system of electric distribution and transmission of power by means of alternate currents, affording peculiar advantages, particularly in the way of motors, which I am confident will at once establish the superior adaptability of these currents to the transmission of power.

To support his claims, Tesla began by using the step-by-step diagrams from his first polyphase patent to explain how two separate alternating currents could create a rotating magnetic field. To convince his engineering audience that the rotating magnetic field exerted a uniform pull on the motor's armature, Tesla offered a brief mathematical analysis of the forces involved. Tesla then described his basic polyphase motor, consisting of a ring with four separate coils for the stator and steel disk for the armature. This motor, he emphasized, could be readily reversed and was also synchronous (*i.e.*, it ran as the same speed as the generator[35]). To bolster Tesla's presentation, Professor Anthony reported during the discussion that "the polyphase motors he had tested had an efficiency of fifty to sixty percent"[36].

Timed to take place just after his patents issued, Tesla's AIEE lecture received extensive coverage in the electrical journals and attracted the interest of George Westinghouse. In contrast to Edison who had focused on DC, Westinghouse had bet on AC, and in late May 1888,

---

[34] NT, *Motor Testimony, op. cit.*, p. 252-253; T. C. Martin, "Electrical World Portraits-XII. Nikola Tesla", *Electrical World*, t. 15, 15 February 1890, p. 106. "The Tesla System of Distribution and Electric Motors for Alternating Currents", *Electrical Review*, 12 May 1888, in I. Vujovic (comp.), *The Tesla Collection: A 23 Volume Full Text Periodical/Newspaper Bibliography*, New York, Tesla Project, t. 1, 1998, p. 11-12. Hereafter cited as TC. The *Electrical Review* article also appeared in *Electrical Engineer*, t. 1, 25 May 1888, TC, p. 28-29.

[35] Tesla's 1888 AIEE lecture has been widely reprinted; it was originally published in *AIEE Transactions*, t. 5, p. 307-324 (September 1887-October 1888) but one convenient source is T. C. Martin, *The Inventions, Researches, and Writings, of Nikola Tesla*, New York, originally published 1893; reprinted by Barnes & Noble, 1995, p. 9-25.

[36] Discussion of Tesla's paper, *AIEE Transactions*, t. 5, p. 324-325 (1887-1888) in TC, t. 1, p. 23.

Westinghouse dispatched two lieutenants, Henry M. Byllesby and Thomas B. Kerr, to Tesla's lab in New York.

Peck arranged for Tesla to demonstrate his polyphase motors for Byllesby and Kerr. Although Tesla offered an explanation of his motor, Byllesby had to admit that "his description was not of a nature which I was enabled, entirely, to comprehend". Byllesby noted that Tesla's motors required more than two wires, indicating that Tesla and Peck were holding back the split-phase designs; after all, why show a potential buyer everything at once? Overall, Byllesby was impressed, and he told Westinghouse that "the motors, as far as I can judge from the examination which I was enabled to make, are a success"[37].

Undoubtedly drawing on his experience with selling Mutual Union to Jay Gould, Peck knew that he would have to "play" Byllesby and Kerr in order to get the best possible deal. Consequently, when Byllesby and Kerr expressed an interest in buying the patents for Westinghouse, Peck informed them that a San Francisco capitalist had offered $ 200,000 plus a royalty of $ 2.50 per horsepower for each motor installed. "The terms, of course, are monstrous", Byllesby told Westinghouse, "and I so told them. [...] I told them that there was no possibility of our considering the matter seriously. [...] In order to avoid giving the impression that the matter was one which excited my curiosity I made my visit short"[38].

Despite Peck's high price, Byllesby and Kerr nonetheless recommended that Westinghouse buy the Tesla patents so as to secure broad coverage of AC technology. However, in order to force Peck to accept a lower price, Westinghouse decided to send his star inventors, Oliver Shallenberger and William Stanley, Jr. to inspect Tesla's work. Perhaps they could persuade Tesla and Peck that Westinghouse was in a stronger technical position and that they should back down[39].

Shallenberger visited Tesla's lab on 12 June 1888 and Tesla demonstrated his motors operating on four wires. Shallenberger had experimented extensively with AC machinery and had independently discovered how to use a rotating magnetic field to create an improved wattmeter. Shallenberger quickly recognized that not only had Tesla discovered the idea of using a rotating magnetic field eight months

---

[37] H. M. Byllesby to G. Westinghouse, 21 May 1888. Quoted in H. Passer, *The Electrical Manufacturers*, p. 277.

[38] *Ibid.*, p. 278.

[39] It appears that Shallenberger and Stanley emphasized their own work in talking with Tesla, but at the same time, they may very well have also dropped hints that Westinghouse would soon control Ferraris' ideas. For instance, after Tesla moved to Pittsburgh Pantaleoni told him that Ferraris's paper might well limit Tesla's chances at securing patents in Europe. See NT, *Motor Testimony*, p. 171.

before he had but Tesla had gone ahead and produced a motor using this principle. Unable to shake Tesla and Peck, Shallenberger returned to Pittsburgh and urged Westinghouse to buy the patents[40].

Shallenberger's trip was followed by a visit from Stanley on 23rd June 1888. Stanley had helped Westinghouse develop single-phase AC electric lighting by designing a practical transformer and confirming the idea that transformers should be connected to the generator in parallel, not in series. To deal with Stanley, Peck decided to go on the offensive, and he instructed Tesla to show Stanley both the polyphase and split-phase motors.

Upon arriving at the Liberty Street lab, Stanley promptly announced that the "Westinghouse boys" had developed an AC motor and were ahead of Tesla. Rather than rising to the bait, Tesla quietly asked Stanley if he would like to see his motor run on two wires – the motor that Tesla and Peck had concealed from Byllesby and Kerr[41]. Impressed, Stanley had to admit that Tesla was indeed ahead of the engineers at Westinghouse. "As far as I know every form of motor proposed by Mr. Shallenberger or myself has been tried by Mr. Tesla", reported Stanley to Westinghouse, "Their motor is the best thing of the kind I have seen. I believe it more efficient than most DC motors. I also believe it belongs to them"[42].

Peck still kept up the pressure on Westinghouse, telling Stanley that he was just about to sell the patents to some other party. With that news, Westinghouse decided that they should not wait any longer, and Kerr, Byllesby, and Shallenberger negotiated an agreement with Peck and Brown[43]. On 7 July 1888, Peck and Brown agreed to sell the Tesla patents to Westinghouse for $ 25,000 in cash, $ 50,000 in notes and a royalty of $ 2.50 per horsepower for each motor. Westinghouse guaranteed that the royalties would be at least $ 5,000 in the first year, $ 10,000 in the second year, and $ 15,000 in each succeeding year. In addition, Peck and Brown were reimbursed by the Westinghouse Company for all of the expenses they incurred during the development of the

---

[40] NT, *Motor Testimony, op. cit.*, p. 330-331; Kerr testimony in NT, *Motor Testimony, op. cit.*, p. 449.

[41] NT, *Motor Testimony, op. cit.*, p. 246-251.

[42] W. Stanley Jr. to G. Westinghouse, 24 June 1888, in *Complainant's Record on Final Hearing. Volume II-Exhibits, Westinghouse Electrical and Manufacturing Company versus Mutual Life Insurance Company of New York and H.C. Mandeville*, US Circuit Court, Western District of New York, p. 592-593. Cataloged in Tesla Museum in Belgrade as NT 74.

[43] Kerr testimony in NT, *Motor Testimony, op. cit.*, p. 449-451.

motor[44]. In whole numbers, the agreement meant that Westinghouse would pay Tesla, Peck, and Brown $ 200,000 over a ten-year period. Over the life of the patents (17 years), Tesla and his backers stood to make at least $ 315,000. Although it was not specified in the written contract, Tesla agreed to come to Pittsburgh and share what he had learned about AC motors with the Westinghouse engineers.

Tesla did not walk away from the Westinghouse deal with $ 200,000 in his pocket; rather, he readily agreed to share the proceeds with Peck and Brown. Since they had shrewdly handled the business negotiations and assumed all of the financial risk in developing the motors, Tesla gave Peck and Brown five-ninths of the proceeds from the deal while retaining four-ninths for himself. In this way, Tesla acknowledged the essential role Peck and Brown had played in developing the AC motor[45].

Westinghouse hoped that one of Tesla's motor designs could be used to run streetcars. To adapt his motors for this purpose, Tesla moved to Pittsburgh in 1888. Over the next year, Tesla and the Westinghouse engineers were frustrated by several problems with Tesla's motors. Because Tesla's best motor required two alternating currents and four wires, it was not possible to add this motor to existing single-phase AC systems; one would need to install new two-phase generators. Although Tesla had developed a number of two-wire motors, these split-phase designs ran best on currents of 50 cycles or less; at that time, the Westinghouse single-phase systems were using 133 cycles so that consumers would not complain about their incandescent lamps flickering. Westinghouse engineers were thus stymied as to how they could combine lights and motors onto a single network.

Led by Charles F. Scott and Benjamin G. Lamme, the engineers at Westinghouse eventually solved these problems by modifying Tesla's motors and developing a new AC system using three-phase, 60 cycle current. The Westinghouse Company dramatically demonstrated this system by building a hydroelectric station at Niagara Falls in 1895 which transmitted large amounts of power over twenty miles to factories in Buffalo. Thus, Tesla's invention of the AC motor and his idea of using multi-phase AC to transmit power thus formed the basis for the standard current distributed in North America today.

---

[44] "Agreement of July 7, 1888" in NT, t. 74, p. 584-587. See also NT, *Motor Testimony, op. cit.*, p. 327.
[45] NT, *Motor Testimony, op. cit.*, p. 326-327.

Developing Wireless Power, 1890-1905

But long before the Niagara plant came on line, Tesla had grown restless and left Westinghouse. He had uncovered the perfect idea for an AC motor, and it was up to others to work out the details. After filing 15 patent applications – many for variations on his split-phase motor – Tesla left Pittsburgh in the summer of 1889.

Drawing on his royalty income from Westinghouse, Tesla traveled in the summer of 1889 to see the Universal Exposition in Paris. While there, Tesla witnessed a demonstration lecture of vibrating diaphragms by a young Norwegian physicist, Vilhelm Bjerknes (1862-1951). It is likely that Bjerknes introduced Tesla to the discovery of electromagnetic waves by Heinrich Hertz. In 1887, Hertz had detected the electromagnetic waves that James Clerk Maxwell had predicted in his theoretical work on electricity and magnetism. Bjerknes had come to Paris to attend Henri Poincaré's lectures on electrodynamics and subsequently spent two years at the University of Bonn as Hertz' assistant. Together, Hertz and Bjerknes studied resonance in oscillatory circuits[46].

When Tesla returned to New York, he went to work in a new laboratory at 175 Grand Street (in what is now Greenwich Village). The lab consisted of one room divided by partitions; Tesla's backer, Brown, complained that the space was too small and inadequate for the work he thought needed to be done[47]. To help with the experiments, Tesla assembled a small team of craftsmen. Along with his old friend Szigeti, Tesla employed another Hungarian mechanic, Charles Leonhardt. He also hired Paul Noyes who had previously helped with the arc lighting system in Rahway. Rounding out the group was F. W. Clark, a skilled mechanic who had worked with Brown & Sharpe and David Hiergesell, a glassblower[48]. In 1892, Tesla enlarged his laboratory by moving to 33-35 South Fifth Avenue (now West Broadway) and probably retained most of the same assistants.

During the early 1890s, Tesla continued to work with the Tesla Electric Company, the firm organized by Peck and Brown. Unfortunately for

---

[46] On Tesla's trip to Paris, see O'Neill, *Prodigal Genius, op. cit.*, p. 99. NT mentions seeing Bjerknes' demonstration in "On the Dissipation of the Electrical Energy of the Hertz Resonator", *Electrical Engineer*, t. 14, 21 December 1892, p. 587-588 reprinted in J. T. Ratzlaff (comp.), *Tesla Said*, Millbrae, California, Tesla Book Co., 1984, p. 22-23. For a biography of Bjerknes, see his entry in the *Dictionary of Scientific Biography*, 2, p. 167-169 as well as http://wwwgroups.dcs.stand.ac.uk/~history/Mathematicians/Bjerknes_Vilhelm.html (viewed 17 January 2005).

[47] NT, *Motor Testimony, op. cit.*, p. 323-325.

[48] L. I. Anderson, *Nikola Tesla on His Work with Alternating Currents and Their Application to Wireless Telegraphy, Telephony, and Transmission of Power*, Denver, Sun Publishing, 1992, p. 12. Hereafter cited as NT, *Radio Testimony*.

Tesla, Peck died in the summer of 1890[49]. Although Tesla continued to consult Brown over the next few years, Brown could not provide the shrewd business judgment that Peck had contributed to Tesla's early success with the AC motor.

In search of a new field to explore in his Grand Street lab, Tesla took measure of the overall development of electrical science and technology. As he saw it, electrical research could move in three major directions: high voltages, heavy currents, or high frequencies. As he observed:

> There were the excessive electrical pressures of millions of volts, which opened up wonderful possibilities if producible in practical ways; there were the currents of many hundreds of thousands of amperes, which appealed to the imagination by their astonishing effects, and most interesting and inviting of all, there were the powerful electrical vibrations with their mysterious actions at a distance.[50]

Of these three, Tesla decided that the most promising was the least investigated, namely high-frequency phenomena. To study high frequencies, Tesla built several alternators in 1890-1891 with hundreds of electromagnets in their rotor and stator; by running these machines at high speeds, he could produce currents with a frequency of 10,000 or 20,000 cycles per second[51].

While developing his alternators, Tesla repeated the experiments of Hertz with regard to electromagnetic waves, for in Paris he had "caught the fire of enthusiasm and fairly burned with desire to behold the miracle with my own eyes"[52]. This enthusiasm led to one of his most famous inventions, the Tesla coil.

In his classic experiments to detect electromagnetic waves, Hertz used a powerful induction coil connected to a battery, a current interrupter, and a spark gap. Prior to 1887, he conducted a series of experiments with an induction coil in which he generated a series of sparks in the secondary whenever the current interrupter opened or closed the primary circuit in his apparatus. As the eminent historian of radio, Hugh Aitken, reminds us, these sparks "represented, of course, a sudden rush of electrical current-precisely the kind of acceleration of current flow, that, according to Maxwell's equations, would generate electromagnetic

---

[49] Will of Charles F. Peck, Bergen County Wills 7893B, W 1890, Wills and Inventories, ca. 1670-1900, Department of State, Secretary of State's Office, New Jersey State Archives, Trenton, NJ.

[50] NT, "Some Experiments in Tesla's Laboratory with Currents of High Potential and High Frequency", *Electrical Review*, 29 March 1899, p. 193-197 and p. 204. Hereafter cited as "1899 Experiments".

[51] NT, *Radio Testimony, op. cit.*, p. 1-12.

[52] NT, "The True Wireless", *Electrical Experimenter*, May 1919, p. 28-30ff. on p. 28.

radiation"[53]. Hertz noticed that whenever the sparks were produced at the induction coil, he could also detect sparks elsewhere in his laboratory using a simple detector or resonator. This detector consisted of a copper loop with a spark gap. By carefully proportioning the diameter of this loop and adjusting the brass balls on either side of the spark gap on the secondary, Hertz was able to show that his apparatus was generating electromagnetic waves that moved through space and were detected by his resonator[54].

In 1890, Tesla repeated Hertz' experiments, and he may very well have been one of the first American researchers to do so. Not satisfied with the apparatus Hertz had used, Tesla altered the experimental set-up[55]. An obvious step was to replace the mechanical current interrupter with his high-frequency alternator. Rather than have the apparatus use the few hundred cycles per second produced by the mechanical interrupter, why not use the 10,000 or 20,000 cycles from his alternator? Tesla soon discovered that, as the frequency increased, so did the amount of heat generated that melted the paraffin or gutta-percha insulation between the primary and secondary inside the induction coil. To address this problem, Tesla made two changes. First, he got rid of the insulation and instead wound his induction coils with an air gap between the primary and the secondary. Second, because the iron core in the induction coil became so hot, he redesigned his version so that the iron core could be moved in and out of the primary coil. By moving the core in and out of the primary, Tesla found that he could also adjust the inductance of the primary[56].

Tesla also encountered problems with the condenser that was frequently used with induction coils. To increase the strength of the spark

---

[53] H. G. J. Aitken, *Syntony and Spark: The Origins of Radio*, Princeton University Press, 1985, p. 52-53.

[54] H. G. J. Aitken, *Syntony and Spark, op. cit.*, p. 53-57. The definitive study of Hertz' work is J. Z. Buchwald, *The Creation of Scientific Effects: Heinrich Hertz and Electric Waves*, Chicago, University of Chicago Press, 1994.

[55] As Tesla wrote in 1919, "Accordingly I began, parallel with high frequency alternators, the construction of several forms of apparatus with the object of exploring the field opened up by Dr. Hertz. Recognizing the limitations of the devices he had employed, I concentrated my attention on the production of a powerful induction coil but made no notable progress until a happy inspiration led me to the invention of the oscillation transformer". NT, "The True Wireless", p. 28.

[56] For a discussion of these problems, see NT, "Alternating Currents of Short Period", *Electrical World*, Vol. 17, 14 March 1891, p. 203, in TC, Vol. 2, p. 138 and NT, "Experiments with Alternate Currents of Very High Frequency and their Application to Methods of Artificial Illumination", a lecture delivered before the AIEE at Columbia College, 21 May 1891, in Martin, *Inventions, Researches, and Writings, op. cit.*, p. 145-197 (hereafter referred to as "1891 Columbia lecture") on p. 170-171.

produced by the secondary, investigators (beginning with Fizeau in 1853) typically placed a Leyden jar or condenser in a shunt around the spark gap of the secondary. With the rapid alterations from his high-frequency generator, Tesla found that this condenser often counteracted the self-inductance of the secondary coil and burned out the coil. In response, Tesla moved the condenser in his apparatus to between the alternator and the primary. He also made this condenser adjustable[57]. Tinkering with the arrangement of the condenser and coils was quite natural for Tesla; in developing his split-phase motors, he had used novel combinations of induction coils, resistors, and condensers to split the incoming current.

Tesla now realized that, with careful adjustment of the condenser and induction coils, it was possible to boost the frequency coming from his alternator to even higher levels. Electrical scientists had initially assumed that when a condenser discharged, the electricity simply flowed from one plate to the other, much like water running out of a reservoir. However in 1856, the prominent British physicist, Sir William Thomson, had discovered that condenser discharge was instead vibratory. Just as a vertical weighted spring bobs up and down when released, so the electrical charge flows back and forth between the plates in the condenser until the stored-up energy is dissipated. Taking advantage of the vibratory character of how condensers discharged, Tesla was soon able to produce a current that alternated up to 20,000 times per second[58].

Together, these three changes – the air gap, the adjustable primary, and the adjustable condenser in the primary circuit – constituted an invention that allowed Tesla to produce larger and more varied sparks. Tesla called this invention his oscillating transformer, but as it came to be widely employed by other investigators, it became known as the Tesla coil. The oscillating transformer was fundamental to much of Tesla's subsequent work on wireless power, and he felt that it was one of his great discoveries. As he recalled in his autobiography: "When in 1900 I obtained powerful discharges of 100 feet and flashed a current around the globe, I was reminded of the first tiny spark I observed in my Grand Street laboratory and was thrilled by sensations akin to those I felt when I discovered the *rotating magnetic field* (Tesla's italics)"[59].

Underlying Tesla's oscillating transformer was the phenomenon of electrical resonance. Just as sound waves emanating from one tuning fork can cause another tuning fork to vibrate in sympathy, so electrical

---

[57] H. G. J. Aitken, *Syntony and Spark, op. cit.*, p. 54; NT, "Alternating Currents of Short Period", and NT, "The True Wireless", p. 28.

[58] O'Neill, *Prodigal Genius, op. cit.*, p. 90.

[59] NT, *Autobiography, op. cit.*, p. 75.

resonance refers to the idea that one electrical circuit can be made to respond to another. But rather than responding to sound waves, the circuits can be adjusted to respond to electromagnetic waves by giving each circuit the right capacitance and inductance. In his oscillating transformer, Tesla adjusted the condenser and primary coil so that they resonated with the incoming signal and then boosted them to ever-higher frequencies and voltage. Using this insight, Tesla built extremely large oscillating transformers and produced sparks over 135 feet long. At the same time, Tesla realized that resonance opened the door to tuning radio signals. If one gave the transmitter a particular capacitance and inductance, it would generate signals at that frequency; likewise, if one placed the same capacitance and inductance in a receiving circuit, then it would respond to signals at that frequency. For Tesla, electrical resonance became the grand idea that informed much of his work over the next fifteen years.

Intrigued how his oscillating transformer took advantage of reso-nance, Tesla now began to study the properties of high-frequency currents. When researchers start investigating new phenomena, they often start by using existing experimental techniques, and then develop new techniques as they become familiar with the phenomena. Since a Tesla coil is an extensive reworking of a Ruhmkorff coil, Tesla repeated many of the usual demonstrations performed with a Ruhmkorff coil. One popular demonstration performed with a Ruhmkorff coil was to use electric sparks to render gases incandescent. To conduct this experiment, investigators used special glass tubes from which most of the air had been evacuated. Known as Geissler tubes, these tubes had two platinum electrodes, and when connected to a Ruhmkorff coil, the high voltages caused the gas to ionize and become luminescent.

Working with Geissler tubes, Tesla made an important discovery. When he attached the terminals of his oscillating transformer to two spheres, the spark jumped at the point where the gap between the balls was the smallest and then climbed up the sides of the spheres, only to be extinguished at the top and to start again at the closest point. Modern experimenters refer to this demonstration as "Jacob's Ladder", and it is often seen in the apparatus used by mad scientists in monster and sci-ence-fiction movies. However, what Tesla found startling was that whenever the spark generated by the coil was blown out – such as at the end of a climb between the spheres – Geissler tubes lying nearby and not connected to the circuit were illuminated and extinguished in unison with the spark. He also noticed that the tubes did not light up when they were at right angles to the terminals of his induction coil; to be illumi-nated, the tubes had to be parallel with the terminals and the spark. This suggested to Tesla that the tubes were lit up as a result of the electric field produced by the spark. Tesla repeated the experiment with vacuum tubes without any electrodes and was amazed to find that these too became illuminated.

Tesla quickly realized that the implications of this experiment was that it might be possible to use high-frequency AC to develop wireless electric lamps; rather than getting power via wires, lamps could now be designed to simply pick up power when placed in a strong electrical field. To help people appreciate the full potential of high-frequency AC for electric lighting, Tesla created a breath-taking demonstration that he included in his public lectures. Two large zinc sheets were suspended from the ceiling about fifteen feet from each other and connected to the oscillating transformer. With the auditorium lights dimmed, Tesla took a long vacuum tube in each hand and stepped between the two sheets. As he waved the slender tubes, they glowed, charged by the field set up between the plates[60].

This demonstration created a sensation and was featured in many of the articles published subsequently about Tesla's lectures in 1891 and 1892. Enthralled with the idea of illumination without heat or flames, Joseph Wetzler in *Harper's Weekly* predicted that Tesla's lamps would "bring a fairy-land within our homes"[61]. "It is difficult to appreciate what those strange phenomena meant at that time", Tesla recalled in his autobiography, "When my tubes were first publicly exhibited they were viewed with [an] amazement impossible to describe"[62].

Having now tapped into new phenomena, Tesla had to decide how to shape his discoveries into a commercial opportunity. While we now know that electromagnetic waves produced by a Tesla coil can be used for wireless telegraphy or radio communications, this application was not obvious to Tesla or other early investigators of Hertzian waves. Indeed, historian Sungook Hong has argued that the Maxwellians – the British scientists who developed the mathematics linking Hertz' experiments with Maxwell's theory – were not particularly interested in existing telegraph practice in the early 1890s and hence not prepared to convert Hertz' discovery into wireless telegraphy[63].

Instead, Tesla decided to develop his high-frequency inventions to serve the applications that he knew best and that were clearly in demand in the early 1890s, namely lighting and power. To complement his

---

[60] NT, "1891 Columbia lecture", p. 187-190.
[61] J. Wetzler, "Electric Lamps Fed from Space, and Flames that Do Not Consume", *Harper's Weekly*, t. 35, 11 July 1891, p. 524, in TC, Vol. 3, p. 104-106.
[62] NT, *Autobiography, op. cit.*, p. 82.
[63] S. Hong, *Wireless: From Marconi's Black-Box to the Audion*, Cambridge, MIT Press, 2001, p. 5-9.

wireless lamps, he fashioned a motor that ran with only a ground con-nection[64]. Tesla quickly scaled up his demonstration apparatus with the two zinc plates by replacing one plate with a large cylinder and the other by grounding the circuit. With the large cylinder placed on the rooftop (much like an antenna), Tesla found that he was able to transmit and receive waves throughout the building at Grand Street. A few years later, he tested his system further by using antennas suspended by balloons over his downtown laboratory and his hotel in uptown Manhat-tan. In the course of these experiments, Tesla strove to increase the luminosity of his lamps as well as the total amount of power transmitted.

Tesla thought about his evolving high-frequency system in terms of what we call "generations" of technology[65]. For Tesla, the first genera-tion of electrical power technology was the DC incandescent system pioneered by Edison. A second generation was the AC power systems that he had helped Westinghouse to develop. And high-frequency AC was going to constitute the third generation of electric power.

To attract public attention and new investors for this next generation of electrical technology, Tesla now cultivated an image of being a brilliant, even eccentric, genius. Tesla delighted in showing off his wireless lamps, and after elaborate dinners at Delmonico's restaurant, he would invite celebrities such as Mark Twain to late-night demonstra-tions in his laboratory. Capitalizing on the success of his 1888 lecture on his AC motor, Tesla gave public lectures on high-frequency AC in New York, London, and Paris in which he mixed literary references, scien-tific theory, and dazzling demonstrations. Just as newspaper reporters had covered Edison's exploits at Menlo Park in the 1870s, so they flocked to Tesla's laboratory in the 1890s to cover his sensational discoveries. Like Edison, Tesla delighted in telling lively stories and promising great results for his new inventions. Anxious to put a human face on the profound changes taking place in American society as the result of technology, reporters eagerly covered Tesla's inventions and predictions, and Tesla became a staple of the Sunday feature sections.

In terms of filing patents for his high-frequency system, Tesla seems to have followed a pattern he gleaned from the negotiations with West-inghouse. While Westinghouse bought in 1888 all of Tesla's polyphase patents – covering both motors and the entire system – what initially attracted Westinghouse were the specific patents for the motors. It was

---

[64] NT, "Experiments with Alternate Currents of High Potential and High Frequency", lecture delivered in London, February 1892, in Martin, *Inventions, Researches, and Writings*, p. 198-293.

[65] See NT to Edward Dean Adams, 2 February 1893 and 6 February 1893, in Western New York Historical Materials, National Grid USA, Syracuse, NY. I am grateful to Robert Dischner for making these materials available to me.

only later, after 1892, that Westinghouse came to appreciate that Tesla had not only given him control over the motor but also the rights to the entire system. Consequently, in patenting his high-frequency inventions, Tesla first filed patents for various components of his new system, followed a few years later by systems patents. While several of the component patents featured new lamps, he also introduced an electro-mechanical oscillator. Designed like a typical steam engine, Tesla's oscillator used a reciprocating piston to move an electric coil rapidly up and down through a magnetic field. While Tesla developed the oscillator to generate precise electromagnetic waves, he also promoted it as a revolutionary new way for efficiently generating power. In taking this approach – component patents followed by systems patents – Tesla was following a "wedge" strategy. Just as the motor patents had brought in Westinghouse initially, so now Tesla hoped that the lamp and oscillator patents would attract investors since they could immediately exploit these component patents. Later on, they could make the major commitment and support the development of the entire system.

Through 1893 and 1894, Tesla seems to have assumed that the combination of his lectures and extensive newspaper coverage would attract individuals who would want to buy or license his new patents for high-frequency AC components. This was a reasonable assumption since in 1892, Tesla successfully negotiated licenses for his motor patents with several major European electrical manufacturers[66].

However, no entrepreneurs stepped forward and offered to license or buy his high-frequency patents. In large measure, Tesla was stymied by business conditions. In the five years following the Panic of 1893, the American economy suffered a severe depression, second only in magnitude to the Great Depression of the 1930s. During the mid-1890s, both the existing electrical manufacturers and utility companies were not especially profitable. If the companies developing the first and second generations of electrical technology (DC and AC) were not earning money, why should investors take a chance on Tesla's next generation of high-frequency AC?

To develop high-frequency AC, Tesla next sought the help of one of the architects of the second generation of AC power, Edward Dean Adams. A New York financier who had studied engineering at MIT, Adams had made a name for himself in reorganizing bankrupt railroads and trusts. Moreover, he was the driving force behind the promotion of

---

[66] See "Tesla Motors in Europe", *Electrical Engineer*, 26 September 1892, p. 291 in TC, Vol. 5, p. 149 and NT to George Westinghouse, 12 September 1892, Tesla Papers, Library of Congress, Washington, DC, Reel 7.

the giant hydroelectric power plant at Niagara[67]. At a critical moment in 1893 when his company had to decide between using AC or DC for Niagara, Adams had sought Tesla's advice[68]. Impressed with Tesla, Adams decided to promote his new inventions, and together with Tesla's old business associate Brown, they launched the Nikola Tesla Company in February 1895. The company planned to "manufacture and sell machinery, generators, motors, electrical apparatus, *etc.*", and the directors planned to issue stock to capitalize it at $ 500,000[69]. If fully subscribed by investors, this level of capitalization would have certainly provided Tesla with the funds he would need to develop his inventions. However, it would not have been sufficient to undertake manufacturing on a meaningful scale. Hence, Adams' strategy with the Nikola Tesla Company was a selling strategy; once the technology had been perfected, then either the patents or the entire company could be sold. Although Adams eventually spent about $ 100,000 on Tesla's work, I think Adams saw himself not as an investor but as a promoter, someone who made his fortune by organizing Tesla's technology and other people's money into a successful enterprise. This is what he had done for various railroads and trusts.

Together, Tesla and Adams waited for other investors to join the Nikola Tesla Company, but they unfortunately did not materialize. While part of the problem was the ongoing business depression, another part of the problem may have been Tesla himself. Having launched a new company with the stated purpose of putting his inventions into use, the next step was to begin to convert these inventions into commercially feasible products. In this phase – commonly called development – the inventor has to know when to shift from generating lots of alternative designs to focusing on perfecting the most promising version. In other words, the inventor needs to shift from divergent to convergent thinking[70]. For both geniuses and mere mortals, convergent thinking is not as

---

[67] E. E. Bartlett, *Edward Dean Adams*, New York, Privately printed, 1926; E. D Adams, *Niagara Power*, 2 vols., Niagara Falls, Niagara Falls Power Company, 1927.

[68] See the following letters from NT to Adams in 1893: 9 January, 2 February, 6 February, 12 March, 21 March, 22 March, 26 March, and 11 May in National Grid USA collection.

[69] Quote is from "The Nikola Tesla Company", *Electrical Engineer*, 13 February 1895, p. 149, in TC, Vol. 9, p. 109. While the *Electrical Engineer* reported that the company was capitalized at $ 5,000, a majority of the directors ran a notice in the *New York Times* on 4 February 1895, p. 11, calling for a meeting to raise the capitalization to $ 500,000.

[70] For a discussion of divergent and convergent research strategies, see W. B. Carlson, "Thomas Edison as a Manager of R&D: The Development of the Alkaline Storage Battery, 1899-1915", *IEEE Technology and Society*, Vol. 12, December 1988, p. 4-12.

much fun as divergent thinking; it's a lot more enjoyable to dream up new alternatives than to face up to the difficulties associated with making a device reliable, efficient, and cost-effective.

Tesla, I suspect, had a genuine problem in making the shift from divergent to convergent thinking. In the crucial period from 1894 to 1898, Tesla seems to have put off doing the essential work of development. In his public lectures, he was never satisfied with demonstrating just a few of the most promising versions of his lamps; rather, he felt compelled to show several dozen variations. Moreover, every few months Tesla would let reporters visit his laboratory and they would write up his "latest" discovery. Tesla may very well have thought that sheer variety conveyed the power of his genius, but it actually may have sent the wrong message to investors. If they are going to risk capital on an inventor and his patents, investors need to feel confident that the inventor is willing to shift to convergent thinking and get down to the nitty-gritty of creating a marketable product.

Several factors contributed to why Tesla was unable to make the jump from divergent to convergent thinking in a timely fashion. A straightforward factor was that his laboratory was destroyed by fire in March 1895, and he lost his apparatus and notes. Although he set up a new lab on East Houston Street (again in Greenwich Village), the fire nonetheless set him back materially and emotionally.

Another factor, which is harder to document, is that Tesla suffered from bouts of depression. Throughout his adult life, Tesla clearly had periods when he was filled with energy, bursting with ideas, and extremely optimistic; hints in his correspondence suggest that these upbeat periods were followed by dark periods in which he retired to his hotel and did not see his friends for weeks at a time. If he indeed was depressed in the mid-1890s, then Tesla would not have had the energy needed for the development work. One indication that something was wrong in this period is that Tesla filed no patent applications whatsoever in 1894 or 1895.

A final factor influencing the shift from divergent to convergent thinking is Tesla's relationship with his promoters. As the motor story shows, Tesla received a great deal of guidance from Peck and Brown. Brown made sure that Tesla developed not only the ideal polyphase motor but also the more practical split-phase designs. Peck insisted on getting expert help in writing up Tesla's patents, in making contact with the technical press, and superbly managing negotiations with potential buyers of Tesla's patents. In contrast, during the development of the high-frequency AC, Tesla did not work closely with either his old associate Brown or Adams. Neither man seems to have guided Tesla in terms of focusing his work on the most promising designs; no one played the role that Peck had played in the development of the motor.

Unable to attract investors using business connections, Tesla turned to using his social connections. In the mid-1890s, Tesla had begun to dine regularly at the elegant Delmonico's restaurant, in order to be seen by the rich and powerful of New York. One of the people Tesla encountered there was John Jacob Astor IV. The heir to a huge fortune, Astor had published a science-fiction novel, patented several inventions, and served as a Lieutenant Colonel in Cuba during the Spanish-American War. Astor was undoubtedly familiar with Tesla's work since he was a director of the Cataract Construction Company, the firm that had built the Niagara power plant. After visiting the Colonel and his wife at home, Tesla convinced Astor in January 1899 to underwrite his development, particularly for a new lamp and his oscillator. In joining up with Astor, Tesla bought majority control of the Nikola Tesla Company and Astor put up $ 100,000 for 500 shares in the Tesla Electric Company.

Significantly, Tesla's strategy was still to develop his patents to the point where they could be sold profitably. "Sooner or later, he told Astor, my system will be purchased by the Whitney syndicate [who were developing electric street railways], General Electric, or Westinghouse, for otherwise they will be driven out of the market"[71].

With the funds supplied by Astor, Tesla shuttered his New York laboratory and moved temporarily to Colorado Springs where he built a new lab at the foot of Pike's Peak. While Astor expected to him to concentrate on perfecting his lamps and oscillator, Tesla instead tackled in 1899 what he thought was the important application for electromagnetic waves: the wireless transmission of power around the world. During the late 1890s, it seemed as if all of America was being wired; while AT&T and other telephone companies were installing exchanges in nearly every town and city, electric utilities were expanding everywhere to deliver power to businesses and homes. With the demand for electricity appearing to be insatiable, Tesla dreamed of pulling an end-run around the wired networks by developing the means for distributing information and power without wires.

Tesla's dream was again based on the grand idea of electrical resonance. In his wireless work, Tesla had come to regard the circuit between the transmitter and receiver as consisting of two parts. First, the transmitter sent radio waves through the air to the receiver. Then because both transmitter and receiver were grounded, a return current passed between the receiver to the transmitter through the earth. Think-

---

[71] NT to John Jacob Astor, 6 January 1899, quoted in Seifer, *Wizard, op. cit.*, p. 211.

ing again like a maverick, Tesla decided to focus not on the radio waves passing through the atmosphere (like everyone else investigating wireless) but rather on the earth current. Why not, wondered Tesla, have the transmitter send waves through the earth to the receiver and then use the atmosphere for the return circuit? Ideally, Tesla thought that it should be possible for a transmitting station to pump electromagnetic waves into the earth's crust until the earth's electrical resonant frequency was reached; then, with the whole planet pulsing, it should be possible to tap this energy at receiving stations located all over the world. To test this theory, Tesla built several extremely large oscillating transformers at Colorado Springs, which he thought successfully transmitted power around the world. Tesla also thought that signals from his magnifying transmitter had reached Mars and that he had received a return message from the Martians!

Satisfied in his own mind that power could be transmitted around the world without wires, Tesla returned to New York in 1900. Confident that success was imminent, he moved into a suite at the luxurious Waldorf-Astoria Hotel. Certain that investors would flock to his magnificent project, Tesla spurned the scientific press and announced his accomplishments in newspapers and popular magazines. Determined to show how all his inventions constituted a grand intellectual scheme, Tesla wrote a sixty-page article entitled "The Problem of Increasing Human Energy" for *Century Magazine*[72]. Tesla illustrated this article with spectacular photographs showing him sitting calmly in the midst of a lightning storm unleashed by his giant coils.

Tesla's promotional efforts paid off. While Astor declined to invest further, J. P. Morgan in 1901 agreed to put $ 150,000 in Tesla's wireless power project. Eagerly, Tesla purchased a large tract of land on Long Island, and he asked the architect Stanford White to design the laboratory building. Sparing no expense in equipping this new lab at Wardenclyffe, Tesla quickly spent the money advanced by Morgan. With no positive results in hand, Morgan refused to invest any more money in the project. Certain that he would find other investors among the elite of New York City, Tesla added an elaborate 187-foot steel tower to Wardenclyffe. With the tower, Tesla boasted that not only could he distribute electric power anywhere in the world but also broadcast news, transmit telephone calls, and send facsimile messages.

But despite his contacts with the rich and powerful in New York, Tesla was unable to raise the funds needed to complete Wardenclyffe. The stress of finding investors caused Tesla to suffer a nervous

---

[72] NT, "The Problem of Increasing Human Energy", *Century*, June 1900, p. 175-211, in TC, Vol. 15, p. 19-55.

breakdown in 1904 or 1905. Supremely confident that he was basing Wardenclyffe on a perfect idea but distraught at not having the money to realize his ideal, Tesla fell apart. Over the next twenty years, Tesla worked on a bladeless turbine and automobile speedometers, but he was never quite the same again. He died penniless in New York in 1943.

Tesla's experience with both the AC motor and wireless power transmission offers insight into the nature of the innovation process in the electrical industry since the mid-nineteenth century. Perhaps the most obvious insight is that it reminds us that the development of technology involves two closely related but nonetheless separate activities: invention or idea generation and development or engineering[73]. All too often in writing about innovation, we downplay one activity or the other. Studies of inventors dwell too much on the Eureka moment, and overlook the hard work involved in converting an invention into a product. Equally, much of history of business and technology gives the inventor short shrift and dwells on the details of manufacturing and marketing. Yet both invention and development are essential for technological change.

While it would be easy to imagine that creative people in technology would be capable of doing both invention and development, the reality seems to be that these activities involve two different sets of skills, two different ways of thinking. In all likelihood, one of the few individuals that could actually do both was Edison, and that's one of the reasons why he accomplished as much as he did.

In popular jargon, inventors are folks who are good at thinking "outside the box" – of imagining what might be possible. At the same time however, the introduction of new technology also requires people who are good at bringing new ideas "inside the box" – figuring out how to manufacture and market a product, given the existing state of production technology and business practices. More often than not, the work of getting ideas "inside the box" is done by an organization, not so much because the profits are there but because development involves coordinating so many different activities. An innovative society, then, needs both idea generators (inventors) as well as developers (engineers and managers).

As Tesla's story shows, when it comes to idea generation, inventors can have a competitive advantage over large firms and laboratories.

---

[73] The notion that invention and development are distinct activities is not a new idea. In his books on Elmer Sperry and electric power, Thomas P. Hughes consistently emphasized that technological change involved both invention and development. What is new here is the idea that these activities require different skills and may be best done by different individuals or organizations. See T. P. Hughes, *Sperry, op. cit.* and *Networks of Power*, Baltimore, Johns Hopkins University Press, 1982.

Unencumbered by the practical constraints of production and marketing, inventors are able to explore new ideas and new ways of doing things. As the economist Joseph Schumpeter suggested years ago, inventors are able to follow subjective rationality – to take something that they know deeply inside and impose it on the outside world[74]. Tesla had a vision of a rotating magnetic field in the early 1880s and he manipulated alternating currents until he found a way to realize this vision. To do so, he had to do something that no practical electrician was willing to do at the time – run four (or more) wires between the generator and his motor. In contrast, because they had to keep a close eye on the competition and the needs of their customers, the engineers at Westinghouse would never have been willing to design a four-wire motor.

Tesla gained this competitive advantage in several ways. Obviously, it helped that he worked in a small laboratory with a handful of assistants; in a small group setting, it was easier to keep focused on a complex task such as developing a motor or wireless power system. But even more importantly, Tesla's promoters contributed to maintaining the focus. Peck, as we have seen, was able to provide guidance and encouragement. Brown helped Tesla by introducing the real-world constraints at the right moment – that a practical motor would need to run on two wires – and then challenging Tesla to come up with his split-phase designs. Drawing on his previous experience in the telegraph industry, Peck knew that the game to play was licensing or selling patents to the highest bidder, and he played the game exceedingly well on Tesla's behalf. Hence, to have a competitive advantage, I would argue that inventors need promoters who can help guide the invention process and facilitate the transition from invention to development.

While the motor episode reveals what promoters can contribute to the innovation process, the wireless power episode illustrates what happens when they fail to do their job. We should be impressed that Tesla ambitiously sought to create the next generation of electric power technology, but such dreams require tremendous skill to make meaningful links with the worlds of finance and business. After Peck died in 1890, Tesla never again had an effective promoter who could help him forge these links. Brown and Edward Dean Adams seem to have been unable to help Tesla strike a balance between generating new devices and converging on the most promising versions. In the depression following the Panic of 1893, they were unable to find entrepreneurs willing to buy Tesla's patents. And Tesla's own mental state did not help matters. In some ways, what is surprising about Tesla's grand scheme for wireless power around 1900 is that he got as far as he did

---

[74] I am grateful to Margaret B. W. Graham for suggesting this point to me.

with the money from Astor and Morgan; that at Colorado Springs and Wardenclyffe he was able to chase his dream so far without being tethered to capital or markets.

In the end, then, Tesla's story reminds us that innovation is very much a social and economic process. Behind every great inventor is undoubtedly a promoter who serves as an intermediary between the dream world of the inventor and the practical world of investors and users. The interaction of the inventor and the promoter are crucial to the form that a technology takes and the timing of its introduction. Equally, we need to understand the business strategy of inventors and promoters. We should not simply assume that inventors plan to manufacture their creations but that strategies of selling and licensing patents inform their creative work. This means that we need to look at how the patent systems in different countries inform the business strategy of inventors. Only by comprehending factors such as these can we come to understand why people produce the technology that they do and how we might guide the innovation process toward the future needs of society.

Recherche et innovation dans les PME

L'industrie suisse des câbles électriques (1870-1970)

Alain CORTAT

Chargé de cours et collaborateur scientifique à l'Université de Neuchâtel

L'objectif de cet article[1] est d'analyser comment deux petites entreprises de l'industrie suisse des câbles ont organisé leur R&D et comment, malgré l'absence de très grands laboratoires, elles ont continué à innover et à suivre les principaux développements de leur secteur. L'hypothèse développée postule que ces entreprises se sont lancées dans diverses formes de coopération qui permirent de pallier leur petite taille et leurs moyens financiers limités. Cette coopération passait par les écoles polytechniques et les universités, puis par l'achat de brevets à de grands groupes industriels (Bell, Siemens[2], Philips) et par la coopération technique à l'intérieur de cartels. La coopération à l'intérieur du cartel constitua, à partir de la fin des années 1960, l'essentiel de la stratégie en matière de R&D[3].

Ce texte aborde chronologiquement la création de laboratoires de R&D et leur organisation dans deux PME. L'un des premiers éléments analysés concerne la technologie : comment une nouvelle technologie – ici les bobines d'induction ou bobines Pupin – influe-t-elle sur la créa-

---

[1] Cet article s'appuie sur les archives de deux entreprises : la société anonyme de Câbleries et tréfileries de Cossonay (SACT), dont les archives sont déposées aux Archives cantonales vaudoises (désormais ACV) et la Société d'exploitation des câbles électriques, système Berthoud, Borel & Cie (SECE), aujourd'hui intégrée au groupe Nexans. La direction de l'entreprise m'a laissé un libre accès aux archives (désormais ASECE) jusqu'au début des années 1970.

[2] Pour Siemens, voir B. Dornseifer, « Strategy, Technological Capability, and Innovation : German Enterprises in Comparative Perspective » in F. Caron, P. Erker, W. Fischer, *Innovations in the European Economy between the Wars*, Berlin, New York, Walter de Gruyter, 1995, p. 216-220.

[3] On constate une situation similaire en ce qui concerne la cartellisation précoce d'un secteur dans l'aluminium, F. Hachez-Leroy, *L'aluminium français. L'invention d'un marché, 1911-1983*, Paris, CNRS Éditions, 1999, 376 p.

tion d'un laboratoire de R&D (1918-1921) ? Un second point tentera de montrer comment un retard pris dans une technologie – des produits défectueux – donne aussi naissance à la R&D et à l'application d'une démarche plus scientifique dans le travail de l'entreprise (1920-1925). Après avoir étudié ces deux points, nous mettrons en évidence la volonté d'indépendance des ingénieurs des laboratoires par rapport à la production et notamment par rapport aux contrôles de fabrication[4], qui sont essentiels pour une câblerie, en raison de la sécurité et du coût élevé de la pose. Cette situation conduit les deux firmes étudiées à mettre en place une organisation spécifique des laboratoires : on les maintient proches de certains ateliers, mais, dans le même temps, on centralise tous les laboratoires en seul lieu. Notre texte soulèvera aussi la question des liens avec les institutions publiques de recherche[5]. Nous montrons comment une école d'ingénieur est à l'origine d'une entreprise et le développement de la collaboration entre firme et laboratoire public au moment où la firme lance ses premiers travaux de R&D.

Nous analyserons aussi ces liens dans la longue durée et nous montrerons que lorsque l'entreprise dispose de son propre laboratoire, les rapports se distendent et que seules se maintiennent des relations personnelles. Ces dernières jouent toutefois un rôle important pour les ingénieurs des laboratoires, c'est du moins notre hypothèse.

Enfin, nous aborderons la collaboration entre firmes dans l'espace national[6], mais aussi la collaboration internationale. Cet aspect est spécifique à l'industrie en question, dans le sens où elle est organisée en cartels au niveau suisse depuis le début du XXe siècle et au niveau international depuis le milieu des années 1920. Or, ces cartels se caractérisent par une stabilité élevée[7] ce qui permet aux firmes de les prendre en compte dans leur stratégie à long terme. Dès les années 1960 les plus

---

[4] M. Le Roux, *L'entreprise et la recherche : un siècle de recherche industrielle à Pechiney*, Paris, Éditions Rive droite, 1998, p. 89.

[5] Pour une comparaison avec un autre secteur, voir en particulier : N. Chézeau, *De la forge au laboratoire. Naissance de la métallurgie physique (1860-1914)*, Rennes, Presses universitaires de Rennes, 2004, p. 92 s.

[6] Pour une vue plus globale sur l'innovation en Suisse, voir H.-J. Gilomen, R. Jaun, M. Müller, B. Veyrassat (dir.), *Innovations. Incitations et résistances des sources de l'innovation à ses effets*, Zurich, Société suisse d'histoire économique & Chronos, 2001.

[7] Cette stabilité s'explique en partie par le fait que les principaux clients sont des régies contrôlées par les états, qui tendent à favoriser les entreprises nationales. On peut aussi citer le fait qu'il y a un petit nombre d'acteurs et le coût d'entrée élevé. Pour une étude sur la durée des cartels : P. Z. Grossman (ed.), *How Cartels Endure and How They Fail : Studies of Industrial Collusion*, Cheltenham, Edward Elgar Pub, 2004, 324 p. et en particulier l'article d'introduction : P. Z. Grossman, « Introduction : What Do We Mean by Cartel Success ? », p. 1-8.

importants travaux de R&D des câbleries suisses sont menés par le cartel et non plus de manière indépendante par les firmes.

Trois entreprises se partagent le marché des câbles en Suisse[8]. La première société est fondée en 1878 par Édouard Berthoud, un horloger neuchâtelois, et François Borel, un ingénieur de l'École polytechnique fédérale de Zurich. Ils installent leur société à Paris en 1879 mais la liquident suite à la faillite de la banque l'Union générale en 1882. Dès 1883, ils reviennent en Suisse, à Cortaillod, et leur société prend dès lors la dénomination de Société d'exploitation des câbles électriques, système Berthoud, Borel & Cie (SECE). À la fin des années 1890, deux autres câbleries sont créées, Aubert, Grenier & Cie qui devient dès 1923 la société anonyme de Câbleries et tréfileries de Cossonay (SACT) et enfin les Câbles de Brugg. Depuis 1923, la SECE possède une participation de 51 % dans la SACT. De plus, la SECE a créé deux sociétés à l'étranger, une à Lyon (1896), dont elle cède très tôt le contrôle à des partenaires français et qui est reprise par la Compagnie générale d'électricité (CGE) dès 1912 et une autre à Mannheim (1899) avec d'autres partenaires auxquels elle cède la majeure partie de sa participation. Ces trois entreprises sont les seules, en Suisse, à fabriquer des câbles papier-plomb, qui servent au transport de l'électricité et à la téléphonie.

Depuis 1907, ces trois câbleries sont organisées en cartel. Elles se sont engagées à s'annoncer mutuellement toutes les grandes commandes et à respecter un niveau de prix. Ces accords se prolongent jusqu'à la fin des années 1920, avec une interruption durant la guerre. En 1928, la création d'un cartel international incite les trois câbleries à signer un accord plus complet, ceci en vue de s'intégrer à la nouvelle entente internationale, l'International Cable Development Corporation (ICDC)[9], qui est active jusque dans les années 1980, avec une interruption durant la Seconde Guerre mondiale. La convention cartellaire signée en 1928 fixe les prix et introduit un contingent pour chaque firme. Cette convention, modifiée sur des points de détail, est prorogée jusqu'en 1943. À cette date, un nouveau contrat est signé, contrat qui introduit une première coopération technique, notamment la standardisation de certaines pièces. Elle est ensuite reconduite à deux reprises pour dix ans, en 1953

---

[8] Pour une histoire de l'électricité en Suisse, voir en particulier : S. Paquier, *Histoire de l'électricité en Suisse. La dynamique d'un petit pays européen, 1875-1939*, Genève, Passé Présent, 1998.

[9] A. Cortat, « Entreprises suisses et cartels internationaux : le cartel international des câbles (1928-1980) » in *Relations internationales et affaires étrangères suisses après 1945*, Lausanne, Antipodes, 2006, p. 147-164 (actes du colloque CUSO 2005). Et pour une étude plus détaillée : Alain Cortat, *Un cartel parfait. Réseaux, R&D et profits dans l'industrie suisse des câbles*, Neuchâtel, Alphil, 2009, 623 p.

et en 1963 et elle est renouvelée en 1968. Ce nouvel accord introduit pour la première fois des organes officiels et il renforce la coopération technique ; il est à l'origine de la création de plusieurs sociétés communes, notamment pour l'exportation et pour la R&D[10].

Recherche et développement : l'atelier (1875-1918)

Les premiers travaux de recherche et développement (R&D) en matière de câbles électriques en Suisse furent conduits par François Borel. En 1878, il mit au point sa fameuse presse à plomb qui lui permit de fabriquer des câbles électriques souterrains. Dès 1879, il travaillait dans l'entreprise qu'il avait fondée en tant que directeur technique et responsable du développement des produits. Pendant longtemps, il fut le seul ingénieur de l'entreprise et il effectuait tous les travaux de pose, de vérifications techniques et de développements. Il s'entoura toutefois d'ingénieurs qui prirent en charge la pose et une partie de la production, alors que lui-même se spécialisait dans les travaux de R&D. Toutefois, lorsqu'il prit sa retraite en 1904, il ne fut pas remplacé et la R&D ne fit plus l'objet de travaux spéciaux, excepté les améliorations continuelles introduites par les responsables de la production.

À la suite du départ de François Borel, le conseil d'administration envisagea à plusieurs reprises la construction d'un laboratoire ou le recrutement d'un ingénieur de laboratoire, mais aucune action concrète ne fut entreprise. Seule l'ancienne filiale lyonnaise créa un laboratoire[11]. Lorsque la Première Guerre mondiale éclata, les Câbles de Cortaillod disposaient d'un laboratoire de contrôle de fabrication, mais ils n'avaient pas encore mis au point une véritable R&D.

En 1898, une seconde câblerie est créée à Cossonay dans le canton de Vaud, elle s'intitule Aubert & Cie et dès 1902 Aubert, Grenier & Cie. Si les archives ne nous éclairent pas sur sa création, le contexte de sa naissance nous permet toutefois de souligner l'influence de l'École d'ingénieurs de l'université de Lausanne (EIUL)[12]. Le fondateur, Jean Marcel Aubert, est un jeune diplômé de l'EIUL, il n'a que 23 ans et il a fréquenté deux grands spécialistes de l'électricité et de son transport en Suisse : Adrien Palaz et William Grenier, tous deux professeurs à l'EIUL qui le soutiennent dans son projet.

---

[10] Pour une vue générale sur l'histoire des cartels en Europe, voir H. Schröter, « Cartelization and Decartelization in Europe, 1870-1995 : Rise and Decline of an Economic Institution », *Journal of European Economic History*, n° 25(1), 1996, p. 129-153.

[11] ASECE, PVCA 18 août 1906, 19 décembre 1906, 30 janvier 1907, 31 janvier 1907 et 20 février 1907.

[12] Cette école devint l'École polytechnique de l'université de Lausanne (EPUL) en 1946 puis l'École polytechnique fédérale de Lausanne (EPFL) en 1969.

Les archives de l'entreprise, très éparses jusqu'aux années 1920, ne nous permettent pas de comprendre comment s'effectuent l'innovation et la R&D durant cette période. On peut émettre quelques hypothèses à partir d'indices. Très tôt, comme à Cortaillod, un laboratoire de contrôle des produits finis est mis en place. Il est certain qu'il est utilisé pour la R&D, mais celle-ci ne semble pas être organisée d'une manière spécifique. Tout ce que l'on peut constater, c'est que plusieurs ingénieurs et contremaîtres allemands sont engagés pour développer certaines productions (caoutchouc, appareillage électrique, etc.). Les nouveaux produits sont en principe développés par les responsables des ateliers. La R&D est donc le fait des ateliers et non d'un laboratoire spécifique[13].

De l'atelier aux premiers laboratoires de R&D (1918-1930)

Deux événements vont contribuer à la création des laboratoires de R&D à Cossonay et à Cortaillod après la Première Guerre mondiale : l'introduction d'une nouvelle technologie, les bobines d'induction[14], et des problèmes de qualité de certains câbles. Il faut y ajouter un facteur évidemment favorable avec l'importance des bénéfices réalisés durant la guerre.

Aubert, Grenier & Cie (SACT dès 1923) à Cossonay : une nouvelle technologie à l'origine du laboratoire de R&D

Michael Pupin, l'inventeur des bobines d'induction avait signé en 1902 un contrat de licence avec Werner von Siemens pour tous les pays du monde, à l'exclusion de l'Amérique du Nord et de l'Amérique du Sud, où le brevet était exploité par la Western Electric. Or, à la fin de la Première Guerre mondiale, ce brevet tomba dans le domaine public et pouvait dès lors être exploité par d'autres compagnies. L'enjeu de cette technique était énorme, car dès les années 1920, toutes les lignes téléphoniques à longue distance en furent équipées. En Suisse, la construction des lignes interurbaines équipées de bobines Pupin ouvrit un marché colossal aux fabricants de câbles. Au terme de la Première Guerre mondiale, les trois câbleries cherchèrent à acquérir cette nouvelle tech-

---

[13] Muriel Le Roux a montré une situation identique dans l'aluminium où la recherche reste très longtemps dans les mains des ingénieurs de production. M. Le Roux, *L'entreprise et la recherche : un siècle de recherche industrielle à Pechiney*, Paris, Éditions Rive droite, 1998, p. 80-89.

[14] Afin de transmettre les communications, la voix est transformée en signal électrique qui parcourt les câbles et qui s'affaiblit avec la distance. Pour compenser cet affaiblissement, on pose tous les 1830 mètres des amplificateurs qui se présentent sous la forme d'une bobine électrique avec un circuit magnétique que l'on appelle bobines Pupin, du nom de son inventeur Michael Pupin (1858-1935).

nique et, après avoir essayé de s'entendre pour produire ensemble ces bobines Pupin, chacune développa sa solution[15].

La société Aubert, Grenier & Cie choisit de produire ses propres bobines et dès la fin de la Première Guerre mondiale, elle créa un laboratoire de recherches. Ce premier laboratoire était dirigé par Kurt von Wysiecki, un ingénieur allemand, secondé par deux compatriotes[16]. Deux autres ingénieurs suisses collaborèrent à ce projet, Édouard Tissot, ingénieur électricien de l'EPFZ, né à Genève en 1896 et fils d'un membre du conseil d'administration, et qui travailla dans l'entreprise de 1920 à 1922, ainsi que Max de Reding, qui quittera l'entreprise en 1921 pour travailler dans une câblerie concurrente. Ce laboratoire fut installé à Lausanne et non pas dans l'usine à Cossonay, en raison de la proximité avec le laboratoire d'électricité de l'EIUL. En fait, la direction de l'entreprise et celle de l'école d'ingénieur ont passé un accord : les ingénieurs pouvaient utiliser les installations de l'EIUL contre le versement de 200 000 francs pour le développement du laboratoire (1918)[17]. À cette époque, l'entreprise et ses ingénieurs collaborèrent régulièrement avec un professeur de l'EIUL, célèbre pour ses travaux en matière d'électricité, Jean Landry (1875-1940)[18], diplômé de l'EPFZ (1898). Il a travaillé à la Compagnie de l'industrie électrique à Genève (futurs Ateliers de Sécheron) aux côtés de René Thury, puis avait créé, en 1903, avec René Neeser, un bureau d'ingénieur-conseil. Parallèlement, il commença à enseigner à l'EIUL en tant que professeur extraordinaire de construction électromécanique. En 1916, il devint professeur ordinaire, poste qu'il occupa jusqu'en 1940. Il dirigea la construction du barrage de la petite Dixence et il fut l'initiateur de la société anonyme de l'Énergie de l'ouest suisse (EOS) qui érigea un réseau de lignes de transport d'électricité, afin de relier les différents réseaux suisses romands. L'EOS devint petit à petit un fournisseur d'électricité par l'acquisition de barrages et par la construction de celui sur la Dixence[19].

---

[15] ASECE, PVCA 17 décembre 1919.

[16] ACV PP 632/7/4, Les Pupins.

[17] ACV, PP 632/16, Lettre de Aubert, Grenier & Cie aux Usines métallurgiques suisses de Dornach, du 13 mai 1918. Dans cette lettre, le conseil de surveillance d'Aubert, Grenier & Cie qui négocie la fusion avec les Usines métallurgiques de Dornach, exige que ce don soit effectué.

[18] Serge Paquier, « Une étude des relations entre hautes écoles techniques et performances d'un secteur industriel en Suisse (1880-1914) » in *La naissance de l'ingénieur-électricien. Origines et développement des formations nationales électrotechniques*, Paris, Association pour l'histoire de l'électricité en France/PUF, 1997, p. 271.

[19] Serge Paquier, « La SA Énergie-Ouest Suisse de 1919 à 1936 », *Bulletin d'histoire de l'électricité*, n° 13, 1989, p. 63-82 et Serge Paquier, « Contribution à l'histoire des

Jean Landry cumule à l'époque les postes de directeur de l'EIUL et de directeur du laboratoire d'électricité. Il est aussi ingénieur conseil d'Aubert, Grenier & Cie où il se rend près d'une fois par semaine pour surveiller la production. En 1914, il avait permis à l'entreprise de remporter la pose d'un câble téléphonique d'un nouveau type entre Bâle et Zurich, le câble Krarup. Jean Landry revenait alors d'un séjour aux États-Unis où il s'était intéressé à cette nouvelle technique.

À la fin de 1919 ou en 1920, le laboratoire de la SACT fut transféré de Lausanne à l'usine de Cossonay et des ingénieurs issus de l'EIUL furent engagés, en particulier Eugène Foretay (1895-1968), qui avait travaillé dans le bureau d'études de Jean Landry et au laboratoire d'électricité industrielle de l'EIUL avant d'entrer à la câblerie (1920). Avec le développement des bobines Pupin, c'est la première fois que l'entreprise disposait d'ingénieurs qui s'occupaient exclusivement de R&D. Les nouveaux ingénieurs vont petit à petit étendre leurs travaux à l'ensemble des produits de l'entreprise, c'est-à-dire aux câbles à courant fort, aux fils isolés pour machines, etc.

La SECE à Cortaillod : la R&D pour combler les difficultés techniques

Dans la seconde câblerie à Cortaillod, les choses évoluent différemment, mais le résultat sera le même à savoir la création d'un premier laboratoire de R&D au début des années 1920. Pour les bobines Pupin et les câbles à courant faible, la SECE choisit de produire selon les procédés de la Western Electric. Elle signa un contrat de licence avec cette dernière qui fournit son savoir-faire et mit des ingénieurs à disposition pendant quelques semaines. De son côté, la SECE envoya deux ingénieurs et deux ouvriers se former aux États-Unis et elle n'engagea pas de programme de R&D en la matière.

La création du laboratoire de R&D à la SECE fut liée à la qualité de câbles posés au début des années 1920. En fait, un câble livré aux CFF et posé dans le tunnel du Gothard fonctionnait à la moitié de la tension prévue et des tronçons claquèrent. L'affaire était d'importance puisque 500 000 francs étaient en jeu. L'entreprise dut alors entièrement revoir la composition de ses câbles et la qualité des produits isolants utilisés (papier, huiles, résine, etc.) ainsi que chercher de nouvelles techniques de fabrication en vue d'assurer une meilleure qualité[20].

Afin de résoudre ces problèmes, le conseil d'administration engage un ingénieur chimiste pour contrôler la qualité des produits et « un

réseaux électriques romands de 1880 à 1936 : l'exemple vaudois », *Revue historique vaudoise*, 1992, p. 129-172.
[20] ASECE, PVCA 30 janvier 1918, 25 février 1920. Et ASECE, PVCA 18 mai 1921.

ingénieur qui s'occupe uniquement des recherches »[21]. Le chimiste n'est autre que James Borel (1896-1948), neveu de l'ancien directeur François Borel, docteur en sciences, chimiste, qui prit ses fonctions en août 1921 et fut chargé du contrôle qualité des matières premières. Le second ingénieur, engagé en 1922 et spécialement chargé de diriger un « laboratoire d'essai », était Walter Schmidt. Avant d'occuper ce poste, il avait travaillé dix ans au laboratoire de Brown Boveri. L'arrivée de Walter Schmidt représentait bien plus que le simple engagement d'un ingénieur, il s'agissait de la mise en place d'un véritable laboratoire de R&D, avec une réorganisation complète des fonctions, l'engagement de personnel auxiliaire et des investissements pour les appareils techniques. Dès lors, le directeur technique Arnold Borel dut se cantonner à la production, alors que le nouveau venu fut chargé des recherches. Un système pour regrouper et faire circuler l'information fut mis au point En fait, pour la première fois, comme l'exprime l'un des membres du conseil d'administration, il y avait « une distinction entre la fabrication et les essais et travaux de recherches »[22]. Dès lors, l'entreprise distingua les laboratoires de fabrication (contrôle des produits finis), d'essai et de chimie.

Les démarches de l'entreprise ne s'arrêtèrent pas à ces mesures et la direction se mit en rapport avec les Câbles de Lyon, en vue de travailler en commun sur les problèmes des câbles. L'usine de Lyon disposait à ce moment-là d'une avance technique sur la SECE, en raison de la mise sur pied d'un laboratoire de recherches quelques années auparavant. Plusieurs voyages furent effectués à Lyon et les techniciens de la SECE améliorèrent leurs connaissances des câbles à haute tension grâce à ces échanges. Très rapidement, les techniciens de Cortaillod prirent conscience de la nécessité de compléter leur laboratoire et de mettre au point des méthodes de travail nouvelles. Ainsi Louis Thormann, ingénieur et membre du conseil d'administration, ne manqua pas de souligner, après une visite à Lyon, la nécessité de compléter le matériel du laboratoire et de « former des dossiers complets permettant de savoir exactement à quels effets aboutit chaque méthode de fabrication »[23]. En 1927, le contrat de Walter Schmidt ne fut pas reconduit[24]. L'entreprise rencontra des difficultés pour trouver un nouveau chef de laboratoire et le poste ne

---

[21]   ASECE, PVCA 30 novembre 1921. Voir aussi : ASECE, PVCA 18 mai 1921, 30 novembre 1921.

[22]   ASECE, PVCA 19 avril 1922. Voir aussi : ASECE, PVCA, 21 décembre 1921, 28 juin 1922, ASECE, PV du bureau 10 février 1922.

[23]   ASECE, PVCA 17 mai 1922. Voir aussi : ASECE, PVCA 18 mai 1921, 15 juin 1921, 19 avril 1922.

[24]   ASECE, PVCA 18 février 1925, 19 décembre 1927, 20 mars 1929.

fut pas renouvelé ; dans les faits, James Borel prit la direction du laboratoire de R&D.

La nouvelle organisation de la R&D porta ses fruits puisque, lors d'une discussion à propos d'une commande pour le Gothard en 1925, le directeur put répondre au conseil d'administration :

> Dès que les premières défectuosités eurent été constatées des recherches approfondies furent entreprises pour déterminer de manière scientifique les conditions scientifiques d'une fabrication qui jusqu'alors s'était poursuivie d'une manière quelque peu empirique. Le laboratoire qui a été développé dans ce but a permis de préciser les matières à employer et surtout celles qui doivent être écartées. Aujourd'hui on peut admettre qu'on sait où l'on va.[25]

Développement des laboratoires et séparation entre contrôles et R&D (1930-1955)

Les années 1930 sont marquées par la modernisation des laboratoires et l'introduction de nouvelles méthodes de travail des ingénieurs chargés de la R&D. À tour de rôle, les deux entreprises augmentent la capacité des laboratoires à tester les tensions des câbles. Ces installations doivent en premier lieu servir à contrôler les produits finis avant leur pose, mais elles vont aussi servir à la R&D.

Un homme joue un rôle clef dans la modernisation des méthodes des laboratoires de Cossonay, c'est Robert Goldschmidt (1902-1984), qui fuit le régime nazi et est engagé en 1933 par la SACT. Il est diplômé de l'École polytechnique de Karlsruhe (1924) et il a travaillé au laboratoire des télécommunications d'AEG. Il fait toute sa carrière dans les laboratoires de la SACT et dès 1946, il consacre une partie de son activité à l'enseignement à l'EPUL. Dès son arrivée, il introduit de nouvelles pratiques, ses démarches aboutissent à la rédaction systématique de rapports de recherches, à la création d'un service de documentation et au repérage systématique et régulier des brevets (tous les six mois un ingénieur est envoyé au bureau fédéral des brevets)[26].

Du milieu des années 1930 aux années 1950, deux éléments président à l'évolution des laboratoires. Le premier concerne la volonté, longuement revendiquée par les ingénieurs, de séparer les contrôles de fabrication et la R&D. Le second touche à la création de laboratoires spécialisés qui assurent de nouvelles tâches. Dans ce chapitre nous

---

[25] ASECE, PVCA 21 octobre 1925.

[26] ACV, PP 632/139, Rapport mensuel, 1er novembre 1933, Atelier Pupin. Le fait que le rapport soit en français pourrait laisser penser qu'il n'est pas de la main de Robert Goldschmidt. Dans tous les cas, son arrivée semble fédérer les énergies au sein de l'entreprise, à cela s'ajoute la construction récente du laboratoire de câblerie, qui est probablement un élément important de cette réorganisation.

traitons essentiellement du cas de la SACT, car les archives de la SECE pour cette période ont été détruites. Toutefois, les deux entreprises se trouvent dans une situation identique à la fin des années 1950.

Dans les câbleries, le rôle premier des laboratoires a toujours été le contrôle de la fabrication. Logiquement, les équipements des laboratoires sont d'abord utilisés pour les contrôles et ensuite seulement pour la R&D. Les ingénieurs des laboratoires revendiquent donc constamment la séparation des fonctions et la possibilité de se consacrer à la R&D. Dès son arrivée en 1933, Robert Goldschmidt sépare le laboratoire des bobines Pupin en deux secteurs[27]. Le chef des laboratoires, Eugène Foretay envoie plusieurs rapports à la direction pour revendiquer cette séparation et la création d'un véritable laboratoire de recherches[28].

Les ingénieurs des laboratoires n'obtiendront pas satisfaction avant le milieu des années 1950. Toutefois, pour atteindre leur but, ils vont passer par une étape intermédiaire, la création de laboratoires spécialisés. C'est une fois de plus de Robert Goldschmidt et du laboratoire des bobines Pupin que vient le changement. L'un des enjeux cruciaux de la fabrication des bobines Pupin est le noyau central, qui doit être miniaturisé, tout en conservant son effet d'impulsion (magnétisme). Les recherches de Goldschmidt dans ce domaine lui font très vite prendre conscience de la nécessité de contrôler les matières premières. C'est pour cela qu'il met en place un embryon de laboratoire de chimie en 1940[29]. Peu de temps auparavant, en 1938, un laboratoire de mécanique est mis en place. Ce laboratoire réunit l'ensemble des machines de contrôle des métaux qui étaient antérieurement disséminées dans l'entreprise. De ce laboratoire naîtra durant les années 1940 un laboratoire de physique. Ces créations permettent surtout de nommer un responsable, le plus souvent un ingénieur qui n'est plus accaparé par les contrôles des câbles.

Cette évolution, d'abord informelle, donne lieu à une structure de laboratoires, qui est officiellement réorganisée en 1951, avec la coexistence de sept laboratoires aux attributions distinctes : physique, mécanique, chimie, haute fréquence, courant faible, courant fort, études et

---

[27] ACV PP 632/139, Rapport des travaux de l'atelier Pupin, pendant le mois de novembre 1933. Rapport n° 3398.

[28] ACV PP 632/157, Rapport du laboratoire, Foretay, 5 août 1938, n° 38077.

[29] ACV PP 632/7/4, Les pupins, 1919-1973, p. 31. Ainsi que : PP 632/148, *Programme de renouvellement, d'amélioration et d'augmentation des moyens de production et de contrôle de la fabrication et d'essais des matières premières*. Rapport du département 13, n° 4529, Fernand Chalet, 16 juillet 1945. En particulier l'annexe avec la mention des appareils de laboratoire achetés « tout spécialement pour le laboratoire de contrôle des matières premières ».

recherches, ainsi qu'un département des bobines Pupin qui développe les fameuses bobines et qui collabore avec les laboratoires cités. S'y ajoute un laboratoire des plastiques dans les années 1960. Depuis la fin des années 1920 jusqu'au milieu des années 1950, la grande évolution des laboratoires est la professionnalisation. Alors qu'auparavant la recherche était aux mains d'ingénieurs de production, on assiste à l'émergence de professionnels qui se consacrent presque exclusivement à la R&D[30]. Cette évolution donne lieu à des revendications de statuts dans l'entreprise, les ingénieurs de la R&D étant souvent privés de titres, alors que les ingénieurs de la production bénéficient de titres de chef d'atelier, fondés de pouvoir, de sous-directeurs, etc.

L'emplacement des laboratoires dans l'usine

La disposition des laboratoires résulte de la nécessité de la production. Les laboratoires sont disséminés dans l'entreprise, le plus souvent à proximité des ateliers, de telle sorte que les contrôles de fabrication puissent s'effectuer sans difficultés. Ainsi, les laboratoires des courants faibles et des courants forts sont à proximité des ateliers de fabrication des câbles téléphoniques et des câbles d'énergie. De même, le laboratoire de mécanique est à proximité de l'atelier de tréfilerie[31]. L'emplacement des autres laboratoires est la plupart du temps déterminé par la place laissée vacante lorsqu'un nouveau bâtiment est construit pour un département[32].

Or, dès la fin des années 1940, l'entreprise envisage la construction de nouveaux locaux pour les laboratoires, en raison de l'achat d'équipements techniques qui exigent de grands espaces. La question classique de tels projets est soulevée : faut-il laisser les laboratoires à proximité des ateliers ou créer un bâtiment *ad hoc* ? La solution choisie par la SACT est un compromis entre ces deux alternatives. Eugène Foretay, chef des laboratoires explique clairement ce choix :

La condition primordiale pour un bon travail est une collaboration étroite entre tous les laboratoires ; elle est facilitée si les laboratoires se trouvent près les uns des autres. Ceci nous amène à proposer une centralisation des laboratoires. Le centre « Laboratoire » doit-il être distant ou au contraire aussi près que possible des ateliers de fabrication ? La première solution, si elle présente l'avantage de faciliter des agrandissements successifs, allonge et complique les transports des produits à examiner et diminue les contacts avec la fabrication. Dans l'idée que l'agrandissement prévu aujourd'hui de-

---

[30] Muriel Le Roux, *L'entreprise et la recherche : un siècle de recherche industrielle à Pechiney*. Paris, Éditions Rive droite, 1998, p. 221 s.

[31] *Ibid.*, p. 80 et p. 173.

[32] Bulletin SACT, n° 12, décembre 1955.

vrait suffire pour plusieurs dizaines d'années, nous préférons placer les laboratoires au centre de la fabrication, c'est-à-dire entre la câblerie et l'atelier des fils isolés.[33]

Cette solution, qui est réalisée en 1955-1956, permet la centralisation des laboratoires et des échanges entre ingénieurs, tout en permettant de contrôler les câbles sans difficultés et sans transport.

Organiser la R&D

Pour des PME telles que la SACT et la SECE, disposer de laboratoires de R&D et d'une équipe de recherche d'une quinzaine d'ingénieurs (environ deux personnes par laboratoire), ne suffit pas pour rester à la pointe de la technique. À l'étranger, les concurrents potentiels sont de grands groupes d'électrotechnique tels que Siemens & Halske et Pirelli ou des câbleries implantées dans plusieurs pays tels que Felten & Guilleaume. Dès lors, se pose la question des stratégies mises au point pour se maintenir à la pointe de la technologie.

Les réponses données par ces PME sont diverses, mais la principale, celle qui détermine toute la stratégie des câbleries depuis les années 1960 est le cartel. Nous y reviendrons. Ces entreprises développent d'autres solutions : la coopération avec les laboratoires publics, les échanges avec d'autres câbleries ou sociétés nationales et internationales et le recours à des bureaux d'études.

La coopération avec les laboratoires publics et les écoles techniques

La collaboration avec les laboratoires publics, en particulier ceux des universités et des écoles d'ingénieurs, prend deux formes : des échanges réguliers formels et informels entre l'entreprise et des professeurs, ainsi que l'utilisation ponctuelle d'installations publiques.

Nous avons déjà montré l'importance de l'EIUL pour la création d'Aubert, Grenier & Cie, à travers l'utilisation du laboratoire d'électricité de cette école après la Première Guerre mondiale, les travaux de Jean Landry comme ingénieur-conseil et le don de 200 000 francs en 1918 pour le laboratoire d'électricité.

Dans les années 1920, les relations avec l'EIUL et l'EPFZ deviennent plus distantes. Toutefois, il ne faut pas négliger l'importance des réseaux et des relations personnelles. Plusieurs indices montrent que les entreprises restent en contact avec certains professeurs de ces écoles. Jean Landry, qui est l'initiateur d'EOS, est, par exemple, probablement

---

[33] PP 632/81 Divers, *Centralisation et agrandissement des laboratoires*, 15 mars 1955.

en contact régulier avec les responsables de la production des lignes aériennes à Cossonay. Dans les années 1930, ces contacts se resserrent. Robert Goldschmidt visite régulièrement des professeurs de l'EPFZ à Zurich[34], notamment à la fin de la décennie, lorsque des câbles à haute fréquence sont mis au point pour la télévision. De même, lorsque, à la même époque, les plastiques font leur entrée dans certains mélanges d'isolation, des contacts sont établis avec un chimiste de l'École de chimie de Genève[35]. Enfin, les rapports de voyage des ingénieurs font systématiquement référence à des rencontres avec des professeurs de l'EPFZ et des autres universités lors de journées scientifiques en Suisse[36] ou à l'étranger (par exemple lors de la Conférence internationale et annuelle des grands réseaux électriques)[37]. Enfin, dans les années 1940 et 1950 les liens entre la SACT et l'EPUL sont renforcés par la nomination de Robert Goldschmidt comme chargé de cours (1946), puis professeur extraordinaire (1954), bien qu'il continue à travailler pour l'entreprise. De même, le responsable du laboratoire de la câblerie, Jean-Jacques Morf (1922-2003) quitte l'entreprise en 1954 pour un poste de professeur à l'EPUL.

Bien que les contacts soient réguliers entre les ingénieurs des câbleries et les scientifiques, ni la SACT ni la SECE ne confient de grands mandats aux laboratoires des écoles polytechniques. Elles ont recours à quelques reprises par décennie à ces laboratoires, mais uniquement lorsqu'il s'agit d'utiliser un équipement très spécifique pour un test[38]. La situation est identique en ce qui concerne les grands laboratoires publics tels que le Laboratoire fédéral pour l'essai des matériaux et l'Institut de recherche pour l'industrie, la construction et les arts et métiers, plus

---

[34] ACV, PP 632/142, 3802, Rapport de l'atelier 21, Reise Zürich, 5/6 II, 1938.

[35] ACV, PP 632/141, Rapport de l'atelier 21, pendant le mois d'octobre 1937.

[36] Kunststofftagung, 5/6 1938 où à l'assemblée générale de l'Abteilung für Industrielle Forschung AFIF, un institut de l'EPFZ en partie financé par l'industrie privée ou encore à la section de physique de la Société Suisse des sciences naturelles lors de sa journée annuelle, etc. ACV PP 632/140, *Concerne l'assemblée de la Société Helvétique des Sciences Naturelles à Soleure, du 28 au 30 août 1936.* Rapport de l'atelier Pupin, n° 3619. ACV PP 632/144, *Assemblée de l'AFIF à ZH (ETH) du 1er février 1940.* Rapport de l'atelier 21, n° 4001. ACV PP 632/142, *Reise Zürich, 5/6 II, 1938. 1. Kunststofftagung Zürich, 5/6 février 1938. 2. Cyclotronvortrag Prof. Scherrer, 6 février 1938. 3. Besprechung mit Dr. Frey, Ciba Basel, 5 février 1938. 4. Rücksprache mit Prof. Tank, HF-Kabel. 5. Rücksprache mit Prof. Forrer, Nationalausstellung 1939.* Rapport de l'atelier 21, n° 3802.

[37] Voir en particulier les publications annuelles de la CIGRE avec la liste des participants.

[38] ACV, PP 632/161, 47276. Essais mécaniques de plomb. Rapport du laboratoire, Eugène Foretay, le 20 février 1947.

connu sous son acronyme allemand EMPA[39]. La SACT ne lui confie que quelques tests dans les années 1940 et 1950 lorsqu'elle ne dispose pas des appareils de laboratoire nécessaires[40].

Les échanges avec d'autres câbleries ou sociétés nationales et internationales

Les câbleries de Cossonay et de Cortaillod forment ensemble, au niveau suisse, un grand groupe industriel avec de nombreuses participations dans d'autres sociétés de leurs branches. Elles contrôlent environ les deux tiers de la tréfilerie des métaux non-ferreux, de la fabrication des câbles, de la transformation des métaux non-ferreux et elles sont propriétaires d'un des plus grands fabricants d'appareillage électrique en Suisse, l'Appareillage Gardy à Genève. Pourtant, aucune recherche commune n'est organisée, aucun laboratoire central n'est construit. Les ingénieurs des laboratoires visitent de temps à autre les installations des entreprises partenaires[41]. Ces visites servent soit à régler des problèmes ponctuels, soit à examiner les installations pour la création d'un laboratoire ou pour le renouvellement d'un équipement.

Les deux câbleries collaborent régulièrement avec des entreprises étrangères. Cette coopération prend diverses formes. Ainsi, la SECE met au point avec les Câbles de Lyon une collaboration technique très étendue. En 1935, les deux entreprises signent un accord en vue de « l'amélioration de la fabrication des câbles électriques [...] [et] l'étude de la fabrication et de la pose des câbles à courant fort (câbles à huile exceptés), ainsi que toute recherche relative à ces câbles »[42]. Cet accord donne lieu à des réunions régulières des directeurs et des ingénieurs de

---

[39] EMPA : Eidg. Materialprüfungs- und Versuchsanstalt für Industrie, Bauwesen und Gewerbe.

[40] ACV PP 632/169, *M. Werdenberg, (Complément à mes fiches 4 & 5 du 12 juillet 1951).* Sans cote, sans auteur. Probablement rédigé par le responsable du laboratoire des matériaux ou de chimie de SACT.

[41] ACV PP 632/164, *Visite aux usines métallurgiques de Dornach, Cristina, le 14 décembre 1948.* Rapport du laboratoire phys. chimie n° 48377bis. ACV PP 632/165, *Visite aux laboratoires de contrôle de matériaux des PTT, Cristina, 30 avril 1949.* Rapport du laboratoire de chimie, C49396. ACV PP 632/165, *Visites à Bâle et Dornach, Eugène Foretay, 28 mai 1949.* Rapport de voyage n° 49400. ACV PP 632/165, *Visite aux laboratoires de l'ASE. Cristina, 22 novembre 1949.* Rapport du laboratoire de chimie n° 4906. ACV PP 632/164, *Visite à la câblerie de Cortaillod. Foretay, laboratoires, 17 juillet 1948.* Rapport de voyage n° 48358. ACV PP 632/163, *Visite à M. Sandmeier, PTT Berne. Eugène Foretay, 25 avril 1948.* Rapport de voyage n° 48340. ACV PP 632/166, *Visite aux laboratoires de l'ASE, Cristina, 22 novembre 1949.* Rapport n° 49431bis.

[42] ASECE, dossier Lyon-Cortaillod, *Annexe au Procès-verbal de la 5e séance du C.D. et de la 6e séance du C.T. Lyon-Cortaillod.* Cortaillod, le 8 février 1937. Accord portant la signature des directions des deux sociétés.

laboratoire (tous les trois mois environ), à Cortaillod ou à Lyon et souvent à Genève. Dans un premier temps, ils comparent les techniques et les méthodes en usage dans les deux sociétés et ils effectuent une mise au point de l'état des recherches passées et en cours. Il s'agit en fait de permettre aux « services techniques [...] [d'] apprendre à se connaître et de prendre l'habitude de travailler en commun ». Un des premiers éléments de cette coopération consiste en l'étude du laboratoire des Câbles de Lyon, inauguré en 1930, par les ingénieurs de Cortaillod qui travaillent à la création de leur laboratoire pour les courants forts, construit de 1936 à 1937. Le second élément de cette coopération est l'échange de licences et le lancement d'études communes, chaque partie s'occupant d'un aspect des recherches[43].

De 1936 à 1940, la collaboration est fructueuse. Les deux entreprises décident en commun le lancement de programmes de recherches et se partagent le travail. Les études portent sur tous les aspects techniques des câbles et de leur fabrication : composition des alliages des métaux, composition des isolants, techniques de pose des isolants, études des boîtes d'extrémités, etc. Les procès-verbaux de ces études fourmillent d'échanges de comptes-rendus d'essais[44].

Cette collaboration est très importante et implique fortement les deux usines. Les Câbles de Lyon investissent près de 250 000 francs par an dans ce programme. Ce programme est interrompu en décembre 1940 et il reprend après la guerre, sans que nous puissions en évaluer exactement l'importance. S'agit-il de simples échanges de brevets ou d'une coopération aussi étendue que dans les années 1930[45] ? Un projet de convention, sans date, mais que l'on peut situer entre 1948 et 1958, entre la SECE et les Câbles de Lyon prévoit le renouvellement des échanges des années 1930.

De son côté, la SACT entretient des relations avec plusieurs sociétés étrangères. Avant la Seconde Guerre mondiale, elle effectue un transfert de technologie en faveur de la Conduttori Elettrici ed Affini-Torino SA (CEAT), une société italienne fondée en 1924 appartenant à la famille

---

[43] ASECE, dossier Lyon-Cortaillod, *PV 5ᵉ séance du comité directeur & de la 6ᵉ séance du comité technique « Lyon-Cortaillod », Genève, 20-21 janvier 1937.*

[44] ASECE, dossier Lyon-Cortaillod, *PV de la 3ᵉ séance du comité technique Lyon-Cortaillod, Lyon du 1-3 avril 1936.*

[45] ASECE, dossier Lyon-Cortaillod, *Lettre des Câbles de Lyon à Cortaillod, le 12 avril 1938. « Collaboration technique Lyon-Cortaillod ».* Et ASECE, dossier technique, *Séance du 2 mai 1946 avec les Câbles de Lyon.* Et ASECE, dossier Lyon-Cortaillod, *Lettre de Cortaillod à Câbles de Lyon, le 9 mai 1949.*

Tedeschi[46]. Cette société verse à la câblerie suisse d'importants droits de licence. Après la guerre, la SACT collabore surtout avec des sociétés anglaises. Dès 1946, des ingénieurs se rendent en Grande-Bretagne et ce voyage devient une tradition bisannuelle. Il s'agit de visiter des fabricants de machines ou d'appareils de laboratoire. Mais très vite ces relations débouchent sur des échanges de brevets avec deux sociétés de câbles et d'électrotechnique, la General Electric Co (GE) et la Telegraph Construction and Maintenance Co (Telcon Works)[47]. Des échanges de postes pour quelques mois se mettent en place entre les ingénieurs. Ce partage de brevets et d'expériences de fabrication est possible en raison de l'existence d'un cartel international, l'International Cable Development Corporation (ICDC), qui réunit près de 80 à 90 % des câbleries européennes et qui interdit la concurrence dans les pays respectifs. Dans ces conditions, les entreprises ne craignent pas de vendre ou d'échanger leurs brevets, c'est même la seule solution de gagner de l'argent avec l'étranger.

La R&D est prise en charge par le cartel

Dans l'industrie des câbles, la stabilité des cartels nationaux et internationaux annihile la concurrence. Cela conduit les câbleries à coopérer non seulement au niveau économique, mais aussi technique. Ainsi, de 1930 à 1938, plusieurs câbleries européennes[48], dont la SACT, engagent un ingénieur, Otto Klein, chargé de développer et d'introduire de nouveaux procédés de fabrication, avec toute liberté d'importer et d'exporter ces procédés d'une usine à l'autre. Otto Klein passe quelques mois par an dans chacune des entreprises et transmet ses expériences. Ce contrat restera en vigueur pendant près de huit ans[49].

En Suisse, la coopération technique entre les câbleries est initiée par la convention du cartel de 1943. Dans un premier temps, il s'agit surtout d'une politique de normalisation et de mise au point de cahiers des charges communs. Concrètement, cela se traduit par des réunions entre les ingénieurs en vue d'apporter des solutions techniques communes à des problèmes spécifiques. Néanmoins, ces rencontres restent rares

---

[46] Le fondateur de la CEAT est le grand-père de Valeria et Carla Bruni Tedeschi. Leur père a revendu l'entreprise dans les années 1970 pour se consacrer à la musique (compositeur).

[47] Ces entreprises sont les plus importantes avec lesquelles des échanges techniques sont organisés, mais nous pouvons aussi citer Philips et ponctuellement de nombreuses autres sociétés, par exemple, les LTT à Conflans-Saint-Honorine en France.

[48] Notamment Les Câbles Grammont qui sont intégrés aux Tréfileries et laminoirs du Havre SA.

[49] ACV PP 632/23, PVCA 17 juin 1938.

avant les années 1960[50]. Lors du renouvellement de la convention en 1968, les trois câbleries collaborent plus étroitement. Elles s'engagent par exemple à ne pas introduire de nouveaux produits sans l'accord des autres, à partager tous les brevets, à développer un pôle R&D commun, etc. Projets entièrement réalisés.

La normalisation

Dans la continuité de ce qui a été réalisé depuis 1943, les trois partenaires accentuent la normalisation des produits dès 1968. Ils établissent notamment des normes pour les boîtes de jonction des câbles et ils les fabriquent selon un modèle unique, avec un sigle commun, BCC (Brougg, Cortaillod et Cossonay). Ils lancent aussi sous ce même sigle une revue technique, qui paraît semestriellement à partir de 1973. De nombreux autres éléments des câbles sont ainsi standardisés.

Le laboratoire hors les murs

Dans la plupart des pays producteurs de câbles, les grandes câbleries ou les distributeurs d'énergie, disposent de stations d'essais grandeur nature où les câbles et leurs accessoires sont testés dans des conditions de service plus sévères que dans la réalité. Ces tests intéressent les câbleries suisses car ils permettent de rassembler de précieuses expériences et connaissances pour le développement des produits. En 1969, les trois fabricants de câbles suisses décident de créer un centre d'essais de ce type. Deux ans plus tard, ils louent aux Services industriels de Genève une sous-station inutilisée située à Verbois et pourvue d'un transformateur haute tension avec tout l'appareillage disponible. Ils y mènent de nombreux essais et se partagent les résultats[51].

La collaboration avec l'Institut Batelle et le câble téléfloc

À la fin des années 1960, les câbleries cherchent à étendre l'utilisation des plastiques aux câbles téléphoniques qui étaient jusqu'alors isolés au papier. Toutefois ils sont confrontés à un problème majeur : lorsqu'un câble plastique subit un dommage, l'eau pénètre et se disperse le long du câble. Les longueurs à réparer sont donc importantes et les coûts élevés. Les PTT refusent ces câbles. L'avantage des câbles papier c'est qu'en cas de dommage, le papier gonfle et bloque la migration de l'eau et circonscrit les dégâts. Toutefois, ces câbles ont d'autres défauts, dont leur coût et leur capacité.

---

[50] ACV PP 632/182, Séance de discussion concernant les manchons de jonction des câbles 3 X 150 mm2 18 kV des SI Genève. Eugène Foretay, 19 novembre 1954. Rapport n° 54934.

[51] Bulletin SACT Printemps 1974.

Pour résoudre ce problème, les câbleries font appel à une entreprise d'ingénierie américaine qui a installé un laboratoire à Genève, l'Institut Batelle et qui maîtrise très bien les matières isolantes artificielles[52]. Les câbleries s'accordent avec cette entreprise de R&D pour développer et mettre au point un câble, qui prend le nom de téléfloc. Il s'agit d'un câble dont l'isolation composite est formée d'une mince couche de polyéthylène expansé dans laquelle sont implantées des fibres de cellulose. Les caractéristiques propres aux isolations plastiques et papier sont réunies. De 1971 à 1974, les trois câbleries versent 490 000 francs pour ce projet à l'Institut Batelle et d'autres projets sont confiés à cette société[53].

La fibre optique et le laboratoire Cabloptic SA

Au début des années 1970, les laboratoires de la firme Corning mettent au point la fibre optique, qui permet de remplacer avantageusement les câbles en cuivre des réseaux téléphoniques traditionnels. En octobre 1977, les trois câbleries suisses décident de se lancer dans cette technologie. Elles créent pour cela une société commune exclusivement chargée de la R&D, la société Cabloptic à Cortaillod. En huit ans, les trois partenaires consentent un investissement de 21 millions de francs ; en 1985, Cabloptic emploie 52 personnes, essentiellement des ingénieurs et des techniciens[54]. De 1985 à 1987 une nouvelle usine est construite à Cortaillod pour 15 millions de francs (usine 7)[55].

De nombreux autres projets sont lancés sous l'égide du cartel, dans les années 1970 et 1980. Presque tous les nouveaux projets de R&D sont menés par le cartel ou par les entreprises, mais toujours sous l'égide du cartel. Ainsi, même l'installation de nouvelles machines très coûteuses est étudiée par le cartel et pour chaque projet, une câblerie est désignée en tant que pionnière, avec l'obligation de partager ses expériences.

Pour les deux firmes analysées, la création du premier laboratoire de R&D résulte non pas d'une stratégie définie à long terme, mais bien de l'état de développement des nouvelles technologies. Dans un cas, ce sont les bobines Pupin qui donnent l'impulsion à la création du laboratoire. Dans le second cas, c'est l'évolution générale de la technologie, qu'une firme n'arrive plus à suivre, qui déclenche le processus de

---

[52] ACV PP 632/200, *Technique de câbles en Europe. Conférence de M. K. S. Wyatt de Philips Dodge devant la Detroit Edison Company, le 29.8.1960. Robert Goldschmidt, 18 novembre 1960.* Rapport n° 60862.

[53] ACV PP 632/234.

[54] *Électronique*, magazine édité à Aarau, n° 6, p. 37, juin 1985.

[55] *Le Toron*, n° 28, été 1979.

création du laboratoire de R&D. En fait, les exemples pourraient être multipliés. Chaque fois qu'une nouvelle technologie apparaît (utilisation des plastiques pour l'isolation, développement du câble téléfloc ou des fibres optiques), les entreprises mettent au point de nouvelles stratégies (création d'un laboratoire de chimie, recours à un institut de R&D externe, création d'une société de R&D dans le cadre du cartel) pour maîtriser les nouvelles techniques.

Les relations directes et effectives avec les laboratoires publics des écoles d'ingénieur et des universités sont l'exception. L'épisode de 1918-1920 où la SACT a recours au laboratoire de l'EIUL n'est jamais reconduit. Dès que l'entreprise engage du personnel pour la R&D, elle doit leur fournir des équipements adéquats, qui rendent inutiles le recours aux laboratoires publics. Par contre, même si c'est un élément difficile à mesurer et à prouver, les liens entre chercheurs des entreprises et professeurs des écoles d'ingénieurs sont importants et permettent de nombreux échanges. Nous n'avons pas évoqué certains aspects de la correspondance de François Borel, où l'on voit qu'il échange de nombreuses idées avec des professeurs de l'EPFZ, mais aussi avec une personnalité telle que Theodore Turrettini. De même, Robert Goldschmidt est en contact permanent avec des professeurs. Sa nomination à l'EPUL, au-delà de son talent, s'explique probablement par ces liens. On peut donc conclure à ce propos que les instituts et les laboratoires publics sont importants pour l'émulation, mais qu'ils jouent un moindre rôle pour l'utilisation des équipements et les projets de recherches concrets.

Pour ces firmes, l'organisation des laboratoires et de la R&D est dépendante de l'industrie dans laquelle elles sont actives. L'importance des contrôles de fabrication conditionne fortement l'implantation des laboratoires et influe ainsi sur leur organisation.

Dans le cadre de cet article, nous avons limité la démonstration concernant les cartels, il faut toutefois souligner que depuis la fin des années 1920, les cartels jouent un rôle fondamental en matière de stratégie commerciale et financière. Et à partir des années 1940 ils intègrent la coopération technique. Dès lors, et surtout dès la fin des années 1960, toute la stratégie en matière de R&D est définie par ceux-ci. Ils permettent à ces petites firmes de soutenir les importants investissements nécessaires aux nouvelles technologies. Aucune des trois câbleries n'auraient pu durant les années 1970 investir les 36 millions nécessaires au développement et à la fabrication des fibres optiques, mais ensemble elles y sont parvenues. Ajoutons, sans le démontrer ici, que les bénéfices réalisés grâce au cartel dégagent des marges qui permettent les réinvestissements dans la R&D. En fait, le cartel a été fondamental dans la survie financière et technologique de ces firmes[56]. D'ailleurs, lorsque les cartels sont démantelés dans les années 1990, les deux firmes sont fusionnées puis intégrées dans le groupe Alcatel, puis Nexans.

L'histoire des laboratoires des grandes entreprises est de mieux en mieux connue, toutefois, les études portant sur les PME restent peu nombreuses. Les laboratoires de ces dernières n'ont souvent pas produit des « premières », c'est-à-dire la mise au point de fabrications totalement nouvelles, qui suscitent la fascination et des études d'historiens. Par contre, ces entreprises sont parvenues dans bien des cas à s'adapter aux nouveautés et à mettre sur le marché des biens qui soutiennent la concurrence. On pourrait répondre que pour atteindre ces résultats, certaines PME – c'est le cas pour les entreprises étudiées ici – ont bénéficié de protections, telles que des commandes de l'État ou d'une loi favorable aux cartels. Mais cette situation est identique pour certains grands groupes. Les Bell laboratories, par exemple, bénéficient aussi du monopole de leur maison mère dans les télécommunications aux États-Unis. Les historiens ont longtemps négligé l'histoire des PME, or, dans le tissu économique d'un pays tel que la Suisse, ces entreprises jouent un rôle fondamental et malgré leurs budgets modestes en matière de R&D, un grand nombre d'entre elles restent innovantes.

---

[56] Peter Z. Grossman (ed.), *How Cartels Endure and How They Fail : Studies of Industrial Collusion*, Cheltenham, Edward Elgar Pub, 2004, 324 p. et en particulier l'article d'introduction de ce livre : Peter Z Grossman, « Introduction : What Do We Mean by Cartel Success ? », p. 1-8.

Le cheminement international d'une innovation majeure

Le transport d'énergie électrique sur longue distance de Francfort-sur-le-Main

Serge PAQUIER

Université de Saint-Étienne

Avec François Caron, on ne peut que souligner la rapidité avec laquelle l'électricité passe de la marge au centre du système technique, globalement en une quinzaine d'années entre 1880 et 1895[1]. Ce résultat ne peut être que le fruit d'un brassage d'idées, de concepts et d'expériences diverses impliquant plusieurs acteurs à l'échelle internationale. Une firme aussi puissante soit-elle, une haute école d'ingénieurs, un cabinet d'inventeurs et encore moins un innovateur indépendant ne peuvent prétendre à la paternité d'un réseau technique aussi complexe. Dès lors, et plus particulièrement lorsqu'il s'agit d'une innovation majeure, comme le transport de courant électrique sur longue distance présenté en 1891 à l'exposition de Francfort-sur-le-Main, il ne faut pas s'étonner si elle est le résultat de la mise en commun de moyens et de compétences de deux entreprises, localisées de surcroît dans deux pays pilotes de la deuxième industrialisation : l'Allemagne et la Suisse. Il convient d'emblée de préciser qu'il s'agit là d'un partenariat ponctuel, exprimé dans le cadre particulier d'expositions. Depuis le début des années 1880, celles-ci fédèrent les énergies en agissant comme catalyseur pour les candidats à la présentation d'une percée technologique du fait de l'écho qu'ils sont susceptibles de recevoir. Les pratiques parfois déloyales utilisées par Edison pour s'imposer à Paris en 1881 face à ses concurrents, qui ont été mises en évidence par Robert Fox, montrent

---

[1] Voir notamment François Caron, « Introduction générale » in François Caron, Fabienne Cardot (dir.), *Histoire générale de l'électricité en France. Tome premier : espoirs et conquêtes (1881-1918)*, Paris, Fayard, 1991, p. 11-14 et notre étude, *Histoire de l'électricité en Suisse. La dynamique d'un petit pays européen (1875-1939)*, vol. 1, Genève, Passé Présent, 1998, p. 57-124.

bien l'enjeu de ces expositions[2]. Ces grandes « messes industrielles » présentent encore l'avantage de réunir les multiples acteurs de l'innovation : créateurs de réseau, fournisseurs d'équipement, experts techniciens et scientifiques chargés de statuer sur les résultats annoncés par les exposants ; une liste à laquelle il convient d'ajouter les collectivités publiques impliquées dans l'organisation des expositions. Et parmi les visiteurs, combien de financiers intéressés à investir dans la nouvelle technologie et de consommateurs potentiels ? Ils sont certainement nombreux.

La dimension internationale du transport d'énergie électrique de Francfort se mesure également par les attentes fortes sur plusieurs grands chantiers d'édification de stations centrales hydrauliques à la recherche de la solution la plus efficiente pour produire l'énergie en grande quantité, la transporter et la distribuer à plusieurs catégories d'abonnés répartis sur de vastes espaces. C'est le cas à la frontière entre le Canada et les États-Unis, aux chutes du Niagara, où il est question d'aménager 50 000 CV[3], sur le Rhin à Rheinfelden dans le cadre d'un grand projet téléguidé dès 1889 par l'Allgemeine Elektrizitäts-Gesellschaft (AEG), encore sur le Rhin à Laufenbourg où le pionnier britannique Sebastian Ziani de Ferranti envisage d'édifier une centrale de 30 000 CV[4], et sur le Rhône en aval de Genève, une ville qui se distingue parmi d'autres dans la création de réseaux d'énergie aux côtés de Munich, Francfort-sur-le-Main, Londres, New York, Paris et Berlin.

Par rapport à ce brassage international, la Suisse dispose de plusieurs atouts. Sa participation s'inscrit dans un mouvement plus large d'appropriation de ses industries de réseau qui démarre dans le sillage de l'implantation des réseaux charbonniers gazier (années 1840) et ferroviaire (années 1850)[5]. Comme nous le verrons, le processus prend,

---

[2]   Robert Fox, « Thomas Edison's Campaign : Incadescent Lighting and the Hidden face of Technology Transfer » in *Annals of Science*, 53, 1996, p. 157-193.

[3]   Voir Edward Dean Adams, *History of the Niagara Falls Power Company (1886-1918)*, 2 volumes, New York, 1927.

[4]   Bruno Meyer « Das Kraftwerk Laufenburg. Eine Pionnierleistung der Technik » in *Vom Jura zum Scharzwald. Blätter für Heimatkunde und Heimatschutz*, 59 (1985), p. 1-35.

[5]   Voir nos études, notamment : Serge Paquier, Olivier Perroux, « Naissance et développement de l'industrie gazière en Suisse. Approche nationale et exemple genevois (1843-1939) » in Serge Paquier, Jean-Pierre Williot (dir.), *L'industrie du gaz en Europe aux XIXe et XXe siècles. L'innovation entre marchés privés et collectivités publiques*, Bruxelles, PIE Peter Lang, 2005, p. 509-529 ; Serge Paquier, « Options privée et publique dans le domaine des chemins de fer suisses des années 1850 à l'Entre-deux-guerres » in *Revue suisse d'histoire*, 56, 2006, n° 1, p. 22-30 et du même auteur « Naissance et développement des services publics en Suisse. Le cas des deux réseaux charbonniers au XIXe siècle » in Hans-Jörg, Margrit Müller,

dès la fin des années 1850, une nouvelle dimension créatrice autour de l'élaboration de systèmes techniques (câble télédynamique, air comprimé, eau sous pression, puis électricité) capables de convertir en énergie utile « l'immense réserve de force à bon marché que renferment les fleuves et les rivières » selon les termes employés en 1858 par l'ingénieur genevois Daniel Colladon (1802-1893), ancien professeur à l'École centrale des arts et manufactures de Paris[6]. Autour de cet enjeu national se mobilisent fournisseurs d'équipement, créateurs de réseaux, promoteurs privés, municipalités et hautes écoles techniques. C'est ainsi que se constitue en Suisse dès le milieu des années 1880 un rouage essentiel du mécanisme de création des grands réseaux électriques, avec une rapide spécialisation dans les génératrices à forte puissance et son corollaire le transport d'énergie à haute tension, soit le cheminement obligé pour tirer le meilleur parti possible de ses abondantes ressources hydrauliques. Comme nous le verrons, ces compétences helvétiques sont particulièrement recherchées dès le milieu des années 1880. De plus, la place de la Suisse au carrefour de l'Europe et sa double culture latine et germanique sont des facteurs qui facilitent les contacts avec des partenaires de diverses provenances alors que sa petite taille et sa neutralité freinent les méfiances à caractère nationaliste.

Dans ces circonstances, il ne faut guère s'étonner si plusieurs laboratoires hors les murs et spécialisés dans l'électricité fonctionnent en Suisse dès la deuxième moitié des années 1880. Nous verrons qu'entre 1886 et 1888, Français, Allemands et Suisses alémaniques unissent leurs efforts sur le Rhin à Neuhausen pour mettre au point un procédé de fabrication d'aluminium, alors qu'à Vallorbe, en 1889 et 1890, l'inventeur indépendant français, Henry Gall, coopère avec des ingénieurs et des fournisseurs d'équipement romands pour y établir la première fabrique d'engrais chloratés en Europe[7]. C'est donc dans un contexte de partenariat international que prend place en 1890 et 1891 le transport d'électricité de Francfort, fruit de la collaboration entreprise entre le géant berlinois AEG et les Ateliers de construction Oerlikon.

Laurent Tissot (dir.), *Les Services. Essor et transformation du 'secteur tertiaire' (15ᵉ-20ᵉ siècles)*, Zurich, Éditions Chronos, 2007.

[6] Daniel Colladon, *Notes et considérations générales sur l'utilisation de la puissance motrice des rivières et des fleuves*, manuscrit, Genève, 1858. Bibliothèque publique et universitaire de Genève, salle des manuscrits : Ms 3758.

[7] C'est à cette occasion qu'est fondée la Société d'électro-chimie. Voir Association amicale des anciens élèves de l'Électro-chimie (ed.), *Mémorial de la Société d'électro-chimie (1889-1966)*, Lyon, 1991.

L'immersion des techniciens suisses dans la longue durée en matière de transport et de distribution d'énergie

L'héritage de l'hydromécanique (années 1800 aux années 1880)[8]

L'analyse de l'innovation dans le domaine du transport et de la distribution d'énergie montre que plusieurs générations de techniciens suisses se sont investies dans un domaine qui revêt une importance toute particulière dans le pays, puisque les infrastructures hydromécaniques représentent la possibilité d'obtenir un service de force motrice sans devoir importer un charbon absent du sous-sol helvétique.

Une première étape est franchie dès les années 1800, alors qu'il faut répondre aux nouveaux besoins en énergie mécanique générés par la mécanisation de l'industrie textile. Des fournisseurs locaux d'équipement, d'abord d'anciennes entreprises de filature mécanisée (Escher, Wyss & Cie à Zurich, puis Rieter & Cie à Winterthour), commencent à installer des roues simples, puis évoluées sur les modèles de l'Anglais Fairbairn à Manchester et du Français Poncelet. À partir de 1830, les fabricants de machines hydrauliques se tournent vers la turbine inventée par le Stéphanois Benoît Fourneyron, mais lui préfèrent dès les années 1840-1850 les Jonval et Girard[9].

Le mouvement s'accélère à partir des années 1850 sous la pression de l'élargissement des besoins en énergie à d'autres secteurs et de l'élévation du coût du charbon. L'ingénieur genevois Colladon nous dit encore en 1858 que « le coût du combustible de la plupart des pays

---

[8] Selon nos études : « Un facteur d'explication de l'électrification rapide de la Suisse : l'expérience acquise en matière d'hydromécanique au XIXe siècle » in *Bulletin d'histoire de l'électricité*, 16, 1990, p. 25-35 ; *Histoire de l'électricité en Suisse*, *op. cit.*, t. 1, p. 303-382 ; « L'utilisation des ressources hydrauliques en Suisse aux XIXe et XXe siècles. Une approche systémique dans la longue durée » in Hans-Jorg Gilomen, Rudolf Jaun, Margritt Müller, Béatrice Veyrassat (eds.), *Innovationen. Voraussetzung und Folgen-Antriebskräfte und Widerstände/Innovations. Incitations et résistances – des sources de l'innovation à ses effets*, Zurich, 2001, p. 99-119. Voir également Cédric Humair, « La force motrice hydraulique au service du développement économique helvétique. L'exemple du réseau d'eau sous pression à Lausanne (1868-1914) » in *Revue suisse d'histoire*, 56, 2006, n° 2, p. 127-151.

[9] L'usage de la turbine Fourneyron ne convient pas au contexte suisse. On note seulement quelques installations dans les années 1830-1840 qui ne donnent pas satisfaction. Les turbines Jonval utilisées pour les petites chutes connaissent un grand succès tout comme les Girard. Un recensement effectué en 1876 pour l'exposition de Philadelphie compte une puissance installée de 11 444 CV développée par les turbines Jonval et de 11 855 CV pour les Girard. Selon Weissenbach, « Die Wassermotoren der Schweiz für die Internationale Ausstellung in Philadelphia 1876 » in *Die Eisenbahn/Le Chemin de fer*, 1876, p. 8-11, ici p. 8.

européens suit une pente ascendante » et précise que dans le département du Rhône, il « est d'environ deux tiers supérieur à sa valeur moyenne de 1800 à 1850 »[10]. C'est à partir de ce moment que des techniciens helvétiques conçoivent les premières stations centrales hydromécaniques, soit des systèmes combinés originaux élaborés sur la base de techniques de transport et de distribution de force motrice conçues à l'extérieur du pays, mais adaptées au contexte suisse par des créateurs de réseau et des fournisseurs d'équipement nationaux. Les cheminements sont diversifiés. C'est la solution la plus simple des transmissions à câble télédynamique, mise au point par les frères alsaciens Charles et Ferdinand Hirn, qui est adaptée aux stations centrales de Schaffhouse (1866), Fribourg (1870) et Zurich (1878). Les solutions plus coûteuses en premier investissement, car consistant à élaborer un système secondaire d'énergie, sont également retenues. Dès le début des années 1850, le Genevois Colladon mise sur l'air comprimé pour percer les tunnels ferroviaires du Mont-Cenis et du Saint-Gothard après avoir écarté le câble proposé par le Belge Maus. L'air comprimé, une technique originaire de France et d'Angleterre, présente non seulement l'intérêt de fournir la force motrice aux perforatrices, mais encore de ventiler le tunnel et de servir de force de traction au matériel roulant utilisé pour transporter les ouvriers et les matériaux. Enfin s'installe dès le début des années 1870 la solution plus performante de l'eau sous pression. En s'inspirant de solutions adoptées dans les ports et les gares français et anglais pour la manutention des marchandises, plusieurs villes suisses adoptent dès le début des années 1870 des services combinés de distribution de petite force motrice et d'adduction d'eau. L'eau sous pression est moins dangereuse que le câble (ce qui évite de concentrer les usagers sur un espace donné), avantageuse en maintenance et permet de comptabiliser l'énergie distribuée aux abonnés. Genève se distingue en édifiant sur le Rhône entre 1883 et 1886 la centrale hydraulique la plus performante de l'époque (Coulouvrenière). Elle permet dès 1891 à son maître d'œuvre, Théodore Turrettini (1845-1916), d'occuper un siège à la Commission internationale pour l'aménagement des chutes du Niagara.

Force est de constater que de par l'ampleur et la complexité de projets et de travaux ambitieux qui s'étalent sur plusieurs années, voire une quinzaine d'années, l'implication de promoteurs privés (Heinrich Moser, horloger enrichi à Schaffhouse ; le centralien Guillaume Ritter à Fribourg) et des municipalités (à Genève, Zurich et Berne), la combinaison des savoir-faire qui mêlent le génie civil pour édifier les retenues d'eau, les fournisseurs d'équipement (Escher, Wyss à Zurich, Rieter à

---

[10] D. Colladon, *Notes et considérations générales, op. cit.*

Winterthour, Benjamin Roy à Vevey), les hautes écoles d'ingénieurs du pays en matière d'expertise et/ou de participation directe à l'élaboration des réseaux (Paul Piccard, ancien professeur de mécanique industrielle à l'école d'ingénieurs de Lausanne, conçoit les moteurs à eau sous pression de la Coulouvrenière), ces chantiers de stations centrales constituent déjà de véritables laboratoires hors les murs qui annoncent ceux de l'électricité. Des centrales préélectriques au transport de l'électricité, il n'y a qu'un pas à franchir qui ne se limite pas au territoire helvétique comme en témoigne la localisation à quelques kilomètres au nord-ouest de Francfort-sur-le-Main, à Oberursel, d'une des six centrales à câble télédynamique recensées en Europe par le spécialiste anglais en transmission d'énergie Charles Unwin[11].

La Suisse et la progression du transport de l'électricité (1881-1891)

Alors que les techniciens suisses restent longtemps en retrait des principales innovations dans le domaine de l'électricité tant sur le plan de la production d'énergie (dynamos) que de celui des premières applications cantonnées à l'éclairage, ils commencent prudemment à émerger au début des années 1880 dès lors que la progression de l'électricité vers un système technique complet présente l'opportunité de tirer parti des ressources hydrauliques. Le succès de Francfort en 1891 s'inscrit directement dans le prolongement d'expériences accumulées depuis le début des années 1880. À partir de 1886 démonstration est faite que les techniciens suisses sont devenus des partenaires dont il faut tenir compte dans l'élaboration des grands réseaux électriques.

Trois centres de compétences sont d'emblée à l'œuvre : genevois, bâlois et zurichois. Les filières les plus précoces sont celles de Genève et de Bâle. Nous pouvons constater que l'innovation est un processus qui repose tant sur des firmes existantes que sur de nouveaux entrants comme François Caron le suggère dans ses travaux[12]. Les filières genevoise et bâloise sont le résultat d'un essaimage commun à partir d'une entreprise existante. La Société genevoise d'instruments de physique fondée en 1858 avait entrepris dès la fin des années 1870 une timide diversification dans la nouvelle énergie en tentant de concevoir sans

---

[11] C'est la seule centrale de ce type en Allemagne, trois autres dont il a été question se situent en Suisse, une à Bellegarde en France voisine de Genève aménagée conjointement par le créateur de réseau Colladon et le fournisseur d'équipement Rieter & Cie et une en Italie à Tortona. Cawthorne Unwin William, *On the development and transmission of power from central station*, Londres, 1894, p. 111.

[12] François Caron, « L'innovation » in Hans-Jorg Gilomen, Jaun Rudolf, Margrit Müller, Béatrice Veyrassat (dir.), *Innovations. Incitations et résistances, op. cit.*, p. 19-31, plus particulièrement p. 25-31.

grand succès une génératrice de sa propre conception. L'ancien apprenti René Thury, formé pendant plusieurs mois au laboratoire d'Edison de Menlo Park, ainsi que le contremaître et ingénieur Emil Bürgin, quittent dès 1881 l'entreprise mère pour valoriser leur savoir-faire dans de nouvelles firmes spécialisées. Le premier se fait engager comme technicien dans une petite entreprise d'électricité genevoise (Cuénod, Sautter & Cie, précurseur de la Compagnie de l'industrie électrique, puis des Ateliers de Sécheron) alors que le second parvient à se hisser au rang d'associé lors de la création à Bâle d'une nouvelle firme, Bürgin & Alioth, spécialement conçue pour s'imposer sur le marché de l'électricité[13].

L'entreprise bâloise est la première à jouer la carte de la coopération internationale. Elle choisit l'Angleterre, plus particulièrement Chelmsford, où elle réalise en juin 1881 ses premiers essais sur les terrains du fabricant de dynamos R. A. Crompton, le partenaire d'un temps. Puis en juillet et en septembre de la même année, elle en entreprend d'autres à King's Cross sur la base d'un transport de courant destiné à alimenter des lampes Swan[14]. Jusqu'en juin 1882, elle ne concrétise pas moins de quatre transports de force avec des génératrices de sa propre conception. Il ne s'agit que d'infrastructures encore modestes, puisque la plus importante transporte 4 CV nets avec un rendement de 65 %. La firme bâloise et son homologue genevoise présentent également des transports d'électricité en 1883 dans le cadre de l'exposition nationale de Zurich[15]. L'année suivante, l'entreprise genevoise, dont l'activité se limite au territoire national, réalise le premier transport permanent de force motrice électrique dans le pays. Une puissance de 12 à 16 CV est transportée sur 1 200 mètres par une ligne aérienne formée de deux fils de cuivre de sept millimètres de diamètre jusqu'à Bienne pour mouvoir deux moteurs électriques[16], l'un installé dans un laminoir d'argent et l'autre dans une fabrique d'horlogerie où la nature du travail exige une vitesse absolument constante.

Dans la région zurichoise s'illustre Charles Eugen Lancelot Brown (1863-1924), le futur lauréat du transport longue distance de Francfort.

---

[13] Voir notre étude, *Histoire de l'électricité en Suisse, op. cit.*, t. 1, p. 430-462.

[14] *Die Eisenbahn/Le chemin de fer*, 16, 1882, p. 149. Il s'agit de la revue éditée par l'École polytechnique fédérale de Zurich (EPFZ). Elle devient *Schweizerische Bauzeitung.*

[15] Voir le rapport établi par le professeur de physique à l'École polytechnique fédérale de Zurich Heinrich Friederich Weber, « Dynamomaschinen und deren Verwendung » in *Bericht über Gruppe 32 : Physikalische Industrie, Schweizerische Landesausstellung Zürich 1883*, Zurich, 1884, p. 52-54. Pour l'anecdote, Weber a été l'un des professeurs de physique d'Albert Einstein, avec lequel il ne s'est pas du tout entendu.

[16] *Schweizerische Bauzeitung (désormais SB)*, 3, 1884, p. 84 ; Gisbert Kapp, *Transmission électrique de l'énergie*, Paris, 1888, p. 4.

Le mérite de ce pionnier s'explique largement par son appartenance à une famille immergée depuis une génération dans les milieux du progrès technologique. Cette dynastie d'innovateurs évolue au niveau des techniciens qui manquent, comme René Thury à Genève, de moyens financiers. Les Brown doivent donc mettre leurs compétences au service d'une entreprise sans parvenir au rang d'associé. Le père, l'ingénieur Charles Brown (1827-1905), qui s'était formé dans la région londonienne à Brixton chez le fabricant de machines Maudsley, décide de valoriser son savoir-faire en émigrant en Suisse selon un parcours qui privilégie la mobilité. D'abord engagé par l'une des premières fabriques de machines Sulzer frères, localisée à proximité du centre d'affaires zurichois dans la ville industrielle de Winterthour[17], il participe ensuite dans cette même ville en 1871 à la formation de la Fabrique suisse de locomotives et de machines, plus connue sous son abréviation alémanique SLM (Schweizerische Lokomotiven und Maschinenfabrik). Toujours dans la région zurichoise, mais dans l'autre ville industrielle d'Oerlikon, il se fait engager aux Ateliers de construction Oerlikon avec ses deux fils formés au Technikum de Winterthour : Sydney et Charles Eugen Lancelot Brown[18]. Ce dernier accède à la direction de la nouvelle division « électricité » créée pour diversifier l'activité de l'entreprise dans le nouveau secteur porteur.

Le jeune directeur se fait rapidement connaître dans le milieu spécialisé du transport d'énergie en réalisant en 1886 un transport permanent destiné à alimenter une fabrique de vis et une minoterie. Si 20 à 30 CV sont transportés sur une distance encore modeste, huit kilomètres, les résultats sont à la hauteur des espérances, puisque cette infrastructure obtient le rendement inégalé jusque-là de 75 %. Ce résultat, qui place l'électricité largement devant ses concurrents à câble, à air comprimé et à eau sous pression dont la rentabilité chute très considérablement après cinq kilomètres[19], est non seulement confirmé par une commission de spécialistes présidée par le professeur de physique à l'École polytech-

---

[17] La position acquise par l'innovateur britannique se lira plus tard dans la place qu'il va occuper dans l'un des premiers ouvrages anniversaire consacré à une entreprise industrielle. Charles Brown y trône auprès des fondateurs Sulzer et des grands managers de l'entreprise. La réputation internationale acquise par son fils joue certainement un rôle dans la mise en scène de son père. Selon Conrad Matschoss, *Geschichte Gebrüder Sulzer Winterthur und Ludwigshafen A. Rh.*, Berlin, 1910, p. 15-16.

[18] Votre notre étude, *Histoire de l'électricité en Suisse, op. cit.*, 1, p. 465-476.

[19] Pour le câble : 60 % à cinq kilomètres, puis 37 % sur dix kilomètres ; l'eau sous pression : entre 40 et 45 % sur cinq kilomètres, puis 35 à 45 % sur dix kilomètres ; l'air comprimé : 50 à 55 % sur cinq kilomètres. Selon A. Beringer, *Kritische Vergleichung der elektrischen Kraftübertragung mit den gebräuchlisten mechanischen Uebertragungssystem*, Berlin, 1883, p. 49, 56-78, 86 et 94.

nique fédérale de Zurich Heinrich Friedrich Weber[20], mais encore largement relayé par la presse technicienne. La revue éditée par l'École polytechnique fédérale de Zurich, la *Schweizerische Bauzeitung*, lui accorde quatre articles[21]. Sans doute, l'une des qualités essentielles à mettre à l'actif du jeune directeur consiste à ne pas se focaliser sur un système avec lequel il a pourtant obtenu un succès, il va quitter le courant continu pour se tourner vers son concurrent, l'alternatif, tout en valorisant l'expérience acquise comme nous le verrons.

Dynamique de la coopération interfirmes

Le groupe AEG et la firme d'Oerlikon unissent leurs compétences dans un *pool* destiné à fabriquer par électrolyse de l'aluminium en grande quantité et à bas prix. Il réunit entre 1886 et 1888 sur la rive suisse du Rhin à Neuhausen, le Français Paul Héroult, l'Allemand Kiliani de l'AEG et les Ateliers de construction Oerlikon en charge de concevoir, d'installer et de faire fonctionner les génératrices destinées à alimenter en énergie le procédé d'électrolyse[22]. Suite au résultat positif obtenu, l'AEG et les Ateliers de construction Oerlikon décident de préciser leur coopération. La firme d'Oerlikon vient de montrer ses compétences dans le transport de courant électrique avec la réussite de Soleure et l'AEG souhaite profiter de cette expérience pour appliquer les hautes tensions à des transformateurs triphasés. En échange, l'AEG apporte les capacités de l'ingénieur Michael Dolivo-Dobrowolsky (1862-1919)[23] dans les moteurs triphasés depuis qu'il a été engagé par la

---

[20] Heinrich Friedrich Weber « Die Leistungen der elektrischen Arbeitsübertragung zwischen Kriegstetten und Solorthurn » in *SB*, 11, 1888, p. 1-7 et 9-15.

[21] *SB* 8, 1886, p. 156-158 ; *SB* 9, 1887, p. 27 ; *SB* 10, 1887, p. 47-48, plus la référence indiquée en note précédente. Voir également Unwin, *On the developement and transmission of power, op. cit.*, p. 264.

[22] Voir Direktorium der Gesellschaft (ed.), *Geschichte der Aluminium Industrie Aktiengesellschaft Neuhausen (1888-1938)*, t. 1, Zurich ; Paul Morel (dir.), Grinberg Ivan (coll.), *Histoire technique de la production d'aluminium. Les apports français au développement international d'une industrie*, Grenoble, 1991, p. 33 et 37 ; concernant la rencontre des Suisses et des Français, voir Paul Toussaint, *La Compagnie des produits chimiques et électrométallurgiques Alais, Froges et Camargue. Première partie : les quatre sociétés constitutives. Titre IV La Société Électro-métallurgique française (SEMF)*, sans lieu, 1953, p. 18. Archives Péchiney 00/8/11 247. Voir également Michel Caron, « Paul Héroult (1863-1914). Un grand inventeur original » in *Cahiers d'histoire de l'aluminium*, n° 4, p. 69-81, plus particulièrement p. 71-73 et Muriel Le Roux, « Les premiers laboratoires d'Alais, Froges et Camargue (1866-1931) : deux stratégies » in *Cahiers d'histoire de l'aluminium*, n° 5, p. 53-66, ici p. 54.

[23] Pour le rôle de cet ingénieur dans les machines polyphasées, voir Thomas Parke Hughes, *Networks of Power. Électrification in Western Society (1880-1930)*, Baltimore/Londres, John Hopkins University Press, 1983, p. 119.

firme berlinoise. Particulièrement qualifié dans la problématique des champs tournants, il crée dès le début de 1889 un premier moteur développant cinq CV sur la base d'une substitution de l'anneau Gramme, utilisé alors dans la partie primaire des moteurs triphasés, par un enroulement en tambour. Cette coopération technique entre le géant berlinois et la firme helvétique peut également s'appuyer sur un facteur humain. Il se trouve en effet que les deux présidents de l'AEG et d'Oerlikon, respectivement Emil Rathenau (1838-1915)[24] et Peter Emil Huber-Werdmüller (1836-1918)[25], sont tous deux diplômés de l'École polytechnique fédérale de Zurich[26]. Le mouvement engagé débouche sur la conception d'un groupe de production d'énergie triphasé mû par une machine à vapeur rapide, l'une des spécialités des Ateliers de construction Oerlikon. Le système est présenté en 1889 tant à Berlin où se tient l'exposition allemande pour la protection pour les accidents, qu'à Paris lors de l'exposition universelle[27].

Dynamique des expositions internationales

Nous venons de constater le rôle joué par plusieurs expositions industrielles, celle de Zurich en 1883 et celles tenues dans les deux capitales européennes en 1889. Il faut encore tenir compte du fait que l'irruption de l'électricité peut s'appuyer sur la tenue régulière d'expositions spécialisées. Après celle de Paris en 1881[28], viennent celles de Munich et Londres (1882), Vienne (1883) et Turin (1884), puis celle de Francfort-sur-le-Main (1891) qui nous intéresse plus particulièrement. Il convient de préciser que les expositions de Londres et de Turin font considérablement progresser le transport de courant électrique en inaugurant la solution des courants alternatifs. À Londres, puis à Turin, le Français Lucien Gaulard associé à l'Anglais John Dixon réalisent deux transports de force, le premier sur 25 kilomètres et le second sur 40 kilomètres en utilisant des transformateurs en fin de ligne qui permettent d'abaisser la tension pour distribuer le courant. Si les tensions utilisées, entre 2 000 et 3 000 volts, tout comme les résultats, restent encore modestes, ces exhibitions retiennent toutefois l'attention des milieux spécialisés comme en témoignent non seulement l'attitude du

---

[24] Ulrich Wengenroth, « Emil Rathenau » in Wilhem Treu, Wolfgang König (eds.), *Berlinsische Lebansbilder Techniker*, Berlin, 1990, p. 193-209.

[25] *Biographisches Lexikon verstorbener Schweizer*, vol. III, 1950, p. 223 ; Fritz Rieter « Peter Emil Huber-Werdmüller dans *Schweizer Pionniere der Wirtschaft und Technik* », 7, 1957, p. 61-84.

[26] Comme le souligne Hughes, *Networks*, *op. cit.*, p. 131.

[27] Fr. Schoenenberg, *Maschinenfabrik Oerlikon*, Zurich, 1927, p. 93.

[28] Voir l'analyse de Fabienne Cardot « L'exposition de 1881 » in Caron, Cardot, *Histoire générale de l'électricité*, *op. cit.*, p. 19-33.

ministre français des Postes et des Télégraphes qui envoie deux ingénieurs à Londres pour se tenir informé, mais encore l'écho que leur accorde en Suisse la *Schweizerische Bauzeitung*[29].

Le créateur de réseau bavarois Oskar von Miller est appelé en 1890 par les organisateurs de Francfort pour centrer la future exposition sur les progrès que peut apporter l'électricité à l'artisanat et à la petite industrie[30]. L'ingénieur von Miller peut s'appuyer sur un parcours qui l'a conduit à établir des liens avec plusieurs créateurs de réseau, fournisseurs d'équipement, experts scientifiques et techniciens et même avec des financiers spécialisés dans les industries de réseau, comme le banquier des chemins de fer Henry Villard. Il convient de rappeler que von Miller a compté parmi les organisateurs de l'exposition de Munich où un transport de courant électrique sur une cinquantaine de kilomètres a été entrepris par le spécialiste français des courants continus : le professeur au Conservatoire national des arts et métiers Marcel Deprez (1843-1918)[31]. Le Bavarois est ainsi entré en contact avec les milieux novateurs de l'industrie électrique aussi bien européens que nord-américains. En Europe font désormais partie de ses fréquentations les Siemens, Hopkinson, Ferraris, Mordey, Swinburne, Swan et Gisbert Kapp l'un des meilleurs spécialistes de la transmission d'énergie. Après l'exposition de Munich, von Miller a effectué un fructueux voyage aux États-Unis où il a visité les usines des fournisseurs d'équipement, les chantiers d'élaboration de réseau les plus ambitieux, dont le site des chutes du Niagara, ainsi que le laboratoire d'Edison à Menlo Park. De retour en Allemagne, le patron de l'AEG, E. Rathenau, lui a proposé un pont d'or pour prendre en charge l'installation des réseaux électriques. Puis il a quitté l'AEG pour s'établir comme ingénieur-conseil à Munich, une activité qui a conduit ce créateur de réseau à concevoir et à installer une importante usine hydroélectrique à Heilbronn pour le compte du cimen-

[29] Voir notre étude, *Histoire de l'électricité en Suisse*, op. cit., t. 1, p. 105-106 et *Schweizerische Bauzeitung*, 1883, p. 6 et 149-150 ; 1884, p. 132.

[30] Nous nous basons surtout sur Rudolf Pörtner, *Oskar von Miller. Der Münchener der das Deutsche Museum erfand*, Düsseldorf/Vienne/New York, 1987, p. 9-17 ; Walther von Miller, *Oskar von Miller nach eingenen Aufzeichnung, Reden und Briefen*, Munich, 1932, p. 31-32. Voir également Hughes, *Networks*, op. cit., p. 131-134.

[31] Von Miller, *Oskar von Miller*, op. cit., p. 18-30 ; Kapp Gisbert, *Transmission électrique de l'énergie électrique, sa transformation, sa subdivision et sa distribution*, Paris, 1888, p. 358 ; Fontaine Hyppolite, « Transmission électrique, renseignements pratiques » in *Note extraite du Bulletin technologique de la Société des anciens élèves des écoles nationales d'arts et métiers*, Paris, 1885, p. 55-60.

tier Portland avec l'option de distribuer l'énergie dans la ville voisine de Lauffen. Pour la première fois le système triphasé a été adopté[32].

Devant travailler la question d'un grand réseau capable de distribuer de la force motrice à l'artisanat et la petite industrie dispersés sur de vastes espaces, von Miller pense d'emblée à l'hydroélectricité, au courant triphasé et aux hautes tensions. Ce dernier point pose problème, car sachant qu'il ne sera pas possible d'obtenir des tensions élevées directement par des génératrices qui ne supporteraient pas cette contrainte, s'impose dès lors à ses yeux la conception de transformateurs qui puissent élever la tension du courant électrique, condition nécessaire pour limiter le coût du transport, puis l'abaisser pour le distribuer. Dans un premier temps, l'ingénieur bavarois calibre l'expérience en fonction du transport d'une cinquantaine de kilomètres qui avait été réalisé par le Français Deprez à Munich[33]. Mais comme son intention d'utiliser une usine hydroélectrique localisée au sud-est de Francfort entre Würzburg et Aschaffenburg ne se concrétise pas. Il se tourne plus au sud en direction du site d'Heilbronn où il s'avère possible d'installer une nouvelle génératrice triphasée à haute puissance dans un espace laissé vacant pour l'extension ultérieure de la centrale. Se pose dès lors la délicate question du transport de l'énergie sur la distance considérable de 174 kilomètres. Après quelques calculs, von Miller estime qu'il conviendra d'utiliser trois fils de cuivre de quatre millimètres de diamètre qui devront fonctionner sous la tension considérable de 25 000 volts. Il interroge les milieux spécialisés allemands, mais ces derniers restent fort critiques.

Le rôle des Ateliers de construction Oerlikon[34]

Pour son affaire de Heilbronn, von Miller s'était adressé aux Ateliers de construction Oerlikon. À cette occasion, le Bavarois avait rencontré le jeune directeur de la division électricité : Charles Eugen Lancelot Brown. Le Bavarois lui demande s'il s'avère possible d'envisager un transport à 25 000 volts et Brown évoque les essais réalisés par Swinburne au Chrystal Palace de Londres où des tensions relativement élevées ont été obtenues en utilisant l'huile comme matière isolante. Le Bavarois accorde sa confiance, car il a lui-même assisté à la démonstra-

---

32 Cette station centrale est décrite par E. Hospitalier, « Transport et distribution de l'énergie électrique par courants alternatifs simples ou polyphasés » in *L'industrie électrique*, 1, 1892, p. 315-321.

33 Hughes, *Networks, op. cit.*, p. 131.

34 Nous nous basons principalement sur Ch. E. Müller, « Le cinquantenaire de la transmission à courant triphasé » in *Bulletin Oerlikon*, n° 231, 1941, p. 1438-1443 et n° 232, p. 1446-1452 ainsi que *Schweizerische Bauzeitung*, 17, 1891, p. 28-29. Voir également Hughes, *Networks, op. cit.*, p. 131-137.

tion de Swinburne. Brown ajoute qu'il a déjà procédé à des essais avec l'huile et lui montre les installations qu'il a déjà réalisées pour tester l'isolation des courants à haute tension. Dès lors persuadé que les courants à haute tension peuvent être produits et transportés comme il le préconise pour son projet à Francfort, l'ingénieur bavarois entre en contact en juin 1890 avec son ancien patron de l'AEG, E. Rathenau, en soutenant l'idée que sa firme doit coopérer avec les Ateliers de construction Oerlikon. L'accord n'est pas difficile à obtenir, car comme indiqué plus haut, les deux firmes coopèrent déjà depuis 1886. Elles conviennent d'une répartition des tâches. Les Ateliers de construction Oerlikon doivent fournir la génératrice à courant triphasé destinée à la centrale hydroélectrique d'Heilbronn et des transformateurs, alors que l'AEG s'engage à fournir les moteurs triphasés de type Dobrowolsky, des lampes à incandescence, le tableau de distribution et également des transformateurs[35]. De son côté, Ch. E. L. Brown doit conduire une série d'essais sur les courants à haute tension. C'est ce laboratoire hors les murs qui nous intéresse maintenant.

Le laboratoire hors les murs

Le processus est engagé et la firme suisse monte une installation d'essai, annonciatrice de ce qui sera appelé « système Oerlikon de ligne à longue distance » pendant l'exposition. L'originalité du système consiste à ne plus utiliser seulement les transformateurs pour abaisser la haute tension fournie par les génératrices au bas voltage exigé par le service de distribution, mais il s'agit cette fois d'utiliser les transformateurs pour élever la tension fournie par les génératrices jusqu'aux très hautes tensions nécessaires au transport. Jusque-là, les lignes de transport étaient alimentées par la tension directement fournie par les génératrices. Vers 1885, afin de limiter les pertes en ligne, les pionniers augmentent toujours plus la tension pour construire des génératrices qui produisent 3 000 à 4 000 volts. En 1889, le Britannique Sebastian Ziani de Ferranti va même jusqu'à concevoir des alternateurs de 10 000 volts pour sa centrale londonienne de Deptford[36]. Le problème devient rapidement insoluble, car plus la tension produite par un alternateur s'élève, plus son rendement diminue si bien que les gains obtenus par l'élévation de tension lors du transport ne compensent plus les pertes des génératrices. Si les pionniers parviennent rapidement à obtenir des rendements

---

[35] *Schweizerische Bauzeitung*, 17, 1891, p. 57 ; *Elektrizität. Offizielle Zeitung der Internationalen Elektrotechnischen Ausstellung Frankfurt am Main 1891*, Francfort-sur-le-Main, 1891, p. 29, 597 et 825 ; Müller, « Le cinquantenaire », *op. cit.*

[36] Voir J.-F. Wilson, *Ferranti and the British Electrical Industry (1864-1930)*, Manchester/New York, 1988, p. 25-51 ; Hughes, *Networks*, *op. cit.*, p. 234-247.

élevés avec le transformateur, il reste à résoudre la question de son isolement.

Bien décidés à surmonter ce problème, les Ateliers de construction Oerlikon construisent un transformateur monophasé d'essai. Il présente un bobinage cylindrique monté sur un noyau magnétique d'une section qui se rapproche autant que possible de la forme circulaire. L'enroulement à haute tension est placé à l'intérieur, celui à basse tension à l'extérieur. Le tout est placé dans un bac en fonte, rempli d'huile résineuse. Depuis les essais effectués par Brook, on sait en effet que l'huile est un bon isolant. On l'utilise ici comme diélectrique homogène capable de remplir tous les interstices et de protéger les enroulements contre l'humidité et la poussière.

Le transformateur d'essai, conçu en vue de sa commercialisation, est d'un démontage facile. Le bobinage est de fabrication aisée ce qui implique un coût réduit, une grande sécurité d'exploitation ainsi qu'une bonne protection contre les contacts accidentels. Le circuit d'essai de dix kilomètres, construit près d'Oerlikon, est composé d'une ligne de cuivre de quatre millimètres de diamètre fixée à l'aide d'isolateurs de dix fois huit centimètres, avec gorge circulaire remplie d'huile, montés sur des poteaux distants de 25 mètres. Ce type d'isolateur à glaçure brune avait prouvé ses capacités lors du transport à courant continu de Soleure. Nous pouvons une fois encore constater le rôle de l'expérience acquise, même lorsqu'il s'agit de procédés différents.

À partir de la mi-novembre 1890, des essais et des mesures sont réalisés quotidiennement dans des conditions atmosphériques les plus diverses. Les tensions utilisées, qui atteignent le niveau considérable de 40 000 volts, ne provoquent aucun phénomène anormal aussi bien dans les transformateurs que sur la ligne. Les pionniers prennent garde de s'occuper des dysfonctionnements que pourraient entraîner le transport de l'énergie sur les lignes téléphoniques, car le tracé projeté doit suivre la ligne du chemin de fer Lauffen-Francfort, le long duquel courent de nombreuses lignes téléphoniques. Pour ce faire, à Oerlikon, les expérimentateurs fixent une ligne téléphonique sur les mêmes traverses que la ligne à haute tension à une distance de 30 centimètres seulement. Il s'avère que le courant alternatif de la ligne de transport d'énergie trouble moins les conversations téléphoniques que les dérangements causés par les lignes télégraphiques.

Il faut surmonter plusieurs obstacles avant que les organisateurs de l'exposition obtiennent enfin l'accord des nombreux *Länder* concernés par le tracé (Wurtemberg, Bade et Hesse). Il s'avère encore indispensable de s'assurer le concours des *Reichstelegraph* afin que l'opération puisse être réalisée par des employés du Reich, alors au bénéfice de la meilleure expérience dans le domaine des câbles aériens en cuivre. Bien que les essais d'Oerlikon aient démontré qu'il est possible d'isoler totalement des courants électriques à 30 000 volts, les représentants de la *Reichspost* ne s'estiment pas satisfaits, car les éventuels dérangements sur les lignes téléphoniques ne sont pas encore bien cernés par les promoteurs du projet.

Dans le but d'obtenir les autorisations et une participation financière, une démonstration est faite en janvier 1891 à Oerlikon. Après avoir présenté les performances, on simule des accidents pour dissiper les craintes. On court-circuite la ligne à haute tension en jetant un fil métallique sur les conducteurs. On simule encore une pluie torrentielle en aspergeant les isolateurs et on provoque des arcs à la terre et des étincelles. Sous l'influence de la pluie, l'intensité qui était précédemment de dix ampères, s'élève seulement à onze ampères, sans troubler le service et les courts-circuits ainsi que les décharges à la terre ne provoquent que la fusion des fusibles en plomb. Afin d'éviter qu'une rupture de conducteurs ne mette en danger les personnes, on envisage de couper automatiquement la génératrice à l'aide d'un interrupteur munie d'un relais à courant minimum. Les autorités du Reich et les administrations d'État promettent leur appui, alors que l'empereur d'Allemagne, soupesant les enjeux économiques et nationaux offre 10 000 Reichsmarks. La Chambre de commerce de Francfort accorde une somme identique et la firme Hesse & Söhne s'engage à fournir gratuitement les câbles de cuivre.

Les organisateurs ne sont pas certains de voir les installations prêtes à fonctionner pour les débuts de l'exposition à fin mai. von Miller en arrive à espérer les inaugurer seulement à la veille de la clôture en automne. Parfois, des difficultés administratives qui paraissaient contournées resurgissent. Ainsi le gouvernement de Bade refuse un temps d'accorder l'autorisation de connecter les lignes pourtant terminées à ses frontières. Mais les constructeurs « font le forcing » et la ligne est mise sous tension pour la première fois fin août. Le 25, 600 lampes à incandescence s'allument, le 26 le moteur de 100 CV fonctionne et le 30, 1 000 lampes sont allumées trois ou quatre heures durant, matin et soir. La ligne, qui fonctionne pour la première fois à pleine charge le 12 septembre, alimente les lampes à incandescence et l'installation de pompage de la cascade artificielle.

Deux jours plus tard, les installations germano-suisses sont visitées par plus de 100 invités dont plusieurs délégués envoyés par divers pays. Le président de la Confédération Welti et le conseiller fédéral Schenk représentent les autorités helvétiques. Les plus grands spécialistes sont aussi présents, parmi lesquels les Français Deprez et Hospitalier, l'Italien Ferrari, le Genevois Turrettini et l'Anglais Thompson.

Compte tenu des enjeux, l'établissement du rendement des installations suscite de nombreuses discussions. La commission d'évaluation réunit des professeurs, des industriels et des spécialistes de plusieurs pays. Elle est notamment composée des professeurs Dietrich, Stenger, Teichmann, Voith, Weber, des docteurs Feussner, Heim, Kopp ainsi que des ingénieurs Nizzola et Schmaller[37]. Des premières analyses démontrent que des rendements de l'ordre de 72 à 75 % sont atteints, pour des puissances oscillants entre 100 et 200 CV[38]. Toutefois, les résultats officiels ne sont rendus qu'en 1894, soit trois années plus tard. Ces derniers sont quelque peu revus à la baisse, à 68,5 % lorsque la puissance transportée est faible (78,1 CV), mais sont maintenus à 75,2 % lorsque la puissance est élevée (126,6 CV). La tension utilisée, entre 7 700 et 8 650 volts, se révèle nettement inférieure à celle que proposait l'organisateur de l'exposition[39].

Cette percée technologique est sans aucun doute représentative des capacités des nouveaux pays pilotes que sont la Suisse et l'Allemagne à saisir les opportunités offertes par les hautes technologies de la deuxième industrialisation. On peut admettre l'hypothèse que dans ces pays, la convergence entre recherche fondamentale et recherche industrielle serait précoce et efficace. Cela reste à démontrer, tout comme les parts respectives de la théorie, de la science, et de la recherche empirique.

Une autre question se pose : après ce partenariat, faut-il pour autant croire que les protagonistes de Francfort vont travailler main dans la main ? Force est de constater le contraire. Après le temps de la coopération vient celui de la rivalité[40]. Il est vrai que la donne change radicalement avec le départ de Ch. Brown des Ateliers de construction Oerlikon parti valoriser au mieux son savoir-faire auprès du nouvel entrant Brown, Boveri & Cie, créé après l'exposition de Francfort en automne 1891. Cela se fait au grand dam de son ancien patron, P.-E. Huber, qui n'hésite pas à déclarer au Crédit suisse que la nouvelle firme fera banqueroute dans six mois[41]. Les Ateliers de construction Oerlikon auront beaucoup de peine à se remettre du départ de Ch. Brown. L'entreprise stagne en effet jusqu'à l'adoption en 1916 de son système de traction sur grande ligne à courant monophasé par les Chemins de fer fédéraux. De

---

[37] Hospitalier, « Transport et distribution d'énergie », *op. cit.*, p. 267-268.

[38] *Ibid.*, p. 268, *Schweizerische Bauzeitung*, 18, 1891, p. 162-164.

[39] *Offizieler Bericht über die International Elektrotechnische Ausstellung in Frankfurt am Main 1891. Band II : Arbeiten der Prüfung-Kommission in deren Auftrag*, Francfort-sur-le-Main, 1894, p. 361.

[40] Nous nous basons sur notre étude, *Histoire de l'électricité en Suisse, op. cit.*, t. 2, p. 659-722.

[41] Selon Fritz Funk, « Gründung der Kommanditgesellschaft Brown Boveri & Cie, Baden, in deren ersten Jahre », dactylographié, sans date, sans lieu, p. 12.

son côté, la firme Brown, Boveri & Cie s'engage dans une progression continue qui la situe au niveau des *small giants* mondiaux. Malgré les protestations des constructeurs d'outre-Rhin, la nouvelle firme remporte en 1893 le marché de Francfort, puis installe en 1900 à Mannheim une filiale de fabrication de machines. Grâce à quatre autres filiales de fabrication implantées entre 1901 et 1910, en France, en Italie, en Autriche-Hongrie et en Norvège, BBC est présente dans les principaux marchés européens. Si cette expansion s'explique par la réussite du duo formé du technicien Brown et du commercial Walter Boveri (ancien collègue de Brown aux Ateliers de construction Oerlikon), elle doit beaucoup à une présence forte sur le créneau de la production et du transport de courant électrique à grande échelle qui s'exprime dans la continuité du transport longue distance de Francfort. Sur ce segment de marché porteur, d'autres innovations suivent : une turbine à vapeur performante (1902) et le fonctionnement combiné d'usines au fil de l'eau avec d'autres à accumulation saisonnière qui débouche en 1908 sur la grande première qui combine l'usine rhénane de Beznau (Argovie) avec l'usine alpine de Löntsch (Glaris). Le patron de l'AEG, E. Rathenau, échaudé par la réussite du *small giant* helvétique, plus particulièrement dans le domaine stratégique des turbines à vapeur, utilise alors ses connexions financières internationales pour tenter d'en prendre le contrôle au début des années 1900.

Par conséquent, la coopération inter-firmes, surtout à l'échelle internationale, ne semble fonctionner que dans des circonstances particulières, dont celles qui entourent l'exposition de Francfort. On se pose donc la question de savoir si d'autres expériences de ce type existent et dans quelles circonstances.

La dynamique industrielle
d'un laboratoire public de recherche
Le cas du Laboratoire de génie électrique de Toulouse

Marie-Pierre Bès[1]

Cers-CIRUS, Unité mixte du CNRS et de l'Université de Toulouse le Mirail

Notre travail s'inscrit, pour une part, dans les études sur la science qui tendent à montrer que les interactions entre la science publique et l'industrie sont anciennes[2] et qu'elles ont « fabriqué » de nouvelles disciplines scientifiques, appelées aussi sciences appliquées[3]. En analysant les collaborations industrielles du Laboratoire public de génie électrique de Toulouse (LGET) de 1955 à 1985[4], nous montrerons à la fois comment ce laboratoire a participé à l'émergence et à la structuration d'une nouvelle discipline des sciences appliquées (le génie électrique) et comment il s'est développé sur la base de plusieurs collaborations industrielles.

La période étudiée est celle des grands programmes technologiques, caractérisée par le rôle primordial des établissements et entreprises publiques (CNES, CNET, CEA[5], EDF, ELF, etc.), l'existence de financements publics conséquents pour la conduite de travaux d'études et de

---

[1] Ce texte a été relu et corrigé par Robert Lacoste directeur du laboratoire de 1968 à 1978. Nous le remercions vivement pour cet exercice et restons responsable des éventuelles erreurs présentes dans le texte. bes@univ-tlse2.fr.

[2] Nous réfutons les analyses sur l'émergence d'un nouveau mode de savoir et préférons les thèses d'un accroissement de la propriété privée des connaissances, voir D. Pestre, *Science, argent et politique, un essai d'interprétation*, INRA, 2003, 201 p.

[3] Voir les travaux du comité de recherche « Sciences, innovation technologique et société » existant au sein de l'Association internationale de sociologie de langue française, http://www.univ-tlse2.fr/aislf/gt6/index1024.htm.

[4] Les sources d'information proviennent d'entretiens, de rapports d'activité, de CV, de lettres, des thèses des premiers chercheurs du laboratoire ainsi que des cinq directeurs successifs.

[5] CNES : Centre national d'études spatiales, CNET : Centre national d'études sur les télécommunications, CEA : Commissariat à l'énergie atomique.

recherches appliquées aux secteurs qualifiés de stratégiques tels que l'espace, le nucléaire et les télécommunications. De surcroît, au cours de ces années 1960-1990, les entreprises françaises tissent des partenariats longs et forts avec les laboratoires publics de recherche de sorte que l'on qualifie ces relations de système national d'innovation[6].

D'autre part, notre approche se positionne dans les études économiques et sociologiques des réseaux sociaux[7] qui permettent d'envisager de manière étroite les relations individuelles et les relations entre organisations. Nous avons déjà montré que, dans les contrats entre la recherche publique et l'industrie[8], les deux échelles sont partiellement emboîtées. Dans cette publication, nous portons notre attention sur la manière dont l'équipe s'est appuyée sur chacun de ses partenaires industriels et institutionnels (universités, sociétés savantes, associations d'enseignants) pour poursuivre ses activités (nombre de partenaires, longueur des partenariats, type de chercheurs investis, responsabilités individuelles, nature du contact, type de recherche, achat de matériel) et sur les enchaînements opérés entre plusieurs collaborations (passages de relais entre individus, changement de partenaire, rupture ou stabilité des sujets de recherche, arrivée ou départ de nouveaux chercheurs). Cet article suit l'ordre chronologique des travaux du laboratoire après un bref rappel historique des ancêtres du LGET.

Rupture « électrique » en 1955

L'Institut électrotechnique de Toulouse (IET)[9] créé dans cette ville en 1907, concentra ses premières activités sur les questions d'hydraulique. Puis apparurent les premiers enseignements dans le domaine de la radioélectricité et de l'électrotechnique. Mais jusqu'aux années 1940, seule l'activité en hydraulique et mécanique des fluides donna lieu à des relations avec l'industrie du secteur de l'énergie hydroélectrique. En 1942, le professeur L. Escande succéda au professeur Camichel à la tête de l'IET et de l'IMFT (Institut de mécanique des fluides de Toulouse) et quelques recherches en électrotechnique démarrèrent, avec, par exemple, la thèse de doctorat d'État de Jean Lagasse, soutenue en 1952 sous

[6]   B. Amable, R. Barré, R. Boyer, *Les systèmes d'innovation à l'ère de la globalisation*, Paris, Economica, 1997, 401 p.

[7]   Voir par exemple, le n° 103 de la *Revue d'économie industrielle* consacrée à la morphogenèse des réseaux, 2e et 3e trimestres 2003.

[8]   M. Grossetti, M. P. Bès, « Encastrements et découplages dans les relations science-industrie », *Revue française de sociologie*, vol. 42, n° 2, 2001, p. 327-355.

[9]   M. Grossetti et B. Milard, « Une ville investit dans la science : genèse de l'Institut Électrotechnique de Toulouse » in *La naissance de l'ingénieur-électricien : origines et développement des formations nationales électrotechniques*, Paris, PUF, 1997, p. 133-148.

l'égide du professeur Tessié-Solier, directeur du laboratoire d'électro-technique et d'électronique industrielle au sein de l'IET. Entre-temps, l'Institut était devenu une école nationale supérieure d'ingénieurs et l'activité de recherche avait été scindée en trois composantes : l'une centrée sur la mécanique des fluides, une autre sur l'électrotechnique et la troisième sur la radio-électricité.

C'est en 1953, dans ce laboratoire d'électrotechnique et d'électro-nique industrielle, qu'un jeune enseignant-chercheur particulièrement dynamique, Jean Lagasse, provoqua une scission, qu'il justifia par des motifs d'orientation scientifique : « l'électrotechnique classique était une discipline vieillissante qu'il convenait de moderniser, il manquait un esprit d'ouverture vers l'industrie ; je voulais démarrer des enseigne-ments et des recherches dans le domaine tout à fait naissant, à l'époque, en France, des servomécanismes et des asservissements »[10]. Il prônait une autre approche de la recherche que celle menée par le directeur du laboratoire, en souhaitant partir des « besoins » scientifiques des nou-veaux produits et technologies. Cette rupture dans la démarche scienti-fique est confirmée par l'un de ses collègues[11] :

> Jean Lagasse qui était le moteur et moi, qui étais du même avis que lui, nous ne pouvions plus supporter de faire de l'électronique traditionnelle que fai-sait le père Tessié-Solier alors on a dit, bon il faut faire quelque chose, il faut se remuer, on va pas rester là, on va pas rester comme ça et alors au sein toujours de cet ancien laboratoire d'électrotechnique et d'électronique industrielle, nous avons fait une sorte de sécession interne et nous n'avons plus eu de lien scientifique avec notre ancien maître à tous les deux...[12]

Jean Lagasse entraîna une vingtaine de personnes dans sa démarche de rupture ; personnes, qui créèrent un nouveau laboratoire en 1955 : le LGE (Laboratoire de génie électrique) dont Jean Lagasse prit la direc-tion. Parmi ces chercheurs, se trouvait Robert Lacoste – qui deviendra le deuxième directeur du LGE – docteur ingénieur depuis 1951, qui se lance dans la préparation d'une thèse d'État.

Le choix du terme « génie électrique » fit l'objet d'une discussion entre les membres de cette nouvelle formation ; l'idée était de souligner l'aspect appliqué des recherches, de se référer à la démarche « ingé-nieur » et de s'inspirer des modèles plus anciens du génie civil et du génie chimique. Bien qu'à l'époque, les chercheurs concernés n'aient pas de connaissances précises du contexte de recherche américain, ce terme se rapproche de « l'Electrical Engineering » largement utilisé dans les pays anglo-saxons. Pour les chercheurs toulousains, l'idée du terme

---

[10] Entretien réalisé par Michel Grossetti, février 1990.
[11] Robert Lacoste, qui deviendra directeur du LGE de 1968 à 1978.
[12] Entretien avec R. Lacoste réalisé en 2005.

« génie » est d'aller vers les applications et de retrouver la même racine étymologique que celle du terme « ingénieur ».

Dès l'entame de la scission, Jean Lagasse, qui projetait de se spécialiser sur dans les servomécanismes, suggéra à son jeune collègue Robert Lacoste, un autre domaine de recherche à savoir celui des isolants et matériels diélectriques dont il savait qu'il était quasiment vierge alors que les besoins de l'industrie y étaient très importants. Ceci opéra une séparation des thématiques scientifiques :

> Nous avions des préoccupations scientifiques tout à fait différentes eux c'était les servomécanismes ce qu'on appelle maintenant les systèmes et moi c'était plutôt la physique des diélectriques, pourquoi ça conduit pas, pourquoi ça conduit, enfin les semi-conducteurs tout ça quoi et on faisait des expériences de physique bien davantage alors qu'eux c'était l'architecture des systèmes, d'ailleurs le LAAS[13] s'appelle maintenant Architecture des systèmes, eux c'était, comment dire, très proche de l'informatique tandis que nous on appliquait les tensions sur des isolants, on gérait des tensions très faibles et puis quand on a étudié l'action des décharges sur la dégradation des isolants on a étudié les décharges, on est allés voir nos collègues chimistes et nous avions beaucoup plus de rapports avec les physico-chimistes qu'avec l'autre équipe du laboratoire mais la tradition s'était bien installée, on était bien ensemble et on a continué comme ça jusqu'à ce que le LAAS se crée.[14]

À ses débuts, le LGE est donc composé de deux équipes assez distinctes : l'équipe « Automatique et électronique associée » dirigée par Jean Lagasse qui prit dès 1957 des contacts industriels et vit ses effectifs rapidement portés à plus de 30 membres, doctorants compris. Selon Robert Lacoste, de nombreux jeunes diplômés de l'école nationale à laquelle était rattaché le laboratoire sont attirés par ces disciplines récentes :

> Cela vient du fait que vu le recrutement des étudiants que nous avions à la fac ou à l'ENSEEIHT[15], ça fait que les gens étaient plus attirés par l'électronique des bidules, faire des systèmes, des choses qui disent papa-maman, des automatismes, des choses comme ça, que par l'étude un peu plus austère d'un phénomène physique et voilà, car quand on passait sa journée à tracer des courbes de décroissance du courant à travers un isolant c'était pas toujours passionnant, il fallait avoir cette tournure d'esprit donc ça s'est fait tout naturellement.[16]

---

[13] LAAS : le Laboratoire d'automatique et ses applications spatiales devenu par la suite le Laboratoire d'analyse et d'architecture des systèmes.

[14] Entretien avec Robert Lacoste, 2005.

[15] ENSEEIHT : École nationale supérieure d'électrotechnique, d'électronique, d'informatique, d'hydraulique et des télécommunications.

[16] Entretien avec Robert Lacoste, 2005.

En 1968, cette équipe fonda, avec l'appui du CNES, un laboratoire propre du CNRS, le Laboratoire d'automatique et ses applications spatiales (LAAS)[17].

L'équipe « Matériaux diélectriques » du LGE était plus modeste – une dizaine de membres – ses contacts industriels moins nombreux et son insertion dans la communauté scientifique très embryonnaire. Elle est naturellement animée par Robert Lacoste, qui préparait une thèse d'État sur le thème des isolants, comme cela lui avait été suggéré par Jean Lagasse. Ce dernier endossa le rôle de véritable directeur de thèse de son collègue en l'aidant efficacement dans cette entreprise.

> Il nous est enfin difficile d'exprimer par de simples mots tout ce que nous devons à M. J. Lagasse, professeur à la faculté des Sciences. Nous avons voulu cependant reporter à la fin de ce propos le témoignage d'attachement et de dévouement que nous tenons à lui donner. Depuis des années, nous avons le privilège de travailler sous la direction de M. Lagasse ; il a stimulé nos efforts et suivi pas à pas le cheminement de nos travaux ; il s'est ingénié à faciliter notre tâche à la fois par ses conseils et en nous procurant tout ce coûteux matériel, nécessaire pourtant à une étude sérieuse sur les isolants. Nous croyons qu'en retour, il n'est pas de remerciements plus vrais que de l'assurer pour l'avenir de la même fidèle collaboration.[18]

La thèse de Robert Lacoste (1954-1959) s'appuie sur un réseau scientifique et industriel national

Afin d'explorer la thématique, nouvelle pour lui, des matériaux diélectriques et dynamiser l'équipe qu'il rassemble et dirige, Robert Lacoste « entreprend un tour de France des laboratoires[19] et industries où l'on étudiait, fabriquait ou utilisait des diélectriques ou isolants électriques »[20]. Ainsi, il rencontre tout d'abord le professeur Esclangon, enseignant à l'université de Paris et directeur du Laboratoire central des industries électriques (LCIE) jusqu'en 1957. Ce dernier l'encourage vivement à poursuivre son projet scientifique :

> je me souviendrai toujours la phrase d'Esclangon quand je suis allé le voir au Laboratoire central des industries électriques, il me dit « vous avez raison de vous diriger vers l'étude des isolants parce que ça fait 40 ans qu'on écrit dessus et vous en avez encore pour 40 ans » il ne croyait pas si bien dire ».

---

[17]   L'histoire de ce laboratoire est parfaitement décrite dans l'ouvrage de M. Grossetti, *Science, Industrie et Territoire*, Toulouse, Presses universitaires du Mirail, 1995, 311 p.

[18]   Postface de la thèse de Robert Lacoste, 1959, p. 116.

[19]   Le Laboratoire de génie électrique de Paris est créé plus tard.

[20]   Entretien avec Robert Lacoste, 1999.

Le jeune chercheur rencontre également des universitaires grenoblois, comme le professeur Louis Néel qui soutient sa démarche et le met en contact avec le professeur N. Félicy du Laboratoire d'électrostatique de Grenoble qui conduisait une approche similaire[21]. Il se rend également à Bordeaux, Montpellier ainsi que dans des sociétés industrielles comme Merlin-Gerin à Grenoble, Delle-Alsthom à Villeurbanne, la Compagnie électromécanique au Bourget, Alsthom à Belfort, les fabricants de matières plastiques à Oyonnax, etc. Robert Lacoste cite une autre rencontre déterminante, celle du professeur Philippe Olmer et de son collaborateur R. Bonnefille, enseignants à Nancy.

Au cours de cette période, ces enseignants et chercheurs universitaires français se réunissent à l'initiative du professeur Paul Aigrain, titulaire de la chaire d'électrotechnique à l'université de Paris avec l'objectif de faire en sorte que l'électrotechnique devienne une discipline majeure dans les facultés[22]. Louis Néel et Paul Aigrain font partie de ces chercheurs réformateurs qui obtiennent les plus hautes récompenses scientifiques et collaborent activement avec l'industrie ou l'armée[23]. Leurs trajectoires correspondent plutôt au modèle dominant américain qu'au schéma français idéologique méfiant vis-à-vis de l'industrie[24]. En 1954, une vingtaine de personnes réunies autour de Paul Aigrain (dont Philippe Olmer, nommé à l'université de Paris, Jean Lagasse et Robert Lacoste) assistent à la première réunion à Supélec (École supérieure d'électricité) du Club EEA (Électrotechnique, électronique, automatique), chargé de constituer une vitrine démarquée de la physique fondamentale[25]. Le Club EEA atteint la centaine de membres en 1960 et prend une importance majeure pour la concertation des enseignements, des diplômes nationaux et des programmes de recherche. En 1964, les électroniciens se joignent aux pionniers qui travaillaient depuis 1960 dans les domaines de l'automatique et de l'électrotechnique et en 1965, Pierre Aigrain est nommé directeur général des Enseignements supérieurs. De la sorte, le Club devint un « bureau d'études »

[21] Le professeur Félicy avait mis au point, dès les années 1944-1947, des machines électrostatiques, très utiles pour l'armée, la marine, les sociétés industrielles, ou d'autres laboratoires.

[22] Michel-Yves Bernard, « les facultés des sciences et la formation des cadres pour l'industrie ; l'exemple du Club EEA », *La naissance de l'ingénieur-électricien*, *op. cit.*, p. 501-520.

[23] T. Shinn, G. Benguigui, « Physicists and Intellectual Mobility », *Information sur les Sciences Sociales*, vol. 36, n° 2, 1997.

[24] T. Shinn, « Axes thématiques et marches de diffusion, la science en France, 1975-1999 », *Sociologies et sociétés*, vol. XXXII, n° 1, 2000, p. 43-69.

[25] Ils se « battront » pour avoir des sections séparées dans les différentes instances de recherche scientifique afin d'obtenir une reconnaissance spécifique, ainsi que les moyens en hommes et en matériel pour développer leurs activités scientifiques.

officieux du ministère de l'Éducation nationale dans les domaines de compétence de l'EEA[26].

Entre-temps, en 1957, Philippe Olmer, professeur à l'université de Paris, est nommé directeur du LCIE, laboratoire créé en 1881 par les industriels et les pouvoirs publics et spécialisé dans la métrologie, les essais et les études consacrées aux matériels électriques[27]. Bien que l'activité majeure du LCIE soit la conduite d'essais en vue de la normalisation d'appareils électriques, certaines études et recherches à caractère technologique sont également conduites en partenariat avec des chercheurs publics ou industriels[28]. En 1960, Philippe Olmer est également directeur de Supélec[29]. En fait, cet ensemble d'éléments laisse penser que Robert Lacoste n'a pas contacté ces chercheurs ou industriels au hasard mais plutôt que ceux-ci se connaissaient à travers leur appartenance à différents collectifs professionnels en gestation, notamment l'EEA et que, d'autre part, Jean Lagasse, déjà inséré dans cette communauté des électriciens, a dû ouvrir à Robert Lacoste « son carnet d'adresses ». Ce dernier s'appuie donc sur un réseau national de scientifiques et d'industriels déjà constitué mais en voie d'institutionnalisation. Grâce à ces contacts, Robert Lacoste put conduire son travail sur les matériaux diélectriques et les isolants. Pour ses essais, il bénéficia notamment des moyens matériels et humains du LCIE. Il soutint sa thèse de doctorat ès sciences physiques en 1959 sous le titre « Contribution à l'étude de la conductibilité des isolants solides » devant un jury présidé par le professeur Escande (ENSEEIHT) et auquel participaient les professeurs Dupin, Blanc, Tessié-Solier, Lagasse[30] et Olmer. Il devint ensuite chef de travaux – l'équivalent de l'actuel maître de conférences – à la faculté.

---

[26] M. Y. Bernard, *op. cit.*, p. 510.

[27] Le LCIE, a été créé par décret en 1882 pour s'occuper de métrologie électrique, puis devient en 1928 le laboratoire de la profession chargé d'entreprendre pour la collectivité des études sur les matériaux, notamment isolants, en vue d'améliorer leur utilisation et de prévenir les incidents pouvant mettre en péril le matériel électrique dans différents secteurs : machines, câbles, appareillage. Robert Lacoste remercie dans sa thèse Jean Fabre, chef du Service des isolants du LCIE (source : thèse R. Lacoste, 1959, p. 116).

[28] D. Ortonne, « Histoire du Laboratoire Central des Industries Électriques de 1881 à nos jours », mémoire de maîtrise de l'université de Paris X Nanterre, 1997, 154 p.

[29] Lors du 3e colloque international d'histoire de l'électricité qui a eu lieu à Paris les 14-16 décembre 1994, le professeur Olmer raconte de quelle manière il a rénové les enseignements de Supélec avec son collaborateur R. Bonnefille. Voir Philippe Olmer, « La nécessaire réforme des années soixante », *La naissance de l'ingénieur-électricien, op. cit.*, p. 193-197.

[30] Quatre professeurs de l'ENSEEIHT.

Schématiquement, il est possible de présenter le réseau des relations scientifiques de Robert Lacoste au cours de sa thèse, entre 1953 et 1959, en faisant figurer les relations entre individus et celles qui engagent des institutions.

**Schéma n° 1 : Le réseau des relations scientifiques
de R. Lacoste entre 1953 et 1959**

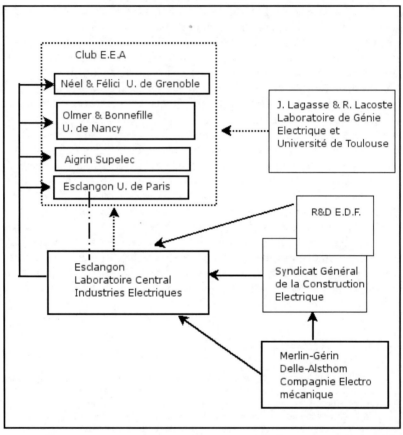

Robert Lacoste s'appuie sur les liens tissés par Jean Lagasse auprès de la jeune communauté scientifique du génie électrique, composée d'un volet enseignement et recherche universitaire (EEA, Supélec, universités de Grenoble et Nancy) et d'un volet recherche industrielle autour du LCIE et d'EDF. Les relations individuelles entre les enseignants-chercheurs de ces jeunes disciplines, co-fondatrices de la section sciences pour l'ingénieur du CNRS quelques années plus tard, se mêlent aux relations existantes entre les différents organismes, tels que par exemple, Supélec, le LCIE et EDF. Cet ensemble forme une véritable communauté professionnelle.

Les premières études du LGE pour EDF : 1960-1966

Dès la nationalisation de l'électricité en 1946, la direction des Études et recherches (DER) d'EDF constitua un laboratoire industriel chargé de conduire et de financer des recherches en vue de moderniser l'outil de production, le transport et la distribution d'électricité. Or, l'appareil industriel français était en retard sur de nombreuses technologies et les incidents de fonctionnement étaient fréquents, par exemple sur les machines synchrones qui fournissaient l'énergie électrique dans les centrales. L'absence de contrôle, de maintenance et de modernisation pendant la guerre, provoqua des pannes répétées sur les machines électriques. La DER engagea donc des études internes sur ces questions, finançant notamment des études sur les matériaux diélectriques et leur vieillissement.

C'est dans ce cadre qu'a été confiée à la jeune équipe « matériaux diélectriques » du LGE, à titre de test, une première étude à peine entamée par le LCIE sur les essais de tenue en tension du matériel électrique. Le travail fut réalisé par un doctorant[31] en électronique dans le cadre d'une thèse de 3ᵉ cycle dirigée par Robert Lacoste. Il montra qu'il était possible de tester valablement l'isolation de matériels en les soumettant aux surtensions imposées par les normes, mais en continu et non en alternatif, c'est-à-dire sans fatigue supplémentaire pour les isolants. Le principe pouvait être alors directement utilisé par les industriels. De surcroît, ce premier travail apporta un réel crédit scientifique au LGE ainsi que l'établissement de contacts directs avec la direction des Études et des recherches d'EDF.

Le deuxième sujet de recherche, fortement financé par EDF à partir de l'année 1960 est celui des interactions entre les décharges et les surfaces et en particulier le problème de la dégradation des isolants sous l'action de ces décharges. En effet, pour isoler les câbles électriques, on a d'abord utilisé des caoutchoucs pendant la guerre, puis, dans les années 1950, du papier imprégné qui posait d'importants problèmes puis on est passé au polyéthylène réticulé chimiquement (PRC) dans les années 1960, qui avait des propriétés beaucoup plus intéressantes mais qui nécessitait de maîtriser cette technologie[32]. EDF a accompagné le

---

[31] Il s'agit de la thèse de 3ᵉ cycle de Bui-Aï soutenue le 30 juin 1960 devant les professeurs Tessié-Solier, Dupin, Lagasse et Lacoste.

[32] Témoignage de Lucien Deschamps (ancien chercheur et chef de division à la direction des Études et recherches d'EDF), au colloque du Comité d'histoire de la Fonda-

processus d'innovation en réalisant un travail de spécifications techniques très précises, très détaillées, pour guider les constructeurs sur la qualité et les essais et en commandant par voie de conséquence des études très précises aux laboratoires. Le Syndicat général de la construction électrique (SGCE) et la direction de l'Électricité du ministère de l'Industrie furent également intéressés par ces travaux[33].

Là, l'équipe se lança dans une étude approfondie de ce phénomène sur le plan électrique (caractérisation des décharges) et sur le plan physico-chimique (caractérisation des dégâts). Le travail porta sur l'analyse des causes de défaillance par l'établissement d'une relation entre, d'une part, le nombre et l'amplitude des décharges et, d'autre part, les produits de dégradation du matériau, qui en sont la conséquence. Ce travail s'effectua dans un cadre bien plus large que la première étude :

– Dans l'équipe, plusieurs chercheurs étaient concernés puisqu'il y aura six thèses[34] sur le sujet, dont les deux plus importantes soutenues en avril 1966. Ils travaillèrent sur l'analyse physico-chimique des nouvelles matières premières des câbles, le polyéthylène.

– Pour effectuer leurs mesures, ils utilisèrent différents procédés spécifiques d'analyse et de mesure nouveaux[35] mais ils utilisèrent aussi les moyens de tests d'un laboratoire spécialisé de l'Armement (GIAT), installé à Tarbes qui possédait des moyens et des matériaux pour effectuer des tests de grande envergure.

– Hors de l'équipe, afin de conduire l'analyse des causes physico-chimiques du phénomène, les chercheurs firent appel à des physiciens des solides et des chimistes de l'université Paul Sabatier de Toulouse[36].

Selon l'un des chercheurs du laboratoire : « l'innovation scientifique a donc consisté, à combiner, pour les besoins du génie électrique, deux procédés auparavant utilisés dans d'autres domaines en ajoutant à l'analyse purement électrique une approche pluridisciplinaire ».

Le schéma suivant présente les relations tissées autour de ces deux études :

---

tion EDF, « Entre l'atelier et le laboratoire. Recherche et innovation dans l'industrie électrique du milieu du XIXe siècle à nos jours », Mulhouse, 8-9 décembre 2005.

[33] Introduction des thèses de Bui-Aï et Mayoux, 1966.

[34] Quatre thèses de 3e cycle (celles de Drujon en 1961, Carayon en 1962, Mendes en 1963, Fieux en 1965), la thèse de doctorat ès sciences physiques de Bui-Aï et également la thèse de 3e cycle de Mayoux. Ces dernières sont soutenues en avril 1966, devant des jurys similaires. Une différence notable est la présence de Bui-Aï au jury de la thèse de Mayoux puisqu'il avait soutenu 14 jours avant sa thèse de doctorat ès sciences.

[35] Par exemple la chromatographie.

[36] Les professeurs Marroni et Lattes.

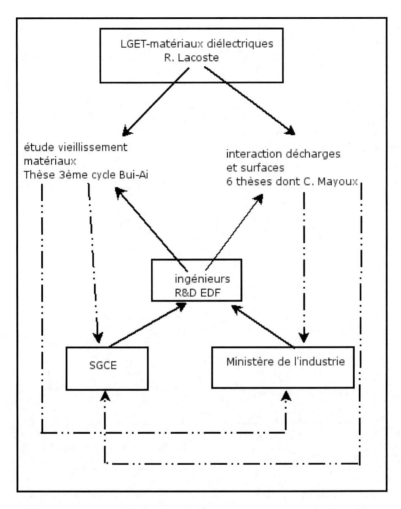

Ces études débouchent naturellement sur des publications de l'équipe et la diffusion des résultats au sein de la communauté scientifique, par exemple auprès de la Société française des électriciens en 1964[37], ou lors d'une conférence à l'École supérieure d'électricité en 1965. Robert Lacoste publia aussi des notes de recherches dans les

---

[37] R. Lacoste, « Étude physique des phénomènes de décharges partielles – Aperçu des recherches en cours et l'orientation des programmes en France », bulletin n° 57 SFE, septembre 1964.

Comptes rendus de l'Académie des sciences (CRAS)[38]. Deux doctorants mobilisés sur cette série d'études, M. Bui-Aï et C. Mayoux obtiendront des postes de chercheurs au CNRS et feront toute leur carrière dans ce laboratoire. L'un d'eux (Bui-Aï) prendra la succession de Robert Lacoste à la direction du LGE. Ainsi, en 1966, le réseau de collaborations de l'équipe de Robert Lacoste est bien plus fourni puisqu'il comprend les laboratoires de l'industrie électrique (EDF, SGCE, LCIE) et la communauté scientifique (Société française des électriciens, Supélec). Il s'est également totalement autonomisé de son contexte de genèse constitué autour du Club EEA et d'autres universités.

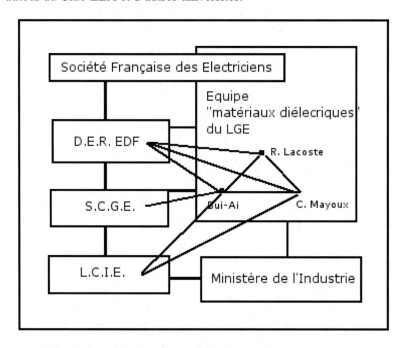

Les activités contractuelles de l'équipe découlèrent directement des besoins croissants de l'industrie électrique, qui cherchait des matériaux d'isolation fiables et conformes à de nouveaux types d'utilisation. L'un des résultats les plus importants pour l'industrie électrique dans cette période concernait la prévention des claquages dans les grandes génératrices synchrones du réseau de production d'énergie électrique. Les résultats des recherches furent normalement diffusés au sein de la communauté scientifique.

---

[38] R. Lacoste, L. Badian, Bui-Aï, « Évaluation de l'épaisseur et du facteur de permittivité de la couche altérée d'une feuille de polyéthylène soumise à l'action des décharges partielles », note aux CRAS, t. 261, p. 2181-2184, septembre 1965.

Les premières études du LGE avec les câbliers (1962-1968)

Les travaux de l'équipe portèrent ici sur les matériaux assurant l'isolation des câbles et les chercheurs allèrent travailler directement avec les fabricants de plastique isolant les câbles[39]. À partir de 1962, ces derniers utilisèrent du polyéthylène (matière plastique) qui posait cependant d'importants problèmes de conductivité, dégradation, phénomènes d'altération, etc.

L'origine des contacts entre le LGE et l'entreprise Atochimie[40], fabricant de polyéthylène, est peu renseignée. D'après le directeur du laboratoire public[41], elle ne découle pas directement des contacts précédents avec l'industrie électrique. En effet, un ingénieur du centre de recherches d'Atochimie en charge des contrats de recherche, aurait pris l'initiative de contacter directement le LGE. Évidemment, Robert Lacoste précise que « La direction des Études et recherches d'Électricité de France, intéressée au premier chef par l'utilisation des câbles, s'est montrée très favorable à cette collaboration ».

L'entreprise Atochimie, qui fabrique du polyéthylène pour des utilisations courantes (revêtements, emballages, etc.), cherche à diversifier sa production vers l'isolation des câbles, ce qui correspond à un matériau à plus forte valeur ajoutée. Les responsables du centre de recherches du groupe pétrolier jouent la « carte locale »[42] et s'adressent aux chercheurs publics. Ils ont besoin de leur expertise pour changer de technologie et s'adapter aux normes de l'industrie électrique. Les dirigeants envisagent de fournir à l'industrie câblière, en l'occurrence l'entreprise Les Câbles de Lyon avec laquelle elle collabore, un matériau « plastique plus noble » en vue du remplacement du papier imprégné dans l'isolation des câbles électriques. En parallèle, l'entreprise SILEC concurrente des Câbles de Lyon avait déjà adopté le polyéthylène comme matériau isolant. Dans la mesure où les compétences des techniciens, ingénieurs et cadres d'Atochimie sont essentiellement chimiques, l'entreprise doit faire appel à l'aide extérieure d'électriciens spécialistes des isolants et notamment le LGE. Pour autant, en interne, l'entreprise disposera rapidement d'un laboratoire de chimie-physique regroupant environ 40 mathématiciens, physiciens, électroniciens, opticiens et atomistes. Ce

---

[39] La première publication sur la dégradation de ce matériau par un membre de l'équipe est la thèse de J. P. Carayon en 1962. On le retrouve dans une publication collective à l'Académie des sciences en 1965.

[40] Filiale de la Société nationale de pétrole d'Aquitaine, SNPA, qui deviendra Elf Aquitaine en 1976 puis Total en 2002.

[41] Entretiens avec R. Lacoste et lettre de R. Lacoste du 14 avril 2000.

[42] Proximité géographique entre les implantations de la SNPA (Boussens en Haute-Garonne ou Pau dans les Pyrénées-Atlantiques).

laboratoire privé traite de sujets divers et met au point de nombreux procédés et appareillages[43]. La collaboration ne comporte pas de relations contractuelles et d'engagement financier, elle porte seulement sur des transmissions d'échantillons de polyéthylène en échange de rapports d'expertise effectués par R. Lacoste.

Dans le laboratoire, tous les chercheurs travaillent sur ces nouveaux matériaux isolants : par exemple, dans sa thèse de 3e cycle soutenue en 1966, C. Mayoux avait annoncé qu'il envisageait de poursuivre ses investigations sur des matériaux plus complexes comme le polyéthylène et d'un usage devenu courant dans le domaine de l'électrotechnique ou de l'électronique. C'est ce qu'il fait grâce à des contrats d'étude avec la direction des Études et recherches d'EDF, le SGCE, la direction de l'Électricité, du gaz et du charbon du ministère du Développement industriel et scientifique et le Laboratoire de physique des décharges de l'École supérieure d'électricité. En 1972, il présente la synthèse des études qu'il a développées depuis 1966 dans sa thèse de doctorat ès sciences physiques sous le titre « Contribution à l'étude de l'action, sur du polyéthylène, des différentes formes d'énergie présentes dans les décharges partielles ».

À la fin des années 1960, intervient la création du LAAS fondé et dirigé par Jean Lagasse, de sorte que le LGE se confond désormais avec la seule équipe « matériaux diélectriques » et devient le LGET[44], associé au CNRS. Il a désormais consolidé les fondations de son activité de recherche : du côté des partenaires, il acquiert la confiance d'EDF et établi des contacts avec la filière câblière (Atochimie, SILEC, Câbles de Lyon). Du côté des lignes de recherche, les trois sujets de recherche évoqués précédemment (vieillissement, décharges partielles et défauts du polyéthylène) seront approfondis au cours du temps, dans le sens d'une meilleure compréhension des phénomènes sous-jacents.

Division du travail et parcours le long de la filière industrielle (1972-1980)

Au cours de la période (1972-1980), le laboratoire est organisé en quatre groupes de recherche regroupant deux enseignants-chercheurs, trois chercheurs du CNRS, quatre techniciens et vingt-cinq doctorants. Au total, quatorze opérations scientifiques mobilisent ce personnel qui se répartit de la sorte[45] :

---

[43] J. Bodelle, P. Castillon, *Histoires de recherche*, Paris, Elf Aquitaine, 2000, 222 p.

[44] Laboratoire de génie électrique de Toulouse ou LGET en 1968.

[45] Les sources d'information de cette partie provenant essentiellement des rapports d'activité du LGET, il convient de garder à l'esprit, tout l'aspect « communication et mise en forme » que comporte ces rapports effectués pour le CNRS. Par exemple, ils

– le groupe 1 « Interactions décharges-surfaces isolantes », dirigé par C. Mayoux (chercheur CNRS), comprend cinq doctorants et un ingénieur et conduit trois opérations de recherche.

– le groupe 2 « Caractérisation des isolants solides », animé par C. Huraux (maître de conférences), formé par quatre doctorants et un chercheur confirmé, travaille sur quatre projets différents.

– le groupe 3 « Isolants sous contraintes extrêmes », dirigé à partir de 1970, par Hoang the Giam (ingénieur de recherche CNRS) comprend neuf doctorants. Trois opérations de recherche démarrent en 1972. R. Lacoste participe surtout à la seconde de ces opérations.

– le groupe 4 « Phénomènes de transport dans les isolants solides » (dirigé par H. Carchano puis par Y. Ségui, attaché de recherche au CNRS) englobe six doctorants. Ces chercheurs conduisent quatre opérations scientifiques différentes.

Les deux premiers groupes se situent dans la suite logique des opérations de recherche, conduites en collaboration avec EDF et Elf-Atochimie. Les collaborations du groupe 1, sont donc centrées sur les phénomènes de dégradation des isolants électriques. Les financeurs sont les institutions publiques (ministère, DGRST[46], CNRS) ainsi qu'EDF. D'après les rapports d'activité du laboratoire, il est possible de dater ces opérations et de les représenter sur un diagramme de Pert simplifié[47] :

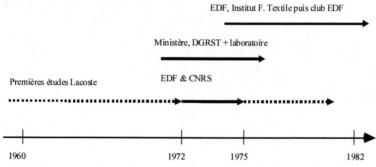

Source : diagramme établi à partir des rapports d'activité du laboratoire (1975, 1977, 1979, 1981, 1983, 1985, 1987, 1991).

---

tendent à rationaliser l'organisation du laboratoire, à cloisonner les différentes opérations de recherche et à surestimer leur volet applicatif.

[46] DGRST : Délégation générale de la recherche scientifique et technique.

[47] Une flèche représente une opération ; son positionnement et sa longueur indiquent les dates de réalisation. Une flèche pointillée suit ou précède une flèche continue dans la mesure où les rapports d'activité indiquent une certaine continuité dans les deux opérations de recherche. On indique au dessus-de la flèche les partenaires financiers ou industriels successifs (il n'y a pas nécessairement d'engagement financier de la part de l'industriel mais il est cité comme partenaire de cette opération de recherche).

Ainsi, souligne-t-on l'importance du soutien d'EDF et des financements institutionnels (CNRS et ministères) pour les recherches à caractère fondamental et méthodologique. Les travaux conduits en collaboration avec l'industrie textile correspondent, pour le laboratoire, à une opportunité d'extension de ces investigations sur d'autres matériaux.

Le groupe 2 du laboratoire « Caractérisation des isolants solides » travaille sur quatre opérations : la première concerne la recherche d'un polyéthylène à faibles pertes pour les télécommunications au profit de l'industrie câblière[48] (Atochimie, les Câbles de Lyon et la Compagnie générale de l'électricité) et du CNET, le commanditaire, qui lance un appel d'offres pour le programme TAT n° 6, télécommunications transatlantiques par câbles sous-marins entre la France et les États-Unis. Les financements institutionnels ne manquent pas pour l'amélioration des câbles : comité « polymères » de la DGRST, comité « matériaux macromoléculaires »[49], etc. Ici, l'enjeu est de développer l'utilisation du polyéthylène produit par Atochimie et de rendre les câbles plus économiques.

Suite aux travaux du premier groupe sur la conductibilité des isolants et sous l'impulsion de R. Lacoste, l'équipe découvre en 1972, l'intérêt d'injecter des anti-oxydants – des chélates[50] – dans les isolants en polyéthylène afin de provoquer un procédé d'auto-extinction des défauts. Elle cherche alors un partenaire pour industrialiser sa méthode auto-cicatrisante des câbles et pense à la société câblière SILEC. En 1975, l'opération est financée par la DGRST mais la SNPA (Société nationale de pétrole d'Aquitaine) et la SILEC en sont les partenaires extérieurs[51]. Deux brevets sont déposés dès 1974 conjointement par les chercheurs du LGET et les ingénieurs de la SILEC « mais la société de câbles traîne les pieds et met deux ans avant de rendre les résultats de tests sur les premiers échantillons fabriqués pendant lesquels le LGET n'a pas pu publier sur ce sujet »[52]. En 1977, EDF s'associe à l'opération, puis Merlin-Gerin en 1979. Entre-temps, le laboratoire a contacté Trefi-

---

[48] Ces sociétés et le CNET travaillent ensemble depuis les années 1940 et ont monté en 1947, une société d'économie mixte pour le développement de la technique des télécommunications sur câbles (la SOTELEC).

[49] Nous ne disposons pas d'éléments sur la composition de ce comité mais il y a fort à parier que des chercheurs plus ou moins proches du LGET y sont présents.

[50] Le terme chimique s'appuie sur le mot grec « χήλή » (« chélé » : pince de crabe) car un atome de métal est pris entre deux atomes d'hydrogène. L'action des décharges sur cette molécule amène sur les parois de la cavité où elle se développe, une couche conductrice qui entraîne leur disparition.

[51] Les rapports d'activité du LGET distinguent les organismes qui financent les opérations de recherche, des partenaires extérieurs, avec lesquels ils échangent des informations ou ils collaborent sans contrat financier.

[52] Entretien avec R. Lacoste.

cables-Pirelli, concurrent de la SILEC qui ne souhaite pas non plus industrialiser le procédé et met en avant le manque de rentabilité du projet. Cependant, quatre doctorants conduisent leurs thèses sur ce sujet, qui s'arrête en 1980 par « manque de motivation industrielle ». Il s'agit d'un cas de recherches appliquées visant à allonger la durée de vie et la fiabilité d'un matériau alors que l'intérêt de l'industriel est au contraire de renouveler périodiquement ses produits.

En 1973, se prolonge un axe scientifique financé par le ministère de l'Industrie et de la recherche, EDF et la CGE sur les décharges superficielles et leur incidence sur les isolateurs de ligne[53]. Les partenaires extérieurs sont des laboratoires : un laboratoire du CNRS spécialisé en physique des décharges[54], Études et recherches d'EDF et la société CERAVER, qui fabrique ces isolateurs. Après plusieurs reconfigurations des financements engagés, cette opération de recherche durera jusqu'en 1987 sous la direction de C. Huraux. Elle est liée à une autre étude sur les phénomènes de durcissement de résines, financée par les mêmes partenaires.

En résumé, les recherches lancées avant 1975 par ce deuxième groupe peuvent être schématisées comme suit :

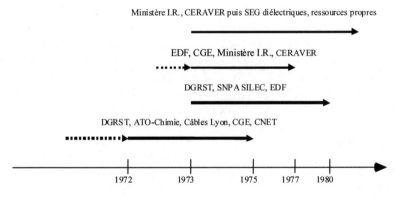

Ministère I.R., CERAVER puis SEG diélectriques, ressources propres

EDF, CGE, Ministère I.R., CERAVER

DGRST, SNPA SILEC, EDF

DGRST, ATO-Chimie, Câbles Lyon, CGE, CNET

1972   1973   1975   1977   1980

Source : rapports d'activité du laboratoire (1975, 1977, 1979, 1981, 1983, 1985, 1987, 1991).

Le groupe 3 « Isolants sous contraintes extrêmes » est lié une activité plus technologique et expérimentale, mise en place en 1970 autour d'un

---

[53] Une note signale que ce programme fait suite à une pré-étude effectuée en liaison avec les laboratoires de la CGE à Marcoussis et en accord avec EDF.

[54] Il s'agit du laboratoire de physique des décharges du CNRS, l'un des premiers laboratoires publics français, partenaire du LGET. Il est alors dirigé par Max Goldman, directeur de recherches au CNRS.

choix d'équipement. Il s'agit d'un dispositif permettant de caractériser le comportement d'un matériau isolant soumis à la superposition d'un champ électrique et d'une forte contrainte mécanique. Ses travaux donnent lieu, pendant cette période, à trois opérations de recherche, dont les deux premières sont complémentaires de celles réalisées par d'autres chercheurs du LGET car liées à la recherche d'un polyéthylène performant. La présentation de ces trois opérations et de leurs financements donne le résultat suivant :

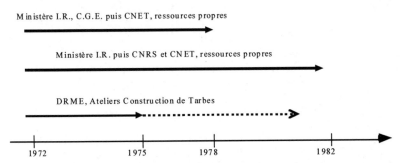

Ministère I.R., C.G.E. puis CNET, ressources propres

Ministère I.R. puis CNRS et CNET, ressources propres

DRME, Ateliers Construction de Tarbes

1972   1975   1978   1982

Source : rapports d'activité du laboratoire (1975, 1977, 1979, 1981, 1983, 1985, 1987, 1991).

Les deux opérations principales concernent en fait l'amélioration des câbles isolés au polyéthylène utilisés dans les télécommunications. De ce fait, elles bénéficient de différents financements publics (ministère, CNRS, CNET).

Le groupe 4, créé en 1970, et animé successivement par Y. Ségui et C. Laurent (deux des futurs directeurs du laboratoire) a comme objectif de réaliser des couches minces de polymères, qui ont des « possibilités d'application nombreuses »[55]. Il a pour mission de fabriquer des couches minces de polymères, à partir de styrène afin d'étudier leur formation et d'entrevoir les possibilités d'application. L'objectif de fabrication ayant été atteint en 1972, l'équipe a ensuite concentré son effort sur le processus de croissance et les mécanismes de conduction. Cette équipe est dirigée successivement par deux chercheurs qui impulsent des travaux différents. On trouve aussi dans ce quatrième groupe, une étude, liée aux travaux des autres équipes du laboratoire. Elle s'effectue dans le cadre d'une recherche coopérative sur programme du CNRS[56] à laquelle participent tous les partenaires français de la filière câble (cinq laboratoires universitaires français, industriels, chimistes, centre de recherches EDF, câbliers). Son objectif est d'étudier sur le plan fondamental,

---

[55]   Rapport d'activité 1975.
[56]   La RCP (recherches coopératives sur programme) du CNRS 370.

l'origine et les premiers instants de la formation des décharges autour d'une électrode ponctuelle. Elle est complémentaire des opérations scientifiques du LGET sur les câbles. Les opérations du quatrième groupe se présentent en résumé de la manière suivante :

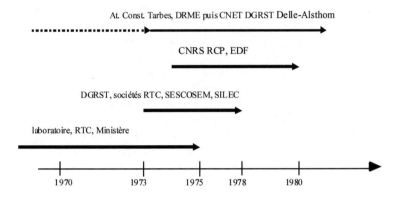

Source : rapports d'activité du laboratoire (1975, 1977, 1979, 1981, 1983, 1985, 1987, 1991).

En regroupant, l'ensemble des quatorze opérations de recherche menées entre 1972 et 1975, il est possible de visualiser dans un tableau récapitulatif, les principaux partenaires mentionnés dans les rapports d'activité :

Type d'organismes partenaires ou de financements	Occurrence des citations (en pourcentage)
Ministère de l'Industrie et de la recherche	18 %
Délégation générale de la Recherche scientifique et technique	20 %
Fonds propres du laboratoire	16 %
CNRS	7 %
DRME (Direction des recherches et des moyens d'essais)	4 %
EDF	17 %
CGE	2 %
Radio technique ou RTC	2 %
ATC Tarbes (Ateliers de construction de Tarbes)	11 %
Institut français du textile	4 %
TOTAL	100 %

Sources : répartition établie à partir des informations tirées des rapports d'activité du laboratoire (1975, 1977, 1979, 1981, 1983, 1985, 1987, 1991).

Ainsi, les supports institutionnels publics couvrent 65 % des opérations, ceux d'EDF représentent 17 % des contrats et 19 % sont soutenus par d'autres acteurs économiques industriels. Sans surprise, les principales relations industrielles du LGET entre 1978 et la fin des années

1980 concernent toujours les secteurs électrique ou électronique et 50 % des contrats d'études proviennent encore d'EDF.

Analyse de la dynamique industrielle du laboratoire :

Le laboratoire s'est déplacé le long de la filière industrielle des matériaux diélectriques jusqu'à devenir un partenaire scientifique important du génie électrique[57]. Il est entré, dans cette communauté, par deux démarches complémentaires : d'une part, en participant à l'émergence d'un réseau embryonnaire d'enseignants et de chercheurs en quête de légitimation sur des disciplines naissantes (automatique, électronique notamment) et d'autre part, en répondant aux besoins d'études et de recherches de l'industrie électrique balisés par EDF et le LCIE. En effet, en 1950, le retard technologique français est important et les incidents de fonctionnement chez les industriels fréquents :

> les industriels, c'est eux qui nous posaient des questions, il y a beaucoup de choses qui n'étaient pas connues, oui c'est sûr, et puis dont on s'occupait au jour le jour, si vous voulez, en essayant de parer au plus pressé par exemple la grosse affaire des machines synchrones qui fournissent l'énergie électrique dans les centrales, n'avaient pas été contrôlées pendant toute la durée de la guerre jusqu'en 1948-1949, ça tournait pas puis ça tournait et il y avait énormément d'incidents et c'est ces incidents qui nous ont fait demander comment peut-on s'en sortir, c'est vrai que c'est de là que cela venait.[58]

Face à ces problèmes électriques, les industriels se tournent vers le Laboratoire central des industries électriques et vers EDF. Cette entreprise publique crée ses propres équipes de recherche mais signe aussi des contrats de recherche avec les chercheurs publics, qui permettent notamment de financer des thèses.

La chronologie des travaux de l'équipe sur les isolants fut donc la suivante : les premières études sur les matériaux di-électriques démarrent en partenariat avec le LCIE et l'assentiment d'un petit nombre de personnes réunies autour de l'idée partagée de faire de la science « utile » (début du Club EEA). Ces derniers forment à la fin des années 1960 un réseau national inscrit dans les universités et écoles d'ingénieur, qui participe au décollage de la jeune discipline « génie électrique ». On retrouve la dynamique socio-cognitive, repérée par Mullins en 1972,

---

[57] D'après M. Bui-Aï (entretien réalisé par Bès et Brugarolas, 1997), le LGET est dans les années 1980, l'un des seuls laboratoires français développant un ensemble complet et homogène d'activités dans le domaine des diélectriques solides avec une interface intéressante vers les composants passifs. Leur homologue français quant aux contrats et aux publications dans le domaine, est le Laboratoire électrostatique de Grenoble.

[58] Entretien avec R. Lacoste, 2005.

dans l'étude de la constitution d'autres disciplines : il insiste sur l'existence de réseaux interpersonnels d'abord informels puis institutionnalisés qui permettent à un paradigme de se développer[59]. Dans cette science « appliquée », la création d'une spécialité est de plus portée par les trajectoires d'amélioration technologique et de normalisation des matériaux rendus nécessaires par les forts besoins en électrotechnique et en télécommunications. Sur la base de nombreuses études très ciblées[60] et à travers des collaborations avec des scientifiques d'autres disciplines, les chercheurs du LGET approfondissent leurs connaissances physico-chimiques des matériaux, ce qui leur permet de proposer directement leurs compétences aux câbliers. Dans les années 1980, le laboratoire travaillera même avec un fabricant de papier pour matériaux électriques (Bolloré).

Les sujets de recherche traités ont essentiellement porté sur les défauts des matériaux industriels et sur des tentatives d'amélioration de ces produits. Les recherches, pilotées par les caractéristiques des produits industriels, ont été le plus souvent conduites dans le sens d'une mise en évidence de propriétés physico-chimiques fondamentales, ce qui a conduit à de nombreuses publications scientifiques. La dynamique industrielle du laboratoire est donc totalement imbriquée à sa dynamique scientifique : l'approfondissement des thématiques de recherche a été possible grâce aux collaborations étroites avec la communauté du « génie électrique » et au souci constant des chercheurs de corriger les « défauts » de fonctionnement des appareils et matériaux. Ceci se heurtant parfois à la logique des entreprises et provoquant des « incidents » dans les recherches de type brevets enterrés, lignes de recherche interrompues, etc.

Cet exemple de laboratoire en sciences de l'ingénieur illustre le régime scientifique « utilitaire » repéré par T. Shinn[61], dans lequel les chercheurs s'engagent sur des thèmes pragmatiques liés à la demande économique et sociale et pour lesquels les référents universitaires restent secondaires. Il souligne que, dans ce régime utilitaire, les axes de recherche correspondent aux besoins techniques, aux sollicitations liées

---

[59] Pour Mullins, l'émergence d'une spécialité passe par quatre grands stades : l'émergence d'un groupe paradigmatique, la création de réseau de communication entre les membres, l'établissement d'un réseau de personnes et d'institutions et enfin l'affirmation d'une spécialité. Voir N.C. Mullins, « The development of a scientific speciality : the phage group and the origins of molecular biology », *Minerva*, vol. 19, 1972, p. 52-82.
[60] Le terme « ciblé » est utilisé ici pour désigner des études dont le cahier des charges est très précis avec des spécifications très détaillées.
[61] T. Shinn, « Axes thématiques et marches de diffusion, la science en France, 1975-1999 », *op. cit.*

aux finalités très concrètes et aux délais de courte et moyenne durée et que les acteurs y sont très hétérogènes : scientifiques, ingénieurs de recherche, d'études, techniciens, etc. Au niveau de l'organisation du travail scientifique, on peut souligner que le trio formé par les trois chercheurs publics[62] présents dès le début des années 1960, gardera jusqu'à la fin des années 1980, la maîtrise des axes de recherche et de la diffusion des résultats. Le travail scientifique fut également réalisé grâce à l'activité de nombreux techniciens de laboratoire autour d'équipements de test et de salles de travail spécifiques. Avec l'industrie (EDF et les entreprises fournisseurs de matériels) s'établiront des relations individuelles fortes facilitant les enchaînements de contrats. De nombreuses thèses ont été ainsi financées[63] et réalisées dans un cadre contractuel.

Cet article consacré à un laboratoire en particulier, avait comme objectif de mettre en évidence les modalités de construction d'une équipe à travers la conduite de recherches « utiles » à l'industrie. Chaque contrat est à la fois, l'occasion de mettre à l'épreuve les travaux fondamentaux portant sur la mise en évidence de certaines propriétés physiques et physico-chimiques des matériaux et de redémarrer d'autres travaux de recherche à partir des problèmes présentés par les industriels. Toutefois, tous les résultats scientifiques ne débouchent pas sur des valorisations industrielles directes et immédiates (dépôt de brevets, utilisation des nouveaux procédés, mise au point de produits innovants).

Deux autres faits ont aussi été mis en exergue : le paysage scientifique a connu une importante logique de spécialisation sur certaines « parties » des produits électriques, qui a accompagné la modernisation de l'industrie française. Les scientifiques des années 1950 avaient de l'avance sur les bureaux d'études des industriels du génie électrique mais ils connaissaient mal leurs besoins et les caractéristiques de leurs produits. C'est sous l'impulsion de la DER d'EDF et du ministère de l'Industrie que cette discipline rencontre la demande industrielle : soit par des contrats directs avec la direction des Études et des recherches, soit en relation avec le Laboratoire central des industries électriques, soit par l'intervention indirecte d'EDF : échanges dans les clubs thématiques d'EDF ou bien collaborations avec les fournisseurs d'EDF en machines et en câbles. Bien sûr, et comme pour de nombreuses relations contractuelles entre des laboratoires et des industriels, les financements publics non affectés à certaines opérations (CNRS, DGRST, par exemple) ont accompagné les recherches sur le génie électrique.

---

[62] R. Lacoste, C. Mayoux et Bui-Aï.

[63] Pour une analyse du travail des doctorants en situation de collaboration avec l'industrie, voir M. P. Bès, « connaissances et relations sociales des jeunes chercheurs », *Recherches sociologiques*, vol. XXXV, n° 3, 2004, p. 123-135.

Sources

Entretiens directs au LGET, avec Bui Ai (avec E. Brugarolas en 1997), entretiens avec R. Lacoste (ex-directeur du LGET), C. Mayoux, C. Laurent et F. Massines en 1999 et 2000 (avec M. Grossetti) et entretien téléphonique avec Béatrice Garros en 1999.

Entretien le 16 septembre 2005 avec R. Lacoste sur une première version de ce texte.

Entretien collectif le 27 février 2001 avec R. Lacoste, Bui Ai (ex-directeur du LGET), C. Huraux, Hoang-The-Giam, Y. Segui (directeur du LGET).

Au LAAS, entretien par M. Grossetti de J. Lagasse le 20 février 1990.

Lettres de R. Lacoste du 16 mars, 17 mars et 14 avril 2000.

The Problem of Permanence

Industrial Research on Steel Magnets by Marie Skłodowska Curie and Sydney Evershed

Graeme GOODAY[1]

University of Leeds

This paper concerns industrial research on the so-called "permanent magnet" in the period 1880 to 1925. Known since ancient times, this artifact only acquired a major economic significance with the rise of electrical power and lighting in the later nineteenth century. Such magnets were widely used in heavy duty technologies for both generation and measurement, especially where electromagnets (current-carrying coils that could be switched on or off) were either too expensive or impractical to use. Yet they were always troublesome: notwithstanding their name, these "permanent" magnets often did not perform to the level of stability presumed by instrument designers and expected by end-users. Such impermanence in behavioral characteristics brought unreliability to devices in which they were embedded, threatening economic loss and technical problems for both makers and users. Moving-coil voltmeters and ammeters using fickle magnets could produce readings as much as 50% too high or too low. At one extreme such dial errors could mislead engineers into unwittingly running supply systems at currents or voltages that could damage to equipment – or at levels well below contract specification, prompting customer complaints[2].

Despite its obvious importance in understanding the rise of the electrical industry, the research and development of the permanent magnet has not previously been investigated by any modern historian. Economic historians have typically not been interested in the internal operations of

---

[1]   g.j.n.gooday@leeds.ac.uk.

[2]   See Graeme Gooday, *The Morals of Measurement: accuracy, irony and trust in late Victorian Electrical Practice*, Cambridge, Cambridge University Press, 2004.

electrical instruments, falsely assuming that all technical problems with such instruments could be resolved just by purchasing sufficient expertise and technical resources. Second for historians of technology, no famous incidents of technological failure or crisis have been attributed to the instability of magnets – so no body of case studies has built up around this subject. For historians of instrument-making, the problem is that manufacturers rarely ever left documentary records of their techniques or problems in magnet-making, these being the subject of trade secrets (permanent magnets being unpatentable); nor did manufacturers ever publicize such problems with magnets, presumably for fear of losing customers through bad publicity. For historians of science, the subject has not been of interest largely because – in contrast to the development of telephony and radio – the solution to making magnets permanent did not come from Maxwellian electromagnetic theory; indeed Pierre Duhem even provocatively suggested that the very *existence* of permanent magnets was a "formal contradiction" of this theory[3]. Finally, biographers of Marie Curie have focused only on her radioactive research not previously noticed the significance of her very first publication on tempered steels as being of international importance to magnet making in the electrical industry.

To recover the research undertaken on permanent magnets in the period 1880 to 1925 we must look at a wide variety of locations and people: academic engineers such as Alfred Ewing (Tokyo and Dundee) and John Hopkinson (Kings College, London), Sylvanus Thompson (Finsbury Technical College, London); instrument makers who specialized in magnets Marcel Deprez (Paris), James White (Glasgow); Sydney Evershed (London) and Edward Weston (New York); metallurgists such as Floris Osmond; US-German geologists Carl Barus and Strouhal; and the early pre-radioactive researches of Marie Sklowodska-Curie in indirect collaboration with Pierre Curie. I show that there was little formal organization of research or systematic culture of publication on this subject until Marie Sklodowska Curie published her wide-ranging study of the magnetic properties of tempered steels "Propriétés magnétiques des aciers trempés" in a variety of British, French and American journals in 1898-1899[4]. This had been commissioned in 1894 by the

---

[3]   In his patriotic attack on "La Science Allemande" in 1915, Duhem criticized those physicists who, like Germans treated Maxwell's equations as "orders" whilst using permanent magnets in their experiments. They thereby invoked "a doctrine whose axioms made the existence of such [magnetic] bodies absurd". Roger Ariew, Peter Barker (eds.), *Pierre Duhem: Essays in the history and philosophy of science*, Indianapolis, Hackett Publishing Co., 1996, p. 268-270.

[4]   Marie Sklodowska Curie, "Propriétés magnétiques des aciers trempés" (1898), reproduced in Irène Joliot-Curie (dir.), *Œuvres de Marie Sklodowska Curie*, Warsaw, Panstwowe Wydawnictwo Naukowe, 1954, p. 3-42.

Société pour l'Encouragement de l'Industrie Nationale but the huge four years project had to be conducted in borrowed space in Pierre Curie's laboratory at the École de Physique et Chimie (Paris) since no other laboratory was available to her to undertake this research. And while Marie and Pierre Curie moved on to studies of radioactivity in the early twentieth century, I show how her widely-read steels paper became the benchmark study for new kinds of industrial research on magnetism.

Evershed Mythologized: the Magnet Problem Solved by Company Research?

[...] recently he [Sydney Evershed] has contributed two papers [1920 and 1925][5], on permanent magnets, adjuncts which, although indispensable in the electrical industry, had previously received little or no attention. The first paper disclosed the scientific basis underlying the design and performance of permanent magnets, matters which until then had been quite unknown. The second paper dealt with the properties and defects of magnets steels and explained the modifications required in steelworks methods in order to avoid the more serious defects. The publication of these magnetic researches has been of great benefit to all who are concerned with permanent magnets, including the manufacturers of magnet steel, who had been working entirely in the dark for want of knowledge of the magnetic side. The investigation of this complicated subject is still in progress at Acton Lane Works, permanent magnets being of special importance in the Company's manufactures.[6]

According to a narrowly ethnocentric British folklore of electrical engineering, the problems of creating permanent magnets were largely solved in the 1920s by Sydney Evershed (1857-1939), elder brother of the eminent astronomer John Evershed (1864-1956). His magnetic researches began in 1885 as a manager of a small electrical instrument manufacturer, Goolden & Trotter in Westminster (central London), as an integral part of the enterprise of designing and refining instruments based upon permanent magnet mechanisms. Evershed's first great success was his development of a portable ohmmeter in 1889, originated by William Ayrton and John Perry in 1882, and specially developed by Evershed for instant "direct" readings of insulation resistance. This work continued through the move to West London suburbs in 1895

---

[5] Sydney Evershed, "Permanent Magnets in Theory and Practice (Part 1)", *Journal of the Institution of Electrical Engineers (JIEE)*, t. 58, 1920, p. 780-825, discussion p. 825-37; "Permanent Magnets in Theory and Practice (Part 2)", *JIEE*, t. 63, 1925, p. 725-810, discussion p. 810-821.

[6] [Anon], *Eversheds: their place in British Industry. How they began and who they are: 1885-1932*, London, Evershed & Vignoles Ltd, 1932, p. 7-8.

when with his assistant he took over and renamed the company Evershed & Vignoles and the company's location from 1903, the Acton Lane Works in Chiswick. In this setting Evershed & Vignoles developed the "Megger" resistance testing set that became world famous – distributed along with the companies ammeters not only across the British Empire but in Argentina, Denmark, France, Germany, Holland, Hungary, Italy, Japan, Java, Spain, Sweden and the US – along with other related equipment.

It was through nearly four decades of intensive work in designing and redesigning such instruments, that Evershed came to produce the enormous amount of information and analysis that appeared in two monumental papers on "Permanent Magnets in Theory and Practice" published by the Institution of Electrical Engineers in 1920 and 1925. The first of these – of 40,000 words length – focused on theory, bringing together macroscopic and molecular theories of magnetism as developed by André-Marie Ampère, James Clerk Maxwell, John Hopkinson, J. A. Ewing, and linking them to more recent electron-based theories as magnetism established by Pierre Langevin (as well as linking to Niels Bohr and J. J. Thomson) and researches of Honda in Japan. The second paper of around 80,000 words focused on the procedural and metallurgical issues of magnet construction, citing the dozen key authors who had addressed the question of the optimum chemical constitution, preparation and heat treatment of magnet steel, the earliest of which was Marie Curie's classic 1898 paper.

The lattermost appeared two years after Evershed retired from inventive work to become company chairman of Evershed & Vignoles. This is no trivial point: definitive research on permanent magnets took a lifetime's work for Evershed to produce – they could only trustworthily be tested in the *longue durée*. In Evershed's first public comment on the subject in a discussion of Deprez d'Arsonval instruments at the Institution of Electrical Engineers in London (November 1891), he commented on the troubled early history of magnets with characteristic wryness: "Some ten years ago, if anyone had been asked if there was anything permanent in the world, he would have said he did not know, but certainly not permanent magnets; but we, most of us [instrument makers], now consider that we can trust permanent magnets if left alone"[7].

---

[7] Capt H. R. Sankey, (late R. E.) and F. V. Andersen, "Description of the Standard Volt- and Ampere-meter used at the Ferry Works, Thames Ditton", *JIEE*, t. 20, 1892, p. 516-590, quote from discussion p. 569-571. For Evershed's life see "Obituary Notices", *JIEE*, t. 85, 1939, p. 775-776 and Graeme Gooday, "Sydney Evershed" in B. Lightman (ed.), *The Dictionary of Nineteenth-Century British Scientists*, Bristol, Thoemmes Press, 2004.

Yet Evershed then confessed that his own trusted permanent magnet tangent galvanometer formerly trustworthy to within 1%, had become much less reliable since the company had relocated to west London[8]. Indeed, the ten years experience of coming to trust permanent magnets by working with them was subsequently countermanded by evidence of the persistent capriciousness of permanent magnets. Suffice to say that, for the next forty years, neither Evershed nor his fellow-instrument makers left such magnets alone in their long-continuing project. Even after producing his two classic papers of 1920 in 1925, Evershed's staff continued to produce research on enhancing magnetic permanency.

The elapse of decades in undertaking such investigation could also have highly distorting effects in judgments of the primacy of recent research. According to the somewhat partisan 1932 company history of Evershed & Vignoles excerpted above, it was Evershed's two papers of that allegedly first disclosed the "scientific basis" underlying the design and performance of permanent magnets – followed by the extraordinary claim that nothing substantial had been known on this subject prior to Evershed's papers. More puzzling still is the company history's sugges-tion that manufacturers of magnet steel had supposedly been working "entirely in the dark for want of knowledge" of the magnetic character-istics of steel. It is most unlikely that such claims would have been published in an official company history without Evershed's personal scrutiny and approval. And the irony increases when one considers – as already indicated – that Evershed's papers took great pains to show credit to previous researchers on the manufacture of permanent magnets. And indeed it was precisely Evershed's synthetic formulation of the theory and practice of permanent magnets by incorporation of *other* previous researchers into a newly comprehensive account that won it numerous accolades; in the discussion immediately after he presented his first paper, Evershed's research was described as likely to become a "classic" as (allegedly) the "first published attempt" to put forward a system of design and predetermination of permanent magnets "usable" by engineers[9].

In what follows I examine the long tradition of research on perma-nent magnets upon which Evershed drew, investigating how successive generations of researchers at widely differing locations across Europe, America and Japan, attempted to attain the seemingly elusive goal of making magnets that were truly *permanent*.

---

[8] Evershed's comments in Sankey & Andersen, "Description of the Standard Volt- and Ampere-meter", discussion p. 569.

[9] Ll. B. Atkinson, discussion to Evershed, 1920, p. 825 and R. E. B. Crompton, *ibid.*, p. 831.

The Secretive Craft Culture of Magnet-making before Sklodowska Curie's Research

The three principal issues in the fabrication of a permanent magnet from steel were the same for Marie Sklodowska and Sydney Evershed in 1894-1897 as they had been for William Barlowe and William Gilbert three centuries earlier. These were: choosing the optimum chemical preparation of steel; using the most efficacious means of heat-hardening and quenching; and its final treatment to stabilize its performance – magnetization, partial demagnetization and heat treatment. In a section of his 1925 paper headed "The Medieval Art and Mystery of the Magnet Maker" Evershed commented lugubriously that the "mysterious" nature of magnetism lent itself to imputations of magical qualities beyond the power of modern science to understand since magnet makers relied on traditions of "art" sanctioned by centuries of inherited and if not always reliable practice[10]. In a similar vein Silvanus Thompson complained in 1912 that magnet makers "have their own procedures" based on the results of their own experiences, so some of the recipes they followed were "quite absurd" such as the age-old use of "stale beer" in the water used to quench harden steels[11].

On the other hand, there was a much more modern commercial imperative for maintaining a "mystery" around the production of permanent magnets, especially in the final crucial "aging" stage[12]. Manufacturers that had developed what they considered to be effective combination of methods for "permanent" magnetization did not patent them – possibly because there was no distinctive unobvious feature of originality in their methods. Thus to preserve their intellectual property, they kept their methods secret. What was at stake was the best and most particular "recipe" for making a good magnet from methods already known. This trade secrecy had the two fold purpose of preventing rival manufacturers stealing their methods, and also of preventing (prospec-

---

[10] Evershed complained that in many respects little had changed since Barlowe had complained in 1616 of the poor "bungerly" construction of compass needles. See citation of William Barlowe, *Barlowe's Magnetical Advertisements*, London, 1616 in Evershed, "Permanent Magnets in Theory and Practice (Part 2)", *op. cit.*, p. 768. For Gilbert see Steve Pumfrey, *Latitude and the magnetic earth: the true story of Queen Elizabeth's most distinguished man of science*, Cambridge, Icon Books, 2001.

[11] S. P. Thompson, "The Magnetism of Permanent Magnets", *JIEE*, 1913, p. 80-142, quote on p. 104.

[12] The aristocratic instrument maker Kenelm Edgcumbe claimed in 1904 that: "The aging process is looked upon by nearly every maker as his own "trade secret", but as a matter of fact every other maker know precisely the method he employs, and is at the same time quite confident that his own method is the only correct and infallible one", Kenelm Edgcumbe, Franklin Punga, "Direct Reading Instruments for switchboard use", *JIEE*, t. 33, 1904, p. 620-668, discussion p. 655-693, quote on p. 625.

tive) customers from critically interrogating their methods. It had the further effect of inhibiting the publication of comparative research on the efficacy of rival materials and methods – until, that is, Marie Sklodowska Curie's paper of 1898 broke the secrecy and brought the whole subject out into the open. But what was the pressing need that eventually forced open the medieval craft of magnet making, culminating in a sense with Marie Curie's paper? It was nearly two decades of dealing with the technological problems of measuring devices for the new electrotechnical industry that followed the arrival of the electric light.

The advent of Jablochkoff arc lights and Edison and Swan's innovative filament electric technology in the period 1878-1880 prompted instrument designers and makers to find new ways of measuring much stronger currents than those encountered previously in telegraphy and telephony. At least some instrument designers, notably Marcel Deprez in Paris, and William Ayrton and John Perry at Finsbury Technical College in London, placed great trust in the power of "permanent" magnets to control the mechanisms of these devices in a trustworthy fashion. As I have written elsewhere, it was Deprez who in 1880 developed the "fishbone" galvanometer that was reworked the following year by Ayrton and Perry in an instrument with linear readings that they christened as an "ammeter". Although widely used, both instruments proved rather wayward in practice[13]. For example, if a current to be measured were increased and then decreased repeatedly, such instruments tended to give readings too high while descending, and readings too low while readings were increasing.

Writing in *La Lumière Électrique* in 1884, Deprez defended his instruments, claiming that such magnet – induced variation in his instruments was "*très petite*" – and when it was more than that this problem would only have "peu d'influence sur les indications de l'instrument". Indeed since the introduction of tungsten steel magnets first displayed at the Paris Electrical Exhibition of 1881, French magnet makers and instrument designers had good reason to trust their instruments (see below for further discussion)[14]. Ayrton and Perry, however, fast became embarrassed by their "permanent magnet" instruments, Perry himself admitting in 1885 that they could be as much as 37% in error. The aristocratic free-lance engineer James Swinburne claimed in 1887 that such errors could be as great as 50% owing to the phenomenon of

---

[13] Gooday, *Morals of Measurement, op. cit.*, chapter 4.

[14] M. Deprez, "Sur les instruments destinés aux mesures électriques industrielles", *La Lumière Électrique*, t. 12, 1884, p. 3-10; see English translation of abstract by "PH" in *Minutes of Proceedings of the Institution of Civil Engineers*, t. 78, 1883-1884, p. 524-525.

magnetic "memory" – a phenomenon I discuss below. Like many other instrument designers, Ayrton and Perry thus soon turned to researching other means of securing a trustworthy controlling force in their instruments (non-magnetic proportional springs). Some, such as R. E. B. Crompton and Gisbert Kapp chose to trust instruments that used springs or electromagnets rather than permanent magnets[15].

Deprez persisted, however, in the use of permanent magnets, notably in the widely used Deprez d'Arsonval instruments. By 1890, such was the apparent progress in the form of these made by Edward Weston in New Jersey that one devoted user, Edward Colby, from the "Electric Club" in New York wrote to the British *Electrician* in December that year to argue against "the general distrust of permanent magnet instruments". Results with Weston's d'Arsonval devices that were typically reliable to within 0.1% in laboratory work and 2% in engineering work furnished, in his view, "substantial evidence of a reformation of the past character of instruments of the permanent magnet type"[16].

How then had such apparent – if not quite complete – improvement in magnetic reliability been accomplished? We can find little documented evidence in the publications of research laboratories prior to Marie Curie's 1898 paper. The "research" that generated this enhancement seems to have involved mostly the extension of traditional craft techniques. What we can recover of such practices in magnet making before Curie's paper come from those who favoured permanent magnet devices and sought to reassure customers and users that these devices were trustworthy for everyday use, without divulging trade secrets. One particular area discussed was the third stage of magnet making. It had long been known that older magnets were generally rendered more stable in their behaviour, if slightly weaker, than younger magnets. Thus magnet makers typically tried to speed up this up by a process known as "artificial aging" – maturing magnets from a capricious and potent adolescence to a sturdy, if slightly diminished, adulthood. In practical terms this meant exposing new magnets to the range and intensity of mechanical, thermal and magnetic forces normally encountered over a decade or so, so that ten years of magnetic maturation could be accomplished artificially in a very much shorter time period (weeks rather than years).

---

[15] See discussion in James Swinburne, *Practical Electrical Measurement*, London, Alabaster & Gatehouse, 1888. p. 25-56.

[16] See "Notes", *The Electrician*, t. 126, 1890, p. 128, and Edward F. Colby, "Permanent Magnet Voltmeters", letter to Editor of *The Electrician*, December 19th, 1890, from the Electric Club, New York, *ibid.*, p. 279.

Following traditional methods of "artificial ageing" by heat treatment employed in the textiles industry, Sir William Thomson reported in 1888 that instruments produced for him by James White's Company in Glasgow had the controlling magnet aged as much as possible by subjecting it to "rough usage", mostly by repeatedly boiling and then cooling it. In the same year the freelance electrical consultant James Swinburne reported that other common techniques of artificial ageing magnets included hammering them, dropping them on the floor, various kinds of heating and exposure to other magnets to partially demagnetize and then re-magnetize. As a dedicated user of permanent magnet measuring instruments, Swinburne's aim was to combat what he called the long-standing "prejudice" that these devices could not be trusted owing to the fluctuating strength of their magnets[17]. Yet neither Thomson nor Swinburne divulged the exact temperatures, configurations and durations of the processes involved since that would have enabled rival makers to reconstruct their trade secrets.

Indeed no scholar or industrial researcher in the 1880s attempted any general surveys of the three key processes of magnet making. For example Barus & Strouhal's 1885 study of magnetization undertaken on behalf of the US Geological Survey in Friedrich Kohlrausch's laboratory at the University of Würzburg focused only on the chemical composition and heat treatment of steels and iron carbides[18]. By contrast, when the Parisian metallurgist Floris Osmond presented "Considerations on Permanent Magnetism" to the Physical Society of London in April 1890, he investigated thermal and metallurgical aspects of the production process, but not the important differences to the magnetic properties of steel caused by adding carbon small quantities of manganese and tungsten. He was thus criticized for not assessing the particularly marked effect of even small amounts of tungsten by then characteristic of the best French magnetic steels[19].

This criticism reveals perhaps a British anxiety that French magnet makers were not sharing newly discovered techniques in magnet-making. In the January before Osmond presented his paper, the Post Office Chief Electrician William Preece raised alarm at the Institution of

---

[17] Swinburne, *Practical Electrical Measurement, op. cit.*, p. 27. For his views on the artificial "aging" of instrumental components see William Thomson, "On his new standard and inspectional electrical measuring instruments", *Proceedings of the Society of Telegraph Engineers & Electricians*, t. 17, 1888, p. 540-556 and discussion on p. 556-567; quote on p. 545.

[18] C. Barus, V. Strouhal, "The electrical and magnetic properties of iron carburets", *US Geological Survey Bulletin*, t. 14, 1885, p. 1-238.

[19] Floris Osmond, "Considerations on Permanent Magnetism", *Proceedings of the Physical Society of London*, t. 10, 1888, p. 382-386.

Electrical Engineers about the deteriorating quality of British magnets used by telegraphists under his jurisdiction[20]. He reiterated this concern at the meeting of the British Association for the Advancement of Science at Leeds during September 1890. This suspicion was borne out by his research that compared five magnetic steels from leading Sheffield manufacturers and one from a steelmaker in Crewe with two French steelmakers Marchal and Clemandot obtained for Preece by his counterpart, M. Trotin, in the French Telegraphic Administration. Preece found that the mean inductive power and retentiveness of the French magnets was significantly greater than all British samples, Marchal steel performing 50% better than the best native samples. John Perry thus speculated openly that certain French steel makers had a "secret" technique of tempering steels as yet unknown in British practice[21].

One of the principal accomplishments of Marie Curie's research in the ensuing decade was to overcome such suspicions and make public the best methods of magnet makers.

Hysteresis Curves: Theoretically Articulating the Form of the "Best" Permanent Magnets

While Curie's research could only rely on a very small body of published empirical research on magnet-making up 1898, at its very heart was well publicized research on the phenomenology of magnetization. As Matthias Dörries has shown, during the early 1880s the engineer Alfred Ewing in Tokyo and physicist Emil Warburg in Berlin developed theories of the inelastic historicity of materials. With reference to the magnetic "memory" that so plagued Ayrton and Perry's instruments, Ewing adopted the Greek term "hysteresis" to characterize the temporal "lagging" of effect behind cause in magnet-bearing instruments[22]. He worked with his cohort of Japanese assistants to develop the hysteresis diagram that characterized the cyclical "inelastic" behaviour of metals undergoing magnetization and demagnetization[23].

[20] William Preece in "Discussion of the President's address on Magnetism", *Electrician*, t. 24, 1890, p. 320-321.

[21] William Preece, "On the character of steel used for permanent magnets", *Electrician*, t. 25, 1890, p. 546-549; comments from Perry on p. 549.

[22] Matthias Dörries, "Prior history and aftereffects: Hysteresis and Nachwirkung in 19th-century physics", *Historical Studies in the Physical and Biological Sciences*, t. 22, 1991, p. 25-55.

[23] James Alfred Ewing, "On effects of retentievness in the magnetisation or iron and steel (1882)", *Proceedings of the Royal Society*, t. 34, 1883, p. 39-45; "Experimental Researches in Magnetism (1885)", *Philosophical Transactions of the Royal Society*, t. 176, 1886, p. 523-640. Ewing spent five years in Japan, 1878-1883 before returning to Dundee University and then proceeding to become professor of engineering at

As Curie clearly knew from the outset of her research, such diagrams helped to specify what physical characteristics were required of the steels used to make good permanent magnets, and thus to differentiate them from the ideal performance of steels used in other magnetization processes. Moreover, in applying this framework to magnets in 1885, John Hopkinson formalized the requisite technical vocabulary: firstly, the residual or remanent field (*l'intensité d'aimantation rémanente*) that measured the strength remaining in the magnet after it had been exposed to a magnetizing force; and secondly the coercitive force or field (*le champ coercitif*) – the strength of field that could completely demagnetize it. On Hopkinson's extension of Ewing's account, an ideal permanent magnet would maximize these parameters – i.e. be as strong as possible and as difficult to demagnetize as possible, thus ideally having an almost rectangular form[24]. The opening section Curie's 1898 paper shows this classic hysteretic form of a permanent magnet. After the metal is magnetized to saturation and the magnetizing force then taken away, the strength of the "permanent" magnet is shown by the remanent magnetism at the intercept on the vertical axis OB; the coercitive field that would need to be applied to demagnetize it – was represented by OC[25]:

---

the University of Cambridge in 1890; see R. T. Glazebrook, "[Obituaries] Sir Alfred Ewing", *Electrician*, t. 77, 1935, p. 889-890.

[24] John Hopkinson, "Magnetisation of Iron", *Philosophical Transactions of the Royal Society*, part II, 1885, p. 455-469 reproduced in Bertram Hopkinson (ed.), *Original Papers by the late John Hopkinson: Vol. 2: Scientific papers*, Cambridge, Cambridge University Press, 1901, p. 154-177. In contrast to permanent magnets for instruments, ideal dynamo magnets had a much "taller" thinner form as they were very easily magnetized to a considerable strength; steels used in transformer steels ideally showed very little hysteresis, i.e. a nearly linear hysteretic curve.

[25] Such empirical hysteresis curves bore out what industrial magnet makers had known for a long time: any magnet could be demagnetized by a magnet much weaker than itself.

Soit ABCDB′C′A (fig. 1) la courbe qui représente l'intensité d'aimantation I en fonction du champ magnétisant H, pour un circuit magnétique fermé,
tel qu'un anneau d'acier. Le champ est produit par un courant circulant dans
un fil enroulé régulièrement autour de l'anneau. Le champ variant d'une façon
continue de $+ H_1$ à $- H_1$ et de $- H_1$ à $+ H_1$ l'intensité d'aimantation prend

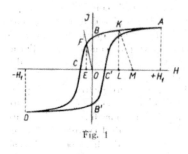

Fig. 1

successivement les valeurs représentées
par les ordonnées des branches ABCD,
DB′C′A de la courbe. Quand le champ
H a sa valeur maximum H_1 *l'intensité
d'aimantation induite* a sa valeur maximum I_m représentée par l'ordonnée du
point A. Quand le champ est nul,
0 a *l'intensité d'aimantation rémanente*
$I_r = OB$. Le champ étant négatif pour
une certaine valeur $OC = H_c$, l'anneau
sera complètement désaimanté. H_c sera
le *champ coercitif* (cette quantité est
souvent appelée force coercitive). La connaissance complète du tracé de
la courbe est nécessaire pour définir les propriétés d'un acier au point de
vue magnétique. Cependant, les trois grandeurs: Intensité d'aimantation
induite maximum I_m; intensité d'aimantation rémanente I_r; champ coercitif
H_c, suffisent déjà pour caractériser assez bien la nature de l'acier à ce point
de vue.

Source: Marie Sklodowska Curie "Propriétés magnétiques des aciers trempés" (1898),
reproduced in Irène Joliot-Curie (dir.), *Œuvres de Marie Sklodowska Curie*, Warsaw,
1954, p. 4.

Like all others pursuing the instrument makers' holy grail of the truly
permanent magnet, Marie Sklodowska aimed to find the methods that
maximized the remanent magnetism and coercitive field of magnets,
whilst also stabilizing them. That is to say, to prepare the steel so that, as
far as possible, after it left the manufacturer's workshop it was resilient
to such dangerously demagnetizing phenomena as heat, collision and
contact with other magnets. This was the research problem that she
addressed for three years 1894-1897.

Marie Sklodowska's First Research on "des bons aimants permanents"

Just as she was finishing her studies at the Sorbonne, in 1894, with
few employment prospects open to her, Marie Skolodowska secured a
commission from the *Société pour l'Encouragement de l'Industrie
Nationale* to study the best techniques and materials for producing
"good permanent magnets". As she later explained the SEIN research
project, in characteristically modest language that understates both the

enormous scale and originality of her project as the first systematic survey of industrial magnetizing processes:

> Ce travail a été fait en vue d'étudier l'influence de la composition chimique des aciers sur leurs propriétés magnétiques à la manière dont ces propriétés sont modifiées par les conditions de trempe. Les aciers qui peuvent servir à faire des bons aimants permanents ont été étudiés plus complètement. Enfin, j'ai étudié l'effet d'un faible recuit sur les mêmes aciers et l'influence des secousses et du temps sur leur aimantation.[26]

This commission was secured through the patronage of Gabriel Lippmann and it was in his Sorbonne laboratory that she began this research, using the training she had received there to magnetize steel with electromagnets and determine a magnet's strength using Gauss's comparative magnetometer. Henry le Chatelier, Paris's leading chemical metallurgical expert, at the École des Mines, helped her procure forty seven samples of relevant samples from seven leading manufacturers of magnetic steel around France, and arranged for their chemical analysis. Marie also got advice from metallurgist Georges Charpy on metallurgical furnaces – very different to the heating techniques used by Pierre in his contemporary doctoral research on paramagnetism.

Soon, however she found it very difficult to maintain sufficient space in Lippman's laboratory, and within a few months Marie was looking for new premises at which to conduct her research project. Through a mutual acquaintance Joseph Kowalski she soon met Pierre Curie[27] and secured his approval to take some space in a corridor of his laboratory in the École de Physique et Chimie where they would later collaborate on radioactive researches.

As there are apparently no extant notes of her steel researches we have to rely on the internal contents of the paper to reconstruct her activities. In the first part of her paper she examined which chemical constitution and which species of heat treatment would furnish steel magnets with the largest remanent strength and coercivity. In so doing she undertook a survey of entirely unprecedented scope: among the forty seven types of steels she studied there were nine chemical variants, a selection of carbon-steels, and steel alloyed with boron, chromium, copper, tungsten, molybdenum, nickel, manganese & silicon. Her work confirmed the prevailing wisdom amongst French instrument makers that tungsten steels furnished magnets with optimum properties. She went beyond this, however, to specify the optimum percentage of tungsten to be 5.5% – and this figure, or one near it, certainly became standard in composition for magnets in the UK thereafter. However, her

---

[26] Sklodowska Curie, "Propriétés magnétiques des aciers trempés", *op. cit.*, p. 3.
[27] Eve Curie, *Madame Curie*, Paris, Gallimard, 1938, p. 102.

most novel claim was that the best steels for making permanent magnets were alloys with a content of 1.2-1.7% molybdenum. This was a striking finding because molybdenum steels were not commercially used for magnet making at the time, and were produced by only one manufacturer: Châtillon et Commentry. So far as I can tell and was evidently a quite unexpected finding, and her advice about this was not immediately widely taken up (but was so much later).

Marie's next claim was more radical, but was in some sense a synthesis of diverse existing researches. Magnet makers had long got the best results from steels hardened by being plunged from at least red-heat into a cold liquid (quench-hardening, usually in water). More recently (1890) John Hopkinson had shown that when heated above a particular critical temperature, magnetized steels suddenly lost a large portion of their remanent field[28]. And in his doctoral thesis of 1895 Pierre Curie made a generalized wide-ranging study of how ferromagnetic materials became (paramagnetic) or "faiblement magnétique" above a critical transition temperature, regaining this magnetism at a slightly lower critical temperature[29]. What Marie claimed was that to produce the best permanent magnet (with highest coercivity and remanence), the steel had to be heated to the upper critical point and then quenched before it cooled to the lower critical point[30]. To prove this she presented new data on all forty-seven steels to show the comparative effects of quenching above and below the critical temperatures, and how such critical temperatures depended on carbon content. Her claims about the strict *necessity* of hardening steels above their higher critical temperature were at first contested by the French metallurgist Floris Osmond and the American Henry Howe[31].

---

[28] John Hopkinson, "Magnetism and Recalescence", *Proceedings of the Royal Society*, t. 48, 1890, p. 442-446.

[29] Pierre identified two temperatures, the upper Curie point at which metals lost their ferromagnetic properties, the lower Curie point being the temperature at which cooling metals returned to ferromagnetic condition. See Pierre Curie's 1895 PhD thesis published as "Propriétés magnétiques des corps à diverses températures" in *Œuvres de Pierre Curie*, Paris, Gauthier-Villars, 1908.

[30] Although she attended his viva voce examination in spring 1895, Marie nowhere explicitly mentions Pierre's research. A connection is perhaps hinted at in her specification that it was necessary to harden magnet steel whilst it was "faiblement magnétique" – in its "weakly magnetic condition", in other words that it should be quenched in water after being raised above its upper critical temperature but before it cooled to the lower critical temperature.

[31] Osmond complained that Marie has failed to mention any of his work in her paper, and he like the American Henry Howe also challenged Marie's claim that it was necessary to heat steels to a non-magnetic condition to attain permanent magnetism. They effectively disagreed that this procedure was necessary to *optimize* the properties of a magnet. See correspondence in *The Metallographist*, t. 1, 1898, p. 266-270;

The final phase of Marie's research concerned the third phase of pre-paring new magnets, building on what little had been published for the US Geological Survey in 1885 by Carl Barus and Vincent Strouhal[32]. For ordinary purposes they recommended reheating hardened steels at about 100 degrees Celsius for long periods *before* magnetization and then again for a short period after magnetization[33]. By March 1897 there were new constraints on her attempts to improve upon Barus and Strou-hal's paper as she suffered daily pregnancy-related attacks of dizzi-ness[34]. When she could she spent many days baking and hitting a variety of steel magnets to find which strategy of stabilizing performance by artificial ageing least harmed their coercitivity and remanent magnetism. Her eventual recommendation was that steel should be heated at no more than 60-70 degrees Celsius for about 48 hours, magnetized to saturation and then demagnetized 10% by non-percussive means. For magnets to be used in precision instruments she recommended that they be reheated to 60 degrees, (just as Barus and Strouhal had specified). At the very end of her paper she apologizes that she has not completed any long-term trials on the permanency of her magnets. She does show, however, that for the months of July to September magnets made to her specifications did not detectably change in strength – the last such measurement taking place on September 18th, four days after giving birth to Irène, her first child with Pierre[35].

The Response to Marie Sklodowska Curie's Research on Magnetic Steels

On receipt of her work in December 1897, the SEIN immediately announced that her paper was "important", publishing all 40 pages of it in three distinct forms over the next 4 years. It was soon abstracted and translated in journals of metallurgy and electrical engineering in France

---

Marie Curie's paper was published in edited translation in that volume in three in-stallments under the title "Magnetic Properties of Tempered Steel", p. 107-124, 229-242, 274-289. The journal's editorial staff criticized her for oversimplifying the met-allurgical transitions that occurred at critical temperatures; Howe and Osmond wrote in to criticize her results after the second installment.

[32] Barus, Strouhal, "The electrical and magnetic properties of iron carburets", *op. cit.*

[33] H. Du Bois, E. Taylor Jones, "Magnetisirung und Hysterese einige Eisen- und Stahlsorten", *Electrotechnische Zeitschrift*, t. 17, 1896, p. 543. The recommended instead magnetization and then partial demagnetization by repeated shocks e.g. by dropping on the floor.

[34] Susan Quinn, *Marie Curie: a life*, London, Heinemann, 1995, p. 130 (March 2nd 1897).

[35] Marie finished writing up her paper in the next two months and submitted it to the SEIN. With both a baby and now also a recently bereaved father-in-law to support, the Société's 1,500 francs fee was of especial utility. *Ibid.*

Britain and the USA[36]. Notwithstanding such efforts, Marie did not thereafter discuss her steels results in public, nor did she defend them against criticisms – let alone try to establish a canonical authorial account of what was original about them. In any case given the quasi-secretive culture of magnet-making, commentators who held diverse localized views about existing best practices of magnet making were not likely to concur about which features of Marie Curie's work were significantly original in relation to *their* practices.

In London, the *Electrical Review* described her paper in January 1899 as one of "the most important" of recent contributions to the subject while being somewhat ambivalent about her originality, writing condescendingly:

> We take this opportunity of complimenting Mme Curie on her patient and systematic work. It does not appear that she made any new departure, or any particular discovery, and her methods are such as most of us are familiar with; but her information is more extensive, varied and exact, than anything we have previously seen on this subject. It is probable that makers of instruments, in which permanent magnets are used, have discovered rules for treating magnets similar or equivalent to those proposed by Mme Curie, but they have not made them public property.[37]

Remarkably, however, such suspicions that Curie had merely revealed well-attested but hitherto private magnet-makers' wisdom did not inhibit this journal from extensive editorializing on the significance of her work or reproducing at great length a nearly complete translation of her paper over the following three weeks.

The unresolved significance of her work on steels continued after Marie won her first Nobel prize (with Pierre Curie and Becquerel) in 1903. This is instanced in the response to the paper the following by year Kenelm Edgcumbe (later the Earl of Edgcumbe) of the company Everett-Edgcumbe and his assistant presented a paper on electrical switchboard instruments at the Institution of Electrical Engineers. They spoke as if the secret trade problem of permanent magnets had been

---

[36] The SEIN published an abstract for its *Bulletin* for December 1897, followed by the 40 page paper in 1898. Such was it enthusiasm that the SEIN also published it as an independent monograph in 1898. A short version of the paper focusing on the comparative merits of tungsten and molybdenum steels was published in *Comptes Rendus*, t. 125, 1897, p. 1165-1169, and the Académie des sciences awarded her a prize for the paper. See also version in Metallographist published above and in "Magnetic Properties of Tempered Steel", *Electrical Review*, t. 44, 1899, p. 40-42, 75-76, 112-113; it was also send to the *Journal of the Iron and Steel Institute* and noted in its 1898 volume, p. 504-505.

[37] Editorial (January 13 1899), "Steel for Permanent Magnets", *Electrical Review*, t. 44, 1899, p. 33-35.

solved, but without specifying how, when or by whom, making no mention of Marie Curie anywhere in their paper[38].

In the ensuing discussion of Edgcumbe's paper, two commentators pinpointed her work as crucial to solving the problem. Rookes E. B. Crompton, veteran of Indian colonial service and dynamo manufacturer who had anathematized permanent magnets twenty years before, saw much of value in her analysis of critical temperatures:

> All instrument-makers are deeply indebted to Marie Curie for the excellent work she has published in regard to the saturation and persistence of magnetism in steel bars. Madame Curie has pointed out how much depends on the exact temperature to which the magnet steel must be heated before being plunged [into water], and if her directions are closely followed excellent and concordant conditions invariably follow. The work that she has given to the world in this respect is almost unique in its character and accuracy. This accuracy in the production of permanent magnets has been a great boon to instrument makers.[39]

The other positive comment on Marie Curie's work was Sydney Evershed. From his experiences of developing the "Megger" ohmmeter he now claimed Marie Curie's results to be "very valuable" if insufficient to prepare magnets which maintain their permanence. Importantly he was rather guarded about revealing what – if anything – needed to be added to her methods, clearly upholding the tradition still of trade secrecy in such matters[40].

The most powerful endorsement of Curie's work came from Silvanus Thompson in a paper he read to a meeting of the Institution of Electrical Engineers (IEE) in Glasgow in 1912. Thompson knew Marie personally, and was highly sympathetic to women's participation in electrical work[41]. As a reflection of this he cited her paper frequently his lecture being especially impressed by the originality of her analysis of alloy steels, especially with regard to molybdenum and tungsten varieties. Like Evershed and many others he concurred that her recommendation of 6% tungsten steel as ideal, and like Crompton, reiterated her advice about the importance of heating steels to the critical temperature and the

---

[38] Edgcumbe, Punga, "Direct Reading Instruments for switchboard use", *op. cit.*, p. 625.

[39] *Ibid.*, discussion p. 656-657.

[40] *ibid.*, discussion p. 663-664.

[41] As President of the IEE in 1900 Thompson had overseen the election of Hertha Ayrton as its first woman member. See Jane Smeal, Helen Thompson, *Silvanus Phillips Thompson: his life and Letters*, London, T. F. Unwin, 1920; Evelyn Sharp, *Hertha Ayrton: 1854-1923: a memoir*, London, Arnold, 1926.

need for rapid quenching thereafter[42]. After Thompson's piece was reprinted in the IEE's London journal the following year, it became the major standard reference work on permanent magnets. Ironically, however, most authors thereafter referred to Curie's results as published by Thompson rather than referencing Curie's original paper[43].

Sydney Evershed's two monumental papers on "Permanent Magnets in Theory and Practice" that eventually replaced Thompson's piece as the canonical treatment were the last to cite Marie's name explicitly on magnet. Evershed not only cited Curie's recommendations about tungsten steels, but drew from it further information that informed his important new recommendations on the relationship between carbon content and critical temperature. Indeed Evershed's main point, going beyond Curie's account was that the key to permanency in magnetism lay in distributing carbide molecules within steel to prevent the orientation of microscopic magnetic elements deviating from their mutual alignment[44]. In reputedly solving the major problems of permanent magnetism, Evershed's papers relied both on Marie Curie's results and her practice of open publication. Yet after his death in 1939, studies on permanent magnetism referred to the name Curie only to point to the importance of the critical temperature in hardening magnets, and this "Curie point" was named after Pierre Curie not Marie.

Finally we should note that notwithstanding the efforts of Marie Curie, Thompson and Evershed, the problem of making magnets "permanent" was still not fully resolved even after Evershed's classic paper. His paper concluded by discussing the limits he had uncovered to ever making magnets completely stable: carbide molecules within the steel would not stay in the position so crucial to magnetic stability. As Evershed observed stoically of a lifetime's research on the subject of permanence:

> Looking back on all this and seeing the elaborate molecular pattern slowly falling to pieces, it is only natural that the word permanent, as applied to

---

[42] Thompson, "The Magnetism of Permanent Magnets", *op. cit.*, p. 85, 87-88, 106-107, 110-111, 127-128.

[43] In 1914 Dr. Margaret Moir, research fellow at the University of Glasgow, published a piece on the use of tungsten and chromium in permanent magnets that she presented primarily as a response to Thompson's work, whilst presenting measurements that purported to improve upon Marie Curie's; Margaret Moir, "Permanent Magnetism of Certain Chrome and Tungsten Steels", *Electrician*, t. 74, 1914-1915, p. 385-386. Conversely in treatise on electrical instruments that Kenelm Edgcumbe revised in a second edition on return from war duty in 1918, he cites Curie's data on Tungsten steels but gives Thompson's lecture as his source instead, Kenelm Edgcumbe, *Industrial electrical measuring instruments*, London, Constable, 1918, p. 66.

[44] Evershed, "Permanent Magnetism in Theory and Practice (part 2)", *op. cit.*, p. 799-800.

hardened steel, should lose something of its force. But after all, even perma-nence is relative. It may be said that a permanent magnet is nothing apart from the man who makes use of it, and from that point of view perhaps it is enough the magnet should be rather more permanent than the man.[45]

Conclusions: Understanding Industrial Research on Permanent Magnetism

The permanent magnet is a classic example of a technology that needed adaptation and adjustment for its effective application to the needs of fin de siècle electro-technology. Thus it was the subject of detailed research in various forms by companies than trusted their techniques for rendering their magnets permanent. Of course there were quite a few companies who did not trust permanent magnets to be "permanent" and did not research the subject at all, trusting rather to electromagnets or proportional springs to govern the mechanism of their measuring instruments. Yet for those companies which did use perma-nent magnets, much research was conducted in a commercially-prudent craft culture of secretiveness – until Curie's work emerged c. 1898-1900. In the absence of research documented in company publicity, let alone published in research journals, it is very difficult for historians to recover what investment – if any – electrotechnical companies made in funding or labour to solve the problem. Most seems to have waited over the *longue durée* to see whether their magnets did behave with the degree of stability desired, indeed perhaps settling down to a mature imperturbability.

However, until the time of Marie Curie's research on the subject from 1894-1897, the kind of research publicly available was limited either to general academic studies of the magnetic behaviour of iron – notably by John Hopkinson as a freelance consultant for Edison, latterly from 1890 as a Professor of Electrical Engineering at Kings College London – or to individual reports on the performance of magnets made from a particular variety of steel reported in trade journals. It seems likely that such individuals invested their own funds magnetic research-es on limited ranges of steel samples, and then published them in order to win the attention and sponsorship of manufacturers; and in the 1880s and 1890s there were many young prospective experimenters who, like Marie Sklodowska, earnestly sought such forms of industrial patronage to support a research career.

By contrast, Marie Curie's contribution to the field was precipitated by a major private French industrial body *La Société pour l'Encourage-*

---

[45] *Ibid.*

ment de l'Industrie Nationale soliciting a very broad and *exhaustive* research project that would unequivocally establish how the *best* permanent magnet should be made in order to benefit the whole electrical industry. By supporting this commission with access to the samples of all the major steel manufacturers in France, via industrially well-connected scholars, Marie Sklodowska made sure she would not miss any existing form of steel with near optimum properties. Nevertheless, neither the SEIN nor the Sorbonne provided Curie either with laboratory facilities needed for her project, nor did they finance any assistance for her; this obliged her to undertake all the research en seule in fortuitously borrowed space in a corridor in Pierre Curie's laboratory. Only *after* she produced her results after four years of work did interest in her highly systematic and entirely open approach to the issues of magnetism grow to the point that manufacturing firms and academic institutes became prepared to pursue intensive research on a similar scale and for a comparable duration, and even to publish it too. And only given *that* effective precedent could Sydney Evershed's company have dedicated so much of its resources and site space to the decades of research that enabled him to publish his two definitive papers in 1920 and 1925.

Finally we should note that whilst Marie Curie did not publicly discuss her magnetic research after she began her doctoral thesis on radioactivity in 1898, her subsequent experiments with radioactive metals borrowed closely the open and large scale approach to research adopted in her steels project. Her second published paper in 1898[46] surveyed dozens of metal ores to compare their radioactivity with uranium obtained using the same skills of networking and patronage employed in 1894 to secure steel samples from across France. Ironically, however, working with Pierre Curie to diagnose by magnetic deflection the nature of the rays emanating from polonium and radium, neither of them ever seems to have used a "permanent magnet" – only the more trustworthy electromagnet.

---

[46] Marie Curie, "Rayons émis par les composés de l'uranium et du thorium", *Œuvres de Marie Sklodowska Curie*, 1898, p. 43-45.

Externalisation et internalisation
de la recherche

Le cas de Clément Ader, entrepreneur d'inventions

Gabriel GALVEZ-BEHAR

Université Lille 3 (IRHiS)

Penser que les dynamiques de l'innovation à la fin du XIXe siècle, et en particulier dans le domaine de l'électricité, reposèrent pour une part essentielle sur l'activité de structures de petite taille, indépendantes des grandes firmes, est aujourd'hui un acquis que partagent sans doute l'ensemble des participants à ce colloque. Un tel postulat conduit cependant à s'interroger sur les rapports entre ces acteurs de l'activité inventive et les firmes qui assument alors la mise en place des premiers réseaux électriques. Dans ce contexte, les firmes se contentent-elles de repérer les inventions susceptibles de les intéresser, de les acquérir et de les exploiter ? Au contraire, parviennent-elles à aller au-delà de cette démarche, en orientant, voire en suscitant l'activité inventive ? Si tel est le cas, comment procèdent-elles ? Ces questions se posent avec d'autant plus d'acuité lorsque la recherche est extérieure à la firme, c'est à dire, lorsque son orientation ne dépend pas tant d'une relation hiérarchique que d'une transaction et d'un contrat entre deux parties autonomes[1]. Ce sont ces problèmes que nous souhaiterions aborder aujourd'hui à travers l'exemple de Clément Ader.

Si la postérité a fait de Clément Ader l'un des pères de l'aviation, c'est aux dépens de ses autres travaux, puisque l'on oublie généralement

---

[1] Cette communication prolonge certaines analyses développées dans ma thèse, *« Pour la fortune et pour la gloire ». Inventeurs, propriété industrielle et organisation de l'invention en France, 1870-1922*, thèse de doctorat sous la dir. de J.-P. Hirsch, université Lille 3, 2004 ; sur l'innovation dans l'industrie électrique, cf. notamment, Robert Fox et Anna Guagnini, *Laboratories, workshops and sites. Concepts and practices of research in industrial Europe, 1800-1914*, Berkeley, Office for the History of Science and Technology (Université de Californie), 1999 ; et pour une revue de la littérature récente, *id.*, « Sites of innovation in electrical technology, 1880-1914 », *Annales historiques de l'électricité*, juin 2004, n° 2, p. 159-172.

qu'il fut l'un des acteurs majeurs de l'essor de la téléphonie en France[2]. En outre, son cas s'avère tout à fait significatif des relations, telles que nous pouvons les analyser à travers les archives, entre un inventeur indépendant et une grande entreprise de la fin du XIXe siècle, la Société générale des téléphones. Même si ces archives laissées par Clément Ader sont assez éparses, elles renferment un certain nombre d'indications relatives à ses contrats et à leur négociation. Elles permettent de mieux caractériser ce commerce entre un inventeur et une grande entreprise. Nous nous attacherons donc à rappeler les grands traits de cette collaboration entre Ader et la Société des téléphones et à montrer en quoi Clément Ader peut être considéré comme un « entrepreneur d'inventions ». Nous décrirons ensuite les moyens utilisés par la Société des téléphones pour l'encadrer, avant de faire le bilan de cette relation qui dura plus de vingt ans.

« M. Ader, ingénieur-conseil de la Société des téléphones »

Rappelons brièvement quelques éléments chronologiques avant de commencer à décrire précisément les relations entre Ader et la Société industrielle des téléphones. Né en 1841, Clément Ader fut un inventeur à la fois précoce et prolifique. Dès l'âge de 25 ans, après des études techniques à Toulouse, il prit ses premiers brevets relatifs à de nouveaux modes de transport[3]. Souhaitant assurer la promotion de ses inventions, il fit au ministère de la Guerre une série de propositions rejetées après avoir été examinées par le Comité des fortifications[4]. Un tel échec ne découragea pas l'inventeur, qui mit au point, en 1868, des roues en caoutchouc pour les vélocipèdes. Afin d'exploiter son invention, Ader créa une petite entreprise dans ce domaine, ce qui ne l'empêcha pas d'être attiré par d'autres industries, et avant tout par l'électricité.

Cet intérêt pour cette toute nouvelle industrie précéda de quelques années l'exposition universelle de 1878. Ses relations avec l'académicien des sciences Théodose du Moncel lui permirent d'acquérir des connaissances dans ce domaine et d'approfondir ses recherches sur un

---

[2] L'une des meilleures biographies d'Ader est sans doute celle du général Pierre Lissarrague, *Clément Ader, Inventeur d'avions*, Toulouse, Éditions Privat, 1990. On pourra également consulter Claude Carlier, *L'affaire Clément Ader. La vérité enfin rétablie*, Paris, Perrin, 1990.

[3] INPI, brevets n° 71031 et 73281 des 15 avril et 30 octobre 1886 relatifs à une machine pour relever la voie ferrée dans les chemins de fer et au chemin de fer amovible. Cette dernière invention est considérée comme une préfiguration de l'utilisation de chenilles pour le mouvement des chars : le chemin de fer est amovible car le train porte avec lui, sous forme d'une chaîne, les rails sur lesquels il roule.

[4] Centre de documentation d'histoire des techniques (CDHT), fonds Ader, doc. 2336.

problème qui lui tenait à cœur : la transmission de la parole[5]. En 1878, Ader déposa ainsi ses premiers brevets relatifs à un système de correspondance vocale dénommé « Électrophone »[6]. Un an plus tard, il s'associait avec Frederic A. Gower, un ingénieur électricien et collaborateur de Cornelius Roosevelt, le représentant de Bell en France[7].

Dès lors, Ader devint l'un des acteurs du développement de la téléphonie en France, travaillant pour la Société générale des téléphones avec laquelle il coopéra dès le début des années 1880. Résultant de la fusion de la Compagnie des téléphones, détentrice des brevets de Gower et de Roosevelt, et de la Société française des téléphones, qui possédait quant à elle des brevets Edison, la Société générale des téléphones avait été fondée en août 1880[8]. Elle se distingua lors de l'exposition internationale d'électricité de 1881, avec la mise en place dans l'enceinte de l'exposition d'un « théatrophone » permettant d'entendre les spectacles donnés à l'Opéra ou à la Comédie Française[9]. Inventeur et maître d'œuvre de ce système qui fut l'un des clous de cette exposition, Clément Ader fut récompensé par une médaille d'or et, quelques temps plus tard, par la Légion d'honneur. Ce succès contribua à renforcer les liens entre Ader et la Société générale des téléphones. En effet, c'est au cours de l'année 1881 que cette dernière devint propriétaire des inventions de Clément Ader et qu'elle s'assura sa collaboration exclusive en matière de téléphonie[10]. Durant la première moitié des années 1880, cette collaboration fut intense et, en 1884, Clément Ader était à l'origine de près de 74 brevets et certificats d'addition[11]. À la fin des années 1880, Ader entamait des recherches sur les récepteurs des transmissions effectuées grâce aux câbles sous-marins. Elles aboutirent en 1887 à la

---

5 Dans une lettre écrite en 1921, Ader évoque son intérêt pour la téléphonie : « J'étais un ami de du Moncel ; un jour, c'était quelques années avant l'exposition de 1878, il me montra un article d'une revue américaine où on parlait vaguement pour la première fois de téléphone. En même temps, il m'apportait un de ces livres : *Exposé de l'électricité*. tome III, Hachette 1856. Ouvert à la page 110 – Transmission électrique de la parole – (Pour votre édification, il est indispensable que vous lisiez cet ouvrage dans l'intérêt de l'honneur français) Vous voyez, me dit-il, on y pensait avant vous et avant les américains ». CDHT, fonds Ader, doc. 2343.

6 INPI, brevet n° 125782 du 23 juillet 1878.

7 Pierre Lissarague, *Clément Ader*, *op. cit.*, p. 55 ; Pierre Aulas, *Les origines du téléphone en France (1876-1914)*, Paris, ADHE, p. 37.

8 Centre des archives du monde du travail (CAMT), 65 AQ Q 3038 et 3039.

9 Sur l'exposition de 1881, cf. François Caron et Fabienne Cardot (dir.), *Histoire générale de l'électricité en France*, tome 1, *Espoirs et conquêtes, 1881-1918*, Paris, Fayard, 1991, p. 18-33.

10 CAMT, 65 AQ Q 3039, rapport du conseil d'administration à l'assemblée générale ordinaire du 14 avril 1881.

11 CDHT, fonds Ader, doc. 2370, « Liste de brevets pris pour les inventions de M. Ader ».

mise au point par Ader d'un nouveau système nommé « Phonosignal »[12]. En 1898, Ader déposa un brevet pour des perfectionnements destinés aux voitures et aux moteurs[13]. Deux ans plus tard, lors de l'assemblée générale de la Société industrielle des téléphones, le 15 décembre 1900, le rapporteur déclarait : « Notre ingénieur-conseil, M. Ader, dont le nom fait autorité en électricité et en mécanique, a combiné et construit un moteur très intéressant »[14]. L'automobile devint alors le champ d'une collaboration nouvelle entre Ader et la Société.

Pendant près de vingt ans, Clément Ader fut donc un collaborateur essentiel de la Société des téléphones. Toutefois, ce rapide résumé ne suffit pas à expliquer la durée de cette relation qui perdura bien que, de son côté, Ader demeura toujours à son propre compte. C'est précisément ce qui nous incite à chercher quels furent les compromis qui rendirent cette coopération possible.

Ader, entrepreneur d'inventions

La longueur de cette relation est d'autant plus frappante qu'Ader, tout au long de cette collaboration, resta autonome vis-à-vis de la Société des téléphones. Trois arguments permettent d'étayer ce constat : l'éclectisme des recherches d'Ader, leur localisation et la défense de son autonomie par l'inventeur.

Un court examen des dates marquantes de la vie d'Ader permet de constater le caractère concomitant de ses recherches sur le téléphone, le télégraphe et l'aviation. Ader entama ses recherches sur l'aviation quelques mois après avoir signé son contrat avec la Société générale des téléphones en 1882. En 1894, un an après la reprise de ce contrat par la Société industrielle des téléphones, il signa un accord avec l'armée sur la mise au point d'un appareil de locomotion aérienne. L'année 1897 est sans doute la plus significative de la dualité des recherches de Clément Ader. En mai 1897, Ader supervisait les essais de ses récepteurs de télégraphie sous-marine qui avaient lieu à Marseille[15]. Quelques mois plus tard, en octobre, il dirigeait les essais de l'*Avion n° 3* à Satory. Au cours de l'année 1897 Ader avait donc mené plusieurs activités de front,

---

[12] INPI, brevet n° 181786 du 24 février 1887 relatif au mode de réception des courants électriques aux extrémités des câbles souterrains et sous-marins.

[13] INPI, brevet n° 278138.

[14] CAMT, 65 AQ Q 3040. La Société industrielle des téléphones est l'héritière de la Société générale des téléphones, liquidée entre 1893 et 1895 à la suite de la nationalisation des réseaux téléphoniques.

[15] CDHT, fonds Ader, doc. 2367, rapports de M. Rossel, chef du laboratoire Ader et de M. Meyer May.

dont certaines n'avaient aucun rapport avec les activités de la Société des téléphones.

Cette capacité à mener un double programme de recherche s'explique par le fait qu'Ader parvint à cloisonner ses différentes activités. Ce cloisonnement reposait tout d'abord sur une distribution spatiale des différents projets. Grâce au contrat signé en 1881, Ader avait pu acquérir un hôtel particulier au 68 rue de l'Assomption à Passy[16]. C'est là qu'il mena l'essentiel de ses recherches sur la téléphonie, dans son laboratoire particulier, où la Société des téléphones – dont le magasin était situé 2 rue des Entrepreneurs de l'autre côté de la Seine – lui livrait le matériel électrique nécessaire[17]. Les recherches aéronautiques étaient menées quant à elles, rue Pajou, puis à partir de novembre 1891, rue Jasmin, les deux emplacements offrant l'avantage d'être tout proches de l'hôtel de la rue de l'Assomption. Cette distinction et cette proximité des lieux de l'activité inventive offraient à Ader la possibilité de mener à bien ses projets sans qu'ils interfèrent entre eux.

Ce cloisonnement des activités était en outre renforcé par l'emploi d'équipes distinctes. Ainsi, Rossel, « chef des laboratoires Ader », n'appartenait-il pas à l'équipe des vingt ouvriers qui, dans la seconde moitié des années 1890, s'affairaient autour de l'*Avion n° 3*[18]. En fait, loin de la mythologie le présentant comme prisonnier de la solitude de l'inventeur, Ader s'avérait être un véritable entrepreneur de l'invention, à la tête de plusieurs dizaines de salariés répartis sur plusieurs sites.

Cette caractérisation pourrait surprendre dans la mesure où une longue tradition schumpéterienne nous a appris à distinguer l'inventeur de l'entrepreneur[19]. Au mieux s'applique-t-elle aux inventeurs de la trempe d'Edison et il peut paraître bien naïf de comparer la rue de l'Assomption à Menlo Park. Pourtant, à y regarder de plus près, l'activité d'Ader correspond bien à celle d'un chef d'entreprise qui coordonne plusieurs projets en supervisant une pluralité d'équipes. La négociation

---

[16] CDHT, fonds Ader, doc. 2305, Ader verse un acompte en décembre 1881 et emménage dans son hôtel à l'hiver 1882.

[17] En effet, dans une lettre adressée à Léauté, Ader déclare : « Tous les essais préliminaires de mon invention ayant déjà été faits chez moi dans mon laboratoire particulier on va pouvoir construire immédiatement les appareils définitifs à l'atelier et j'ai bon espoir pour leur réussite ». Le laboratoire particulier est donc au domicile d'Ader. CDHT, fonds Ader, doc. 2369. Lettre de Léauté à Ader du 16 avril 1895. Par ailleurs les factures relatives au matériel délivré par la Société générale des téléphones font état de livraisons rue de l'Assomption. CDHT, fonds Ader, doc. 2306.

[18] CDHT, fonds Ader, doc. 2311.

[19] Cf. Joseph Schumpeter, *Théorie de l'évolution économique. Recherches sur le profit, le crédit, l'intérêt et le cycle de la conjoncture*, Paris, Dalloz, 1999 (1re éd. allemande : 1911), p. 126. Schumpeter y déclare : « La fonction d'inventeur ou de technicien en général, et celle de l'entrepreneur ne coïncide pas ».

du contrat de 1887 entre Ader et la Société générale des téléphones vient d'ailleurs le confirmer de manière éclatante. Collaborateur depuis plus de six ans avec la Société à laquelle il avait permis de prendre plusieurs brevets relatifs à la téléphonie, Ader mit au point, on l'a vu, un nouveau système de réception des signaux électriques à l'extrémité de câbles sous-marins. En février 1887, il proposa à l'administrateur de la Société générale des téléphones cette nouvelle invention pour laquelle il avait déjà pourvu « aux premières dépenses de laboratoire »[20]. Il proposa de continuer à payer les essais, si nécessaire, mais entendait également partager les bénéfices auxquels pourrait donner lieu l'exploitation de son invention.

Plusieurs mois furent nécessaires à la rédaction d'un traité entre les deux parties. Le 22 avril 1887, la Société proposa à Ader de lui ouvrir un crédit de 1 000 francs pour commencer à financer les essais complémentaires et avancer les frais relatifs à la prise de brevets tant en France qu'à l'étranger. À la fin de la période d'essais, Ader s'engageait à rembourser la moitié des frais d'essais et de brevets. Enfin, en cas d'exploitation commerciale, la Société des téléphones suggérait un partage égal des bénéfices comme des pertes[21]. Aussitôt Ader répondit par la négative. Autant il lui paraissait acceptable de rembourser la moitié des frais d'essais et de brevets, autant il lui semblait totalement inenvisageable de partager les pertes éventuellement occasionnées par l'exploitation commerciale[22].

Le 27 avril 1887, dans une lettre probablement adressée au directeur de la Société, Ader donna une explication transparente de son refus :

> Cette invention m'a déjà occasionné d'autres dépenses, que je ne songe pas d'ailleurs à réclamer, car comme vous savez j'ai un laboratoire particulier qu'il me faut entretenir de personnel, d'outillage et de fourniture. Je sais que vous traitez les affaires d'une manière pratique, aussi j'ai la certitude que vous me donnerez raison. Voyez dans quel embarras je me trouverais s'il me fallait solder un déficit. Je suis inventeur et non capitaliste.[23]

Cette courte citation apporte une lumière qui éclaire l'activité de Clément Ader dès 1887. Loin d'être un inventeur solitaire, Ader se trouvait être à la tête d'une affaire, reposant sur un laboratoire outillé où travaillaient plusieurs ouvriers et dont l'objet était de produire des inventions. Si Ader acceptait de prendre le risque d'essais infructueux, il

---

[20] CDHT, fonds Ader, doc. 2382, brouillon de lettre du 23 février 1887 d'Ader à Wallerstein.

[21] CDHT, fonds Ader, doc. 2382, lettre du 22 avril 1887 du directeur de la SGT à Ader.

[22] CDHT, fonds Ader, doc. 2382, lettre du 23 avril 1887 à la Société.

[23] CDHT, fonds Ader, brouillon d'une lettre du 27 avril 1887 d'Ader à un destinataire inconnu (le nom est illisible).

refusait de mettre en péril son entreprise en l'exposant à des revers commerciaux. La tâche d'affronter les aléas du marché revenait au capitaliste ; à l'inventeur incombait celle de se confronter aux vicissitudes de la technique. En dernier ressort, les logiques de l'entrepreneur capitaliste et de l'entrepreneur d'inventions n'étaient pas les mêmes. Des compromis étaient donc bien nécessaires à leur collaboration.

Encadrer l'inventeur

Cette différence entre les logiques de l'entrepreneur d'inventions et celles de l'entreprise commerciale est à la source d'incertitudes que les parties tentent de réduire. Pour la seconde, l'indépendance de l'inventeur représente un risque puisqu'elle n'a guère d'assurance que ses fonds seront effectivement investis dans une activité inventive conforme à ses intérêts. Elle doit donc encadrer l'inventeur. Cet encadrement repose sur la contractualisation de la relation, elle-même renvoyant à un financement limité des essais, à un contrôle de la propriété industrielle et à une surveillance du conseil d'administration de l'entreprise.

Plusieurs contrats ponctuèrent la collaboration entre Clément Ader et la Société des téléphones. L'existence d'une pluralité de contrats révèle en fait le caractère séquentiel de cette relation. Aussi faudrait-il parler de plusieurs phases de collaboration, et non pas d'une seule, les règles du compromis pouvant changer d'un contrat à l'autre. Concernant la première période de collaboration, entre 1881 et 1887, nous ne disposons malheureusement pas du premier contrat liant Ader à la Société générale des téléphones. Ce contrat signé le 3 novembre 1881 fait cependant l'objet de mentions dans des documents ultérieurs qui permettent d'en reconstituer partiellement le contenu[24]. Le point de départ de cette convention était constitué par les deux brevets d'Ader de 1878 et de 1879 protégeant respectivement un récepteur « électrophone » et un récepteur téléphonique[25]. En cédant ses droits sur ces brevets, Ader s'engageait également à apporter à la Société des perfectionnements à la

---

[24] La première de ces mentions est contenue dans le rapport, déjà cité, du conseil d'administration lors de l'assemblée générale ordinaire de la Société générale des téléphones le 14 avril 1881 : « Enfin, c'est sur son avis [de la Commission technique de la Société] que nous avons tranché une question mal définie, restée litigieuse entre votre Société et un de ses fondateurs et qu'en conséquence, nous sommes devenus propriétaires des inventions de M. Ader, en même temps que nous nous assurions la collaboration exclusive de ce dernier. Cette solution nous paru d'autant plus satisfaisante que M. Ader est certainement un des ingénieurs français qui a fait faire le plus de progrès à la téléphonie ; son concours sera précieux pour votre Société ». CAMT, 65 AQ Q 3039. En revanche, dans lettre écrite en 1894, Henry Léauté, administrateur délégué de la Société industrielle des téléphones, mentionne « la convention du 3 novembre 1881 ». CHDT, fonds Ader, doc. 2369.

[25] INPI, brevets n° 127180 du 28 octobre 1878 et n° 27 février 1879.

téléphonie. Ainsi, en vendant ses premiers brevets pris à son nom, Ader entamait une collaboration plus large mais limitée à un objet, la téléphonie.

C'est une séquence identique sur laquelle on en sait un peu plus qui caractérise la seconde phase de collaboration entre Ader et la Société. En effet, la liquidation de la Société générale des téléphones en 1893-1895, conséquence de la nationalisation du téléphone en 1889, donna lieu à une abondante correspondance entre Ader et le liquidateur de la Société, correspondance assez instructive sur l'état de la relation entre les deux partenaires. Là encore un brevet, relatif aux câbles sous-marins et pris au nom d'Ader en février 1887, fut à l'origine d'un nouveau partenariat de recherches. Un contrat lia par la suite Ader et la Société le 5 mai 1887[26]. Il prévoyait le paiement de redevances contre la cession automatique de licences des brevets qu'Ader continuerait à prendre à son nom ; la Société générale des téléphones, quant à elle, prendrait à sa charge les frais nécessaires aux recherches d'Ader et au paiement des annuités[27]. On le voit, les règles du compromis avaient été quelque peu modifiées par rapport au premier contrat puisque la prise de brevets ne se faisait plus de la même manière. En négociant plusieurs contrats instituant des collaborations relatives à des objectifs distincts, les parties gardaient la possibilité de modifier les règles au regard de leurs expériences et de leurs résultats antérieurs.

Malgré ces modifications, l'encadrement de l'inventeur par la Société laisse toutefois apparaître des préoccupations constantes. La première porte sur le caractère limité et conditionnel du financement des essais réalisés par l'inventeur. La Société ouvrait ainsi à Ader un crédit déterminé grâce auquel Ader menait ses recherches et achetait son matériel d'expérimentation à la Société, tout en lui facturant en retour l'ensemble des frais afférents à ses expériences[28]. En outre, selon les termes du contrat, Ader pouvait être conduit à rembourser les frais d'expériences si ces dernières n'aboutissaient pas à une exploitation du système projeté[29]. Si Ader pouvait ainsi bénéficier des avances nécessaires à ses re-

---

[26] Ce contrat ne figure pas dans le fonds Ader mais est mentionné dans une lettre du 21 février 1895 (CDHT, doc. 2383) et dans un autre courrier du 16 avril 1895 (CDHT, doc. 2369). Sur l'industrie du câble sous-marin, cf. Pascal Griset, *Entreprise, technologie et souveraineté : les télécommunications transatlantiques de la France, XIX*e*-XX*e* siècles*, Paris, Éditions Rive Droite, 1996.

[27] En revanche, il semble que les brevets afférents au matériel téléphonique aient été pris au nom de la Société générale des téléphones.

[28] Ader conservait donc toutes les pièces comptables pour la détermination de ces frais. Une partie d'entre elles sont conservées dans le fonds Ader du CHDT (doc. 2308).

[29] Cette disposition est rappelée dans une lettre du président de la commission de liquidation de la Société générale des téléphones à Ader, du 21 février 1895. CDHT, fonds Ader, doc. 2383. Ce remboursement est plafonné à 5 000 francs.

cherches, l'entreprise s'assurait cependant de ne pas les financer à fonds perdus et tentait de responsabiliser l'inventeur en lui faisant supporter une partie des conséquences découlant d'un éventuel échec. En d'autres termes, la recherche externalisée avait pour avantage de faire partager les risques de tout investissement dans l'activité inventive.

Dans la perspective d'un succès, il était cependant nécessaire d'établir de la manière la plus nette possible la détention des droits de propriété sur les inventions. De ce fait, un contrôle de la propriété industrielle s'avérait nécessaire et, on l'a vu, les contrats prévoyaient des modalités précises quant à la prise de brevets. En outre, la Société des téléphones n'hésita pas à imposer son propre agent de brevets, Armengaud, par ailleurs un de ses administrateurs. Cela n'empêchait pas Ader de se montrer loyal et très soucieux de voir poursuivie une stratégie cohérente en matière de propriété industrielle[30]. En outre, Ader tenait à ce que son nom soit mentionné dans les titres des brevets, afin de faire établir la paternité de ses inventions, fût-elle symbolique. La contractualisation de la recherche supposait donc que fussent mises en place différentes modalités de reconnaissance de l'invention. Ce contrôle de la propriété industrielle par la Société permet aussi de souligner le rôle crucial du conseil d'administration de la Société des téléphones, qui fut un lieu de décision essentiel dans l'orientation des recherches menées par Ader. Non seulement le conseil d'administration autorisait ou non la prise d'un brevet ou le paiement des annuités, mais il était également amené à accepter ou à refuser les propositions techniques de son inventeur en titre. Bien souvent, Ader devait chercher à convaincre les membres du conseil d'administration de l'intérêt de ses inventions, notamment en les incitant à les expérimenter eux-mêmes. Ce fut le cas en 1884, avec la mise au point d'un téléphone d'intérieur qu'Ader proposa d'installer chez plusieurs administrateurs afin qu'ils puissent témoigner de son mérite auprès de leurs collègues.

Ce dialogue entre Ader et le conseil d'administration était facilité par la personnalité de l'administrateur-délégué de la Société, Henry Léauté. Centralien, élu dans la section de mécanique de l'Académie des sciences en 1890, Henry Léauté fut un interlocuteur constant et bienveillant à l'égard de Clément Ader. En tant que savant, il était à même de comprendre, voire d'expertiser, les propositions d'Ader, d'autant qu'il était secondé par un comité technique. En tant qu'administrateur il pouvait répondre auprès de ses collègues du sérieux du collaborateur de la Société. La relation entre la Société des téléphones et l'entrepreneur d'inventions nécessitait donc qu'un acteur puisse, en interne, évaluer l'intérêt et la consistance des inventions proposées.

---

[30] CDHT, fonds Ader, doc. 2369, lettre de Léauté à Ader du 26 mai 1895.

La présence de Léauté permettait enfin d'offrir à Ader des récompenses symboliques complétant sa rémunération financière. Outre les redevances fixées par chaque contrat, Léauté profita de sa position académique pour conférer au collaborateur de la Société des marques de reconnaissance qu'Ader était sans doute loin de mépriser. Ainsi, en 1897, Léauté n'hésita pas à user de son influence pour faire entendre à l'Académie des sciences une communication d'Ader, tout en s'assurant que cette dernière recevrait un écho médiatique important. La collaboration entre l'inventeur et la Société des téléphones dépassait donc le seul domaine d'une transaction purement commerciale pour s'inscrire dans un système d'échanges se jouant dans une pluralité de champs.

Une relation conflictuelle mais positive

Dans le cadre d'une relation dont on mesure la complexité, les conflits ne manquèrent pas. L'une des sources de divergence porta sur la pertinence de l'exploitation des inventions mises au point par Ader. Dès la signature de la convention de 1887, des brevets relatifs au « Phonosignal » avaient été pris dans près d'une dizaine de pays étrangers, dont la Belgique, l'Allemagne, la Grande-Bretagne et les États-Unis[31]. Pourtant, tous les brevets étrangers furent abandonnés en 1891, la Société ne voyant pas l'intérêt de les maintenir et d'en payer les annuités. Ader fut ainsi fort irrité de voir que « la Société générale des téléphones n'a rien fait pour tirer parti commercialement de [son] invention » alors même qu'il avait fait « techniquement tout ce qu'il fallait pour rendre le système pratique »[32]. L'inadéquation des logiques commerciale et technique rendait toujours plus difficiles les relations entre la Société générale des téléphones et son inventeur.

Le versement des redevances pouvait également être source de difficultés. La liquidation de la Société générale des téléphones conduisit à la création d'une société nouvelle en octobre 1893, la Société industrielle des téléphones[33]. Forte d'un capital de 18 millions de francs et d'un portefeuille de 18 brevets, la nouvelle société avait pour objet la fabrication et la vente de tout matériel ayant pour but une application quelconque de l'électricité, en particulier la pose de câbles sous-marins[34].

---

[31] CDHT, fonds Ader, doc. 2351, liste des brevets concernant la télégraphie sous-marine établie par le cabinet Armengaud jeune.

[32] CDHT, fonds Ader, doc. 2383. Cette analyse est produite quatre années après les faits. Ader en fait part, cependant, dans d'autres courriers.

[33] CDHT, fonds Ader, doc. 2381, statuts de la Société industrielle des téléphones. Les archives du Crédit Lyonnais disposent, elles aussi, d'un dossier sur la société : ACL, DEEF 23999.

[34] CDHT, fonds Ader, doc. 2381, statuts de la Société industrielle des téléphones. Sur les dix-huit brevets, trois brevets sont l'œuvre de Clément Ader.

Dès le mois de mars 1894, la Société industrielle des téléphones manifesta le désir de poursuivre la collaboration avec Clément Ader en reprenant à son compte les contrats signés entre ce dernier et la Société générale des téléphones[35]. Le début de cette coopération fut cependant difficile, Ader s'évertuant à demander à la nouvelle société qu'elle réglât les redevances dont l'ancienne entreprise ne s'était pas acquittée, à tort selon lui. Le comité de direction de la Société industrielle des téléphones repoussa les réclamations d'Ader, au point que Léauté exhorta l'inventeur à se mettre au travail en ces termes :

> Je ne puis que vous répéter à ce sujet ce que je vous ai déjà dit dans nos entrevues ; nous désirons travailler avec vous, dont nous apprécions la valeur ; remettez-vous à la téléphonie, faites du nouveau, prenez des brevets et nous serons enchantés de recommencer à vous payer pendant quinze ans des redevances.[36]

Peut-être l'âpreté d'Ader s'expliquait-elle par les coûts en temps et en argent qu'occasionnaient ses recherches sur l'*Éole*. En tout cas, la Société industrielle des téléphones n'était pas prête à payer plus que nécessaire. Elle n'était surtout pas prête à payer pour les inventions personnelles d'Ader.

Pourtant, la Société allait profiter de la diversité de l'activité inventive d'Ader. Quand Ader prit, le 3 septembre 1898, un brevet relatif au perfectionnement des voitures automobiles et des moteurs, la Société industrielle des téléphones vit là l'occasion d'une diversification de ses propres activités[37]. Par un contrat en date du 2 février 1900, elle et Ader précisèrent les fondements d'une nouvelle coopération. Par bonheur, nous disposons de ce document qui permet d'en savoir plus sur le lien entre ces deux partenaires[38]. Selon les dispositions du contrat, Ader devait garder « la direction des études, inventions, recherches, relatives aux automobiles », avec un droit de contrôle sur le service de construction et en étant membre de droit de toutes les commissions que la société pourrait mettre en place pour prendre des décisions dans l'affaire des automobiles. Par ailleurs, Ader apportait à la société son brevet du 3 septembre 1898 (ainsi que tous ceux qui s'y rattachaient) et s'engageait à « faire profiter exclusivement la Société industrielle des téléphones, [...] de toutes les inventions et de tous les perfectionne-

---

[35] CDHT, fonds Ader, doc. 2383.
[36] CDHT, fonds Ader, doc. 2369, lettre de Léauté à Ader du 19 avril 1894.
[37] INPI, brevet n° 278138 du 21 avril 1898.
[38] CDHT, fonds Ader, doc. 2393. James M. Laux ne mentionne ni Ader ni la Société industrielle des téléphones, cf. James M. Laux, *In first gear. The French automobile industry to 1914*, Liverpool, Liverpool University Press, 1976. Jean-Louis Loubet ne fait guère qu'une brève allusion à Clément Ader dans son *Histoire de l'automobile française*, Paris, Le Seuil, 2001, p. 21.

ments » qu'il apporterait dans l'industrie concernant l'automobilisme. En contrepartie, Ader recevrait pendant quinze ans une part du produit net encaissé des ventes[39]. Les brevets seraient pris au nom de la Société, qui rétribuerait pour ce faire une agence de brevets, agréée par les deux parties. Si elle demeurait libre de prendre les brevets qui lui sembleraient utiles, la Société industrielle des téléphones devait prendre à sa charge les procès de toutes natures auxquels les inventions pourraient donner lieu, étant entendu qu'Ader déclinait toute responsabilité en cas de déchéance ou d'annulation des brevets pris à la suite de ses recherches. Une commission fut donc instituée pour évaluer les recherches d'Ader et procéder à des études et des essais qui firent l'objet de véritables programmes[40]. Mais l'affaire échoua et, en 1902, l'accord signé deux ans auparavant fut remplacé par une convention rendant leur liberté aux deux partenaires[41]. Au final, la Société des téléphones et Ader avaient su dépasser tous leurs contentieux pour parvenir à reconduire, sur des terrains différents, leur collaboration.

L'étude des relations de Clément Ader avec la Société générale des téléphones puis avec la Société industrielle vient tout d'abord relativiser la distinction entre recherche interne et recherche externe. En effet, la première est supposée reposer sur les ressources humaines et matérielles propres à l'entreprise alors que la seconde devrait relever d'inventeurs indépendants, extérieurs à l'entreprise. Au final, une telle typologie s'avère fort peu pertinente pour rendre compte de la relation d'Ader avec les différentes sociétés évoquées. D'un côté, les recherches d'Ader furent effectuées hors de la Société des téléphones et firent l'objet d'une véritable transaction, permettant ainsi à cette entreprise de se défausser d'une partie du risque que comporte l'activité inventive. D'un autre côté, Clément Ader ne fut pas un inventeur totalement indépendant et les règles de la transaction eurent une influence non négligeable sur son activité inventive. Le refus de Société générale des téléphones de payer à Ader un certain nombre d'équipements eut ainsi une incidence directe sur le cours de ses recherches[42]. De même, le fait que la Société industrielle des téléphones ait pu prendre certains brevets proposés, les abandonner ou les défendre, voire soumettre les travaux d'Ader à une commission technique, tout cela montre bien que la recherche de l'inventeur indépendant peut être orientée par les règles définies lors de la transaction.

---

[39]   Ader devait toucher 4 % sur la vente des automobiles complètes et 5 % sur la vente des pièces détachées.

[40]   CDHT, fonds Ader, doc. 2390, notes relative à l'automobile.

[41]   CDHT, fonds Ader, doc. 2393, contrat du 29 décembre 1902.

[42]   CDHT, fonds Ader, doc. 2369. Ader rappelle ce type de déboires dans une lettre à Léauté du 18 mars 1895.

Recourir à un inventeur extérieur à l'entreprise offre cependant à cette dernière l'avantage de partager le risque de l'activité inventive tout en l'orientant. À cet égard, le statut d'entrepreneur d'inventions constitue l'une des conditions de possibilité de cette relation. En poursuivant ses propres objectifs en matière d'invention, en dirigeant plusieurs équipes de techniciens engagées sur des projets différents, l'entrepreneur d'inventions qu'était Ader offrait à son client une garantie importante : celle de vouloir produire assez de résultats dans leur domaine commun pour pouvoir financer d'autres projets auxquels il tenait. En s'adonnant uniquement à des recherches sur la téléphonie, il n'est pas du tout certain qu'Ader eût été en mesure de partager les risques de son activité avec la Société industrielle. Le recours à un entrepreneur d'inventions reconnu, travaillant sur des projets diversifiés, était sans doute l'un des meilleurs moyens à la disposition de la Société des téléphones pour promouvoir des formes d'innovation tout en en maîtrisant le risque.

Dans ce processus, le rôle du brevet d'invention et de la propriété industrielle apparaît dans toute sa dimension. À travers la gestion des droits de propriété, c'est en effet une véritable organisation de l'invention qui est alors établie. Savoir qui doit prendre le brevet, jusqu'à quand l'entretenir, quand et comment le défendre, en quels termes le rédiger, toutes ces questions constituent les éléments de stratégies complexes en vue de maîtriser et d'orienter l'activité inventive. Là encore, les objectifs de l'entreprise et de l'inventeur peuvent diverger, la première restant bien souvent attentive à la rentabilité de ses actifs tandis que le second se soucie par ailleurs de sa propre renommée.

Enfin, cette importance des tractations qui ont lieu autour des brevets d'invention et la richesse des relations entre l'entreprise commerciale et l'entrepreneur d'inventions conduisent à redéfinir le rôle du laboratoire, traditionnellement considéré comme un reflet fidèle de l'organisation de l'invention ou de la recherche industrielle. On ne peut déduire, en effet, de l'absence d'un laboratoire au sein d'une entreprise une carence en matière de recherche lorsque l'essentiel de l'activité inventive est susceptible d'être mené hors des locaux, dans les ateliers ou dans le laboratoire particulier d'un inventeur. En fait, non seulement le défaut de laboratoire de recherche ne signifie pas le défaut d'activité inventive de l'entreprise, mais il ne signifie pas non plus l'absence d'organisation de cette activité.

Ainsi, dans un contexte où l'invention semble être l'apanage de l'inventeur individuel, l'organisation de l'invention repose sur une pluralité d'acteurs, qui ne sont pas nécessairement concentrés en un seul et même lieu, ainsi que sur une série de procédures visant à partager les fruits de l'activité inventive. Dès lors, chercher à décrire l'organisation de l'invention à la fin du XIXe siècle à travers le seul cadre d'analyse hérité des heures glorieuses de la *Big Science* est une entreprise périlleuse. Pour reconstruire les cadres de l'invention, il convient avant tout de prendre en compte la diversité de ses manifestations.

Conclusion

Pascal GRISET

Université Paris IV Sorbonne / IRICE-CRHI

Conclure ce colloque consacré à la recherche et à l'innovation dans l'industrie électrique n'est pas une tâche aisée, en particulier parce qu'il faut trouver une manière originale de parler du colloque sans reprendre les parties du colloque, mais en parlant de tout. Cependant, quand on est l'un des organisateurs et que l'on adopte, dans la conclusion, un autre plan pour parler du colloque cela signifie que le plan que l'on avait décidé n'était pas le bon. L'organisation du colloque était une excellente entrée. Il faut aboutir, maintenant, à des « sorties » c'est-à-dire se demander de quoi nous pourrions profiter à la fin de ce colloque, quels en sont les acquis ?

Nous pouvons retenir une approche générale fondée sur les dynamiques car la plupart des communications ont eu pour point commun, et je m'en félicite, d'insister sur les dynamiques et les échanges. Autour de ces dynamiques je retiendrai deux points principaux : les dynamiques liées à l'élaboration des savoirs et les dynamiques liées, non pas à la diffusion car le terme est mal choisi, mais aux flux qui sont liés à ces savoirs. Si cette distinction est un peu artificielle, elle permet néanmoins de clarifier les choses. En termes d'élaboration des savoirs je retiendrai deux points principaux. À travers les différentes communications, l'approche de recherche proposée et acquise dans ce colloque est une perception des articulations des domaines mais également d'une articulation des structures.

Pour les articulations des domaines, Robert Fox a évoqué d'emblée ce thème dans l'introduction en utilisant la notion de « porosité ». Il a évoqué naturellement les travaux de Wolfgang König. Nous pouvons également parler d'articulations des structures, dans une vision peut-être plus statique, mais avec des débouchés extrêmement dynamiques. La communication faite par Alain Cortat est sans doute significative, avec un débat autour du rôle des cartels qui devrait être repris, de la question de l'articulation des entreprises les unes aux autres. Nous avons pu voir comment un cartel pouvait même être organisateur de la recherche. Ce point a été particulièrement contesté, même en-dehors de la salle, et restera, par conséquent l'un des débats de ce colloque.

Le lien entre recherche et contrôle technique, notamment pour le milieu du XXe, est un sujet important, puisqu'il a constitué l'une des bases du développement de la recherche de haut niveau dans les télécommunications en France. À partir du moment où le contrôle technique a été associé à la recherche, celle-ci s'est particulièrement bien développée. Dans d'autres analyses, on présente l'émancipation de la recherche des activités de contrôle ou de vérification comme la condition *sine qua non* de développement de la recherche. Dans ces articulations, il existe des parcours et des contextes différents qui rendraient illusoires l'existence de recettes de réussite.

On a également reconnu les articulations parfois difficiles entre deux communautés, celle des électromécaniciens et celle des électroniciens et puis entre les entreprises françaises et les entreprises américaines.

Ces articulations et zones de contact débouchent sur des flux, sur des mouvements. Des flux d'échanges ont tout d'abord été identifiés à travers des vecteurs spécifiques identifiés, à travers des processus. Ainsi, dans la communication de Graeme Gooday nous avons vu le rôle de Marie Curie. Cette contribution, véritablement passionnante, illustrait la manière dont Marie Curie a joué ce rôle de « passeuse » entre un savoir caché, tenu secret au sein des entreprises, et un savoir qu'elle a révélé, amélioré, embelli, et rendu cohérent. Elle a donc joué un rôle extrêmement important en révélant et regroupant ce qui était caché. Marie-Pierre Bès, dans son intervention, a également mis l'accent sur l'importance des réseaux sociaux et des réseaux personnels comme vecteurs d'innovation.

De manière plus générale, des flux sont liés aux circuits économiques donc à ce qu'il y a de plus spécifique à ce nous dénommons l'innovation et à son histoire. La présentation de W. Bernard Carlson nous a montré l'importance de cette monétarisation de l'échange de ses enjeux économiques à travers les relations entre les grandes entreprises américaines et les entrepreneurs indépendants de l'Amérique de la fin du XIXe siècle dans le cas de Nikolas Tesla. Serge Paquier nous en a aussi fait part avec son exposé dans lequel j'ai particulièrement retenu l'expression utilisée à propos de l'un de ses acteurs, qualifié de « rassembleur de connaissances ». Par une position sociale, institutionnelle et par la manière dont ces personnes savent créer les réseaux, ces acteurs s'installent dans une situation de carrefour, devenant ainsi des « rassembleurs de connaissances » avec tout ce que cela permet en termes de dynamique et de synergie.

Le papier de Gabriel Galvez-Béhar s'articulant autour du domaine de la téléphonie a montré l'existence de cas très particuliers, en évoquant celui de Clément Ader. Ces notions de contractualisation, de durée, ont permis de démontrer l'aspect fondamental revêtu par les problèmes d'argent et de négociation. Malgré nos connaissances, les papiers chiffrés et argumentés permettent de mieux saisir cette importance. J'ai retenu une des expressions employée dans son exposé, celle « d'entrepreneur d'inventions ». Je trouve l'expression très belle. Elle correspond effectivement à une notion sensiblement différente de celle d'innovateur, et que je trouve efficace en termes de conceptualisation.

Je conclurais en reprenant l'expression de Jean Monnet, citée par Alain Beltran : « le Plan c'est un crayon et surtout une gomme ». Nous pourrions reprendre cette expression pour l'organisation d'un colloque, où après avoir commenté les interventions et les acquis qui en découlent, nous terminons, tout de même sur un certain nombre de critiques. À mon avis, nous pouvons regrouper les manques de nos travaux en deux approches transversales.

La première été soulignée par Christophe Bouneau et je me rallie à sa remarque. Nous constatons un manque, dans les différents papiers, de dimension spatiale. Le sentiment qui prévaut est celui de l'absence de papiers qui traiteraient, non pas directement, mais prendraient compte les implantations, les domaines et l'architecture. Nous n'avons pas eu d'interventions sur l'organisation concrète, presque physique, d'un laboratoire. Par conséquent, j'ai particulièrement apprécié les papiers dans lesquels des photographies évoquaient ces laboratoires en nous les montrant.

Ma seconde remarque est peut-être plus personnelle. Il m'a semblé qu'à travers la plupart de nos débats, nous portions un regard assez aseptisé, oubliant que ces histoires d'innovation et d'économie, sont autant des guerres impitoyables, avec des victimes, avec des gens qui souffrent, avec des exploiteurs, des exploités. Je force sans doute le trait, mais l'histoire de l'innovation est marquée par une structure pyramidale. L'intervention de W. Bernard Carlson nous en fournissait un bon exemple, mais il n'a pas été explicitement exprimé. Nikola Tesla « se fait manger la laine sur le dos, année après année par un grand groupe ». Ce processus se déroule ainsi car il existe une économie, que j'avais essayé de décrire dans une partie de ma thèse au sujet des innovateurs des radiocommunications, où l'on voit de grandes entreprises tirer tout le parti possible d'innovateurs individuels. Je crois que le système actuel entraîne les mêmes processus avec une sorte d'écologie de l'innovation.

Collection « Histoire de l'énergie »

La collection « Histoire de l'énergie » est née du constat de l'éparpillement des publications sur le thème de l'énergie, au moment même où les approches sont en train d'être profondément renouvelées. Le projet scientifique de la collection consiste à rendre compte, par la publication de thèses, d'actes de colloques ou de travaux de recherche, de la diversité des approches scientifiques. L'objectif est de proposer une vaste réflexion sur les différentes énergies, tant pour ce qui est de leur production que de leur consommation. Les acteurs (entreprises, États, consommateurs), les marchés, les modes de vie conduisent à privilégier une approche globale dans laquelle les différentes énergies sont toutà la fois concurrentes et complémentaires.

En adoptant ces perspectives volontairement larges, la collection « Histoire de l'énergie » entend servir de point d'ancrage à des travaux académiques et faciliter leur diffusion.

"History of Energy" Series

The series "History of Energy" is the result of the diversity of academic publications on energetic questions, at the time when the academic approaches are being deeply renewed. The scientific purpose of this series is to show the variety of the thoughts by the publication of PhD, conference papers or research works. The objective is to propose a vast reflection on the various energies, both for the production and for the consumption. Actors (companies, States, consumers), markets and lifestyles induce a global approach in which the various energies are, at the same time, rival and complementary.

By adopting these voluntarily wide perspectives, the series provides an outlet for academic works which offer a recent and original contribution to history of energy.

Visitez le groupe éditorial Peter Lang
sur son site Internet commun

www.peterlang.com

Peter Lang – The website
Discover the general website of the Peter Lang publishing group:

www.peterlang.com

Thanks to my mum for giving birth to me and then continuing to give me everything she could (and sometimes stuff that she couldn't) always. You're fiyah! I love you. Thanks to dad for always being proud of me. Thank you to my Uncle Melvin, the Godfather, for always being there for me. I hope I continue to make you proud. Thank you to my Aunty Dot for her constant love, to my Aunty Yvey for *getting me*. Thank you to my Uncle Fred for being a first-class hype man. Thank you to my Aunty Billie and my Aunty Marcie for all their support and to all my uncles and grandparents; it took a crew to raise Levi, and it took a village to raise me. Thank you for being my village. Shout-out to my cousins whom I cherish; watching you grow up is such a privilege. Shout-out also to my Irish family, who have accepted and supported me like one of their own.

To Saffy, who makes me laugh until I wheeze; being your sister is my favourite job. I am so proud of you.

To Alice and Lara: you two are my pillars and my rocks and I am so grateful for you. I don't say it enough.

To Ingrid, who I see a lot of myself in (LOL, sorry) – never underestimate how smart, funny and capable you are.

And, finally, to my Michael. Thank you for building this life with me. I'd sail into the mist with you. I love you.

in writing *The Map That Led To You*, I hope I at least raised some interesting questions.

I want to thank Steph, Grace, Izzy and the team at Curtis Brown for always having my back. I am so lucky to be represented by you! I want to thank Polly and Gen Herr at Scholastic for their creative insights, sensitivity and faith in my storytelling. I want to thank Yasmin for her support and encouragement. Thanks to Jenny for her copy-editing and incredibly generous feedback, and thanks to Sarah Hall for her diligent proofreading. Thanks to Wendy Shakespeare for her incredible oversight. Thanks also to Harriet, Hannah Love, Hannah Griffiths and Ellen: your hard work is so appreciated and I always have the best time when we get a day together. And a massive shout-out to the whole Scholastic team for all their love and support.

To my writer girlies! When I debuted, I didn't have any writer friends. I am so thrilled that I have you now! You're all an endless well of support, positivity, inspiration, dedication and fun. From writing sprints to lots of wine – I adore you.

I want to thank Natasha Bowen for writing *Skin of the Sea* and *Soul of the Deep*; you're a true role model. And I also want to shout out to the late great Benjamin Zephaniah. Thank you for showing me everything that poetry can be.

To my friends for their patience when I'm writing, their enthusiasm for going out when I'm not and for their endless reassurance – love you. Thank you for being my people; I couldn't do this without you. Special shout-out to Emily and the Shetas! Before the empire of adulthood swept in, your house was the pirate republic of my adolescence. Adore you.

Acknowledgements

This book is a coming together of many things that I love and is an exploration of many things that I don't. It was such a joy to spend time in a world of pirates, mermaids, seafaring stories and queer romance. I had such a wonderful time researching this book and for that I must thank all the staff at the Maritime Museum in Greenwich. Writing this story also meant that I spent a lot of time in the world of Caribbean folklore, so a big shout-out to the Scholastic Classics *African and Caribbean Folktales, Myths and Legend* by Wendy Shearer. A big shout-out also to my grandma, my OG source of Caribbean mythology, who first introduced me to the River Mumma and is also just the best – love you.

At the heart of these stories is a tension; as a British Jamaican woman who has grown up in London, whose whole experience of Jamaican-ness is diasporic, I am no stranger to tension. My existence, my place in this world is inextricably linked with one of the worst atrocities humanity has ever commited – the transatlantic slave trade – the effects of which are still felt by people and nations globally. What does it mean to be British, while loathing so much of the legacy of Britain? What does it mean to be "from" a place that you've never inhabited? What is home? There are no answers, of course. But

X

To all my fellow weird kids; I hope you
find something special in these pages.

And to you, who charted a course without
a map. The stars are watching.

The Prophecy

Nigh is the time of the witch who burned,
Nigh is the time that stars will fall,
Nigh is the time of the mermaid's son
Who'll destroy his home to answer a call.
Nigh is the time of sixteen suns,
Nigh is the time of poison root,
Nigh is the time to find lost things,
For witch's blood bears fertile fruit.

Prologue: To Live

The Seer from Persea was born powerful. She had entered the world with her eyes wide open, devouring each sight as though she'd been starved in the darkness.

Persea was her coven. Her mother smiled into her babe's eyes in those bloody, tired moments, and gave thanks to Yaa, the great goddess of their land, which was known as Xaymaca.

"Yvane," her mother whispered reverently. "You are Yaa blessed." The baby gazed with precocious clarity. To be a Seer was a great gift and a heavy burden. It was understood that when she came of age with her sixteenth sun, she would see the great truths of Xaymaca. Her little sister, who will die at the end of this chapter, was not so gifted.

Not that Nubia ever accepted this. Where Yvane saw more than any one being could ever wish, Nubia sought more than any witch might have dared. Nubia would venture beyond her coven's eastern grove and plunge into the depths of the great forest. She would lie down on the soft blanket of green, gaze at the stars, and the stars would gaze back. When Yvane would unfold nervously at Nubia's side, lowering her back to the grass, Nubia's eyes would light from brown to gold in wicked amusement and she would clutch at her sister's arm to illicit a shriek of surprise. It is here that we find our Seer and her sister, the silvery light of the tenth moon pooling blue on their dark faces.

1

"Oh, great Seer of Persea, quite blind in the dark, quite unseeing of her sister's tricks!"

"My skin prickles." Yvane rubbed her arms.

"It is only natural. It is the Sankofa. And you are sensitive to the currents of the world."

"I know." Yvane followed her sister's gaze, turning her eyes skywards. "It is strange, is it not? Every witch celebrates their own birthday but it is their sixteenth Sankofa that really matters."

In Xaymaca the sun and moon would certainly wax and wane, but Time had a magic, had a voice, a soul of her own. The Sankofa was a point of consistency, though, always occurring on the first full moon after the late equinox. It was thought that despite distance or difference in name or language, on this night, witches everywhere raised their eyes to the heavens in reverence and so magic flared brightest in the world. On this night, witches who had celebrated their sixteenth sun that year would come into their full power.

When the River Mumma and Yaa, the goddess of the land, came together in what was known as the Great Bonding, a rainbow had arced crossed the sky. This happened in a time that predated memory. Together they had overcome the true darkness of chaos, drawing it out, out and away, into the depths of the sea. But what is taken must always be replaced, and so magic flowed back into the land until it was absorbed by its natural vessel, the witches whose coven was called Persea.

As the darkness left, some of their shadows remained – the fraying, blurry edges that mediate with the light. From these silvery diplomats, the Anansi spiders were born.

The Anansi spiders were large and shadow-coloured, their masses moving in clusters through the forest, spinning silk that could find truths, knowing how each thing connected to the next and the next and passing them from elder to youth. They had no names, for what need had they of such individualizing things?

Not like the faeries, who valued the opalescent glimmer of each distinct wing. The faeries had arrived not long after the spiders; the air created by the magic in the plants had formed their light, weightless figures with skin that glowed bronze and copper. Mmoatia was the only faerie queen that Yvane and Nubia had ever known. Where the spiders preferred the cool dark corners of the deep forest, the faeries preferred the rolling hills and lush valleys of the west of the island. The air was elderberry sharp; they were creatures formed for catching breezes, for drifting with thin currents. They avoided the forests and groves, could not understand the language of their slipstreams and told resentful tales of faeries whose wings had been shredded on sharp branches and thorns. They, led by their queen, Mmoatia, built wide, airy halls and chambers above Favour Falls, a waterfall as clear and sparkling as the eyes of Mmoatia herself.

"Are you nervous? About tonight?" Yvane asked her sister. The River Aphra, the watery source of the land's magic, murmured nearby, laughing at the haste of youth. Tonight the veil was thin and magic coated the air.

"No," came the typical response, and though Yvane could taste the lie, she chose to ignore it.

"You can be honest with me, Nubia."

"I am. I am not nervous. I am just … frustrated."

3

"Why?"

Nubia wriggled her shoulders. "It's the … the noble sacrifice of it all. On your sixteenth Sankofa, you cease to be who you were before, become someone new. And you don't decide. *Yaa* does."

"That is not true." Yvane frowned. "I am still who I was before my Sankofa."

"But you *always* knew you would be the Seer. You were born more powerful than most. And even of you, that is not quite true. You are more worried, more burdened."

"The burden of sight is one I am willing to bear for Persea, for my coven and land."

Nubia snorted. "Well, I am happy as I am, thank you. I do not wish to change. I do not *want* a burden. I defy it. Not for Persea, not for Xaymaca would I give up a chance to live *as I am.*"

Nubia threw the words across the forest, skipping them like stones across the river.

And the river spoke back.

"Who you are will change, defiant child of Persea."

The River Mumma sat before them. Her seaweed-coloured tail rippled idly. Had she been listening all along? An ancient and powerful mermaid, she was feared and revered. It was said that she guarded the river, protecting the source of the land's magic, and showed herself only to those considered worthy. Her dark green hair was lost in the relative gloom of the forest, so like it in shade and texture. Her skin shone smooth and brown and her eyes, the blue-grey of a stormy sky, seemed to glow in the darkness.

Nubia glared back. She was, perhaps, the first living thing

4

to dare to do so. "I know I will," she countered, as though the ancient river mermaid had been sitting with them all evening. "I simply do not see the point in living my life for anyone else. It is my life. I want to live it and live it for me."

The River Mumma's eyes sparkled with amusement. She did not have Yvane's proficiency for prophecy but she did, of course, know things. She was older than they could even comprehend.

Yvane regained her voice, though it trembled in awe, interrupting before her sister could say something else offensive. "You are worried. I felt the same before my sixteenth Sankofa. I feel the same tonight, with all the eyes of this world upon us. But tonight is more than just a party or some rite we are compelled by duty to perform. It is a celebration of who we are. Who you are."

"I know who I am!" Nubia was indignant. "I am me! Nubia! I don't need to be affirmed by anyone, not even Yaa."

The River Mumma chuckled, snapping the witches' heads towards her. "I like you, witchling. I'm sure Yaa does too. But some things are meant for you, Nubia. There are some wills that you cannot live in defiance of."

Nubia shivered. *How did the mermaid know her name?* The river frothed and foamed and the water closed over the River Mumma's head as though she'd never been there.

Yvane gazed at the place she had vanished for a few moments. The River Mumma was so rarely seen and yet she had chosen to present herself on the night of her sister's sixteenth Sankofa. *What did it mean?* Two years after answering her own call, she knew that to see was not always to know. But she had the gift of sight and she could not shy away from it. It was as

5

the River Mumma had said to Nubia: she could not always live in defiance.

And now, from the depths of the forest, she could hear the faint beginnings of music. A wild, pulsing drumbeat, both unearthly and entirely of the earth, as though the land itself had begun to dance. But even as Nubia stiffened, ears pricked towards the sound, Yvane the Seer heard something else.

A familiar whispering. A song that only she could hear.

A prophecy.

Turning from the river, Yvane trod lightly up the bank towards the watery bower where the willow trees dipped their heads in silent prayer.

Yvane pressed her hand to the bark of a willow tree and felt the familiar light-headedness that spread in a tingling throughout her body, until she was so thin and glittering that she could become part of the tree, could dissolve into bark and stem and root. What she saw sent her careering back into her body, her breath catching in her throat.

Fractured pieces of future, some vague, others certain, but the whole of it a puncture through her heart.

*

Nubia would think often about Yvane's face that evening. The press of her cheek against her neck as she had emerged from the willow bower, a fresh prophecy bubbling like blisters on her lips.

The Sankofa had called them deeper into the forest and Nubia remembered the feeling of the tug, the musical cry of the call as she was swept up and lost.

The coven had assembled, hundreds of witches dancing and singing and drinking and eating – all eyes trained on her, the sister of the Seer, waiting for her to take that first step on the path laid out before her—

No!

Her body surged in response to the music and magic around her but even though it was anathema to everything she knew, she stopped dancing. She fought the pulls and tugs, her body longing to twist and arc but she fought it still, jerking until she came to a painful standstill. Something was building in the air around her, a gathering pressure, a storm about to break. Nubia's bones shook, her teeth grinding as though her jaw might splinter, her feet bore into the cool moist grass beneath her.

And then a release, clear and dazzling, as though the twinkling of the stars had been given a voice. *Hello, Defiant One.*

The call she had been waiting for, primed for all her life. The voice of Yaa, soft and sweet and immovably demanding an answer. Her body reached towards the presence of her goddess, and she fought it, even as she began to suspect that it was a fight she had lost long ago. All around Nubia, bodies continued to move and blur but all was mute and grey. Because the stars were twinkling at her. Winking and calling and laughing until her *No!* became the song that beckoned to her from far away.

And the newly named Nubia of Defiance had no choice but to open her heart, and answer Yaa's call.

Fate claimed her as it claims us all. Afterwards, when Yvane shared her prophecy and her suspicions about the witch that would burn, Nubia was almost deaf to her speculation. Even when the faeries and spiders gathered to discuss, coven, court

7

and cluster, murmuring of the River Mumma's dangerous future son, of what it all might mean, the call of her future was loud in her ears, drowning out all other sound. While part of her clung to her old defiance, another part of her, the part of her that was bright and permeable, had already reached into the sky and answered.

*

Two suns passed and Nubia could resist no longer. She could not deny what was written in her stars.

Yvane wrung her hands, swollen with worry. "You must not go!"

Nubia grasped them in her own. "You will rub them raw," she chastised gently. "I will miss you terribly. But the stars, they call me, Yvane. I hear their song in the mortal world and I must answer."

"Yaa named you Nubia of Defiance! So defy this!"

"I can't defy this any more than you can see a way to be free of the responsibility of your sight. We are Persean witches. With our many blessings come burdens. You taught me that. And our people do not fear goodbyes."

"I fear that world, Nubia. It is far away and different. I hear whispers of it from the trees. It is as though everything that exists beyond the material there is … dying. Magic is not wanted there, *Xaymacans* are not wanted there. I think of my prophecy and worry that you will never be by my side again."

*

Later, as Nubia burned, she played those words over and over in her head. She was unsure, as the first of the flames licked her feet, how she could have avoided this moment. Her cry of pain was a whisper as the smoke scratched at her throat. She was weakened, vulnerable after the hours she had bled and sweated to bring her baby into the world. She thought of the sweet cherubim face she had known only for a day and a half before they had taken him from her arms. Pain was pushing at her consciousness; distantly she was aware that she was screaming but she was far away from her body now, as gentle hands stroked her brow and a musical voice intoned, *Hello, Defiant One*.

The rage that burned in Nubia's chest cooled the fire, now encasing her body, to inconsequentiality. Her fury at the injustice of this dance that she had been led down, of this end, was hot and deadly, a supernova exploding to swallow the world around her. She would not go grateful or obsequious. She would not die thanking Yaa for whatever any of it meant – for what did it matter anyway? She would not see it. She would be gone and her son would never know his mother. She was Nubia of Defiance, and she would not be noble.

Where she burned and became ash, the earth was fertilized by her flesh and bones and a tree of blistering, blazing danger shot up in her wake.

The *"NO!"* Nubia of Defiance sent out into the ether with her dying breath tore through the skies with such force that it rattled the stars themselves.

And slowly, falteringly, one star in particular – one that had watched too closely and twinkled too bright – began to fall.

9

Part one

Port

NEW SHETATOWN

Someone, somewhere, far away
is calling out your name.
You are one of ours, they say,
Your eyes are so familiar.
Your blood is burning bright.
You know the language of the trees,
You hear them in the night.
Inexact but with intent,
You know the song we sing,
Hear Her voice, find your place,
Brown girl in the ring

There's a brown girl in the ring
Tralalala
There's a brown girl in the ring
Tralalalalala
Brown girl in the ring
Tralalala
She looks like the sugar in the plum

Many things had to begin long before your story started. Without all that went before, you might have been frozen in the prologue of your existence or, perhaps, never past act two.

You always have had a sense of beginnings being significant, but despite that, you have never really liked birthdays, and today is no different. Celebrating the day of your birth is not an entirely comfortable occasion in your house given that it happens to coincide with the day your mother died. You don't remember her, of course. Not as she was. She haunts your house now, an unacknowledged spectre, a flitting shadow of resentment, laughing at your father's jokes and knocking over your photos. She brought you into the world, the first girl in your dad's family – "And you thanked her for it by killing her. Some feminist you are!"

That's the joke your dad, Five, often makes.

According to him, he has a "famously dark sense of humour".

Five is the cartographer of New Shetatown, Sheta Island's small, solitary port town. The map-making company is a family business and unsurprisingly successful, given that naval paraphernalia, marine research and navigation are what the island is best known for. The monopoly over what is technically a successful industry in the island's capital has given him, in your opinion, a rather inflated sense of self-importance. That and the repeated refrain "dark sense of humour" often feel like an excuse for the hurt he throws at you, casual and small, dropped like pennies for you to pick up.

School-day birthdays are a blessing. They feel like any other day, even though your mother's ghost gusts more coldly through the house. Going to school means avoiding her bitterness. Though it does not avoid the modest "Happy

birthday, Reggie" from your dad, a card handed over while he downs his coffee and reminds you that he'll be back late.

Although loneliness sometimes gnaws at the edges of your daydreams, you have found freedom in the independence of being a solitary figure, the "weird girl". You watch your peers playing at social politics in your classes, arguing, kissing, making up, lying. You have witnessed in fascination, have built up an understanding of how people work from the outside.

When you were eleven, you and the most popular girl at school, Chloe Johnson, kissed behind the bike shed in her garden. Her father the pastor walked by, and that had been the beginning of the end. You can still remember the heat of your body, the plunging sickness, the way you had recoiled from yourself in the initial days after your first brush with shame. In abject mortification, Chloe told all the girls you were a "pervert" even though neither of you knew what that word meant, and a "weirdo who had killed her mother". You didn't hang out in her garden after that.

Later that year when all the girls lined up at church in their pretty white confirmation dresses, you had simply refused, much to your zealous father's embarrassment. You did not want a heavenly father, your earthly one caused you enough tense stomach cramping.

When you were fourteen, you'd shaved your head. All the other girls had started braiding their hair, or chemically straightening it with relaxer, but Five wouldn't pay for you to visit a salon. Nobody had ever shown you how to comb and oil your thick afro. Before you were a teenager, Five had sent you to a knowing neighbour but by thirteen you'd felt you were too

old to sit against knees and be fussed over and inquired into. You had taken Five's clippers and given yourself the same style you'd seen him give himself hundreds of times; number two all over. It had not occurred to you to feel apprehensive when Five came home; you were used to the *look*. Disappointment and resignation and something worse. But this time his face split into an unexpected smile and he had called you "a chip off the old block".

That was the year you had learned what the word *ambivalent* meant and had been thrilled by the validation its existence conferred. Five could love you and not love you all at once and that wasn't a thing that you'd made up because there was a word for it. This made perfect sense to you because there have always been things about Five that are best described as contradictions. His full name, for example, isn't Five, it's Diego Hornigold the Fifth. Your family are men of tradition. Five loves tradition and he hates his nickname, even though people have always called him Five. When you'd asked him why he hated it, he said, "Five is what people call thieves sometimes. Because they get five-finger discounts, see?"

You had shrugged. "But you're not a thief."

"I know that!" he had snapped. "I just don't appreciate the association."

You sort of understand. Five has lots of friends in the island's small police force, he wears shoes that shine and he changes his voice depending on who he's speaking to. He wears neat suits and keeps his fingernails clean and never lets his stubble progress past a five o'clock shadow. He runs a "business of unimpeachable reputation". Decent, respectable, upstanding. That's Five.

You reflect on that moment now and stifle a laugh which morphs into a yawn. You have always been a restless sleeper, a vivid dreamer and often wake gasping, reaching out for something or someone who is not there. Lately, though, the dreams have been even more vivid, a clarity and brightness, images that linger with you long after you wake. Often the sea, sometimes a forest, lush and dense and green, burned into your retina.

You shake off the strange longing sensation that descends and rinse out your bowl and your dad's mug which is still warm where he poured, stirred and downed it.

On the counter next to the open birthday card – five words and some money, Five's gold standard – is a leaflet, junk mail. A garish splash of orange, blue and yellow boasting Sheta Island's new Aqua World: *Within the cluster of coves on the eastern shore, where local legend claims the great sea dragon Leviathan once dwelled, a new legend is about to be born – AQUA WORLD! COME RIDE THE TIDE! Scan the QR code now for discounted early bird entry!*

There had been much excitement about this at school, but you have your reservations. Into the bin it goes. Aqua World have a reputation for poor pay and you'd heard that a local over-sixteens' club where drag artists performed was being asked to move to make space. You'd mentioned it in conversation with Five. "Sinful squatters," he'd barked. "You know they don't even have permission from the local council to be there. They've been trying to move that dive for ages but somehow it always falls through."

You head upstairs to feed the stray cat in your room that

refuses to leave. Five hates cats. He claims he's allergic but you've been secretly tucking Bast (named after the goddess) into your bed every night for months and Five has not sneezed once, despite the fur that clings to you, invisible because you dress in black to match her. Five still gives you an allowance to ensure that you never ask to come and work in the cartographer's, and so you even saved to get her spayed and vaccinated. You lock your door but keep the window open when you leave for school. She's never once made a mess.

You tuck her under your chin and gently wave her paws in time to a round of *"Happy Birthday"*. She butts her head against you, purring.

As you get ready for school, the shimmering veil of the dream falls back over your mind, light as the sun on water. A headache threatens. *Come on, Reggie, don't mope, it's your birthday.* You dress in your own unofficial uniform, wispy layers of thin black mesh, tulle and, today, chiffon. You line your eyes and apply red to your lips. You try and find pleasure in the smooth darkness of your skin, the soft fullness of your nose and mouth. You want to look pretty for you. After all – you don't turn sixteen every day.

*

Your school is on the outskirts of town. It's busy today. Heat waves off the pavement, sticks glistening to strangers' skin as they hustle. You like this part of your small port town. The golden light beating down, turning the sandstone to rich ochre, the smell of sun cream. Beyond the walls and talk, vast and

promising, is the sea. A boundless blue contradiction, constant but ever changing. Your eyes roam the freedom of the horizon while the waves lap at the shores. All the roads are hilly and yellow-bricked, full of steep acclivities and swift descents, and ultimately lead here, to the town centre at sea level. You like to get lost in the crowd. The lanes of shops that twist up and away from the centre are well stocked with local fare; salt lamps and cowry necklaces, wooden masks, finely carved and painted, creamy Guinness punch fudge. Spoonfuls of a blended culture, from a time before, when pirates, the persecuted and the enslaved found a shared home on your island, outside of imperial rule.

Then there are the recent developments. The tourist office was first, part of the governor's modernization project. You remember seeing him on the news, making a speech.

"Sheta Island has a rich and diverse culture and a fascinating history. Pirates and empire, republics and revolutions, a dream destination for any keen historian. Not to mention tropical weather, beautiful beaches and a quaint community spirit. There is no reason that in a few years' time, Sheta Island shouldn't be a popular location for holidaymakers."

His statement had excited you initially. The promise of a changing wind blowing in new people, diversifying the doldrum. Your dad gets more business than ever and the local museum got a cash injection. But your certainty has begun to wane. The greengrocer's and the butcher's have been overtaken by a supermarket chain, the shiny neon sign promising convenience to everyone but the locals, who have found the price of bread and meat rising while their wages remain the same. The

governor got re-elected after promising affordable housing along the cliffs, and then announced that he'd sold them to a private company for holiday homes.

Miss Gibbers, your history teacher, once said that the island replaced magic with faith but always remained superstitious: "one foot in the church and the other dancing the hempen jig", which is what pirates used to call execution by hanging. But the authenticity is lagging. The fairy tales of witches and sea dragons are moulded into plastic toys and worn as costumes by sulky twenty-somethings handing out flyers for the newest bar.

You can feel the hot haunting of what you had loved about your home slipping away from you with each passing year, and you are slipping with it.

The Birth

The land would become Xaymaca,
	but in the beginning
	there were no words –
there were no names.
There was Light and Dark
but, without their titles,
these existed together,
an agonizing push and pull.
In this chaos were glimmers
of magic made from separation;
when either became singular they
pulled power from the other,
self-identifying among the everything
that was all that had ever been.
One was never able to truly dominate the other –
they were evenly matched and so
tussled on.

But then,
	from fissures in foundations,
	an impact.
	She had no name,
	no real memory of much at all,

just knew that she was ejected
full-formed, rejected,
unknown by the world of her
creation
and then she was *here*,
pulled through the in-between.
She was made of so much of
her surroundings that
for a long, long time
she was unable to discern between
the mottled weeds that drifted by
and the dark green of her billowing hair,
could not see how the swift steel of the
ripples around her
differed from the thrashing
quicksilver of her tail.

When she broke the surface
she realized
to her surprise
that she could *feel* the dazzling rainbow of
world,
a thousand different views,
a thousand different blues,
and so much sensation,
each shade part of her.
Day turned to night turned to day again,
gold razed by pink, blinded by orange,
fading to an indigo inky hue.

A thousand different views,
a thousand different blues
until – *land*.

She had never known land before
but knew it immediately for
what it was;
anathema to herself and
yet something
she could not be wholly separate from,

for what is water without land
against which to define itself?
As she approached it
she bent back
waves smacked
crested against a crack
a split she hit
against the rocks and
fit
into the island's gaping
mouth, it would eat her whole,
surely devour her alive,
surely she could not survive,
but then – *peace*.
A world of wood and water.
Since she had first found herself
in this heaving world of
light and sound and feeling,

the pressure abated
as though the currents waited
breath baited
for her to realize that she was *home*.

The Sea Dragon

The world is dark and cool
but not hostile,
the gentle cool of a pillow
turned on a hot night,
the cool of a shadow in the
glare of the sun,
cool is comforting,
cool is kind,
cool is a caress, is an embrace,
is a half-forgotten whispering voice.
"Where your old cradle lies,
your first home burbles by.
The first sight held in your bright eyes,
the first ears rent with your new cry,
now only hears the drummer..."
The voice ebbs and flows like the tide,
he is up and down,
he is lost and found,
he is home but far, far away—

"LEVI! I swear on the *locker itself* if you don't wake up in the next five minutes I will cleave ye to the brisket and roast you on the poop."

Levi's eyes stung as they adjusted to the bright marigold light streaming through the portholes of *The Sea Dragon*. He tasted the salty tang in the air, and felt something pressing gently on his abdomen. He rubbed his face, calloused palms anchoring him to reality far more surely than the training sabre currently resting on his midriff. He closed his eyes briefly, straining his ears for the voice that lapped against his memory. But whatever, whoever it was, was gone. He focused instead on the person immediately in front of him.

"For God's sake, Levi, stop staring at me like some gormless paper-skull and *get up*!"

Vega, Levi's adopted sister, looked quite serious about the cleaving and roasting. Standing in her loose white shirt and fitted leather trousers, she was dressed for practice – her thickly curling cadmium hair was tied back with a bandana he recognized as belonging to their father.

"Paper-skull? That's new. I didn't think Tally could teach you any more insults." He grinned at her sleepily, stretched his long limbs into the streaming sunlight.

Vega glared at him. "I've been waiting *ages*!"

"Come on, Vega," Levi yawned. "What's the point, really? You're extraordinarily fast and stronger than anyone aboard the ship, including me and Pa."

He was not exaggerating. It was a simple fact – his sister was extraordinary. She had, after all, been found in an extraordinary way, by their father and crew. A toddler bobbing in the middle of the sea, in a cradle of rock and sky matter. She had twinkled like a beacon in the dark and Ezi, pirate prince and captain of *The Sea Dragon*, had been rendered helpless. He knew what

she was, spoke her name, though how he had known it he could never say, and had immediately placed her in the cot with his son, Levi, who had been but a few moons old. It was uncommon, in this time, for stars to fall from the sky and walk the earth, but not entirely unheard of. In this golden age of gods and monsters, stranger things had happened. The crew of *The Sea Dragon* had nicknamed the star-child "driftling" and so she was, Levi's extraordinary sister.

He squinted up at her now, bright face gold and glowing, competing with the sun, and felt not a little resentful at always being so outshone. "What more can you possibly have to learn? Anyway, no one has sprung upon the crew of *The Sea Dragon* in years. They'd not be stupid enough to try it now."

"You're a paper-skull indeed, hatchling!" Vega was not known for her patience. "We must always be prepared! Tally says the winds are changing so we'd better batten down the hatches. Now move it!" Talani, or Tally, was the helmsman. Ever since the first pie-bird had arrived, its black-and-white plumage stark against the clear blue of the sky, Levi had indeed heard her say this at least twice a day.

Only the Nubian Brethren, the five pirate captains who had led the founding of the Republic, used pie-birds as messengers. Their father was one such captain. Most landlubbers thought of pie-birds as omens of sorrow but pirates had other superstitions and knew them to be incredibly reliable. Captain Ezi, their pa, had set sail for the open seas not long after the Republic had been established.

"When can we visit the Republic, Pa?" they had asked repeatedly over the years. Ezi's reply was always the same.

"The Republic is no place for children."

It had seemed to Levi and Vega that they would never see the famous Pirate Republic of Sheta Island, a land of freedom and adventure that existed outside of the tightening grip of the Empire. But lately, with the sudden influx of missives, Levi and Vega had reason to hope that this might change.

Levi sighed and eased himself out of bed. He strolled over to the washbasin, suppressing his laughter as Vega's eyes narrowed at his leisurely pace, foot tapping. "It's *hours* past first light! There isn't even any breakfast left. *Come on!*"

"Sink me, Vega, don't tell me there's naught to eat?"

She stopped her tapping, torn between the reprimand and the rush before saying, "No, obviously I saved you some" – Levi grinned – "but I'll not tell you where I'm keeping it until *after* you've worked up an appetite."

He dipped into a graceful bow. "Sister" – he flourished his hand – "accept my most humble apologies for my tardiness." He grinned at her and then lunged to the right, reaching for his training sabre. Vega's expression did not change as she parried his attempted hit, sending his sabre clattering to the floor. He chuckled, stretching again, the picture of nonchalance, and her face softened somewhat. "Sink me, you look like Pa when you stretch like that."

Levi had inherited much of his father's appearance, the long limbs, the wide grin, the thick, heavy dark hair that Ezi himself had twisted into locs when Levi was just a boy. The only differences were his eyes, the blue-grey of a stormy sea, his slightly darker complexion and his lack of *ichi* – facial scars of his father's royal family. He had been told that even their expressions

were similar, though Ezi's had long since lined with brooding.

Levi's mind wandered past his father's face, past Vega's impatience, returning, as it so often did, to his plan to sneak off for a swim later. Maybe he could persuade Tally to let him out of their lessons early. He yearned for the salt and clarity, the endless stretch of possibility – the sea connected every land, every shore holding potential for exploration and adventure. Levi wanted to see them all. Perhaps this was why his dreams, always vivid, were all the more so after a swim. Though lately they had developed a darkness, a persistent tug, a pulsing kind of urgency that he couldn't ignore but couldn't articulate when he woke.

"Levi, are you even listening?" Vega's sharp tone pulled him out of his reverie.

"Sorry."

"I *said*, I finally twisted Tally's arm and got her to tell me some part of the pie-bird's message."

Levi paused. "Well?"

"It's to do with people leaving the Republic. Pirates – other crews."

Levi looked at her blankly. If falling stars were rare, their father receiving messages by pie-bird was rarer still. He and Vega had spent weeks speculating on what mysteries it contained. But this was disappointingly mundane. "Why would Pa care if pirates leave the Republic? Pa always said as long as a crew didn't sell the rest of their comrades out to the Empire, and swore to return and defend the island if needed, they could come and go as they liked."

"*Exactly.*" Vega's tone was heavy with unknown meaning.

"Why would the crew care? I asked Tally more but all she said was that it seemed that a voyage to another island was being organized and it *boded ill*."

"Did Tally say anything else?" Levi rubbed his face. It was unlike him to care much for scuttle but this felt different.

Vega shook her head. "Not really. I asked her why it 'boded ill' and she said that just because all the pirates on the Republic are technically our allies, it doesn't mean that they're all our friends."

Levi nodded thoughtfully. "So maybe whoever is leading this … voyage … is no friend of *The Sea Dragon*."

"Maybe. Whatever it is, Pa's got more pie-birds in the last two moons than he has in our whole lives. It rings like a cry for help to me." She raised an eyebrow, her chin set at a cocky angle. "It would make sense. There's no crew alive that matches the strength of *The Sea Dragon*."

Levi snorted. "And I suppose you hope to fight this mysterious threat too, do you, driftling, when the time comes?"

Vega grinned, the gold in her brown eyes flashing, exhilarated. "Of course. We shall both fight. Pa knows it's inevitable, that's why he's always insisting we train."

Levi rolled his eyes. "Vega, Pa will never let us fight. He won't even let us haul booty when we come about on a navy's lone caravel."

"He will." She straightened again, swinging her hips from side to side, arcing and stretching. "We're already the best fighters aboard the ship and we've never even seen combat. At some point Pa will have to use us." Levi wondered if she was genuinely concerned about the Republic or simply keen to show

off. "Besides," she continued, "I'm basically indestructible and you're … well, you're not exactly normal either, hatchling." Levi blinked, bemused. He had no real concept of *normal*. Perhaps if he had lived on land he would have known he was different to other boys his age but he did not know any other boys his age. Even the youngest swabbies and deckhands were at least a decade older than him. Vega moved for the door. "Now hurry, it's nearly nine and Pa will give no quarter if we're not on deck."

Her footsteps retreated down the corridor and up the stairs. Levi swiftly tied up his locs with a bandana. On top he added a tricorne stolen from the quartermaster, Able. It was a lifelong game of his and Vega's, stealing small items from members of the crew. Items were always immediately returned when they were noticed missing – but a currency had developed between them, scoring each small trinket according to a complicated system of judging, based on everything from cost to colour, the story of how the original owner came to possess it and, of course, how daring and dastardly the thief had to be to sneak it away.

Vega was right: their father would wear his guts for garters if he was late again. Levi glanced around the cabin he shared with Able before he left. *The Sea Dragon* had been modified for equity. Able and Talani often spoke about his father who, after formally renouncing his title as a prince, had his own grand captain's quarters turned into multiple cabins so that the junior members of his crew did not have to sleep on deck.

Most of the crew slept five or six to a cabin, stacked on top of each other in precarious bunks, nailed and railed to prevent drunken pirates flying out as the ship moved, or hung higgledy-

piggledy in hammocks, which rocked with the vessels motion. Levi, son of the captain, only had one cabin mate. It was the only special treatment Ezi afforded his children. The furniture was all old but ornate, carved wooden tables the relics from Ezi's past life as part of a royal family Levi had never known. Levi paused, glancing out of the window at the bright sun, wondering if it was too warm for his favourite skirt, a dark cobalt violet overlay, lustrous in velvet.

He thought of Vega, in her sleeveless loose white shirt, and opted for just the muslin layered petticoat. It was his father's rule that they train in what they were most likely to be wearing if ever sprung upon. Levi spent most of his time in an underskirt, with a thick, richly coloured and decorated overlay in cooler weather, sometimes worn *retroussé dans les poches* for extra volume and flair. His father approved of flair. Levi remembered the moment he became aware that not everyone felt the same.

They had docked just off the coast of a wealthy port town. He could not remember if it was his first time disembarking from The Sea Dragon *but if he had before he could not recall. He was seven or eight years old. It was strange to feel the ground beneath them remaining still and rooted while they walked, the noise of life on land, the bodies that jostled in their inconceivable numbers.*

"Right, Levi, Vega." They had looked up at the seriousness of their father's tone. "Stay close, keep your chins up and when people stare, you just give them a long hard look until they turn away, savvy? And, Levi, none—"

"—of my daydreaming," Levi interrupted, voice half-singing along to a very familiar melody. "I know, I know."

It didn't occur to Levi to think that the staring that Ezi had

warned about was for any reason other than the jewels that hung
about the necks of the crew, the glinting sabres at their sides.

"That's Ezi, prince of pirates!"

"Captain of The Sea Dragon!"

"My, isn't he handsome!"

"My, isn't he fierce-looking!"

"They say he's visited magic islands!"

Ezi had raised an eyebrow at Levi and Vega, stifling a chuckle
as they turned from him to their onlookers and back again. Smart
ladies and gentlemen lounging outside eateries selling sugared
confectionery, clucking like appreciative geese as Ezi walked by,
dressed in all his finery, royalty and stolen riches combined.

Their pa had always told them he was famous, the crew had
bragged of their adventures, but to Levi and Vega they were a
motley bunch of callous-handed nannies and their world was so
small that they couldn't really comprehend what fame meant.

"They say he's been blessed by sea gods!"

"They say all royals of his kingdom bare scars shaped like
the sun!"

"I heard that's because the royals in his kingdom are
descended from gods!"

"Descended from gods, Pa!" Levi and Vega had crowed with
laughter.

Ezi had merely shrugged, saying, "A stopped clock is right
twice a day," his voice low and mysterious, and they had laughed
harder.

"Who are those children straggling along behind him?"

"They say he has love children on every continent!"

"Look at them, though! Those aren't ordinary ship urchins!"

33

"Well, they can't be his, look at their rags!"

At this last comment Ezi had frozen, and his amused expression slipped. He had rounded on the clucking, quacking geese. For a moment Levi thought he would gut them right there. But Ezi merely fixed his gaze and allowed the onlookers to see how depthless those black eyes could become.

Then he took his children's hands and led them into a boutique.

"I need a trunkful, fit for a prince." Ezi had dropped a jangling bag on the counter and the tailor had sprung into action. It was only when Levi, admiring the black-and-gold damask sheet of hanging fabric, felt a needle jab his side, that he had realized he was the prince to which Ezi referred.

"Which print, hatchling?" Ezi had asked and Levi had picked out the brightest and most flamboyant; intricate silver stitching, lace-cuffed coats, and the damask, of course.

"Pa, didn't you have a coat like this when you fought the dread Pirate Redbeard and freed all those stolen children?"

"I did indeed."

Vega had sighed longingly at his neat breeches and waistcoat. "Pa, Pa, can I have some too?"

The tailor had looked askance. "Now, little miss, I think these are more appropriate for your brother. I'm sure your papa will take you to the dressmaker down the road after."

Vega had looked scandalized. "I'm not a little miss! I'm a pirate! And Levi and I always wear the same thing!"

"Well, I think—"

Ezi had cut him off with a brusque "I'm not paying you to think, man. Nor am I paying you to parent my children. You do your job and I'll do mine, savvy?"

34

The tailor had fallen silent immediately.

Vega smiled, vindicated, but Levi felt his face heat. Was there something wrong? Why shouldn't he and Vega wear the same thing? They always had – he didn't understand.

The store from which he and Ezi had purchased their wares had been a serious place, it made shopping a serious business. Everything was dimly lit and darkly wooded, but not like The Sea Dragon which, despite being worn and shabby in places, had flair. Perhaps you would call it camp, but Levi did not know that word in that context. The store that he and his father had shopped in was the very opposite of camp and even though Levi could not specifically identify this, he knew the lack of it made him feel more at sea than he had ever been.

Vega's shop was not so afflicted. Such wonders! The colours, the textures, the shapes, the patterns. The dresses! There was delicate filigree jewellery in glass cases and glass mirrors lining every wall.

Levi was entranced.

Vega was not.

"Must I wear these, Pa?" Her mouth was a thin straight line. Even at ten, or eleven, or however old Vega was, no one had ever been sure, that rebellious look held power. Even Ezi did not often go toe to toe with Vega when she had that expression on her face but this time there was no arguing with him.

"Yes, driftling. I don't want people saying that Ezi, the captain of The Sea Dragon, the pirate prince, can't clothe his own."

"But why can't I wear what Levi wears?" Levi said nothing but turned his eyes to Ezi hopefully. Maybe if Vega could wear the clothes he had just been bought, he would be able to buy something

35

here instead. The skirts and dresses, colourful and majestic as polly-birds, hung temptingly on racks to his right. Levi's stomach twisted. His body ached to fill them.

"Well, because those are boys' clothes." Two pairs of eyes had widened on Ezi's face. Brown flecked with golden sunshine. A storm flecked with silver stars. The lady who owned the store, a pink-and-white-crinolined walking powder puff, was listening in with interest. Ezi looked uncomfortable.

"But I always wear what Levi wears." Vega was confused. How could they be "boys' clothes" when she happily wore them? Levi was similarly bemused.

"Well, maybe you shouldn't. Maybe you should wear what other little ladies wear."

"But I'm not a little lady. I'm a pirate."

Ezi couldn't argue with that. He took a breath.

"That's true. When you're on The Drag, you're a pirate, and when you're a pirate, you can be whoever you want, go wherever you want. It is our home and you can be free there. But when we're on land" – he cut a glance at the powder-puff lady who quickly busied herself with one of the many glass cases – "we have to perform a version of ourselves so that the world sees us a certain way and doesn't bother us. I wear all of this," he gestured at his plum velvet coat, full pantaloons and shining black boots, "so people say, 'Look out! There goes Captain Ezi, prince of the pirates!' I'd rather be in a shirt and leathers too. But they don't always protect me. Sometimes this costume is better than any armour, savvy?"

Levi and Vega looked at each other. Then Vega said, "So these dresses are like my armour and when I wear them I won't be bothered?"

36

Ezi paused, then, "Not exactly. It's different for girls. You will have to be especially guarded. But you'll look the part of the pirate prince's daughter, not some port-side blowsabella, and that's powerful."

Vega thought some more. Then said, "OK, Pa. I'll wear the dresses on land. And on the ship I can wear my shirt and leathers." Ezi opened his mouth to agree, but Vega hadn't finished. "And one day," she pressed on, "when I'm big and strong and dangerous like you, I'll wear what I want to wear. I won't need to look like your daughter, because people will fear me for what I can do, no matter who my pa is. I'll be Vega, the world's best navigator, Vega of the Seas and Skies, and anyone that bothers me, I'll slice nose to navel!"

Ezi erupted in a roar of warm laughter. "Fair enough, driftling."

Once they were back on The Drag, and she and Levi had unpacked their many bags and parcels, Vega was disdainful as she spread her bounty on the bunks.

"Look at all these ruffles. It's so heavy I can barely move. I'm glad Pa said I was too young for a corset."

Now alone, with no one but Vega – who he trusted above all others – Levi felt free to loose his admiration. "But they're beautiful, Vega." He ran his hands over one, a flowing oxblood dress with a separate petticoat.

"Sure enough, the shoes would make scaling the lookout post tricksy, but imagine how fine you'd look raiding enemy stores in this!"

"What about you, though?" Vega had countered enviously, shrugging out of the layers and saffron-coloured slip she'd been

heaved into by the powder-puff lady. "Your new leathers are fine indeed!" She held the leathers to her face and inhaled deeply.

"Sink me!" She had sighed and pulled them on, admiring herself in the ancient spotted mirror. "I'm never taking these off, even if it means I never leave The Drag ever, ever again!"

Levi yearned for her relief. He itched on the inside and scratched at the internal nettling thing, until he had picked away at what had covered it and said aloud to Vega, "You know. You wear leathers onboard, and so does Tally and all the other women in the crew. But men never wear skirts and dresses. I wonder why?"

"Well, skirts and dresses are a bother. Imagine swabbing the deck or mending the sails wearing this." She raised and limply dropped the petticoat on the bed. "And besides, Pa wears his cloth wrapper sometimes, so he's not always in pants."

But Levi shook his head. "I like Pa's wrapper more than leathers, but this" – he stroked the layers lovingly – "this is so ... extra. Pa would never wear a skirt, none of the men would. How come you get both and we get half?"

Levi would always remember the beat that followed. Remember the way Vega had paused, pursed lips, reminding him of their father, masticating words.

Then she said, "You're right. It's stupid and unfair." She had held out the skirt to Levi – "Swapsies, savvy?" – and had slipped into the lush black-and-gold damask velvet coat, strutting the cabin with pride.

Levi imitated her, ignoring the stays and stomacher, tucking his ruffled shirt into the oxblood skirt and arranging the layered petticoat underneath. Vega assisted and after adding a tricorne,

a jerkin and crowing with delight at her own artistic genius, she declared him to be quite perfect. Levi improvised with a matching set of brooches found in one of the many chests of neglected booty, pinning up some of the skirt to create a pleasing ruffled look, for he agreed with Vega that tripping during a duel would be highly embarrassing and, "Besides, there's so much petticoat that it's a waste for no one to see it."

They had emerged on deck with their chests puffed with pride, not noticing the descending hush, the surprise and confusion.

But Ezi had said, "Well, whelps. Swapsies, is it?" with perfect calm, and in that moment had indicated that for the crew to laugh would have invited a trip to the locker. And so, nobody had.

The wind arced as though craning to listen, caught the sails and The Sea Dragon sped up.

Father and son met each other's gaze. Levi swallowed, his stomach suddenly tight. Then, "Very well, hatchling. Same rules. Your frock is fine for The Drag. But you will practise duelling in the biggest petticoat I can buy so that one day this can be your armour, so that one day you too will be able to slice any cur from nose to navel without my assistance, or my name" – here he'd paused and flashed his teeth, a grin of pride and defiance – "and without spoiling the muslin. This is our home. You can be free."

The Bonding

Y ou would call her a mermaid,
　　　but she did not know that word yet.
　　　All she knew was
Light and Dark and Light again
as above the island, chaos reigned.
Time here meant little; she did not know
how long she watched,
the Light and Dark had no respect
for
Night and Day
and so on they warred,
until – *a change.*
From within the flashes of Light,
something like a hand
moving towards her,
not to snatch but in supplication,
reaching, beseeching,
please.
She did not know why she did the thing
she did next,
the thing that would change everything
for ever –
but she reached back.
Sent a hand of her own,

pulled a current up from the sea
and extended it like a life belt
and where the two fused,
where cobalt mixed with
gold,
the world split into a rainbow.
Hand gripped hand in a firm embrace.
She could feel the Light passing something
to her,
something raw and hot and hungry
that she could not hold for too long
lest it feed on her,
and so she passed it on and out,
out along her currents, out to the
teeming eternal wine-dark waves,
where it would surely get lost in the
thousand views of a thousand hues,
where it hissed, was stubbed out,
where the white froth foamed and spat at it
in contempt
and it was reduced to nothing.

This may have lasted seconds,
it may have lasted millennia.
Slowly the mass of Dark
shrank, siphoned out to sea
and the thing that was Light grew,
formed into a shape that she
recognized,

as something not unlike herself.
This new something or someone
smiled at her,
she was so big and bright and beautiful
that it hurt to look at
her.
Greetings, Great Mermaid. What do they call you?
She did not know how to answer.
So she did not.
Simply stared.
The one made of Light smiled.
An ancient enemy has been here defeated,
banished and restrained far away –
it could not have been done without your aid.
Yaa thanks you.
The mermaid smiled.
Yaa inclined her head.
I would call you friend and grant you blessings in
    gratitude.
The mermaid inclined *her* head,
Yaa spoke:
Something has been created where you stand,
something has been imprinted,
spearing through existence
and staking your place there
eternally.
If there you remain, you will do so
safely,
with great power.

42

You may be older than everything but
you are young here.
From our Great Bonding
comes a Source;
the time of magic is nigh,
the time of life and mortality and more,
the time of creation, of channelling
what we have back to
the land –
turn your breast to the mouth of this
Great River
and you will find home.
Pause,
the world stilled, frozen
between possibilities.
The mermaid nodded.

Her dark skin,
    the closest brown could be to
    onyx while still reflecting the
    light, prickled with
    the change.
    Yaa repeated:
    Friend, what do they call you?
    The mermaid spoke,
    her voice cracked with
    never-use,
    "They don't."
    May I name you?

"Yes."
Yaa opened her mouth and all
the light of all the worlds
spilled forth like ore,
a thousand different hues
a thousand different views:
"Ata," said the goddess and the mermaid as one,
and her name arced over the rainbow and the sun.

A Piece of the Pie

Their Republic had not formed out of a press-gang or any kind of conscription. A witch called Nubia from a faraway land was put to death for her magic. When lit at the stake she was said to burn so brightly that all those who stood in solidarity with her were able, that night, to fight back against the naval officers and constables in charge of what was then simply known as Sheta Island.

The Republic of Sheta Island was formed, a land of pirates set apart from the rest. Vicious and deadly, yes, but with a kind of honour and an abhorrence for the new wave of society that was sweeping the world, calling magic heretical and piracy barbaric while turning people into cargo and raping their homelands of all resources.

Before Levi and Vega, before fatherhood, Ezi and *The Sea Dragon* were famed for the lengths they went to, upholding this code of honour; they freed the enslaved and offered them a place aboard *The Drag*, they never harmed women or children, they never killed if surrender was offered. Despite this, they were merciless in their conquests; some of the fiercest buccaneers of the day fell to Ezi's swift sabre and cutlass and organized, loyal crew. Pirates of the senselessly pillaging kind were robbed, slavers were slaughtered and made a bloody and brutal example of. In his youth Ezi was lit by a righteous fire, creative in his

45

cruelty, and once decorated a mile of coastline with the spiked heads of men of the Empire. He made sure all of their hats were visible, and had laughed a laugh heard across the horizon, as his colours waved among them.

Levi blinked up at these colours now, the white dragon against the black background, straining his eyes once more under the sharp attention of the sun. Members of the crew wove past him, sluggishly repeating, "Mornin', lad." The usual to-ing and fro-ing rocked him like the ship, the familiar cries of "All hands!" settling his soul like a cradle song. His crew, his family – washing clothes, scrubbing the deck, smoking.

Talani and Able were bickering, as usual, standing at the helm as Vega watched, impatiently waiting to begin training. Tally, sepia-skinned, with a shaved head and limned with muscle, spoke quietly because she never needed to shout.

Able, ruddy-faced, beer-bellied and peg-legged, by stark contrast, shouted loudly and was never heard. "What kind of landlubber would take to the high seas without a map? The key to being a good navigator is preparation and—"

"Maps aren't always accurate. Printers plagiarize and seek profit and many have no nautical nous at all." Talani's tone was weary, as though she'd been battling Able in this way for decades which, Levi supposed, she had. "Besides, maps are scraps of paper, they are easily destroyed. The stars are the only reliable guide at sea."

"Aye," Levi said as he approached. "Didn't a gully-bird steal a map from your hand once, Tally? When you were navigating the eastern gulf after plundering that naval man o' war?"

Talani laughed. "Levi, I swear, you have a memory for stories and dreams and nothing else."

Levi grinned.

"*I* wouldn't need a map," Vega interjected. "See, this is why you really ought to let me navigate, Abe. As long as I know the destination, I just listen for star-song and—"

"Now, now, young Miss Vega, Tally and I have been steering this ship right since you were naught but a twinkle in the sky. I think we're managing just fine."

Vega harrumphed, "I'm older than half this crew were when they joined and, besides" – she looked slyly at Abe's greying hair – "you're getting on, Abe. If you let me navigate, you'd have plenty of time to take a caulk or do something else about as useful as you." She was gratified to see Able swell with indignation. Vega loved ruffling his feathers. Before he could respond, however, a warm growl rumbled, "Now, driftling, none of your disrespect," and Levi turned to see his father, swinging himself down from the lookout post with the agility of a man half his age.

"Captain!" The cry was echoed around the deck, but Ezi waved an enormous hand and the ebb and flow of work continued.

"I don't know what's worse," Vega scowled. "'Young Miss Vega' or 'driftling'."

"'Driftling' is better than 'hatchling'," Levi said as Ezi strolled across the deck to them. At almost six-and-ten years old, Levi stood as tall as his father, but he was still lean, still had something of youthful roundness about his face. Ezi's was weathered but the rakish handsomeness of his youth hardened

into something undeniably appealing. He looked as though he had been carved from the ship itself, scars adorning his face like fine craftsmanship.

"Oh, aye, and thanks for joining us, Your Highness, good of you to arise at last!" Vega narrowed her eyes at her brother and began to strap her wrists in strips of leather.

"Apologies." Levi was serious now he was in front of his father. He hated disappointing him. "Sleep did not wish to loosen her grip on me."

Ezi's heavy brow furrowed and he reached for Levi's face, cupping his jaw and scanning the features that merged his own with another's. "What's the problem? Hmm?"

"No problem, Pa," Levi said quickly. "Strange dreams is all."

Ezi held his gaze a moment longer, even as Able tutted about how soft the captain was on his children.

No one ever discussed how Levi had come to be aboard the ship. It seemed to Levi that he had been formed like the stories they told as the sun died and rum flowed freely around lanterns, his birth not a mystery exactly, but something between legend and reality. He was the son of the captain, his mother had died when he was a baby, that was that. A little time later, they had found Vega the star – she had lit up his nursery and had been dazzling them ever since.

In the time after, Ezi was more cautious. He plundered only when necessary for the financial security of the crew and kept the children locked in his cabin with two of his fiercest buccaneers for protection. Able had scoffed and called him a 'grandsire sailor' but did not disobey orders. On occasion they would be come upon by another ship, bright navy colours

waving the far-reaching arm of a distant monarch, or fellow pirates with the blackjack hoisted high. These ships had heard of the pirate prince's strange new seafaring and sought to take advantage. Perhaps they regretted this, but dead men tell no tales, and Ezi was not one for last words.

Ezi released Levi now and reached for the bandana tying Vega's hair back. "Did you think I didn't notice this was missing from my trunk?"

Vega opened her mouth to explain but Ezi merely said, "You can keep it, driftling. It suits you." Vega smiled, her brown eyes flashing briefly gold, and picked up her practice sabre. The old wood of the deck creaked underfoot, groaned as it rocked through the briny blue, *The Sea Dragon* sang its tired sea shanty. The sails caught the wind, billowing outwards like the wings of a great white storm-bird.

"Right, whelps." Armed and stretching, Ezi began a variation of his usual pre-sparring-practice speech, as though they might forget from one day to the next. "The world is changing. Daydreaming is nary an option" – here he fixed Levi with a beetle black eye and said – "Aye, hatchling?"

Levi, who had been staring out to where the waves tossed like white-headed horses, responded, "Aye, sir!"

Vega rolled her eyes. "Pa, can we please get started? The day's half-gone and Tally needs help with the binnacle, it's drifting again."

Ezi leaned back, his broad shoulders resting against the port-side ballast. "Tally can wait, Vega, this is important. Things are happening, out in the world. Our way of life will not last for ever."

Levi was listening now. Vega threw a glance in his direction and took a deep breath, before saying, "Pa – Tally told me a bit about what the pie-birds' letters said."

"Oh, aye? What did she tell you?"

Vega swallowed. "That some buccaneers from the Republic are embarking on a voyage and that it ... *bodes ill.*"

The crew continued their chores though a quiet fell. Ezi looked towards Talani at the helm. Her back was to them but she was clearly listening. Ezi lit a cigar. "Aye, well, that's true enough." He puffed, chewing his words, deciding what to divulge. "Leaving Sheta Island is nary a cause for concern normally ... but the last of what magic we once had is dying. The Empire is closing in on the Republic and buccaneers leaving presents greater risk. As far away as we are, we cannot hope to remain unaffected. As numbers dwindle, we must replenish them."

"So we *will* get to fight!"

Ezi sighed heavily. "Aye, 'tis likely, Vega." He paused, eyes meeting Levi's. "Would that I could spare you from it."

His words skittered along Levi's spine.

"Pa..." Levi would not miss the opportunity to ask questions, not when Ezi answered them so rarely. "If this ... voyage means that the Empire might weaken the Republic, why are the crews allowed to go?"

"The Republic is a free land, Levi. People may come and go as they please."

"But why would they *want* to go?" Vega exclaimed. "And leave their home vulnerable?"

"That" – Ezi pointed at her with his cigar – "is an excellent question, driftling."

Levi threw caution to the wind. "Why don't we go, then? To the Republic? Shouldn't we help?"

Levi thought he saw a flicker of something in Ezi's eyes, thought the deck quietened imperceptibly once more, but Ezi simply shrugged and repeated his old refrain: "Perhaps we will, eventually. But the Republic is no place for children. And I've not been back in eight-and-ten years, Levi – there are no guarantees that I will be welcomed by everyone. I'd rather keep you both free and clear of all of that until absolutely necessary. Now. No more delays. *En garde.*"

They began. Vega was swifter, stronger, the superior swordsman. She anticipated Levi's every move before he made it, training sabre a blur through the air. She was sparkling, burning, ferocious. Levi redoubled his focus, fighting to ignore all that sought to distract him; this whispering of the waves, the seductive scent of the salt, the calling of more than rehearsal and routine. He caught his skirts in one hand and used their size to his advantage as Ezi had once advised him, throwing them out as if he meant to move in their wake, feinting and landing his first hit on his sister's sword arm. Levi glanced over his shoulder to see if his father had noticed, but Ezi was looking out at the horizon. Levi's diverted attention cost him and Vega rained down blows upon him until he was forced to cry out, "Quarter, quarter!" and jolt Ezi out of his reverie.

"You lost focus, hatchling."

"Well, so did you."

"I was not the one with a sabre pointed at my gut."

"You're meant to be teaching us. You said this was important."

"Trying to best Vega is better than any lesson I can teach

you, Levi. I won't always be there to offer improvement. Keep up and keep alert. That's all there is to it."

Levi opened his mouth, retort quick on his tongue, but Davies the lookout appeared, thudding down from the lookout post and sprinting across the deck.

"Man overboard! Man overboard off the starboard side!"

Levi and Vega whirled round, eyes squinting. There was a moment of still as the whole crew turned its attention starboard. Then Levi and Vega rushed to where Davies had pointed, leaning over the rail.

"Come about!" Orders rang out. Ezi would rescue first and ask questions later – he would never leave a man's life to the fickle judgement of the sea. If they *were* an enemy then they would die like all enemies of *The Sea Dragon* – with a cutlass at their neck, knowing who it was that wielded it.

The ship gained on the dark floating mass, tacking against the westerly wind, until they were close enough for Levi to make out features on a face. Reddened from exposure to the sun, lips cracked and salted. The Jacob's ladder was thrown over and Levi could have sworn that the man hesitated before taking it. Even as he climbed, his face was not the mask of relief one might expect from a man who could not have hoped to last another day out on the open water.

Ezi eyed him warily as he was hauled over the side, taking in the empty belt round his middle, the torn shirt and sodden bandana. This was no landlubber. Though he was immediately given a skin of water to drink from and pulled out of the sun's glare, into shade, Davies and his bunk-mate Aleck did not loosen their hold on him.

"Capt'n." Shock stretched the singular vowel and Davies pointed with his left hand to the man's arm. Where his right hand gripped him, his shirt had ridden up. Tattoos were powerful among pirates, identifying and protective, a way of swearing loyalty to a crew or person. Every member of *The Sea Dragon* was inked with an image of the creature for which their vessel was named, twisting across pectorals or shoulder blades. Ezi's was tattooed right over his heart and Levi longed for the day his father would let him do the same.

Levi took in the details of the faded ink on the man's arm; the insignia of a coin with a male profile on it. Levi heard Vega's muted murmur of "*The Sterling*".

The Sterling fleet belonged to Captain James Johnson, a member of the Nubian Brethren and a founder of the Republic, just like Ezi. As far as Levi's lessons had taught him, *The Sterling*'s crew were still docked at the Republic.

So what was he doing here, floating in the middle of the sea?

Ezi's dark eyes were guarded. The crew murmured to each other, a confused hubbub.

Ezi held his hand for silence. "Well" – and the man looked up panting, licking his dry lips – "as you bear *The Sterling*'s mark, I dare say you recognize our colours."

The man took in the colours, his eyes snagged on Ezi's *ichi*, on the sea-dragon tattoos of Davies and Aleck nearest to him.

"Captain Ezi," he croaked.

Ezi sketched a mocking bow. "And how do you come to be floating in the middle of the briny?"

The man laughed raggedly. "Too much whisky, too much wine, too little balance."

Murmurs of contempt from the veteran crew but Ezi looked almost pitying. "You are young. Is this your maiden voyage?"

"Aye," the man rasped. His eyes scanning the deck with a bitterness that belied his performed humour. "They tell so many stories about you. I wonder which are true."

Ezi shrugged, leaning against the mast. "A stopped clock is right twice a day."

"On the Republic … they say you died. That *The Sea Dragon* foundered and is no more."

Levi shared a glance with his sister, her expression carefully impassive, a mirror of his own. They said nothing but could feel each other's brimming questions. It didn't make sense. If the pirates of the Republic believed Ezi dead, then who had been sending the pie-birds?

"Well, scuttle isn't fact," Ezi said wryly, but the man pressed on,

"Even Ó Néill and Hook said you must be dead. They said you must be dead because you'd never betray the Republic."

Ezi's voice remained calm, light. "Are those the only two options? I am neither dead, nor am I a traitor."

The man laughed a dry, hacking sound. "I don't think most on the Republic see it that way."

"Watch your mouth!" Talani's tone was the harshest Levi had ever heard it.

The man took another swig of water, licked his lips. "Eight-and-ten years and not a word to anyone. You sail off into the sunset, chasing a witch's tale and a dream, off to find a magic island…"

54

"What of it?" Ezi relit his cigar and puffed. "I was free to leave. I swore to return to defend the Republic, should I be needed. I have not been needed."

"Aye." His voice was vicious and probing. "Maybe you have better things to do these days, Captain Ezi. Maybe the Republic isn't worth your while. A land where everyone gets a piece of the pie… Maybe you found a new pie and you didn't want to share it. Did you get a little piece of that pie, Ezi? I bet pie in Xaymaca tastes real sweet…"

What echoed through Levi was not the strangeness of the word that he had never heard before, but the familiarity of it. *Xaymaca*. It rippled around the deck, a frisson that made the hairs on the back of his neck stand up.

Ezi continued to puff on his cigar, regarding the man, face closed. "And that's what they're saying on the Republic, is it?"

The man grinned again. "Oh, aye. Captain Johnson has heard all about it. You're not the only one with friends in strange places, Pirate Prince. He sent me to scout ahead, you see. They say you found wonders and didn't want to share. Magic lands … witches and spiders and mermaids… Well, now it's Captain Johnson's turn! And he'll, er … *sample the local wares* too," he giggled. "He'll even help himself to a piece of your pie, Pirate Prince. He's always been a fan of seafood—"

Levi had no idea what was going on. It all sounded like dehydrated rambling to him – but every single member of the crew froze at these words. And then Ezi was crossing the deck in three swift, long strides. He struck the man round the face. The crack reverberated through Levi's bones. He thought he had seen his father lose his temper. But in observing the flat

55

darkness of his glare Levi realized he had merely seen the tip of a very large iceberg.

The man was laughing again, the dry sound maniacal, he was talking but more to himself than any of them, a strange singsong tone that made Levi sure he was of their reality no longer. "Witches and spiders and mermaids... I'm going to free the faeries ... I'm sailing on the westerly wind ... bewitch a witch, entangle the spider, catch a mermaid, can I ride her..."

"What did you say?" And Levi thought that the quiet menace in Ezi's voice was possibly the most terrifying thing he had ever heard.

The scout laughed again. "The westerly wind, the westerly wind, free the faeries, Ezi's scary, the sea's a good servant, the sea's a bad master, fuck a mermaid, trap her after..." And he was off again.

There was a flash of silver, the singing of metal and air, a wet definite slicing—

And then the man's head was on the ground.

The reality of it did not register. The head bounced absurdly across the deck. The blood seeped into the worn, stained wood, darkening it like spilled wine. It reminded Levi forcibly of the time that a drunken Able, having spilled his cup, cried, "Waste not want not!" and made as if to lick the deck clean. He stifled a laugh, stifled revulsion and retching, kept his face still and calm and unreadable.

And so Levi came to know death for the first time.

The crew around him, so hardened to such things that their unconcern was likely not a performance, had already moved into action like a well-oiled machine. He turned to his sister.

Her face was also a carefully composed mask but her breaths were shallow.

"Did he have to?" Levi asked quietly.

"If he did not, he would not," she replied, equally quietly.

He nodded. He knew his father's reputation but until now it had all been stories or muffled cries outside doors he and Vega had been locked behind for safety. But now ... his brain was foggy, snippets of the strange conversation twisting with the wet slicing sound.

"What did he mean? Magic and mermaids and pieces of the pie ... and, Vega – what's *Xaymaca*?"

But Ezi was walking towards them, barking orders as he went.

"Talani, Able – to my cabin."

"Aye, sir!"

"Davies – dispose of him."

"Aye, Capt'n!"

"You two" – he turned to Levi and Vega. Levi expected him to bring them with him, to offer further explanation, but – "continue with your practice and then to your chores. We'll talk later, savvy?"

Levi stared, composure slipping, and even Vega's eyes widened slightly. "But, Pa—"

"Your captain just gave you an order, hatchling. Don't argue with me."

He fixed them both with the kind of look only parents can give before grasping them to his broad chest in an embrace so tight it left them breathless. Then he released them and stalked below deck. Silence teemed in his wake.

Wishing on a Star

Over the millennia,
faces appeared – slowly
at first,
then swiftly, suddenly,
multiplying.
The witches called Persea with their halo
of hair,
absorbing through their roots
all that Ata fed back into the
land,
and naming her home,
a land of wood and water,
Xaymaca.
Then the spiders;
as terrible darkness was drawn out of the land,
out, out to sea.
Sweet darkness was left –
the dark of a sleepy lavender night,
the cool of shadows after a scorching sun,
and so the spiders came to populate them.
Finally the faeries,
drifting fragments of air and light,
delicate and winged and clear.

To them she was vast and powerful.

    More ancient than even their most aged.

    And so they all kept away,

    unsure what they'd have to say

    to a goddess among them,

    and simply called her the River Mumma,

    and her name remained hers alone.

    Occasionally her loneliness was soothed;

    she stole a whispered word or two and –

    on a night she would never forget –

    talked with two witchlings on the bank,

    like they were as old as she.

    She would often think about them –

    the Seer she saw occasionally;

    greeting her willowy friends,

    bowing her head as though the burden

    of her gift weighed heavy.

    The youngest one she did not see again.

    She was said to have journeyed far away.

    Ata offered up questions to Yaa

    but Yaa was everything

    and everywhere

    and everyone –

    was an infinite loop of cause and effect.

    She rarely answered questions.

And so it was that one night,

    a night spent thinking of the witchling,

    that real moment of connectedness

that she heard the murmurs of her currents
and *knew* – from somewhere
way out there.
She felt the flare,
sensed fire in hair,
a white-hot glare
sent back at the skies,
gold in the eyes
of one who dares,
one who defies.
Ata saw the impact.
And suspected who was behind it.
A rattled star began to fall.
It teetered, it tipped,
the worlds, they ripped
and she felt the strange new one
against her skin,
its muted metal tones,
its magic in decay, too sweet and rotting.
She reached for it,
she couldn't help herself,
she brushed her finger along the edge,
thought of the dying witch
and *burned* with her aloneness,
so tight and sharp that in that instance
she prayed for absolution.

Reached for a balm to soothe her burn,
  formed antidote to her yearn.

The star was falling true,
tearing through the night,
and with it Ata grew
more certain of its flight –
she knew that something *new*
was just beyond her sight.
So Ata threw her wish
at the star with all her might.

*

Two turns of the sun passed Ata by
And were gone in a blink of her immortal eye.

*

Down was up and
    up was down,
    there were sobs of
    merriment,
    delighted frowns.
A man is lost
but also found,
everything he knew,
beneath him drowned,
a singing, burning, rushing sound.
He is not alone, he's with his crew,
they gasp and pass through
something strange and shifting,

air met air, the same on sight,
water met water, the difference slight,
a layered cline, a thin divide—

Then they burst through,
fresh and new,
wiping fear from their faces
they could not hide
their wonder at what they saw before them.
Paradise.
Verdant, velvet to their eyes.
Anchors dropped,
cool water splashed against
skin, soothing that which
the sun and sky and sea of an
angrier world had chafed.
Boots were tossed joyfully into sands
warm and fine as faerie dust.
Captain Ezi, the pirate prince,
had never before –
and never since –
seen such wonder.
But he and his motley crew –
not that any of them knew –
had followed a wish from afar.
The dust-tail of a shooting star,
through the fabric of worlds they sailed,
through tingling cold and burning hot,

		to where on their map
		an X marked a spot.

And so a heart beating in the shadows,
		river mouths – delta mangroves,
		love and life lying in wait,
		the wide-eyed gaze of their fate.

X Marks the Spot

Levi abandoned the prospect of an afternoon filled with chores and made swiftly for the plank. His father had been gone less than a minute – perfect. He shirked his layers along with his responsibilities, already aching for the sweet oblivion found only beneath the surface.

"Where are you going?" Vega had no intention of being so excused and was tightening her leather wrist supports. "Pa said to keep practising!"

"Pa won't notice if I slip for a dip."

"But we've chores!"

"I'll swing the lead as I go." He reached for it, the weighted rope used to ascertain the depth of the briny blue below. Quite the easiest task and one that Levi, now balancing on the plank and preparing to dive, benefitted from.

Vega grabbed his bare ankle. "And how can I practise alone?"

"Sink me, Vega! Need you practise? Go fix the binnacle like you said, or else push Davies out the crow's nest. The sky is your home and you're a finer lookout."

The compliment soothed her somewhat, pulled at her mouth's corners. She did not relinquish her grip on his ankle, however. Vega was anxious of the sea. Perhaps it was the endless stretching time she had spent in it, sheltered only by the sky matter and stone that she had collected on her descent to earth,

but she did not find Levi's peace. He was right – the sky was her home.

"Just … just take care, all right. Feed not the fishes."

"I'll catch us dinner and make sure they feed *us* instead."

Vega spat on the floor, a precaution against bad luck.

She let go and Levi bounded forward, the spring of the plank rebounding as it launched him into the air. The whoop that ripped from him was instinctive, in spite of all they had just seen. How could he not whoop when so free and strong? He turned two somersaults before impact, twisting and graceful. When he hit the water he rippled but did not splash, folding between the waves as if he'd found indiscernible spaces. Vega marvelled for a moment, as she always did, and then, sighing, left her brother where he was happiest, and headed to the helm to inspect the binnacle.

Levi sank like a stone. He did not fight for air, let his body go heavy and willed further plummet, down and down and down into that gentle dark. He felt the calm descend, felt safety and a welcome restfulness wrap around him. He sat in this moment, let out a bubble or two but did not fear that his lungs would fail, for they never had. He enjoyed the suspension of time and place and being, he was part of everything, he was barely a droplet in this immense ocean, but also was vast and expansive, made up, in turn, of a billion trillion droplets.

He began to propel himself forward. Ghostlike he moved through the water, surprising himself, as he always did, at his clarity of vision. Here, Levi understood his singularity. He felt it tremor through his bones with the currents that brushed his skin and maybe it was the memory of the dream, brought to life

by the familiarity of the water, or maybe it was something more lucid, but he thought he could hear that calling voice again,

> *The world is dark and cool,*
> *cool is comforting,*
> *cool is kind…*
> *Find the place*
> *where rainbows fill the sky …*
> *she is waiting…*

The words themselves he could barely make out, an indistinct rushing like the sound of the sea heard through a shell. He strained to hear more but the tide was pulling away, present and then gone. He kicked his long legs and swam on. Vague curiosity had been gnawing at him since the pie-birds had first begun appearing in the sky but with the afternoon's events fresh in his mind, he knew he needed answers. Levi had spent his whole life hearing stories about his father and his crew, considered himself an expert on *The Sea Dragon*'s history.

So how, in the name of Davy Jones himself, had he never heard mention of faeries or spiders or – and his stomach gave a peculiar lurch – *mermaids*? There was only one way to find out.

He was going to eavesdrop.

*

To eavesdrop on a pirate captain came with only one rule: do not get caught. Eavesdropping was a crime punishable by having one's ears cut off, and even though Ezi was no tyrant,

Levi did not expect preferential treatment. If Ezi saw him… It did not bear thinking about. Levi rounded the hull of the ship, coming to bob and rest at the aft, behind the poop deck, where the windows of Ezi's cabin cast light dancing across the surface above him. He rose a few inches and allowed his head to break, feeling cool salty air on his forehead, across his eyes, replacing the water in his nose. He chanced a glance up and saw with satisfaction that he was right where he planned to be; directly under the open window of his father's cabin.

He was low and close enough that where the stern peaked and curved up and out, he would only be seen if someone were to lean so far out of a window that they risked falling. He kept close to the water, relying on the eddying waves and shadows that rippled from the rudder to hide him further and thanked the heavens for the strangely superior hearing that he had, for some reason, been blessed with. Voices drifted down to him like thick white snowflakes and he strained to catch the words before they were melted by the wind.

"Scum! Vile bleedin' scum, the lot of them!"

Levi started. It was rare to hear Talani so enraged. Brawn and bluster were Able's attitude and her fury was quiet – keenly felt but not often heard like this.

"Peace, Tally, it is not news." That was his father's voice, even and measured, if strained, as though he was keeping a tight leash on his temper.

"Nay, Captain! Marianne's pie-bird spoke of Johnson's voyage and we had reason enough to be suspicious, but this…"

"We knew we could not trust Johnson, Tally. Davy's locker, we've always known it. Marianne's missive said that Johnson

was running round the Republic reclaiming our story, the X and the map, all of it," Ezi scoffed. Levi could hear the contempt colouring his father's tone. "As if Xaymaca would ever call for the likes of Johnson."

And there it was again – *Xaymaca,* that name. A tremor through Levi's skin, his flesh, his bones, which rippled outward sending waves and currents roiling beneath the mostly calm surface of the sea.

"Aye, Captain." Tally's voice was still warm with fury. "He was never a friend, I always thought he was a puffed-up buffoon, but… We thought – hoped – he was … bluffing. But now it seems that he *has* found a way to the island and his intentions are not as ours were!"

"How can this happen?" Able erupted, startling Levi. It was a marker of how deeply the quartermaster must have been thinking because it was the longest Levi thought he'd ever gone without speaking. "Oaths were sworn! Many of us were there that day! It has not yet been a score since we watched our dear Nubia burn, heard her final cry, and *felt* the undeniable surge of power propel us forward. And now – what? *Bewitch a witch, entangle the spider…*"

"If the scout speaks true, I do not think Johnson has made his plan known to anyone outside of his crew." Ezi was tense and musing and Levi heard his father's footsteps *rap rap rap* as he paced the wooden floors. "Marianne's letters speak only of preparations made and scouting crews sent out—"

"How many in the scouting crews, Capt'n?"

"About two hundred buccaneers." And there was genuine fear there, as Ezi spoke the number.

"Did the letter mention … mention what is … said of you? On the Republic now?"

"No. Though that is not surprising. Marianne is not the type to put pen to paper and write of how my name has been dragged through the mud. It's worth knowing, though."

"Is it? Johnson nary had a good thing to say about you."

"Nay, Able. It confirms what we suspected. However Johnson has been called to Xaymaca, it was not by the same means as us."

Another silence and then Talani's voice. "You … you haven't heard from … from *her*, have you?"

"No." Ezi was gruff but there was an unfamiliar tightness to his voice. "Not since we left. But she would never speak about me that way. Whatever Johnson has heard of my time on Xaymaca, he has come by the information from another source. Besides… *Catch a mermaid, can I ride her?*" Levi had never heard his father sound like this – soft, sickened.

"Ah, *Captain*." Able's voice, gentle in sympathy, again unfamiliar. A beat, a quiet held-in comfort.

For a few moments, Levi could hear nothing but his own breathing. Then the lapping of the waves against the hull, against his fingers as he unconsciously continued to tread water, competed with the roaring, rushing in his ears.

Then Ezi said, slow and thoughtful, "Johnson has not been told … about Levi."

Levi's heart leaped. *Told what?*

"His scout did not seem to pay him any mind, no, Capt'n."

"But … the comment about the pie, Capt'n … and …

69

seafood..." The words died on Tally's tongue as though she herself killed them, hated them.

Ezi hummed thoughtfully. "It's clever. Someone on Xaymaca contacted Johnson ... whoever they are, they're pulling the strings... They have mentioned Levi's mother, painted me as ... lecherous, and used the promise of such things to entice the likes of Johnson ... but didn't mention Levi himself."

With each mention of his name, Levi's breath caught in his throat. *His mother? He had a mother?*

"They know he is a threat?"

"Aye. Better to discredit me and encourage others to keep this from me, isolate our crew. But there is a plot afoot and they don't want Levi involved – and should Johnson find out about him, he would fly as the crow for us. It could be ... catastrophic." Another beat. "Well, that's something at least. He and Vega can remain out of this. For now."

"Capt'n, in light of these events ... maybe it is time to tell the boy ... who ... what he is. Where he is from..." Able's tentative tone was ever softer as he added, "About the prophecy—"

"No." Ezi cut him off abruptly. "No, Abe. We swore when we left that the truth would burden him. I know all too well how heavily such responsibility can weigh, I do not want that for him."

"But his six-and-tenth birthday approaches, Capt'n. You know the traditions there... Is it not ... riskier? To keep him in the dark?"

"The truth is riskier, Tally. If he doesn't know, his age won't matter."

"But, Capt'n, he is a man now—"

"But he is not, is he? That's the point, isn't it? He isn't a *man* at all. He is something else entirely. It is not just the burden of the truth that I fear, it is the danger of it. It is not just that I want to protect him from the world. I want to protect the *world* from *him*."

Levi couldn't breathe. His father's words twisted themselves around his mind, writhing like serpents.

And then Talani, sudden, urgent, a bolt of sudden realization and Levi wished he could see her face: "*Captain!* A *western* wind, Captain."

A silence. "Freeing the faeries," Ezi said slowly. "Sink me."

"Do you really think…" Able's disbelieving breath was drowned out by Tally's growl:

"Abe, nary a day passed that the Capt'n didn't warn us all about Mmoatia."

"I never trusted her." Ezi let out a whistle. "I would never have thought she'd sink to this, though."

"Johnson likely has his own agenda too, though, Capt'n."

"Mmoatia's not stupid. She's the furthest thing from it. I'd wager every move Johnson makes, she has a hand in." Ezi's voice was low and grim. "So. The island of Xaymaca has been betrayed."

"What of the other captains of the Brethren?" asked Talani, who had been quiet for some time. "Ó Néill, Hook … should we not send pie-birds to them?"

"As far as they're aware, Johnson is leading what could be a lucrative voyage. I'm sure he's told them he'll form powerful –

potentially magical – allies and bring back bounty. With the Empire closing in, I'm sure they think it a canny idea. How do we prove what we know? We've been gone eight-and-ten years, and cannot account for why – not without risking Levi. They will not trust us."

"What about … the map, Capt'n?" Able had picked up the line of enquiry now, hushed and uncertain, probing gently. "It remains … unchanged?"

"Yes."

Ezi sighed heavily. From the clink and jangle Levi knew that his father had pulled out his set of keys, ancient and wrought and always on his person.

Levi listened closely. Clink, jangle, the scrape of a drawer being opened. Then a rustle of paper and a low whistle from Able.

"It looks exactly the same as I remember."

"Well, it would for us. But there's one key detail missing, isn't there?"

"Aye, Tally."

"'Tis true enough. You can't see it any more, can you, Capt'n?"

"No." Beat. Levi did not breathe, though the moment did.

Another sigh. "And once again I must choose between the two lives most dear to me."

"We don't know that she is in danger, Captain."

"Don't we, Tally? If Johnson's crew reach her and outnumber her… If she has been betrayed by those who know her defences…"

72

"It all connects to Levi somehow." Tally's voice was urgent. "He is here for a reason. Nubia always said there are some things we cannot live in defiance of. Maybe we've been wrong to keep so much from him."

"Defiance was Nubia's very being," Ezi said, almost impatiently. "She fought her fate so hard she rattled the stars!"

"And maybe *that* was her purpose."

A pause and Ezi's tone was thoughtful. "She ... Levi's mother ... once told me ... the star that fell that night Nubia formed the Republic. Well, she believed that she ... she wished upon it."

Something was reverberating deep in Levi's chest, a heavy clanging, like a gong in the darkest part of the sea. A mother. He had a mother. He reeled as it sunk in, and momentarily dipped back beneath the water, steadying himself. And his father feared she was in danger? Then another thought – *was hers the voice he'd been hearing?* He strained for it now but there was only silence, cloaking him like night.

When he re-emerged his father was speaking and Levi knew his father had never said these words aloud before.

"... She noticed a ripping, as though far away something tore through the fabric of the world. She had known Nubia and knew ... as I suppose she can know things, that something terrible had befallen her. Through that tear, though, she saw a star teeter and begin to fall. She sent a bolt of feeling out towards the star."

"Was it—"

"Aye. And not long after – a couple of years at most – we arrived. I told her the feeling was ... loneliness."

73

More silence. Levi's throat felt very tight.

"We were right to leave, Captain." Able's voice was soothing. "And if we return to Xaymaca with Levi now, the risks being what they are, then these six-and-ten years might well be for nought."

"I know that, Abe. I have no intention of returning. Even if it wasn't such a risk, we have no means of getting there. The map is still … just a map." The scrape, jangle, clink again. Another rustle. Another exhalation. This time Levi heard the hollow-cheeked deep breath and sensed his father returning from wherever his recollections had taken him, back to his role and responsibilities.

"Give the orders to come about. *The Sea Dragon* can shirk its duty no longer. We must return to the Republic. But when we dock – Levi and Vega will stay aboard."

"Aye, Capt'n." Under the heavy step and thunk of Able's footsteps, swift despite the gnarled wood of his left leg, Levi, still bobbing below, nearly missed Talani's quiet murmur. "Levi is more like you than you think, Captain. I see him staring out as if he can see beyond the horizon, just as you once did. You expect him to captain this ship one day, but he cares more for swimming and finery. He's a dreamer, as you once were. Perhaps we are wrong, not teaching him to harness his full potential."

"Tally, his full potential could well damn us all!"

"Or save us! You remember what they said about him…"

"What they said about him is the reason we left!" Ezi took a breath. "I know my son, Tally. I know that there is much to prepare him for. But he is fast and strong and a better

fighter than most on this ship – save for Vega. He does not need anything more than that, than this. I will speak with the Brethren and Levi and Vega will stay on *The Drag*. Whatever this business is, I will keep Levi out of it. That was always the plan. What we have learned today does not change that."

"And … and what of … his mother, Captain?"

Levi clung to the ship, stretching his torso out of the water straining to hear. He ignored when his arms were scratched by barnacles. They would heal swiftly.

"We have all had to make hard choices, Tally. She made hers and I made mine. We are here and she is not. And we have no way to reach her. All we can do is find Johnson and stop whatever it is he's planning. That's it. Savvy?" Beneath the hardness, there was a profound sadness in his father's voice. "We won't make port for at least another week, with a fair wind. We have much to be at before then."

It was a clear dismissal and Tally must have heard it too because after a few moments her quick footsteps retreated above him.

Levi lingered in the water a long time after. He pictured his father, sitting above him at the old claw-footed rosewood desk, brooding with his head in his hands. Levi's body felt too small, his skeleton too tight, constricted by the grip of all that had been kept from him. It was as though a door had opened, just a crack, and through it lay all the truths that he did not know were being kept from him. He could not be easy until he had pushed it wide. He allowed the rhythm of the currents to rock him, the salt to soothe the itching, burning panic of his skin, fighting the urge to explode out of it entirely, and rip himself to shreds.

THE WEIRD SISTER

You are sixteen and you have history this afternoon, and that, you realize, is the best birthday present you're going to get. You move through the corridors quietly yet you disrupt the peace. It is worse than usual today. The mutterings, the snide remarks, the sniggers. Perhaps you shouldn't have worn the red lipstick.

"Hey, horny vag! Happy birthday!" You start. Not at the stupid nickname – the petty portmanteau of your name. (Regina could sort of sound like vagina, if one was cruelly reaching. Your surname, Hornigold is just, well, unfortunate.)

"How do you know it's my birthday?"

"Well, it's the same day every year, right? I always remember my friends' birthdays."

Chloe Johnson, the pastor's daughter, is not your friend. You were friends between the ages of four and eleven – up until the bike-shed incident – and you regret every secret you've ever told her.

Her long braids, pulled up into a high ponytail, swing as she angles her head.

"Oooh, that's why the lippy, right? And which lucky lady will you be kissing?"

She raises her eyebrows and smiles and your skin crawls. You never know how to play it with Chloe. She knows the moves to a dance that you were never taught.

"No kissing."

"No? No special birthday plans?"

You turn, busying yourself at your locker, but she doesn't leave.

"I'm planning some spell casting," you say, deadpan. "It's a full moon. It can't be an equinox a week before halloween. I'll be charging my crystals and hexing my enemies."

She steps back, looking unnerved. You're joking, of course, and Chloe knows it. But there's enough of an ineffable *something* in your expression and she flips her long braids defensively and smirks. "Weirdo." She stalks off.

You eat on your own at lunch, your nose in a book. It's a good book, so you can ignore the part of you that would like to sit with a chattering group of girls if it were not for the fear of being laughed at.

After lunch, in the history classroom, a painting is projected on the bright white of the interactive whiteboard. A blazing splash of orange and red, a woman tied to a stake. The paint, with its streaks of white and yellow, looks alight. You are impressed. In the shadows beneath the woman, picked out in navy and grey and brown, a battle rages. Half the forces – the half who appear to be rushing in from the sea – are uniformed, the rich blue and red and white of their coats blending into the chaos. The other half are not uniformed and yet are united by their tricorne hats and curved cutlasses. *Pirates.*

Miss Gibbers' footsteps sound in the hallway. Chairs scrape the wooden floor. You all stand.

"Good afternoon, Miss Gibbers!"

"Good afternoon, girls. You may sit." You like Miss Gibbers.

She's young and smart and not from your small, strange town. She had come here to study the local history at the university and never left. You know you'll be away at the first opportunity, but you can also see the appeal of three hundred and forty days of sunshine.

"Right, you all know what today is – I'm going to give you your coursework. You'll all have the same initial assessment objective, but I'll tell you now that any plagiarism attempts will receive zero marks. Originality of thought. Unique perspectives. Well-argued points. That's what I'm looking for." A pause, then, "You will get the entire term to work on it, so I'm expecting five thousand very high quality words." Groans. Complaints. A swell of noise.

"What? Come on, miss, *five thousand words*? We have other coursework and exams too!" Chloe's best friend Grace, whose name has always struck you as ironic as she's a sore loser and never says sorry, is complaining loudest of all.

Miss Gibbers simply waits for everyone to realize complaining won't change the curriculum. The class falls quiet again.

"Right, as this is our last lesson before the half-term break, let's recap. As we've learned, the Empire colonized many nations in its first two hundred years. It had a particular interest in islands in the southern hemisphere where the land was fertile and resources were aplenty. Who can tell me the Empire's most profitable export during this time?"

Hands in the air.

"Cotton?"

"One of, but not quite."

"Tea?"

"No."

"Sugar."

"No."

You put up your hand.

"Yes, Reggie?"

"People."

Miss Gibbers nods gravely. "Precisely. The trading of people into slave labour enabled the Empire not only to profit greatly from the produce you have all just correctly named but, crucially, they lost no money on pesky things like salaries." She raises an eyebrow sardonically. "The Empire, with the royal family at its head and heart, was able to expand and build extraordinary wealth, the wealth they still live off today. The island nations affected, like this one, still call the Empire's monarchy their head of state and the Empire still benefits from things like our taxes, our army and our navy."

Now Miss Gibbers turns to the picture, bright on the board. "There was a period, however, almost three centuries ago now, during the height of the Empire's rule, when something remarkable happened. Something like … revolution."

The hairs on the back of your neck stand up. You follow her gaze to the picture.

"The history gets murky here, confused by superstition and fears of heresy and the occult. And so we have to rely on myth, myths I'm sure many of you know, to make our informed deductions.

"The revolution began with a woman named Nubia who was burned for witchcraft, the last witch to burn on Sheta Island. They say that after she died, a toxic manchineel tree grew on the

same spot. Certainly, a manchineel tree exists on Sheta Island today. It's on the green beside the library. The library used to be a church so it is not beyond the realm of possibility that a stake for witch burnings would have been there, in the centre of town. It is said that Nubia had allies – pirates. They sought revenge for her death. In one night, they gained complete control of Sheta Island, expelled the Empire and founded a pirate republic."

You know this story, of course, but hearing Miss Gibbers lay it out before you, clearly with no embellishment, you feel a hitch of excitement in your chest. *It's such a vibe.*

"This Republic of Pirates existed for almost twenty years. The international accounts of this time state that it was a dangerous and lawless place, filled with devil worship and deviancy. But we must remember" – she hesitates – "who is telling us that story. Could it be that those influential voices were threatened by a way of life that contradicted their own?"

You catch Chloe and Grace smirking sideways at each other because you're sixteen and all sincerity is amusing.

Miss Gibbers reaches over to her desk and picks up a book. "The Republic did fall, eventually, as you all know. It has since remained under the rule of the Empire, as it is today. But how did this happen? Why did this happen? I'm sure you'll find a variety of answers – destroyed by a sea dragon?" A few titters. "That's the most popular myth, of course. Or washed away by the sea in an act of God? Betrayed by those loyal to the Empire? Or … a complicated combination of all of the above? Do you see, girls? Myth and history, history and myth.

"For reading, I'd recommend *The Republic of Sheta Island*. There's little else written about what those twenty years without

Empire rule were actually like. Its author is unknown but it's a sort of compendium of accounts from many of the port's inhabitants – pirates, barmaids, shipwrights, all sorts, as well as extracts from texts of the time that were banned or destroyed. I have a copy here."

She holds it up. "There are other copies in the town library, as well as old naval records and captains' logs that will come in handy. There's very little on the internet, so you will have to – *gasp* – read a book."

Chloe and Grace share another look and you snort internally. You doubt that either of them have ever visited the library.

"And so that is the purpose of your coursework. Five thousand words on the lost Republic. It will be heavily research-based and I'm expecting a high level of analysis. What happened in those twenty years? How did the Republic rise and fall? Who were the key players? There will likely be many answers with many lines of inquiry. Consider yourselves historical investigators – proper *historians*! This will count towards your final exam grades and for those of you looking at colleges for next year, this could well be instrumental."

There are only two colleges in Shetatown, one that specializes in more academic subjects and one that specializes in vocational ones. Limited options that mean you'll probably end up with some combination of the same students you've spent every day of your education with so far. It is not an appealing thought, but neither is starting work with your dad.

"For the rest of your lesson I'd like you to go through the textbook and begin sketching a skeleton timeline using what

we know so far – or think we do." Miss Gibbers flicks through the textbook. "I would start at chapter three, *The Weird Sister*."

You open your book, dig out your notebook and pencil.

"Miss!" Grace's hand is in the air again.

"Yes, Grace?"

"Miss, what's a weird sister?"

You don't like the way she says the word *weird*. It turns tangible in her mouth, bounces against your hunched back.

"A good question. So, *weird*, a word I'm sure you're all familiar with, comes from 'wyrd' meaning 'fate'. Originally the phrase 'wyrd sisters' was used to refer to the fates in classical mythology. It got picked up by Shakespeare who used it as a nickname for his three witches."

"Interesting" – Grace stretches the word with feigned sincerity, "that there were three of them –" You can hear her turn in her seat. "So even weirdos should have friends."

Your stomach sinks at the titters.

"Once you begin reading," says Miss Gibbers calmly, "you will see that the term *weird sister* is often used to refer to a woman who is seen different – be that for her intellect, her demeanour or her ability to piss off men."

The mild swear word is enough of a distraction and the class, determined not to look impressed or shocked by a teacher swearing, temporarily forget about you.

Everyone is quiet then, pens scratching across paper.

A few minutes before the lesson ends Miss Gibbers calls for attention.

"Before we finish, a last piece of housekeeping. As this will be a lot of work, you'll be pleased to know that I am allowing

you to work in pairs. This is *not*" – Miss Gibbers raises her voice slightly to be heard over the swell of claiming cries – "an opportunity for laziness. Working as an independent thinker while being part of a team is a key element of the study of history and you will be marked accordingly." A sigh and then, "But, yes, you may pick your own partners."

The usual fanfare. You don't look up. You'll go with whoever is reluctantly left out.

"And so finally we'll have … Reggie Hornigold and Maeve O'Neill."

You look round. Maeve was new at the start of this term. Her dad is in the navy and was posted to Sheta Island, so they'd moved in with her aunt, a woman you are only familiar with because she works in the bakery and has a permanently disapproving disposition. You've not spoken to Maeve much. She flies under the radar, though you know that she turned sixteen back in July – school years are different wherever she's from – and her grades have been as good as yours. She'd attracted some brief interest in her first week as the shiny and new thing, but having failed to sufficiently dazzle your classmates, the collective gaze had quickly returned to Chloe and Grace.

You turn to her now, feel yourself go hot when you find she is already looking at you. She smiles, tentatively. You smile back.

*

After school, Maeve taps you on the back of the shoulder. She somehow manages to find the gap between your layers,

her fingers brushing your skin. Goosebumps rise – you can't remember the last time someone touched you … well … at all really.

"Are you busy this weekend? I thought we could go to the library?" Her accent isn't a million miles away from your own. Rolling hills instead of sliding sand dunes. "It's open late on Saturdays, isn't it? If we go in the afternoon or evening we'll be less likely to see… Well, it'll be quieter." The unsaid lingers briefly like a bad smell, *We'll be less likely to see people from school and leave me further socially stranded.* You can't blame her really – weirdo is contagious.

"Unless you have plans? It's Halloween, isn't it?" she adds. You keep your face neutral. Her hair is a copper coil twisted tight round her finger like a spring.

"I don't have plans."

"Saturday at five, then?" Maeve asks and you nod before you both walk away. You try not to bump into people as the image of her finger, purpling under the burnished russet of her hair plays over and over again in front of your eyes.

Pirates Punished

They still could not say
    what had happened that fateful day,
    when on Ezi's ragged map they saw
an X that had not been there before.

On Xaymaca Prince Ezi explored;
    there was much to discover.
    The Great Forest hummed and sang and sparked,
    a land where nights were bright electric dark,
    where faeries flew high above,
    where spiders spun webs of silk
    and witches dwelled within a grove.

For Ezi and his crew,
    each day brought new
    excitement and discovery,
    this place spoke in the language of dreams,
    sang with the sound of stories.
    Of many, one people,
    they all would say.

They had heard from campfire songs
    of the mermaid that belonged
    to the land's magic –
    some said she
    guarded the Source
    some say the magic came from *her* force
    and others spoke of a Great Bonding,
    a joining of her hands with Yaa's
    to create all that they were given.

Some of Ezi's crew became consumed
    by the mermaid in her bower—
    They thought of stranded
    peach and cream bodies
    prostrate on rocks;
    they could not comprehend a threat
    in the form of a nameless local water mother;
    water is a good servant but a bad master is the
    first
    thing all able sea-folk must learn,
    but if too late, the lesson comes when
    tears and blood stain the stern.

They wanted her.

And so they went into the forest
    in groups of maybe six or five
    to catch a mermaid for her magic.
    Not a single one returned alive.

After a dozen or maybe more
    were lost to the river floor
    a song whistled down the river,
    so all with ears would stop and shiver;

    Where our Great Forest lies,
    a river quietly burbles by.
    Willows drape the earth and skies,
    weeping and with magic cry,
    as dawns the sun of summer.

    Underwater, over stones,
    the land's power will pulse on loam,
    fishes swim, nymphs they roam,
    all things return to the watery home
    of the River Mumma.

She guards the magic of the land,
    she protects its treasures from violent hands,
    all our fears she understands.
    She watches all from the sands
    and basks in heat of summer.

    She is neither foe nor friend,
    you will find her at the rainbow's end.
    The land's Source she must defend,
    while mortality she must transcend.
    Beware the River Mumma.

Many foolish men have tried,
have ignored the mermaid's wrath and pride,
have pulled and hauled against the tide,
when on hot days her beauty spied,
at the surface in the summer.

But they have suffered for their greed,
of my warning they did not heed,
and though they beg, though they plead,
down into the river they are heaved
by the River Mumma.

Her skin is dark, her hair is green,
her eyes are grey and silver gleam,
but if you see her, hear her scream,
darkness descends, a watery dream,
and death forgets the summer.

Do not catch her, do not try,
the earth will brown, the river will dry,
her children, all the fish, will die,
she is older than the sea and sky.
Respect the River Mumma.

One day Ezi followed them
    deep into the Great Forest.
    "I'm going to bewitch a witch!"
    "I'm going to entangle a spider!"
    "I'm going to catch a mermaid,
    do you think she'd let me ride her?"

He could have caught up to them, perhaps,
    but they had sickened the rest long enough.
    Magic was inexact but always intentional,
    so all the Xaymacans said,
    but on nights like tonight
    he could hear the hum,
    the throb of strange magic,
    hubris about to be humbled.

He hid behind the willow trees,
    watched his men crouch to their knees.
    She emerged after only moments,
    of their presence seemingly unaware
    as she gently finger combed her hair
    which climbed and filled
    the heavy air,
    her breasts were bare –
    his men lunged,
    the mermaid plunged,
    she vanished beneath the surface.
    The foolish men scrabbled at the loam
    and the river began to foam,
    to froth and heave and toss and churn,
    all because they did not learn,
    did not listen when they were warned
    about the River Mumma.

She rose from the hissing, spitting white,
    some of the men collapsed on sight,

her beauty was terrible, her body gleamed,
she burned silver-gold, the water steamed.
You dare?
Her voice choked the air
from their throats, and her hair
lifted and swirled about her face.
You dare?
I am the River Mumma, goddess from the sea,
I am the Great Mermaid, bonded with Yaa,
as ancient as sun and moon and star!

The river burst its banks,
seething with rage and teeming,
to carry his men towards her –
they had tried to take
what they could not own.
All things return to the watery home
of the River Mumma.

Then they were gone.
Ezi's heart was loud in his chest.
The river began to calm and rest,
a violent rage subsiding to
burbling hiccups. He backed away but –
Do you think I do not see you,
mortal prince?
He froze.
Captain Ezi of The Sea Dragon. *Stand and face the*
    River Mumma.

He faced her but did not stand.
He did not ask how she knew his name.
He sank to his knees, stretched his arms,
prostrate and unthreatening.
"I did not mean to see you, oh great
mermaid.
I wanted to call them back but it
did not seem worth the risk to myself.
I mean you and this land no harm,
I would ask for your mercy."

The silence was charged.
What will you offer me,
in exchange for your life?
He had not expected that. He still did not
look up,
did not challenge that fierce gaze with his
own.
"Anything! Anything you want. I am not
fool enough to say
no
to a goddess."
She laughed, and even as fear near
blinded him,
the sound snaked along his spine,
tickled his skin like gentle nails
and he shivered.

She stilled at the movement.

He sensed her primal focus,
    her head angling with curiosity,
    he basked in her ferocity
    and waited.
    Then – *I would have stories.*
    Stories of land.
    I have heard all the stories of the sea,
    all its creatures and currents whisper to me
    but of land
    I know little.
    Bring me things I have not known of,
    teach me something new
    and I will spare you.

He sagged with relief–
    before daring himself to look into her eyes,
    just in time to see the river rise.
    "I am your servant, great goddess."
    She laughed again as she vanished beneath the
        bubbling banks,
    molten metal met brown –
    her eyes
    never left his own.

Later,
    as he told the remaining crew of her kill,
    he felt as though she watched him still.

Strange Dreams

Levi headed back to his cabin and sank on to this bed, watching the light dipping past the rim of the porthole, casting shadows that morphed and shifted into strange unknown creatures across the worn wooded floors.

Levi is a threat…

It is not just that I want to protect him from the world. I want to protect the world from him…

He isn't a man at all. He is something else entirely.

His father was afraid. Of him.

For the first time, Levi became aware of the shape of his past, saw it stitched together – and where it could all come apart. He ran his mind along those edges, thinking about a mysterious land called Xaymaca, a map – and a mother. Mermaids and witches and treacherous pirates.

How did he connect to all of it?

He closed his eyes. The salt prickled where it glittered on his skin.

The world is dark and cool

he had spent too long in the water

cool soothes the sting

but he wanted to see, he wanted to pull at the thread

cool is comforting

and understand

cool is kind
he wanted to follow the stitching and
unravel the seam,
rocking still
the weaving current of what had been
lost
not still at all
and forgotten
"Where your old cradle lies,
your first home burbles by.
The first sight held in your bright eyes,
the first ears rent with your new cry,
now only hears the drummer.
I am here and you are there,
you have love and nought to fear,
you are more than you appear,
my currents' song you can hear,
storms always split the summer."
"Levi!"

He awoke with a gasp, air pouring into his lungs, feeling closer to drowning than he ever had in water. Able was shaking him, firm but gentle.

"Are you quite well?" Levi looked up at him. He had known Able his whole life. Levi wondered just how much of it had been a lie.

He forced a smile on to his face. "Strange dreams, that's all."

"Right, well. Cook's called. He wants your help with the saltfish – there'll be extra doughboy for you." Able was still eyeing him somewhat anxiously.

94

"Grand!" Levi stuck his bare feet into his boots. "Sink me, I'm starved!"

*

Over the next few days, Levi continued to sleep fitfully.

Deciding to make the best of his insomnia, and in order to avoid his father, Levi volunteered himself for the night shift. He was not sure, should he be around Ezi, that he could hold back the tide of his hurt and anger. On more than one occasion he considered marching into the captain's cabin and demanding answers. But he never did. This was in part because there was every chance that Ezi would simply lie again. But it was more complicated than that; for all his rage, Levi admired his father greatly. To stand in front of him and see the fear he had heard in Ezi's voice cloud his face, to look at him and hear him say, "You are dangerous, you could damn us, you are something *other.*" Levi did not think he was ready for that. And so, he sat with his musings, on deck of *The Sea Dragon*, staring out at the spilled ink of the world.

For the first time in his life, Levi felt lonely.

*

As dawn broke on the fourth morning since *The Sterling* scout had lost his head, Levi did not go back to his cabin after the shift as usual. This was because today marked his six-and-tenth birthday. And he wanted to see his sister's face first.

He passed Talani, however, on his way down and she

squeezed the back of his neck. "Levi. Six-and-ten! Sink me, nary a day has passed since you and Vega were mewling pups, small enough each for Ezi to hold in a hand. Now look at you!"

Talani was not maternal but she was the closest thing to a mother he'd had. But he did have a mother. And she had known it all along. He wondered if this was true of the whole crew. For a moment, an accusation formed on his tongue. Then he caught it. Talani was not the captain. She had been following orders, had even suggested his father tell him the truth and been denied. He forced a smile on to his face, a playful roll of his eyes. "Now, Tally, none of your wet-nursing today."

She laughed, the gentle rasp of her callouses against his skin soothing and familiar. "Are you coming up? Cook's making your favourite – cornmeal and cackle." Porridge and eggs, you might call them. But Levi shook his head. "He said he'd do breakfast for dinner as I'm on night shifts this week."

"Breakfast for dinner! Must we start calling you princeling now instead of hatchling?"

"A real brat, aren't I?"

"Aye, well, you're always arse upwards!"

"Well, we all are." Then he pressed, "We're all lucky to be part of this crew. We trust each other."

"We do." Tally's eyes misted but Levi did not know if this was guilt or something else. It happened sometimes. Levi had once asked his father why Tally was prone to tears. They had watched salt tracking her cheeks as she steered, never faltering, even as Able patted her back.

Ezi had replied, "Tally cries to wash her eyes. There are things that she has seen that sometimes she can't look

away from. Her tears clear her sight and bring her back to us again."

People's pasts were not often or readily discussed on *The Drag*. It was only now, as Talani blinked rapidly, that the realization occurred. Talani and other members of the crew did not talk about their pasts because they were painful. They kept their secrets because it hurt to share. So what of his past? Was it kept secret for the same reason? And who would it hurt, if it were shared? He squeezed Tally's shoulder despite himself before stepping back. "I'm exhausted. I'm going to say good morning to Vega."

Talani departed for the deck and Levi knocked on her cabin door.

Twice.

Then, "Levi?"

He pushed open the cabin door.

Vega looked up, grinning. "Happy birthday, hatchling. Not such a whelp now, are you?"

"How'd you know it was me?"

"I know your footsteps, I know the rhythm when you knock the door, I know the way you breathe—"

"What do you mean *the way I breathe*, how do I *breathe*?"

"I just knew, savvy?"

Levi thought about it, then nodded. He would know Vega's knock anywhere too. "We need to talk." He lowered himself on to Talani's bed opposite. His dress fanned out wide around him, dark cerulean, high necked and layered with long ruffled sleeves. He smiled slightly at the sight. It really was a delicious shade.

"That dress suits you," Vega acknowledged. "Pass it to me when you're changing for bed, would you? The skirts are nice and big."

She smiled and looked back to her lap where she was unpicking the hem of her – no, Levi realized, with a flare of horror – his – jacket.

"Is that my black-and-gold damask? Sink me, Vega, you better have a good reason for this!"

"I'm taking precautions."

Levi watched as she took a handful of bounty from the overspilling trunk in the corner and began to tip jewels into the lining of the jacket. Shining ruby rings, medallions of smooth silver, gleaming pieces of gold. Then she sewed over them, neatly folding the treasures into the seams until they were undetectable.

"I don't understand. If you want to add jewels to our jackets, what's the good of putting them where no one can see?"

She rolled her eyes. "Precautions, as I said, or have you filled your ears with water again?"

The memory of the last time he'd been swimming filled Levi's head.

He shuffled his thoughts into a line as neat as the row of jewels Vega had on the bed, but she continued, "Tally was telling me of how landlubber women aren't taught to protect themselves like we are. She said if you don't have a rich or powerful pa or brother or husband to look out for you, there's danger. Beatings and theft and worse. Apparently it's customary for some to sew their earnings into their dresses. If

you ever have to make a run for it, all you need are the clothes on your back."

"And are we likely to have to make a run for it any time soon?"

Even as he said it, the twisting serpents of his father's words slithered back through his mind: The Sea Dragon *can shirk its duty no longer. We must return to the Republic.*

"Perhaps not. But something is ... off. Wrong. And it's not just Tally's superstitions, Levi. First the pie-birds, then *The Sterling* scout. I can feel it, Levi, the stars are ... wary. And Pa is—"

"Has he said something to you?"

His tone made her look up again. "No? Why?" She peered more closely at him, the gold flecks in her brown eyes catching shadows. "You know something."

It was not a question.

Levi leaned back on Talani's bed. "Well, *know* is probably too strong a word."

He relayed what he had heard, uncharacteristically succinct in his storytelling. When he had finished, she regarded him in silence. Then she began to sew again, needle flying.

"Oh, hatchling. This is heavy talk for a birthday."

"I know. So ... have you heard of this ... *Xaymaca*?"

"There are legends, of course. Lost lands, paradise islands that sink beneath the sea or vanish in the mist. But Xaymaca? No, I've never heard of it. And apparently that's where you were born?"

"Apparently it's where my *mother* is so ... seems it."

They looked at each other. Vega chewed her words; Levi could almost see her mind similarly masticating, sorting through everything he had said. "So Pa already knew of Johnson's involvement."

Levi nodded. "But the letters the pie-bird brought only spoke of a ... lucrative voyage. Alliance and treasure – nothing more."

"The scout spoke of ... bewitching witches and catching mermaids. Well, it's hardly diplomatic, is it? It's ... violent. And Pa thinks someone on Xaymaca is helping him? Has betrayed the land, and so the people there – your mother perhaps included – are in danger?"

"In enough danger that Pa wants to come about and make full sail for the Republic."

"But ... who is your mother? Pa's never spoken of her and now suddenly he's willing to sail to the Republic – something he's always avoided – because she might be in trouble?"

"I know. I can't make sense of it." His thoughts darted – he'd reach for them and they'd leap away like so many tiny flickering fish. "Why can't Pa read the map any more? What's the *prophecy* – what does it say about me? *Who am I, Vega?*" Levi heard the edge of panic creep into his voice.

Vega angled her head, kept her voice calm. "You are Levi, son of Ezi, prince of pirates, captain of *The Sea Dragon*. You are my very well-dressed baby brother." She paused, then, "You are someone who is *meant to be here*."

This warmed him, but the glow sputtered and died as he thought again of his father's words.

His full potential could well damn us all!

"You've seen all of the ship's maps, haven't you, Vega?"

100

"I thought so. But then what's one more lie among so many?" Her tone was bitter and Levi felt relieved. He had been worried that she would berate him for his resentment. "What did they say again? About the map?"

"They said the map was *just a map*. But it sounded like it somehow linked to how they'd found Xaymaca in the first place."

"We need to do some digging. All of this speculating, we're rabbit hunting with a dead ferret." Another one of Talani's favourites. Usually hearing Vega repeating a line from their beloved collector of phrases cheered him. Today the words jarred. "They lied to me, Vega. To us. All of them. This crew have sailed with Pa for years. They're all in on it."

"I know" – she looked up at him again, lips pursed – "but … but they love us, Levi. That we know to be true. Whatever they did, they must have done for our own good."

"And who are they to say what our own good is?"

"They love us, Levi," she said again, insistent.

Levi wanted to believe her.

But he could not forget his father's voice, the slight breathlessness, the stuttered fright –

It is not just that I want to protect him from the world. I want to protect the world from him.

He sighed and avoided his sister's gaze as he said, 'It sounded like Pa was afraid of me."

His sister scoffed. "The great Captain Ezi, afraid of a mewling pup like you?" He looked down at her but her eyes were not as light as her words and she said, more softly, "Well, I will never be afraid of you, Levi. Savvy?"

He felt better then.

Tiredness sagged against him, but he thought, for the first time in a while, that he may sleep properly. When all else was chaos, Vega was fixed and constant. *How lucky was he, to have a star for a sister?*

Vega finished stitching the jacket she had been working on and faced him again.

"So what is it you want to do? We could just ask Pa?"

That was Vega. All action. But Levi shook his head. Their shared childhood of mischief spread like a smile before them, bright and wicked, and he said, "A bit of birthday fun. Our old game. I'll let you do it, though – you're better than me. Gods, I really must be old and wise now."

She blinked. Then understanding, she touched her hand to their father's bandana, a twin grin to match his.

"You want me to steal the map."

The Mermaid and the Pirate Prince

Ezi's invitation did not allay
his trepidation but anticipation
propelled him anyway –
he wanted to see her.

He had not forgotten the snake
of her laugh,
the dark green of her hair,
how her breasts had been bare,
the burnished metal of her stare.

"I have returned," he announced.
I can see that, mortal prince.
What have you brought me?
"My own tale, if it pleases you,
great goddess."
She rose out of the water
and he rose to meet her.

Up close the silver-grey glow
of her eyes was shocked

with the blue of stormy seas.
Up close he could see the gentle
undulating of her tail,
green-grey as reeds and weeds.
Up close her locs were of a similar
complexion but richer –
oxidized like the green of the forest.
She came to rest,
half on land and half in the water,
bare breasts pushing against
slick shining arms –
he did not know where to look.
Fear mingled with something
else—

Does my nakedness concern you?
   The few males I meet are witch or fae,
   they always look away
   but I have come to know that
   mortal men look
   too much.
He did not know what to say,
so simply replied,
"I have seen breasts before."
And she laughed once more. *Tell me your story,*
mortal prince.
Ezi met her gaze,
insides ablaze –
and began:

"I am keen-eyed and searching,
I am never still,
I am always yearning,
I cannot eat my fill.
Born to a king,
the dreaming second son.

When I became a man
I took to the seas,
to explore every land was my
greatest dream –
and so I bought a brigantine
and named it *The Sea Dragon*.
I gained quite the reputation,
and much to my royal parents' consternation
I formally renounced my title.

I freed the enslaved
where they were shackled,
raised my white dragon
and cackled
when those in bondage,
bruised, bloodied, left for dead,
rose on shaky sea legs
to fight for me instead.
I have women on my brig
which many said was unlucky
but I am not superstitious,
I find women pirates plucky –
and I need their fierce hearts.

In this land where magic was fast dying,
    I still found myself trying
    for more;
    when a witch was burned at the stake
    I was filled with fire, helped take
    back that island
    from the clutches of Empire
    and so founded the Republic.
    Some moons of building,
    of laying the cornerstones of freedom and then

    One day on an old
    yellowing map
    I saw
    something that had not been there
    before.
    An X.
    I am grateful my crew trusted me,
    followed an X only I could see,
    all in the name of adventure.

We raised the anchor,
    the cockswain crowed.
    We planted coins and flowers,
    out we flowed with the tide.
    It had not happened before,
    it has not happened since
    but that X seemed to say,
    Come follow, pirate prince.

The River Mumma wondered
    about her wishing star;
    she thought about the way her insides
    had twisted,
    she fisted pebbles in her palms,
    thinking of those black sails on the horizon.
    How the burning had
    eased. Lessened.
    She searched for it now, for the internal rawness,
    but it was soothed somehow.

Ezi was reaching towards her.

He presented to her a
    yellowing map, deeply creased,
    lined like palms,
    holding many fortunes.
    "*This* is where the X appeared."

The River Mumma reached for where
    he pointed – and she recognized the stamp of
    her magic.

She sank back beneath the surface,
    intoning,
    Come again. I would hear more.

Each rainbow that sprawled
    after a storm

when the sun grew warm
so too would the pirate prince
as he hurried through the forest
to meet the River Mumma.
He did not share one-sidedly,
listened aghast to her Great Bonding,
heard an immortal's account of mortality,
a millennia of life on this land.

I am made of seas and storms,
I am part of the vast primordial flow.
Sometimes a squall lets me know just how small
I am.
Sometimes I roar back.
Ezi could not imagine any gale or hurricane
more
powerful than she and the sweep of her
force doused him –
but he could master his fear.
She liked this about him.

I have many creatures for company,
all those who belong to water
belong to each other
– but once I felt something new.
I wished for a balm
and then saw you sail into my
bay. I do not know what ailed me
but I am … glad. That it has gone
away.

"You were lonely?"

The River Mumma considered.
> *If I have been lonely, I did not know it*
> *until now.*
> "You need never be lonely again."
> He feared he had overstepped ...
> would she take his concern for
> disrespect?

But she met the moment,
> saw him chewing the words
> he could not take back and *smiled*.
> Then she surged forward,
> a wave cresting the shore,
> extended her hand and *touched him*.
> Her fingertips skimmed his temple
> to his jaw and,
> as though she wanted more,
> continued to his collarbone.
> And the pirate prince,
> who had known many women
> and known many men,
> had never been touched
> so intimately.

Tally's Tale

Levi bumped into his father on his way back to his cabin.

The pirate prince was smoking a fat cigar in one of the nooks and crannies *The Drag* was made up of. He had his eyes closed, the shadows under them thrown into sharp relief as he rested his head against wood. The colour was so close to his skin, dark brown and worn, that Levi once again imagined that his father and the ship were one. He could not dream of Ezi without *The Drag*. Without one, the other simply did not exist.

And now it seemed, both were tired.

"Pa?"

Ezi started, puffing smoke, looking in that moment like the very creature for which his vessel was named.

"Hatchling! Happy birthday! Going to bed?"

"Aye."

"You not breaking your fast? There's cornmeal and cackle, your favourites."

Levi shook his head. "I'll fall face first into my plate if I try. But I'll be up later. Wouldn't do to miss dinner on my birthday, would it?"

They looked at each other. Unsaid things filled the alcove, forming shapes in the smoke.

Ezi inclined his head, gesturing with the pipe, but Levi took in those dark circles again, the weariness and worry,

and hesitated. Asking Ezi anything would mean confessing to eavesdropping – the thought of which sent Levi's stomach keelhauling. Besides, he and his sister already had a plan.

So instead he said, "I – I'm sorry I've been so ... so away with the fae, lately. Well, not lately really, always. I'll – I'll do better."

Ezi sighed, standing slowly, stretching. "No apology needed, hatchling. I'm tough on you. But you're stronger, smarter and more able to defend yourself than anyone on this ship." A beat. "Except perhaps me."

"And Vega."

Ezi chuckled. "Yes, and Vega."

"Sometimes ... well, I know you want me to captain *The Drag* someday. But really, Pa, I think Vega would be better."

Calloused palms and deep lines, Ezi's rough hands gentled Levi's face before gripping his chin. Not hard, just firm enough so that Levi could not avoid his gaze.

"You remind me so much of myself at your age. I didn't think I'd be a captain either. I wanted no responsibility at all. The wayward second son of a king... Sailing the high seas was my way to be free of all that. And it was that longing for adventure – for freedom and justice – that got me the loyalty of this crew. Vega will be a superb helmsman, she will be the world's best navigator. But you, Levi ... you *know* the sea. You will look for magic and new lands and people, you will always search for more. The captain of *The Sea Dragon* should be a dreamer. Should always have an idea of where this ship is going. And Vega..." He grinned, looking in the direction of her cabin. "Vega will know how to get there."

Something tight and hot was expanding in Levi's chest. He

grabbed his father in a tight embrace with a muffled "OK, Pa" and staked the feeling into his memory – Ezi's arms around him. His beard scratching his forehead as he dropped a kiss there.

They pulled apart and Ezi headed towards the stairs, back to the main deck.

"Pa?"

Ezi turned.

"Why d'you call me hatchling? Driftling for Vega makes sense, but why...?"

Ezi paused. His face was unreadable, clouded by cigar smoke. "I suppose... I suppose most creatures aren't ... without their mothers at such a young age. But hatchlings ... well, they have their eggs. The egg just needs to be kept warm and safe and, well... Well, anyone might do that. Even a pirate prince."

A shared smile. Ezi's rich brown eyes, warm as earth. Levi did not have Ezi's eyes. He wondered if he had his mother's. The tight, hot feeling cooled. If Ezi had secrets, then he, Levi, could have them too.

*

Levi did not go straight to sleep as he had told his father he would. He had much to be at. He returned to his cabin that afternoon and by the time he awoke, the sun had set.

He headed to the stairwell, thronged with other members of the crew, and those he had not seen yet that day called out glad tidings for another year. Emerging on deck he could see Vega, in position already, barrelling to the front of the dinner

queue, swearing, feigning her moon cycle and the subsequent bottomless pit of hunger. This was not uncharacteristic and so her presence was simultaneously noted and avoided. Exactly as she intended. The crew gathered as Levi took his own plate of cornmeal and cackle – breakfast for dinner – and cup of wine. Able's voice boomed across the deck and heads turned in his direction, recognition of the old favourite tune pricking ears and clearing throats. They picked up the response to Able's melodic call, stamping their feet and laughing:

> They called him the monster, great of the seas!
> Yo, ho! The dragon will roar!
> He was here 'fore the stars and the trees!
> Oh, ho! The dragon will roar!
>
> And when time has wound to an end?
> Yo, ho! The dragon will roar!
> He'll unwind it and start it again!
> Oh, ho! The dragon will roar!
>
> Hoist the serpent, colour the sea!
> Yo, ho! The dragon will roar!
> He is the life of the firm and the free!
> Oh, ho! The dragon will roar!

Levi caught sight of his father, sitting beside Talani on an upturned keg. With no tricorne atop his bandana and his shirt sleeves rolled up, he looked younger, slurping his cornmeal and singing, like any member of his crew. The wind lifted their

voices, expanding them, stretching them, so they filled the air with a great sheet of sound which puffed, billowed and settled around them. Quiet fell. Able began:

"Young Miss Vega reminded me this morning, lest I forget, that we have a most important occasion to mark!" Vega gave Levi the faintest nod before she melted into the ship and Levi's heart began to race. "One among our number can no longer be counted a child." Stamps, cheers, faces beamed at him. "Many happy returns, young Levi. To mark such an occasion, I thought of a seldom recounted story, one of the few, perhaps, that you have not heard.

"'Twas many years ago, when our captain was but a whelp, the youngest pirate captain to sail the seas. They say he's descended from the gods for a reason!" The crew cheered and under the cover of the noise Levi felt a warm breath at his neck, heard a quiet voice order "Quick!" as a hand pressed into his back, where he leaned by the stairwell. He carefully passed Vega the key he had swiped off his father earlier. They had made sure that Ezi had not had a moment to return to his cabin and discover its absence – fraying ropes, faulting the binnacle and what felt like a hundred other small nuisances to keep their pa busy.

Vega slipped down the stairs as Able continued, "Now this was long before the days of the Republic and long before your birth, young Levi. Trouble was coming towards us, twenty-two knots in a fair wind."

He glanced at Talani, who raised her tankard, as if in salute. Able went on, "A vessel, name o' *Volunteer*. Cargo ship. With the human kind of cargo aboard." A chill skimmed Levi's

spine. Talani's face was in shadow. The crew hissed and the sound, the rage and disgust, prickled his skin with gooseflesh. "Now if there is one thing that this crew and its captain can't abide, it's *slavers*." The crew stamped their approval. "Whether they'd come upon us by chance or seen us and thought to try their luck" – the stamping intensified – "we'll never know. But I remember the rage and death in our captain's eyes as he raised his cutlass and gave his orders."

Able adjusted his stance, spreading his arms as he embodied the young pirate prince, and the stamping became a fierce drumroll that vibrated through Levi's body. "*All hands! Free them all. Any who wish to fight may join us. Any who wish to flee may be given the means to commandeer that ship. Give no quarter, show no mercy. Those who put such little value on human life can hardly value their own! And so we will see how they scream their worth!*"

The crew erupted into stamps and cheers and Levi was transported, imagining the same cheers to those same words. He looked at his father, for once not brooding, smiling almost ruefully at his bloodthirsty righteousness.

Ezi said, "I have lost my flair for the dramatics but I don't regret a single kill I made that day."

Able went on, "They were beside us in a moment and their men were leaping on to our ship, just as our crew were leaping on to theirs, and it was only then that we raised our flag, and as the night is dark I saw regret dawn upon them at the sight of our white dragon. We killed our way across that deck, slashing throats and opening insides like it was sport." Levi's stomach lurched at the image of a blood-slick deck, the deck where he

now stood. He regretted how quickly he'd eaten his cornmeal. "We went below and came to the poor kidnapped souls, sick and shivering and crammed so many to a cabin as to make our quarters look luxurious. The capt'n gave his orders: *All aboard this vessel are dead or fleeing. Come with us and fight or commandeer this ship and find somewhere safe.*

"Understandably, most opted to stay where they were, many were sick or wounded and why would they risk our company? A pirate is a pirate, after all. But a few ... a few had vengeance in their hearts and wanted justice.

"Back on *The Drag* the freedmen joined the fray, with many of the poor bastards being almost immediately slain. But they died with honour in their hearts, on their own terms. But one ... one wee lass ... wee scrawny thing, she was. Dressed in rags, not a lick of fat on her, head shaved not half so neatly as it is now..." Cheers, and Levi felt a jolt of recognition, realizing whose story was being told.

Talani raised her tankard with a wan smile but her voice was strong. "Blimey, Abe, I couldn't let those scurvy knaves ruin such an attractive and convenient style for me, now, could I?" and they all laughed, cheered some more.

"Tally the Dread, we ought to have called you, after that day. She cut through the remaining men like taking a sickle to wheat. She can't have eaten in days but she said, *The reaper won't be having me today, so he can take you instead.* And when she was done and the blood and bones of those who had so foully wronged her lay at her feet, what did Tally the Dread do? Only asked if she might have a bath."

Laughter, whooping, the stamping of boots and, under

cover of the frenetic jostle of excited bodies, Levi noticed Vega slipping back up the stairs, weaving through the crowd. She leaned in to drop a kiss on Ezi's cheek and Levi saw her hand drift to where his jerkin was strewn over an empty barrel. It was artfully done; if Levi hadn't been looking out for it he would not have noticed the flash of metal as Vega slipped the key into their father's pocket.

He met his sister's gaze and she nodded tacitly. She had the map.

Levi relaxed somewhat. And as the crew's shared voice rose to fill the sails once more, Levi sang along with them, allowing the familiar tide to wash him towards the shore of his family.

The First Storm

Ata had never felt this way before,
like she was made of mangroves,
like she was forest nectar, roots drinking and thirsty,
giving *lush* to water woods.
She had never felt her veins so crystal glittering,
so wealthy, so mineral rich,
but such hunger.
She licked her fingers and tasted
the memory of him,
the pirate prince,
and again came the yearning,
the fire was burning inside her
and none but he could quench it.

Some storms occurred of their own volition,
others came when she called.
But this time, when the storm arrived,
it rolled in heady and pulsing, enthralled
by the knots at her breast,
the pain at her chest,
the swift sucking
at her surface,
the crackling of

lightning in the air –
it thrilled against her skin.

She broke the surface to watch what she had created.
　　Something was building above her,
　　something fierce and fathomless.
　　She thought of Ezi's stories of storms,
　　outrunning them at sea,
　　dropping anchor and battening down the hatches,
　　yelling into the wind and laughing as
　　it stole the sound.
　　Rainbows broke through before
　　the squall had shrieked itself into exhaustion,
　　sun and rain warred,
　　twisting the sky with dazzling colour,
　　entwining as lovers
　　tangle sheets.
　　Even after millennia,
　　the mermaid was amazed.

His footsteps were all but silent,
　　her storm was so loud
　　and quite suddenly he was there –
　　lightning struck trees and the trees raged back,
　　the rain lashed down
　　filling his ears and nose and mouth,
　　the land raged against itself,
　　and now
　　　that she could see him,

mortal and fragile,
she was afraid.
This fear of what she'd started
only served to whip the winds more harshly,
and she cried out a warning.

It happened then,
the thing she had dreaded,
the magic that was threaded through her
and the land
snapped loose momentarily,
inexact but intentional and untethered,
her river burst its banks
and claimed him.
His eyes never left hers,
brown on molten metal,
the same colour as the charged air that surrounded
them.
He moved against his will and
those legs and feet,
that had seemed so delicate,
were now so stupid, so ineffectual.

She would not allow this.
No one sank beneath her surface
without her permission.
She fought to regain control,
grappled for the threads,
gripped tight to her currents

and pulled, reins on white horses.
They bucked and reared
and she wrestled with them,
throwing her force against them
as she calmed and shushed her mind.

The storm lashed on but the river
    quieted somewhat and she swam
    beneath the surface.
    Where was Ezi?
    Her tail propelled her faster
    than any land legs
    and she saw him, sinking like a stone,
    drifting for her sub-aquatic graveyard,
    coming to rest beside
    the partly devoured corpses
    of the crew he had forsaken.
    She was glad of his closed eyes
    but not ashamed of her
    nature;
    it was her nature that enabled her to save him.
    She lay him on her riverbed,
    sucked in magic and air from the water –
    and pressed her lips to his.
    She loathed the stolen kiss
    but this,
    this transfer of magic and air
    to him felt fair,
    she could not let him die.

The shift she wrought was unexpected,
    even by her immortal standards,
    she felt warm and loose against
    his mouth
    and saw his lungs swell in response
    as his body, so strange,
    began to change
    into something familiar –
    and finally his promise was enacted
    as the pirate prince reacted
    to her magic and
    the River Mumma was alone no more.

He took a breath, he saw her face,
    could breathe and speak in this dappled place,
    he reached for her, surged like a wave
    and the motion of his movement startled him.
    He looked down at where his legs had been,
    gasped bubbles at the flashing blue-green,
    the solid muscle and shimmering scales
    of his new flicking fins and merrow tail.
    His hands found her body,
    he pressed her close,
    he gave her what necessity had bade her
    take –
    their mouths met, parted, shared.
    She shuddered in his embrace,
    he relished in her taste.

And so beneath the surface, loneliness lost,
the mermaid thought of the star that came
to grant her wish, whatever the cost,
she breathed in and out, "Ata is my name."

His landlubber legs seemed so
    slow and clumsy to him now,
and though they returned to him when
    high and dry,
he found himself staying long in
    the River Aphra.
He slipped through ripples,
    supple and smooth,
he rode currents to meet her and
    heard her snaking laugh
    along
    each one
until she was there before him,
    tangling with him.
They explored each other's bodies –
    felt the newness and fell deeper,
    and deeper still,
    a life saved and changed
    through sheer will.
Skin to skin and scale to scale,
    fin to fin and tail to tail,
undulating with each tremulous crest,
the mineral taste of salt on lips and chest,
they delighted in each other.

Found peace beneath their surface,
in rocky coves and shady banks
celebrated in laughter,
crowed their thanks
for what they were together.
But in moments of peace,
a pinprick in the weather –
wind blows one way and cannot last,
we cannot avoid the future or the past,
the scent of lashes, the whistle of whips,
the looming of a long eclipse.

The Third Storm

"Well?" Levi asked. "You did it, right?"

"Do fish pee in the sea?"

"I don't like to think about it, to be honest."

"They do."

"Ugh."

"You swim in fish piss."

"Stop it, Vega."

"Probably fish shit too."

"I said stop!"

She laughed. "You're such a princess!"

They headed belowdeck. The revelry had continued late into the night and they'd had to wait for Ezi, Able and the others to get good and flawed, staggering off to bed, before they could confer.

"Well, our father is a prince," Levi replied.

"Aye, true enough. And one day, so shall you be!"

"I think princess suits me better."

"Well, the pirate princess you'll be. You'll be captain, you can call yourself a pirate *queen* if you like."

Vega slipped inside her bunk, silent-footed, so as not to wake the sleeping Talani, and to retrieve the map from where she'd stashed it. Levi waited for her.

The night wrapped around them, a muffling blanket, the

star-studded sky protecting them and keeping their secrets. Levi could smell a storm in the distance, though as neither Tally nor Vega had warned of it, it likely wouldn't move in until morning. Plenty of time to batten down the hatches.

Vega returned, swinging a lantern in front of her, and they went down another level of stairs, deep into the dark bowels of the ship. They hurried to a corner, nestling themselves among stacks of grain and sitting cross-legged. Vega spread the map before them.

A velvety-black queen stretched from the shadows, green eyes glowing. There were always cats aboard the ship, they kept the rats at bay. She bumped her head against his leg, purring, and then curled in his lap, settling among the folds of the green velvet skirt he was wearing.

Levi's first instinct was disappointment. It looked like an ordinary map, no different from many in Vega and Talani's collection, though old and yellowing. At the centre was the Republic of Sheta Island, shaped like the turtle which had given Sheta Island its name, for Sheta had meant turtle in an ancient, local culture. Peninsulas protruded like flippers, the head was a jutting headland where a dock was marked. It was fairly unremarkable and he was just wondering if it had been worth the stealth and risk of a walloping, when something extraordinary happened.

A soft green glow began to seep across the page in a thin line. Levi's breathing quickened as he looked. It was as if an invisible fingernail traced itself across the inked markings of the sea, forming an X on the parchment. And around it, a shape, unfamiliar and yet unmistakable.

An island.

"Sink me!" he murmured. Levi looked at his sister.

Vega looked at him blankly. "What?" she said.

"What do you mean, 'What'? Look, driftling! X marks the spot!"

But Vega was looking from him to the map in utter confusion. "What do you mean, 'X marks the spot'? What X?"

For a beat they stared at each other, comprehension dawning.

"You can't see it?"

"Can't see what?" She was impatient now and Levi had to swallow a smile. It was rare for him to understand something that Vega didn't.

"The green island that just appeared on the map?"

"What in Davey's name are you on about?"

"It's as though someone's traced the shape of an island in shimmering sea green," he traced his finger over where it appeared, "and then … an X." He ran his finger along it and felt a pulse, a pull. His heart stuttered.

Vega's eyes widened. "Levi. As your older sister and your future navigator, let me make it clear that I will cleave ye if you're running a rig."

"As if I would!" Levi snarled, offended, and pointed again at where the markings continued to glow brightly in the dark, casting a green light across their skin. So strange that Vega couldn't see the way his hand looked as if it was lit from under water.

He looked back at the map.

"An island. Do you think it's… Is it Xaymaca?"

"It has to be. It's too much of a coincidence."

"Pa and Abe and Tally … said there was a key detail missing on the map. Something Pa could see before but can't see now."

"But…" Vega chewed her confusion. "But if the detail is this island, this X … why can you see it and Pa can't?"

"Maybe" – the words came without permission – "maybe it's not for him to see this time."

Levi shook his head trying to clear it but Vega was nodding. "What did Pa say? That he was … *called*. And he didn't believe that someone like Johnson could be. And that it's to do with a *her*, your mother, perhaps… Maybe … maybe if you're really from here … you're being called home."

Levi thought again of the voice lapping at the edges of his dreams, weaving in and out of the slipstreams as he swam.

"But … *this* is my home, Vega." *The Sea Dragon* had always been his home, his world. He felt that too-tight feeling, that sting and itch, as though he wanted to shed his restrictive skin. He wanted to go swimming but he'd never risked the ocean at night and didn't think now, on little sleep, was the time to try it.

Vega interrupted his train of thought. "Will you tell him? Pa, I mean. What you can see on the map?"

Levi exhaled through his nose, rubbed his eyes. "I don't know. Telling him means admitting to eavesdropping and stealing."

His father's words continued to twist in his mind, over and over. *His full potential could damn us all.*

"But not telling him means that he makes port in the Republic, instead of going straight to Xaymaca."

"Maybe I'll talk to him tomorrow. Perhaps this will stop him locking us up like mewling babes."

Vega sighed again but nodded, folding up the map. "If you're sure, then I'll take this and sew it into my jacket. Just in case."

He nodded and stood, stretched. The cat, that he had all but forgotten about, leaped lightly from his lap with a disgruntled meow, but returned to purring as he scooped her up. She could share his bed tonight.

He said goodnight to Vega and headed for his bunk, tucking the queen in beside him, careful not to wake a loudly snoring Abe. He gazed out of the porthole, weary but defiant, daring the night and its secrets, wondering where amid the wash of cobalt and coal was that bright green X made manifest.

As Levi fell asleep, the clouds contended with the stars and the storm rolled in.

> *Too tight and too small,*
> *too quiet, her call,*
> *too far you have roamed,*
> *come home, come home!*
> *She calls to you, so awake!*
> *Leviathan! Hear mortals quake!*
> *Leviathan! The call of fate!*
> *She cannot wait, she cannot wait!*

Something was stirring beneath Levi's skin. Something that was at once bright and dark, hot and cold, burning ice, hoar frost and sea fire, he couldn't move though he thrashed, his skeleton was restrictive, too tight, he would suffocate—

The world is dark and cool,
cool is comforting,
cool is kind,
cool is a caress, is an embrace—

The song of the sea, that ancient, strange – familiar – lullaby was a war drum in his soul, keeping tempo with the deafening thrumming of his heart; it was too loud, the world too full of sound, an assault on all his senses, smashing into his ears, forcing itself down his nose and mouth and throat –

he is up and down
he is lost and found
he is home but far, far away,
floating just out of her reach—

Levi was screaming now, though he could not hear it. Sea fire ignited his world and *The Sea Dragon*, his Drag, the centre of everything, was burning, burning green and vicious blue, the white-hot centre of a driftwood flame—

She cannot wait,
she cannot wait,
she cannot wait!
LEVIATHAN!
LEVIATHAN!
LEVIATHAN!

Levi did not know where or who or what he was. He did not

know if he was dead or alive or something else entirely. He felt everything so intensely that it felt like nothing at all, nothing beyond intense sensation. He was made of so much of his surroundings that he was unable to discern between the thick supple movement of his body and the smooth swift currents that rippled across him. He could not see the shimmering scales of sea fire, nor detect the lava like streams of water that ejected again and again from his hot nostrils or his gaping maw. He could not smell the stench of burned flesh, of singed hair, of death and fear. The world was screaming and heat, the white-hot flame centre of pain, the sharp metallic panic scattered among a thousand different blues. A thousand different views. And his heart, his home, turned to ash.

And then, an anchor. A fixed point – a north star. Amid the chaos – a calm. A solid, glowing, golden strength. He clung to it, steadfast and gentle; it was fragile, he did not want to shatter that piece of peace. That glittering gold.

> *Find the place*
> *where magic does not die*
> *where rainbows fill the sky*
> *where the river bends*
> *where the ocean ends*
> *she cannot wait*
> *she cannot wait*
> *she cannot wait*
> *Leviathan – awake!*

The Prophecy, Revisited

Time passed in its way
    and Ezi's crew enjoyed their stay.
    One sun rose, fell and another
began to swell –
and Ata's stomach did as well.
A child was born.
Ata the mermaid, the River Mumma,
and Ezi the prince, the pirate captain,
were filled with inconceivable joy
by the birth of their baby boy,
who swift displayed remarkable power
within the hour
of his birth.

Ata heard his name,
    felt it sung along currents and
    flow into her mouth –
    Leviathan.

And when she called it,
    filled it with the force of the sea,
    their babe in their arms
    ceased to be;

his dark dimpled flesh
shifted to shining scale and wing,
he twisted and morphed
while lit by a flame
and in that moment
he filled his true name –
Leviathan.

Born of a goddess and a pirate prince,
a union not seen before or since,
what else could he be
but a powerful King of the Sea?
And so splashing in the river,
where mother and father lay,
a baby sea dragon began to play,

The Leviathan's earliest moons
were filled with laughter and love,
until a convergence from above.
A Xaymacan assembly
of Cluster, Coven and Court,
who remembered the prophecy
the Seer of Persea had brought
from the trees.
Said Mmoatia, faerie queen:
"Look, I really don't mean to be mean
but Yvane the Seer has seen what she's seen—
*Nigh is the time of the mermaid's son
Who'll destroy his home…*

Your boy puts us all in danger here."
Said Yvane the Seer,
"What I see is unclear.
We cannot be *sure* there's danger here—"
But Anansi the spider interrupted her gently,
"You saw destruction in his wake,
the risk is too great to take.
River Mumma, great mermaid,
for forgiveness we pray
but we do not think your son can stay."

Ata wanted to squall and shriek,
    she wanted to bring Xaymaca to its knees.
    Millennia and millennia she had served and given
    asking for nothing
    and now she had *something*, something for
    herself,
    they were asking her to give it up.
    Her rage was terrible,
    waves crashed at the bank.
    They shrank back in fear,
    they felt her magic tear
    across their skin,
    stinging with salt and sediment.

But then – a light,
    she found Yaa in sight,
    asked, "Dear friend,
    what answers can you give me?"

Too few, came the reply. *And at once
too many. Endless possibilities.
Pleasure and pain inevitable.*

"Do not make me give up my heart,
  do not ask for this sacrifice,
  do not wish it that we part."

But Yaa said,
  *Do not forget, great mermaid, that I named
  you in love and friendship –
  you are Ata to few but River Mumma to all,
  and you named yourself as such
  in their service.
  You are tasked with the
  protection of this land,
  you are mother to fishes and currents wild.
  You are not simply the mother of this child.*

ALL HALLOWS' EVE

You have always loved the library. It is your safe place, your port in a storm, your door to a thousand different worlds. Five would drop you here when you first started refusing to go to church. It's cool enough to walk and so you follow the footprints of these memories into town, down the high street and across the green, towards Maeve who is standing, waiting for you.

She is wearing a black high-necked tank top, a black miniskirt and black boots. A black rucksack hangs from her shoulder. The outfit casts the red of her hair into sharp relief. Your heart feels quick and light in your chest, a frantic butterfly.

"I like your outfit."

She grins back at you. "Well, it's Halloween and I knew you'd be dressed for the occasion. I couldn't turn up in my yellow sundress, though it's definitely warm enough. Where I'm from, it rains about two hundred days of the year!"

Your eyes widen. "Are you kidding? Two hundred?"

She gestures at her face, her pale skin. "Clearly it's what I'm built for," and you both laugh.

"But your family are from here, right?"

"Sort of. I think we date back a few hundred years. Family legend is that an ancestor was a pirate involved in the Republic, but my family are ... well ... put it this way, my aunt is friends with Chloe's family. Thinks Chloe is a *proper young lady*."

She makes a face that you don't expect, the kind of face people rarely make when talking about Chloe.

You head inside, appreciating her expression as she takes in the rows of books, the round shining of her eyes as she spots the gleaming stained-glass window at the back. The library had been a church before the Republic and, according to Miss Gibbers, it was made a library during the eighteen years without Empire rule. When the Empire reclaimed the island, they had built a new church, believing that the old building had been "defiled by satanic texts".

"Miss Gibbers said that many people wanted the library destroyed, burned or knocked down after the Republic fell," Maeve murmurs. Her voice is reverent, awed.

"Must be Nubia's wrath, keeping it standing." You wiggle your brows at Maeve but you're a little bit serious. Everyone on Sheta Island is a little bit serious when talking about Nubia.

Vega, the librarian, is stalking towards you. "Well, now, Reggie. Is it a trick or treat you've brought me this All Hallows' Eve?"

She is smiling, arms filled with books. The rich gold of her skin is as smooth and shiny as the varnished shelves, her vivid violet and vermillion two-piece complement the red of her hair. You blush. You have loved her all your life. From picture books to *Paradise Lost*. As you grew through children's literature and graduated to YA and classics, your love grew to lust which grew again, sometime around bell hooks, to a kind of coveting. Now she is simply everything you want to be when you grow up.

She puts the books down on her desk and pats your face gently. You grin. "Vega, you see through tricks like glass, I wouldn't be stupid enough."

Maeve is still staring at the grandeur of the building but eventually holds out her hand. "Hi, I'm Maeve O'Neill."

Vega shakes it. "Quite the collection we have here, no?"

Maeve nods keenly. "It's a huge library for such a small island."

Vega smiles. "It's my pride and joy."

"How long have you worked here?"

"Erm." Vega purses her lips in thought. "About sixteen years or so?"

Maeve blinks. "Wow. You don't look old enough!"

Vega grins, eyes flashing gold. "Oh, I'm at least three hundred, I just have good genes."

Maeve laughs.

"So what can I help you both with, or are you just browsing?"

You explain the school project. Vega listens with interest. "So that's why Anna Gibbers took out a copy of *The Republic of Sheta Island*. I always liked her. She gets it – what history really is, a weighing up of different opinions. Not just the story of whoever is in power."

Maeve nods. "History is written by the victors."

"Yes," Vega agrees. "But it's more than that. What is and isn't history is *defined* by the victors. Somehow, on this island, there has still been resistance. Even the most devoted church goers tell their children stories of witches and pirates."

You snort. "Yes, as examples of how the devil works. They even say the fall of the Republic happened because the town was destroyed by a sea dragon! I mean that's some seriously Old Testament shit, Vega."

Vega laughs. "So what you're *asking* is – *to what extent has*

Sheta Island's relationship with religion revised its history? That is an excellent line of enquiry. Very nuanced and complex."

"Is it?" You fight the urge to roll your eyes. "Or did Sheta Island go the same way as a lot of the islands and fall to the Empire's gorgeous colonial combo of slavery, religious zealousness and money?"

Vega shakes her head, her eyes taking in the layers of knowledge that surround you. "This place is different. It has lived a long time balancing its two truths, its two identities, Republic and Empire, home of pirates and naval officers. Magic and religion. For centuries the church here has preached the hell fire and brimstone of the Republic ... but wouldn't dare attempt to cut down Nubia's manchineel tree. Who would risk the witch's wrath, after all?"

"Right." Maeve claps her hands excitedly. "Vega, we might steal your question if you don't mind? *To what extent has Sheta Island's relationship with religion revised its history?* Where should we start?"

"Well, all of the copies of *The Republic of Sheta Island* are out on loan – with your classmates, I assume." She pauses. "I do have my own well-thumbed copy at home, though. I can bring it for you—" A wry smile. "I must warn you both, my books are my babies. I will be trusting you with my baby. Please don't lose it."

You and Maeve assure her wholeheartedly.

"I suggest you start with the navy's version of things, and work backwards. It's easier to know what you're missing when you know what you have. First floor, third section on the right."

*

You and Maeve sort through old naval logbooks, adding to the timeline you started in class and making notes of anything else that might be useful. Maeve writes Miss Gibbers' instructions on a sticky note: *Informed deductions. What happened in those eighteen years? How did the Republic rise and fall? Who were the key players? Rigorous research… Well-reasoned arguments … unique thought processes.* You like that she does this, her shameless diligence twitching your lips. She smiles sheepishly. "Sorry." And then, by way of an explanation: "Aquarius moon. Virgo rising."

You raise your eyebrows. "So you're an avoidant control freak?"

You worry momentarily that this will sound harsh, but Maeve laughs. "Yes, but my sun is in Cancer so if anyone other than a Scorpio called me an avoidant control freak, I'd probably cry."

"How do you know I'm a Scorpio?"

She blinks at you, surprised. "It was your birthday on Monday."

You'd forgotten. "Oh, yeah." You realize this probably sounds a bit sad, so you hastily add, "Well, yeah. Scorpio. Aries Moon. Capricorn rising."

It's Maeve's turn to raise her eyebrows. "Damn. So your whole aloof bitch who's so above it all thing isn't an act?"

Your laugh is breathy with surprise. "Savage."

Her eyes sparkle. "Virgo and Capricorn rising, though? We're literally going to come top of the class."

"I mean, I didn't need our birth charts to know that."

It is the nicest afternoon you've had in years.

At nine o'clock Vega calls up for closing. You head downstairs and squeeze her goodbye. She hugs Maeve too and Maeve looks delighted.

The streets are still busy, the lamps lit, the town flickers with orange. All Hallows' Eve is taken very seriously on Sheta Island. Every year a carnival of sorts takes place. The streets are full of people in costumes, lit jack o' lanterns adorn every corner and shops stay open late, hosting revellers in a variety of events from apple bobbing to Make Your Poison workshops (cocktail-making classes). Five hates All Hallows' Eve. He always refused to take you when you were little and you couldn't go alone. And then you'd grown up and had no friends to go with. But now…

"Do you … want to look around for a bit?" you ask tentatively. Maeve smiles, nods.

"Be right back," she says. She vanishes into the crowd and after a minute or two of waiting you wonder if she's made a run for it. But as the thought forms, Maeve returns, with two toffee apples and two hot spiced ciders.

"Happy birthday, Reggie. For Monday, I mean."

"I hope it's not poisoned," you quip, but you honestly think it's the best birthday present you've ever had.

She hunches over, her voice husky. "A sweet red apple … just one bite for the princess…"

You give a shout of laughter. You think about the Maeve you see in class, quiet in her corner. She's comfortable enough with you that she's coming out of her shell. This warms you more than the cider.

You loop round the green, chatting about everything and nothing, taking in the evening activity, until you are back at

141

the library, the darkest point in town. The lights in the church opposite are out. The green of the grass that stretches between the two buildings is black with shadows, a no man's land between two opposing forces.

"So this is where they say the witch Nubia burned?" Maeve asks.

"Yep. Burned at the stake outside the church that's now the library." Feeling suddenly daring, you say, "Do you want to see the exact spot? The manchineel tree?"

Maeve bites her lip, then nods.

You cross the green.

The shadows envelop you, inviting you in. Your head has started to ache, probably the alcohol and sugar, but you ignore it, distracted by the feel of Maeve next to you in the whispering dark.

The tree is broad and defiant. A ring fence to protect it.

"I feel like … like the other trees are watching us," she breathes.

You look up at the palm trees towering over you and snicker. "Like disapproving aunts, with their big coconut cleavages."

The shared laugh makes you giddy. It invites transgression as you lie down on the grass beside the DANGER and WARNING signs.

"Manchineel trees are the most poisonous in the world," you tell her. "From fruit to bark, like, just lethal all round. I've always been surprised that it doesn't get cut down."

Maeve shakes her head as she lies down next to you. "I mean, who would dare? Where I come from, we have faery trees. Hawthorn or ash. It's considered dreadful bad luck to disturb

one, or cut one down. It's not that everyone believes in faeries, but sure, why would you risk it?"

Her tone is so serious, her eyes wide, glowing in the dark, and you feel something catch inside you.

You smile at her. "Right enough. Why indeed?"

The silence lengthens. You're aware of the way her freckles have become tiny shadows.

The moment is shattered by a cry of "Well, well, where else would we find a witchy weirdo on Halloween?"

Chloe is dressed in a white mini skirt with a floaty white tank top, white feathered wings and a halo. It's so ironic it's not even clever. Grace is dressed as a cat because ... well, of course.

"Reggie, you don't help yourself, you know. Everyone in our year is dressed up enjoying the carnival, and you're lurking outside the library under the poison tree like some Tumblr goth."

"At least you wore a costume," Grace smirks. "Oh ... wait."

They both laugh. You sigh, getting to your feet. "Can we help you, Chloe?"

Chloe turns to assess Maeve, who is straightening up, brushing grass off her skirt.

"The poor new girl. Maeve clearly doesn't know what a loser you are, Reggie, or she would have asked Miss Gibbers to work on the project alone."

Maeve stares at the grass. It's a bit disappointing, if you're honest.

"Yeah, Maeve, why don't you join us for the rest of the evening?" Grace gestures to the group. "We're going for prinx – pre-drinks" – she explains it as though she personally coined the

stupid portmanteau – "and then back to mine for a party. It'll be fun! Plus, Adrien has a thing for redheads."

More titters. Adrien Samuels, the devil on Chloe's left, raises his mask and pushes his floppy blond hair out of his eyes in a way that's probably supposed to make you swoon but actually just makes you queasy. "That is true. I do."

You all look at Maeve. Maeve looks panicked. Eventually, she mutters something about having to get home because her aunt will be expecting her.

"No worries," Adrien says smoothly. "But can I have your number? For another night?" He is holding out his phone to her.

A pause that is, frankly, painful.

And then – she takes it. Even in the gloom you can see that she is bright red in the face, but as she types her number into his phone, she sort of smiles.

You feel a bit sick. The pounding in your head is enough now that you place a hand to your temple.

Maeve is handing Adrien's phone back but she looks at you with concern. "Are you all right?" she asks.

You don't want her concern. You understand avoiding conflict but you see Adrien's smug smile in your peripheral vision, and take a step back.

"I'm fine." Your voice is curt, even as your vision suddenly starts to blacken at the edges. "This lot and their bullshit give me a migraine."

Chloe's laugh is too loud, too delightedly contemptuous. "You always were such a drama queen, horny vag."

You can't even think of a stinging retort because you can feel your knees weakening, your legs are about to give out and

you don't want to faint in front of them. What is going on? It's come on so quickly, you don't even have any painkillers on you. You stagger, your hearing is strange, muffled, a ringing, a singing? Who's singing—

> *There's a brown girl in the ring*
> *Tralalalala*
> *There's a brown girl in the ring*
> *Traaalalalalala*

You think they're laughing but you're not sure. You think you can hear Maeve calling your name, but you're not sure. You stagger again, your body arcs and twists and you are powerless to stop yourself.

You crash through the barrier around the manchineel tree, your hands splaying against the bark. Something firm and fierce grips your hands, seizes them with the force of a white-hot light. You close your eyes against its retina-burning power, and you sag where you are, slumped against the tree, knees in the grass, nose centimetres from its root, your hands still pressed to the tree.

> *Brown girl in the ring*
> *Tralalalala*
> *She looks like the sugar in the plum*

You can hear screams and yells, they may be your own, you are not sure because you are rising up and away. You are thin and far apart, you are the poisoned sap, you are the bright light.

Someone, somewhere, is calling your name.

Hello, Defiant Child. It has been a long time since I have seen one like you.

The voice is musical and quiet, so quiet you almost can't hear it because someone, somewhere, is calling your name—

You are to seek and *to see, it seems. It is time to go home, Defiant Child.*

Someone, somewhere, is calling your name.

The quiet, musical voice fades.

You become aware of your surroundings. Maeve crouched on the floor next to you. Chloe and Grace a little way off, torn along the line of how much they care and the drama.

"Reggie? Reggie!"

You gasp and return to yourself. "I'm sorry," you pant. "I'm fine. It must have been the cider."

"It's OK, don't apologize. Are you all right?"

You are dazed and suddenly exhausted. You are confused and sweating but can feel a chill creeping up your extremities. Your jaw is involuntarily chattering.

"We should take you to the hospital," Maeve says, holding out her hand. But you are staring at your own, looking at where your palms touched the poison tree. They should be blistering, weeping, torn by the toxic sap. But they're fine. You don't understand.

You get slowly and wearily to your feet. The night is coming into sharp relief around you. "I don't need a hospital."

The revellers are rowdier than when you first left the library. People have moved on from hot apple cider. You check your watch. You just want to be in bed with Bast.

"I'm going home."

"Let me come with you!" Maeve moves after you. "Make sure you're al—"

"No." You bite out the word. "I'm fine." You are remembering how she didn't stick up for you in front of Chloe, her smile when she gave Adrien her number. You know you are probably being unfair but you don't care.

"Such an attention seeker," you hear Grace mutter, as you stalk past, willing your legs not to wobble.

"See, I told you, Maeve," you hear Chloe say. "You should hang out with us. She's so weird."

Maeve says nothing. Your feet pound the familiar pavement, unfeeling and cold, marking the steps away from her.

The Second Storm

Ezi is running,
he's calling her name,
he should be more careful with it,
but he isn't to blame –
he's afraid.
He smelled change on the breeze,
felt a storm in the air
and knew something was wrong.
And so Ezi is running to find his love.

He slips into her waters and shifts,
only in *her* water can he do this,
he calls her name, he calls for his son,
they are in his arms, for a moment,
just one,
he holds them close.
And she shares what she has heard.

Ata is serious as she touches his face.
"You must leave this place,"
she whispers.
"While our son is here, he will never know peace,
the people of this land fear him."

"This prophecy would seek to separate you from your
        child!
This prophecy would force you to choose between
        two parts of yourself!"
"I am the River Mumma first, Ata second, Ezi."
"No! You were Ata first! You are both!"
"I exist to serve Xaymaca."
She thought of Yaa, of her bright-white light
and hated her for being right.
"I cannot defy my nature, Ezi."
"Bullshit! I have defied mine!"
Before her he was bare-chested and tailed –
he was so changed. For her.
"And you should not have had to.
The gulf between us is too great.
You are mortal and human and your life
will be over in a blink of my eyes."
"Then do not blink!" He reaches for her.
"Keep your eyes open. Do not look away from me.
We are meant to be together,
I swore to stay, I swore to for ever."

The old burning is barely a sputter,
        a candle in a guttering wind
        next to this vicious injustice,
        this shredding ache,
        oh, she had not known her heart
        could break!

She presses her son to her chest,
    inhales his scent.
    Etches each dimple into her mind,
    each eyelash –
    then a flash –
    he shifts and she repeats.
    Each scale, each nail, each kink in his tail –
    his tiny huffing snout,
    his eyes dart about – and meet hers.

She passes Ezi their baby.

Her chest is heaving,
    her heart is cleaving,
    the air is grieving –
    their son is crying, grabbing,
    reaching for his mother.
    The River Mumma reaches for Ezi.
    Their lips meet, their breath is sweet,
    she does not wish to sour it with words.
    So she simply says,
    "Go quickly. My soul howls and the skies will open.
    Go while I am still in control."
    Ezi leaves his lover
    and their shared tears salt the river.

He returns to the beach, the white sandy shore
    that had tossed him out all of those moons before.
    He is so changed.

He feels the charge as he breathes and picks up
    speed,
        giving orders to cast off. The loyal crew spring into
            action
        immediately.
        New horizons. New adventures. New undiscovered
            corners.
        The wind wails and howls and Ezi chokes back
        an answering cry; his crew all understand why
        but simply ask,
        "Will we outrun the storm, Captain?"
        Ezi nods curtly. He wishes the
        storm would catch them,
        would smash them against the rocks,
        would take away the choice he
        had not even been able to make.
        His son cannot stay with his mother,
        his son is the reason he'd lost his lover –
        he is wretched.

The sails are full, he holds his son close,
        he would not let him become a danger,
        then one day they might return,
        Ata would not be a stranger,
        he would be again a balm to her burn,
        he would keep their son tame,
        he would dampen his flame,
        he would keep him safe,
        he would quell his name.

And where the mouth of the Aphra
    opens in a scream,
    a keening mermaid could be seen,
    watching the black sails shrink and shrink.
    The thunder claps –
    Ata does not blink.
    The storm gathers as she tears at her hair,
    a lightning flash – and they are no longer there.

Part two

Starboard

The Republic of Sheta Island

The first thing that Levi was aware of was how dry his skin felt. Flayed and raw and itching.

He swallowed and came up panting and thirsty. Shards of glass behind his eyelids. Warm, buttery light temporarily blinding him as he moved to sit up.

First the familiar smell of salt and horizon mingled with new scents, fish and fragrant cooking spices barely overlaying the too ripe people smell, bodies and waste and sweat. Then the sand beneath him, soft but harsh against his sensitive skin, and the steadiness of the ground, so different from the worn rocking wood of *The Sea Dragon*.

Next, the sounds – imperious shouts in unfamiliar voices, hammering and creaking, and the mournful cries of many gully-birds. Neither Levi, nor his father, liked gully-birds. They were said to carry the souls of dead sailors and cry with their grief and regret. And indeed, their frantic *aeh aeh aeh* set something cold and dark descending over Levi, like a kind of dread.

He forced himself more fully upright, dragging his eyes open, and noticing he was naked save for a cloth around his middle. Gentle but firm hands held him.

"Easy." Vega's voice.

Levi looked around, his eyes growing accustomed to the light. He was sitting in the entrance of a sort of cave, the cool grey stone sheltering him from the blistering sun.

His eyes found Vega's. And again that cold, dark dread sluiced over him. Her face was wan and waxy. She had dark circles under her eyes. The edges of her mouth were pinched, restraining some unknown emotion, and her shine, her star-bright glow, had gone out entirely.

"Vega?" His voice was hoarse and cracked. His gaze *flick flick flicked* over her face again. *Aeh aeh aeh*, cried the gully-birds.

She was wearing what he had last seen her in, her shirt and trousers, but they were torn, tattered and even in some places *scorched*. She was sitting on, he realized, his own black-and-gold damask coat, the one that she had been stitching.

"Vega, where are we? What happened?"

For a long time she just looked at him. Long enough for Levi to see silver replace the gold in her eyes.

"There was a storm," she whispered. And her mouth loosened and opened in anguish.

Levi watched her as she gripped his arms before collapsing, breathing great, shaking gulps.

"What can you remember?"

Levi's seeking soul strained against the memories, but they were weighty, dragging him back. He remembered screaming and splintering and the smell of burning flesh. His mind recoiled.

"I was asleep." His voice was shaking. "I was sleeping, dreaming, having more strange dreams and then…" His voice

quailed to a whisper. "Was there a fire? What happened? Where's Pa?"

She dragged her eyes to meet his. He hated what he read in them.

"You have to know," she began. "It is not your fault."

"Tell me," he choked. An iron hand had his throat in a vice-like grip and was squeezing tighter and tighter, but he said it again, "Tell me, Vega."

And so she did.

"I was in my cabin, finishing the sewing. A storm blew in, so quickly, as if out of nowhere. It raged outside but it felt … I don't know. Something was wrong. Normally I feel peaceful at night, even during storms, but my skin prickled. Like the stars were warning me. Then I smelled smoke, like burning but that felt wrong too. I woke Tally and she said we should rouse the others and head on deck but when we opened our door there was smoke everywhere. And there was fire racing down the passage from your cabin. It wasn't ordinary fire, Levi, it was blue and green and white and silver and so bright it hurt my eyes. I could hear you screaming and calling out. I wanted to go to you but Tally told me to run for Pa so I did… She headed towards your cabin, calling for Abe.

"I got to Pa's cabin and banged on his door but he was already up and…" She was fighting to speak now, tears tracking down her cheeks, but she pushed on. "And he said, 'I should have known better, driftling, I should have known better than lies and shame. *I did not prepare him with this name.* I should have known better,' he kept saying. And then he said, '*He will never be lost with you, Vega, you're the future, you're his North*

Star.' Then he ran towards you, towards your cabin and the fire."

She was trembling so hard Levi could barely hold her. "There was a blast – heat and sound and strange fire, it swallowed everything. I saw our world explode. I saw Abe and Tally and Pa … and Pa … and Pa—" Her cry bounced off the walls of the cave. And the gully-birds cried with her.

It's not your fault.

Eventually Vega spoke again. "I was lucky. I did not burn. I hurled myself into the sea and found some of the wreckage to stay afloat. Driftling by name…" She hiccupped. "And that's when I saw … rising up out of the water. Myth and legend made flesh. Twice the size of *The Drag*, covered in shining blue and green scales – and that strange fire. A snout like a sea horse snorting steam and hot water, with vast wings. A sea dragon. A real one. It was you, Levi."

No.

He scrabbled away from her, shaking his head, denial ringing his ears. *No no no no no.*

"It can't have been me, Vega."

"Levi—"

"No, Vega, *it can't have been me!*" He closed his eyes. He could not look at her. "*It can't be, it can't be, it can't be,*" he intoned over and over again.

She reached for his hand and gripped so tightly that he could not let go. "You're my brother. I always know that it's you, remember?"

Levi didn't reply. He would not accept it, he would not hear what she was telling him. He was hunched on his knees now, chanting still: *It can't be, it can't be, it can't be…*

"You were thrashing around. I could tell you were scared. I called to you – and you went still. Like you were waiting for me to tell you what to do." Vega hiccupped again, half-hysterical. "I knew we weren't far from the Republic." Her voice broke. "The stars sang and I followed and you followed me. I paddled on my driftwood to the nearest shore. As soon as we were on land, you turned back into … into yourself."

He shook his head again, shook it hard as if to shake himself, to rattle the world until the pieces of his life fell back into place. He tried to breathe but the air was dense and heavy. He thought that if he unclenched his teeth, his fists, he would come undone entirely, he would scream until he ripped apart, until he burst from his skin, until he burned and burned…

A sudden acute fear of himself gripped his innards tightly, digging fingernails into every soft weeping place, forcing pained restraint. But he could not stop the muffled keening, it came from a deep place that could not be silenced.

Vega's face was twisted, her eyes closed. Levi knew that they were all filling her mind, Cook and Davies and the vessel herself, the proud *Sea Dragon*…

And Able and Talani and Pa. Their pa. Ezi, prince of the pirates, survivor of a hundred wars and raids, never beaten, never defeated.

All of them, everyone they had ever loved, their crew, their family, their home.

Gone.

There were no words for a long time after that.

Eventually, Vega got stiffly to her feet, and stood framed in the entrance to the cave, staring out at the sea and sky. The first stars would start to appear soon.

Levi raised his head from where he lay curled like a child. "Vega? Is this the Republic?"

She nodded. He closed his eyes.

Despite his years of trepidation, the last course Captain Ezi had set was for Sheta Island. Stories about this land were as much a part of their childhood as shells are a part of the turtles who bear them, carrying *home* upon their back. Levi remembered lying in his bunk with Vega and whispering excitedly of the land where all those who shared the spirit of adventure lived freely and equally.

They had imagined docking *The Sea Dragon* and swaggering ashore, dressed in their finery, cutlasses sharpened to deadly points. Levi would wear a black skirt that billowed and ruffled with his linen shirt and matching linen petticoat. He would wear his black-and-gold damask, and a jewelled pendant around his neck, and hoops in his ears and a tricorne to match his father's – but the finery wouldn't weigh him down – oh no! – because he was Levi, son of Ezi the pirate prince, and was swifter and stronger than any that dared to challenge him.

Loss speared him again.

It's not your fault.

Levi realized that it was the first time that his sister had lied to him.

Vega was unpicking her stitching on the hems of the

damask jacket. She had crammed more jewels and gold coins in there than he had realized. Tally had told her to do that. Tally, like the rest of the crew, had spent her life teaching them, giving them useful advice, sharing lessons from decades of stories. But Tally was gone and there was no one left to guide them.

"We should probably find somewhere else to sleep. An inn or something," Vega suggested.

Levi shook his head, fear gripping him. What if he transformed again? Hurt more people? "I want to stay here."

She looked, for a moment, like she might argue, then she nodded and said, "I'll get us some things. Food and ale. I found somewhere while you were... And you need clothes. Shirt and skirts and boots and—"

"No!" Levi said it quickly, his eyes flying open. "No skirts. Just ... just a shirt and pants."

He could not bear the thought of feeling so like ... like himself. She scrutinized him and then nodded, gathering some coins into her pocket, pulling her boots on. Before she left, she reached her hand out. "Here. I sewed this into my jacket after we looked at it yesterday. It's a wonder it didn't get wet. It really must be magic."

It was the map. Even with the awkward angle, he could see the glowing sea-green of the markings. The far-off island, marked by an X.

He felt as though years had passed since he and Vega had sat against the stores and ballast, whispering secrets in the crannies of *The Drag*, as they had done so many times throughout their lives. Levi thought of the cat, her small warm

161

purring body curled up beside him. Had her death been quick, lying beside him as he'd become a human inferno? Had any of theirs? Fresh guilt and horror washed over him. He retched but his stomach was empty. He crouched there for a long time, heaving into the sand.

*

Over the next few days, time was warped and strange. Neither of them slept much, drifting into a fitful doze before waking with starts. The cave was, according to Vega, beside the docks and beneath stalls where vendors bartered, and an inn where people drank and sang and laughed.

How could it be that life continued?

Around them the sea flickered blue to black and on some nights even glowed as though lit from beneath. Each time he saw this, the fingers of fear gripped Levi tighter, squeezing until he could not breathe. He did not understand what had caused the initial transformation and he could not think through the haze of smoke and loss to speculate. The faces of his family loomed before him, the twisting serpents returning to writhe their words through his mind.

I want to protect the world from him… His full potential could well damn us all.

That was what his father had said. And now he knew why.

The gully-birds wailed on.

After the first few days, Vega began fighting forward again, finding structure and routine. She sold one of the jewels she had sewn into the damask, a gold necklace inlaid with rubies,

hung fat and glistening like drops of blood. With several coin purses full and clinking she had immediately bought a knife and returned to the beach, glancing over her shoulder. But stealing on the Republic was rare enough, despite being inhabited by pirates – on Sheta Island no one went without, so no one need take what wasn't theirs. She would wake early to go to the docks to buy them breakfast and would spend a few hours lingering around shops and inns, scooping for scuttle.

She did not cry in front of Levi as he sat and stared at the sea in silence, barely eating or drinking.

On their fifth day, however, Levi was skimming stones, keeping out of sight of the main docks, when he heard a *gasp hic gasp*. He turned a corner formed by heaped rocks and saw Vega with her head bowed. He felt worse than ever then. She was grieving because of him, hiding that grief because of him, was sleeping in a cave because he was a risk to others. He was the cause of her suffering.

There was talk of Johnson's voyage at every watering hole. Vega told her brother of experiencing the strange frequency phenomenon; it was disconcerting having never heard the name *Xaymaca* before a few days ago, to land on the Republic and discover that the story of the magical island visited thus far only by *The Sea Dragon* was ubiquitous.

"Their greatest adventure," Vega said, passing her brother a warm wrapped bundle. The afternoon sun had already begun its protracted departure and Levi had not eaten all day but he didn't move to take a bite, despite the tempting aromas. "The thing they're famed for here. No wonder P— they kept us from this place. We'd have found out about Xaymaca in a heartbeat."

Speaking Ezi's name might one day be possible, but *Pa* was too sorrowful an epithet, too close to a gasp of pain to be said aloud.

"Is that why he kept us from here? Or was it because he feared that one day I'd turn into a dirty great monster and destroy it?"

"What happened wasn't your fault, Levi."

"Then whose fault was it, Vega?" His voice was dull and hollow.

Vega did not answer immediately. She dug a small well in the sand and bit the cork off an ale bottle, securing it before taking a bite of warm fresh bread, a generous slab of cheese, some slices of salted meat.

"I don't think seeking blame is helpful. What good does it do when your intent was never to hurt anybody? Point a finger forward, hatchling. Not at yourself. Or to the past."

"Forward where?"

"Well … where do we go from here?"

Levi looked at her. Looked past her. It required monumental effort – grief was a millstone round his neck, dragging his gaze down and in and back. But for her he tried.

"He – they – the crew … wanted to keep us … me … from Xaymaca. And we don't know why. But we also know that they set course for here, that they were suspicious about Johnson's journey and his intentions."

"Well, they were suspicious before, but whatever the scout said made them damn near certain that something was amiss."

Levi thought back over what he'd overheard, beneath the cabin. He found that if he focused on the facts, the specifics of what he could remember, the sharp impact was lessened.

"*Bewitch a witch, entangle the spider...* And there was something about ... about faeries."

"Aye, the scout said, *free the faeries*, or something? Didn't he? Maybe the faeries are in danger?"

"No, the scout said Johnson *wanted* to free the faeries—"

"Did he? But why would that be a bad thing?"

"Damned if I know." Levi paused, stretching, reaching for his thoughts and then stopped abruptly at the expression on Vega's face. "Erm – they mentioned letters from someone on the Republic called Marianne. We should find out who she is. There was another name too, someone they didn't trust, someone on Xaymaca they thought was allied with Johnson, *pulling the strings...* I think it was another M, but..." Levi shook his head regretfully. "No. It's gone."

Vega tore off a mouthful of bread, washing it down with a gulp of ale. "Well, Johnson plans to sail in two moons, he's waiting on supplies and seeing about gathering buccaneers from other crews."

"Who told you that?"

"Emabelle, the innkeeper in the Freeman's," and when Levi looked at her blankly, she explained. "The inn I've been visiting. It's the busiest, the best for scuttlebutt."

It was strange. In the space of a few days, Vega had familiarized herself with much of this town. Guilt and shame swelled again, accompanied by loneliness. There had never been a place or person that Vega had known that he hadn't also known. It was strange, being still on land for so long. He missed *The Drag.* He missed freedom and sword practice and shirking chores to swim. He missed his pa. His eyes stung but he stared

through the hazing of his vision, out to the horizon. Breathed. If Ezi were here, what would he do?

"Hatchling?"

Levi jolted out of his reverie. "If Johnson sails, my … my mother might be in danger."

"Aye."

Beat. Another fractured piece. *His mother.* The many things to be considered hung in the air around them. Levi could almost see them, interweaving threads of life and story. Impulsively, he tore off a piece of bread, a piece of cheese, a piece of meat and made a little pile in his hand before pushing it into his mouth. He still had no appetite but he thought he might be able to swallow whatever he was feeling along with it.

"Before … the last thing *he* said to you … was something about names?"

"I did not prepare him with this name."

Levi took a breath. "Remember I said I'd been having strange dreams?" Vega nodded. "Well, in those dreams I could hear something, a singing, a weird water song. I felt I knew it but couldn't remember how or where from." Levi swallowed. "I think it might have been my mother. Calling me somehow."

"Your mother? But how?"

"I don't know. But I think … given what's happened, we can probably assume that she isn't … human."

Vega rolled her eyes. "Sink me, do you really think?" Levi's mouth twitched. She almost sounded like her old self. "What did she say? Can you remember?"

"Not really. Bits … water riddles and current whispers and talk of … of a home. But there's something else. The voice

kept calling out a word, a name. Vega, we never thought that Levi might be short for something but … the voice, it called me *Leviathan*."

Maybe it was because Levi had braced himself this time, or because he harnessed the word as it wrapped around his tongue, or maybe it was because he was so spent and depleted that anything more than a juddering beneath his skin was impossible, but the worst did not happen. And then Vega gasped. Looking down at his hands he saw thin, wispy tendrils of smoke rising off his body and a faint flickering of blue-green sea fire.

"Did you see that?"

"Aye."

A beat. Levi stared at his skin, ran his fingers along his arms. But they remained the same, ordinary. Dark skin, smooth, shining in the sun, flecked with sand.

"What was it?"

"I think it was what happened before only I haven't the strength to fully … change."

Beat.

"Do you think … do you think that's your … real name?"

"Aye," Levi answered from a place of truth that went beyond a conscious decision to reply. "When I hear it, something happens. I feel … like I might burst out of my skin or something. But I don't know what it means."

"Perhaps your name is the trigger for the transformation? Do you feel that feeling at any other times?"

Levi strained to think. He had been so drained the last few days, so numb, that he had barely felt anything at all. He thought back further.

"Before … before that night, I'd felt something like it. But quieter, softer. And her voice, the singing, that was quieter too. But then that night, the night of my birthday…"

Another piece of the conversation that changed everything came back to him.

"In the cabin, they spoke about my birthday. My age and some tradition. Maybe … maybe on Xaymaca, something happens when you turn six-and-ten. Something that, when combined with my name…"

It is not just that I want to protect him from the world. I want to protect the world from him.

Vega sighed, thoughtful. "I wonder if there's anything been written about Xaymaca at all. There's a library here, you know. Well, it was a church. Remember the crew told us that the old church was used for storing books and logs when the Republic formed?"

Levi remembered. "Aye. The one with Nubia's tree outside it?" The crew had told them this at least; the story of how the witch Nubia's defiance as she burned at the stake had created a surge of rebellious power. As her allies among the pirates had fought off the naval men of the Empire, her body had become a tree that still burned with her rage.

"The manchineel tree." Vega nodded. "There's a fence around it. It's fierce poisonous. We should take a look at it."

Levi knew he couldn't avoid the Republic for ever. His father had a plan – a plan he could no longer carry out – but he was still their captain. He had told Tally and Abe that *The Sea Dragon* could no longer shirk its duty. Levi would not shirk it now. But uncertainty lay ahead. He stared at his hands, his

arms. His skin remained comfortingly brown but his body felt foreign and unpredictable. He looked up at Vega. She glowed faintly gold in the setting sun. She hadn't glowed in days but now, with something like a next step, she seemed almost herself again. Almost.

"I'm scared," Levi murmured.

Vega opened her mouth to reply but another voice spoke from directly behind them. "Fear won't make you feel more in control. Knowledge will, though."

They spun round to see the outline of a person standing before them in the dying light.

FACT AND FICTION

Someone, somewhere far away,
is calling out your name.
Whispering leaves, beckoning song,
aren't you glad you came?
Shimmer silver, gold and blues,
chart the course and check the cost,
find the tree and share its power.
They know you're hurt, they know you're lost,
find the star that once did roam.
Shimmer silver, gold and home…

There's a brown girl in the ring
Tralalala…

You are grateful for the half-term break. You spend your mornings with Bast and your afternoons with Maeve. After the incident under the manchineel tree at Halloween, your stomach is leaden at the thought of seeing her. You're not sure how to vocalize the feeling of betrayal, not sure if you even have a right to feel that way at all. You've not known Maeve for very long; it's understandable that she wanted to avoid conflict with Chloe. Everyone wants to avoid conflict with Chloe.

Perhaps that's why you immediately accept her hastily

mumbled apology, cutting off her explanation ("I'm not good at conflict, I'm working on it, I—") with a swift "Seriously, don't worry about it, I'm used to it, seriously, it's fine."

The beat that follows is awkward and you search for a way to dissipate it. This new friendship is an early-blooming thing, you don't want it to wilt under Chloe's malicious glare.

"Did you ... did you get home all right?"

Maeve nods, still looking worried. "Did you?" and then more hasty tripping words: "Were you OK? I'm sorry, I should have gone after you, you touched the tree and collapsed and I was worried but—"

You cut her off again. "I'm honestly fine, Maeve. Promise. I touched a poisonous tree, I fainted, I went home and took some painkillers and went to bed. No big deal." And when the pinch of her brow does not release, you insist harder, "I'm *fine*." You almost believe yourself. But suspicion has twined at the corner of your mind, creeping dark tendrils connecting what happened with the tree to your recent strange dreams and the song stirring your blood. You push the thought aside.

"Come on, let's get a basic pumpkin-flavoured something before we start." Maeve smiles her acquiescence and you are relieved.

The library, as ever, is your haven. You walk there after lunch every day. It is autumn now, and though the temperature only drops by one or two degrees, you enjoy the fresh briskness of the wind off the sea, stirring up the resinous scent of peat and earth.

You and Maeve work well together. You fall into an easy rhythm. She is quick and sharp but sweet like the tonic wine you

steal from your dad and you're angry at yourself for not trying to make friends with her sooner. You say as much but she brushes it off. "There's nothing wrong with liking your own company. I've envied that about you, to be honest."

You're sitting at your usual corner table, books spread out before you, next to the two pumpkin-spiced lattes that it is absolutely too hot for but Maeve insisted you try. It's nice. You've never had coffee with anyone.

"Really? I didn't think you'd even noticed me."

She laughs. "Of course I've noticed you. You're hard not to notice."

You're perplexed. "How do you mean?"

"Well, for one thing, you give off this totally unbothered, brooding, rich interior life thing. It's sort of ... well, I'm kind of in awe."

"You're ... in awe of me?"

She is getting flustered. "Yes, I mean like the way you are with Chloe. You're not bothered by all of her nastiness, all that repressed sexuality, jealousy and insecurity."

You blink. "Repressed sexuality?"

"Obviously."

"How do you mean?"

Maeve sighs. "Look, I'm new here. So there's a lot of context I don't have. But I've heard the rumours and Chloe targets you for a reason. With stuff like this it's normally jealousy. She's the pastor's daughter, she has all this pressure to be a certain way and clearly that way does not involve kissing girls. And then there's you, and I mean I don't want to assume anything about who or what you like but it just seems

like you have no interest in being someone you're not just to make someone else happy."

"Well … I don't." You say it like it's the simplest thing on earth, but you know it isn't.

"Well, there you go, then."

You like the way Maeve sees you and for a second you glow under her gaze. But, as she said, she doesn't have context.

"It's not that I don't care though." You're thinking as you speak. This intimacy is a rare and lovely thing for you. "It's just that … well, for whatever reason, I just don't really fit in. Most of the people in our year don't like me or think I'm weird or whatever. And the amount of effort it would take to try and convince them otherwise doesn't seem worth it, and if I did try, they'd probably laugh at me more for trying anyway. Like when we were younger, Grace used to tease me for being this skinny kid with knobbly knees. Then puberty hit and I got bigger, bigger than her, I got boobs first and everything. And then she teased me for that and called me fat. So I learned pretty quickly that there was no point. I just … don't think I've found my people." You trail off, swallow, shake yourself. "Sorry, please feel free to tell me to shut up."

"I don't want you to shut up." Maeve's bewilderment is tender. "We're having a conversation!"

You're self-conscious then; you don't really know how to do this and when you begin to think about it, you doubt yourself.

"What about you?" you ask. "Your friends back home?"

Maeve shrugs. "Yeah, they were all right. Nice, mostly, though I get what you mean about feeling like you haven't really found your people. I always felt like … I don't know,

as if I was the butt of some unknown joke." You nod, keen in shared experience, and she continues, "I was always pretty … introverted. I think of all the funny, smart things I could have said when chatting to people but I think of them too late or get tongue-tied in the moment."

"So you like your own company too?"

"God, no!" Maeve laughs. "I'm so easily bored of myself but am too shy to do anything about it. Hopeless, I know."

"You don't seem that shy right now."

You don't know where this tone has come from. You think you might be flirting but you're not sure, you've never done it before.

Maeve grins, her cheeks rosying again, she meets your eyes. Her lashes are so blonde they're almost white, thin strands but many of them, how you imagine snowflakes. "I guess you're just easy to talk to."

The rest of the afternoon passes. Warm cheeks, fingers smudged with ink, acute observations and strange truths. She reads graceless Grace so savagely your eyes bulge. ("Fascinating how she thinks her parents' money is a substitute for her having a personality.") You tell her about your secret cat, showing her pictures of Bast on your phone. She believes in ghosts. You tell her about your parents and she tells you about hers. She swears that she saw faeries at the end of her garden, you tell her about your unusual recurring dreams – but don't mention your inkling that the tree is connected, that you didn't just faint. She is intrigued enough by them without that added information, says she wants to look up what they mean in her dream book because of course she has a dream book. You agree to read her

tarot sometime. You like she way she says *sometime* like the two of you will have all the time. You like the way she twines her hair round her finger when embarrassed or excited. You like the way her lips form a perfect pink tulip when they open in surprise. She catches you staring at her mouth. You look away, mortified.

*

By the end of the half-term break you've finished the naval logs and move on to Vega's copy of *The Republic of Sheta Island*. She has underlined a lot of the things that are useful to you. Adrien texts Maeve a lot. You can tell because her phone lights up and she goes pink. Whenever it happens something dark begins to flutter between your stomach and chest.

One day, as you make notes, Vega comes to join you.

"Yeah, we had pirates in my family," Maeve is saying, standing to relieve Vega of the cups of coffee she carries towards you. The library is, as always, almost empty. "Apparently there was a Captain Ó Néill here during the time of the Republic. I asked my aunt and she said she was some great-great-something-or-other of ours, but she got all weird and cross about it."

"That's right." Vega sits, sipping her coffee. "Cora Ó Néill, captain of *The Queen Áine*. She was said to be fierce and honourable." She gestures towards the book in front of you. "She was one of the Nubian Brethren captains to first establish the Republic, and when it did eventually fall, she refused to yield to the Empire. She was executed." Vega sighs. "A noble death."

"Why is your aunt ashamed?" you ask Maeve. "She sounds like a badass."

Maeve shrugs. "Doesn't like the association."

You turn a page of the book. "This account of the pirates is so different to everything else we've read. They aren't vicious and violent, except when they need to be."

"Maybe not all pirates are bad," muses Maeve, leaning over your shoulder to read. Her proximity sets gooseflesh squawking, she smells sweet and sharp, of berries and blossoms. Her phone buzzes. She glances at it, smiles slightly and puts it away.

"Well, some were," says Vega thoughtfully. "Some looted, some raped and murdered. Some betrayed their comrades. But some simply ... wanted an existence outside the tide of empire that was rolling across the world." Her voice was almost wistful. You don't notice it now but later, much later, you'll think of the expression that filled her eyes. They're very similar to your eyes. Similar enough that when you were small you used to fantasize that Vega was actually your mother, mysteriously kept away from you.

"Yeah, here." Maeve turns a couple of pages and leans away to scribble. "*Those fleeing slavery were known to find a home on the Republic, where they were able to claim their freedom. They were as likely, then, to be promoted to positions of high status as any person. The case of Captain Lotte Hook, of* The Cleopatra, *is an example of this.*"

You pull the book towards you with interest. "Wow. A former enslaved woman who became a pirate captain? Now that's badass. I wonder what happened to her."

"Much of what became of her is unknown but she's

mentioned later on, if you keep reading. I'm sure Miss Gibbers warned that myth blends with history very often in the tale of the Republic, particularly when looking at its origins. You've read the prologue, yes?"

"*The Myth of Xaymaca*? Yes!" Maeve's eyes are shining. "Witches and mermaids and spiders and faeries. I'm obsessed!"

"It's been a really useful starting point for us," you say, flicking to the page. "Two different islands, both homes of the witch Nubia, both utopias of a sort. One that fell to an empire and modernized, one that vanished into myth and memory."

You imagine it for a moment, the island from the prologue. A place of freedom and magic and equality.

A sharp ding from downstairs and Vega rises to attend to the people who are waiting at the front desk, saying, "Find the chapter called *The Leviathan*. There's mention of Captain Hook there, I believe."

You do as she instructs, hands bumping in your eagerness, the touch sending your coffee swooping around your stomach. "Here!" You point to the chapter and, together, begin to read:

Before Sheta Island fell once again under the rule of the Empire, after nearly nineteen years of a republic, there was a little known and much mythologized conflict. It was said that the Empire sent a fleet, several thousand men strong, to reclaim Sheta Island. They arrived swiftly and believed themselves to outnumber the Republicans ten-to-one. However, they were met, unexpectedly in the bay, by the Leviathan, a great sea dragon of ancient marine legend, who tore the naval ships to shreds. The

Republicans sustained many losses, though thanks to the Leviathan, they were ultimately victorious. However, their depleted numbers left them vulnerable to more attempts by the Empire to reclaim the island. The Leviathan was said to be from Xaymaca, like the great witch Nubia. He longed to return. The grateful Republic presented him with ships and crew under the captaincy of two members of the Brethren, Captain Jacques de Casse and Captain Lotte Hook, to ensure his safe passage.

It is said that they accompanied the Leviathan through the mist to that island. What became of them remains unknown.

Vega returns as you finish reading and you both look at her excitedly.

"I've heard the stories, of course, about a sea dragon," you say. "The new water park will have a whole ride with a sea monster. But I was always told that the reason the Republic fell was because the sea dragon *destroyed* it. Did he really defend the pirates?"

Vega smiles mysteriously. "Who can say for sure? I suppose it comes down to whether you believe in monsters." She raises an eyebrow. "Or in magic."

"I do," says Maeve. She launches enthusiastically into a detailed explanation of her tarot practice, of pagan nature rituals and her crystal collection, kept secret from her family. Your mind keeps returning to the manchineel tree. You think of your strange dreams and the voice that calls you again and again.

"I do," I say, breaking in. They both turn to you. "I believe in magic." You think about the line of inquiry you and Maeve had

agreed upon: *To what extent has Sheta Island's relationship with religion revised its history?* "We should have a section about it in our coursework. How the island's history of believing in magic was revised. And erased."

"Yes!" Maeve cries. "I love that idea! We could start by researching the witch burnings … the sea myths…"

And she's off, ink smudging her hands and forehead, pushing her hair out of her eyes.

If they want weird sister, then that's what I'll give them, you think.

*

School starts again, a familiar monotony that is strangely soothing. Your dreams have intensified, the light musical voice loud in your ear, your mind nightly replaying the white-hot flash of the manchineel tree over and over, so bright that it burns your retina, and you wake even more blurry-eyed than usual. Maeve's presence beside you in most of your lessons improves things. You walk to the library after school every evening. And almost every evening Chloe and Grace try to make something of it.

"Is 'the library' code for some lesbian shit now?"

"It sounds like it would be."

"Mind where you change before netball tomorrow, Maeve."

You ignore them, of course. But you hate the way it pinches Maeve's face, the way she turns flush with embarrassment.

"I'll remember that the next time you post a rainbow saying 'happy pride' on Instagram, Chloe."

The hallway falls quiet around you.

"I'm literally such an ally." Chloe's expression of hurt is so insincere that you can't fathom how everyone else doesn't notice. "I just think that if Maeve is … that way inclined, then she can do better." She smiles her shark's smile at Maeve, sharp white teeth making daggers of the fluorescent overhead lights.

"I'm not," Maeve mumbles. "Erm, that way inclined, I mean. Not that there's anything wrong with it." She throws an apologetic look at you. You arrange your face, keeping it neutral, disinterested, though something in your sternum splinters, leaving behind tight, sharp needles.

"Of course," Chloe swoops in smoothly. "Of course there's nothing wrong with it. You just … aren't."

You and Maeve leave school together without another word.

Once in the library though, holed up in your corner on the second floor, with Vega bringing you tea and biscuits, the awkwardness dissolves and you fall back into the rhythm that has started to feel so natural. Maybe the people you are in school are not the people you are in the library. The niggling disappointment remains though. Perhaps Maeve senses this or perhaps she's genuinely interested because she says:

"I know I asked you … if you were OK, after Halloween. But we've still not really talked about … what that was."

You freeze, uncertain how to proceed.

"Yeah, we have. Like I said, I fainted, no big deal."

"You fainted?"

"Yes. I touched a poisonous tree and I fainted. It's no great mystery, Maeve."

She winds a coil of copper around her finger, tucking it

behind an ear and angling her head, the movement the epitome of scepticism. "OK. You fainted. Sure. Except, I've been doing some more reading about manchineel trees. Most people who touch them don't just *faint*, Reggie. They die. Often pretty horribly."

You look at her. You are floundering internally. "What do you want me to say?"

Hurt flashes in response to your defensiveness. "I don't know. I thought we'd been... I mean, I thought we were friends. I thought you might want to, like, confide in me. If something is going on?"

Confide in her. The thought had honestly never crossed your mind.

You take a breath. "Do you promise you won't laugh?"

"I cross my heart hope to die."

"Well, don't die, I'd only get half a grade on this coursework if you did." She pinches you lightly, her smile encouraging.

"So, remember those weird dreams I mentioned?" Maeve nods. "I think... Well, they started around my birthday. And ever since Halloween, when I touched the tree, they've been ... vivid. It feels real, Maeve, I don't know how else to explain it."

To her credit, she isn't laughing. She frowns instead. "OK..." But her long vowel isn't sarcastic, it's thoughtful. "Well, what do you think the dreams are trying to tell you?"

You think back. It all feels very vague, an honest but deceptive kind of language that you don't understand yet. You try to drill in on specifics. *Whispering leaves, beckoning song. Find the tree and share its power...*

"I think that ... I need to go back to the tree."

Maeve nods again, slowly. "I can see why you'd … feel that way. But, Reggie, the manchineel tree is like the most poisonous tree ever. I'm not even exaggerating, it literally is. I don't want you touching it again."

You relish her sweet concern and wish you could agree to her terms. "No, I know. But I … I don't think it will hurt me, Maeve. It didn't before and … I don't think it can. Honestly, I can feel it."

Her brow is twisted in reluctance, her rosebud mouth pursed, but all she says is, "We'll stay and help Vega close and go after. It'll be dark and quiet then."

You cannot believe how calmly she is taking all of this, returning to her notes as though you haven't just told her that you are potentially having magic dreams and can commune with trees.

You huff a laugh. "I can't believe that you don't think I'm weird or crazy."

She looks up, a crooked smile, mischief and something flirtatious. "I do think you're weird. But, no, I don't think you're crazy. Didn't I say I believed in magic?"

At nine o'clock, you help Vega tidy up, clearing away books that have been left out and locking up the front.

"Will you girls get home OK?"

"Of course, Vega—" You roll your eyes. "The only crimes that happen here are tourists trying to shoplift tacky pirate shit."

She chuckles and makes to walk you to the edge of the green, before she stops, realizing you're not following.

"What?"

"We think we're going to stay and … look at the tree for a bit."

She peers at you. "Oh… Oh!" Her eyes become full of meaning, her grin a little too broad. "Understood. No worries at all."

Realizing her error, you go to correct her, but Maeve squeezes your arm and you say nothing. You don't understand her. She was so quick to assure the others at school that there was nothing even close to romantic between you two. But now here she is, allowing Vega to believe it, waiting with you in the dark green to see if you sense a spark of magic.

She is walking over to the manchineel tree and you follow her, looking up at its strange twisting bark and branches that reach up, arms thrown to the sky.

You look at each other. "What if I really do get poisoned this time?" But even as you ask it, you can feel something behind your skin. Your head doesn't pound like it did last time, but you can definitely feel *something*. The tree is alive to you. It emanates a vibrancy, a current of energy. You reach out, and place your palms against the bark.

There is brightness but there is no flash or burning; that was the threshold and now you are through the door. You breathe and you feel the tree breathe with you, a synchronized inhalation and exhalation. Without quite understanding why, you begin to sing. The *brown girl* song from your dream floats up from inside of you and you whisper-sing it to the tree. And the tree sings back. You can hear it. Not like you can hear other things – Maeve's breathing, the occasional passing car, the opposing metre of the sea, a *whoosh* and *ahhh* far away – but

more like you can hear your thoughts and your pulse and Maeve's earlier laughter.

And then – words. They seep into your blood and lick up your skin, clear and distinct.

> Nigh is the time of the witch who burned,
> Nigh is the time that stars will fall,
> Nigh is the time of the mermaid's son
> Who'll destroy his home to answer a call.
> Nigh is the time of sixteen suns,
> Nigh is the time of poison root,
> Nigh is the time to find lost things,
> For witch's blood bears fertile fruit.

Along with the words come images, some blurred as if seen through fog or smoke. Flickering flames of silver and blue, pinpricks of light in darkness. Some are more clear. You see yourself, not as you are, but some other kind of self, liquid and sparkling and part of the tree. You see a small dusty chest. A street lined with bluey-purple flowers. And a familiar door with a familiar shiny gold plaque above it: *Hornigold's Navigation and Cartography Services.* The last thing you see before jolting back to your body of solid flesh and bone is a pair of familiar flashing eyes, brown flecked with gold.

The Pull

Acute and infinite,
her grief and groaning,
so great was it and she –
a force unconstrained
an explosion of pain
grin and bear it,
she would not wear it,
it formed itself anew
her grief,
it took on shape and sinew,
her grief
became salt and mist and dew,
her grief
at that great parting,
the loss of her love and son,
was *felt* into being,
until – a Being.
Faraway and off the shore
as she grieved and cried and stormed,
and in response
the Great Energy formed –
a creature of sensation.
A water spirit drifting

on an errant breeze blown or
with a current lifting,
befriending, upending,
experiencing, rejoicing,
tasting, wasting
beloved and alone.
But even one born of feeling
cannot exist, indefinitely freewheeling,
and so they responded to each little pull,
a nudge towards
something more, a
part of them yet unknown
a song unsung, calling them home,
and so each meal, each sip, each taste,
each new lover and each new face,
sent Kano the nymph eddying with glee,
lusciously untethered,
sumptuously free
and yet, on occasion,
a bolt from above,
a shafting sunlight question,
and the answer?
Love.

New Tides

"Who are you?"

At the sound of the voice, Levi and Vega had reached for their cutlasses but, of course, found nothing at their waists. Levi swallowed uneasily.

He had never seen a person such as this before. They were lithe and graceful and moved like water. Their hair was an oil slick falling to their shoulders and their eyes were the grey of summer clouds. Their face, sharply featured and finely angled, was pale and lit with an internal iridescence so that even as the evening gathered around them, they seemed to glow. Silver in the way Vega was gold. Their chest and feet were bare and they wore something that resembled a loose skirt, made of linen.

Vega was eyeing the newcomer, her gaze wary. "Who are you and what are you doing in our cave?"

They blinked at her. "The first question has an easy answer – I am Kano. The second question is harder respond to… I am here because I am one who follows the Great Energy and I've never been steered wrong before." Their voice was soft, mellifluous, waves lapping against the shore.

Vega was not impressed.

"The great … *what*? What are you on about? And how did you just" – she clicked emphatically – "*appear*?"

"Well, this is a place of air and water, my shifting is all the more fluid in such spaces."

"Do you only know riddles and games?" Vega snapped.

The person called Kano hummed, eyes glowing in the shadows. Levi thought for a moment that this stranger might look amused by his sister. *Brave.* "I've not spoken to anyone in so long. Let me start with what I know to be true. I was born from the Great Energy. When a powerful creature feels a strong emotion, it can force the Great Energy into a single compact point, fusing into something almost solid. That almost-solid is I. The closest human word I have found is nymph."

"A nymph?"

Kano nodded. "Yes. There aren't many left in this world. Magic is dying here."

"So we've heard."

"So you just washed up here?" said Vega suspiciously. "Where did you come from?"

"Another difficult question." Again, that amused glimmer. Kano caught Levi's eyes briefly before they continued, "I have always drifted between states, water, air, this physical form. But I, like others of my kind, am pulled by the Great Energy. I have lived at sea and on land, shared stories with humans and secrets with the currents and occasionally came across one not unlike myself. But the further away I moved from the place of my birth, the fewer and fewer of my kind I have found."

"So why are you here now?" Vega pressed impatiently. Levi noted her hand clenched in her pocket and remembered the knife she had bought on their first morning.

"I saw you shift." A beat. Silence. Kano continued, "I was

drifting nearby, riding the white-water horse spirits that gallop ahead of waves, when I heard the blast and saw the fire. Then I saw … you. You." They nodded at Levi. "You were…"

"I know," Levi spat. "A monster."

Kano's eyes widened. "You were … beautiful. Glittering. And the water horses, the spirits, all the eddies and currents, they whispered a name … *Leviathan.*"

Levi had a split-second to be prepared for the shudder that quaked beneath his skin, the feeling of being on the precipice of ripping free of his flesh. Vega cried, "No!" But it was too late.

He saw the blue-green flames as his flesh ignited. He flung himself towards the sea, legs crossing the sand with inhuman speed, taking his danger away from them. He felt the shift, felt his muscles morph and expand into something strong and sleek and twisting. He moved through the air, so fast the world around him seemed slow. His skin shed in flakes and replaced itself immediately with scales and he noticed Kano moving behind him, almost step for step.

He dived beneath the water. It was the first time since the wreck of *The Sea Dragon*. He braced himself for dread but as the salt and sea moved over his new body, his scales swift and supple, the torment, the sharp ache snatching at his chest, eased. He stretched and his vast membranous wings followed. The ocean around him was vast and infinite, and in it Levi could hear the voices of the currents, singing and sighing with every story ever told, every moment he had spent at sea. His whole childhood was here. The reunion was both sweet and agonizing, a remembrance he was not ready for.

Then a voice. "You could control it you know." Kano.

"Where are you?"

"Here and everywhere. I am air, I am water."

"How?"

"I am a nymph. I am the place where the sea meets the shore. I am the spendthrift that catches the sky. I am good at shifting between states. I could show you, if you like. It would be good for you."

Levi snorted and was startled by the jet of warm water that huffed out of his snout. "You do not know me."

"I do actually," came the reply. "Water spirits have whispered of you. You are the Leviathan. You will be a legend."

Levi snarled. "I do not *want* to be a legend. I just want to…" He trailed off. He did not know what he wanted any more. "I want to change back."

"So, shift." Kano's voice made it sound so easy.

"How?"

"Think of what you want to become."

Levi tried. He conjured an image of his body, the lean limbs and face that so resembled his father. His father had known about this. His father had gone and could no longer answer his questions. His father had feared him – and yet had wanted him to captain *The Drag*. He, Levi, had never really wanted to be captain. He had just wanted freedom – the sky and the sea and vast potential.

The captain of The Sea Dragon *should be a dreamer. Should always have an idea of where this ship is going. And Vega will know how to get there.*

But *The Sea Dragon* would never go anywhere again. And he and Vega were lost…

190

"Easy. That is not the way." Kano's voice was soothing, gentle, but Levi could not hear it. He wanted to burn and burn until he was ash, until he dissolved between the waves, until he was with his family once more. But beyond the sea fire consuming him, burning through his magic and strength, Levi felt a formless weeping, a dousing sympathy, extinguishing where he could not. Kano pulled him back from the brink of his grief, back to himself, as Levi drifted into unconsciousness.

*

Night descended. A chill breeze that swayed and bent the palm trees that lined the beach. Kano stayed in their human form to help Vega carry Levi to the Freeman's Inn. They all needed rest and Kano assured Vega that Levi was too spent to be a risk. Vega made Kano dress in the same shirt and pants and boots to match hers and Levi's; she thought their bare chest may attract attention. Emabelle, who ran the inn and knew Vega by now, gave her a good rate on rooms and did not ask questions about the "drunk brother" slumped in Kano's arms.

There were only two rooms left, on the top-floor landing. The doors faced each other, as did Kano and Vega.

Vega held out her arms for Levi, but Kano did not yield. "I should share a room with him."

Every line of Vega's face was etched with suspicion. "Why would I let you, a stranger, share a room with my unconscious brother?"

"You saw what happened on the beach." Kano's voice was calm, their face open. "You saw what I did. I'm the only one that

can dampen that sea fire if something happens. We know his name is a trigger, but we don't know that it is the only trigger. Have there been other times … times when he has felt as if he might" – they cast around for the right phrase – "burst out of his body?"

Vega pressed her lips into a thin line, saying nothing.

Kano nodded. "If something happens, I can help." Their hair was slick off their face and in the lamplight Vega could now see that it was actually dark blue, inky as the sea at night.

"Listen, *nymph*" – she flicked her knife out of her pocket and took a step closer to them – "I don't care if you become a tidal pool or a sea breeze – you don't know who or what I am. If anything happens to my brother, on the locker, I swear there is no form you can take that will escape me – savvy?"

Kano nodded and kicked the door open. "I don't expect you to trust me right away," they said, looking back. "But I do believe that I was meant to find you. I will be a loyal friend, always." Vega stared at them for a moment, reading their face, listening for star song. But the stars were silent. She could not feel their ringing warning and Levi's face was surprisingly peaceful in Kano's arms. So, sending a silent prayer up to her kin, she nodded and closed the door to her room.

*

Levi found Kano and Vega eating breakfast downstairs in the main room of the inn. He had awoken, warm and rested in bed, and for a moment was unsure where he was. Then he noticed a clean shirt and leather pants draped over a chair in the corner.

Undergarments lay on top as well as a bandana, his black-and-gold damask jacket and Kano's skirt.

Levi had picked the skirt up thoughtfully for a moment, imagining the shape it would make as he moved. It then occurred to him that it had not been Vega's cool body lying next to him that had tempered his fever in the night. He put it down and pulled on his shirt, pants and boots. The room was low-ceilinged and small, shabby but clean. A worn woven rug was spread across the centre and the large four-poster bed replete with moth-eaten umber hangings was set against the wall opposite, next to a small, wobbly bedside table. A small window let in light bright as starflowers and a view over a cliff, the sea sparkling crystal far below. He splashed his face with cold water from a jug and bowl set atop a chest of drawers, hewn from the same wood as the bed, the handles spotted with rust. He revelled in the rousing *slap slap*, and for a moment he felt clearer than he had in days. It did not last long. How quickly would all that warm, worn wood ignite if he had another dream, if the voice – his mother? – called him once more? He thought of the other times – the times before his birthday – that he'd felt that stretching, juddering beneath his skin, the times he'd been stressed or drifted too close to the truth. A spotted mirror sat beside the bowl and jug but Levi did not glance at his reflection as he tied his locs back with the bandana.

"Cornmeal and cackle?" Vega said by way of a greeting, gesturing to her bowl. Levi sniffed appreciatively but was then confronted with the mental image of Cook's ruddy face, of Tally with deft fingers peeling his eggs when he was small. He shook his head, working to swallow past the lump in his throat, and said hoarsely, "Just bread and cheese is fine."

He sat and eyed Kano warily. In the daylight, Levi too noticed the inky spill of their hair – underneath a bandana identical to his – and the sweet silver of their complexion, but even as he looked, the air around them shifted and their shimmering dulled until, in their white shirt and leather pants, they seemed almost human.

"How did you do it?"

"Do what?" Kano asked, eyes wide and innocent.

Levi kissed his teeth the way Tally often had. "You know what."

Kano shrugged. "Shifting? I wanted to and so I did."

"You can choose? You can be one thing or another or somewhere in between?"

Kano considered. "Choose is the wrong word. I *am* all of the things that I can become. The choice is how and when I express them. When I want to be seen less, to drift freely, then I will become as light as air or as fine as dew. When I want to move fast and hungrily I become like the currents of the sea…"

"And now?"

"Now I want to be rooted. Solid and material. And so I look human. Sort of."

Levi allowed a wry smile. "Aye. Sort of." He felt wistful for a moment. "It sounds very freeing."

Kano nodded. "It is. It is very hard to trap a nymph. But not impossible. We all have things that we are in opposition to. Fire, for instance."

Levi's eyes widened. "Fire?"

Kano nodded. "I am made of water and land and air. Fire eats those things. It dries me out, stops me from shifting. It's

the rare time my solid form is stronger than any other shape. But even then, I am vulnerable."

"But my fire didn't—"

"Your fire is sea fire. It is made of magic and whatever else creates beings such as us. I am talking about the red and yellow variety. It is infinitely human in a way I will never be, for all my imitating."

Even dressed like everyone else in the dining room, Kano dazzled Levi. Their smile was broad and open, rugged almost, but the way they moved, angling their shoulders, holding their cutlery, was delicate, precise. In the sunshine that streamed in through the windows, the nymph's eyes were pearlescent, set apart from the whites by a darker, smokier colour. Even their magic could not mask the dew and mist that glimmered there.

Levi realized he was staring.

He cleared his throat, as Vega returned with a plate of bread and cheese, and a mug of thick, rich coffee. "Why did you bring me here? How do we know that I'm … that I'm safe?"

Vega and Kano exchanged a glance that halted Levi as he reached for his food. "What?"

"It would seem," Vega began slowly, not taking her eyes from the silver-and-blue of the nymph's face, "that Kano can … put out your fire." The dining room wasn't busy but she lowered her voice even further, so Levi had to lean across the table to hear. "Last night, when you transformed, you shifted back much quicker. And the fire was far less … explosive. Apparently, the nymph had something to do with this. They kept watch last night."

Kano shrugged. "It's not entirely surprising. We are both

195

of the sea. You are fire and I am water and air." They paused. "Perhaps that's why the Great Energy brought me here. To help you."

"So you'll be staying with us?" She sounded less combative, Levi noted, and wondered what had happened when he was unconscious.

Kano nodded. "I think I could teach you to control your shifting as well. I can show you what it is like for me?"

"Are you sure? You don't have to."

"I would be happy to help you, Levi."

Something twisted in Levi when Kano said his name. He noted the way their tongue touched the roof of their mouth to form the L, the way their teeth bit their bottom lip on the V. He swallowed.

"Why do you think it's saying my full name that … that causes it?"

Kano was quiet for a moment. "I … I think it's a truth of yourself that you cannot escape. A call that you have to answer. Just like if Vega or I were to yell 'Levi!' now, you'd look around."

"This is what it all comes back to." Vega drummed her fingers on the tabletop and sipped her coffee. "It's as if this Xaymaca place is calling you. Calling you home. I want to know why. And why now? Your strange dreams, Johnson's plans, the map, the shifting. There's something *off*."

"So what are you thinking? You have a plan, Vega, I know you."

"It's not a plan, exactly. I want to find this Marianne you heard mentioned, ask her what she knows. It seems she's the only one who recently wrote to … the crew. Maybe she

knows why they were so sure that Johnson's intentions can't be trusted."

"Marianne," Kano said slowly. "I have heard this name often. Surely there will be many so called on this island."

Vega angled her head. The gesture was cocky, all piratical swagger, and Levi's heart ached. "It's all about your sources." She nodded towards where Emabelle was busy with customers. "If there's a Marianne associated with the Brethren in any way, Emabelle will know who she is. And if we want to get close to Johnson, Emabelle will know how to do that too."

Levi took a bite of his breakfast and the room in more fully. The atmosphere was easy, even jovial, a loud familiarity. From almost every table Levi heard Johnson's name. The inn was full of talk of his voyage to the magical island that would become their ally, that would help the Republic of Sheta Island face down the Empire. Naked of knowledge and armour, Levi felt vulnerable. Buccaneers and tradespeople alike wore swords and rapiers like accessories. "We should acquaint ourselves with our surroundings, stock up on supplies. I don't like being unarmed, we need to remedy that. And we should get some decent clothes," he added as an afterthought and twitched a smile in Vega's direction, his first in days. "Don't want to look like some *port-side blowsabella*."

*

The bustling port town was full of activity. The lane which housed the inn paved the eastern cliff path and twisted into one of many cobbled streets. The scent of warm bodies permeated

the air and Levi's keen sense of smell was overwhelmed as he and Kano followed Vega through the town, trying not to attract too much attention.

They stopped at several shops and stalls, Vega picking up shirts and undergarments, while Levi and Kano drifted to the next store, an armoury. Ramshackle structures blended with wooden-shuttered shops, which became more permanent-looking the closer they drew to the hive of the docks, giving the town the look of a place that had expanded very quickly.

Levi weighed swords and cutlasses in his hands as he waited for Vega, swished a sabre.

"Take care." Kano's light, musical voice. "We don't want anyone marking you out as a threat just yet."

"Just yet?"

"Oh, I'm sure they'll realize who you are and what you can do eventually. But you're not ready for that." Their head was angled, their gaze appraising. Levi swallowed and nodded, but paid for the cutlass and sabre, before belting them both at his side.

"Can you use a sword?" Levi asked the nymph.

They shook their head.

"Well, you'll have to learn. Right now blending in is your armour but it won't always be. You have to be able to defend yourself. If you teach me what I need to know" – Levi glanced at the man counting his coins behind the rickety table piled high with weapons – "I'll teach you too."

Kano grinned, their head at that angle again. "A fair exchange."

Levi and Vega picked out weapons for Kano and then

continued on towards the centre of the town. The walk, down a fairly steep hill to sea level, was not long but the day was warm, and Levi, now he was moving again, now he had a plan and a direction, relished the activity.

The atmosphere of the Republic unnerved him and for a little while Levi could not identify exactly why. Loud laughter and brash greetings, scuttle and gossip, a song on the wind. A town built upon a brotherhood and bound by a comradery of nearly two decades. It was precarious in nature but fundamentally scrappy. People met in the streets, called greetings or good-hearted insults, listened to local musicians playing wooden flutes and violins. It was only as he walked past two women, sitting playing cards in the sun, that he realized. For all its strangeness, it felt familiar. It reminded him of *The Drag*.

In the centre of town, where the shops had high-arched thresholds, they found the library. It was made of red brick and wood. Its sloping roof and stained-glass windows identified it as having clearly been a church. Next to it was a still scorched patch of grass and a tree with a red X painted on to its bark. The manchineel tree. A wooden railing encircled it but to Levi this was unnecessary – the tree pulsed threateningly. Daring one to touch it, promising pain, swearing vengeance.

The library door was ajar, a light shining from within. They looked at each other, toying with the idea of going inside, the cumbersome parcels making them hesitate. Before they could decide, a shout went up across the square.

"The map!"

"He's got the map to Xaymaca!"

Levi's stomach dropped and for a second his hand flew to

the pocket of his shirt where his own map was kept. He dropped several packages but was rewarded with the rustle of paper against his chest. Now even more curious, he collected up his parcels and led Vega and Kano towards where a small crowd was gathered, eyes on a young red-faced man, rolled-up sleeves bearing a familiar tattoo. A coin with a man's profile on it. *The Sterling.* A member of Johnson's crew.

"Go on, Alfie, show us!"

"What did Diego say?"

"Is it really magic?"

The three of them lingered towards the back of the crowd. A few curious glances shot their way but their attention was quickly reclaimed by the young man, Alfie. "Well, it's like this. The capt'n says to me, 'Alf, my boy. Eight 'n ten years ago, an X appeared on a map belongin' to Captain Ezi—'" The steady pulse of talk turned disgruntled. There were boos, even hisses. Vega growled quietly and Levi felt his blood thrum with fury. "'And now the magic of Xaymaca has found us, and an X has appeared on a map of ours. And we will not keep all that land has to offer to ourselves, oh no! We will not forsake the Republic, like Ezi the Absent! We are a more worthy crew than *The Sea Dragon*! We will share with our comrades on Sheta Island!'" Cheers, whistles, scattered applause, scattered thoughts, Vega's twisted face. Levi reeled and nausea surged. *Ezi the Absent.* To hear this, to witness this contempt of those he had loved, it was intolerable.

Cool fingers squeezed just above his elbow, soothing reassurance. Kano. The world came into focus again, but not before a memory surfaced.

Ezi was peering into his face, peering down because he was

200

small, no more than seven or eight. Every moon – sometimes more, sometimes less, Ezi would call him to his cabin. There he would spend an afternoon talking him through the job of the captain.

"I thought captains were elected," Levi had said, and Ezi's eyes had gleamed.

"They are. But I am not like most captains and you are my son, my blood. It is expected that you will be elected."

Levi dreaded these times. He loved listening to his father talk, but he preferred the tales of adventure, the glow of his father's face, ichi like rays of the sun across his cheeks, as he pointed to the horizon. These lessons weighed him down. He did not want to be responsible for a crew, he did not want to plan and organize and fight. He wanted to swim and seek and taste the world. He did not want to be captain. Hearing word his father had sent for him, he'd darted away. His quick excuses and little lies were slick as he slipped free of his father's grasping, paternal desires and into the welcoming arms of the water. But now he was caught.

"What is it you want, hatchling?"

He'd toed the dust, avoiding his father's pinning gaze. "I dunno," he'd said with a shrug. "What do you mean?"

"Well, you lied. There is a want behind every lie."

He heard these words again. What was the want behind these lies?

Alfie was still speaking. "This is the map with the X that leads to Xaymaca. We know it works, so we do, but the other captains of the Brethren have their reservations. 'Well, that's only fair,' says Capt'n Johnson. Only he can see the X, o' course they have some questions. Captain Ó Néill wanted

201

us to take the map to Diego. See what an expert cartographer made of it."

"What did Diego say, Alfie?"

"Well!" Alfie inflated even further, swelling with the imminent climax of his news. "He said, *'It looks just like any old map to me!'* and I says to Diego, 'Well, that bodes well. Because that's exactly what everyone said to Capt'n Ezi!' Our scouts have been sending word, we know they reached Xaymaca safely – and we know Capt'n Ezi did too. And now we know that the map's magic is the same as Capt'n Ezi's, you see?" With a flourish, Alfie drew the folded canvas from his shirt pocket. With deliberate and dramatic slowness, he unfolded it before them.

It was a sage trick, Levi realized. The crowd gasped and murmured at the ordinary map – for it was indeed an ordinary map. But the crowd had been told that the map, in appearing ordinary, was extraordinary, and so they reacted accordingly. Levi was sure that by dinner time every table on the Republic would be discussing the mysterious X that no one could see, as hard proof of the veracity of Johnson's voyage.

But there was no glimmering green X to be seen. Captain Johnson was lying. And he was doing it very well.

The Queen Áine

Maybe it had something to do with the fact that he had now spent more time on land than ever before in his life but Levi's strange dreams, the shushing, melodic watery sigh had dulled to silence. He missed the voice. Without it, his nights were filled with dreams that tore pieces from his chest, invaded his nostrils with the scent of burning flesh and set his skin singing with blue flame. He would awake panting, sweating, embarrassed, as Kano became cool mist and dampened the sea fire that threatened to explode out of him, soothing the sting and itch.

Despite this, routine imposed itself easily over the next few days. Sharing a room with Kano did not feel as alien as it should have; perhaps this was because Levi had always had a bunk-mate. All the same, he maintained a careful distance between himself and the nymph as they lay side by side, even as they talked well into the night.

"What was Vega like, as a child? I cannot imagine it."

"Much the same as she is now, only smaller. She has always been better than me at everything. Well, not everything. Not swimming. Or cards. Or cooking, actually."

"You would cook? But I thought sons of princes never did such things."

A laugh, the tightness of bittersweet memory. "Pa..." A cough, a vocal absence, but such things were permitted in Kano's

quiet dark, and Levi tried again. "Pa was not that sort of prince. He gave up his money and title to sail the seas as a pirate."

The burning sensation intensified but Levi breathed through it. "Cook used to let me help sometimes. I'd make fried saltfish. Vega loved it."

"I should like to try it sometime. I love salt fish. I remember tasting some on an island surrounded by coral so bright the whole ocean seemed orange."

"Oh! I remember a place like that! Pa and I swam together around it and Vega hung the jib for days at being left out."

Kano laughed, picturing a small, scowling Vega. "Well, she missed quite a sight. The fish glittered like nowhere else I've seen."

"Aye!" And Levi's mind's eye conjured so many places that he'd seen with his crew, his family. His chest tightened further, but he kept speaking. "Well, actually I once saw ice glitter. I had never seen ice before. I had to ask Vega what it was. She'd read about it but even she didn't think it would be so pretty."

"I was terrified when I first saw an ice plain," Kano confessed. "I had always thought I understood water. And then, there it was, frozen solid. Totally stuck. I wept for it, so confined and imprisoned."

Levi laughed then, the tightness in his chest easing.

Kano laughed too.

Levi, Vega and Kano would arise with the sun and break their fast early, in the downstairs dining room of the Freeman's. They preferred the quiet of the near-dawn. They could plan the day's training and indulge in lengthy discussions about Johnson without being overheard.

"We need to speak to Brethren captains."

"Vega, it's too risky. They're allies of Johnson's, they're in favour of his voyage!"

"We don't know that for sure."

"Everywhere we go, people are singing his praises. They think he's a hero. Why would they believe us? And P— The crew ... their name's mud here too."

"If *our* crew didn't trust Johnson, who's to say all of the others do? If we speak to the captains, give some ... some reason for our misgivings, maybe they'll pull support for his voyage. We have to start somewhere, hatchling."

Returning at night for dinner, when the inn was busy, they noticed, with each passing day, more looks in their direction, more murmured questions.

Emabelle, who had become particularly close with Vega, was excellent at these times, diverting attention and starting singsongs. She was pretty and soft, dark-skinned with sweet brown eyes, thick hair coiled on her head. Levi felt a momentary flare of envy at the pink-and-green play of her dress.

"Pay 'em no mind." She poured them more ale. "They're harmless. You're shiny and new, they'll get bored soon enough."

The day after they'd seen Alfie with the map, Emabelle was pouring their coffee at breakfast when Levi threw Vega a look of intent. She caught it and turned to the landlady. "Emabelle, you wouldn't know a Marianne, would you?"

"Marianne?"

"Aye. Someone in the Brethren, maybe?"

She paused, pouring herself a cup of coffee and sipping thoughtfully. "Hmmmm. No one springs to mind. I think

Ó Néill might have a granddaughter called Marianne? She's probably about ... three?"

"No, it's not her we're thinking of. Anyone else?"

Emabelle thought some more then shook her head. "No. No one I can think of. I'll let you know though."

"And also ... the captains?" Vega paused, a momentary debate before deciding on directness. "What if we wanted to talk to one?"

Emabelle snorted sceptically. "You three, talk to a captain? Why would a capt'n bother with you odd folk?"

"We're not odd; odd is just what people call that which is new to them." Kano's musical intonation sufficiently undermined their point, so too did the trailing of their elegant fingers through the dust motes illuminated in a stream of sunlight through the window behind them. Levi gently caught their hand and placed it on the table, ignoring the jolt of contact.

Emabelle's forehead creased, a silent *I told you so*, but what she said was, "Well, your best bet is to chat to one of their secretaries. They frequent this place more often than their captains. I'll point 'em out to you next time they're in. I wouldn't count on any kind of meeting though. The captains are busy with all this Xaymaca business." She looked around her inn, draining her coffee, readying herself to return to the floor. "This place has always been the final frontier – of freedom, of adventure ... of magic. But maybe we're not the final frontier after all. The threat of the Empire looms larger every day – an alliance would be sweet." Her eyes shone with hope and she moved off, leaving the three of them to ponder her words.

"It must all seem so … silly and human to you." Levi cocked his head at Kano. "All this fighting over land and place, when you can move so freely."

Kano shook their head. "The more time I spend with … humans, the more I understand it."

"Understand what?"

"Home," they murmured, looking after Emabelle. "And the lengths people will go to to make one."

*

After breakfast each day they would take various long routes through the bustling port town to the beach where they had first arrived. The coves there provided shelter enough to train. As they walked, they learned to identify various crew members by their tattoos, keeping their eyes open for the captains, using the little information Emabelle had provided.

"That's one of Hook's," Levi said one morning, a few days after their arrival, pointing to a woman with a tattoo on her forearm, a thin snake in the shape of a hook. Emabelle had told them it was for the queen their vessel was named after, *The Cleopatra*, who, according to legend, took her own life using a snake bite after her lover had been murdered. She was laughing with a tall and handsome man and, as he turned, Levi noticed a red horse inked across his brown skin. He caught Levi's eye and smiled. Levi couldn't help but smile back.

Kano raised an eyebrow. "And who would that be?"

Levi shrugged. "One of Ó Néill's men, I assume. Red horse for *The Queen Áine*. That's right, isn't it, Vega?"

"Aye." Vega nodded. "Áine is a faerie queen in Ó Néill's homeland. I read it in one of my old books. She's the goddess of summer and wealth. Her symbol is a red horse."

"Maybe we should talk to him."

"Why?" Kano asked sharply.

"Well, that Alfie, Johnson's man with the map, he said that Ó Néill was the one who had reservations and wanted the cartographer – Diego, was he called? – to look at it."

"That's true," Vega agreed. "We need an in with the Brethren somehow. Ó Néill seems like a good place to start." She assessed the handsome stranger. He glanced Levi's way again, smiled again, and she raised an eyebrow. "Well, he clearly likes your pretty face, hatchling. Go and win him over."

Levi made to move away but Kano grabbed Levi's arm, a strange expression on their face. "No! What I mean is ... we should discuss this more. Isn't it risky approaching him in front of someone from another crew?"

"Not really." Vega was perplexed. "So she'll tell Hook that three obnoxious whelps want to talk to captains? She'll probably just think we're interested in joining a crew. What harm is it?"

"Er – I – I just think – I just feel..." As Kano stuttered, the man from *The Queen Áine* clapped the woman from *The Cleopatra* on the shoulder and departed, throwing another grin in Levi's direction. Levi turned and felt Kano bristle beside him.

"What is it?" He had only known Kano a few days but felt as though it had been longer. The musical lilt of their voice, their quiet wisdom and kindness all felt so familiar. But this ... this was new. For the first time, they seemed angry.

"Kano? Why have you taken the owl?"

"What owl? I do not know what that means!" they snapped. Levi and Vega exchanged a look. Kano scowled and it was suddenly awkward between the three of them for the first time. And perhaps they realized it because after another moment they deflated.

"Apologies." Now Kano was shamefaced, confused even. "I do not... I do not know what that was. I am sorry."

Another beat. Levi looked to Vega again, expecting to see his confusion once more mirrored by his sister, but instead it rather seemed as though she was trying not to laugh.

*

Kano was strongest at the point of their Great Energy's origin, where the sea met the shore, and it was there, tucked away in the rocky cove that Levi and Vega had stayed in those first few days, that they began Levi's lessons. It was not going well.

"Lie here beside me," Kano said today, lying at the convergence, so that the insouciant tide lapped over them. Here at this nexus of their power, Kano could not dull their otherworldly beauty. They were radiant and Levi felt humbled lying beside them.

"So," Kano said, eyes closed. "Tell me how your heart is?"

Levi's eyes flew open. "Wha— How d'you mean?" he stuttered.

"Exactly what I said." Kano's eyes were still closed. "How is your heart? How does it feel?"

"Why?"

209

Kano opened their eyes. "Because it is important. You've shifted twice now and both times have had the potential to cause you serious harm. You let whatever it is that wars in your heart consume you. You will not be able to shift safely until you have made peace with it."

Levi lay back in the sand and stared at the cyan sky. "Maybe I'll never be able to shift safely because I am not safe."

"Why do you think you are unsafe?"

"My father said so." Levi told them what he had overheard the day that he had eavesdropped. And then found himself talking on – telling Kano about his strange dreams, about stealing the map, about what he had seen on it, about the catastrophic events of that night. He did not know how much Kano had seen or overheard in the cave, but he found he did not care. He needed to talk and Kano listened. He did not cry. He felt hollow and dry inside, but his throat was tight as he said, "You asked how my heart is? My heart is broken, Kano. I do not think it will ever mend." Levi felt the words hang. He knew himself to be irrevocably changed and did not know how to process this.

"Hmmm. Now you have said this, I do not think your heart is the problem." Kano was thoughtful. "I do not think it *needs* to be mended. But you must learn to live with all its pieces, and it is *this* that I believe to be your problem."

Gooseflesh prickled Levi's skin as Kano placed a hand across his chest, the heart line of their palm meeting the gap between his ribs. Cool, soothing contact. Levi felt lighter.

"Beneath your heart, there is something else. Something that tethers us all to the Great Energy that gives us life and

purpose. I have heard humans call it a soul or a spirit, I do not think the name is important. What is important is that it is *ours*." Levi let their words wash over him, soft and lulling. "We must learn to love it, to be at peace with all its pieces. But right now … you cannot do this. Your father sounds like a great man, who loved you and did for you the best that he could. The crew were your family and followed your father's suit. I am so sorry that you lost them in the way that you did."

Levi closed his eyes. He had been wrong. He was not dry on the inside.

"And I am so sorry that you have to accept and make peace with this," Kano continued. "But they failed you, Levi."

Levi sat bolt upright, glaring at Kano.

"They didn't fail me!"

"They did. They did not tell you the truth about who you are or where you come from, and in doing so split you from you." They reached out their hand and touched the place beneath his heart once more. Levi stiffened but did not pull away. "I am not saying what happened to them was not the worst thing a person can go through, because it is. I am not saying that it was their fault … but it most certainly was not yours." Kano's voice was low and insistent, their hand rubbed gentle circles and Levi felt his breath slowing once more, syncing with the motion of their hand. "It is not your fault. To shift is to employ gentle, loving manifestation. To move from state to state, you have to be aware of all of your possible states, not just be aware of them, but love them. Each of them. Separately and as part of a whole. To be at peace with your multitudes."

"I can't." Barely a breath, a whispered word, a half-gasp. "I

can't be at peace with the part of me that … that took everything away from the rest of me."

"I will help you," Kano promised.

*

A few days after they had seen the tall, handsome member of *The Queen Áine*, Levi felt a persistent prickling on the back of his neck while sitting at dinner with Kano and Vega. The Freeman's was as rowdy as ever. He turned to find the handsome man smiling at him through the crowd and returned the warmth, before nudging Vega. She looked round with interest.

"Oh, grand. Go and talk to him, Levi, use your charm."

Levi nodded and moved towards him, only to find himself blocked by Kano. Levi raised his eyebrows, almost exasperated. "*What?* First you take the owl, and now you hang the jib. Is there something you're not saying, Kano?"

"What owl? What is a jib? I don't know what these things mean!" And there it was again, that sullen tone and expression, so at odds, so *human* that they were incongruous.

"Kano." Levi looked round but Vega did not seem confused or frustrated. Her tone was kind. "Come now. What's the worry?"

"Nothing!" they sighed. "No. Nothing."

Kano frowned into Levi's face. It stirred something in him. He squeezed Kano's hand, then dropped it, drifting across the room to the tall handsome man whose smile seemed so offensive to Kano.

Half an hour later, Leví was back, grinning broadly, a bottle of wine swinging celebratorily from his hand.

"Well?"

"Well, what?"

"Well, what did he say?"

Levi sat down and leaned in, using the pouring of the wine into their glasses to mask his surreptitiousness. "Captain Cora Ó Néill keeps lodgings north-east of the library. She has a big family now – lots of children and even some grandchildren. Her husband looks after them mostly but her offices are attached to the main house. Ameyro" – Levi jerked his head back at the handsome young man, now talking to some friends but still occasionally glancing over – "is her secretary and says she runs her family as if they're her crew and her crew as if they're her family. They are all incredibly loyal and somewhat concerned about what Johnson's voyage will mean. Apparently she's particularly worried that so many able fighters sailing to Xaymaca will leave the Republic vulnerable to the Empire. Which is a fair point." He looked from Kano to Vega with the air of one savouring the last, juiciest titbit. "But we can find out more about that when we meet with Captain Ó Néill, savvy?"

"What?"

"We're meeting with Captain Ó Néill? A rig, surely?"

Levi beamed even wider and shook his head. "True as the ale is wet. Day after tomorrow. We're to be at her offices by eleven o'clock!"

"How in Davy's name did you manage that?"

Levi's eyes flicked unbidden to Kano's face for a fraction

of a second, before he winked at Vega and said, "I think ... I think I flirted."

Kano dropped their glass.

*

"Nubia always said Sheta Island was different to other lands because it's so close to the horizon, to where the air grows thin and turns to magic. She once told me that Xaymaca was a land just out of reach of mortal hands but it was still Sheta Island's neighbour. She told me that the stars bade her come here..." Captain Cora Ó Néill trailed off, staring out of her office window. Her home topped the rear flipper limb of the turtle-shaped island, which curved out to form a narrow peninsula with stunning views of the sea.

Levi, Vega and Kano had walked the eastern stretch of coast that morning, from the Freeman's which was situated above the turtle's fore flipper on the same side. Where this flipper curved into the jutting headland that formed the turtle's head, a bay of tucked coves and uneven rocks kept the sea's secrets. This was where Levi and Vega had come ashore and where Levi and Kano practised shifting. Though the Freeman's was slightly further inland it was still in sight of the sea – but then, Sheta Island was small enough that almost everywhere was in sight of the sea, an expansive cerulean inevitability. *A good servant but a bad master, The Sterling*'s late scout had said. Even at the time Levi had thought this strange – to him the sea was neither. The sea was a friend, a collaborator, unpredictable but ultimately a member of the crew. But watching the easy-breathing blue

214

become spiteful and spitting the closer it came to shore before smashing into the rocks far below, Levi thought he understood, for the first time, what the sea was to those who were not of it.

Now they sat in Ó Néill's office, the sounds of her children at play and her crew at work drifting in through the open windows. Down in the bay below, *The Queen Áine* fleet was docked – five ships, each with a dedicated crew of fifty to a hundred. Even though Ó Néill had not left the Republic in almost twenty years, she still saw to it that her vessels were kept in top condition, routinely patrolling the shore on rotation with the fleets of the other three captains. She was a fearsome woman, buxom and broad, red hair beginning to grey at her temples, a lined face pale but scattered with freckles, showing a temperament prone to both frowns and smiles. Her dress and apron and rolled-up sleeves made the belt of weapons slung around her waist seem all the more impressive. Off duty, but never off guard. She had greeted them civilly enough, glancing from Ameyro's eyes, which shone in Levi's direction, to the strange trio. She'd appraised them impassively before inviting them in and calling for her valet to bring tea and cakes, which she called "wee buns".

Vega had immediately begun their rehearsed spiel; they were fishermen's children, who'd grown up hearing tales of the Republic and had wanted to see it for themselves. Now, having heard of Johnson's voyage to a mysterious and magical island, and having heard some of the things being said in the various alehouses about Captain Ezi, they were concerned.

Levi could immediately tell that Ó Néill did not believe them. And yet, she did not send them out on their ear. Her

eyes drifted over his face and he thought he saw a glimmer of recognition there. He cursed his own stupidity.

Everyone aboard *The Drag* had always said that he was the image of his father when he was young. And Captain Cora Ó Néill had known his father when he was young.

"Why should ye care for Captain Ezi's reputation?" she asked. There was something shrewd in the purse of her lips and Levi felt beads of sweat prickle the base of his neck.

"He docked a few times, in the small port from which we hail," Vega replied smoothly. "He was not like other pirates, or other princes. He was fierce but … fair. Generous even. He overpaid our parents for their catch."

"That sounds like Ezi," Ó Néill said wryly and Levi's heart leaped.

"So you … you don't believe it? What everyone's saying?" Vega squeezed his leg, a pinch of caution, and Levi worked to temper his face. He could not seem too eager, like he cared too much about this pirate prince he had, ostensibly, met only once or twice. But this was about more than just potentially preventing Johnson's journey. His father was seen as one who had betrayed his ideals, had found riches on a magical island and refused to contribute to the Republic, to maintain contact with his comrades in the Brethren. And it was his fault. Levi knew that if it wasn't for him, his father would have returned to the Republic. Would have been hailed a hero with magical allies. Would still be alive.

"Well, I don't know what to believe. Certainly Johnson's version of things does not match the Ezi I knew. But then I've not laid eyes upon the Ezi I knew for more than eight-and-ten

216

years. Indeed he is known as Ezi the Absent here. And Johnson has a direct line to Xaymaca, it seems."

"I have travelled to many lands," Kano interjected, "with my ... parents. In most places the belief in such things – witches and magic – is dying out. Is seen as superstitious nonsense. And yet here..."

"Oh, aye, there are some here that believe it to be superstitious nonsense, who think Johnson must be mad with his maps and the like," Ó Néill said, sipping her coffee. "Wee ones who did not know Nubia, or Ezi. Who have only known the freedom we fought for."

"Well, you can hardly blame them," Vega probed. "No one here has ever seen Xaymaca, have they?"

That look of shrewd appraisal once more.

"What is it you're asking me, wee girl?"

Vega bristled at being so addressed but kept her tone polite, stuck to the well-rehearsed lie. "Well ... when *The Sea Dragon* docked in our port, my brother and I" – she nodded at Levi – "we overheard a conversation between our father and the quartermaster. Able."

"Aye. I know Abe."

"He did not say much about Xaymaca. He just said that it was best left alone. That what they had found there was trouble and his captain had no desire to bring trouble to Sheta Island."

Ó Néill pondered her words for a moment, chewed her bun. Then she said, "You know, we here all have curiosity upon us. Those of us that knew the witch Nubia best – we Brethren captains – have all wondered about Nubia's homeland. We were ... good friends in our youth. Well, Johnson and Ezi were

often at each other's throats. But regardless. We heard stories of witches and mermaids and faeries ... magic rivers, and giant spiders and dark wicked mountains and would whisper around firesides at the magic of it. And the real magic, the spark of spell that charmed *this* place? Her land had no Empire. No ruler, no one in charge. A land where things were divided equitably, where beings played to their strengths for the greater good. That is what we have here, on this Republic. Everyone who can work, does. Those who cannot, don't. None are hungry, none are cold, none are a slave. We captains assumed control, yes, but we formed the Nubian Brethren to remain accountable. To our crews, to our families, to all who wish to live here. Any issues are brought to our gathering and we solve them as a community." She bit, chewed again. "It would not surprise me that Johnson would seek to belittle Ezi's legacy. But I cannot believe that he would send his own crew into danger, or sail knowingly into danger himself."

"But what if he does not know that he sails into danger?" Kano probed softly. "We would not, of course, assume to accuse a captain of the Nubian Brethren of anything untoward. But if Able told my uncle that Xaymaca is best left alone, then maybe it is."

Ó Néill's head dipped, *left right*, a gesture between a nod of acquiescence and a shake of denial. Then she sighed. "Listen. I appreciate ye telling me this. I do not believe that you've told me the whole truth" – she looked them each in the eye, hard, her gaze a physical force – "nor do I believe that your intentions are malicious. But the fact remains you've no proof for what you say. Johnson is a Brethren captain. He is free to make his

own choices. And the Republic is vulnerable – the Empire is expanding and a time may come, sooner than most think, when we will have to fight for our existence. If Johnson's voyage to Xaymaca gives us even the slightest advantage then I must support it."

Levi and Vega looked at each other. Her logic was sound enough – there was not much more they could say to convince her without revealing themselves.

"It sounds as though the witch, Nubia … she was your friend," Kano said suddenly. Levi looked round. Their eyes were full as the moon and their voice was thick, humid air and no breeze.

"She was."

"Then I am sorry that you lost her."

Ó Néill blinked. "Thank you," she said quietly. "It was a hard time." She regarded them pensively. "Was there anything else ye wanted to ask me?"

Levi sorted through his thoughts like a deck of cards, shuffling them into place, not wanting to waste the opportunity. He considered mentioning the elusive Marianne but decided against it. If Emabelle, who knew the name and position of every crew member of every Brethren fleet and most of their families to boot, had not known her, then perhaps she did not want to be known. Perhaps his knowing of her would give something away, like how he'd heard the name in the first place.

"Has anyone else ever tried to find Xaymaca?" Vega asked tentatively. "To track down Nubia's birthplace? To see if it's real?"

Ó Néill snorted. "Has anyone tried to find a place

unmarked on any map and relatively unheard of? Come, girl, I did not have you pegged a dull-swift. Nay. 'Twould be a pitiful waste of strong hands and resources. And Sheta Island needs strong hands and resources."

Vega nodded and glanced at Levi. Her brow was furrowed and he was sure she was thinking what he was – they had talked about preventing Johnson's voyage and had underestimated the enormity of the task, had not grasped the way that respect and trust and status could be carefully worked to one's advantage in a society such as this. Well, they had never really lived in a society before.

"Captain Ó Néill. Thank you for meeting with us. You have given us much to think on."

They stood. Shook hands. She stared in Vega and Levi's faces, seeing familiar unknowable things. They prepared to leave, but she said, "I feel we will have need of ye."

They turned back.

"Sorry?"

"You said you wanted to see the Republic. Well, should ye wish to stay and join a crew … you would be welcome."

Levi was surprised. "Just like that?"

"You three are … unlike others. I trust my instincts on such things."

"Forgive me, Captain Ó Néill." Vega's tone was slow with curiosity and confusion. "But with all that has happened lately … are you not worried that we might be Empire spies? Sent to, I don't know, prevent the Republic gaining strength and allies? Do you not want to … have us followed or something?"

Levi looked at his sister, alarmed that she should have

put this idea in Ó Néill's head, but to his surprise the captain laughed. She looked almost motherly to Levi, though of course Levi did not consider that most mothers aren't armed to the teeth while they bite their buns.

"No, wee girl. I am not worried that you might be spies for the Empire – or for anyone at all, for that matter." She chuckled again. "You three are far too conspicuous."

Watercourses

Never never never before
had Xaymaca seen such a pour
but a dam had burst and the mother of water
could not be contained.
She raged at the faeries for forcing her hand.
She raged at Yaa and the spiders and the land.
She raged at the witches for their future sight.
She raged and raged with all of her might.

Until one day she could not rage any more.
Never never never before
had Ata felt so drained
and yet she reined herself in,
spooling like she'd seen the spiders do,
winding in her silver self
and sighed.

Never never never before
had Ata spent so much time on
the forest floor.
She lay on the banks and breathed in the
earth,
imagined Ezi's stories; a house and a hearth,

the Map that Led to You

ELLA MCLEOD

■ SCHOLASTIC

Published in the UK by Scholastic, 2024
1 London Bridge, London, SE1 9BG

Scholastic Ireland, 89E Lagan Road, Dublin Industrial Estate,
Glasnevin, Dublin, D11 HP5F

SCHOLASTIC and associated logos are trademarks and/or
registered trademarks of Scholastic Inc.

Text © Ella McLeod, 2024
Cover illustration © Adriana Bellet, 2024

The right of Ella McLeod and Adriana Bellet to be identified
as the author and cover illustrator of this work have been asserted by them under the
Copyright, Designs and Patents Act 1988.

Pages 409 to 410: Wikipedia contributors. "Vega". *Wikipedia, The Free Encyclopedia*.
Wikipedia, The Free Encyclopedia, 8 Jan. 2024. (Accessed 24 Jan. 2024.)

ISBN 978 0702 31385 1

A CIP catalogue record for this book is available from the British Library.

All rights reserved.
This book is sold subject to the condition that it shall not,
by way of trade or otherwise, be lent, hired out or otherwise circulated
in any form of binding or cover other than that in which it is published.
No part of this publication may be reproduced, stored in a retrieval system,
or transmitted in any form or by any other means (electronic,
mechanical, photocopying, recording or otherwise) without
prior written permission of Scholastic Limited.

Printed and bound in Great Britain in Clays Ltd, Elcograf S.p.A.

MIX
Paper | Supporting
responsible forestry
FSC
www.fsc.org   FSC® C018072

Paper made from wood grown in sustainable forests and other controlled sources.

1 3 5 7 9 10 8 6 4 2

This is a work of fiction.
Names, characters, places, incidents and dialogues are products of the author's
imagination or are used fictitiously. Any resemblance to actual people, living or dead,
events or locales is entirely coincidental.

www.scholastic.co.uk

her family of three
a simple fantasy
a life she knew she was not made for but
the picturing was a salve all the same,
a balm to the burn that had started again – oh—

Never never never before
    had Ata been so stinging sore,
    the yearning was churning was burning once more,
    and she could not see past the *missing them*.
    She could not remember how she'd filled her days,
    snapped at her fish for their fishy ways;
    hated the held-hands of the fluffy ones,
    or the shimmering scales so like her son's,
    until Yaa, in light and colour,
    reached down to remind her
    of the peace she had once known.

Never never never before
    had normality seemed such a chore,
    time warped and stretched as Ata had not known it.
    And she waited. And waited.
    She did not know what for.
    She called herself foolish,
    berated that more human part
    for giving a human her immortal heart –
    because now she hoped and waited for a return
    that she knew could not come for she herself had
        forbade it.

Never never never before
had Ata so lost who she was at her core –
for she was the River Mumma.
For almost six-and-ten years
the River Mumma's mortal tears
blinded her to immortal truths –
that her son would bring danger to her land.
That her son could never hold her hand,
things she *knew* but was afraid to know,
afraid to wish for –
lest they come true. Lest they never do –
that her waiting would not be entirely in vain,
that *The Drag* would return again.

The Seams of Things

As the days wore on, Levi found he could access that tranquil, in-between state more easily, the lapping of the tide as the sea inhaled and exhaled, the warmth of the sun loosening his bones and gumming his skin. This was how they worked. Levi and Kano, lying side by side in the sand, Levi talking as he carried out Kano's orders; to feel along the seams of himself, to see what had been sewn over where, what had been stuffed into pockets out of sight, to understand that it all connected together into one beautiful *Levi*.

In between these sessions, when their voices grew hoarse or Levi needed a break from his own thoughts, he would teach Kano swordplay. Kano had never used a sword – "What use would a nymph have for a sword? They're heavy and would slow me down" – and Levi had never taught anyone anything. But he afforded Kano the same patience Kano afforded him and the nymph was able to master the basics quickly. Infuriatingly quickly, as a matter of fact. Levi found himself increasingly put out as Kano cultivated their practice from basic sabre work, to a two-handed sabre and cutlass style, to being able to shift between states, mist, dew, rain, a wave, while duelling.

"I cannot believe I spent my whole life being trained by the best pirates in the world *and* training alongside Vega, who can

outmatch them all easily, and here I am having my arse kicked by a nymph novice."

Kano laughed and flicked their sabre at Levi, so that it smacked him lightly on the aforementioned arse. "When you master shifting and learn to control your sea-dragon form, you will be unstoppable."

Levi pouted. "So unfair. Not my fault I'm a better teacher than you are."

Vega would often help, sparring with Kano while Levi meditated in the sand, trying to conjure up the image of the Leviathan encircling his body, without flinching away from it in horror. Otherwise she would pace between the library, the Freeman's, the markets and other popular establishments, keeping abreast of any news, keeping her eyes and ears alert to any mention of the unknown Marianne. She was becoming restless. This became clear one morning when she suggested they take Ó Néill up on her offer of joining her crew.

"And what use would that be?" Levi had snapped. "*The Queen Áine* aren't likely to sail to Xaymaca. We'd end up stuck here, defending the Republic. We'd have duties, responsibilities, someone to answer to. How long before people start asking questions about us?" He pushed his breakfast aside, no longer hungry. His pique had startled all three of them and Vega did not broach the subject again. Levi wanted to tell her the real reason that he did not want to accept Ó Néill's offer, but pain blocked his throat with reticence. The idea of being on a deck that was not *The Sea Dragon*'s, of hearing *"All hands!"* cried by a crew that was not his own … he did not think he could bear it.

And so Levi and Kano practised, because they did not

know what else to do. They had no idea of how to prove to the Brethren that Johnson's claims were false and Levi knew that even an attempt to purchase a small sloop and sail for Xaymaca themselves could be thwarted in an instant if he could not control his shifting.

Occasionally, very occasionally, when the twisting serpents were sleepy, when he was laughing with Kano or looking out at the heaving breathing sea, Levi felt something fall away just out of his reach. It was only ever brief, the many folds of a sail being shaken out, a ripple of hope and love and grief and bright power, his full name on sweet-smiling lips calling to him from a great distance. For a moment then he would see it, the manifestation of his greater self, a huge, glorious skin waiting to be slipped into. But then doubt would wash in, the sails would catch fire. The image of his father's face would fill his mind. Kano would always encourage though, always notice. And so Levi began noticing too. The fresh morning-dew smell of their skin. The way he felt a particular kind of peace around them. The way they made Vega laugh. The gestures of friendship, tiny instances of care for his sister that squeezed Levi's insides, new undiscovered muscles flexing awake. They always stopped to buy her favourite coconut macaroons from the stall by the docks if she was spending a day in the library. Levi noticed.

*

Vega had always loved reading. It had been a luxury on *The Drag*. There were few books, as books are so easily damaged at sea, and she tore through them so swiftly that she often had to

go many moons with no reading material at all, waiting for the ship to dock and her father to replenish her supplies. It was no wonder that the simple Sheta Island library awed her. It was just a collection of books really, with no categorization or librarian to act as custodian of the place. The single column of pews was stacked with scrolls, leather-bound books, loose sheafs of paper. Shelves of all different sizes lined the walls and at the front, where the altar would have been, two bookcases were bathed in rainbow shafts of light, streaming in through the stained-glass windows. But it wasn't just that. Even Vega, who had visited very few libraries and even fewer churches on her travels, felt the insistence of something *more* here. Whether god or magic or Kano's Great Energy, she didn't know. She just knew *more*.

It was their third week on the island. Vega was sequestered in a favoured corner. She had, in her short time there, made something of a nest for herself – a couple of holey blankets borrowed from Emabelle and a steady supply of macaroons from the stall she and Kano discovered while Levi had been pretending not to admire skirts in a window of a boutique. Her book contained absolutely no useful information whatsoever – in fact it was a *novel*. She'd never had a novel before, had not supposed she'd like such a thing – Levi was the dreamer. But with the imagining laid out before her, the dream of another sprawling for her to immerse herself in, Vega found a rare enjoyment, one she had not felt since the last time she'd stood in the crow's nest, vivid hair ignited by her kin, the sun. She'd had precious little opportunity to feel this way lately – cosy and warm with potential – and the simple pleasure momentarily distracted her from grief or productivity.

She heard a creak then and the door swung open. Vega looked up. So few people came in here.

A figure was silhouetted in the threshold, momentarily blocking out the sun that streamed in through the open door.

The woman who stood there was lean and muscled. It was almost impossible to guess her age; she could have been as young as five and thirty or as old as five and sixty. Something in her stance reminded Vega of Tally; they looked nothing alike and yet she was similarly coiled, a lithe spring. Unlike Tally, who had dressed in pants and a shirt like most of the crew, this woman wore little more than scraps of leather, cut precisely and studded with bolts of brass, wrapped to protect vulnerable places. She had many gold earrings in her ears and one in her nose and her bare arms were freckled with many finely swirling tattoos which, even at this distance, she could see covered the brutal striping of scars. Vega suspected, taking in the curving hooked cutlass and two sabres, the glinting jewellery and intricately braided hair that crowned the woman's head, that this was not some underling.

The woman's brow was furrowed in thought and she was scanning the pews that served as shelves. Vega bit her lip. On one hand, she could continue reading. On the other, hiding and potentially startling someone armed to the teeth was foolhardy in the extreme. She decided to announce herself, straightening to her feet and moving forward.

Just as she opened her mouth, the woman spoke, her back still turned. "Are you going to introduce yourself, whelp, or were you planning on skulking in that corner all day?" She turned to face Vega, an eyebrow raised. As she did so, Vega

229

noticed that one of the woman's tattoos twisted familiarly – an asp in the shape of a hook. *The Cleopatra.*

"You're Captain Hook," Vega breathed.

Hook turned away, uninterested. "Blimey. And they say the youth of the day are so focused on fashion and fancy that they don't notice things."

Vega's face heated. She was not used to being embarrassed or intimidated. She grit her teeth, overcome by a sudden desire to impress.

"Well, I know little of fancy and fashion," she said composedly, "but I've come to know this library fairly well. As there's no librarian here to mind it, I've been doing some organizing. Maybe I can help you?" Vega walked between two pews, gesturing to where she had begun to group texts by category. "These here are naval logs – this side are the logs from buccaneers for the Republic. These" – another pew – "are what I assume were books left from a time before the Republic because, from what I've read, they're very pro-Empire. There's more general history, geography, tales of world leaders here. And *these* are novels." She stood in the centre aisle, looking around at what had become, she realized, her small slice of the Republic. Hers but also everyone's.

Hook was nodding slowly. "All right, whelp. I stand corrected." She was looking at Vega, really looking at her, and Vega realized her error along with Ó Néill's words. *Conspicuous.*

"I was wondering," she said quickly, as though small talk might distract the captain from her scrutiny, "how all these books and logs and things came to be here?"

Hook shrugged, looking around. "Like most things on Sheta Island, I imagine. Bought, smuggled, lost, abandoned and left over from the days of the Empire." She considered, then added, "A few were probably given intentionally. Gifted to the Republic, to be freely enjoyed by all those who freely lived." Hook eyed Vega thoughtfully. "This is impressive."

Vega thrilled at the words. There was something about Hook's prowling gait, the ripple of her muscles beneath her bands of leather and brass; she was fierce in a way that was familiar. It awoke something inside her, the intense buzz of validation. Perhaps it would have seemed strange to Levi, believing as he did that Vega excelled constantly, that she should still need to be praised. But she did.

"You know, driftling, you can read these nautical charts almost as well as I can."

Vega grinned up at Tally, where she stood at the helm. The navigator was not wrong; her young protégée could tell when a map was drawn based on its rhumb lines, could point out the contour lines and estimate fathoms without even having to swing the lead. Dusk was falling and the sky was bleeding, scarlet staining the blue violet. The sun hung juicy and sanguine, the colour of her hair, the evening star appeared, winking a familial greeting. She winked back from where she was sitting cross-legged on deck.

"But, Tally, I don't understand something."

"Aye, what's that?"

Vega frowned down at her compass. "The compass is s'posed to point north?"

"Aye, 'tis."

"But the compass is pointing" – Vega squinted at the compass – "about eight degrees west of Polaris."

Tally nodded. "Mmm, yes. That happens sometimes. It's called a magnetic declination. The poles of our world change, savvy? Slower than the tides but ceaseless. So the magnetic north, the north the compass points to, isn't always the same as true north – the north of Polaris, our North Star. It depends where in the world you are and it doesn't happen often." Tally smiled down at her. "You see, driftling? Charts are wonderful, but stars are our only constant."

"But why?" Vega chewed her words. "What's the point of a compass if it doesn't direct you right?"

Tally chuckled. "Well, driftling. A few degrees out is the best we mere mortals have." Then she frowned at the horizon. More stars had joined the first, a bright twinkly evensong. "Aye, the stars are better than maps, more constant. But our world's position in the sky is in flux, just like everything else." She looked back at Vega, her eyes inscrutable, the lights of a thousand more constants reflected in them. "Thousands of years ago, Polaris wasn't the North Star. Alpha Lyrae was. She was one of the brightest stars in the sky. It was thought that she would be the North Star again, some day."

Vega's eyes were round. "What happened to Alpha Lyrae? Where did she go?"

Tally hesitated. "Who can say? Stars flare and burn and die, they fall and walk among us." A shared smile. "But you don't need to worry about this, driftling. Not all of us are natural navigators like you – we can't all hear the song of the stars."

Vega glowed under the praise. She was a natural navigator.

She *would not be led astray by deceptive compasses or maps, or celestial shifts. She was Vega of the Sea and Skies and she had her Tally, her very own Polaris, to guide her true.*

"Hang about. You're the wee whelp who saw Cora last week. She's disappointed not to have heard from you." The flicker of realization in Hook's gaze was the light Vega followed back to the present.

She began to stutter an explanation but Hook cut her off. "And I said, Cora! God for*bid* your crew are so aged that you're pining over three whelps who have not even shown you what they can do." She laughed again. "Cora did not like that!"

Hook moved then, so swiftly, an adder about to strike, unbuckling her cutlass at her belt and holding it *en garde*. Vega barely had time to register the movement or register that she herself had, a split-second later, imitated Hook, so that she too was armed. One second her sabre was lying discarded in its belt on the nearest pew, the next it was in her hand. Their swords crossed – not a move of combat but an assertion of readiness. The clang rippled along the hairs of Vega's arms. Hook's nostrils flared. The light that filtered through the windows was shafted, sequentially dim, coloured and bright. It played across her face, throwing her impassivity into sharp relief. "I hear you've been raising some concerns. About Johnson and his voyage."

Vega's heart raced. If Ó Néill had shared the details of their meeting with Hook and Hook was a friend of Johnson's...

But if that were the case, wouldn't someone have come to interrogate them earlier? Vega wasn't sure how dissent was managed on the Republic. It was a land of freedom – all the

233

same, her eyes flicked from the tip of Hook's cutlass to her intent gaze.

"We came across Captain Ezi and the crew of *The Sea Dragon* in our childhood. He advised that Xaymaca be left alone. We simply wanted to pass that on."

The tip of Hook's cutlass twitched. "If you're going to be expressing vocal opposition to a voyage that may allow the Republic to prosper, may even hold off the Empire, then you'd best be ready to defend that position. Johnson's word is very trusted on this island. If I were a member of *The Sterling*, for example, and I heard what you, an outsider, had to say on the matter, I might think you didn't want the Republic to benefit from this alliance. I might ask why it is you trust the word of Captain Ezi, a man no one's seen in years, over a trusted veteran of the Republic."

Beat. Vega kept her sabre raised and her eyes trained on Hook's.

"But I'm not a member of *The Sterling*, am I, whelp? I'm captain of *The Cleopatra*. And I can spit further than I trust Johnson." Hook relaxed, slinging her cutlass back into her belt. "And Captain Ezi ... is ... was a friend. And a good man."

Vega lowered her sabre too but remained wary. "I thought that Captain Johnson was your ally?"

Hook glanced around the empty library. Then strode to the door and pulled it to, before facing Vega once more. Vega's whole body tensed as the room darkened somewhat, but Hook said, "Allies aren't always friends." She sighed. "The times are strange. No one has spoken of Xaymaca since Ezi left – not beyond shanties and sea stories. And now Johnson

claims to know how to reach the spot marked by the X. The X that nobody has seen. And at the same time, three strange whelps arrive on the Republic, requesting an audience with a Brethren captain and claiming to know of *The Sea Dragon*'s adventure after she left Sheta Island." Hook grinned. It was a wild, menacing thing. "Strange times indeed. But heed me, whelp; this is a free land, you can say what you will about who you are. It matters little whether you're believed. What matters is the want behind the lie. If what you want is in line with our ideals then be welcome. But if what you want falls afoul of this Republic's great purpose" – her cutlass was suddenly in Vega's face again, swifter and closer than before, the gap between its vicious tip and Vega's throat shorter than the length of her own sabre – "well. Let's just say, you'd be a fool indeed to be reading in a library with your sword discarded across the room. Savvy?"

Vega nodded.

Another beat.

Hook lowered her cutlass, turning abruptly back to the pews. "I'm looking for books on the weather."

Vega swallowed. "The weather?" Her heart still thrummed alarmingly. What damage a cutlass could do to a fragment of the heaven made flesh, Vega did not know. But there was something in the flash of Hook's eyes that made her grateful that today would not be the day she found out.

"Aye." Hook walked to the lone two shelves at what had once been the altar, scanning Vega's handiwork. "Do you know how long Captain Ezi had to wait to sail to Xaymaca? After he found the X?"

Vega shook her head.

"Two weeks."

"Why?"

"The doldrums."

Vega frowned. *"The doldrums?* But we're not near enough to the equator for that. Anyone sailing off the coast of Sheta Island should pick up a trade wind easy enough." *The doldrums* was typically the term used to refer to the stretch of ocean near the equator. The *trade winds*, swift currents from the north-east and south-east would converge and cancel each other out, leading to a windless calm belt dreaded by all who sailed. But Vega didn't understand. Sheta Island wasn't geographically placed to experience such an issue.

Hook was scanning her face, an eyebrow raised. "You're fair knowledgeable. Spent much time at sea, have you?"

Vega shook her head quickly, too quickly, perhaps. "I just like reading," she muttered.

Hook didn't press the issue, simply said, "Aye, well, right you are. And yet Sheta Island experiences very little in the way of swift wind. The seas are calm, the weather perpetually balmy – we get an occasional breeze, but that's all. Other islands in the region experience heavy storms, monsoons. But not Sheta Island."

"Oh. But if you know all this, why do you need to read about the weather?"

Hook scrutinized her for a moment. Vega could tell that she was deciding how much truth to tell her.

"Johnson's first scouts sailed three days after he claims to have seen the X," Hook said bluntly. "Not only were they suspiciously well prepared, but a westerly wind picked up,

236

almost as though … as though Johnson had called it to him." She shook her head. "The wind doesn't work that way. Not around here. It's one of the reasons so few actually leave Sheta Island. Most don't want to, but many can't be bothered to wait for a fair wind. By the time their sails can be filled, they're settled here. Content. An island for blow-ins who couldn't be blown out again."

A westerly wind. Interesting. The scout had mentioned a westerly wind. Vega tucked this information away to tell Levi and Kano later, and replied, "I see. Well, I've not seen anything that will help you here. There's nothing on Xaymaca either – I suppose no one wrote down the stories that Nubia told."

"No. We didn't. It didn't occur to us that we might need to." Perhaps if Vega had not lost so much so recently she would not have noticed the spasm, the imperceptible flicker across Hook's face at Nubia's name. But she had, so she did. It had been almost twenty years and yet, like Ó Néill, Hook still mourned their friend. Had they seen her burn? Did they too know what singed flesh smelled like? Could Hook still hear the way flames swallowed screams? Vega had a sudden impulse to ask, a desire to know if the consumptive, engulfing loss that woke her in the night and left her gasping for air ever diminished – but she held back, of course.

"Maybe if it's a nautical log of wind activity in the area then the cartographers would be better? What's his name—"

"Diego. Perhaps. But Diego doesn't … doesn't care much for talk of Xaymaca, to be honest."

"Why not?" Vega was perplexed. She couldn't imagine anyone on the Republic not wanting to talk of Xaymaca. Sheta

Island was a mortal land but it seemed to her that magic still boiled somewhere in its blood, bubbling beneath the surface. With word of Johnson's voyage, it was heating and rising like a fever.

Hook hesitated then said, "The revolution that formed the Republic was as brutal as it was triumphant. Many innocent lives were lost. Including those of Diego's mother. Xaymaca and mention of the witch Nubia serve as a reminder of it. I would have to be subtle."

Vega snorted with unexpected mirth. Hook raised a brow. "Something funny, whelp? Do I not seem subtle?"

"Well, your name is *Hook*." Vega spoke without thinking and immediately regretted it. She took in Hook's namesake and briefly wondered again if she was about to see an eponymous retaliation. Then Hook threw back her head and laughed.

"Right enough! True enough!" She laughed again. "When I fell into this world, whelp, I could not afford to be subtle. I had to forge my reputation in blood and wear it on my sleeve." She pointed to the tattoo that she shared with her crew before starting back towards the door. She pushed it open. Sunlight illuminated her once more. "It was Vega, wasn't it?"

Vega realized she had not even introduced herself but was unsurprised that Hook knew her name. She nodded.

Hook hummed, abrupt as a sudden thought. "Interesting. Well, Vega. You are not … inconspicuous." She studied Vega's unique golden glow, the strange colour of her hair. "In some ways this is a good thing – people who are noticeable arouse less suspicion. No one could ever think *you* would be an imperial spy. And this is, in many ways, a safe place. One of justice

and fairness. But times are changing. People have agendas. Be wary."

Vega nodded.

Hook left.

THE JACARANDA

TREES

"I can't believe I've never been down this street before, it's gorgeous!"

"Yeah, it's OK."

"Reggie … are you kidding?"

Maeve's tone is disbelieving but her face is delighted as she takes in the glowing canopy of amethyst, sunlight streaming through the boughs of the purple-blue jacaranda.

You shrug. This street holds twisted confusion and painful loneliness, so too does the little green door, the last building at the end. The same memory that the manchineel tree showed you. Five's cartography office.

"I wonder why I saw this place." You are thinking out loud. "I never really came here. Even as a child."

"Maybe your father knows something. About the Republic and magic and everything."

You snort. "Unlikely. Five likes to think of himself as being very *enlightened*. He goes to Pastor Johnson's church, of course, because that's, you know—"

"The done thing," you both say in unison and chuckle.

"But otherwise," you continue, "he's a … material sort of

man. Thinks any spirituality that isn't his own is all woo-woo and hippy nonsense."

The sides of Maeve's mouth dip wryly. "I think our fathers would get on very well." She looks around. "Still, it's a great spot for a family business."

You look around the street, taking in the cobbled walkway, the neatly painted doors, peer up at the purple that lines the centre of the street. "I've always preferred daffodils," is all you say.

She laughs. "Of course you have."

"I'm not trying to be contrarian." You are defensive. "The jacarandas are nice, obviously, but in books daffodils always mean spring and hope, and I know we don't exactly have seasons here but I like the idea that after months of cold and frost their funny little faces are the first thing you see."

She is looking at you. It is soft, that look. The expression picks out sage shades among the wooded hazel of her eyes. "I'll find you some daffodils."

You stutter without thinking. "Well, don't let Adrien near them," and douse cold water on the sun-kissed moment.

"Why would I let Adrien near them?" Maeve asks, confused, embarrassed. A flush creeps across her neck and chest, the exact same shade of delicate pink as the camisole she's paired with her long denim skirt.

You kick yourself internally. Hard. You had spoken mostly from jealousy, the image of Adrien's name on Maeve's phone floating unbidden into your mind, dragging an old hangnail of hurt along the fresh sting of your feelings for her. You try and laugh it off. "Oh, no, it's just a stupid thing, from when we were

kids, he probably won't remember." But she is questioning, expectant. You sigh. "It's honestly nothing, I feel stupid for even bringing it up, I literally don't know why I said anything, I just, we were talking about flowers and" – you sigh again – "basically when we were in primary school, I had a pet daffodil." You pause, waiting for her to laugh, but she doesn't. "Five – I mean my dad – he doesn't really like to have flowers in the house because, well, he associates them with my mother's grave or something. Anyway, this daffodil was in the school playground and it was the only one there; it had been a really hot spring and all the others must have died but this one was resilient and I … I sort of got attached to it and made it my mission to keep it alive, and watered it and…" You can feel heat creeping up your face. "And talked to it and stuff. When I was feeling lonely. And one day Adrien told me to give him his lunch and I said no, and I went to the toilet and when I came back he'd torn the head off the daffodil."

You feel the moment acutely still, staring at the soil and the broken, decapitated stem. Her petals had been trodden into the concrete, yellow smearing with the chalk of the hopscotch. You had sobbed as though your heart would break, right up until home time. Five had tried to explain to you, patiently at first, that "sometimes flowers die". This had not worked and he had grown frustrated. "For goodness' sake, Reggie, it wasn't a person." This had only made you sob harder and eventually he had shoved a lollipop in your mouth, which had muffled your wails of anguish until you fell asleep, exhausted by the effort. Perhaps some of this shows on your face because Maeve's lip begins to wobble dangerously.

"Oh, Reggie, that's … that's so sad. I'm sorry."

"No, no" – you hasten to right the tone of the day – "don't be sorry, I'm sure he's not like that any more. It was just a daffodil." You continue to make placating noises until you reach the little green door. You hesitate briefly but master yourself; the tree showed you this door, this place. There must be something here that you're meant to find.

"Hi, Fi— Dad."

He starts from behind the counter and for a moment you think he's forgotten that you said you'd be coming today, and is going to bark at you. But then he notices that you're not alone and says, "Oh, Reggie, darling, hello. And this must be Maeve O'Neill?" The "darling" lands clumsily in your ears but you don't react. He shakes Maeve's hand and you look around the shop. It's familiar, so perhaps you have indeed been here before, or perhaps you've imagined it enough that it feels like you have. Five kept you away from this place, kept his work and home lives distinct and separate, as though he could keep some part of himself safe from the grief of his wife's death.

Dark panelled wood, shelves with expensive books line the walls, glossy expensive ones, leather-bound antiques, and, above them, framed navigation charts, some as old as the fifteenth century. The back wall of the small room is split between a cabinet full of strange curiosities, nautical equipment, globes, compasses, and a spiralling staircase of wrought and twisted iron. Five leads you up it to the room off the mezzanine. It might be a decently sized second showroom but has been used for storage for so long and is packed so high, that it looks as though it hasn't been sorted and organized in

centuries. This is mostly unlike your father but you can see how even he would be overwhelmed. You've no idea where to begin and are, frankly, worried about what furry scurrying things might be lurking among the hundreds of boxes, some of which are piled high as the ceiling.

"Feel free to have a look around," he says nervously. "I'm afraid I can't let you take anything with you but you can take photos and … and make notes and such. This is for your … your school history project, yes?" Even though it's a lie, it is embarrassing how much he has to strain to remember.

"Yes. On the Republic. How it formed and fell. We're looking at the role magic has played, how it's been lost, overwritten by religion and propriety."

Five rolls his eyes. "Of course you are," he says drily. "Well, the front half of the left wall is everything from roughly the time that you're looking for. Everything else is pre- and post-Republic. Eras of Enlightenment."

"You mean of Empire."

Beat. He descends back down the stairs and you and Maeve set to work, looking for the box you saw when you touched the tree. While you search, you keep an eye out for anything that might also help with your coursework, taking photos and making notes, as Five suggested. The walls are a jumbled mess of rickety wooden sets of drawers, 1980s style filing cabinets and many cardboard boxes.

"I understand it, you know."

"Understand what?"

"What it's like for it to just be you and your da."

You register what she's said. "Yeah. I know you do. And at

least I only have Five to deal with." You make a half-hearted attempt at joviality. "If I had a Karen of an aunt too, I think I'd go mad."

Maeve smiles. "Yeah. Sometimes I wish my mother had been more open to motherhood. I wonder what my life would look like if she hadn't left."

"I don't understand it at all." You speak without thinking, you cannot resist the sad dip of her chin. "I don't know how anyone could leave you, could not want to be around you all the time."

Her earlier flush returns, deepening. "Well, as cool as this place is I can't understand why Five squirrels himself away in here instead of hanging out with you. But at least" – she wrestles the words and desire wins – "at least his loss is my gain. And we have each other, in the evenings." She bites her lip, as though she regrets being so bold…

You smile. She stole your sentiment and you have never been so grateful to a thief.

Her phone buzzes. She doesn't even look at it. Your smile widens and you return to the stack of papers in your hand. The island in the maps that you peer at is familiar in its shape and landmarks. The cartographer's is where it always has been; the docks have, unsurprisingly, not moved; what is now a five-star hotel is marked as *The Freeman's Inn*.

The room is dusty and warm and you oscillate between fear that you'll fall sleep and fear that you'll suffocate. Two hours tick by. You stand and stretch, crossing the room, wondering about opening a window. You try the one on the far right and fail. The windows have been blocked for so long that you can't

even reach it. You turn to walk back towards the door, hoping to inhale the slightly fresher current of air from downstairs when you let out a gasp and a yelp, as your foot sinks partially through the floorboard.

The sight of you wobbling, one foot through the floor, sends Maeve into peels of laugher. You try to look annoyed but it is impossible and you join in.

"Your face!"

"God, Maeve, don't just stand there laughing – help me!"

Still cackling, Maeve obliges, carefully crossing the weak rotting wood and gripping your hand and forearm to hoist you out. You avoid a splinter and are grateful for your black knee-high socks. It takes a few tries as Maeve is smaller than you but eventually your foot comes loose and you stagger together.

"My dad's going to kill me," you say regretfully, looking at the hole.

"Wait a second, Reggie…" Maeve is peering into the dark space, previously occupied by wood and nails. "What's … *that*?"

You see the treasure-chest style box almost immediately and your heart thuds. Reaching into the dark dusty space, thinking, with some apprehension, of mice and spiders, you pull it loose. As it emerges into the sunlight you gasp a jubilant "Yes!"

It's exactly the one that you saw.

Your face falls slightly. It's locked.

You scan the room for a key without much hope. "Damn," you mutter, "and I'm hardly going to have a hairpin on me, am I?" You gesture to your cropped cut.

"No, but I do." Maeve's grin is mischievous. "Picking the lock on your da's secret cabinet. Very on brand, Reggie."

You take the pin. "I mean, I've no idea how to pick a lock. But I have YouTube and 4G."

The lock is old-fashioned, rusty and easily picked. It springs apart in less than twenty minutes.

You open it. A rolled-up piece of paper, wilted and yellowing, sits inside. You unfurl it and spread a map out before you.

For a moment you're a bit disappointed. Other than the fact that it is dated nearly three hundred years ago, it's a fairly ordinary map. And as the daughter of a cartographer, very old maps aren't particularly exciting.

"It's a map," Maeve says.

"No shit."

"It's a map of the Republic and the surrounding islands, as they were marked then."

You think about the timeline. "It's dated just before the forming of the Republic. I wonder whose it was?"

"And why it's in a locked chest, beneath the floor in your father's office?"

"This place has been in our family for generations. Judging by the date it would have belonged to" – you rock back on you heels, thinking, counting – "Diego Hornigold the First, at least."

"Is that who your father is named after?"

"Yep. He and four others."

"So traditional"

"Well, it's—"

"The done thing." You laugh in unison but you remain confused.

"I wonder why they hid it, though?"

"I wonder why the tree showed it to you?" Your mind feels

stretched tight, thin and taut, and the too hot room is suddenly suffocating.

"Let's get some air." You get to your feet. Blood rushes to your head and you feel momentarily lightheaded.

"Reggie? Are you OK?"

You nod. "Yeah, just didn't eat any breakfast and it's hot and this is ... there's been a lot to process lately."

Maeve smiles, her eyes wide. "It's very surreal, for sure." She pockets the map and takes care to return the dusty chest to beneath the floorboard. She covers the hole over with other cardboard boxes, full of old books and paperwork, centuries of tax returns. Hopefully Five won't notice. You both head downstairs, shouting hasty goodbyes to Five, who barely looks up from the trade magazine he's reading, and emerge into the bright sunlight.

You walk slowly over to a bench, covered slightly by the vivid shade of the jacaranda, and sit down, folding the map carefully into a pocket

"I feel like someone is calling to me. Asking me for help. But I don't know why."

Maeve's hand squeezes yours and you squeeze it back, you never want to let it go. "You can't know everything, Reggie." She pauses. "I have to say, it's not that I didn't *believe* you – I mean I saw the manchineel tree *not* poison you – but I just couldn't believe it. Like when you said, 'I think there's a secret chest hidden my dad's office,' I thought ... but sure, what are the chances? Now though ... well." She shakes her head. "I don't suppose you would want to ask your da about it?"

You scoff. "I doubt he even knew it was there. There's no way

248

he'd have something that old in the back room without trying to sell it to some antiques collector. He would just be annoyed that I took it and make me give it back. And then I'd never get any answers."

"You could go back to the tree? See if you see anything else?"

You nod, somewhat reluctant. You cannot put into words what you experience when you touch the manchineel tree. It is as though you've been struck by lightning, charged like a battery, a current of energy that isn't quite yours and doesn't quite answer to you, running through you. You feel defiant and dangerous. You feel exhausted.

"Bet you're regretting being paired with me," you say. "From history coursework to this."

"Why do you do that?" Her shoulders move in jerky frustration. "Reggie, I like spending time with you. I think this island has many questions and not many people seeking answers … but you … you seek things, you seek the truth. I like that about you."

You squirm, your face is warm, you deflect. "You're such a Cancer."

"And you're such a Scorpio!"

"The witchiest of all the signs," you agree, and then: "Maybe it's connected to Nubia in some way. The stories say where she burned, the manchineel tree grew. If she really was a witch…"

A beat of understanding. "Then maybe the tree is … magic." Maeve's eyes are wide. She leans forward, whispers, "Maybe you're magic, Reggie."

You laugh and it is a breathy sound. You like the way she sees you. You like the way she says your name. She is not looking at

you like you're crazy or weird, she's looking at you like … like she likes looking. Her eyes dart between your own and your mouth in a heady back and forth. She captures you with her gaze, but you are willing. The perfect pink tulip of her lips blooms before you, her neck is feather soft beneath your fingertips. You arch and brush together, like the jacaranda blooms above.

A Whisper on the Wind

There is a breath on the breeze,
A westerly whisper on the wind,
A tempting tickle 'til you sneeze,
A restless shiver down a limb.

Come to the land of pirate hoards,
Come and tangle with a spider,
Come and catch a mermaid whore,
Have a go, try and ride her.

Come and set the faeries free,
Xaymaca offers a piece of her pie,
Come live as rich as man can be,
Prince Ezi shall laugh if you do not try.

He saw all this paradise holds,
He took and took and would not share,
Bewitching witches and mounds of gold,
Of his comrades he did not care.

Wretched is your land and town,
Inevitable is your disaster,
For some ideal will you drown?
Don't be a servant, be a master.

Of Sea, Of Stars

"This is starting to feel like a waste of time!"

Levi had been lying on his back, trying to find his sea dragon form for over an hour. Feeling along the seams, tugging at threads, unearthing memories of childhood joy and worry. Able's lessons, Talani's tears, his father's stories, stealing trinkets in the game with Vega. But no matter what folds of Levi he pulled back, he could not find Leviathan anywhere.

He felt far away from himself. Kano was patient and unhurried. Levi found himself wondering if his consistent failure was, in part, due to the fear of what would happen if he did succeed. Would Kano leave? Levi could not imagine the dark of the night without Kano's silk skin and hanging dew beside him. The thought sent a twanging though his midriff, as though clinging to the phantom of Kano's touch.

"Why can't you just say my name? That would probably do something."

But Kano shook their head. "This work that we do is to give you control over your power. Right now it controls you. We avoid your true name like it is a dirty word—"

"It is a dirty word!"

"It is not. It is a beautiful word and it is who you are. It is a beautiful word *because* it is who you are."

"No, it's the name of a fucking monster."

"And that belief is why you cannot shift."

Levi sprung to his feet and stalked away. He was taking his frustration out on Kano. He knew they didn't deserve it, but could not help himself. It was easy for Kano to say. Their shifting had never been discovered, it had always just been. They became air and mist and a gentle sea breeze. Something sweet and beautiful and necessary. He became a monster.

"I don't fancy sword practice this morning," Levi threw over his shoulder at where he knew Kano had remained rooted by the shoreline. "You don't need it anyway. I'm going to get lunch."

He stalked back to the Freeman's, not waiting to see if Kano followed.

The inn was always busy at lunchtimes. Those who worked at the docks crushed themselves into the hours between noon and two. Levi squeezed through the press of bodies, forcing his way towards the welcome prospect of a meal. He would feel better once he'd eaten.

"Hatchling!"

He turned. Vega sat at a table, tucked in the corner by the window. He knew by her face that something had happened.

"What is it?"

She took a breath – then she stopped short.

"Let's go outside."

Levi doubted anyone would hear their conversation over the din of the lunchtime rabble but he did not argue. He took a platter of bread and cheese from Emabelle, wrapped it in a handkerchief and followed his sister out on to the street.

He caught up with her at a quiet corner, a cliff path where the tracks were sandy, wending the long way down towards

the markets at the docks. She had settled down but was looking ahead into the middle distance as Kano strode swiftly towards them.

"Kano, I brought you lunch." Vega offered a third bundle to the nymph who accepted it, before pressing Vega's fingers to their lips affectionately. It did not improve Levi's mood.

"Well, count not the waves, Vega, what is it you wanted to say?" He could not keep the bite of impatience out of his voice. Vega raised her eyebrows in Kano's direction, slightly mocking, including them. Levi yanked the cork out of his bottle of ale with a vicious snap of his teeth.

"I was reading in the library. And Captain Hook came in." Levi sat down heavily beside her. "And?"

She told them what was said, replaying their conversation in her usual meticulous detail. When she finished, she swigged her ale in relief, her throat parched from talking in the dry heat.

Levi chewed his bread thoughtfully, staring out at the sea. It was so clear today that were it not for that indefinable line that created the illusion of a severe drop, he would be unable to tell it apart from the sky above.

"Did Captain Hook say that she was trying to stop Johnson leaving?" Kano was stretched out on their front at Vega's feet. "Or just that she shared our worry?"

"Aye, the latter," Vega mused. "No one can really *stop* him. Not without very good reason and firm proof. This is a free land, remember. It's their most sacred ideal."

"But she knew … the crew," Levi said slowly, "was friends with them. So everything Johnson has been saying about them makes her wary. Even more mistrusting." It was hopeful.

Perhaps if they learned more about Xaymaca they could find some proof of Johnson's agenda. Hook sounded like she might believe them. And maybe then Ó Néill would too.

"I wanted to raise something again, too." The hesitation in his sister's voice made Levi look round. She chewed her words. "Maybe we … we ought to think about trying to join a … another crew." She held up her hand as Levi opened his mouth in protest. "No, listen to me, Levi. I know you didn't want to sail under Ó Néill. But you want to get to Xaymaca. To do that you need a boat, resources. And everything from the smallest sloop to the largest brigantine is spoken for."

"I still haven't mastered my shifting and no captain other than Johnson has plans to leave the Republic."

"But when you have … perhaps, if we join up, we could convince them. Think about it, hatchling, what other options do we have?"

Levi did not want to hear it. How could she not see that it was impossible for him? He would be betraying *The Sea Dragon* all over again.

"Why? Did Hook make you a good offer or something?" He could hear it, the defensiveness, the tightness, the kind of rearing ugliness that can only precede picking a fight with a sibling.

"No." Vega's forced calm sounded patronizing. "But I think she would. And Captain Ó Néill did, so—"

"What did she say? Why do you think she would? What – did she call you a *good girl* and *very quick* and praise your knowledge of the sea and skies?" He was being nasty, and he knew it; the scathing words scraped his tongue on the way out

and he regretted them instantly. Because Levi understood the temptation. He could not deny the appeal of asking a grown-up. Of telling everything to someone older and wiser, someone who had known their father and their crew. But they were the grown-ups now.

Vega stood abruptly. She was angry and the otherwise empty cliff path seemed to fill with her, eclipsed by her scorching rays. "Why are you taking the owl and speaking to me this way? I'm trying to help!"

"No, you just want to be back on deck, being praised and called a *star*, taking the egg again!"

"Taking the egg?" Her voice rang with outrage. "It's not a fucking contest, Levi!"

"That's easy for you to say when you always win!" He was on his feet too. He had not had a fight with his sister in years and it felt good, a heady rushing, a mortal release. "Perfect driftling, marvellous Miss Vega, Vega our *star*! Who fell from the sky and blessed us with her presence! Not like her murderous, monstrous brother, who destroys everything he touches!"

Her teeth were bared and her eyes were shining, gold and silver, rage and heartbreak and pity. "We're on the same team, hatchling!" She ground the words out, her chest heaving. "It makes *sense* to join another crew, we can't do all this alone. We can't stop Johnson, we can't set sail, we haven't even found out who *Marianne* is! Pa joined the Brethren, but that didn't stop *The Sea Dragon* from being a crew too. And so are we! A crew of three!"

She had not said *Pa* in weeks. She had not even noticed. But Levi had.

They stared at each other, breathing hard. He almost reached for her, almost clung to her.

Then she said, her voice slightly gentler, "So? What say you, Captain?" and the word turned his insides to ice.

"Oh, I'm the captain now, am I? Sure you wouldn't rather Hook or Ó Néill?"

Vega swore ferociously and stalked away. A steady stream of curses followed her like a bad smell, sending nearby people leaping out of her way.

He looked down at Kano. The nymph was gazing into his face, wordless but so very loud.

Captain. Levi's eyes stung with the certainty that he did not deserve that title.

*

Vega retreated to the library after her fight with Levi. She was so full of feeling that she had to force herself to slow her pace lest she begin to walk beyond the bounds of what was normal for a human and be even more conspicuous than she was. She pushed open the door and inhaled, the sweet smell of worn paper soothing her. She knew that Levi was struggling – with his shifting, his guilt, his grief. But she wished he would remember that she was struggling too. She tucked herself into her nest. The book she had been reading that morning, before meeting Hook, was where she left it and she picked it up, resolving to lose herself in it and forget all about Levi and the argument.

As she reached though, she felt a rustle behind her and at the same time felt something hard dig into her back. She twisted

to find another book, placed deliberately so that she would find it. A fold of separate parchment poked out of it. She turned to the page the parchment marked and held the book open as she read the note. It was short. Eight words in large jagged swoops:

> *Whelp,*
> *I thought you'd find this page interesting.*
>   *Hook*

The leg of the *k* kicked defiantly, curving like the cutlass of its scribe. Vega smiled slightly, and looked down.

She recognized the navigational chart, an old map of the sky, printed across the double page spread of the book. It was dated some years before she had been found by Ezi, before the forming of the Republic, and was older than any of the maps she had seen aboard *The Drag*. She peered at it. After a few minutes' perusal, she frowned to herself. Something was wrong and she could not immediately put her finger on what.

Then it came to her. There was a star here that shouldn't be. A star she'd never seen before. She was confused. She turned the page and found another map, one dated a few years after the first. The sky as she knew it. She turned the page again and found what she was looking for, a printed explanation, details of the stars and constellations shown. She scanned down until a line leaped off the faded page, claiming her attention.

> *The star Alpha Lyrae, which appeared as part of the con-*
> *stellation Lyra, and vanished soon after Sheta Island was*
> *reclaimed as the Republic.*

Alpha Lyrae. Vega remembered Tally's lessons and read on eagerly – was this the answer to what had happened to the missing star?

> *Navigators note strange occurrences in the night at this time.*
> *Explanations have interwoven with local legend and those*
> *that inhabit the Republic, those who saw the witch's death,*
> *believe that her burning caused something strange and un-*
> *heard of. Seafarer legend postulates that stars may fall to*
> *earth and walk among us as beings like people; and so it is*
> *believed that the witch's defiance rattled the heavens, shak-*
> *ing a star loose. Alpha Lyrae was believed by astronomers to*
> *be the North Star of the future, that one day it would have*
> *been the star to guide home those lost at sea. Those who saw*
> *the light hurtling towards earth sent up many wishes, in-*
> *cluding those wishes for this island and a well-fated future.*
> *What really happened to the star, none can say.*

And beneath this paragraph, an addendum,

> *Alpha Lyrae was also known as Vega.*

Vega felt all of the air leave her lungs. She blinked once, twice, but it was as though she was looking at the page through warped glass. She was on her feet in seconds, moving for the door, forcing herself once more to slow down so that the world did not see her as what she was – a comet-bright blur of red and gold, a sight more in keeping with the vast achromatic night, born to light an infinite nothingness.

"What in Davy's name are you on about?"

Vega leaned against the rocks that formed the cliff face and breathed sharply through her nose and out of her mouth. Levi and Kano had paused their sword practice, which they had returned to after lunch in an attempt to distract Levi from his bad temper. They looked at her now, bemused, atrabiliousness arrested.

"The star that went missing when the Republic formed, *Alpha Lyrae*, the star that everyone said Nubia's rage shook from the sky!"

"Yes, what about it?"

"Its name was Vega!"

They stared at each other.

"No…"

"Yes!"

"Are you sure?"

"Certain!" And she was. "I can feel it, Levi. I can feel it with all that I am! The truth, it itches beneath my skin, savvy?"

He understood. Stared at her some more. Perhaps to someone other than Levi, knowing *which* star his sister had been, which space in the sky she'd claimed, would matter less than having a star for a sister. But it was not simply that she had fallen the night the Republic formed, it was all that had happened after.

"Do you think Pa knew?"

She paused. Then nodded. "Yes. Remember what the last thing he said to me was? *He will never be lost with you, Vega,*

you're the future, you're his North Star. The book said that the star, Alpha Lyrae, Vega, whatever, was thought to be the North Star of the future. That it, not the Pole Star, would guide home those that were lost. And I…"

"You are a navigator." Kano was sitting at the shoreline, half in and half out of the water. They looked perfectly calm.

"You think she's right?" Levi faced them.

Kano rolled their eyes and the expression was so new, an imitation of himself or Vega, that Levi laughed despite himself.

"Of course. A defiant witch was burned at the stake and threw the last of her magic into the heavens. Her cry rattled the stars, one plummeted to earth and landed in the sea. Who can say what the stars are made of, or what can happen when their matter meets what the *ocean* is made of – magic and spirit and force?" Kano smiled at Vega. "You've spent every spare minute since we arrived at that library near the spot that Nubia's life ended. You came to your family with your name. You came to Levi for a reason." They laughed suddenly, a gay, bubbling sound, and lay back in the sand and salt. "It is not just I, it seems, being pulled along a path by the Great Energy!"

Levi and Vega stared at each other. For a few long moments they just stared. Then they started laughing. Once it started, they could not stop. It had been so long since they laughed this way. Bent double, clutching each other, smearing sand along each other's skin.

Eventually, when the tears had dried on their faces and their stomachs ached, they collapsed in the sand beside Kano. A thought occurred to Vega and she said, "The day you

eavesdropped on Pa. He said something about … something about your mother. Wishing on a star."

Levi met his sister's gaze. "Aye. He said a star fell and she wished on it and it brought Pa to her."

"Perhaps you were always meant to find each other," Kano said with an absent smile.

"Perhaps we all were." Levi looked at the nymph with a soft smile.

Vega grinned. "A fallen star, a nymph and a sea dragon!"

"Sink me, what a ridiculous trio!"

And they laughed some more.

*

They trained for a couple of hours more, running drills along the shore before heading back to the Freeman's.

Vega reached for her brother's hand, squeezed it, and he reached for Kano's hand and squeezed it and for a little while they walked like that. The last few weeks had been so full of feeling and Levi wondered if part of the problem with his shifting was his inability to separate them all. They formed a jumbled mess of grief and joy and longing, tangled, knotty threads; it was a knotty mess, this life of his. But as he looked at his sister and saw the assuredness in her gaze, he thought that maybe it did not need to be untangled. Maybe just accepted for what it was. A life in pursuit of a dream. A life of love.

"I am sorry for how I spoke to you earlier, driftling."

"Forgiven, hatchling."

"We've always been told that I would be captain. That it's

my job to know where we are going, and your job to get me there. But I have been … fearful of the journey. Of what it means. Pa…" He swallowed. Saying the epithet in front of Vega drew him up short and he cast her a darting look. But she had opened this door, he was merely stepping through. "Pa was worried about my mother. He feared she was in danger and he wanted to help somehow. I want to help too." A plan had formed as they'd drilled parries and thrusts, the kind of work of the mind that can only occur when the body is occupied. Their conversations with Ó Néill and Hook had made one thing very clear: they would not be able to stop Johnson's voyage without very good reason or proof of ill intent.

"There's something I think we have to do."

"What?" The star and the nymph turned to their reluctant captain and he sighed.

"Break into Johnson's offices."

Star Quality

The docks that formed the humming hub of the Republic had rapidly expanded in the years since the Empire had held Sheta Island. Markets sprung up, winding stalls and narrow alleys bridging the gap between the fishermen and shipwrights and what had once been the "smart part of town". Now that money was distributed more evenly, there was no "smart part of town". The townhouses that had once been owned by members of the upper crust were taken over when the upper crust flaked and dissolved into the sea. They fled back to their imperial motherland on ships weighty with jewels mined and stolen from other colonies. It was on a few of these formerly smart streets that the crew of *The Sterling* now lived. Slightly central and fairly west, the townhouses were made of sandstone with sloping grey rooves and wide bay windows. The street had the air of a place that was usually quiet, but today it was alive with excited activity.

The equinox had arrived. Everywhere across the Republic signs of imminent festivity appeared. Street parties and strewn flowers, plates of sweet treats carried to and fro by harassed-looking bakers. The air was electric with excitement but Levi's spirits did not lift. The equinoxes were his favourite festivals aboard *The Drag*. Vega preferred the solstices but Levi was enthralled by the rightness of it, the unity of the whole world

in alignment, the sun and moon perfect in the steps of their infinite dance.

It was another scorcher on this island of few seasons and Levi found himself longing for the springtime rain, for the heady petrichor and the fat droplets of *familiar* on his face.

"So, are we all clear on the plan?"

"Aye."

Levi turned to Kano. "Are you sure about this? I still think I should be the one to—"

But Kano offered a rare interruption. "No. You might be seen. I will shift and go unnoticed."

Levi nodded reluctantly. "Vega, have you worked out a signal?"

"Aye." She opened her mouth and cawed like a gully-bird. It was haunting in its accuracy and, for a moment, nausea rose in Levi and he heard again the screams of his family, heard that blood-curdling call, smelt the scent of burning.

"Is something on fire?"

Vega glanced around. "It's just the candles and incense. Standard equinox fare."

"Levi?" Kano was looking at him, a V of concern etched between their brows.

"Sorry." Levi shook himself. It would not do to lose focus now. "So, everyone in the house will be going to this ... equinox party, aye?"

Vega nodded. "Emabelle said most streets will have parties and everyone in all the houses gathers. Even the Freeman's is hosting a sort of ball. I think she was disappointed we wouldn't be there."

"Maybe we'll make it back in time," Kano suggested but Levi met Vega's eyes and knew she was no more in the mood for such reminiscent revelry than he was. He opened his mouth to say so, but Vega nudged him and pointed as a door at the very end of the street swung open. They drew back. Men and women dressed for the occasion emerged from the house laughing, some in linen, some in light muslin, others in silk ball gowns in pale pinks and yellows. Where Levi saw flashes of ink on arms, he noted the coin with the side profile of a man's head and remembered Emabelle's scoffing tone. *Only Captain Johnson would think to make his crew's tattoo a coin with his own face on it.* From a few paces away, the sounds of drums and whistles, a band of pipes and percussion beginning to set up. The street filled, along with the tables, piles of cakes and breads and platters of meat and fruit and cheese. The music began in earnest, a sudden swell of lively sound that made Levi want to dance for the first time in weeks.

"Look." Vega drew his attention once more and he turned as a man who could only be Captain Johnson – because he looked exactly like the kind of man his father would have disliked – emerged, finally, from the house. Tall, pale-haired, with the walk of someone accustomed to ownership.

Levi turned away and found Kano and Vega watching him, awaiting instruction. The assumed responsibility made him uneasy but he squared his shoulders. It was his plan, after all. "Right. Vega, watch the house. I'll keep eyes on Johnson. Kano – hang back another ten minutes or so, see if anyone else comes out. And then—" He swallowed, his throat suddenly contracting beneath the grip of what Kano – sweet, soft

Kano – was about to do. He shook himself again. He thought of the barely-there dew and mist he had seen Kano become. They would be fine. "Get inside. Find his study. Search for anything – papers, letters, anything. Then get out."

They all nodded and Levi moved off behind Johnson.

Levi made sure to keep a few paces behind his quarry, allowing the tide of people to ebb and flow between them as Johnson took a plate from a stack and filled it with food. The wind picked up, changing direction and carrying the scent of fresh fruit and sweet wine. Levi inhaled deeply, watching Johnson holding court among the crowd. His booming voice and rounded vowels carried above the music and laughter, drowning out the chatter and the cawing of the gully-birds. "So I said to Ezi, *The Sea Dragon*? Why on earth would you call it that? It sounds like a terrible omen! Never has there ever been a ship called *The Kraken*! And it seems I was right, doesn't it?"

"So they've really foundered, Captain?"

"Aye, so it would seem. The second scouting ship to Xaymaca found evidence of a wreckage a couple of days east. Strange, though. They reported it out at sea, so what it foundered on I couldn't tell ye."

Levi sickened, his blood pumped with frigid fury. He knew Johnson had been no friend of his father's but to hear him speak so casually of his death, contemptuously throwing around news of his family's watery grave like mere scuttle. Hatred pooled in his stomach. It felt good to have someone to direct it at that was not himself. He stepped unsteadily backwards, keeping Johnson in view but retreating to where the sounds of music and dancing feet muffled Johnson's gossip and shielded Levi's

shredded heart. He stood lost in the sound for a few minutes, wishing he could shake off all that had been and dance as freely as the bodies whirling around him. He watched a little boy spinning in his mother's arms, legs dangling gleefully. Ezi had told him that the Republic was no place for children. Another lie. Children laughed here, played in the streets. What Ezi had meant was that the Republic was no place for Levi. *It's not just that I want to protect him from the world. It's that I want to protect the* world *from him.*

"Levi! Levi!" He looked round. Vega was at his side. Her eyes were wide, nostrils flared, skin of her face stretched into sharp angles of anxiety.

"What?"

"I was calling you!"

Levi stared at her, cursing himself. How had he allowed himself to lose focus so quickly?

"What's happened?"

"I don't know how no one else has noticed yet but – they will and – Levi, I thought Kano would come out when I cawed but they haven't and … Levi, there's a fire!"

A wave of nausea. *A fire.* He was choking on panic, it stuffed itself up his nostrils and shoved its fingers down his throat, coating his tongue and fogging his brain. And then he heard the commotion behind him, the shouts and calls, "Fire!"

"Captain!"

"Captain Johnson, sir!"

"Fire!"

"A fire in your house!"

"We don't know how it started!"

"It's a dry day, it must be all the candles!"

Levi was shaking his head, eyes wide, jaw slack. Screaming and cracking and the smell of burning flesh. Singed hair and wood. Greedy fire consuming and taking and not stopping.

I am made of water and land and air. Fire eats those things. It dries me out, stops me from shifting. It's the rare time my solid form is stronger than any other shape. But even then, I am vulnerable.

The truth beat a horrible tattoo against his skull.

Kano was in grave danger.

*

The horizon was ablaze. The sky above had become the faded periwinkle of a new bruise. The air was crisp and crackling, dry wood snapping, the smell of food and bodies. And under it, new and subtle but to Levi's nose so distinct he wondered that he had not smelled it before, the unmistakable acrid sting of smoke. He couldn't think, he couldn't breathe. He could hear the screams of his family, smell their flesh as it melted from their bones, the sulphurous odour of hair as it caught, lit, burned to the scalp, and somewhere beyond Vega was crying, pleading, calling his name—

"Levi! Levi!" His sister's vice-like grip on his arm brought him back to himself.

"Kano is vulnerable to fire." His voice was calm now, authoritative and sure. He knew what had to be done. "They are born of air and water and land. Fire traps them in their

human form, weakens them. They won't be able to shift or flee unseen and they probably won't be strong enough to climb out through a window unaided either. We have to help them." Beat. He weighed their options, his mind a pendulum between what he wanted to do and what must be done. Then he swallowed all competitive pride and said, "Vega, can yo—"

"Of course, I'll go, hatchling. I'm a better climber."

And then she was gone.

*

Vega speared through the crowd, a flame-bright ray that began to attract attention, but she was gone before it could settle on her. She noticed an alley on her right and veered down it, following her instincts. As she moved she tuned out the world around her, the shouts of people running for buckets and water and her anxiety for Kano, who in the few weeks she had known them, had made her feel soft and cared for in a way she had never been. She focused on her pulse, her even breathing. It was not quite night, the sun had just begun to slip away, but the stars were never invisible to Vega. She wound out of the alley and began to run down a street parallel to the one where the party and fire fought to rage. It was empty – clearly all of the revellers from this street were partying with their neighbours – and she took advantage of the desertion to break into her full sprint, swift and startling. Birds nesting in trees, neatly manicured and lining the street, spiralled into the air, shrieking. She ran faster, until she drew to a screeching halt at the end of the row, facing the house that backed on to Johnson's.

A brief moment of assessing. The townhouses were built close together, high-walled gardens lying end to end like dominoes, narrow alleyways running vertically in between. To reach the back of Johnson's house, Vega would have to dart down the alleyway of the house now facing her, the house whose garden backed on to Johnson's. Then she would climb Johnson's garden wall and scale the side of the house, using the gutters, the trellises, the window sills, clinging to the alley shadows and praying that no stray flash of gold would give her away. *Easy.* Vega snorted to herself before glancing around and slipping into the shadows.

About halfway down the alleyway the brickwork in the wall on her right changed slightly, marking where the first garden ended and Johnson's began. She jumped for the top of it, swinging her legs up lightly, remaining low while she found her balance. She ran along the wall in a crouch, noticing how dry the gardens were, the grass yellowing in places, the flowers wilting for lack of rain or moisture in the air. No wonder the fire, however it had started, now raged so intensely. The crew must be back with buckets of water by now – this would make extracting Kano unseen even harder. She could smell the inferno and the part of her that burned similarly could sense it. It had not yet reached the top floor but it was reaching up the stairs with hot hands. Kano must be trapped. She knew where they were, had seen the slight flicker of movement in the top-floor window with her keen eyes and marked the room as being Johnson's study. The fire had cut off their escape down the stairs and they were too weakened to jump from a window.

The sky had darkened now, the stars blinking their eyes

open to watch her fully. She felt calm as she began to climb, hand over hand, foot over foot, wall to gutter, to trellis.

Up and up.

She put her hand on a window ledge and instantly pulled it away again at a flash of movement inside. She clung to the wall, one foot in a groove left by a broken piece of sandstone, another braced against the sheer vertical face of the wall, a hand on the gutter above, so close to the roof now, and the other, incriminating hand clenched in a fist in her mouth. She waited as one of Johnson's underlings swung the window open.

The moment stretched, so tense it dizzied her.

Vega didn't dare breathe.

The buccaneer leaned out of the window, looking down. All she had to do was turn her head to the right, lean a little and she would see Vega, hanging frozen from the gutter.

A few, heart-stopping seconds passed. Then the head retreated and the window closed.

Vega breathed a sigh of relief and swung her other arm up to join the first, before scrabbling her feet up on to the roof. The crew of *The Sterling* were nearly at the top floor. Kano's gentle, summer-cloud eyes filled her mind. She reached the window of the attic at the side of the house and peered inside. It was indeed the study, spacious, stretching out over most of the top floor of the house. There was nothing, no movement. She looked closer and her stomach dropped. Smoke furling under the door.

Vega weighed her options, clenching and unclenching her jaw, chewing each decision. If Kano was in there, the fire was all that was between them and discovery. If they weren't… Vega did not let herself think it. Throwing caution to the rare

wind she swung a long leg awkwardly round, lined up the toe of her steel-capped boot with the window and kicked. The glass gave way and she slid herself along and down, before dropping inside.

She swiftly surveyed the room. It was swelteringly hot, the heat from the floors below rising to render the study a furnace, but she was not sweating. It was full of smoke, the air grey and impenetrable, but she could breathe fine. At her core she was made of hotter stuff. A large writing desk was stacked neatly with papers, quills in pots, bookshelves filled with Johnson's personal literature. Everything was perfectly in order. Either Kano had not been able to search at all or they had put everything back exactly as they found it. As she thought this, a dry cough sounded from somewhere in the room, followed by a rasp of "Vega?"

Crumpled on the floor beneath the desk was a creature that spoke with an approximation of Kano's voice and possessed very little of their appearance. Their normally dewy complexion had dulled to ash, their opal eyes foggy, their skin wrinkled and shrivelled.

"Kano?" She reached for them, feeling sickened by their strange new texture. "Come on, quickly, let's get you some air. I'll carry you until you can shift and—"

"No, wait!" Their voice was hoarse. "The desk … there's a letter on top … take it … seal of the Empire…" They collapsed against her, a dry hacking cough shaking their frame. Vega moved round the desk, scanning the stack of papers. The waxed seal of the Empire leaped out at her, three lions each wearing a crown. It was broken where the letter had been opened. She did not stop to read it, just slid it inside her pants where it would

not come loose and fall in the climb, and returned to Kano. She lifted them easily and carried them over to the window. They grasped the frame, not caring about the shards of glass that sliced their skin, gulping down the cool night air, grateful for the drop in the temperature.

"Hold on tight and don't let go, savvy?"

"Aye, Vega," Kano panted. "Thank you. For coming for me. In all my life, I've never had … such a friend."

Vega's throat squeezed, but what she said was, "Thank me when we've both got our feet back on the ground."

As she took one last look around the smoke-darkened room she heard the door give an ominous creak and then a loud crack. "Shit."

She slung Kano on to her back, moving as quickly as she could, and hoisted herself up back through the window and on to the roof. The stars hid themselves behind clouds, nudging the moon to do the same, and she silently thanked them for the darkness. She was about to begin her descent down the side of the building, back into the alleyway below, when it happened.

There was a loud BANG, like a cannon, followed by a smashing, screams from below, the sound of falling debris. The heat of the inferno had blown out the windows. The slates of the roof shook and Vega, midway between transferring her weight to the unstable gutter, lost her grip. It was so sudden, so quick, but she could see everything in perfect detail, her scrabbling hands, too close to her feet for her to balance with Kano on her back, the sickening lurch and tilt of her vision.

She twisted sideways, aiming for the chute formed by

the alley, narrowly avoiding smacking Kano's head on the townhouse next door.

"SHIFT, KANO! SHIFT! NOW! SHIFT!"

For a heart-stopping moment she thought they could not hear her, so fried internally by the fire that they had lost consciousness. Then they were gone. Vega knew only cool, grateful moisture kissing her cheeks before she hit the ground with a sound like the earth splitting.

For a few seconds she lay there stunned. Then Levi and Kano were beside her, asking if she was OK, urging her to move lest they be discovered, hands helping her to her feet. There was a sizeable dent in the compact earth and stone of the alleyway and, as battered as she was, she worried about what people would think when they noticed and hoped the sound was attributed to the fire. She felt as though she'd been in the worst fight of her life, but the thought of actually having a bruise for the first time, a properly purple and green thing instead of the rapidly fading marks she was used to, cheered her. She limped to where they were waiting for her.

They headed immediately for the beach, for their cove, a silent understanding carrying their footsteps to the shore, where Kano would regain their strength. They collapsed in the sand, panting. Levi ran his hands anxiously over Kano's face even as they began to regain their usual appearance. Then he squeezed his sister so tightly that she gasped.

"Well, driftling, I'd say you've won the game for good."

Vega laughed breathlessly. Then leaned up just long enough to reach into her pants and pull out the letter with the Empire's seal that she had found on Johnson's desk. She tossed it to Levi

275

and flopped back down. Levi unfolded it, eyes scanning, his features slowly freezing in place.

"This is a letter of marque."

Vega sat bolt upright, staring at him.

"What?" Kano's head swivelled between them, following the beam of their shocked gaze on each other's faces.

"It's a … a kind of pardon. From the Empire. It's sent to known pirates and buccaneers, offers clemency in exchange for important information and work as a privateer. Basically a pirate under their employ, a kind of paid mole."

Kano's eyes widened. "But Johnson's a captain of the Nubian Brethren."

"Maybe … maybe he was sent it? And refused?" Vega cast around, searching for logic to ease her disbelief.

Levi's mouth was set in a grim line. "But if that's the case, why didn't he burn it? Why wasn't he offended? Why – why did he keep it?"

*

They had sat on the beach talking until Vega's head had begun to nod between sentences. Then she and Kano dragged their weary bodies, heavy and exhausted as the rush of the evening left their bloodstream, into the sea. They scrubbed away the detritus, watching soot dissolve into the water around them. Levi waited on the shore. Kano floated on their back awhile, breathing deeply. Vega trod water in the shallows beside them, the gentle lapping soothing her bruises.

"Thanks again, Vega. You saved me."

"You'd have done it for me."

"I would have."

They smiled at each other, and Vega added, "Anyway – I have much to thank you for, too."

"You do?"

"Yes." She looked at them, their face glowing purest silver in the moonlight. "Thank you for all you've done for my brother. I know him better than anyone. And – well – he and I have never discussed such things but – you bring him peace."

Kano's grin was wide as the quarter moon and they ducked under the water, turning to large bubbles that burst delightedly in Vega's hair.

Do Not Catch Her, Do Not Try

The River Mumma on her banks
watched six-and-ten years drift past
and came to find grace and thanks
for the way a river *lasts*.
Each ripple of the yielding reeds,
the dappled jewellery of her scales,
the river knows her every need,
until one day she sees the sails.

They inhale and billow caught in the wind,
they swell like hope in her breast.
She is swift and flicking-finned,
her hair a seaweed wave she crests –
and watches. Eager eyes bright
and scanning the decks
for any sign or any sight.
They're too far away but still she checks –

Have my family returned?

But the river is an open mouth –
    When she, the teeth, forgets her bite,
    vulnerable is a goddess who has yearned
    and is not prepared for a fight.
    It was not *The Sea Dragon*,
    or her son's reaching hands,
    these were the kinds of men
    she had purged from her lands—

And the strange new pirates found her
    armed they came,
    not bearing swords
    but bearing a name—

"Ata! Ata! It's me, Ezi! Ata!"
    And, Yaa damn her, she did not hear
    the deceit, see the line on the bait,
    until she was hooked, until much too late.
    Who had told them? How did they know?
    That to that name she would always go?
    Net after net,
    rope after rope.
    There were so many she thought she might choke,
    she did not have the breath, she did not have the voice
    to summon a storm, she did not have a choice –
    and so
    the River Mumma was taken.

La Liberté

The next morning dawned even hotter than the last. Levi awoke beside Kano, as usual. Today, though, Levi became aware that the careful gap between them, the gap that had been shrinking with each passing night, had vanished entirely. Cool limbs tangled with his own, the smell of fresh morning dew, the feel of cool silk skin. Levi felt his face heating and carefully separated himself. Kano stirred but said nothing of their new closeness. Merely greeted him with the accustomed "Good morning, Levi", their light musical voice heavier from sleep and still slightly raw from yesterday's fire. They dressed and headed for breakfast, bumping into Vega on the stairs.

They were all relatively quiet over their cornmeal and coffee. The dining room was busier than usual – it was so late in the morning that the lunch rush was beginning and they didn't want to discuss anything with so many ears scouring for scuttle. They bantered lightly about nonsense before Vega left for the library. Levi was surprised; he assumed she would want to come with them, so as to properly discuss the best way to expose what they had discovered in Johnson's study without revealing how they had discovered it. But she mumbled something vague about "research" and sped off.

Levi had the strangest feeling that she wanted to leave the two of them alone.

Kano and Levi drifted down to their usual cove, treading their familiar path through markets and docks, down to the shore, through the sweet-scented gorse. As they began to descend the slope towards the beach, Kano suddenly tugged Levi's hand so they both went tumbling. The prickly plants stuck to their shirts, caught in their hair, leaving them smelling like a coconut pretence. They landed on the beach, narrowly avoiding a rocky outcropping, sand clouding around them. Levi spat some out of his mouth and looked at Kano, where they lay paces away, chest rising and falling, staring at the sky.

"Why d'you do that?"

Kano turned their head to look at him. "I thought you could do with shaking loose."

"Could you not have just asked me to stretch?"

Kano laughed. "When you stretch you are in your body, when we work you are in your head. It is good, sometimes, to be out of both."

"I don't find it so easy, stepping out of my head and body."

Kano grinned. "Obviously. Or we would not need this practice."

"How do you do it?" Levi asked, pulling himself up to sitting, pushing his locs out of his face. "How do you shift the way you do? Suspend yourself between states?"

Kano straightened to half-mast, arms wide behind them. Their eyes were closed. "I do not know, really. It is all I've ever been. Yesterday, during the fire, was the first time I'd felt so ... constrained. It was strange. And scary." They opened their eyes and looked at him. "I am sorry. If that is how you feel

281

always. It made me think, though…" They paused, head cocked thoughtfully. "I do not overly attach my sense of self to my body. I am grateful to my body, for all it gives me, speed, strength, sensation, but I am more than my body. And there is different speed and strength and sensation to be experienced in different states." They sat up suddenly, a smile forming, part-mischief and part-flirtation. Levi was immediately wary.

"What?"

"Close your eyes."

Levi was past asking why at this point, and did as he was told.

"Think about what you can feel, in every part of your body. The breeze in your hair, the sun on your eyelids, the warmth and freshness of the air in your nose…"

Kano's hand came to rest, as it had before, on the place between his ribs.

"Now breathe in and with each breath out … expand. You are more than this body, you are more than each sensation."

Levi fell into the rhythm of his breath. After a time he found he was not thinking of anything at all. The salt and coconut of the air intensified with each inhalation. The warm hand placed against his sternum seemed to heat the skin around it, pulsing, stretching, filling. He was aware of something opening, falling loose, and relaxed. Distantly he found himself noticing the way parts of himself interacted – joining, separating, working together. One part of himself trying to protect another, petals folding over a soft, vulnerable centre. He thanked it, that protective part of himself, and a strange quiet descended. It tasted like a kind of peace.

He flickered his eyes open to find Kano's face inches from his. The smooth seashell of their lips curved, deliciously soft, inviting. He was beyond thought, was pure aesthesis, calm and tingling bliss, he leaned forward—

Kano gasped.

The sound was enough to root Levi back in his body with a rush of flight or fight until he realized that Kano had gasped at him. At the shimmering sea flame that had momentarily appeared and the brief flicker of shining scales. They vanished as quickly as they had come but Kano looked triumphant.

"That was close! So close! I think we're getting somewhere!"

Levi's heart sank slightly. Had that – that brief, electric moment – been nothing more than a way of getting him to shift?

*

After lunch – for which Vega remained mysteriously absent – Kano and Levi headed back towards the south-eastern coves, taking the long way past market stalls of jewellery and boutiques selling flamboyant skirts and dresses. Levi paused, aching. He could not deny that he still noticed the glory of texture and shade, but each time he reached for the joy it would usually bring, he would shy away, afraid that joy would mean he was callously forgetting what he had done.

He stretched and turned away, looking for Kano who had drifted away to the stall that sold the coconut macaroons. A familiar hotness prickling the back of his neck alerted Levi to the fact that he was being watched. He glanced around. The street was quieter here, but even if it had been busy, Levi would

have noticed the man who watched him. Levi, with his keen sartorial eye, knew luxury when he saw it. The man was dressed impeccably, in a waistcoat and breeches all made of the finest silk in various shades of rose and burgundy. The embroidery was detailed in silver and gold, swirling curves shaped like seashells and waves, speckled with sequins. His shirt was thin linen and his heeled shoes shone. The man was smoking a clay pipe carved like a dragon. Well, he had been. The pipe was resting on his bottom lip, precariously so, as his mouth had slackened and was, presently, hanging open. For some moments the man just stared at Levi.

Then he walked towards him. Levi stood, unsure. The man did not seem threatening, with his finely kept moustache and serious dark face and eyes, but Levi's hand drifted towards his cutlass anyway. It was only when he was close that Levi noticed a tattoo peeking out from behind the sequinned hem of the sleeve on the man's left arm. A seated woman holding a torch, wearing a crown with seven distinct rays. *La Liberté.* Levi met the man's eyes again, took in the thick shoulder-length hair braided back in a low ponytail, and allowed himself to acknowledge the spark of recognition in the man's eyes. He had become aware, over the weeks they had been on the Republic, of the way his resemblance to his father had intensified. He had taken pains, initially, to keep his face clean-shaven. Levi thought back to the morning that had changed. He had reached for the razor and soap and caught the flicker across Kano's face.

"What?"

"What?"

"You're hanging the jib."

"No, I—"

"You are, what is it?"

"I just … like it as it is." The nymph's face had heated.

"All right," he had said. "As it is."

He had not shaved his face since.

And staring into the face of Captain Jacques de Casse, Levi was beginning to regret his decision.

De Casse cleared his throat. "*Pardon*. Would you mind coming with me?"

His accent was throaty and rich, short, sharp vowels that shone against the velvet of his consonants. Levi swallowed, glancing towards the macaroon stall. But if trouble was brewing, he did not want to drag Kano into it. He looked back at de Casse and nodded. De Casse turned on his heel and Levi followed, winding west through the streets, past Johnson's part of town where the smell of smoke still hung in the air, and west still, until the shops and houses began to thin. Levi realized, as the sea came once more into clear view, that they were somewhere by the fore western flipper of the turtle, the cliffs jutting out to the peninsula that was almost symmetrical to the eastern flipper that was home to the Freeman's. De Casse did not speak or turn back, just continued walking swiftly, until he reached the part of the cliff path that sloped down towards the beach and a cove not unlike the one Levi and Kano had spent every day at. He wondered if Kano was worried, if they had gone back to the inn or to find Vega in the library. He hoped Vega did not act rashly.

They turned a corner and Levi halted abruptly. There, behind a rocky inlet, away from the main town, stood a beached boat. In the shallows was a small dock and three more boats. Painted in clear white letters, clearly frequently maintained, were the words *La Liberté*, followed by a number from one to four. Two brigantines and two galleons. Captain de Casse's fleet. The gangway on the beached ship was down and, judging by the wooden slats around it forming solid ground, and the wooden posts with washing lines and clothes hung between them, it had been so for a long time. Here, away from the main town, de Casse had clearly formed his own little shanty. Levi took it in. The crew bustled around, sat on chairs on deck or on land, playing cards, drinking. In a far cave strewn with rugs Levi saw several small children having a story told to them by an older man with a wooden leg. He thought of Able, and then remembered why he was here. He looked around for de Casse and found him on deck of the beached boat, holding two goblets, watching him.

He took the ale de Casse offered but did not drink. Merely waited.

"Why did you follow me?" de Casse asked curiously.

Levi raised an eyebrow. "You asked me to," he replied calmly.

"And you usually do everything you are asked?"

"No." Levi shrugged. "But if a captain of the Brethren asks you to follow, only a fool would say no."

De Casse nodded. "So you know who I am, *oui*? That hardly seems fair. I do not know who you are."

"Oh?" Levi's heart was punching his ribs as though

desperate to escape and he fought to give nothing away. "Do you usually ask strangers to drink with you?"

De Casse barked a laugh. "Sometimes. But I do not think you are a stranger. I have a feeling. And my feelings are rarely wrong."

"A stopped clock is right twice a day." Levi had intended to sound flippant but as de Casse's eyes widened and he remembered who had taught him that particular figure of speech, his heart stopped beating entirely, before its pace ratcheted dangerously.

"Levi," de Casse breathed.

Now it was Levi's turn for his eyes to widen. His breathing became shallow with shock. He reached for his cutlass but de Casse held up a hand.

"Peace, *s'il vous plaît*. I am no enemy. I am ... a great friend of your father's." Levi froze but did not move his hand from twitching distance of his weapons.

"Why should I believe you?" Levi was wary. "Pa... Pa spoke very little of his time here. He said that there were enemies even among allies."

Despite the tension, de Casse snorted. "*Oui*, that sounds like Ezi. *Attendez!*" He hurried down some steps and it took Levi a moment to understand that de Casse was ... excited. He returned moments later holding a scroll of parchment, curled at the edges, but otherwise smoothed flat as though it had been read over and over. He handed it to Levi. "*S'il vous plaît!* Read! Go on!"

Keeping his hand still close to his belt, Levi passed his goblet back to de Casse, took the parchment, and began to read.

My dear Marianne,

I know I have much to apologize for, much I promised that I did not fulfil. A man's heart bears many secrets and mine is no different. I promised to tell you if I found the land that Nubia spoke of, and I did not. I promised to write you every week and I did not. I promised to never love another, and I broke that promise also. I would not insult your pride by asking your forgiveness, nor would I insult your intelligence by not asking for your understanding. I have made decisions I regret and am spared self-flagellation only by the knowledge that I would have regretted the alternatives also – a stopped clock is right twice a day and I can only hope that I have been so lucky as to be right twice. I pray that writing this letter is one of those times and that in reading it you might know the meaning of my absence and distance.

I am a father now. A daughter, Vega. She is my pride. And a son, Levi. He is my hope. He will do great things. But danger will follow them – rather, danger will follow my boy and, where he goes, his sister will follow. I will not say more here as, having read your latest missive, I believe that it may not be long now until we are reunited. But I could not dock at the Republic having not given you time to prepare yourself for the person I am now. And for my asking this final request – the last thing I shall ever ask of you. In times ahead my family will need friends. Can we count on you? For all that I have betrayed you, I would not betray your dignity so. I have no petty excuses but if you have loved me, consider this: if an octopod has three hearts, could not a dragon have two?

*If this pie-bird flies true then this should reach you
before we do.* The Sea Dragon *will return and I am glad
of it. There is much to discuss.*

I love you. Know it.

Drag

"Who is Marianne?"

De Casse chuckled. "Oh. *C'est moi.* Me." He indicated his
tattoo. "The lady *Liberté* is sometimes called this name. It was
a ... special name between Ezi and me. I was Marianne. He was
Drag, the dragon."

Levi nodded and looked back down at the letter. It was dated
his birthday. The day his father had died. Along with the rest of
the crew. His thoughts crashed into each other and for a moment
his didn't breathe. He found Kano's face in his mind's eye amid
the churning emotion and remembered their lessons. He looked
at de Casse and wondered how he was going to tell him that the
man he had waited for would not return. He swallowed.

"There was ... a storm. A very bad storm. My sister and I
... survived. The crew ... Pa ... did not."

De Casse's hands shook on his goblet.

There was one moment, one ringing moment, where Levi
did not know if the man would howl or rage or collapse. All
the air was gone, and for the first time in weeks, Levi felt his
father's loss as keenly as he had in its immediate aftermath.
Then it was over. De Casse called for wine and two chairs
from his cabin.

"Your father trusted me, Levi. You can too. Please. Tell me
how I can help you."

289

Levi sat and assessed the man in front of him. He was tempted to tell him all about Johnson, about the letter of marque, about what they suspected. His father had loved this man. But his father had also lied to him for years. And how would de Casse react to the knowledge that they had broken into Johnson's house? Would he go straight to Johnson? This had been his, Vega and Kano's biggest concern; that if they told anyone, Johnson would have an opportunity to explain, to use his status within the community to assuage all justified mistrust. So instead, Levi told him about the scout. De Casse listened in silence. "My father had reason to be wary of Johnson, the seeds of doubt already sewn when he read your letters. But whatever the scout said troubled him, gave him reason to worry about Xaymaca. And the safety of those there. Including … my mother. We think. We've been looking for information but there's precious little here. Can you think of *anyone* who might know something?"

Levi felt a pang of guilt in saying his mother's name, a reference to the other who had claimed his father's heart, but de Casse did not react. Simply said, *"Oui.* There is someone. But he is mistrustful and does not like speaking of such things." He called for parchment and ink and a quill, on which he scrawled a few words before passing it to Levi. "The cartographer. Diego. Give him this. He does not know much more than I do, but what he does know he might share – with you. You have much in common, it is worth you meeting."

Levi read the note. There were only a few words.

D,

> *This is a friend. Help him if you can, he can be trusted.*
>> *In your mother's name and with all my best,*
>> *– JDC*

"His mother?"

"*Oui*. Most believe that Nubia burned with her son inside her. But these falsehoods were spread by the Brethren captains to allow Diego to live as normal a life as possible. She died the night he was born."

So he wasn't alone. There was another – another boy, born of a Xaymacan mother, who had not known her. Levi reeled. *Was it always this way?* he wondered. Could *home* only exist in its singularity? And to forge more was to wield a greedy hammer in a furnace of loss and fear and grief? Are we each only of one place? And where is home for those who claim many?

"You will seek the island too, *oui*?"

Levi returned from his reverie and nodded.

"You have the map?"

Levi hesitated. And then nodded once more. "But I need a crew," Levi said slowly. "A crew and ship and resources. To sail to such an unknown place without one would be foolish."

De Casse poured more wine. "For Ezi's son, I can provide the latter two. But a crew, that must be earned, *no*? Won, *oui*? I cannot make people respect you, follow you. To have their true loyalty, they must choose." He looked out at the proof of this, the activity of those who loved and trusted him bonded by a promise to fight and die together. "But I will tell you this" – his

face was suddenly grim – "once you find them, your crew, bid them take the mark. Loyalty in the way all true buccaneers bear it. Swear it in ink and blood and flesh and may ill fortune befall those who are tattooed with their pirate's promise and break it. These are ... strange times."

Levi let the silence settle for a moment.

De Casse drained his cup and suddenly smiled, shaking his head. "Your father believed that you were great. His hope and his pride. Ezi was a man of great hope and pride." His voice caught and Levi knew that he should soon leave the man to his grief but de Casse composed himself and continued, "He did not say such things lightly. Know that." He got to his feet. "Know also that his last request to me was to be a friend to his family." His eyes misted then. "I could never deny Ezi anything. I do not intend on starting now."

*

It was twilight. The sun had dipped below the horizon, the sea a silk sheet tucking it into bed, and Levi envied it. After his talk with de Casse he had tracked down Kano and Vega at the library and relayed what he had learned, showing them the note to Diego. It had felt strange, relaying the details of his father's love letter. Intrusive. Vega had blinked several times, rapidly, when Levi had spoken the words *my pride* but gathered herself enough to say that Levi had handled the thing well.

"See, hatchling. Told you you'll make a fine captain."

Levi had smiled wanly. He was hungry. It had been long enough after lunch that the wine had rushed to his head and

he wanted some of Emabelle's cheese-baked bread and a cold pitcher of water. But he steeled himself. He had mulled over de Casse's words on the walk to the library and an idea had formed.

"Aye, funny you should say that, driftling," he grinned at her. "There aren't any books on tattooing here, are there?"

*

After searching through every book and log on the subject, they made a quick visit to the apothecary before it closed for a special black pigment. Hours later, after a lengthy chat with the various crew mates of *The Queen Áine* and *The Cleopatra* who were drinking in the Freeman's that evening, Vega was stretched out on her bed and Levi's hand was cramping. He stood up, admiring his handiwork.

"Right, you're done, savvy? What do you think?"

She craned round to look at the back of her left shoulder in the mirror. "Sink me, Levi! If buccaneering fails I think you could just stay here and spend your days inking sea dogs."

"Aye, it's right and fair, isn't it? It's because I did mine first, I got the hang of it."

"Ah," Vega said shrewdly. "So Kano's will be the best, will it?" Her eyes twinkled as Levi smiled softly at the nymph.

"Yes. It will."

"Well, why don't you and Kano finish up in your room? I'm baked."

Levi raised his eyebrows at her total lack of subtlety but did not protest.

Back in their room, Levi turned to Kano. "Now, you'll have

to hold off shifting for a few days. The moisture in your mist will ruin my masterpiece."

Kano nodded. "I was thinking maybe here?" They pulled their shirt over their head and pointed to the spot directly over their heart. Levi's mouth dried. He nodded. Wordlessly he placed the makeshift stencil, bowl of ink, rag and needle on the bedside table and slowly pushed against Kano's chest until they were lying down. The nymph didn't move. They barely seemed to breathe. Levi sterilized the needle with matches once again, before pressing the stencil into Kano's skin. The ink glistened, black against silver moon over their heart, the same image Levi had imprinted twice already. The simple outline of a dragon, like that of the crew of *The Sea Dragon*. But this one had a crown on its head. This last addition had been Vega's suggestion, a reference to a joke she'd made what felt like a lifetime ago.

"You're such a princess!"

"Well, our father is a prince."

"Aye, true enough. And one day, so shall you be!"

"I think princess suits me better."

"Well, the pirate princess you'll be. You'll be captain, you can call yourself a pirate queen if you like."

Slowly, carefully, he began the process again. Ink, needle, prick the skin. He felt the cool silk of Kano beneath his fingers, felt their breath on his hair as he worked, their heart beneath his palm. The silence stretched between them taut with something unnamed. Levi wanted to call it focus. Levi knew it was not focus. Kano lay prone in their undergarments beneath him. The room was warm and dark, but Kano was cool and light, Kano was always cool and light.

294

"I wonder when de Casse will have a ship for us?" Kano said after a long time, when Levi was nearly finished. Their voice was slightly breathless.

"I don't know." Levi tried to ignore the way Kano's sensitivity to fire, sparked by the nearby candlelight, and the short sharp pain of the needle sent what felt like tiny little pulses along their skin, sweat beading. Levi imagined tasting it and the thought was so unravelling that he stood quickly and went to take a sip of water. "I didn't ask."

"Maybe we should in a few days. If we're to return to Xaymaca, we'll need to know how long we have to practise and pack and—" Their words cut off slightly as Levi resumed, the edge of his palm grazing their nipple. Their throat worked in a graceful undulation.

Levi's breath hitched. "We?"

Kano looked at him questioningly.

"You said 'we'."

Kano looked confused. "Yes? So?"

Levi stood. "You're finished."

Kano looked down, crossed the room to admire Levi's handiwork in the mirror.

"Beautiful," they said. Their reflected eyes found Levi's behind them.

"Yes," Levi agreed. He coughed. "I… I didn't realize… Well, I didn't want to assume that you'd…" Levi could feel his face heating.

Kano chuckled then, returning to the bed, slipping between the sheets, the moon replacing the sun, stealing away for intimacy, and held out a hand, inviting him in. "Levi." They

295

said his name like a promise. "I just let you tattoo me. I'm part of this crew, savvy?"

Levi's chuckle at the imitation was not a distraction from the internal eddying. He lay on the bed beside them, fought for control over the moment. "But there's still so much world for you to see. What if ... what if where I'm going is not what the Great Energy intends for you?"

Kano was shaking their head. "I think you are what is intended for me. I don't know ... how exactly. But I feel it. Wherever I've gone, whoever I've been with, I've always been pulled onwards or elsewhere. But now I am ... peaceful."

Their faces were close. Soft seashell, petrichor warmth, somewhere in Levi a flame was burning but this gentle flicker was not consumptive, was sweet heat, a pleasurable pooling; they melted together.

"Silly nymph," said Levi quietly. "You said return to Xaymaca. You can't return if you've never been."

"I am starting to realize that ... everywhere you have been I have been. So if you were once in Xaymaca, then so was I. Once upon a time or a dream. Where you go, I go." They threaded their fingers through Levi's and at the same moment, he leaned forward. Their lips met. Salt and hope and horizon. Levi's toes were cold, the dark unknown depths of the great pelagic to which they both belonged. He ran them over Kano's legs and they shivered, tangling with him, seaweed catching currents. The stars came out to witness, bright and watching. Salt and hope and wide, open horizon.

The Nubian Brethren

"Do you think he's up?"

"It's very early." Levi yawned and stretched, then knocked again on the dark green painted door of the cartographer's office and store. The shiny gold plaque above it read *Hornigold's Navigation and Cartography Services*.

"Tired?" asked Vega, as Kano too yawned.

"A little," they answered, somewhat sheepishly. They avoided Levi's gaze in a way that Levi knew his sister's sharp eyes would not miss. They *flick flick flicked* between them both, *brown gold brown gold* initial concern at the thought of flames and nightmares sharpening to something pointed and amused.

"Did something keep you from your sleep, hatchling?" Levi's face heated.

"It was hot," he mumbled.

Vega raised an eyebrow but Levi was spared further interrogation by the green door swinging open. The man who stood on the threshold was tall and handsome with ebony skin and eyes, not much older than Levi himself. His hair was short, cropped close to his head. He had a beard, but it was trimmed precisely, almost too precisely, as though he had used one of the many measuring instruments that Levi could see lining a shelf behind him. His suit was as neat as the rest of his appearance, black and understated.

Whatever Levi had expected of the son of a witch, it was not someone so … well, *normal*.

"Can I help you?" His voice was low and calm, polite, professional. The exact opposite to almost everyone they had met on the Republic so far.

He and Vega exchanged a glance. "Erm – yes. Are you Diego? The cartographer?"

"I am."

Levi did not know where to begin, how to ask this cool, formal, figure about the witch mother he'd never known and a land of magic that he'd never seen. He swallowed. "May we come in?" he asked, imitating the polite tone. "We have some … questions for you."

Diego's face was unreadable. He scanned the three of them and Levi wondered if he was assessing their strangeness, anticipating the line of enquiry. But he nodded and stepped aside. The room was small and panelled in dark wood. The walls were hung with charts and maps or were lined with shelves full of books and rolling tubes, containing maps, Levi supposed. The back of the room was divided between a bookcase that Levi had glimpsed through the door, where sat many curious objects – spinning globes, telescopes, strangely shaped compasses, a gilded oval mirror – and a staircase that twisted up into a mezzanine with one door. Levi supposed this was a back office.

"Tea?" Diego's face was fixed in a smile of polite interest, and he gestured up to the office.

Levi glanced at Vega. He did not think he'd ever been presented with such nice manners, it was like a dance with

entirely new steps and he was thrown. But Kano stepped forward, easy, graceful, placidly smiling. "Oh, that would be lovely," they said. "Milk and sugar, please."

Diego nodded and walked primly to the stairs. Vega and Levi looked round at the nymph, who shrugged.

"I have travelled widely. I have had ale with some and tea with others."

They could hear Diego upstairs, the whistle of the kettle, the tinkling of china. They examined the room while they waited. It was once of those establishments that clearly predated the forming of the Republic. Levi watched Vega scan the dates printed on the ends of the rolled tubes, awed.

At last, Diego returned, placing the tea down on the large writing desk under the mezzanine and indicating that they draw up the chairs that were artfully strewn about the space to encourage the clientele to peruse the merchandise.

"So," he said, that same polite smile on his face. "How can I be of assistance?"

"Well, I am Levi. Son of Prince Ezi, captain of *The Sea Dragon*. This is my sister Vega and our friend Kano." Diego raised his eyebrows but said nothing, watchful eyes expectant. Levi hesitated. He had not spoken his full name aloud in many weeks, avoiding it like the other name, in fear and guilt. It drew him up short, but he mastered himself. He pulled out de Casse's note and passed it across the table, taking his tea while Diego unfolded it and scanned the words.

His face froze and his eyes were immediately sharp, wary.

He looked up at them. "I knew when I saw you that it would be something like this. I had a feeling – and I don't get those

often. But I'm afraid I shall be of little use to you. I don't know very much."

Levi bit his lip. He did not want to push it, and yet... "That's all right. Whatever you know, even if it's little, will be helpful. I guarantee, it's probably more than we know." He hesitated and then, "I am glad to meet you. I feel ... we have a lot in common."

Diego snorted but there was no real humour in the sound. "What would give you that idea?"

"Well." Levi floundered, glancing at Kano for support. They squeezed his leg in reassurance and he continued, "I have reason to believe that my mother is also from Xaymaca. And I have never known her either, have always wondered ... wondered what the whole of me is. Where I'm from."

"I know where I am from." Diego frowned. "I am from Sheta Island. The fact that my mother was from some place that few have reached, that is noted on no maps, with no routes charted, is immaterial."

Levi did not know what to say to this. This was not going how he had expected.

Vega jumped in. "Were you never curious? Did you never want to see Xaymaca?"

"Again, that is immaterial." Diego's tone was still polite, but there was a bite to it, a hard edge made of neat, straight lines like his beard and hair and clothes. "No map of mine was ever marked with an X like Captain Ezi's or Captain Johnson's. I have never received instruction as to how to reach the land of my mother's birth. I cannot say why. Maybe it does not want to be found. At least not by me."

Vega too fell silent. The air was heavy and awkward. She slurped her tea, the sound disconcertingly loud.

Then Kano said, "What about your father?"

Diego's face cleared somewhat. "What about him?"

"Was he from Sheta Island? Did you know him?"

"Oh. Yes." He nodded to a miniature in a brass frame at the corner of his desk. A man and a boy, near identical; the older sat holding a scrolled map, the younger stood holding a compass. "He raised me, owned this place. It was how he met the Brethren captains. And my mother. They were quite the motley crew, so I'm told. Full of tales."

"Nubia's tales? Tales of Xaymaca?"

"Yes, some of them. Though my father did not relay many. It … pained him. To speak of her. My mother."

"Where is he now?" asked Vega.

Diego's eyes flickered, his throat worked. "He sickened and died. A year ago."

"I'm sorry."

Diego nodded, accepting it. He sipped his tea and sighed, seeming to realize that providing information would end this conversation most efficiently. "As I said, he did not tell me many of my mother's stories. Vague bits and pieces here and there. Talk of the faeries and their palace above Favour Falls, I believe it was called. Then there were the spiders, who lived in the forest – and the witches, of course, my mother's kin. Their coven was – is – I don't know – called Persea. He told me that magic took a person fully when they turned six-and-ten." A jolt of understanding and Levi realized then why the transformation had happened on his birthday. But that meant that his mother

301

might have been calling him for weeks before that. The idea made him uneasy, but Diego was still speaking. "I don't know if that's true of just the witches, but I know their magic is more prominent in the maternal line, that sons with power were rare. A shame," he added bitterly. "Perhaps if I were a daughter, I could have saved him."

Sympathy struck Levi like a physical blow. He could see through the chinks in Diego's gaze, the formality he wore like armour. He knew what it was to only be given half-truths, to take those broken pieces of information and puzzle them together to form something that was uglier than the intended picture.

He reached into his pocket and pulled out the map. He did not know why he did it, but he handed it to Diego.

"My father ... our father. He died too. Almost a full moon ago. This was his map. The one that led him to Xaymaca, to my mother, to the land of our mothers. Would you like to look?"

Shadow and light raged across Diego's face and for a moment Levi feared he would snatch the map and tear it to pieces. Then he nodded, his bottom lip briefly tremulous, betraying the truth behind the internal conflict.

He studied the map. Levi could see the flicker of eagerness, a faint glow of hope – before his face closed in again, folding over on itself.

"Can you see it?" he asked Levi. "The X?"

Levi did not want to answer. He looked to Vega and Kano, almost hoping for an indication that he should lie. But the truth was clear in their expression and Diego could see it too.

"Yes," he said.

Diego nodded tersely, his unspoken questions hanging in

the air. *Why not me? Why haven't I been called home? Why don't they want me?*

"Would you mind if I held on to this? And took a closer look? Just for a couple of days?"

Levi did not want to say yes, he could feel Vega and Kano straining against their refusal beside him, but he could not look into those flat, dark eyes and say no. Not when Diego had already been denied by so many.

"Aye. All right. I'll come back for it in a couple of days."

"Thank you." A small smile. "I'll try and remember anything else my father told me. There were other things. The magic trees and flowers, for example, and the nymphs—"

Kano's lowered his teacup from his mouth. "The nymphs?"

"Yes. Let's see, what did he say? That they were created from some kind of Great Energy."

"What kind of Great Energy?"

"I could not say. It's been so many years since I've heard such tales..." He pondered a moment. "I do remember him once saying that ... my mother had told him that nymphs were very rare because for one to be born it would require immense feeling from an immensely powerful being. And few such beings exist."

"Powerful how?" Vega urged.

"A deity, perhaps. My mother would pray to a goddess, apparently, Yaa. And there was a water goddess too. I think she was called ... the River Mumma."

Levi froze as the words coursed through him.

He felt rooted to the spot and at the same time as though he was floating high above his body.

"The what?"

"The River Mumma." Diego eyed him curiously. "Supposedly she guards the great River Aphra and is an ancient and terrifying mermaid, as old as Xaymaca itself."

Levi could not speak. The truth struck around him, lightning in the eye of a storm. He could hear the others talking, hustling him out of the shop, saying their goodbyes. He imitated them like a polly-bird until they were on the street again, heading for the comfort of the shoreline, for water lapping wide, the blue of his home.

*

Levi lay beside Kano at the shoreline. Their hand rubbed circles over the point where his ribs met each other. Levi focused on it. Focused on his breath, in and out in time with Kano's hand, in time with the lapping tide. He inhaled with the world, and exhaled to expand, feeling his body ripple and flex. He could feel the shift there, just out of reach, as though he was thinning to dew and spindrift. He was hovering above that canvas of self, seeing all the seams, criss-crossing and interweaving, but this time he wasn't so close, wasn't unpicking with his nose pressed to the thread, he was further away, could see the whole beautiful picture of Levi. A sea dragon son, a Leviathan, born of an ancient mermaid and a pirate prince, on a faraway land that no one could find.

She had been calling him, he could see that now. Was she in danger? Was he failing yet another parent? He mentally shook himself. He was not the only one who had learned a great truth today.

"So … what do you think?" He turned on his side to face

Kano. They were alone there, Vega had headed back to the Freeman's for lunch but Levi was not hungry.

"What do I think about what?" the nymph replied. Their hair absorbed the sun, their skin bright against the sand.

"What Diego said. That … that maybe you were born because … of some great feeling … of the River Mumma."

"Of your mother."

"Yes."

Kano shrugged. "It is interesting, I suppose. But it does not change much."

"Doesn't it? Have you not wondered about the timing of it? If it's because…"

"If it's because of you? If the River Mumma having you … or losing you is what forced the Great Energy to forge my existence?"

"Yes."

"Yes."

"Yes, what?"

"Yes, I have wondered that."

"And?"

"And what?"

"You're being infuriating."

Kano laughed and it took Levi by surprise. The last thing Levi felt like doing was laughing. He had just been starting to feel … well, not normal, but steady. But with today's revelation it seemed that his very existence was an agent of chaos, throwing danger into the lives of everyone he loved.

"And if that is the case, then fine. All I take from this is that we are meant to be together."

"But … but what about choice? Would you have … chosen this? Chosen … me?"

Kano reached for Levi, sweeping fingertips down his face, soft as a breeze. "I choose peace. You are peace for me. Why that is, is irrelevant."

They kissed him them, and Levi tasted that peace too. And for a moment, just one, suspended and shining, he imagined what it would be to stay here with Kano, on the Republic. To leave Xaymaca to those who knew it, to ignore the way the map and the sea and his mother called to him.

But that was not his peace.

"Levi! LEVI!"

He sat up, turning. Sliding down the slope, his fine silks – green today – incongruous with the scrubby brush and gorse surroundings, came de Casse, his face taut with anxiety.

"Captain de Casse?"

Levi and Kano sprung to their feet and de Casse hurried towards them. "I wanted to tell you myself. To give you time to decide how to act." He caught his breath. "I shall not be able to give you a ship and resources. For I will need them. The Nubian Brethren assembles tonight. We have just had word: they are coming. A Republican scout has spotted the naval fleet of the Empire, not a night's sail away."

Levi felt his insides pitch and list. The Empire? Here? Now?

"You should know. If there is no elected replacement, the child of a late captain may speak in the Brethren in their stead. I understand if you do not want to, this is not your fight, not your home, that you have other things to worry about. But should you wish to stand up and answer the call, I shall support you."

He hurried away. Levi and Kano looked at each other, a thought shared. Levi had never thought he would find a home that wasn't *The Sea Dragon*. But he had been wrong. And so was de Casse. They had been on the Republic for almost a full moon – but there was something here worth defending. Magic in the mortal world was dying but this was a place where people still believed, where no one went hungry or cold, where everyone got a piece of the pie. Nubia had known it, and Ezi had known it. And Levi knew it too.

*

Levi and Kano dressed. For the first time since arriving on Sheta Island and entering the Republic, Levi dressed as himself. He donned the billowing, wine-dark skirt that Kano had bought him, pinning it up with a brooch as he had aboard *The Drag*, as Kano pulled on the same set in livid blue-grey. They wore white shirts with ruffled collars, their back leather boots polished to a high shine and shiny black tricornes atop their hair, grown longer in the weeks on the Republic, pulled back in bandanas. Their weapons were belted round their middles and hung at their sides. Despite the heat, Levi pulled on the black-and-gold damask jacket that he had not worn since his birthday, and looked at himself in the mirror. His father stared back, though with specific distinctions; younger, darker and softer jawed, skin bare of the facial scaring denoting a family and culture to which Levi had never belonged. He wondered fleetingly if he should have sought them as hard as he sought this other part of him, but he shook

the thought loose. His father had left that royal family, and they had never called.

Kano kissed him lightly. Levi sighed against their mouth. His mind was clear. He knew what he had to do.

Downstairs the hum was beginning to dwindle and quiet to a low murmuring. There was a knock on the door. Vega stood on the threshold. She wore a new leather jerkin in a black-and-gold damask almost identical to Levi's jacket over a loose white shirt, tight leather pants and shiny boots.

They looked at each other, remembering a time a moment and a lifetime ago, in a cabin of their home, when they had properly *seen* each other for the first time.

"Sink me, driftling. You look fiercely yourself."

Vega glinted gold. "Sink me, hatchling, but you look like a captain." She smiled at their shared tattoos. "And so the pirate princess becomes the pirate queen." Levi laughed.

Dressed as they were, standing as they were, together as they were, there was no mistaking them for ordinary. They were an indefinable more, shining and beautiful and deadly.

They had decided not to draw attention to themselves too soon, to come forward only when the time was right, and so they descended the stairs on silent toes, avoiding the creaking steps almost instinctively, having ascended and descended them many times now. They drew to a halt on the second landing, which overlooked the heavy beams of the main room, and pressed into the shadows. The room was heaving, with hundreds of people. Some were older, those who remembered the forming of the Republic. Others were young, not much older than they were, who perhaps had never known the sting

of Empire. Emabelle stood in a corner, sharp eyes missing nothing, her presence a silent order that peace be kept in her establishment. As Levi, Vega and Kano watched, the quiet murmuring stilled to silence and Captain Lotte Hook stood. Her mouth was set in a determined line and her muscles bulged around the pieces of leather that made up her lightweight armour. Around her, rippling away from her, the pirates of the Nubian Brethren began to stamp their feet in a slow, rhythmic beat. The ritual was so achingly familiar that the breath caught in Levi's throat as Hook began to sing,

> *Swing low,*
> *Sweet chariot,*
> *Coming forth to carry me home,*
> *Swing low,*
> *Sweet chariot,*
> *Coming forth to carry me home.*

Her voice reverberated readiness and it skittered down Levi's spine. She let the song sit in the silence a while and then spoke. "I, Lotte Hook, captain of *The Cleopatra* and a buccaneer of the Brethren, do call an assembly in the name of the great witch Nubia, in protection of our freedoms against the imminent threat of Empire. How do you answer?"

"Aye!" a great shout from the many pirates assembled. The beams rumbled.

"We here gather in deference to our code and honour of our way of life. We stand here opposed to the tyranny of Empire, the brutality of slavery" – a great stamping of feet and tankards on

tables – "and in favour of the eradication of oppression, where freedom and adventure may prosper. We sing the song of the enslaved in acknowledgement of those lives lost and what we, the Nubian Brethren, still seek. Fellow captains of the Brethren, how do you answer?"

Captain Ó Néill stood. Her skirts were pinned like Levi's own, her waist synched across her dark grey dress by her belt hanging with many knives.

"I, Cora Ó Néill, captain of *The Queen Áine* and a buccaneer of the Brethren, do honour the life of the great witch Nubia. She burned for her courage and her wisdom. She came to Sheta Island, bringing with her the spirit of her home Xaymaca. In doing so she set our world alight and from the ashes came a revolution and our good Republic. We answer the call!" And her crew stamped their approval.

Then de Casse, lean and moustached. His eyes darted around the room as though looking for someone – him? – but he spoke with a voice full of emotion. "I, Jacques de Casse, captain of *La Liberté* and a buccaneer of the Brethren, do honour the life of the great witch Nubia, and the lives of all members of the Brethren, past and present. For nigh on a score we have stood together, and we will stand still, from this breath until our last. We answer the call." More stamping and shouts.

De Casse sat and turned towards a movement across the room. The candlelight flickered across the face of Captain James Johnson. Levi felt Vega shift beside him and he squeezed her arm. *Easy.*

"I, James Johnson, captain of *The Sterling* and a buccaneer of the Brethren, do honour the life of the great witch Nubia

and seek to lay my life, as she lay hers, in protection of this Republic." He cleared his throat and when he spoke again the metre of his words told Levi he had learned them by heart, that he had been preparing for this moment. "Comrades, this invasion occurs at a most inopportune moment. The voyage to Xaymaca is well prepared for, we are but a few weeks away from being ready to set sail. The alliance was supposed to give us the leverage we needed to remain stalwart against the threat of the navy. But, alas, time has made fools of us. And so I have a proposition, one that will see our Sheta Island safe from the inevitable death and bloodshed. I call upon the Brethren to vote on the matter … of parlaying with the Empire."

An uproar.

Captains Hook and Ó Néill were immediately on their feet.

"And I suppose you would nominate yourself to lead these negotiations?" Hook snarled over the swearing and shouting of her crew.

"You would be free to do the same." Even Levi wanted to punch Johnson for the maddening calm of his reply.

"I would never disgrace myself in such a way! And I would rather die than kneel before the Empire, on the soil of this Republic!"

"There would be no need to kneel," Johnson said, a sanctimonious little smile twisting his ruddy face. "We would be their allies, not their colony."

"What's the difference?" de Casse spat in his face. "We would become their outpost again. They would slowly erode everything that we have fought for. Is that what you wish, Johnson? Do you wish to see a return to fine houses and beggars and hangings and whippings?"

"There is no need for the dramatics, de Casse," Johnson sighed as though he was dealing with squalling children. "I believe that if we engage the might of a navy in a fight, we will lose—"

"Then we will die free! I will not live under the yoke of those who killed Nubia!" Hook snarled. "Have you forgotten that, James? Have you forgotten how we watched our friend burn?" She shook her head. "You have been many things. But I never thought you to be disloyal."

"Perhaps Ezi was right about you."

De Casse's voice was frigid and Johnson flared up. "Prince Ezi left before Nubia's ashes had cooled, never to return, and you want to talk to me about *loyalty*? I have only ever wanted what was best for the Brethren, for the Republic, for Sheta Island!"

"Have you?" The words burst from Levi's mouth, pulled forth by the outstretched hand of the moment. He stood and stepped into the opportunity. Behind him Kano and Vega matched his footsteps.

The four captains had frozen in their fight. All eyes were upon them as they descended the final flight of stairs.

"I am Levi, son of the late Prince Ezi, captain of *The Sea Dragon* and the River Mumma, mermaid of Xaymaca."

No one moved. There was no sound. All the air in the room was sucked towards the trio.

"There was an explosion aboard the ship, caused by a storm. My sister Vega and I were the only survivors." He gestured at Vega. "And we answer the call in place of our father and our crew." Beat. The room throbbed. Levi pressed on.

"Captain James Johnson, we have reason to believe you are in league with the Empire, due to your possession of this letter of marque. We rescued a scout belonging to *The Sterling* before the storm who also gave us cause to be concerned for the safety of Xaymaca, for my mother, and to believe that your plans for the alliance between Nubia's homeland and the Republic are not what you say they are." Levi pulled the letter from his jacket and presented it to the room.

Hook hissed and Ó Néill's eyes narrowed. De Casse met Levi's gaze and he saw a flicker of reassurance behind the mask of impassivity.

Johnson was outraged. "The *nerve* of you, whelp! Barging in here, claiming a birthright we've no proof of and admitting to breaking into my home!"

"James, you need only look upon his face to know he is Ezi's son." De Casse spoke quietly from his corner. "As for his mother – I don't see that it really matters. If Nubia can exist, so can the River Mumma. But I second the boy's inquiry. Why are you in possession of a letter of marque?"

Johnson scoffed. "I will not dignify such an insult with a response. I admit the Empire have courted me, offered me pardon. I turned them down. Do I believe that negotiations with them are vital? Aye, I do. We cannot stand against them for ever. Sooner or later they will take Sheta Island back and I would rather it happened before more lives are lost."

"The Empire will only take this island back when we who have sworn to protect this Republic fail to do so. *Parlay?*" Hook growled. "James, I trust not your motives." She turned to Levi. "Whelp, we are in time of crisis. We must rally and act and

313

tradition dictates that as Ezi's child you may do so in his stead. So … how will you answer the call?"

Levi glanced behind him at Vega and Kano. They nodded. "I, Levi, son of Prince Ezi, captain of *The Sea Dragon*, do honour the life of the great witch Nubia. We swear to lay down our lives and swords for this Republic, which has become our home these weeks."

A loud, incredulous guffaw broke the hush. "Hark, do you hear the boy? Standing there offering his sword!" Johnson laughed again. "No, God love him, the salt in the sinking must have addled his brain! Standing in his skirts speaking of his mermaid mother!" The rest of his crew joined in. "Poor Ezi, to have a soft skirted son!"

What Levi would have done next, confronted with that jeering, detestable face, he was glad he would never find out. The pulsing beneath the skin, the falling open of something internal, a loss of control that drew Levi's attention to the ghost of flame along his skin – it was gone before anyone could notice. But at that moment Ameyro, Ó Néill's secretary, crashed into the room. All heads turned towards him, where he panted and gasped into the hush.

"Empire sails, on the horizon, to the west! Just sighted! They're here!"

NEW YEAR'S EVE

Someone, somewhere far away
is calling out your name.
Do not forget the world you lack,
this land is not the same.
Listen well, it's in your blood,
you cannot bear the path alone;
poison tree and fertile fruit
X marks the spot to find your home.

There's a brown girl in the ring
Tralalala…

November bleeds into December, you watch films where the light is cool blue and downy-grey and sigh at the never-changing yellow of your world. Sometimes, when you know Five is working late, Maeve comes over. You let Bast out of your bedroom and she prances down the stairs, tail high, lady of the manor, before leaping on to Maeve's lap, much to her delight. You sit on the sofa, carefully not touching, the distance between your knees charged with the current that flows between you. You talk about school, life, the project. Maeve is fascinated by the origins of the Leviathan myth, but you can't help fixating on the prologue.

"I'm surprised," Maeve observes one such evening, sitting opposite each other on your sofa. You've ordered Chinese food, sticky sweet and sour comfort, her bare foot has come to rest next to your calf but you don't think she's noticed. "There are a thousand treasure island stories or tales from mysterious faraway lands. What is it about this one that gets you?"

You shrug. You're not totally sure. "I don't know. The magic of it is certainly a draw, especially given … my recent weirdness." Maeve rolls her eyes though doesn't interrupt. "But it's more than that. I guess it's the idea of a place being so free. It doesn't seem like, in Xaymaca, people are judged for what they wear or what they look like … or who they love." Your words hang between you, the suggestion and the picture you've painted. A different world. One where weird kids might be welcome, might walk hand and hand in the sun, might kiss with wild abandon.

Nothing has happened between you since that day outside Five's store and you haven't spoken about it. You remember what Maeve said to Chloe about not being into girls and kick yourself internally, repeatedly, and vow not to mention it, to keep whatever it is you may be feeling in check.

This is harder than you anticipated. You spend many evenings after school at the library, Vega first bringing you tea and biscuits but, seeming to suspect the empty houses you are both avoiding, increasingly "just popping" to the takeaway next door and bringing you back stewed chicken and curry goat and ackee and saltfish. As your coursework deadline approaches, you are thrown together more and

more frequently, consolidating your notes and dividing up the drafting between you.

"Reggie?" Maeve has been speaking but you were distracted. She has taken a sip of water and a drop of it has made its way down her throat, charting a course between the blue currents of her veins. She wipes it away and you mentally shake yourself.

"Sorry, yeah?"

She looks at you strangely, her neck flushing under your gaze, but doesn't push it. "I said, did you see my notes on the early trade and property papers?"

"Oh. No, sorry, which folder were they in?"

"The one on the five main captains of the Nubian Brethren."

"The ones who formed the Republic?"

"Right." She pulls her laptop towards her. "So Captain Ezi is a bit of a mystery, from everything I've read. Disappeared a couple of years after the Republic formed and was never seen again. A couple of old naval sources say his ship was supposed to have been struck by lightning or sunk in a storm or something. We've read about Hook and de Casse, and my ancestor Cora."

"The badass, right."

"Right, so then there's Johnson."

"Johnson?" You gape. "What – some great great great of Chloe's? God, her family kept that quiet!" You laugh disbelievingly. You think of Five and all your knowing neighbours. They don't know this, that's for sure.

"Exactly – like my aunt, right, they don't want to be associated with anything other than who they are now. But that's not all. These early trade papers show that some eighteen years after the Republic formed it began trading with the

Empire again. Sugar and tea and cotton. And guess who signed those papers?"

"No way."

"Yep. Captain James Johnson."

Most families in New Shetatown with generational wealth had naval connections but Reggie had never been sure where the Johnsons' money was from. This made sense. "So even the first Johnson was a bootlicker. It's in the blood." Maeve snorts with laughter. You think it's adorable and you silently trill at the sound.

"What does this mean then? That he betrayed the Republic?"

"Let's see…" Maeve scrolls through her notes humming tunelessly. "I don't know. It seems like he signed the papers before the naval battle and that he fought for the Republic in it – then there's no record of him. No record of Captain Hook or Captain de Casse either. There was only one captain of the Brethren left. My ancestor – Cora. I can't find anything that says definitively what happened."

"Maybe they died in the battle?"

"Maybe. Then there were fewer people to defend the Republic or vote to preserve the way of life. And whatever happened to Johnson, he had signed those papers and accepted a king's pardon. So the trade started, then the naval outpost…"

"And the members of the Republic who were left?"

"They either accepted the Empire or were executed for piracy. Like Ó Néill."

You sit back in your seat, thinking. After almost three months of research, of reading about witches and sea dragons

and thinking about magic trees, you had not expected this. Your dreams have led you down a path of imagining – if you can experience such strangeness, then anything is possible. But the conclusion of your essay, it seems, will be far more mundane. Myths and magic and dragons, yes maybe. But ultimately the Republic fell like most things do. Money was the inevitable tide that eroded the ideal, the hand that held history's pen, the noose that tied round the necks of those who stood against it.

*

Christmas arrives on Sheta Island and with it all of the accompanying anachronisms of existing as a tropical nation under a frigid Empire. Songs of snowmen and winter wonderlands blast through the high street, made louder by the shop doors flung open to let in the breeze, a balmy twenty-seven degrees.

The season of giving gives you a headache and social anxiety. Parties you're not invited to, Secret Santas you're left out of, Christmas talent shows you've absolutely no desire to partake in; you're not sure what you're good at anyway.

Maybe you never had a chance to discover your talents. When you were small, Five had enrolled you in a ballet class like all of his respectable friends with their respectable daughters, but the structure and rigour did not suit you and the teacher soon advised Five that maybe you'd be happier in something "more contemporary". Five did not enrol you in something more contemporary and you were left to dance alone in your room, which suited you just fine anyway.

You do this still. Come home from school, kick your shoes off and move in private. Sometimes you play music, sometimes you don't, only feel the stretch of your limbs, the arc of your spine, the sway of your hips. In those moments you are big and small at the same time, your arms reach like trees to the night sky, you are the night's sky, you are the spirits' cry, you are the stars that watch, the ancestors that hear your prayers and are yet to answer. In your room you reach a midpoint between *something more contemporary* and flying. Your scalp tingles, your feet move in time to the song that beats in your heart, you're the *brown girl in the ring* and the voice that calls you tells you so.

You carry all of this with you through the day, feel it warm you from the inside. It is a personal talisman guarding you against the usual catty comments.

"Don't get too close, Maeve, or Adrien will get jealous."

Maeve does not reply but she doesn't step away or turn her back to you either. The kiss hangs between you, neon and flashing whenever you catch eyes.

Just before the bell on the last day of term you hand in your coursework. You're proud of it. Together you selected key events and wove them together with the myths of the island – Nubia, the Leviathan, what the Republic had meant to those who defended it. You leave school with Maeve, who insists on analysing the essay again, worrying at her lip.

"I don't know why you trusted me to write the paragraph about the star, Reggie, it's a really sophisticated point."

"You're going to chew a hole through your lip if you don't stop stressing."

"I just don't know if I made it clear enough, the link between the sea and skies in navigation and marine history..."

"You absolutely did," you say for what must be the hundredth time: "And the metaphor you used, the bit about the stories of Nubia rattling the stars so fiercely that one fell, that was excellent. Perfectly phrased."

"Well." Maeve smiles at you warmly. "I only got the idea because you noticed that discrepancy on those navigational charts."

"Ah, yes," you smile. "Alpha Lyrae. The star that went missing." You don't think you've ever had so much fun doing schoolwork in your life. And you love schoolwork.

You continue up the road, discussing your plans for the Christmas holidays.

She grabs you suddenly, pulls you sideways off the narrow road which leads back into the main part of town, down an even narrower lane and through the hedgerow until you are standing in a field, backed by the five-star hotel, shielded from sight. "I wanted to give you this." She holds out her hand. "Because I don't know when I'll next see you." The box is square and neatly wrapped in sparkly purple paper. "Merry Christmas, Reggie."

You blink. If birthday presents are rare for you, Christmas presents are things of fancy. Sea dragons and witches are more likely.

You reach into your own bag and pull out your own carefully wrapped box. Red and silver wrapping, you had agonized over each perfectly folded corner.

"Merry Christmas, Maeve."

She beams. A beat. A shared laugh and you *tear tear*

together. She beats you and gasps in delight. "Oh, Reggie, it's gorgeous." A moonstone necklace, her birthstone. She puts it on immediately, and it gleams, the same bluish colour of her veins, sitting in the centre of her chest, shining like a heartbeat. You are so enjoying her enjoyment that you momentarily forget your own gift. Your hands quiver slightly. The box is unmarked but when you open it, you take a moment to process what you find. Earrings. Beautiful, shimmering gold, shaped like sea shells.

"I don't know what to say."

She swallows. "Oh, well, I mean, I just saw them and thought … they'd bring out the gold in your eyes and…" Her words die in her throat and you look at each other. The shadows ensconce you, shielding you from the eyes of the world. She pulls you towards her. This kiss is different, thorough and intentional. Your free hand is in her hair, at the small of her back, her fingers flutter from your collarbone to your waist, bare in a crop top, light as bird wings. They rest there, skimming the waistband of your skirt.

*

Ten days pass and Christmas blows through your house on a slightly pine-scented wind, bringing little disruption. You stave off loneliness with a smutty book and ignore the ghost of your mother, never more active than on an occasion when she can demand attention, moving between rooms lamenting what this time of year might have been.

The slamming of the door jolts you out of your reverie where you lie on New Year's Eve, sprawled across the sofa,

contemplating another midnight spent with pre-recorded TV hosts counting down to a moment that, for them, was months away. You had considered texting Maeve but you don't want to appear desperate. You've been texting intermittently all holiday. She's had ample opportunity to ask to see you tonight. She hasn't. And she hasn't brought up the kiss either. You leap to your feet as you hear Five's key in the door. Bast springs up from where she was curled on your chest and you quickly toss her into the garden with a whispered apology.

"Reggie!"

"Oh, hey, Fi— Dad."

He sits on the sofa. "I want to talk to you." Your ears prick at his tone – warmer than usual.

"I've had some wonderful news."

"Oh, really?"

"A job. A really important job, actually. The town tourism board have finally announced that they'll be opening a new museum – and I'm to manage the whole process!"

"Wow, that's really great. When will it be opening?"

"It'll take a few years yet; you'll likely be at university by then. Though I'm sure we'll offer lectures on naval history, astronomy, navigation – just imagine your class coming to see me lecture!"

You don't mention that you have absolutely no intention of staying on Sheta Island for university.

"Will you keep the store?"

"Oh, yes! That little green door is an institution on this island. But I'll be able to hire some staff, and I'll have an office in the museum as well."

You find yourself genuinely pleased for him. "Well, shall I order us a takeaway to celebrate? Get some ice cream, maybe?"

"Ah, no thanks, Reg, some of the boys down at the station want to take me for a drink." You deflate.

You want to keep him a moment longer. You're so rarely able to share joy.

"So … what will the commute be like?"

"No time at all. It'll be where the library is."

Beat. The thudding, clamouring of your heart. The tree. The library. You think you must have heard him wrong.

"What?"

He continues. "Yes, they're pulling down the library and building the museum there instead. A good thing too, that building is an eyesore. I've seen the plans, they're amazing. People from all around the world will flock to see it. It's to be the finest naval institute in the world, it's all planned. It'll rival Greenwich and—"

"But … but they can't tear down the library. I mean … where will people go? For books and research?"

"Come on, Reggie, no one really uses that library any more. People go on the internet." He laughs. "Aren't I supposed to be the boomer here?"

His laugh burns your throat like bile. "*I* go to the library!" *Do not cry, do not cry, do not cry.*

"Reggie," – his tone patronizingly patient – "I have always admired your … your style. The way you dance to the beat of your own drum, etcetera. But it might be good for you to go to the library a little less. You need to experience the world a

bit, make some friends! I mean, it's New Year's Eve! Don't you have any plans? What about that … Maeve? She's Commodore O'Néill's girl, isn't she? He's a very well-respected man. What's she up to this evening?"

You do not answer. He ploughs on. "Come on now. I run a business of repute, I can't be the dad of the local weirdo."

He says it as a joke, that *famously dark sense of humour* again, laughs after the sentence as he always does, but the last word shoots shards of ice through your heart.

"No!" you spit back. "I guess you can't." You storm up to your room, slam the door, fling yourself on to your bed and scream into a pillow. You feel the curious presence of your mother, wondering who it is displaying more rage than she. She is the only one allowed to be angry here. You feel her leave as Bast hisses at her, before nestling in beside you, having wriggled through the ajar window, bumping her head into your armpit. You scoop her up and bury your head in her fur. She licks your forehead with her rough little tongue, vigorously, as if she is cleaning the sad off you.

You pick up your phone and find your chat with Maeve.

Five got a job at a new museum that's opening where the library is.

The reply is immediate.

Shit! Are you OK?

You appreciate that you don't have to explain anything. That Maeve gets it.

Not really to be honest.

What are your New Year's Eve plans?

Lol. Partying with all my friends.

325

Good, meet me in an hour then?

Wdym?

There's a beach party tonight, for the countdown. Come.

I don't think I'm invited.

I'm inviting you. It's the beach, it exists in commons (as stated by the 2nd amendment to the public and commons act, formed in the second year of the second imperial occupation of Sheta Island).

Nerd.

I have all this local history knowledge. Gotta use it somewhere.

Adrien not bothered about local trespassing law then?

Adrien is only bothered about Adrien.

Oooh. Interesting.

Who's going to be there?

Not sure. People from school, a few different groups.

You know this, of course. The New Year's beach party is infamous on Sheta Island. It happens every year and has no organizers; under-eighteens just turn up to drink without being ID'd. Somehow it never gets shut down by the authorities.

I don't think so tbh. Would rather be with Bast than somewhere I'm not wanted.

Typing. Not typing. Typing. Not typing. Typing.

I want you there.

Beat.

OK.

*

Maeve meets you on the western shore of the island, at the rocky outcropping that forms the turtle's fore-flipper. You are wearing a long black dress with subtle sparkly silver threading. She is in black jeans and a green sequinned crop top that sets the green in her eyes glinting. Her bare midriff looks soft as down and for a moment you think of pulling her in, crushing her mouth to yours and skimming that stretch of stomach with your fingers so that she shivers against you…

"I know it's hardly a December frost, but the breeze is chilly out here." She has two takeaway coffee cups in her hands. You take a sip. Hot chocolate with a kick. "This is exactly what I needed."

"Wait!" She pulls a brown paper parcel out of her shoulder bag and produces an enormous chocolate-chip cookie, which she passes to you.

"I love you," you sigh and then freeze, your brain in awkward, embarrassed overdrive. Maeve doesn't say anything but you can feel the heat of her blush. You begin to walk. You tell her what Five said and the validation of her outrage buoys you.

"Damn, did we luck out with family, eh?"

"Bullshit, isn't it?"

"Sometimes you have to make your own family, I guess."

"Yeah," you say and you smile at each other. When you finish the cookies, she takes your hand. Your brain twists in confusion and your heart skips but your fingers tangle so naturally that you don't say anything.

"I actually had a fight with my aunt as well," she admits.

You feel guilty, you have taken up too much oxygen. "Oh, Maeve, I'm sorry, I'm always running my mouth about my stuff and—" She shushes you.

She is patient without being patronizing. "Reggie. This is how a conversation goes. One of us shares something and the other empathizes and also shares something. Sometimes, there will be a day where just you share stuff and sometimes there will be a day where just I do. But you don't have to apologize every time you get in first." She lifts your hand to her mouth. You think she is going to kiss it, but she bites you, playfully but enough to leave imprints of her teeth waxed into your skin. "Every time you apologize for being too much, I'm going to bite you, all right?"

"All right!"

She kisses it better and your stomach jolts again. "Now, as I was saying before you so rudely interrupted me..."

The apology forms instinctively behind your teeth.

"What did I just say?" She raises your hand again threateningly. You grin and mime zipping your lips. "So, yeah. Basically someone who knows my aunt saw us together. And, well, she basically said that I need to *conduct myself correctly in public* if I wanted to *avoid nasty vicious rumours*."

"Shit."

"Yeah."

"What did you say?"

Maeve is avoidant, amused, a sweet little bluster of air. "Obviously I just said *mmhmmm* and went to take the cookies out of the oven. You know I suck at confrontation."

You look at each other. Maeve takes a breath. "Look, I told my aunt that I'm into Adrien and whatever her friend saw she's probably wrong."

The words punch you in the gut, your hand is suddenly

heavy in hers, but you keep your face carefully interested. "Well, that's … sensible. And … I mean … are you? Into Adrien?"

Maeve looks out to the sea instead of at you. It's a crisp night, the coldest you've had in a while. The waves are restless, ceaseless in their toss and turn.

"No. Not at all. It's just easier to say that I am." She swallows. "I've never really given much thought to like … my sexuality or anything. I never really fancied anyone back home. They were all people I'd been in nursery with, you know? But, no, Adrien is … just fine. But I … I'm into someone else, actually."

You don't know what to say, so you say nothing, but the wish feels corporeal between you.

Maeve faces you at last. "I like you a lot, Reggie. Aside from any of the other stuff, you're like, my best friend. But I … I guess I'm just a bit confused and need a second to figure it out?"

You process this. She likes you. She sees you as her best friend. But there's *other stuff*. Is the *other stuff* the same for her as it is for you? You don't know if she finds you as sweet, as funny and beautiful, if she watches the muscles of your throat bob while you drink, or stares at each individual lash, or lies awake at night thinking of all the smart, witty things you said that day…

"That's OK." It is a half-truth. "I have a lot to figure out here too. It's probably best that we don't … rush anything."

She sighs, smiles at you, relieved, and you are glad to make her happy when she makes you so happy.

You reach the sounds of teenage laugher, shouts in voices that aren't really theirs, sweet sips of sticky stuff sending them staggering, careering out of the crowd on the beach, and then back in again, shiny in festive sequins like inebriated whirligig

beetles. You follow Maeve, weaving through the crowd, she is still holding your hand. Light from a large bonfire flickers, casting people in and out of shadow. Someone has brought a speaker and the bass thumps loudly. People are dancing haphazardly, clutching bottles and plastic cups that make you worry about sea turtles and beach clean-ups. Others are talking, kissing, glancing at watches. Excited for the moment. It's already half-past ten.

You've always found New Year's strange. This grand theoretical shift but in reality nothing changes. You prefer equinoxes and solstices. In your seasonless life where time stagnates, the waxing and waning of the moon, the incremental drift of the sun, all seem bigger to you than a confettied countdown and copious amounts of alcohol.

A crowd of people from your school emerge from the gloom and Maeve lets go of your hand. You try not to overthink this. She is immediately waylaid by a group from her literature class. Social panic sets in and you pull her to you, saying into her ear so she can hear over the noise, "I'm going to go and find us some drinks," and hurry off before she can stop you.

You've no idea where to find drinks, of course. Do people just keep their own? Would there be … a cooler somewhere, like in TV shows? You're wandering on the outskirts of the crowd, trying very hard not to look lost, when an unpleasantly familiar voice attracts your attention.

"Howdy, horny vag!"

You sigh. Typical.

"Hello, Chloe."

She is alone for once, seems smaller without her entourage.

Perhaps she is thinking the same thing because she says, "Where's your shadow?" She is clearly drunk. Her voice is too loud. She doesn't slur like most drunk people. Her words are too sharp, their edges too crisp.

"Pardon?"

"Pardon?" she mimics you. You sigh and move to step around her but she blocks your path. "Sorry, I mean your *girlfriend*?"

"She's not my girlfriend."

"That's not what I heard."

"Then maybe you should clean out your ears."

"Oooh, touchy!" You go to step round her again but she once more blocks your path, laughing.

"Chloe. Get out of my way."

"Make me." You push past her, she grabs your wrist, and for an unnerving moment you don't know if she's going to punch you or kiss you. Then you shake her loose and move away.

As it turns out, there is a cooler. You're not sure who it belongs to, if anyone, but there are a few glass bottles of beer on ice. You are looking round for someone to ask when a shadow falls across your path and your second least favourite person looms above you.

"They're mine but you can have one," says Adrien. He pushes his hair out of his face and tries to smoulder but he's drunk and just looks like he has IBS.

"Thanks. Can I get one for Maeve?"

"I'm already getting her one actually, but I'm sure she'll want one later." He picks up two beers and lurches back through the crowd. You also grab two and follow him. No matter your

feelings towards Maeve, she was right. She's your best friend and you are not about to let this drunk slimy bastard slobber all over her. You nearly bump into him as he stops abruptly, a little way away from where you'd left Maeve. You register his slack-jawed open mouth breaking into a grin and slurring, "Is it Christmas again?" You peer round Adrien.

You drop the beer bottles.

Chloe's hands are in her hair and on her face and she is kissing Maeve.

Your stomach bottoms out.

There are whoops from the various nearby boys as they break apart. Chloe flashes her eyes at their little audience. Maeve looks dazed, a little embarrassed, but as Adrien says, "That's the hottest thing I've ever seen," she smiles slightly. She is enjoying the attention. "Kiss again!" another boy yells. And they do.

You move back through the crowd, tripping over the dropped bottles, back past the bass-thumping speakers, away from the loud and the laughing, up the gorse slope, back, back, back to Bast and the bubble where no one can hurt you. Everyone fancies Chloe. *Why did I think Maeve was immune?* As you round the corner on to your street, Chloe's words come floating back to you. *"I just think she can do better."* You feel the sob pushing up through your chest. Why had she invited you tonight if she was just going to do this? You should have stayed in, you should never have gone.

The house is dark and empty when you arrive home. Your mother eats at the emptiness, feeds on the dark, and you turn the lights on. It is no matter, she enjoys your wallowing. You

crawl into bed with Bast to protect you. You put on a film, any film, you're not watching. After a little while, from inside the houses of your neighbours, you can hear the chant begin.

Ten

Nine

Eight

You turn the film up. It's just another night, turning to just another day. It's an arbitrary measure of time, it's made up by Roman men…

Five

Four

You think of Maeve, kissing Chloe at midnight…

Three

Two

One.

You sob into Bast's fur.

Leviathan, Awake

At Ameyro's alarm there was a great surge, the members of the Brethren, flawed and brandy-faced, on their feet with impressive speed and balance.

"Wait!" Johnson's arms were out, his voice fighting to be heard over the tide of men and women, shouting, jostling, seeking out the weapons they abandoned. "We could still parlay, we could still…"

"Johnson, there's nary a buc in here that would run from a good fight," snarled Hook; her grimace was a grin, a battle mask.

"Aye, we are a land of free folk." Ó Néill peered over her shoulder. "We set little stock by foregone conclusions. We fight until the end, as Nubia did."

De Casse was making his way to the door. He passed Levi on his way out and clapped his shoulder. For a moment his warm eyes crinkled close to Levi's. "Your father would be proud. The furnace forges the blade – how will you be made?"

The four captains, with the ease of those who have co-existed for many years, fell in line, barking orders at their crews, pulling out maps of the island. Even Johnson, once it was apparent that no one would be forming an alliance with the Empire today, reluctantly but rigorously joined in swift strategy talks with his comrades. Each divided their crew between those

that would defend the Republic from the shore and those that would hoist their colours and sail out to meet the oncoming naval fleet.

Levi felt his resolve rock. He had never known combat. He had no crew, no ship, no Tally or Abe to instruct, no Ezi to defend him. The internal canvas lay scrunched, crumpled in some dark corner – he could not make any part of himself manifest. He had never been able to shift on command. He was rooted, watching chaos, the frenetic activity: shops boarded up, civilians and children, those unable to take up arms, hidden in cellars, doors locked. He was sewn and threaded with doubt. But then Kano's hand was at his sternum, and their voice was low in his ear. "You are the son of Prince Ezi, captain of *The Sea Dragon* and the River Mumma. You are born for this, Leviathan. Awake." A true name on the truest lips and Levi felt the shudder wrack him. His skin suddenly did not fit his bones and he fought his fear with everything he had. Screams and terror and burning flesh, he acknowledged the jagged memories that cut at him but did not shy away. He stepped out into the darkening night.

"Orders, Captain?" Vega was grinning at him. She was tense but her eyes flashed gold, her hands on her sabre, a fearless fire walking. Suddenly they were on deck, planning future adventures as they practised their sparring. They were born for this. She had been forged in death and defiance, had blazed through the world and sent circumstance eddying. If she did not fear *her* glow, he should not fear his. He took stock of the activity around him, watching people and pirates fall into place.

Ameyro sprinted past and Levi hailed him. "Ameyro!"

"Levi!"

"You said you sighted the ships to the west?"

"Yes, but their sails banked east. We take the docks as our front!" And he was off, following the pounding feet of his own crew.

Levi turned to his sister. "If they break the ranks, I want you to fall back and defend the inn. Kano and I will be strongest on the shoreline. But Emabelle…"

"I won't let anything happen to her." Levi believed her. "The docks, then?" she asked, looking at them both. They nodded. And began to run.

They arrived at the crowded dock within minutes, pushed through the mass of bodies and raced down the familiar gorse slope to the shoreline, startling those who hurried by, carrying weapons or wheeling heavy cannons to line up on the beach at Captain Johnson's instruction.

He scoffed when he saw them. "This is no place for you, whelp, unless you want your skirts soiled with shit and blood!"

Vega bridled, but Kano held her back. "He'll soon see what can be done in a skirt, worry not."

Levi took stock of the shoreline. Closer than he'd have imagined, sails in red, white and blue blotted the ink of the horizon. Eleven, all ships of the line. He counted the guns, sized up their decks, wracked his brains for memories from his lessons with Able.

"Two first rates, three second rates, four third rates, two fourth rates."

Vega tallied, her breath hitched. "Men, likely over seven thousand, guns and cannon eight hundred and twenty-six."

"Or eight hundred and sixty-six, if they're using the four-and-seventy model."

"They likely are; Pa said it had become popular."

"Sink me. Perhaps we're in luck and they're flying light."

They looked at Kano who'd been observing their back and forth in bewilderment. It was endearing and would have amused Levi if peril weren't so close at hand. He scanned the activity before him, a dance of death decades out of practice. Each captain commanded a fleet, but their numbers were small, as were their ships, built for swift manoeuvring and outpacing larger naval vessels. Equipment was as rusted and creaky as those who wielded them, many had not taken to the seas in years.

"And what are our numbers?"

Vega flicked through all she had overheard in the last few weeks, all the logs she had read in the library. "Buccaneers, maybe five hundred, if we're lucky. With those in town able to take up arms, maybe two hundred or so more."

They looked at each other. Levi's resolve fractured but he caught it before it splintered completely. Seven hundred Republicans – and that was being generous. Against seven thousand naval men. Seven thousand strong naval men who were trained and equipped and practised. He breathed in the salt and the smoke of the signal fires lit along the beach, inhaled and exhaled with the tide. He wondered if his father had ever been so outnumbered, at least ten to one. Certainly he had heard stories, but only ones of dazzling victories and daring feats. Never ones of fear and loss. Maybe because his father had never known how to be afraid and be a father at the

337

same time. He, Levi, had not known how to be all the parts of himself at the same time either. Even before the death of *The Sea Dragon* and awakening of the new one, he had been tossed by the waves of self. The dreamer, the future captain; the hatchling in a skirt, the skilled sword fighter; the boy who loved cornmeal and cackle. But he was not that person any more. Who was he now?

"It looks as though de Casse and Hook will sail out to meet the navy. Johnson and Ó Néill are holding the shorelines. And so will we, savvy?"

"Aye, Captain," in two voices.

They turned to face the foe on the horizon, closer now, so much closer, and Levi, with the sharp eyes that had not belonged to his father, could see the faces of individual men, hear their tinny battle cries blown towards him on the wind. Vega's teeth were bared. She had never seen combat but she was a star who'd been handed a sword by a pirate prince and no whelp had ever been more ready. Kano was her opposite, their face calm and clear; they would take no pleasure in bloodshed, not like Vega who burned for the fierce heat of battle. But for freedom and for Levi they would do what must be done. As Levi would for them. For a moment he took them both in, as they regarded him. Unspoken things warmed the air between them, the night was humid and heavy.

*

Closer they came and closer still.

The men who would destroy everything he loved about the

place that had become his home. He thought of the Freeman's, of markets and tiny coconut macaroons and the shops that sold silk skirts and the library.

Closer and closer and closer.

Far to the left, the land dipped in the east and Levi could glimpse their cove. The cove that he had failed to shift in so many times. So many times had he come close to unfolding all of himself only to shy away from what he saw. From the guilt and the grief that he could not face. But Kano had not given up on him, had stayed by his side. Was still by his side.

They were almost upon them. Levi held his position. His knees quaked but he kept them steady. He would not look weak. Not with Johnson at his back. They were leaping from their ships now, smartly uniformed and armed. They were splashing absurdly through the water, kicking their legs up to fight the currents which fought to hold them back and pull them away. There was a roaring in his ears which drowned out the roaring of those around him and, as the first of the navy fell upon them, Levi knew nothing but the instinctive response of his body, the flow of fury and defence.

It was easier to kill than he had expected. The first man died with a swish of his cutlass as he swiped through his neck like butter. He had rounded and impaled another with his sabre before the first man's head hit the sand. Death became a dance, a drum beating on deck, the rhythm of a shanty. He entered a trance, a place between body and beyond, and where each phrase of the shanty began, life ended. He sought out Vega when he had cleared a path around him and saw that she had felled almost twice as many men as he. Her face was splattered with

blood but even beneath the gore he could see the fierce grin, hear the wild laugh over the gurgling screams of slashed throats and the squelches of disembowelment.

Kano moved beside her; they were deadly competent and lethally quick, but Levi saw how anathema this was to them. It was entirely too human, too mortal and earthy. All the same they kept on, flicking between shapes, and each shift into mist and dew and vicious current seemed to offer them brief reprieve, allowing them to gut one more time, decapitate again, take their opponent off guard and wade through blood like water.

Elsewhere, Levi could tell that the Republicans were having less success. The navy were gaining ground, pushing them back inland. Republicans from every crew fell and the brutal reality Johnson had painted not hours before was fast becoming inevitable. Levi redoubled his efforts. If the Republic fell, that was another home lost. If the Republic fell, how would he reach Xaymaca? If the Republic fell, where would they go? Where could a star, a nymph and a sea dragon make a home, in this world of dying magic? He looked up and his stomach became a hard pit. The beach was strewn with bodies, and still the navy came. Even as he watched, a ball blasted through the port-side hull of one of *The Cleopatra* fleet. They were using caravels and galleons and brigantines to fight ships-of-the-line which dwarfed them in number as well as size. They were woefully underprepared for an attack of this magnitude. A cry of pain and rage and Levi saw Ameyro, fighting his way through a tide of red, blue and white uniforms, fall. They fell on him and Levi launched himself forward, cutting down men like wheat

and reaching Ameyro just in time to slice the men before him nose to navel, effectively clearing a space that allowed his fellow buccaneer to stand and fall back.

Panic gave way to something else as the world grew eerily still around him.

They were going to lose.

His father would not have allowed that to happen. And so he could not allow that to happen.

De Casse had said the furnace forges the sword and he was burning, he was pinned in the fiery heat and he could not yield, could not melt and give way to fear. He was no longer the person he had been, he was no longer joyfully self-assured but, finally, after all that had happened, he was … sure. So much of what had happened was not his fault – but what happened now was his responsibility. He could not fail. And in that moment, that shining moment of *sure*, he knew what it meant to be a captain. Ezi had known it too; weighing the threats and making a choice. Even knowing the choice might cost you. Ezi had weighed the danger of him, Levi, to his crew, had weighed whatever threat had made him leave Xaymaca – and had still picked his son. His father had loved him enough to alter the course of his existence, to jeopardize his crew; he could have left him and all that he was on Xaymaca, but he didn't.

Levi meant to make that decision count.

He could feel it now, rushing towards him, within his grasp. He had lost family, he had gained family, he had lost parts of himself, he had found new parts of himself. He had become a master in messy, beautiful contradiction.

"LEVI!" Vega shouted to him from where she twisted and

341

ducked, never missing a beat or an opening. "WHAT ARE YOU DOING?"

He did not answer. Instead he asked, "Why do you think they sang of a sea dragon? Knowing who and what I was?"

Vega stared as though he'd gone mad. "WHAT? I DON'T KNOW! THE SHIP WAS ALWAYS *THE SEA DRAGON*. WHAT SORT OF QUESTION IS THAT AT A TIME LIKE THIS?"

"Some things are meant to be, driftling." Levi cleared a path to Kano and caught them in their human form. A heartbeat, death suspended. Levi pressed his lips to Kano's. The nymph's hand found the place on his sternum. He breathed in the smell of them. In and out and up and out and open breezes, a place beyond, a form of what he could be... Then Vega was in front of him, clearing her throat pointedly. "Hatchling! This is not the time for dreaming!"

"Ah, how wrong you are, big sister."

But she was laughing.

Levi was laughing too as he walked to the shore, laughing as he opened his lungs and filled them with salt and sea breath and certainty. For all the clamour on the beach, the gathering night was still. The stars peeked out, eager spectators. Levi took the tang of smoke and gunpowder and sweat to whet his focus. He held these smells of battle up to an inner eye and peered through it as he looked at his whole self. Levi and the Leviathan. His skin began to heat, pulsing and stretching. *To shift is to employ gentle, loving manifestation ... you have to be aware of all of your possible states, not just be aware of them, but love them.* The dark fog of grief threatened at the corners but he didn't shrink or bat

them away, he greeted them with forgiveness. A sharp breeze tore loose his tricorne and bandana, his locs flew free about his neck and face, his skirts ruffled and billowed. The canvas fell open around him, baring himself to himself.

The Leviathan exploded in a firework of emerald and sapphire flame.

He arced through the air, graceful and deadly, showering the shore in sea fire that sizzled where it hit the water and, as he descended towards the surface, two great wings expanded from each flank. Spiked as his tail and crown, they gleamed in cyan and cobalt, the length of his body and twice the size of a blue whale. The sea dragon twisted once, twice through the air, somersaulting, his softer underside gleaming, and then dived into the water. Where darkened sea had been still, it now frothed and waved, a warning to those still advancing ships, the men aboard them now staggering to keep upright as they rocked in his wake.

"Blood 'n' 'ounds!" Ó Néill gasped. "What is that?"

Kano was grinning broadly. "That is the Leviathan."

Beneath the water Levi was loose and tingling in each nerve and delighted in the kiss of the currents against his skin. He kissed them back in delicious reunion, sent a jet stream out of the nostrils of his snout and flexed the never-ending muscles of his wings and tail. He crested and broke the surface between *The Cleopatra* and *La Liberté*, gazing with each eye at the stunned faces of their captains. The naval ships were gaining on them; in any moment they would begin their onslaught and Levi suspected they only hadn't opened fire yet because his appearance had stunned them into panic. And they were not the

only ones. In his left eye, Levi spied de Casse aiming a musket at his head, his crew gathered around him similarly positioned, some even readying to swing their cannons round.

"Do not waste your ammunition on me, *Marianne*." Levi did not at first recognize the voice he spoke with, for it was the voice of deep trenches and ancient brine. De Casse started at the sound of that name, his gun dipped. "You called yourself a friend to my father. Be a friend to his son. I mean you no harm." De Casse hesitated and then grinned and lowered his gun.

Captain Hook did not have a gun pointed at him but faced him with awe and dread. When he turned both his great storm-blue eyes upon her, she sank to her knees, reverent as if before a god.

The ancient deep voice chuckled. "Now, Captain Hook, this is a republic. You need not bow to me, for I bow to none but the sea." She met his gaze as she stood and her face split in a fierce smile. Levi found this face could not show such emotion and so he sent a jet of steam in the air before turning towards the horizon and saying, "I'm afraid you may be rather bored now." Captain Hook barked a laugh of surprise and Levi vanished beneath the water.

*

In the years to come, much of what came next would be a blur to Levi, and what wasn't would be forever etched into his memory. In the few moments before he came in range of his enemy he felt no fear. He strained to hear the voice, the voice of his mother, the familiar singing, but he could not hear her. He heard other

things, though. Other songs and stories were whistled to him, the beginning and the end, all of life was water and he would have all of life to listen but not now. He was a tsunami of gleaming-gem death in the warm night world but beneath the water he twisted and danced and focused only on his dream, on the open horizon.

And then it was over.

Ship after ship sent to the locker. Hulls torn, sterns shredded. They did not even have time to load their cannons. Those able to flee either surrendered to *The Cleopatra* or were picked off by de Casse's well-aimed musket. Levi did not linger to see their bodies sink, but returned to the shore, cutting through the water and returning within minutes. The crews of *The Queen Áine* and *The Sterling* were slack-jawed and stunned, their captains' swords loose at their sides. Levi opened himself up again, found the part of himself he wished to become, the part of himself that ate cornmeal and cackle and slept in a warm bed beside Kano, and shifted. He made to emerge from the water but, becoming aware of his nakedness, thought the better of it and sank backwards, swimming for their eastern cove. He hoped Vega and Kano would realize why and follow him. He did not focus on his churning emotion and thrumming heartbeat, only on mourning his lovely lost skirt.

*

Levi had not been sure what to expect as he walked back inland. Kano had rushed to him as he'd emerged from the water, clutching a shirt and skirt – this one in dark, lustrous green –

that they had flown back to the Freeman's to retrieve. Kano had pressed him, briefly, against the jagged wall of the cove, hands checking for injury and finding none.

"Was it glorious?"

"Yes," Levi admitted. "Though I can't say I am suited to the occasion. I didn't get that from my father – blood-letting and death is not where my pleasure lies."

"Where does your pleasure lie?"

Levi had laughed shakily. "Later. Let us go and see the damage."

Most of the survivors had congregated at the Freeman's. The mood was sombre. They had won, but barely, were tallying their losses which already numbered over three hundred in buccaneers – almost half of their good fighters. De Casse and Hook had lost two ships a piece. If the Republic had been vulnerable before, its position now was even more precarious.

"They will return," Johnson was saying hotly. "The Empire will return and what then? We let them wipe us all out?" He slammed his fist on the table. "If we'd parlayed we'd—"

"We'd be kissing their Imperial boots right now!" Hook flared up.

"We would not have lost all of those that we did!"

"They died for their Republic, they died fighting for what they believed in!"

"Nubia always said martyrs were the things of Banbury stories!"

"And then she became one!"

"Please." De Casse held up his hand. "You've been having this argument for years. Nothing is ever accomplished. Today is

346

today. We lost and won. We live to fight again." Noticing Levi, he stood and walked towards him. "Before this day, I never thought I would see proof of the things Nubia spoke of. Levi – this Republic is in your debt." He passed Levi a goblet of wine, and raised his own. "To Levi. To the Leviathan."

Levi felt the pulse between his flesh and bones at the name but he did not fear it now. He acknowledged it, raised his glass to it as the toast was echoed around the dining hall, and then soothed it back to its slumber.

"How can we repay ye?" Ó Néill asked seriously, as Vega crossed the room to join them. Levi looked at his sister, his navigator. Her nod was his guidance.

"I need a crew," said Levi. "And a ship and food and general resources. I know that you need every strong fighter you have and you have lost so many. But the Empire will take some time to recover and regroup from this. And I *have* to go to Xaymaca. I have to find my mother. She is the only parent I have left."

"And what of me?" The indignant shout arose from across the room. Captain Johnson. He was unharmed, barely a scratch on him.

Hook eyed him with intense dislike. "*You* have much to answer to, James. The letter of marque is one thing, but do not think it has gone unnoticed that your crew alone sustained no losses."

A beat. All heads turned towards Johnson's reddening face.

"And I find it most curious," de Casse mused, "that our enemies seemed to know exactly when to sail into the wind. The doldrums have been calm for weeks, and just as a westerly wind picks up, the navy appears."

"I cannot control the weather, man, for God's sake!"

"If all you desire, James, is an alliance between the Republic and Xaymaca, then I see no reason that Levi should not be the one to broker it. In fact," she pressed on, as Johnson made to argue, "he is likely to be more successful than you, surely. If his mother is the River Mumma and a goddess of that land."

"I received the summons!" Johnson blustered, his face saturating, red to mauve. "I have the map with the X! How will the whelp navigate the journey?"

"I have my father's map." Levi's voice was level, calm. "I too can see the X." He paused, then added, "And, for what it is worth, I do not believe that your map is anything more than just a map. Your man Alfie brandished it in the street weeks ago. I saw no X. I have no proof of this, but know, Captain Johnson, that I believe you to be a liar."

"You dare—" Johnson's hand twitched towards his cutlass but he stopped himself.

"Regardless," de Casse interrupted with an air of finality, "I am afraid we have enough reason to doubt your loyalty to this Republic. You shall stay here until the people of Sheta Island are satisfied, *oui*?"

Levi felt a thrill of satisfaction. Then he thought of Johnson's scouts, already in Xaymaca. His mother's voice drifted through his memory as did his father's words, *The island of Xaymaca has been betrayed.* There was still much to be answered.

Ó Néill searched Levi's face. "If I were a younger woman and unattached, I would be right at the prow with you. But I have a family, wee'uns I cannot leave." Levi nodded. If there was

348

anything he understood, it was this. "But I will offer ye one of my ships." She turned to her crew fanned out around her. "Who will sail under Captain Levi, the Leviathan?"

Hands raised. Levi's stomach lurched. One spoke. "D'Arcy, Captain Levi," she said by way of introduction. She was grizzled with scars and wore an eyepatch. "Quartermaster. We are in your debt. And we of *The Queen Áine* honour our debts. Your destruction of the naval fleet has bought us some time – they will not return for now and when they do we shall be bolstered by our Xaymacan alliance. We'll muster up your crew."

Levi nodded, his throat tight. "I am grateful to you, Captain Ó Néill."

"A fair price for what you have done." She stood, and turned a fierce eye on Johnson. "I suggest you turn your stores and supplies over to Captain Levi. You'll not be needing them." She left to see to the losses within her crew.

"We will sail with you, Captain Levi." Levi started. Captain Hook stood from her seat, and her crew, peppered behind her, did likewise. "With our last ship. For Nubia."

"As will we." De Casse stood beside her. "For Ezi."

Johnson hissed with contemptuous laughter. "You're all fools." He stormed out.

Levi tried to speak, coughed, and simply said, "I am most grateful." Vega and Kano took Johnson's and Ó Néill's places round the table, making introductions and talking keenly of plans. Emabelle entered, having been called in to assist with the wounded, and set about rustling up some food. Levi watched de Casse and Hook, sombre-faced but moving forward. They would address their own bereaved later. Is that what it meant,

being a captain? Fighting, counting losses, regrouping and moving forward, always moving forward.

Levi watched it all unfurl around him, a map spread out, a new course charted. He was far away and somewhere else, his soul sweet and settled inside him.

He had shifted. He had secured passage. He was going home. The Leviathan had awoken.

The Third Storm, Revisited

Ata was dragged on to the bank,
    she felt the water leave her skin,
    she could not scream she could not shout,
but each droplet pooling was her kin.

The river gasped at the absence,
    it surged and writhed as though fighting for air,
    the mouth a desperate dying abyss
    as it tried to swallow something that wasn't there.

These new pirates came to claim
    and cut Xaymaca's magic at the source.
    The land would soon learn of the loss
    and feel with brutish, barren force.

The river rushed out to sea
    but, with its Mumma gone, saw no reason to return
    and instead would reach and search and call
    for the object of her yearn.

The river would be its Mumma's voice.
    The river too was Ata's daughter.

The river would find its Mumma's salvation,
it need only search through every water.

Primordial flow, a forgotten speak,
we are most ourselves when we're asleep
and reaching into the dark and the deep,
find a mother's kiss against our cheek…

Find the place
where magic does not die
where rainbows fill the sky
where the river bends
where the ocean ends
she cannot wait
she cannot wait
she cannot wait
Leviathan – awake!

Part three

Prow

THE DRAG QUEEN

Someone, somewhere far away
is calling out your name.
Won't you reply, seeking child?
You are not so tame.
You are the fruit of fertile earth.
You are the blood of the witch who raged.
You are the answer to their prayers.
You are what's left of a war that was waged
for those who dreamed of freedom.

There's a brown girl in the ring
Tralalala...

The library opens on 3 January and school resumes; you fall back into your pattern, homework in the library after school and in your room with Bast at night. *It's better this way*, you tell yourself. This is what you're used to. Your cat and Vega for company. The latter asks about Maeve but you evade and she doesn't push it. Maeve has sent you seven variations of *Can we please talk?* You have ignored them all because there is nothing to talk about. She tries to get your attention in every class you share but you, again, ignore her. It wasn't so much that she had kissed someone else so quickly after kissing you, after saying

she wasn't even sure about kissing girls anyway. You understand the rules of exclusivity – nothing formal had been arranged. No one had signed on a dotted line. But it was *who* she had kissed. And why she had done it. You just can't believe that after making it so clear that she considered you her best friend she would hook up with the person who had spent the last six years trying to make your life miserable. You throw yourself into exam prep, you live within your books, you pretend your life is exactly as it was before. But your dreams are as loud as your loneliness. A week or so into February, her name comes up on your phone screen.

Hey. I know I fucked up. But I miss you. Please can we talk about it?

You delete the message.

Amid the Maeve and Chloe drama, you had almost forgotten about the closing of the library. But when you remember, remember the fight with Five that led you to that stupid party in the first place, you decide that New Year's is a cursed holiday.

"Where will you go, though?"

Vega smiles at you, placing a mug of tea in front of you. You are in the library. It's a Friday evening, sitting dunking an excellent selection of biscuits into several cups of warm brew. The ritual alone squeezes your chest more. What will you do without this place?

"I'm not sure. Maybe I can get a job in the museum."

"Ugh."

"It wouldn't be so bad."

You scowl. "You're too good for that museum."

Vega laughs. "Thank you, Reggie. And maybe you're right."

She hesitates. "My family and I have been … talking about moving on actually."

"What?" You freeze, the mug of tea halfway to your lips. You lower it. "What do you mean?"

"Well…" She is speaking carefully. "Well, we've lived here a while. With this job situation, it might be time for a change."

You don't understand. "But … but what about their jobs?" You blink, and then ask, "What family?"

It is dawning on you, suddenly and strangely, that you know absolutely nothing about Vega's family. In all the years you've known her, spent time with her, she's never really spoken about them. You wrack your brains for any other details – but no. Nothing. Have you just never asked? Has she told you and you've forgotten?

She laughs lightly, though you're sure you hear unease underneath it. "What do you mean? Of course I have a family, Reggie."

Your neck prickles. You stare at her. She stares back, her eyes innocent but guarded. Brown flashing gold like yours.

"You know, for years I used to make up that you were my mum. In my head. Because of how similar our eyes are."

Her face softens into kind creases. "It would have been the privilege of a lifetime to be your mother, Reggie."

You don't know why you said it. You'd noticed the similarity before but, now you focused on it, it was stark. The shape, the fringing of the lashes, the threads of gold. All the same you're embarrassed. "You couldn't be my mum, though, you're not old enough." But even as you say it, you frown and look up at her. Exactly how old *is* Vega? She looks to be in her thirties at

an absolute push and even then… But how could that be? She hadn't been a teenager when you met, had she? You think back but time fogs your memory. You look at her again. Since your sixteenth birthday, since the incident on Halloween with the manchineel tree, much has been strange but this unnerves you. Something has niggled you for weeks now, but you've been too distracted by Maeve to pay close attention. Now though…

An image flashes into your mind. The night sky. The map. Brown eyes flecked with gold. Your eyes. *Vega's eyes.*

"Vega?" You're thinking quickly, but keep your tone light, casual.

"Yes?"

"A few months ago … Maeve and I" – you are surprised by how hard it was to say her name but you plough on, determined not to lose focus – "found a weird chest underneath the floorboards in Five's back room."

"Oh, yes?" She is politely interested.

"Yeah." You sip your tea, dunk a biscuit. "It was so odd. It had a map in it. We were a bit disappointed, we thought we might have discovered some long-lost family fortune." You laugh and so does she, but you're sure of it this time, there's a definite edge to the sound. "Anyway, it was basically useless for the coursework but I thought maybe you might know something about it?"

"Why would I know something about it?" A look like a meteor, hot and quick.

"I just meant that you've done a lot of reading about local myth and history. You helped us loads with our project. I wondered if you'd ever come across anything about a lost

map? It was in the chest and is dated sometime just before the Republic formed."

"Erm…" She pauses. "I might have. I'll have to check some old notes. Maybe … maybe you could bring me the map to have a look at? It might … tell me a bit more."

You think about it for a second. Then nod. "OK, I will."

She is scrutinizing you closely. Then she says, "You know … my family and I run a pretty cool over-sixteens club down on the eastern beach."

You are taken aback. How did you not know this? "Oh, your family run that? I didn't know. Five always told me not to go."

"Really?"

"Well, yeah, obviously. Isn't it … well, a club for kids whose parents have basically chucked them out? Five always said it's run by sinful squatters."

Vega throws back her head and laughs. "Well, I suppose, to Diego Hornigold the Fifth, that's true." She chuckles again. "I've never known you to be particularly heedful of your father."

"True, I tend to ignore everything he says." Then you remember something else. "But … isn't that where the water park is being built?"

Vega sighs. "Yes. It is. We've been there for some time but it seems that … well … all roads are pointing to our exit, aren't they?" For a moment her shoulders are tense and then she grins. "We have an event tonight. You should come. It might well be our last and, besides, I think you might like it."

*

You dress carefully, not knowing what to expect. A black mid-length skirt, a sheer black top with a silver bralet underneath, chunky black platform boots. Something tells you that the kinds of over-sixteens at a youth club run by anyone connected to Vega will not be the same kinds of over-sixteens that were on the beach at New Year's. But then who are they? Everyone who's anyone goes to the beach at New Year's. *Well,* you think cynically, *maybe tonight will be full of nobodies like me.* The thought is surprisingly cheering.

You lock the front door. It's Friday night and Five is celebrating his new employment with some Very Important Men from the city council. You head for the eastern shore, walking through town which is humming with pre-weekend activity. Tonight the high street is papered pink and red, hearts and cherubs in abundance. *It must be Valentine's Day.* You hadn't even noticed. The bars are already packed, people spilling out of open doors on to the street, couples on dates, innumerable mouths making promises, puckering to kiss. It does not put you in the party mood. The town feels busier every time you walk through it, hot and heaving.

You follow the road down towards the docks and around, taking the cliff path. You brace yourself as you head for the gorse slope, the smell of salt and coconuts not enough to soothe your anxiety. *At least it won't be as bad as the last party I went to,* you think wryly. *And it's good for me to learn to socialize without Maeve.*

"Reggie."

And there she is.

"Shit."

She is standing against a collection of rocks spilling out of the cliff face, which form a corner along a bend in the shoreline. Her hair is pulled up into a messy bun. She is wearing a white linen two-piece set, a matching vest and culottes, with hoop earrings and the necklace your bought her. She looks so beautiful that you feel furious. She could at least have the decency to look crap.

"I was waiting for you."

You frown. "How did you know I was going to be here?"

She hesitates and then admits, "Vega told me."

Your frown deepens.

"You wouldn't answer my texts or speak to me in school, I didn't know what to do."

"How about leave me alone?"

"Reggie, please."

You go to move past her but she stops you, catches your wrist and it's the wrong thing to do because the gesture reminds you of Chloe and you wrench your hand free and round on her.

"How could you have done that to me, Maeve?"

"I don't know. I'm sorry."

"You don't know?"

"No. I just … everyone was cheering, and Chloe and the boys... Boys never looked twice at me when I was at my last school, but here…"

"You know" – and everything you've been thinking and feeling for six weeks comes flying out – "you know, I would actually have understood if you'd kissed Adrien. Even if you think he's *just fine,* I would have got it. He's good-looking and

people like him and you care about stuff like that. Cool. But *Chloe?* After everything I told you about her and me, after you said to me that you're not even sure about whether you like girls, that you don't even know if… Is it just me you don't like? Because you could have said so!"

"Reggie, please, no, it's not like that." Her eyes are full and her lips are quivering but this just makes you more infuriated.

"Don't you dare cry!" you rage. "I should be the one crying! Don't you dare cry and make me feel bad for you!"

"I'm sorry," she cries, tears spilling down her cheeks. "I really am! You're absolutely right to be angry, I'd be angry, I am angry. It was stupid. I got … got caught up in the attention. Chloe, she … she performs and people like it. And I just, in that moment, wanted to see what it would be like to perform too."

"And then you kissed her again!"

"I know, I know. It seemed … harmless. I wasn't thinking. Then I saw you running away and—"

The image heats your face, wounds your already fragile pride. "I didn't run. I stormed."

"Yes, you did, and you were right to." She dabs at her face with the back of her hand, trying not to ruin her make-up. You make an impatient sound and hand her a tissue.

"Thanks." She takes it from you. Hiccups, swallows. You watch her throat ripple. *Dammit.* "I'm really, really sorry, Reggie. And not … not just as your friend, for kissing the girl who's been so mean to you all these years. I'm sorry that" – she takes a breath – "I've been trying to figure out what it means, the way I feel about you. And I've gone about it badly. And it's upset you and I feel so bad about that. But I do … like you. And

I just want us to go back to how we were … before … when we were just figuring things out."

She is wringing her hands, her face is still damp. Your heart is beating fast. You know her apology is sincere. But you are tender inside. Bruised. And she is still uncertain.

You let the silence linger, let her wring some more.

"You have to promise me that you'll never, ever do something like that again."

"I won't."

"I mean, you can kiss whoever—"

"I don't want to kiss whoever, I just—"

You talk over her. "You're not my girlfriend. I'm not going to tell you who you can and can't kiss. Except for Chloe. And Grace. They take any opportunity to make me feel shit, Maeve. And you don't defend me. And that's fine, I get it, you don't do confrontation. But you can't do that and then kiss Chloe and say you're my best friend. It doesn't work that way for me."

"I understand, I really do, Reg. And, honestly, there is *nothing* between me and Chloe."

You face each other. You're not really sure how to proceed. You feel strangely tired and the last thing you want to do is go and party. But the thought of going and sitting at home alone is also unappealing. Even Bast is probably out hunting.

"Do you still … want to go to this?"

You consider.

"Please," she says. She quirks a half-smile, the final flares of the setting sun turning her hazel eyes as gold as yours. "It's Valentine's Day?"

You sigh. Deciding that, if nothing else, you'll get to find out

more about Vega ahead of potentially showing her the map, you nod. She tentatively holds out her hand towards you. You think about it then shake your head. You need a minute. Hurt flickers but she understands, and reaches into her bag instead, pulling out two water bottles filled with a liquid that is absolutely not water.

"I brought drinks?"

You smile despite yourself. "Thanks." You fall into step beside her and begin to walk down the beach. The silence is not uncomfortable, but it is heavy, each of you processing what was said, what was meant.

You don't know it's there until you're upon it. Then you wonder how you could have missed it. It is as though you've come through a mist, a mist that can be felt but not quite seen. You round the corner fully and are drawn up short. An enormous ship is docked in the sand, though *docked* is too temporary a word for what is clearly a permanent residence. It is buried deep and held fast by many great rocks and boulders. You have lived on Sheta Island your whole life and never before beheld this sight. People are moving around on deck, strolling up and down the gangway that slopes down to the sand. There are chairs, tables, even strings of lights between the ship and the craggy cliff face. The prow and stern are decorated with wreaths of flowers, and a name is painted across the hull: *The Dragon Queen.*

You and Maeve look at each other and walk towards it. As you draw closer you hear the sound of music, laughter. Lamp-light on deck casts the figures that dance there into sharp relief as the sun departs the day, their long gowns lengthened further

by the shadows. Those that aren't dancing talk, kiss, hug, swig out of glasses and bottles. The impossibility of it dawns on you, this marvellous mirage in the sand. It's loud and riotous and yet you've never heard of a party ship on the beach. Is this the seedy den of iniquity Five had mentioned? The over-sixteens club Vega spoke of? You take in the faces. Your town is a small one, there are easily less than ten thousand people, though tourism is steadily growing the numbers, but these can't all be tourists. And yet ... you don't recognize any of them. And you feel you would recognize them if you'd seen them before; tall chiselled topless people in baggy board shorts, large full-breasted people in diamanté bralets, buzz cuts and ballgowns, blonde wigs and biker boots, you can only gape at the range. Something feels tight and sweet in your chest as you watch them all, flitting wraith-like through the night. They are so at ease. Not stoically uncaring like you are, determinedly flushing the water off your more permeable-than-you'd-ever-admit wings. No, these people are *happy*. They're free of judgement and spectators, they're having *fun*.

"Ladies, gentlemen and those of you sophisticated enough to have evolved past the bizarre gender binary – tonight's main even is about to begin!" The crowd of people, numbered at not quite a hundred by your estimation, surge towards the ship, all gazing up at the deck. You grab Maeve's hand without thinking and pull her forward. The person speaking is quite the most beautiful being you've ever seen. Moon-silver skin, hair like spilled ink in the gathering dark. They are bare-chested, wearing a billowing pair of culottes in midnight blue trimmed with silver, and a pair of dizzying silver stilettos. The wonderland opens up

around you amid whoops and cheers. Maeve pinches you as a group of people emerge to take to the stage on deck. They are all dressed differently, dazzlingly, stationary fireworks in the night; vivid fuchsias, bold violets, blazing saffrons. At their head is a man dressed in a stunning ballgown of sapphire and jade, emerald sleeves fashioned into wings. He wears a black tricorne edged with silver atop his long locs. His skin is the polished dark of coffee beans and flecked with silver glitter. He is otherworldly in his beauty.

You reel. The music starts. On deck and on shore, stamping begins, a slow rhythmic beat, gaining and building, a tidal wave of something on your horizon. Over the thrumming of the feet and the beat and the heat of Maeve vibrating beside you, the captain in the gown steps forward. The noise doesn't reduce, it intensifies, but somehow his voice carries over it easily. "Welcome, friends, welcome, family. Welcome to *The Dragon Queen*!"

It's like a kind of variety show but also like nothing you've ever seen before. It is articulate and creative and angry. Each performance speaks to a kind of beauty that the likes of Chloe Johnson and her family would sneer at or maybe even be scared of. A comedian with a buzz cut has your sides split with laughing. A trio with colourful box-braids, in black jeans and T-shirts, play on guitars and sing something that sounds like a sea shanty about a dragon but made, as Maeve puts it, "high camp". Then comes the drag show and it is a revelation. You wonder how long they've been here, running this place, perfecting this art form. They tell stories in the grand gestures of melodrama, they perform lip syncs and dance numbers with kicks and twirls that make your head spin, and each outfit they wear is

so carefully constructed that you wish the show would go on for ever; mermaid tails with each scale a shining gem, faeries' wings stitched from thousands of shimmering strands, and the beautiful silver-skinned someone dressed as a spider with a headdress of eight legs and sparkling silver ribbons attached to their wrists so that as they dance they create the illusion of one weaving an intricate web.

After the drag show, the party begins in earnest. You don't know anyone but they greet you as an old friend. Dancing, singing, riotous joy. Your fight with Maeve pales, not forgotten but forgiven. You are here and you are together, you are both utterly yourselves.

There is a flash of cadmium in the corner of your vision, a blaze of gold and then Vega is squeezing you both tightly. She is wearing a flowing white shirt with leather pants, knee-high boots and a long sleeveless jacket in black-and-gold damask. Her hair is wild about her – where she moves through the crowd, faces turn to bask in her as though she is their sun, and she basks in return as though they are hers.

"I'm so glad you made up!" You both grin at her wildly. "Let me know if you need anything," she says, before being swallowed by the twisting dancing bodies once more. The music is a fast frenetic thing and you feel Maeve moving beside you, her body against yours, so close you can smell the berries in her shampoo, the light floral perfume, the musk of her skin. The rhythm slows and climbs. She is facing you now. The lights flicker across her face, her freckles glow orange. You ache but you pause. *Don't be too much.* She senses your hesitation. Her eyes are burning, her chest rises and falls shallowly.

She leans towards you.

"I think I've changed my mind."

Your stomach swoops sickeningly.

"What do you mean?"

"I said earlier that I wanted things to go back to how they were before."

"Yeah?"

"I don't."

"OK." Even over the music you can hear that your voice is higher than usual.

"I don't think I need to figure things out. I think I've figured them out." She holds her arms out, embracing the night. "I wish I could be this happy all the time."

You laugh nervously. "Yeah, me too."

"Right? And the only thing I experience every day that makes me almost this happy … is you."

Your heart thumps. Her smile beckons you. Your palm cups her neck, you rub a lock of her hair between your thumb and forefinger. Her hands are on your shoulders, her thumbs stroke your collarbones. You kiss until you are both dizzy. You are grinning at each other as you break apart, and as the music swells and the bass drops, you twist and kiss and twirl and kiss until you have transcended dizzy altogether.

*

Perhaps if you hadn't, if you weren't busy dancing and laughing and falling in love, you'd have heard the slightly hushed conversation away from the dance floor.

"Do you see what I mean?"

"She really mentioned a map?"

"Yes. I *knew* the First kept it. We should have demanded!"

"It's a long time ago, no point crying about it now."

"So what do you think?"

"I think she's of Nubia's line. She turned sixteen in October, so the timing makes sense. And she's always been drawn to the library … and … she has my eyes. I think she might be it."

"Witch's blood bears fertile fruit."

"After all this time."

Disembark

"Names have power." It was one of the last things Captain Cora Ó Néill said to Levi, the night before they were to depart. It had taken her just three days to assemble a delegation of her pirates to form a crew for Levi, and between the rest of the Nubian captains – save for Johnson, naturally – they together had pooled food, water, ale, guns, powder and other general resources for their journey. Everything was inexact – they did not know how long they would be at sea. "That vessel has served *The Queen Áine* fleet for many years. But it is of our fleet no more. It would be dreadful bad luck to sail under another's colours. You're the captain now."

Levi thought about it. And then paid a visit to the shipwrights at the docks, to see if they could paint over the old moniker by the next morning.

The Dragon Queen stood ready at dawn, freshly painted for her maiden voyage. Levi had chosen the name in honour of *The Sea Dragon* and *The Queen Áine*. The shipwrights had even found, buried in a workroom, an old flag that had belonged to his father, the familiar white dragon insignia still stark against the black. They had painted a crown atop its head and strung it high.

They cast off with little delay. Levi watched de Casse and Hook standing at the prows of *La Liberté* and *The Cleopatra*.

They wore similar expressions, teeth bared, eyes wide, fierce excitement. They were at sea once more. Levi wondered if they had missed it, had longed for it, or if they felt torn as he did. On one hand the sea *called* him, the smell of salt, the open waves, the grief of the cawing gully-birds, the hope of the horizon. It was his home. But the Republic was his home too now. He had never stayed on land so long, never known so many different people in one place. They sailed away, sails empty initially in the doldrums of Sheta Island, but this was no matter – they were pulled by currents that rejoiced to sense him among them once more.

I'm on my way, Mother.

He watched those on the docks grow smaller, Ó Néill, Ameyro, Emabelle. He would miss the latter especially. His mind filled with the music of the solstice, the hubbub of the markets, the taste of Emabelle's cornmeal. He wondered if he would ever see it again, if the map would show him a way back. He reached inside his pocket for it.

But it wasn't there.

His stomach dropped. Where was it? How could it not be there, it was always there, he was so used to having it there that he'd stopped checking...

"Vega! Vega!"

"What?"

"The map? Where's the map?"

"What do you mean? Don't you have it?"

His mind whirred. Kano came rushing over. "What is it?"

"Levi can't find the map!"

Kano touched his face gently. Levi's eyes were wide with panic and he was trembling more than he had after the battle against the navy. He couldn't have lost it, he couldn't have. Not now. Not when they were so close.

"Where did you last have it?" Kano asked calmly. Levi strained to think. He couldn't remember when he'd last seen it and cursed himself silently – he should have checked every day, no, every hour. He wracked his brains. The last two days on the Republic had been a blur of packing and preparations. He couldn't recall any sight of the map during that time. And before that was the night of the battle – had it really only been three days ago? – and earlier that same day the Brethren meeting, and the trip to Diego the cartographer's...

A hideous realization hit.

"I never got it back from Diego." Levi sank to the floor. "I said I'd go and get it back after he asked to look at it, but then there was the Brethren meeting and the battle and we had so much to prepare..." He felt ill.

But Vega kicked him. Not hard, a light jab with her foot. "Come now, hatchling, don't mope."

He looked at her disbelievingly. "Vega, we've got a ship and a crew and I've mastered shifting and it's all for nothing because I lost the map. I can't believe I was away with the fae *again*!" Ezi had been right to chastise his dreaming. Look where it had got him.

"It's not all for nothing, don't be so dramatic." She was smiling at him, her eyes a touch impatient, her hair caught by the wind, which picked up, as though excited by her standing there so bold and shining.

"Ancient wayfinders and folk of the sea used the stars as their map and guide. And they didn't have the *privilege*" – she gave a cocky little smile – "of being able to ask the stars advice. Well, you do." She looked up. "As long as there are stars in the sky, we can never be lost." Levi's heart swelled. He wondered, not for the first time, at his luck, having her for a sister.

"Point it out on a map to me, describe where the X was. Show me where we're going, and I'll get us there, Captain, don't you worry."

Levi did as she asked and Vega mapped their journey through the stars. She wondered at the boundless unknowns before her, standing next to her brother, the pair of them together, imagining the island that would emerge from the mist before them, the magic in her blood enough to find the way.

*

Levi had never known happiness like that week at sea. He would stand at the prow, skirts sweeping the view, and breathe his world in. As one who had always dreaded the burden of being captain, once confronted with it he found it far more to his liking than he had anticipated. The idea of making his dreams a reality, of moving, under his instruction, towards the horizon that he had so yearned for, was wonderful. The weather was fair and the wind strong and steady. He got to know the other captains too; they drew up and leaped across, spry and agile, often without need of a gangway. They played cards and shared stories, stories of Captain Ezi, stories Levi and Vega had not heard. Hook taught them the "railroad song" as she called it,

more than a shanty, a defiant score sung by those who were enslaved of their hope for freedom.

When he wasn't aboard *The Drag Queen*, as they affectionately called it, Levi was in the sea. He delighted in the reunion, in both his human and Leviathan forms. He would teeter on the edge of the prow with Kano, enjoying the delicious before moments. Sometimes they would lean to kiss him and then suddenly shift, teasing him, daring him into joining. "Do you want to play?" He would hear them laugh from all around him and Levi would leap after them; they would reach for the waves in unison. He would shift as he fell and it was so easy he could not believe he had found it so hard before. Now he could float above it all, look down and see the whole rich tapestry that made up *Levi, the Leviathan*. The sea dragon twisted, racing through the water, the nymph all around him, between states, current, then mist, then crashing foam.

*

"Quarter, quarter! This isn't fun!" Vega threw her cards down, pouting. She had just been beaten at cards by Levi. Again. Levi tried not to gloat. It wasn't captainly and though he had always been better at cards than Vega, she certainly could land a cleaner punch.

Hook and de Casse had joined them on deck and were laughing. "You are so much like your father," Hook chuckled. "He hated losing too."

"And he made the same mistake you do," said de Casse, collecting the cards, shuffling, dealing again.

"What? What mistake? Levi is just better at cards than me, that's all!"

"Is he?" asked de Casse. "Or is he just better at trickery and deceit?"

"Well, Vega tends to act first and think later." Kano grinned at her.

"The nerve of you, *nymphling!*" She was indignant. "That's not true!"

"Vega, you rushed into a burning building to save Kano, you didn't even stop to think of a plan, you just climbed the house and booted the window in."

Hook and de Casse laughed.

"Well!" She was defensive but smiling. "It was urgent! You've not always the time to sit around playing the jaw-me-down. Sometimes you have to just get on with things."

"Aye," said de Casse. "But sometimes you have to keep your cards close to your chest. You reveal your hand too quickly. You should always leave your enemy guessing, savvy?"

Vega shrugged. "Aye, Marianne, but that's more Levi's style than mine."

It had already been decided that as they approached Xaymaca Levi and Kano would not shift. They did not know what state they would find the place in, how they would be greeted. They wanted to be cautious and not give too much away. Levi spent a lot of time thinking about what Ezi would say, what advice he would give. Sometimes his eyes burned at the thought of his previous life on a previous deck, sometimes he caught Vega bowed over the helm, cheeks damp. But he did

not shy away from her now, wrapped his arms about her, rested his chin on her shoulder. She had never blamed him.

"Do you think I should tell them? De Casse and Hook? About how ... how P... About Pa and the others...?" he had asked on one such occasion.

She leaned her cheek into his forehead. "One day, if you're ready. But Pa chose to keep his counsel on many things. I believe it is your right to do the same."

He kissed her cheek in thanks.

At night, in the captain's bunk, he tangled his fingers in Kano's inky hair. His sea fire turned their dew to steam, they hissed and sighed together. Lying in bed at night he dreamed of Xaymaca. He had thought, having returned to the high seas, that his mother's voice would be loud once more. But it was silent and this worried him greatly. He wondered where she was, what she looked like, if she was OK. The currents whispered to him still, when he and Kano greeted them each day. Stories of adventures past, of crews and ships long turned to sediment in the depths below.

*

A fortnight after they had set sail, Vega's voice, a bright peeling bell, called from the crow's nest, "Land ahoy!"

Levi froze where he stood at the helm. Kano, dealing out cards for a game of patience behind him, froze too, then rushed to his side. Vega could glint a needle in a haystack on the moon, but Levi could see it too.

Xaymaca.

Orders, a quickening, a liveliness. Pie-birds sent to *La Liberté* and *The Cleopatra*. The thrill of fear lapping against the shore of ebullience. They sailed on, the wind picking up, urging them onwards. The island loomed in front of them. Trees and sand and golden shore. High up in the rolling hills that emerged from the clouds, the sparkle of water undulated – waterfalls. Levi was sure, even at this distance, he could see a building there, something wide, reaching across the hilltops in a light stone. De Casse with his crew aboard *La Liberté* would sail round the island and scout, while *The Cleopatra* and *The Dragon Queen* would drop anchor as soon as possible. The shallows were in sight, the beach deserted, he was so close. His mother could be watching him approach right now. They dropped anchor.

Down the Jacob's ladder and out into the bay, wading easily, the water falling away from his legs as though consciously clearing a path. Kano at his left, Vega at his right, they moved in a triangle formation, flanked by six of what had been the crew of *The Queen Áine*. D'Arcy, Ó Néill's old quartermaster, was nearest to Levi. They were all armed, cutlasses and sabres, swords and scimitars flexing sunlight like muscles. The rest of the crew of *The Dragon Queen* stayed aboard, along with *The Cleopatra*, where Hook watched and waited. The small landing party reached the shore, and as Levi felt the weight of his homecoming settle on him like a heavy cloak, he took in the island of his birth.

It was a paradise – or it would have been. Fine sand the colour of buttermilk rolled into the treeline, thin young spruces scattering to reveal a penumbral forest.

377

But something was terribly wrong.

Where the forest waned to the west, the trees were lush and green, rolling upwards into hills, the air clear over the sun-kissed valleys. But where the forest waxed eastwards, the trees were dry, almost burned-looking. The leaves were brown and deadened, becoming more frail and ashy the further east he looked. He could sense the echo of life, of a pulsing and breathing that reminded him of the tides, but now it wheezed and hacked as though sickening. No birds chirped, no tiny wings rustled. Above the thickening forest, on the other side of the island, clouded and ominous jagged black peaks cut a menacing line against the sky.

A silver sliver told Levi of a river nearby and it was to this that he attached his attention. He followed it with his gaze, from where it started, high up amid the shimmering frost of the highlands, to where it vanished into the treeline. But the great River Aphra, the River Mumma's home, was silent, even to the Leviathan's ears.

"Orders, Captain?"

Levi tried not to thrill at the way Kano pronounced his title. *Focus, hatchling.*

"We head into the forest to find the River Mumma. We'll try and find the river's mouth and follow it inland. Kano, shift and scout ahead – but not too far, savvy? D'Arcy, replace them on my flank. Vega, stick close and—"

Levi looked around for Vega.

She was staring at the dry, barren landscape, her mouth slightly open.

"Vega, what—"

But the shade shuddered and there was movement in the forest.

A woman emerged from the trees and floated towards them. She was tall, elegant, almost frail-looking. Her skin was the colour of polished bronze and, at her back, fine gossamer-like wings fluttered, splitting the light into rainbows and keeping her a few inches above the ground. She wore a circlet of gold atop her head and pale yellow gauze about her body. Her dark eyes swept the procession. She was accompanied by a few others, similarly bronze-spun winged beings. They were beautiful but she was radiant and Levi knew she must be their queen.

"So this is the Leviathan." The faerie assessed him. Her voice was a clear ringing bell. "Welcome to Xaymaca. We have been waiting for you a long time." She smiled, her face shining cool metal, her gaze hard and bright like flint. "You look a lot like your father. But where are my manners?" She curtseyed low. "I am Mmoatia, Queen of the Favour Falls Faeries."

Levi was caught off guard but did his best not to show it. There was something about her face. He did not know if he was just bad at reading faerie expressions, for their faces were so still and smooth, but there seemed to be something deceptive in her courtliness. *What is the want behind the lie?* He bowed. "Greetings, Mmoatia, Queen of the Faeries. I am Levi, the Leviathan and captain of *The Dragon Queen*. This is my crew – my sister, Vega of the Sea and Skies, and my—" He hesitated. He did not know what to call Kano – *paramour* seemed a rather declarative given their circumstances – so he settled for: "First mate, Kano the nymph."

Mmoatia raised her eyes. "A nymph? How unusual.

I'm sure there is a marvellous story that accompanies such a union."

"Aye, there is." He did not say any more. "If you know who I am, then you know who my mother is?"

Mmoatia nodded. "Yes. She is why I am here to greet you. Naturally, the River Mumma could not walk on land herself, but she has sent us to bring you to her."

Levi frowned. "Why?"

"She has been ... helping us," Mmoatia explained smoothly. "She will explain all herself if you follow us."

Levi remembered then what the scout had said aboard *The Sea Dragon*, something about *freeing the faeries*. He hesitated. But he couldn't really see that he had much choice; he did not know his way around this land. If the faeries could reunite him with his mother more swiftly, then all the better.

"We have reason to believe that a buccaneer of the Republic, a man by the name of Johnson, has had contact with someone on Xaymaca. We are concerned about his motives and for the safety of all those here."

Mmoatia's eyes glittered. "Yes, we know of this. One of his ships landed here three moons ago, and another two moons ago. You can see the damage they have caused." She gestured to the withering treeline, the *wrongness* of the east.

Levi was horrified. "Johnson's crew did that?" He felt a swell of relief that they had acted as they had on the Republic, and not allowed Johnson to sail to Xaymaca and cause even more destruction.

"Where are they now?"

"Engaged in conflict somewhere, with the witches, I

believe. The Perseans have been fighting most valiantly. As I said, your mother has been helping us. There is much to discuss. Perhaps you can help us too?"

She had drifted closer to him, reached out a long thin-fingered hand, her eyes burning black and bright, somewhere between beseeching and demanding.

Something was niggling at him, something rattling behind a locked door in his memory. He looked to Vega, to Kano. Three pairs of eyes met and weighed in silent communication.

If something goes awry, we can easily overpower them.

How else will we find your mother?

De Casse has eyes elsewhere, he'll send a pie-bird if there's something truly amiss.

Levi nodded. "All right."

"I must ask that you only bring these few of your crew. As you can imagine, the denizens of Xaymaca are wary of pirates right now."

Levi nodded. "I understand."

The walk through the forest was eerily quiet. Levi wanted to ask a thousand questions and yet there was something remote and aloof about the faerie queen that killed the curiosity on Levi's tongue. Each tree stood silent sentinel, headstones in the gloom. Levi knew in his bones that this place had once teemed with creatures, smelled sweet with the perfume of a thousand plants, but now it stank of rot, animal flesh decaying in arid air. They walked on, passing tree stumps, whole patches of forest cleared, broken, and severed barks and boughs, trees that had been cut down. Kano shivered behind him, and Levi reached for their hand. *Wrong, wrong, wrong.* All that had once called

this place home had either left or lay dry and brittle as bones, crackling where they trudged.

They broke free of the heavy reek after what felt like hours. The sun had charted a course swiftly across the sky, rushing to light their way up the western slopes. Levi could see the rolling hills, the plunging valleys and the sliver of silver where somehow the River Aphra still ran. *So whatever blight Johnson's crew caused has not yet reached the west,* he mused, and clung to it. Atop the highest knolls, a sweeping palatial structure of gold-white marble, the one he had seen from the bay. It was across a singular level, but vast, sprawling across many hilltops, and Levi wondered momentarily how one reached each structure but then spied what drifted like dust motes above the open-roofed buildings and understood. *Faeries.*

The incline steepened, the palace expanded before them. It was even more spectacular up close. A construction of tiny-tiled beauty and many courtyards adorned with fountains and thinly lashed trees, creating private shadowy corners hidden from view of the light, so bright up here. Nearby a waterfall rushed quietly – presumably Favour Falls for which the faeries were named. Above them, around them, behind the closed lids of the lashed trees, faeries frolicked. There was no other word to describe what they did. They were spun glass, light and waif-like, their wings membranous. They drifted on breezes, were picked up easily by each zephyrean kiss. Looking around at them all now, bronzed and delicate, Levi wondered how they had avoided the devastation that raged in the rest of the land. How the west, where they lived, remained so lush and pristine, how it had not been ransacked by the crew of *The Sterling*.

The answers that formed in Levi's mind fell as though, in asking the right questions, he had opened the trapdoor under that far-reaching part of his memory. His father's voice in his cabin that day. His suggestion that Johnson couldn't be acting alone, must have an ally. *Xaymaca has been betrayed.* He reached for the itch that lurked beneath the surface of his mind, scratched loose those words: *Nary a day passed that the Capt'n didn't warn us all about Mmoatia ...*

His eyes met Mmoatia's. They were cold. Dark and fathomless. Her smile was gleefully cruel.

I never trusted her.

And behind her, swarming into the courtyard before the palace like ants, enough armed pirates to equal *The Dragon Queen*'s full crew. Levi noted familiar tattoos and his head felt light. *The Sterling.* At their head, eliciting hisses of angry recognition from his own crew and sharp expletives from Vega, strolling as though entirely at leisure – Captain James Johnson.

"I did wish to keep you out of all this, Leviathan. I did not tell my dear James about you, was keen for you to sail off into the sunset with your father and leave Xaymaca alone. Imagine my dismay when I discovered that a boy who could turn into a sea dragon was on the Republic, throwing around accusations." The crew of *The Sterling* trained their guns on Levi and his eight companions. "We have met before, you know. But you were just a baby. It was not long after your mother killed my lover that you were born. He was a member of your father's crew, before she dragged him by his ankles into her river. I was with child at the time. Faerie children are rare things – what power would have lain in the blood of my half-

human, half-faerie child!" Her hand drifted to her stomach. "We shall never know. In my grief, the babe was lost. They would have come of age with the last sun. As I marked the day they would have been born, a thought occurred to me. You see, my lover told me that the humans who know of this place believe it to be a paradise of equality. Is that not funny? The River Mumma got her lover and son and I got neither. Does that sound like equality to you?"

"Where is she?" He was surprised by how calm his voice was, how little it belied the turbulence within. "Where is my mother?"

Mmoatia tutted. "You are as arrogant as your parents, I see. Making demands of me in my home." The faeries had drifted over to witness their arrival, curious and murmuring to each other. Levi noted that they displayed no anxiety at the sight of the pirates, and he felt rage trill within him. So much betrayal. Mmoatia addressed them. "My faerie court. On this day, what our loyal friend, Captain Johnson, warned us of has come true. The Leviathan has returned." A ripple through the hovering crowd, surprise, interest, fear. "As you will all remember, the Seer of Persea gave a prophecy some years ago that identified this creature" – she gestured at Levi – "as a threat. Fortunately, we have him apprehended. I assure you, loyal court, I shall not allow him or his mother to get in the way of our plans."

In the chaos of the weeks that had past, in his grief, Levi had almost forgotten about the mention of the prophecy. But he went cold now at Mmoatia's words. A threat? To who? He could feel Vega shaking beside him.

Johnson stepped forward to join Mmoatia. And his face was so smug, so *pleased* with himself. Vega trembled harder, Kano's breath came quick and fast, and Levi absorbed their conflict. *Rage and pity and traitor and shame and grief and fury and fire and flame—*

"Now, no shifting, no silliness at all." Johnson gestured to the men behind him. "Your mummy will suffer for it."

"And that would really complicate our plans," Mmoatia trilled. Her grin suddenly widened, dazzlingly beautiful and utterly horrifying. "This is my island now."

Diego the First

W hen he was just a boy
        He'd begged to hear all the stories
        Of the pirates, of the witch,
Of their many, bloody glories.

His father told him of a custom
        And so, as he grew, his breath was baited,
        For when one turned six-and-ten,
        The magic for which they waited

Would seek them, would send out a call.
        Xaymaca would claim its kin
        And so Diego waited and waited
        – But the magic was not for him.

In time he gave up such hope,
        He lost the language of those dreams,
        Though longed for any earthly power
        To soothe his father's pain and screams.

Magic is what took his mother,
        For magic she did give her life,

Magic became a dirty word and he
Found order to soothe his strife.

By those witches he was rejected,
    And so magic he learned to fear,
    He clung fast to material certainty,
    His sole orbit in normality's sphere.

So when he found the map with the X
    He felt magic must never return,
    He took it, tried to rid the world,
    It would not shred, it would not burn.

So Diego kept it under lock and key,
    He hid it where none would see,
    For nothing at all would ruin his plan
    Of becoming a most respectable man.

The River Mumma

For a moment Levi wrestled with the self-loathing that reared, a thorny bloom fertilized by fear. He had led his crew behind enemy lines, allowed them to become separated from their reinforcements and drastically outnumbered. But it would not do to lose focus now.

"How did you sail so fast?"

Johnson smirked. "Ah, a true mariner's interest, I see!" His pompous tone, the light-hearted joviality enraged Levi further. It was clear Johnson did not perceive him to be a threat. "Well, the sticky issue of the doldrums matters little when your ally is so adept at manoeuvring the winds. The westerly wind answers to the song of the faeries, you know. And they sent it to sing to me. Far better than an X on a map. We could actually converse, you see. Make plans." He turned to Mmoatia. "Splendid job, Your Highness."

Witches and spiders and mermaids ... I'm going to free the faeries ... I'm sailing on the westerly wind ... bewitch a witch, entangle the spider, catch a mermaid, can I ride her...

Levi wanted to spit in the smirking face, wanted to become sea fire and fury and set the traitor's temerity alight. But he kept a tight hold on that canvas, showing only the thinnest sliver of self. "And how did you escape Ó Néill?"

"Oh, she let me go."

"Captain Ó Néill would *never* act against the Republic!" D'Arcy snarled from behind Levi. She had sailed with Ó Néill, known her for decades. "Never!"

"Well, in all fairness to dear Cora, I did leave her with little choice. Or rather, *you* did."

"What do you mean?" Levi snapped. "I did nothing!"

"My dear boy, you took more than half of the Republic's remaining forces."

"What does that matter? The Empire won't be able to rally a new navy for weeks!"

"True, but when my crew took arms against what was left of hers, there was little in the way of defence. I'm afraid dear Cora didn't think I'd be so bold when she allowed your little voyage." He sighed tragically, a smile playing at the corner of his lips. "When it became clear that she was woefully outnumbered, she surrendered, not wanting to leave the Republic without anyone to defend it at all. Not that it hugely matters," he added as an afterthought, "now that I've sent word to the Empire that the Republic is so weakened it shall be back under their control in no time at all. Cora will either accept a letter of marque or die." He snorted. "And if I know Cora, I'd assume the latter."

"Fuck you!" If Levi had not seen Kano's mouth form the words, he would not have believed it was the nymph who spoke them, hurled them across the pristine, sun-drenched courtyard. "You fought the Empire on that beach beside us, you fought them alongside all the captains on the night Nubia died. You have lived on Sheta Island for nearly two decades and now you betray it? What was it all for?"

Johnson sighed heavily "Nubia and her ideals were lovely, but let's speak freely here. The appeal of the Republic was a life outside of the Empire, to do as we pleased. Well, that's no longer possible. They're too big, too powerful. We must be practical! Compromises must be made."

"So you sold out." Vega's trembling voice rang with promised violence. "Both of you." She looked from Johnson to the faerie queen. "You betrayed your lands, your homes, so you can get your pieces of the pie and damn everyone else."

Johnson shook his head patronizingly. "Ah, the piece of the pie. One of Nubia's sayings. The problem is, there really isn't enough pie to go around. Who can blame me for wanting to make sure me and mine eat? I left my family on the Republic, you know. To parlay with the navy when they arrive. If Ó Néill is smart she'll stand with them, secure herself a place in the future. The old word is dying. I will not suffer in denial."

"And this place? What happens to Xaymaca when the Empire learns of where you've gone?" Levi asked the question, fearing the answer would confirm his suspicions.

"Well, my dear boy, you did not think Mmoatia and I would trouble ourselves with all this planning and diplomacy for nothing. Why, I even sacrificed part of my property. Those wind wards you put on my house were a little *over enthusiastic*, Your Highness. Blew a blaze right into my study and didn't even trap the thief." He shook his head and waggled his finger, his pompous disapproval unnervingly incongruous. "No, no. The Empire will make an excellent trading partner with Xaymaca, using Sheta Island as its outpost." He raised his voice slightly,

addressing the assembled crowd of his crew and Mmoatia's court. "As the future Queen of Xaymaca and Governor of the Island, we look forward to a very prosperous relationship."

And the crowd *applauded*.

Mmotia beamed. "Now, despite the unfortunate circumstances, I will of course be treating you as guests. We are not uncivilized. I simply wanted to ensure that you don't get in the way of our plans." Her smile sweetened, showing too many teeth. "Dear James here thinks it might be easier to just kill you all." That hideous, trilling laugh. "Honestly! So tasteless! And such a waste! He lacks my passion for research, you see. The Leviathan, a nymph and a … something." Mmoatia eyed Vega with indecent interest.

"Have you even noticed it?" Vega glared back at her; her face was twisted, she crackled with electricity, and Johnson's men trained their guns on her. "I've been here less than an afternoon! Do you ever remove your head from your arse long enough to see what … whatever it is you're doing has *done* to this place?"

"A few trees are nothing in the name of progress. We are trying to help the island reach its potential." She ignored the disbelieving scoffs. "My lover told me of your world. So has James. Xaymaca has so much to gain, so much progress, and so much to offer human traders – but more must be done, more magic must be harnessed. It is not for me. I truly have no desire for my court to rule this land." The lie was so plain on her face that Levi wondered why she even bothered with the façade.

"And what about everyone else here?" he asked coldly. "Xaymaca doesn't just belong to the faeries. What of the witches and spiders? What do they think of your grand plans?"

Mmoatia stiffened. "The Anansi spiders are wise and are remaining out of this. The Persea coven have made their feelings perfectly clear. If it is conflict they want, it is conflict they shall get."

"They burn witches in our world! Do you know that? Do you think you will be treated cordially by the navy?" Vega glared at the queen in disgust but Mmoatia merely shook her head.

"Captain Johnson has assured me that his is an Empire that *respects* royalty. My faerie court truly means you no ill. We will house you and clothe you and feed you well. The rest of your crew will not, of course, be permitted to stay."

"The crew of *The Dragon Queen* did not sail alone, Your Highness. But worry not, I dispatched a ship to search for *La Liberté* and *The Cleopatra* as soon as you sent word that sails were sighted. *The Dragon Queen* and *The Cleopatra* have thus far evaded us, but we are optimistic. We made short work of *La Liberté*, however. Took them entirely by surprise, barely wasted any ammunition." Johnson smiled at the faerie queen and flicked his fingers at the crowd.

There was a moment's pause and then the sounds of a scuffle. Shouts, curses.

And Captain de Casse was dragged forward by his hair. To his credit, he required four of Johnson's men to subdue him and even then they dodged and ducked as he kicked and struggled. Levi recognized one of them as Alfie, the bumptious young man who had bragged of Johnson's map. De Casse was bound and gagged but Johnson removed the gag from his mouth, smiling down at him in disappointed paternalism.

"What a shame, Jacques. For all I tried to teach you over the years about pragmatism, you were always too fixated on Xaymaca and Ezi the Absent to learn. And now it is too late. Is there anything you'd like to say?"

De Casse spat in Johnson's face.

The faeries gasped, one or two even shrieked.

Mmoatia patted Johnson's arm indulgently. "My dear James, we simply cannot tolerate such disrespect. I think we'd better show Levi and his friends here the consequences of poor choices and bad behaviour."

"Aye, right you are, Your Highness."

Levi knew what was about to happen before it did, knew he was powerless to stop it but still he surged forward, still he tried to reach the man who had loved his father.

It was Vega who held him back, Vega who hissed in his ear, "No, Levi, your mother, your mother!"

Johnson's long blade flashed and the world refracted into splintered pieces but Levi could see de Casse clearly. He stood straight-backed, he would not slump, his eyes were on Levi's face. The pirate captain's lips formed three words, rang them out so that they bounced off the marble. *"For the dragon!"*

The words echoed around the valley, between the hills, louder than the falls, so that de Casse's voice lingered on, even after his head had been separated from his body.

The faeries broke into a smattering of polite applause. Levi swayed on his feet.

"Very good." Mmoatia smiled into Levi's face. "It's only fair, Levi. All we ask for is respect. Now, you will have to be guarded, but you will be given your own quarters."

Levi could not hear her. Only the whistle of Johnson's sword. De Casse's eyes were open, gazing at something Levi could not see. Faeries immediately came to clean the blood, clear the body, regimented as any crew, but Levi just stared into those open eyes. His braid was already sodden, red and dark, but the moustache was still pristine, still perfectly curled. Before the faeries could move the head, Levi broke free of Vega and crouched beside it.

"*The Dragon Queen* is forever in your debt, Marianne. Know it. Tell my pa that his heart beats and his pride will not yield." Levi's throat was tight and his eyes burned. He could hear Vega's shallow breathing behind him, the soft whimper that Kano did not fight to keep in their chest. He wanted to turn to them, to comfort them, but instead he reached out and closed the eyes of Jacques de Casse so that the captain of *La Liberté* looked peaceful.

Mmoatia loomed above him, floating a little way off the ground, her feet and skirts avoiding the pooling blood.

Her gaze locked on Levi's. "I did rather think that you might like to pay someone a visit." She smiled at him, as though sincerely delighted. "How would you like to meet your mother, Levi?"

*

The outhouse his mother lay in was in a slight valley behind the main palace grounds, attached to the slow chugging grind of a watermill. Hills rose on either side, the temperature dropped intensely with the incline. The air was frigid, dry and icy. Her

only source of water was a small pool in the middle of the one room. It was clean, the same gold-white marble, but it was bare, save for a few cushions; the tiny blue-and-green mosaic tiling glittered with frost, mimicking light on water, mocking her. Her locs were a tangle of dark green, her body was thin and wan. Her breasts had been wrapped with thin blue faerie gauze, as if to make her decent. Her gaunt face seemed suspended between sleep and waking, life and death, and Levi saw, looking at her unseeing eyes, the colour of the sea in a storm – *his eyes*.

The guard – one of Johnson's underlings – closed the door behind him, stating that he was right outside, a threat and a promise. Her head turned slowly towards him and he met his mother's eyes for the first time.

"Ezi?"

The words he'd been practising died on his lips.

"No. Levi."

"Levi?" A blue-grey gleam. "Can it be?"

"I…" He struggled, a lifetime of unsaid things. Her face was that of a stranger, he did not recognize her, but he *knew* her. "I've come home. I've come to help you."

Slowly, so slowly, eyes never leaving his face, she swung her tail, so cracked and dull it made him ache to look at it, and sank it into the pool. It only reached midway and so the scutes at the top suffered worse, sore and weeping. The air was so cold Levi was sure the water should have been frozen; perhaps it was her presence that kept it fluid and moving. The pool revived her somewhat and she swallowed, blinking, drinking him in.

"You … you answered my call."

Levi nodded. "Yes. I … I wasn't sure it was you but…" He

struggled again, how much truth to share, how to navigate this moment? "I knew I needed to find you."

She was shivering, a faint tremor. Her hand reached for him. The skin was crisp and thin as parchment. "My boy. My Levi." Her face folded but no tears leaked out. She was bone dry and so Levi cried for both of them. *What have they done to her?* But she smelled like something that danced at the edge of his memory, a forgotten place where the forest was lush and green and he swam with his parents in the cool, dappled shallows...

"How did you do it? How did you call to me?"

"I am the River Mumma. I commune with the currents. I speak the language of dreams."

"Can you not free yourself? Can you not speak to the faeries, in their dreams?"

"Mmoatia does not dream. The faeries have forgotten how." Her paper palm gentled his face. "You look so much like Ezi."

"I know."

"Is he here?"

He could not answer. Instead he stood and opened the door and demanded the guard fetch her some more water. After a moment's hesitation, the guard that had brought him there left the one already stationed and went off in search of a carafe.

"It will not help." Her voice was a whispering rush, the ghost of stones and silt. "They do not deprive me of anything but that which I need most dearly. They bring me food and water and cannot understand why I weaken. They are worried that I will spoil their plans just as they spoiled this land."

"What happened? What has happened here?"

"Mmoatia and those she commands have redirected the

396

course of things. They have melted and hastened what was frozen and slow, they have cut this land off from its source," she choked. "I cannot bear to think what it must look like now."

"But why?" He asked it even though he knew the answer, reaching for her hands again.

"For trade and greed and personal plenty. They want my magic for themselves. They know that I am inextricable from the island and are using the mill to harness me. To keep what I give the land for themselves and use it to become *prosperous*." She said the word like it was a curse. "Mmoatia believes the faeries are entitled to more than they have. What they have has never been a disadvantage; each Xaymacan is powerful in their own way. But Mmoatia is unsatisfied. She intends to use the mill, powered by me, to bring *industry* to the island. That is what James Johnson calls it." Levi burned. *Rage and sea fire and traitor and thief.* Taking what was not theirs, taking more than they were due until there was nothing left for anyone else.

"How ... how did they catch you?"

"I was ... hopeful. And it made me vulnerable. I saw their sails and smelled their human flesh on the wind. I thought they were men of *The Sea Dragon* returned. I should have known better. The crew of *The Sea Dragon* were not cruel. Those that were met their fate at my hands. This is why Mmoatia punishes me. One such man, who she loved, sought to take me against my will and soon learned what it meant to cross the River Mumma. These new ones, the ones who call Johnson captain, are more like him. Ezi told me all about Johnson. He is vindicated. Where is he?"

It would never be easy to say aloud.

"He's dead. Along with the rest of the crew that raised me."

She merely blinked at him, waiting. A tremor passed over her but that was all. He had not known what he expected, he knew so little about her.

"Your face does what his did when feeling many things at once. It is a very human expression."

"Well, I am human."

"You are half-human."

"Half-human, half ... what? I don't turn into a mermaid like you."

"You are half of Ezi and half of me. Half of land and half of sea." She pondered this for a moment and then added, "Though Ezi *chose* the sea over the lands of his birth. That is a powerful thing. And there was always something of the sea dragon about him. Perhaps my immortal blood made that manifest." A true smile widened her cracked lips. "I am sure you are spectacular in the water."

"I am now," Levi said quietly. "I did not start out that way."

She waited again, still shivering. Levi could not dance around the subject any longer. So he told her. Told her how he'd heard her voice, and about his strange dreams and about the pie-birds and the scout and all that had come next. The words poured out of him and flowed on, filling the prison that she had been empty in for so many moons, and he found himself continuing, telling her about the Republic and Kano's lessons, about Tally and Abe and Vega the star. About the kind of father Ezi had been, and the brooding silences that Levi was now sure had been filled with thoughts of his mother.

The jug of water arrived while he talked and she insisted he have some, and he insisted she needed it more, but she insisted

harder and his mother *mothered* him for the first time. His throat was tight as she said, "I want you to know that I loved Ezi very much. And I am so" – that tremor again – "so sorry that he is gone. I have thought about you both every day for sixteen years and hoped we might all be together again. But some things are not to be, and life does not end with death. We are all part of the Great Energy, and to it we all return."

"You sound like Kano."

"Nymphs are often wise." She sighed. "I am sorry for the part I played in all that you have been through. I did not summon you back to this willingly." She paused. "Before you were born, the Seer from Persea, the witch Nubia's sister, delivered a prophecy." She measured him with her gaze before reciting:

> *Nigh is the time of the witch who burned,*
> *Nigh is the time that stars will fall,*
> *Nigh is the time of the mermaid's son*
> *Who'll destroy his home to answer a call.*
> *Nigh is the time of sixteen suns,*
> *Nigh is the time of poison root,*
> *Nigh is the time to find lost things,*
> *For witch's blood bears fertile fruit.*

"The idea that I might have a son who would destroy his home scared many Xaymacans. This is understandable. Mmoatia and her court called for your expulsion the loudest. I think now this was probably out of vengeance." She sighed very deeply. "I had to give you up. I cannot deny my nature and

my nature is to protect this land. I am River Mumma first and your mother second." Once upon a time this would have hurt him, would have sent a dart of rejection through his chest. But Levi had learned a thing or two about what it means to deny ones true nature. "I understand," he said. Then, "Nubia didn't tell anyone. About the prophecy, I mean. She … she must have known that it was about her, that she would die but…"

"Perhaps she had made her peace with it and did not see the need to disrupt anyone else's. Mortals do not handle prophecies well."

Levi considered this. "No. They don't. Pa … he loved me. But he was scared of who I was. He tried to turn away from it and turn me away from it too." He shook his head. "I don't understand why he didn't just chuck me out, like the Xaymacans. He knew the risk."

The River Mumma's eyes flared momentarily, as though lit with strange lightning. "Ezi loved you. We both did. But our positions were different; I was your mother second. But he was your father first. It is why I loved him – well, it is one of the reasons. I saw him hold you as a babe, shifting back and forth, a little, wriggling, scaled thing then fleshy and plump. I saw him look at you and knew that he would choose you over and over, even at the expense of his crew. And himself."

Levi's throat tightened. "He was afraid of me," he whispered. "And so he lied. He was my … my whole world. But he kept secrets. About everything."

She stroked his face, his hair, as if she still could not believe he was real. "He loved you. He loved you the only way he knew how. For we must love what we cannot change, and fight for

what we can. I should have advised Ezi better when you were both in my care." Her face folded once more. "I should have known better."

"That's exactly what he said, to Vega."

"He is mortal, I am not."

"Yes, you're not … so … how old are you?" He had asked the question to ease the grip of grief but found himself genuinely curious. It worked somewhat. Her lips quirked again.

"Such a human question. What is age? What is time? What are years? I am as old as Xaymaca but not so old as other beings, one that here they would call Yaa – what humans might call a goddess. And even Yaa and I are subject to the currents of the Great Energy, a force that is older than shape and form."

"You were here when … this island formed?"

She settled back against the few cushions. "Long ago, a cycle began. Chaos ruled this island, a dance of dark and light. I emerged from the sea and was drawn towards the light, yearned for it, knew I had to be some part of it. I reached for it, sent my power out to it, and it reached for me and our essences met. Where we bonded was somewhere here, above these waters." She splashed her tail gently. "And the light, which was Yaa, became my friend. Together we worked to draw away the darkness, to siphon it out to sea, where it was torn apart by the currents. The stretch of our work can still be seen when there is a storm; a shower of colour tracing the way, from dark to light. A rainbow. Some darkness still remains, dormant, above the mountains in the east. And so we continue to siphon. After a while, the path was forged and the darkness flowed by itself, but I continued to guard the mouth of the River Aphra, the point

where it would leave this land. But all existence is a cycle and for what we took, we had to give, and so we shared the burden, a return cycle of energy back to Xaymaca. This energy is magic. In giving water and light, of which we are made, we created two branches of power. The first in roots of plants, for all roots need light and water, and so the Persean witches, whose magic finds them through the roots of their hair, came to be. Then came the spiders, who gather all that remains, sweet decaying mulch, content in the shadows, for not all darkness is destructive. And of course all planting, all decay creates air and so the faeries found Xaymaca next. Thus we all play our parts."

"But that changed."

"Yes. *The Sea Dragon* arrived on the island. Mmoatia and I both found love with two very different men." Levi realized that she'd taken his hand. "The faeries have always spoken of this land's potential, said that they want more knowledge ... but the witches know things and so do the spiders. And I ... I know many, many things. So it seems they've been tempted by a new type of knowledge."

"And the darkness?" Levi asked. "What will happen to the balance, the dance of chaos, now that you're here?"

The River Mumma closed her eyes. "That is the heart of my fear. I am locked away, put to work watering the soil of the faeries. If I am not guarding my post at the river mouth, if I am not fuelling the source, the great destructive drive that exists in this land will grow strong again. If we cannot temper it swiftly it will become too great for us." She sighed, and Levi noted her exhaustion. The guard banged on the door.

"I am to escort you to your quarters now!"

He got reluctantly to his feet. "I will come back. I will find a way to free you."

She smiled, adoring, drinking him in. "I know you will. My Leviathan."

He acknowledged the tremor of self, the sea dragon beneath, but he was so at peace with it now, that it was no trouble at all to resist the shift. He headed to the door, but a thought struck him. "What … what do I call you?"

Mother sounded too facile somehow and *Ma* downright ridiculous.

She picked the sentence with care. "Names are powerful here. And so … only among ourselves – call me Ata. Because no one does."

FRIENDS WITH THE TREES

Summer arrives early on Sheta Island, baking pavements blasting heat at the end of March. You feel about summer the way you feel about Christmas, that it must be fun for people elsewhere. New Shetatown grows busier and busier, tourists arrive and leave and then arrive and don't leave, the novelty of new accents and languages wears off as more pirate-themed eateries open and what had been the local takeaway next to the library, the place from where Vega had often brought you dinner, becomes a bar called The Burning Witch. You walk the familiar winding streets, watching them become unfamiliar.

You and Maeve spend every minute together that you can and, for the first time, happiness does not feel like something you're just meant to observe. Exams pass in their practised rituals but now you study with Maeve and the time feels sacred. You both get top marks for your coursework. Miss Gibbers calls you "a dream team". Chloe makes a retching noise but you don't care because Miss Gibbers is right, you are. Occasionally, guilt nags at you. Girls in Maeve's literature class don't invite her to their parties. They don't say why, but you are the elephant in the room.

"I've made you a pariah." You say it jokingly, but the words sting so that your smile hurts.

She simply rolls her eyes. "You're not that powerful, Reggie. They're not my people. They're Team Mr Bennet in *Pride and Prejudice*. Such a red flag."

You allow the dig to shake a chuckle from you. "True enough. He's a terrible father."

"And husband! I said in class yesterday that he's a condescending chauvinist and they were all like, *Oh, no, he just doesn't have patience for Mrs Bennet's hysteria.* They actually used the word *hysteria*!"

"Such pick-me behaviour."

"Right?"

The worry persists so you speak it. "But I'm bad for your reputation."

Maeve laughs. "Good! I've decided against having a good reputation. It would mean pretending to be someone else and that sounds pretty shit, to be honest." She grabs your hand and pulls you towards her. You're in the middle of the school corridor. People stare at you but you both ignore them. "Maybe we'll run away to Xaymaca together and vanish into mist and memory!" You laugh too and head towards the gates.

You are so absorbed in each other that you do not notice the group walking towards you until they are upon you and their jeers surround you, filling your ears.

"Well, if it isn't the weird sisters!"

"Off to the library?"

"Off to pray to a tree?"

"That's your latest weird witchy ritual, right? We've seen you

405

hanging around the poisoned tree like the emo you are."

"Yeah, like, and did you not get the memo, Reggie? It's summer now. Or have you been attending the funeral of your social life?"

Crows of laughter. You just smile. "Summer is a season, goth is for ever."

"Oh my *god,* did she just say that?"

"Christ, how cringe!"

"I don't think your dad would be very happy to hear you blaspheming so casually, Chloe."

"I don't think your dad would be very happy to hear about you kissing Maeve O'Neill all about town," she throws back casually. "Sorry, correction, I mean your dad *wasn't* very happy to hear about you kissing Maeve O'Neill all about town."

Your stomach turns. "What do you mean?"

She shrugs. "Well, not all of us keep secrets from our parents. *Some* of us have worked to have trust and honesty. I tell Daddy everything. And he always asks after my school friends. I'm not going to lie to him, am I?"

You feel Maeve freeze and think about her aunt, who you've still never met and have no desire to.

"Well, you're one to talk, Chloe. Or does your goldfish brain not remember New Year's?"

Adrien steps forward and wraps his arm around her waist. You roll your eyes. "So you're a thing now? What a cliché."

Chloe strokes Adrien's face. "He evolved past gingers, and I evolved past girls. Sorry, Maeve."

You open your mouth, the defence on your tongue, but Maeve finds hers. "Oh, piss off, Chloe. I know you're jealous

because you fancy me *and* my girlfriend, but bitter repression is not a good colour on you."

There is a stunned silence. You swell with pride, your chest constricts – Maeve just called you her girlfriend. You don't wait to hear the response, you simply grab her hand and walk away, almost skip away, you are jubilant. She is red-faced and beaming, she is proud of herself and it makes you feel warm. You head back to yours – Five won't be in, as usual – you are talking the whole time.

"I cannot BELIEVE you said that to her!"

"Neither can I!"

"You were amazing!"

"I was, wasn't I?" Her face deserves to be thoroughly kissed and you are keen to oblige.

You get in through the front door, giggling, giddy. Maeve heads up to your room to see Bast. You go to the fridge and bring up two bottles of beer. You don't normally drink Five's supply but this is a momentous occasion. You open them, pass one to Maeve, Bast purring on her lap as she is fed ham from the packet Maeve picked up specially.

"To Maeve O'Néill, who comes from a long line of badass O'Néill women. Your ancestor Cora was betrayed by a Johnson. Today that wrong was righted!"

Maeve clinks, laughs. "Hardly."

"Seriously. Captain Cora is dancing in her grave, cheering, 'You tell her, Maevey!'"

You put on some music, contentment and company seeping into your pores, soothing as a warm bath. Bast switches to your lap and you play with her ears. Your mother's ghost is quiet,

hiding from the happiness, a sucking sorrowful corner in the attic who will never know such peace again. You pity her in these moments, as you watch Maeve flick through your stack of books, settled in your space.

"Reggie, these must be overdue by now." She turns the books over in her hands.

"Yeah, but Vega doesn't care. She says as the library's shutting anyway she has a good mind to steal and distribute the books herself."

"She should!" Maeve is zero to outraged in seconds. "It's shocking what they're doing. The museum is just a propaganda machine, a collection of other country's prized possessions stolen by the Empire. The audacity of them to build another one."

"I know," you agree. "It's wild, isn't it? Most thieves have to squirrel away their stolen goods and pretend they didn't take them. The Empire just puts them on show like, *ta dah,* finders keepers."

"Though speaking of which..." Maeve is holding up another book. "I don't think Vega would appreciate you keeping this." It's Vega's copy of *The Republic of Sheta Island,* the one you used for school.

"Damn, yeah, I forgot. I'll drop it in to her tomorrow. Wouldn't want to be held responsible for the kidnapping of her baby." You laugh but Maeve is frowning at a page. The damaged spine of the book has made the pages fall open at chapter three, *The Weird Sister,* the first chapter you'd ever read.

"What does this mean?"

"What?"

"This section here." She crosses the room and sits next to

you on the bed. You look where she's pointing, at a line about the star that went missing.

> *Those who were there that night claimed that the witch Nubia, as she burned, cried out, "No!" with her dying breath. Her wrath sent a flare of something – a defiant kind of magic perhaps – out into the world. This flare, according to legend, was so powerful that it was said to have rattled the stars so hard that one began to fall.*

The whole section was underlined. You'd noticed it before, but ignored it; Vega always made notes.

"Yeah, I saw that. So?"

"Well, it's just odd. Vega underlines words here and there but never whole sections. In fact, she actively said that was 'poor note-taking' and that there was no point 'highlighting the whole book'."

You remember her saying this. "Oh, yeah. Weird." You skim the paragraph again. "The star must have been Alpha Lyrae, it's the only star that disappears from the navigational charts after that point. Wonder why Vega was bothered?"

Maeve pulls your laptop towards her, pulls up Google, types in *Alpha Lyrae*.

It loads slowly. The results fan down the page and it takes you a moment to process what you're reading. The first result is Wikipedia.

> *Vega is the brightest star in the northern constellation*

of Lyra. It has the Bayer designation α *Lyrae, which is Latinized to Alpha Lyrae and abbreviated…:*

There is a pounding in your head, the ringing of truth in your ears. *Nigh is the time of the witch who burned, Nigh is the time that stars will fall…*

"What the…" Maeve is looking completely confused. "Is she … is Vega named after a star? But it's so weird that she didn't say. We discussed Alpha Lyrae in front of her."

Your mind is whirring. Vega and Alpha Lyrae. Her perennially youthful appearance. Years of vague answers, deflected questions, never mentioning her family…

You spring to your feet. Bast leaps up with an indignant yowl. You check your watch. Just past nine o'clock. If you hurry, you could catch her.

"We're going to the library." Maeve imitates you, picking up the book and hurrying downstairs to grab her things. You go to follow her and then a thought occurs. You reach under your bed and find the box you had put the map in for safekeeping, You pull it out. Then you follow her at high speed, barely closing the bedroom door behind you, tripping over yourself in your haste.

*

"Where did you get this?"

Vega is staring at the crumpled, yellowing parchment like it's priceless.

"It's the one we found – remember I told you? Under the floorboards in Five's office."

Vega sinks slowly into her seat, behind the front desk.

"What? Vega, what is it?"

She looks between the map and you, lost for words.

"Vega?" Maeve takes her silence as opportunity. "Vega, we had a question to ask you."

"Yes?"

"Why didn't you tell us… You never mentioned that you have the same name as the star, Alpha Lyrae. Why?"

Her eyes are wide, her breathing is short and sharp and rapid. You think again of the brown-gold eyes that flickered in the vision the manchineel tree showed you. You know you are on to something.

She doesn't answer Maeve's question. Instead she says, "Names are … very powerful things. Tell me again how you found this map? What do you know of it?"

You and Maeve's eyes touch, like passing a note. Vega catches the look. She stands. "All right. Trust for trust, savvy? I'll make us some tea and bring some biscuits. And then…" She takes a breath. "Then we'll all be honest with each other."

She walks towards the small staff kitchenette. You and Maeve head for the stairs, for your familiar first-floor corner table.

Maeve looks at you, perplexed. "What does 'savvy' mean?"

Vega returns with a pot and plate. Ensconced here, it almost feels like you're doing coursework again.

"All right, Reggie. Please. Tell me what you know."

You look at Maeve. Her eyes are clear and trusting and they

encourage you. *Vega will believe you. Vega won't think you're crazy. Vega is a weird kid too.*

And so you tell her. About your strange sixteenth birthday, about the dreams, about Halloween. You tell her about the manchineel tree and the flashing eyes and the words that pulse with prophecy. Her breath hitches at this last part.

"What?"

"Can I hear it? Can you tell me? What the tree told you?"

You swallow but you have no difficulty remembering at all, it's as though the words are tattooed in your memory.

> *"Nigh is the time of the witch who burned,*
> *Nigh is the time that stars will fall,*
> *Nigh is the time of the mermaid's son*
> *Who'll destroy his home to answer a call.*
> *Nigh is the time of sixteen suns,*
> *Nigh is the time of poison root,*
> *Nigh is the time to find lost things—"*

"*For witch's blood bears fertile fruit*," Vega finishes.

You gape at her. "How ... how did you know that?" She isn't listening. Her eyes have misted over. "We have the same eyes," she says.

"I know." You are exasperated, impatient. "I've said this before. So?"

"Forgive me, Reggie." Her face splits in a wide beam. "All these years I thought that your ... attachment to me was because you needed a mother figure in your life. And I was happy to play that role. But it made me so blind." She gives a

sudden wild little laugh and claps her hands. "Oh, the Great Energy works strangely!"

You and Maeve share a glance and you know you're thinking the same thing. Perhaps it's not you that's crazy.

"Erm, Vega…" Maeve's tone is wary. "Could you please … explain?"

"Yes! Yes. I will. I'm sorry." It's her turn to take a breath. "Where to begin?"

"At the beginning?" you suggest, trying not to sound impatient.

"Indeed." Vega is thoughtful. "But what *is* the beginning of this story?" She looks you in your shared eyes, smiles. "I asked you if you believe in magic once, didn't I?" Vega says slowly. You nod. "You said yes. I was surprised, but it makes sense now. In your school project, you said that your conclusion was that myth and history cannot be separated on this island. Well, you are right. They are one and the same. Fairy tales are histories here, histories are myths." And so she tells you a tale of magic and adventure; of honourable pirates and wise nymphs; of fallen stars and ancient mermaids and selfish, foolish faeries. You take in her honest open face as she tells you again the story of the Leviathan that defended the Republic against the Empire's navy and the tale of the witch Nubia, whose defiance shook the skies and whose brown eyes glimmered with gold. You listen as she recites your prophecy, as told to her by a witch, a Seer, on a faraway island that vanished into mist, as she plays a game of remember.

Twilight claims the day, an ink spill of purple across a page, that scrawls, eradicating the sun, replacing its story with stars.

413

The library lights glow against the gathering dark and you sit in twinkling truth, words you would never have believed had you not felt the blazing heat of the manchineel tree and heard a defiant song sung on a night where the fabric of the world felt thin.

"Why did you never return?" you ask after a few moments of silence. "To Xaymaca?"

"We tried," Vega says sadly. "But we didn't have the map."

"You didn't have the map the first time," Maeve points out.

"No, but we had magic the first time. By the time we were ready to return, magic had died here and a foul darkness had polluted Xaymaca."

"What kind of darkness?"

"The kind that prays on what is already there and makes it so much worse. The years passed, we travelled the world, a ship hidden in a mermaid's mist. Sixteen years ago, we returned to Sheta Island. I could not say why. We took a notion and followed it. Maybe that notion was you." She smiled, and glowed. Of course she was a star, how had you never noticed her glow? "After some time, people began to find us, notice us. The mermaid's mist was clearing; as our magic died so too did hers. Slow but inevitable. But … somehow … the people who found us were the ones who were meant to. The ones who needed a home, a community. Levi says he destroyed many homes but he is at peace with that now he has built this one."

"Maybe they all answered a call too," Maeve said, quietly thoughtful. "Not as loud as Reggie's or your brother's. But a call, nonetheless."

"I wonder why my ancestor stole the map?"

"Stole? Failed to return, more like. I assumed ... we all assumed that the prophecy couldn't possibly refer to him. That another witch would arrive from Persea. We never imagined that centuries later, one of his own would... I mean, he intensely disliked all talk of Xaymaca – out of fear, perhaps. Or a feeling of ... I don't know, rejection?" She looked down at the map in her hands. "Maybe he stole it for you, somehow."

"What? No – I mean, it's just a coincidence really. I can't see an X or—"

"But you've followed it, haven't you? It's led you here."

You ponder all that has been said. "And now ... will you? Return?"

Vega looks at you, her gold eyes silver once more. "I cannot say for sure. But there is a good chance that... The Seer said I would *know the future when she arrived*. You have given me more hope than I have had in a very long time, Reggie."

"But Xaymaca was never your home," Maeve presses. "Not really? You defended it because of the people you loved but—"

"Xaymaca is home to anyone who needs it. Anyone who will love it and give to it. Anyone who believes in magic, and dreams of freedom and adventure. Magic has died in this world. I don't belong here any more."

You don't know where you belong. *Witch's blood bears fertile fruit.* Is that you? Was your life prophesized? Vega had told you that the witches of Xaymaca had a ritual called a *Sankofa*. A young witch's sixteenth Sankofa was a coming of age of sorts. Their goddess, or Great Energy or power or whatever, would call on them. It marked a beginning of their destiny. You think about the Halloween after your birthday, the surge of white-

hot intensity from the tree. Was any choice you made your own? Or was your every action a pre-paved path before you? It does not make you feel important or powerful. It makes you feel like a pawn. You're not some fruit, you're *you*. Regina Hornigold. Dancing to the beat of your own drum. As soon as the thought occurs, you realize that Nubia herself had felt the same, and you become resentful all over again. Her defiance of her fate had been her fate; she burned with it – no wonder the manchineel tree had formed in her wake. No other plant had that kind of fury.

And maybe you don't notice it immediately, because you're thinking of burning. Maybe you think your imagination is so vivid that the acrid smell of smoke is a conjuring. But then you hear Maeve's voice, high and afraid.

"Something's burning!"

The library is filling with smoke. Your brain moves slowly, not comprehending. Somewhere to your left you can see a flicker of orange and gold, sprung up so quickly that you know it wasn't there seconds ago. But this is a wooden building filled with books. A pyre stuffed with kindling.

Vega's voice is clear and harsh and furious. "We have to get out. The bastards have set the place on fire!"

The Leeching

Where the Anansi cluster gathers,
    deep in the forest there is a nest;
    they watch their homeland brown and dry,
discuss in hushed tones what is best.

The Persean witches weaken slowly,
    as the source of their magic is compromised;
    they use their power to feed who they can
    and watch in horror as the river dries.

The spiders could not comprehend
    such baseless greed devoid of shame,
    they shared everything equally,
    they shared their title and shared their name.

The River Mumma, captured and missing,
    dragged through the forest shrieking and bound,
    and since that day the river thinned
    and fish were harder to be found.

Those that caught her used her ill,
    scales from her tail they carved;
    they stole her magic for themselves
    while the rest of their island starved.

Caught

The faerie court prized themselves on politeness above all else. They provided fresh clothes: layered skirts in thin faerie gauze and mesh for Levi and Kano, flowing chiffon pants for Vega, and even presented them with cards for games of patience. The next three days passed in isolation. Levi only saw the others at mealtimes. They were escorted from their rooms (which were as airy and bright as his mother's outhouse, though slightly more furnished) to a large dining hall, open-roofed like all the other buildings. The portions were small, the food too sweet, too light, making Levi's head swim and his stomach sicken. The hierarchy of the hall was strictly enforced, Mmoatia and the closest members of her court dining on a dais set above the rest. Stares of deep intent prickled the back of Levi's neck; the faeries looked at him with cool appraisal. He heard his father's name more than once, faint like the breath of air through chitin.

He thought of the fierce, raging, passionate ocean with longing. A longing shared by Kano. The first night, the nymph had shifted into mist, calcifying at Levi's bedside with a hushed groan. Clinging, limpet-like, to each other, Kano had confessed that they did not think they would be able to make the journey again.

"I am most powerful at the shoreline; home is so far away from here."

"I know." Levi breathed in their smell, home and horizon, the saline solution to all his problems. "The air is too thin, the taste of the water here makes my head ache."

Kano stroked his face. "What was she like?"

Levi did not need to ask who. "Sorely abused and worried for the future of this place. More than human in a way I've never seen… More than just my mother. But … but she is my mother. I feel that she loves me."

Kano squeezed him tighter still. "Of course she does."

Levi told them what she had said of the faeries' plans, his voice hushed beneath earshot of the guard sat outside their door. "She fears that her imprisonment will allow the evil that lies dormant here to rise once more. She said there are worse things than Mmoatia."

"I've managed to listen in on a few conversations. It seems…" Kano trembled. "It seems that they think … they might be able to find a way to harness your magic. Like they have your mother's."

Levi was horrified. He saw himself suddenly in an outhouse, being forced to shift, knives pointed at Kano and his mother. His only consolation was that Vega would be hard to harm, but if she was so outnumbered and so unarmed, what could she really do?

They whispered for some time, their low voices keeping the shadows away, trying to come up with a plan that did not founder on Mmoatia's threat of harming the River Mumma. They shared in murmured grief for de Casse and the crew of *La*

Liberté, and sent prayers of relief for Hook, hoping she remained evasive still. After so many adventures, so many battles, so many stories of the Nubian Brethren captains, what Levi grieved for most was the end of their era. The out-manoeuvring and treachery that they had fallen foul of. Grief turned to rage and they spent a cathartic half an hour vehemently cursing Johnson, swearing a sweet and bloody reckoning. Eventually, the subject changed to nostalgic reminiscence of their time on Sheta Island and, aware that they might not get this time again, they found more hopeful things to do with their mouths.

*

The following night, after a day spent isolated and hungry, sick of solitary card games, Levi gazed at the sidereal canopy above. It was still warm but a chill had settled between his bones; despite how high up he was, the stars seemed very far away. This was the reason, when the shadow first fell across the open roof, that he didn't immediately cry out, drifting somewhere between sleeping and waking.

He stayed very still as a heavy hairy body hovered above him, blocking out the night. It moved as though suspended from the walls, swinging and scuttling at once. A faint clicking sound precipitated each lurch *left right left right*; it scaled the far wall, all the way around to the threshold. It landed lightly on his side of the door and, as it did so, it spoke.

"Greetings, Leviathan. We do not have much time. There are pirates everywhere. I am an Anansi spider. And I am here to help you." Their voice was soft, rumbling, the texture of rest.

Levi rose slowly, regarding them. They were huge. Levi recalled many of the most hardened sea dogs shrieking like babes at spiders aboard *The Sea Dragon*. He dimly registered that this spider seemed more human to him than the faeries he'd been imprisoned by and thought back to Mmoatia's words from the day that they had arrived, *The Anansi spiders are wise and are remaining out of this*. Had she been deceived?

A wary moment. "Can I trust you?"

"Have you much choice?"

Another beat. A weighing. Levi remembered how he had ended up in this predicament in the first place – following a strange creature because he felt like he had no choice. But if he had been without options then, it was nothing compared to the present situation.

"What would you have me do?"

"Open this door when I say – and quietly, so as not to startle the guard outside."

Levi rested his hand on the handle. The door was guarded at all times and so unlocked.

"Now."

The door clicked, a muffled creak, the Anansi struck. A pincer swiped through the gap and back.

"Close the door."

Levi obliged. Mere seconds had passed. Then a soft thud sounded outside the door. Levi stared up into the face. The Anansi was a mass of charcoal and black, blinking at him slowly.

"What now?"

"My poison should render him unconscious for a few hours. Killing him outright would raise the alarm too soon and we

would risk your mother's safety. When he comes round he will not say anything, for fear of being reprimanded for dozing. We should have until they fetch you to break the fast."

"To do what?"

"Free you and your companions. And formulate a plan to free your mother."

Levi's heart leaped. "How?"

"We are here this night to deliver spools of spider silk to the faeries. In the before times, we would give such things as gifts but now, with food so scarce in the forest, we are forced to trade large amounts. But faerie eyes are poor in dim light. We will wrap you in our silk and claim that you are a contaminated spool. We will carry you back to the forest and assemble with the witches and the rest of your crew."

"Do I have to be wrapped up? Can you not carry me out as you came in?"

"We alerted suspicion entering the palace grounds in this direction, feigned disorientation. We will be seen. We do not have much time," the spider repeated.

The prospect of voluntarily being suffocated by a spider like a trapped fly was not appealing but Levi had spent three nights and four days at Favour Falls and had not come up with anything better than the present suggestion. He did not think the faeries would kill his mother – they needed her. But there is pain that makes one beg for death. Levi remembered the cruel gleam in Mmoatia's eyes.

"You said 'we'?"

"My siblings are with your companions now." Levi could not be sure, for the undulation of the Anansi's face was not

entirely readable to him, but he thought he heard something wry and sarcastic as they said, "Likely also being asked many questions." Levi hesitated again, but the spider was right – he did not have much choice.

He lay down and allowed the spider to swaddle him tightly. The first few layers were so light and downy that he was certain the faeries would know it was him, no matter how poor their eyes in the gloom. But with each spooling, each twisting that lifted Levi higher off the floor, the tighter and heavier the silk felt, until he was entirely covered. Each filament was thin enough to breathe through but he felt claustrophobic and very vulnerable. If he had judged wrongly, had willingly crawled into a spider's web, well, it would be just about the stupidest thing he'd ever done. He imagined Vega, bundled up as he was, and fought the sudden urge to laugh.

The Anansi was moving now, lifting him with surprising ease, carrying him back across the walls, out into the gardens behind his quarters. He felt a momentary jolt and then more weight, as the spider's bundles of silk – the ones free of an anxious buccaneer – were piled on top of him. Then they were on the move again. Levi could only hear muffled sounds, but could not see anything at all. He had a vague idea of the direction they moved in, away from the dining hall, towards the front of the building, the entrance they had used upon arrival. He was dimly aware of a colour shift behind his lids, as though it had become a fraction lighter.

Then voices: "Do you have them?"

"Yes." Levi counted nine voices, all low and rumbling. Nine spiders, including his own.

"We proceed, then." A shuffling forward. More light and then more voices, bored, officious.

"Delivery for the court."

A pause. "Put them there." A jostling. Then: "All of them, Anansi."

"These are soiled."

"What?"

"Goods dropped in the forest."

"Every one of you dropped a bundle? Well, they can't all be ruined, let me have a look."

The bottom dropped out of Levi's stomach. The inaction was unbearable, hearing the steps of the faerie moving closer and closer. She was upon him now, so close Levi could smell the cut glass of her skin and the berries from dinner that coated her fingertips.

"By all means take them," his spider rasped coolly. "Our silk is fine and debris is hard to remove, but I'm sure Mmoatia won't mind dirt woven into her tablecloth."

The faerie drew back abruptly. "Very well," she said, "but I'll be deducting the value of the ruined bundles from your overall payment. Return and collect it tomorrow."

All went smoothly after that. At one point he thought he heard one of the crew sneeze, but a spider talked over it, their rumbling voice disguising the sound, and there were no more interruptions. They retreated, out of the palace, on to the path that led back to the forest, and as Levi felt the spiders begin to descend, the sea calling him home, he sent a thought, hot and strong, out into night.

I'll be back, Ata. I'll not leave you again.

The spiders did not stop to unspool them until they had reached a wide glade deep in the forest. There, once free, Levi and the other crew members of *The Dragon Queen* fell upon each other in relief. Levi pressed his face to Kano's, his mouth finding theirs in brief reassurance. They were safe. The assembled spiders watched them impassively. Or perhaps with great emotion, it was hard to tell.

Levi extended a hand to the Anansi he was fairly certain had borne him; he noticed they had a slightly darker ring of coal-coloured hair around their top right eye, which resembled D'Arcy's eyepatch in Levi's mind.

"We are very grateful and much in your debt."

The Anansi extended a thick hairy leg and curved it around Levi's arm. "We are very grateful for your return, Leviathan. Many of us remember you as but a hatchling babe in your mother's arms. We were sorry to hear of Captain Ezi's passing on from this world. It needs him."

Levi jolted at his nickname in their strange mouth but said, "Thank you."

"Can you tell us what has happened in the years since our pa left?" asked Vega.

"It began with the faeries refusing to attend our assemblies. A growing anger, a discontent, a resentment of what we have and what they believe they do not. The wind began blowing strangely, we could smell ill intent in the air. And not long after, the pirates arrived. They seized the River Mumma and we have since all grown weak after the disruption to our land."

"And *we* are relying heavily on the poor Anansi to spy. We are now so outnumbered that we cannot attack openly. A whole

lot of palaver and mess, to be frank." A new voice. The crew of *The Dragon Queen*'s heads whipped round, hands reaching for their weapons and then remembering they had been disarmed when they entered the palace. But the women walking towards them from the eastern side of the glade wore devilish grins despite the circles shrouding their eyes. Levi's eyes fell on one of them. She was tall, dark-skinned and very lovely, thick dark hair hanging in luscious locs. She wore a belt around her middle, buckled in copper. Levi did not have to ask to know that she was a witch. Her grey-gold eyes speared Levi's soul, but it was not to Levi that she looked. Her gaze claimed Vega immediately.

"Who is this?" she asked without greeting. "She bears something of my sister's aspect." Her gaze darted from Vega's face to her coven. "Does she not have my Nubia's eyes?"

There was a rumbling of assent among the witches.

"Who are you?" the witch pressed. "Who is your mother, child?"

Vega drew back in alarm. "I-I have no mother, I… I am…"

"She is a fallen star." Levi had said it out loud so rarely that he had failed to acknowledge how strange it sounded.

The taller witch's eyes widened. "I saw you," she breathed. "*Nigh is the time of the witch who burned, Nigh is the time that stars will fall…*"

Levi recognized the words of the prophecy. So this was the Seer.

"You are … Nubia's family?" asked Kano, looking at the witch. She nodded sombrely, her expression a relief to Levi. At least he would not have to tell anyone else that their loved one had died. "It is I who saw the prophecy about the Leviathan,"

426

the witch said. "I also saw my sister's demise at the hands of humans. And I saw..."

"Me?" Vega blinked rapidly, digesting.

The witch nodded, smiling at her. "You have my sister's eyes. Maybe, when she knocked you down, she gave them to you. She always did see things clearly."

"What is your name?"

The witch smiled. "I am Yvane of Sight, Seer of Persea."

"Please" – Levi spoke suddenly – "if you're a Seer ... was it inevitable? Me destroying my home? Am I just ... destined to hurt the people I love?"

Her gaze was so intense that Levi could not look directly at it. The Seer considered the question and then said, "Nothing is inevitable. But everything is. Does our destiny mould us? Or are we moulded by how we perceive our destiny? Are we all just wanderers, waiting to answer a call? I am sorry, Levi, I do not know how to answer these questions. These are questions that wrack me every day."

She was burdened by what she was. And this was something Levi understood.

"What do you see? Did you see us coming back?"

"That I did not see, no. The land chooses what to show. Magic is inexact but always intentional."

"Was it your sight that showed you where we were being kept?" Kano asked. "Was it you who told the spiders where to find us?"

"No. That was me."

Levi risked snapping his neck entirely. The voice was familiar. He felt his stomach lurch in delight as Captain Hook

crashed through the undergrowth towards them. There were colourful shouts of welcome. Captain Hook passed Levi, Vega and Kano swords and sabres and Levi felt something ease in his chest as the weight of his weapons settled around his hips.

"What happened?"

Hook looked very grim. "Johnson's men. The crew of *The Sterling*. And not the ones who we know sailed here in the scouting parties. Others, Levi."

"Aye, we know." He gestured around the clearing, delaying the inevitable bad news. "Lotte Hook, captain of *The Cleopatra*, the Anansi spiders. And the Persean witches."

Hook stared around in awe. Levi wished he could let her have the moment, enjoy the stories she had heard in her days as a young, daring buccaneer become corporeal in front of her. He did not want to recount all that had happened, but Hook had known de Casse for longer than his own lifespan. She deserved an explanation.

"Captain Hook – Jacques de Casse is dead."

There was a silence, the kind that always follows such a pronouncement. "What happened?' she growled.

Levi collected the pieces of their last few days, laying them out before her, trying not to leave out any details. Where his voice failed, Vega and Kano aided.

When they had finished, Hook's aspect had shifted from grim to downright terrifying. Levi thought she might roar with rage, thought her fury might rip from her chest. But she would not give away their location. She clenched her fists against her knees, bowed her back and shook with the repression of it.

"So, after near two decades of community, he betrays us. Betrays Nubia."

Yvane started. "You knew my sister?" Her voice was soft, a wind through willow trees. Hook turned and, staring at the witch who had addressed her, looked quite as though she had seen a ghost. "You are ... Yvane?"

Yvane nodded, a singular dip.

Hook swallowed. "Aye. She was my friend. You look just how she described. You look a lot like her."

Loss shimmered alive in the clearing and then was shaken off.

"We're so glad you're all safe." Vega's voice sounded stronger than it had in days. "We were so sure ... after de Casse, and with Johnson combing the seas for you..."

Hook tutted shakily, regaining her composure. "Come now, whelp, we are *The Cleopatra*."

"So, how did you do it?"

"We are named for a great queen – do you know the manner of that great queen's death?"

"An asp!"

Hook nodded at Vega approvingly. "Exactly. A deadly snake, silent and quick. Hiding, ready to bite. We had help, of course." She turned, grateful, to the spiders. "You know, I'd never much liked spiders. But even I can be wrong."

"Humans often are," said the Anansi who had carried Levi, and the cluster chuckled as one, a strange rumbling sound.

"Johnson was combing the seas for us – and so he was not searching the land. We beached *The Cleopatra* and *The Dragon*

Queen. Or rather, the spiders did. The strongest creatures I've ever seen. We're camped out in the forest, not far from their nest. We told them that you had followed the faeries, and they knew at once you were in danger."

Levi began to sort through all he knew. "Do you know how Mmoatia's numbers stand?"

"She has her own fighters who number about one hundred," answered one of the Persean witches. "They are quick and airborne but not strong or used to combat. Johnson has four ships – how many is that?"

"It's his whole fleet bar one – he must have left one to protect his family on Sheta Island. So probably between five and six hundred buccaneers."

Levi nodded, scanning the assembled crowd. "Anansi, how many spiders will be able to join us?"

They conferred in clicks and murmurs. "Fifty spiders."

"And, Yvane? What of your coven?"

"One hundred. But we must warn you – we are strong, but our magic is not so effective. Not as long as the River Mumma remains captured."

Levi's and Hook's crews were less than two hundred – combined with the witches and spiders able to fight, they were three-hundred and fifty. And that was being optimistic. They were outnumbered – again – but a plan was forming. Vega and Kano watched it shape his face.

"Orders, Captain?"

Something blazed in his breath and blood, the furore of sea fire but only seen by him. He would not let anyone else die, he would not let anyone else lose a parent or lover or friend.

Not for greed and conquest. Not while he breathed. It occurred to him, that in all of the stories of daring feats upon the high seas he and Vega had been told as whelps, none of them had started with such a motley crew. Grinning despite himself at what his pa would say, Levi began to speak.

*

The western cannons sounded as Levi crouched alone at the edge of the treeline. The bangs were loud, the effect dramatic. *Boom...* Dawn painted the horizon the colour of coral. Levi remembered the tales he and Kano had shared about seas flooded similarly and his heart pounded painfully. Parting had been short, severed by necessity – they'd be missed at the palace soon, they did not have long to maintain the advantage of their escape. Lips and hands and salt and sea and – they were gone. Flying beside Vega, armed and determined, ready to fight alongside their sister and their crew. They could not accompany Levi back so far above sea level where their power was weakest, they would not stay out of harm's way in the forest, like Levi secretly wanted. He trembled to think of the weapons in Kano's hands finding flesh and bone, and comforted himself with the knowledge that they had done it before, were more practised now, and Vega would not allow harm to befall them.

Another *boom*, followed by a swelling swarm. Johnson's men, the ones who weren't patrolling the seas, began to run from their base near the palace, slightly lower in the Favour Falls valley. Levi could hear the jeering; the readiness for blood. They moved swiftly towards the firing at the western shoreline.

Levi shuddered, kept low to the ground, and circumvented their hill, headed for the valley with the outhouse. Leaving the prettily trickling falls behind him, Levi hastened to a sprint until he was flying up the incline, leaving a trail of sea fire in his wake, calling for his mother.

Blood and Water

Kano stood ready at the shoreline. Vega on one side, Captain Hook on the other. Behind them, a delegation of Anansi spiders and Persean witches, those strong enough to fight. An assembly of crew spread the length of the shore. Some remained aboard their ships, ready for Johnson's fleet to enter the fray. Kano's cutlass and sabre shook in their hands, their silver face gleamed with sweat.

"Have you killed many men?" they asked Captain Hook by way of distraction.

"More than I can count."

"And seen many battles?"

"One for each ring in my ear."

Kano counted twenty in one ear, eight-and-ten in another. "So you are not afraid?"

She laughed. "Of course I am afraid. I am mortal. I fear death as any such one of us does. You should not be so afraid, nymph."

Kano shook their head. "We do not know what happens to my kind if they are cut and cut and cut again. Few of us are in one place long enough to try. Battles do not suit nymphs."

Hook smiled at them. "Then you are most unusual."

This felt so different to last time. Last time, Kano had been nervous for themself, for their friends – their family, really – but

knew that it would take a lot to injure Levi or Vega. This time, they had come to like and respect Hook. And D'Arcy. And they had already lost de Casse and his crew. "How do you face it?" A dull roar had started inland, a war drum of feet and voices. "Knowing you may not see another day, knowing that you will take life again and again."

Hook narrowed her eyes towards the sound, tattoos rippling where her muscles flexed. "I have never been one to fight for nothing. It is why those of us who formed the Brethren did so. This life is one of fleeting joy and persistent pain. Pleasure is to be cherished, but ideals – ideals last. When my time comes, I shall not cry nor beg for mercy – I shall face it knowing that if I fall my body may be used as a bulwark against the tide of whatever evil I wished to hold back."

The sound became louder still. "But you cannot hold back the tides, Captain Hook."

Hook smiled. "Can we not?"

Vega crowed from where she stood beside them. "A witch shakes a star from the skies, a boy becomes a sea dragon, a nomadic nymph finds a home and yet you think we cannot hold back the tides?" She was aflame with surety, burning so brightly the air about her turned hazy. Hook inhaled sharply. Vega of the Sea and Skies raised her swords to meet their foe. "They have come to steal our world, Kano. We will not give it up. We are pirates. The treasure is ours."

Kano did not answer. Vega's words reverberated inside them. Hook raised her voice, with her crew, and began to sing.

Swing low, sweet chariot, coming forth to carry me home…

*

The canvas was open. Levi ran and moved swiftly through sensation, throwing up sparks of self in sapphire and emerald and jade. He was a baby buccaneer in a too-big tricorne chasing his sister barefoot on deck, skirts billowing around him; he was a lover, warm and glistening, pressed safe against Kano; he was in his breath, moving like the waves, *in and out and up and out*, he existed between states. He thought of his crew, his family, and there a memory, maybe his first ever, darting like a fish –

"Pa, do you love Levi more?" Vega, small and lisping.

Ezi had stroked her hair. "Now, driftling, how could you ask such a thing?"

"'Cause he's your blood. Blood is thicker than water, Davies said."

He, Levi, had been at his father's feet playing with his ring of keys but at her words the ground vanished from beneath him. His father lifted them both, each in an arm, holding them close. "Davies will get a cuff about the ear for such blasphemy. Thicker than water? Gah! Water is the root of all things! We are water people. Blood may be thicker, but a river is wider, the sea is endlessly vast. No one shall cross us!"

Levi leaned into the memory, he pulled at a thread of self, which shone sea-fire blue-green. His mother was blood *and* water. He pulled on the thread again, followed it like a line on an old yellowing map leading to the X of his mother's outhouse. He was aware of the cold air on his skin but rose beyond it, stepping into where the river flowed into her valley, turning the mill behind the waterfall, a quiet trickling. It pierced his skin like

435

shards of glass but he blew out a breath and shifted, finding that Leviathan form as effortlessly as glancing, turning his attention to another section of canvas. The river was narrow here, he was only just able to move upstream. And there was the outhouse, lit pale pink in the light of the new day; he reared up on his vast wings like an amphithere and dove through the open roof. He was incandescent and alive and where he landed, shaking off fireworks of sea and self, he bathed his mother in light.

She gazed up at him in awe. "Levi?"

He bowed his head. *"Ata."* Her name rumbled out of his mouth and she breathed deep. *"It's time to awaken.* You are more than the River Mumma, than this. You are my mother and I have come to take you home."

She trembled, reached for him. A smile split her face, a radiant inhuman thing.

She climbed upon his back and he took off. Back through the roof, then through the river, towards the waterfall, but this time it was easier. With each second that the River Mumma spent back in her Aphra, the currents picked up, the water flowed more freely, and soon she did not need to hold on to him at all. She swam ahead, she was laughing, the river deepened, whispering to her of things that might have been. Fish flickered by in joyful reunion, the waterfall insisted upon itself and Levi followed his mother through the land of his birth.

*

Vega wondered if her enjoyment of battle said something terribly perverse about her. Kano, a flickering figure of mist,

sea form, harnessed their power and did not fight as one who had only fought once before. But she could see the anguish with each spatter of gore; this was not the song of freedom and defiance that it was for her. She had always known that she was stronger than most, felt right to the end of her nerves in a way few did, but now with a *why* and direction in which to drive each zinging stroke, she was unleashed anew. She rained golden death down upon Johnson's men, each pirouette brought blood and screaming. The faeries flew overhead, shooting arrows and vicious shafts of light, the westerly wind whipped to a stinging frenzy, but the witches threw their own magic back, growing stronger by the minute. Vega wondered if that meant Levi had freed his mother. They were outnumbered but she was the daughter of the pirate prince, so what were numbers to her?

She was not surprised to see the ships rounding the western edge of the beach but her stomach still twisted. Two brigantines, two galleons, enormous cannons. She could not be everywhere at once.

*

They fell through the waterfall together, which swelled to a roar. Levi felt his mother's tension and fear dissolve into the spray; she shrieked with wild glee and he echoed her. He spread his wings and banked before they fell, she caught hold of him in the air and for a few shining seconds Levi flew with his mother's arms around him. Faeries screamed, falling back as the River Mumma and the Leviathan landed, splashing water and sparkle. Where Johnson's men fell upon them from

437

the banks, Levi's spiked tail cleared them away. When faeries took to the air and aimed arrows, he set steaming jets of water from his snout. He would not allow anything to touch his mother. She moved through the water with exponential speed, he struggled to keep up. She was gaining strength, her scales healing, skin regaining its lustre until it was dark and shining, her hair twisting free of matts into individual long dark green locs. She was beautiful but she was more than that; in her eyes pulsed storms above seas, in her veins lay every lambent flicker of shredded silver made by light touching water.

They were in the forest now and he watched as the world changed before him. His mother swam ahead, water rolling out before her like a rug laid for a royal. The great River Aphra filled and so did the earth with moss, the bark with brown, the branches with leaves. Where the mermaid swam, where the sea dragon followed, life teemed once more. He could still hear their pursuers but those that followed found themselves tangled in webs, traps cleverly laid by the Anansi. Those that made it past them crowed with victory at avoiding sticky death, their feet muffled as the dry cracking soil beneath them became sweet and mulchy. They gained on them again; Levi swung his tail and blew steam and boiling water from his snout but was cautious of doing damage to the forest as it healed. He hesitated and the hesitation cost him, one of Johnson's men landing a blow to his neck with a sword that would have fatally pierced thinner skin. Persean witches erupted from the next bend in the river, their magic returning, flowing through their roots, protecting their mermaid and their forest.

The River Mumma grew stronger with each moment,

sending great waves crashing down on those who lunged, but she tired quickly and left the combat to Levi, while she coaxed the currents into hastening as the river widened and widened. At its mouth, she stopped. A storm was gathering swiftly, as if drawn to the sudden flare of magic; the clouds crackled. If there had been hairs on his neck they would have stood up. Around his mother, the sea frothed and foamed, churning as she pulled out and pushed in, reinstating the cycle. A flash lit the sky and Levi looked up, expecting to see lightning, but instead was blinded by a display of colour that made his sea fire seem dull in comparison. A rainbow, vivid, each hue distinct and glowing, lanced across the sky. His mother was pure energy now, drawn up to her full, considerable height in the water, balancing on surface waves with her tail. She was incomparable to the frail, frozen wraith he had met just a few days before.

The rainbow arced again and she shuddered, sending ripples back towards the land – light, water, life. The trees that draped over the river's maw undulated in her gale force. Her eyes snapped open and she looked at him. "Something is terribly wrong. I fear what I have dreaded has taken place."

"What? What is it?"

"Something has arisen, something grim and sneaking is creeping through the land. Something appalling gathers in the east. I have been gone too long. I have left Yaa to hold back the darkness alone and some of it has slipped through." This was the most agitated he had seen her. "Go. Go west and help your friends. While Xaymaca battles on, peace cannot be restored." She pressed her hand to his giant head, once. "Be safe. Shine. Protect."

The water around him twisted and pulled, becoming a fast-moving chute through which he plunged, back into the fray.

*

They were losing. Even Vega could not deny it. She battled two men at once, her teeth bared ferociously, Kano battled four, shifting and darting. They no longer flinched every time metal crunched bone, they danced to a beat Vega could not hear. But the men kept coming, and their crew kept falling. D'Arcy lay bleeding too far away for her to reach, a Persean witch lay still a few paces away. She was aboard *The Dragon Queen* now. Kano and those who remained of the witches and the Anansi held the shore. Despite the wave of nausea at the sight of the spiders kicking on their backs, shrieking as men fell upon them in groups, she and Hook had leaped aboard their respective ships to oversee their defence. Johnson's fleet had surrounded them, and the battle had spread on deck. She whirled her cutlass and sabre, killing her way across to where the cannons were unmanned, those who had been tasked with firing them cut down. *The Sterling* had not fired yet, clearly not wanting to damage their ships in hopes of reaping them as spoils, and their arrogance incensed her. They did not believe them worth the use of their ammunition – well, she would prove them wrong. Storm clouds gathered above her. *The River Mumma.* She shuddered at the memory of the last storm caused by the mermaid's power, but she did not lose focus. They understood it all now, could use it and harness it and their enemies would quake to see it. Witches and spiders;

mermaids and a sea dragons; a nymph and a fallen star – one crew, pirates all.

*

"Pretty games, pretty nymph." Kano slashed and the leering face would leer no more. "Aren't you tired of all your sorcery?" Kano was tired of the taunting and tore out the guts of a man brandishing a broadsword. Killing had become easy, they had fallen into the rhythm, each swift move punctuating three words. *Let. It. End. Let. It. End.* They noticed, dimly, the sprouting of life around them, felt a gratifying surge of strength and hoped that this meant Levi's rescue of his mother had been successful. The bright clear morning had succumbed to dark clouds and a luminescent rainbow raced across the sky. Where the rainbow faded, thunder and lightning took its place.

The heavens opened.

The downpour was immense, rain like no other they had witnessed. Johnson's men slipped and slid but Kano felt *alive*. The rain coated their skin, dripped in their eyes; they had never felt so awake, full of a dizzying, electric fervour.

They let out a wild battle cry, a sound they did not know they could make, and heard it echoed on all sides by their crew.

The fervour only intensified, when, in a shimmer of silver and gold and blue, the Leviathan rounded the bay. A great shout went up among what remained of the crews of *The Dragon Queen* and *The Cleopatra*.

"Captain! It's our captain!"

"Captain Levi!"

"The bloody Leviathan!"

"All hail *The Dragon Queen!*"

They were saved, they were spurred, they could not fail with such a beast in their corner. Levi moved with brute efficiency. He was cut from the storm, he was made of thunder and lightning. His snout set blistering heat across men's backs and faces and they fell screaming. His tail tore through metal and wood, his wings lifted him and he shredded masts to pieces. One ship bubbled and sank in minutes, men swarmed into the water like rats. *The Sterling's* crew were distracted now, unsure whether to fight on when faced with the hulking form of the Leviathan. Three men fell by Kano's hands, then another three and another, and suddenly there was no one left to kill. They staggered in the stained and grisly sand, eyes on the flurry of activity in the sea. There were three ships left and Levi fell on them in a determined purge.

Aboard *The Cleopatra*, Kano noticed a flash of blond; Captain Johnson. He had leaped from *The Sterling* aboard Hook's deck and the two old comrades, captains of the Brethren both, duelled fiercely. Kano's breath hitched in their throat to see Hook so close to death. Johnson's longsword, the blade that had killed de Casse, missed her throat by inches and Kano made to shift but stopped themselves. This was Hook's battle. Win or lose, the reckoning was hers.

Many things happened at once then. Levi, still steadily destroying *The Sterling's* fleet, swung his tail, *THRASH*, and a prow splintered like a chair in a drunken brawl. Wood rained down upon him, immediately charring and dissolving to ash against his hard, hot scales. Again, *THRASH*, and the

442

stern followed suit, *THRASH*, and the whole thing caved inwards. Two more ships standing and Levi showed no signs of slowing.

Kano did not know where to look, their love held their attention, they could not bear to look away from that glorious, vicious form and yet there was Hook, ducking and leaping, moving with the speed and agility of one half her age. But Johnson was stronger. His thrusts were heavier. And Hook staggered once, twice, almost keeling over completely.

No.

Kano could not breathe.

Not Hook too.

She was on the starboard rail now, and Johnson was raining down blows, and she was barely deflecting, taking the full force of them, and Johnson was laughing, laughing in her face, laughing as though it were sport—

And Hook, Hook's eyes were wide with horror, her bottom lip trembling, even at this distance Kano could hear a whimper of fear...

Wait. What was it Levi always said? What was it his father had told him?

What is the want behind the lie?

Johnson had closed in, his left arm slack, so close to Hook now, who sprawled, spent, over the rail, seeming to have no fight left in her. But Kano, far away and below, could see with their inhuman eyesight what Johnson could not see; Hook's hand, flung limp over the rail, gripped tight around her cutlass.

It happened so quickly, Kano almost missed it.

Johnson raised his arm, twisting his wrist in the motion they'd seen him use with de Casse, and Hook swiped.

She drew her arm in and around, a farmhand cutting a golden stalk of wheat. Blood spurted. And Johnson fell.

The cry of triumph and victory escaped Kano's lips and was echoed along the shore.

With their captain felled, those of Johnson's men left fighting scattered. They were made light work of, some escaping into the forest only to be picked off by the rest of the spiders and witches.

And Levi only had one more ship to wreck. At Hook's victory he surged upwards, fuelled by the fire of revenge, and crashed into the port-side stern. His tail moved behind him and took out the prow in seconds. But Levi could not see what was happening aboard *The Dragon Queen*. Vega had been distracted by *The Dragon Queen*'s unfamiliar guns. She was aiming them at the ship Levi had just destroyed, but, just as her action was rendered unnecessary, a blow to the side of the head caught her off guard.

Alfie, Johnson's underling, had clambered his way across from *The Sterling* and now swung the hilt of his sword against her temple. The blow was enough to knock a normal person unconscious – and Vega, sure-footed Vega, stumbled.

Leaving her loaded cannon, pointed towards her brother, open and unguarded.

The cry of warning on their tongue forced Kano towards the shoreline. They shifted before they'd even made the decision to do so, and so watched what happened with perfect clarity, each second suspended before them.

As Alfie fired, Vega found her feet and slashed, *once, twice.*
Alfie crumpled but she did not see him fall, saw only the ball of
lead whizzing towards her brother's soft underbelly.

Levi's eyes somehow found Kano's, suspended in the
spindrift above. Distantly, Kano wondered how they could be
so light when horror had rendered them so solid and heavy.

The cannonball tore through Levi's side and Kano watched
as a flood of scarlet stained the sea.

The Unmaking

The faerie queen fills her wings
　　With the wind with which she sings.
　　She takes her bow and to the skies
Above the forest she fast flies.

The mermaid has broken free,
　　Is swimming for the open sea,
　　The dragon is bright blue with fire,
　　The faerie queen flutters in wrath and

Down below the land inhales,
　　Magic from the mills curtailed
　　And spread once more, turns barren to green,
　　Ruining the plans of the faerie queen.

She sees the mermaid and dragon part
　　And fury spills into her heart.
　　"I am justice, I am strife,
　　I will avenge my lover's life!"

The mermaid hears the thrumming
　　knows the faerie queen is coming,

her wings like frantic distant
drumming.
The readiness is all.
The mermaid breathes in her journey,
the run of every droplet,
the path of every current,
laid out roads full of lessons,
limited until ready to be free,
the river fresh collecting sediment
like wisdom to gift to the sea.
Never since, never after,
has the mermaid heard such chilling laughter,
arrow after arrow whizzing passed her,
the faerie queen shrieking her revenge.
She coats each shaft in shards of light,
calls the wind so they take flight
towards the mermaid below.
But even as she urges them *go*, they somehow seem to
      miss.
The faerie queen,
in ancient pride,
ignored when the mermaid cried at
what must be done.
The faerie queen had forgotten, in all her years,
that she was made of the mermaid's tears.
The River Mumma took no pleasure
in burying another treasure,
one she'd given, but had learned to take,
one she must now *unmake*.

447

The mermaid swells and lightning flashes,
    the rain begins to pour,
    rainbows arc through the sky,
    the faerie flies no more.
    The water at the river's mouth
    climbs and climbs, it claims the sky,
    and that blue, once her friend,
    expels her from where she hovers high.
    She falls into the mermaid's arms,
    sees a vast hand split the scene;
    her wings are limp, her world dark –
    and so ends the faerie queen.

SOME CATTINESS

The fires consumes the library. In what feels like mere seconds the world collapses around you, turns hot and smoky and unsteady. You and Maeve grab your things and begin to run for the stairs. You turn to see Vega moving around at impossible speed, grabbing book after book after book. The smoke is thickening, stealing the flow of oxygen from the room.

"Vega! Vega, please!"

She looks at you, the gold of her eyes flashing. You are struck by the realization of the last few minutes. Vega is a fallen star, a ball of fire made flesh. She is in no danger, the terror in her eyes is not for herself. Because she cannot save all the books. The library, her library, will fall.

She gathers what she can into her arms and follows you down the stairs at a run. On the street outside, the seagulls cry. You, Maeve and Vega spill into the street. It is late, hours past closing, nearly midnight and you were the only ones in there. A small crowd has gathered, illuminated by the swelling inferno. Vega's hands are at her cheeks, in her hair, tears track down her cheeks, her mouth is a firm line, so tight you think her face might implode. Her pride and joy. Her work, her respite, her home of sorts. It had been the same for you too, but for Vega... You grapple with the new knowledge of her vast age.

Maeve pulls her back, taking out her phone to call the fire brigade.

You round on the assembled crowd. "Who was it?"

No one says anything.

"Who was it? Buildings don't just catch fire, WHO WAS IT?"

There is a titter to your left and you feel fury explode out of your chest. Chloe, Grace, Adrien and a few other miscellaneous arseholes are standing in the shadows at the edge of the green watching the fire rage. Their expressions are articulate. Smug, feigned innocence, and those too stupid to look anything other than amused.

You stalk over to them.

"Reggie, don't!" Vega calls, her voice hoarse. "It won't achieve anything."

You don't care. You are beyond reason. "Was it you?"

They laugh. Wrath rises in your blood, you are pulsing, you are razor-sharp and waiting. "WAS IT YOU?"

Your shout catches them off guard but they quickly recover, laughing louder.

Chloe's eyes are narrowed pins of malice. Her mouth twists into a hateful little smile. "Does it matter?" she asks. "They're going to tear it down anyway."

Her words are flint flicking over you, setting light to the flammable things inside you.

There is line of fuel, invisible, tangible to no one else, stretching between you and the poison tree, and it is catching.

It builds and builds, melting the years of neutral expressions and stoicism and the careful construct of don't care, why would I bother, until they are no longer laughing,

are frozen in shock or backing away. You turn from them towards the rest of the street, where onlookers gaze up at the library. And it's the sight of it, the passive observance, the lack of urgency. No one running for water or for the fire brigade, Maeve the only one speaking urgently into her phone. As you watch a cry goes up and you think, *Finally some empathy, finally they care.*

"Chloe, Grace, get away from there!"

"Watch it, kids, she's going down!"

It happens very quickly but you see it all as clearly as if you are watching it frame by frame. The roof pops, the noise is like thunder, the top left corner of the library caves in. The whole building trembles, creaking, beginning to fold inwards. Vega lets out a moan of grief and sinks to her knees. The sound goes through you.

And Adrien, standing behind you, laughs.

Something snaps. The last shred of propriety and pacificity. As your eyes find Maeve's, you see hers widen, she can see it coming before you can. The fiery jet of *NO* comes unbidden but come it does, rushing along the space between the manchineel tree and you, so fierce you don't need contact with the bark to feel the defiance claim your skin, channel through you, upwards and out of you, and with it, satisfyingly salty: "Burn in hell, Adrien!"

He is blasted back by your brightness, the world is white-hot around you and burn he does.

*

451

You don't know what you did. The screams are loud behind you, your street is two corners away, you don't know what you did. Maeve sprints through the night, by your side.

"Are you scared of me?" you pant.

"No."

"Maybe you should be."

"I don't know what you're talking about. You didn't touch him."

"Maeve—"

"What's everyone going to say? That you conjured starlight using a magic tree and then launched Adrien at it like a human Molotov cocktail?"

"That I'm an arsonist and I pushed him."

"You didn't!"

"I wanted to!"

"So did I." She clutches at a stitch. "Really I did. And I've not even been here a year. I don't know how you've never smacked Chloe in the mouth."

"Well, now I might have killed her boyfriend."

"You won't have killed him, he barely touched the tree, he'll just have some serious blisters all over that pretty face of his." She does not sound aggrieved or regretful. You have not seen this wicked streak before and you are freshly thrilled by her.

"Shit, Maeve, that's dark."

"He'll heal." She stops, pulls you close. Your hearts are beating fast against each other, she presses her mouth to yours. Right there, in the middle of your street. Her eyes are wild. "Reggie, let's just fuck off!"

"What?!"

"I mean it!"

"Fuck off where?"

"Where do you think?" She grabs your hands. "*Xaymaca.*"

"Oh my god. I've traumatized you and now you've lost it."

"I haven't, Reggie, I haven't at all, don't you *see?* Neither of us belongs here, neither of us are happy. We're old enough to leave home and let's not pretend like we'll be missed. Have you never dreamed of just … just running away and leaving it all behind?"

It was an almost ludicrous question. "Of course I have! Every day! But we can't just … just pick up and sail away?"

"Why not? *Why not?* Why *not* choose freedom and magic and adventure? *Why not, Reggie?*" She steadies her breathing, captures your eyes with hers. "You're *meant* to go, Reggie. And I … I am *meant* to be with you."

There again, a meteor through you, a bolt of truth that contradicts everything you thought you knew.

"We're sixteen, Maeve! We can't run away together! It's impossible! It … it doesn't make sense."

"Not in this world."

You start walking again, your skin tingles, you feel that the stars are watching. Everything is strange and vivid. You try to think, drag your mind through the thoughts, shuffle them like cards. Your edges are still orange-blue, a burned internal retina from your outburst under the manchineel tree. You know it won't be long until someone comes looking for you. Five may actually be forced to talk to you.

You don't notice the dark shape in the middle of the road until you are nearly upon it. Maeve catches you before you can step on

it and you teeter, almost stumbling over entirely, and it is then, when your eyes are centimetres from hers and they are staring at you unseeingly, that you realize what – who – is sprawled before you. Your shuddering hiss and gasp is enough for Maeve to connect the dots and her arms are around you in an instant.

Bast's body is barely broken. She is stretched familiarly, as if she is apricating in the sun on your bed. But there is a twist in her spine that speaks of hard impact, at speed, and her tail is too limp, too flat. For a moment you kneel there, concrete digging into your knees but you are too numb to feel it. Had she come looking for you? Guilt crests and you follow its wave, lunging forward to cradle her poor broken body, murmuring her name into her fur that still smells, faintly, of your bedroom.

Your tears soak her and your questions form. How was she even out here? Your bedroom window opens on to the garden and all the gardens in your street connect to all the other gardens and those back on to the gardens in the street behind yours. She had never ventured this way before, had no interest in exploring anything beyond the few surrounding gardens, and even then, she only ever really left your bedroom when you feared Five may see her.

Five.

You gather her into your arms. You round the corner into your street, stride for your front door. It bangs open a split second before you touch it and you see Five, standing in the threshold, temper towering.

"Reggie, send Maeve home, we need to talk."

"No."

He swells. "I said, *send her home.*"

"*And I said no!*" You move into the house and Maeve closes the door behind you, chin held high.

Five narrows his eyes at her and storms into the living room. "Fine. Actually, yes, Maeve, stay, seeing as you seem to be a witness to every moment of my daughter's disgrace."

You try to remember the last time Five called you his daughter. "Why have I just received a call from Pastor Johnson, who I already had a *very* embarrassing talk with earlier today about how you've been conducting yourself in public, saying that you pushed Adrien Richard into the manchineel tree? Do you understand the seriousness of this, Regina? He's been rushed to hospital and is being treated for burns! His parents could press charges!"

Doors bang upstairs, your mother's ghost making herself known, a gale of strife blowing through the house, delighted by the discord. Maeve jumps and looks about unnerved.

You hold out the dead cat. "Did you go into my room?"

"Regina, are you listening to me?"

"*Did you go into my room?*"

He throws up his arms in despair. "I am trying to impress upon you the gravity of this situation! Apparently the library is on fire and you were seen there too! As well as I know you would never harm your precious library, you are developing a name as a troublemaker! Your actions affect my reputation and by extension my business – that affects my livelihood, which affects my ability to put a roof ov—"

"DID YOU GO INTO MY ROOM?"

"YES! Jesus Christ, yes, I did! You left your door *and* the window open, do you realize what a security risk that is?"

455

"Did you let her out the front door?"

"Am I talking to a brick wall, Regina? I am accusing you of leaving our house vulnerable to theft, of arson, of assaulting a classmate and of … behaving indecently, and all you can do is ask me about a bloody cat!"

"*Did you let her—*"

"Yes! I did! I've told you already, no pets! I come in and she's sitting there on your bed, bold as brass. And I threw out those bowls and that disgusting food as well. It's a wonder you didn't get mice up there!"

The stupidity of this sentence registers dully but it is not important. "Why?"

"Why *what*?"

"*Why did you let her out the front? Why, when you're always complaining about how fast cars come flying down this road?*"

"I-I—" He is guilty, defiant, you see the reality of who he is then; the neat lines, the order, the absolute zero tolerance for anything else.

"You did it on purpose, didn't you?"

"You are being hysterical and irrational. I could not have predicted that it would get hit—"

"*She!* She! Not *it!* She!" A sob breaks from you and you bare your teeth against it, feel the pulsing rage, the gold flash of your eyes, and think you see him shrink slightly. You know, in that moment, that there is no going back. You will never be to each other what you might have been, you will never even be what you were. You turn to Maeve, ignoring Five, who now swells so large you think he may take off. "Not in this world."

Her eyes grow round. "A place for weird sisters."

"Go do what you need to. I'll meet you at the beach in two hours."

She takes off running, slamming the door behind her, and you fly for the stairs. Five has indeed taken the bowls and the food, but the circular dent in your duvet, flecked with black fur, remains. You place Bast's body on it, her favourite spot. Another sob. You grit your teeth. You begin. This room has played a part and you are grateful. Posters but no pictures, books and jewellery but no gifts. Well, other than your earrings. This room wore its costume well and hid the performer beneath, a sanctuary of closed curtains in which to hide away from prying eyes. You have always felt less lonely on your own, the aloneness in this room always seemed intentional and then you had Bast. You stroke her head and close her eyes. You wrap her in a blanket and place her in a cardboard box. You will not leave her here. You strip the room of its finery until it is naked and bare; you only pack what you need.

"Where the hell do you think you're going?" Five is waiting at the bottom of the stairs, arms crossed, playing paternal for the first time in his life.

"I stole a map," you say by way of reply. "I gave it to a friend who can read it far better than you. It was under the floorboards upstairs in your office. They're rotten, by the way, you should fix them." You clutch Bast's box for moral support. "I'm leaving."

"No, you're not, you're … you're grounded."

It's so absurd. You've never been grounded in your life. You laugh. "You have not been terrible and you have not been good, you have been nothing and it suits you." The moment is here and it is wild; you have dreamed of it and dreamed of

457

it and now you walk through your reverie, you hasten towards your home.

"You … you can't leave! You're sixteen! What about school? What will people say?"

"I have never ever cared what *those* people will say."

"But where will you go?"

You laugh again and it shimmers among the stars. "To a fucking faraway land."

The Language of Dreams

The world is cool and dark,
the cool is a permanent embrace,
the cool is the smile of a familiar face.
"Secrets and lies, I should have known,
my hatchling, how you have grown;
do not weep for we are well,
we salt the sea, we rise each swell
of the waves,
we lounge infinite in lagoon caves –
find us when so cools the clime,
find us when it is your time,
find us when the hour grows late,
we will wait, we will wait…"
The words drift up from below,
as, from above, a conflicting current,
another song sung in a whispering voice.
"Where your old cradle lies,
your first home burbles by.
The first sight held in your bright eyes,
the first ears rent with your new cry,
now only beckons in the summer.

By the forest, by the tree,
you have set your homeland free.
My Leviathan, listen and see,
open your eyes, return to me,
awaken for your mumma…
Strength of the shore, please renew,
return my boy to his crew;
girl of stars, love of dew,
shimmer silver, gold and blue…"
The voices ebb and flow like the tide
around him,
he sinks, rises, bobs,
caught in a thalassic limbo,
suspended—

The mermaid sang to her son, where he lay dying on the beach. On the other side of the great sea dragon, the girl who'd fallen from the stars wept like a child beside her brother. Kano could feel the sand in their boots, the blood stiffening the linen of their shirt, the shock stiffening their joints. They gazed into the half-closed eyes of the boy they loved and wondered if he could see them. If he knew they had won, that he had won the battle for them. The storm had mostly cleared, softened to a light but consistent drizzle. The River Mumma's tears fell sizzling into Levi's sea fire. He was burning out, his fire consuming him. She stroked the great head and snout as though he was a babe in her arms and not many times her size. Hissing and spitting steam, he shifted back, though remained unconscious, blood saturating the sand.

"What can be done?" breathed Kano. "Please, I'll do anything. Go anywhere."

The River Mumma stroked her son's hair, pushed his locs out of his face. "Summon the witches."

"We are here, great goddess." Kano looked round. Yvane stood with an assembly of her coven. As they watched, a few came forward, hands full of leaves and herbs. "I sent for our best healers as soon as I saw the Leviathan fall."

Some moved towards where Hook tended to the wounded, a respectful distance away from Levi and his family. Three healers moved towards the River Mumma, who drew back. Two carried a trunk embossed with swirling runes, a language only they seemed to understand, and pulled ancient-looking texts from it. They examined the wound, murmured in hushed tones. They skimmed, flicked, shook their heads. Then they turned to the River Mumma.

"It would be possible for us to heal him. But we'd need more time."

"Do it, please! We have all the time," Vega begged.

The healers were shaking their heads. "It is not possible. We can staunch the blood flow, slow the internal dying, but ... there is something very wrong in Xaymaca. We feel something strange and malignant stirring. The kind of magic that would interfere with our efforts. While Levi remains here, he will not fully recover."

A rustling at the treeline and suddenly an Anansi was scrambling towards them. This one was pale charcoal, almost silver-grey and smaller than the others, a juvenile, perhaps. They hastily bowed to their elders, the ones who stood and the

461

ones who had fallen – "Yaa bless you all" – before skidding to a halt before the River Mumma. "Great Mother of the River, I bring ill tidings."

"Speak, spiderling."

They drew a shuddering breath. "Your imprisonment has unbalanced all things. The darkness that lies dormant in the east has awakened. Chaos returns."

The River Mumma raised her face to the sky. The sun had begun its descent, drawing the morning around itself and trailing the afternoon, but the blue was wrong. Tinged and bruised. Sure enough, something was building in the east. A black spot marring the horizon. It sent ill ease creeping along Kano's flesh, an alluvion of nausea building in their stomach.

Alarm like a current among them.

"What must be done?" the River Mumma asked the healer witches. But she already knew.

*

Their hasty departure was hazy to Kano and later they would recall vivid moments with sorrow. Hook clasping their shoulder, even embracing Vega and the witches, before dropping anchor. It was later said that she had returned to Sheta Island, hoping to aid Ó Néill. But the Republic was already lost and she did not make port. She was not seen again. Hers is another story. The rain fell, the sky darkened and Levi slipped in and out of consciousness, clinging to his mother with his little awareness. To have rescued and reunited with her, only to leave again, dark green locs and wet cheeks pressed against his. To have rescued

Xaymaca, only to leave it once more in danger. The goodbye was bittersweet.

"We will bring him back to you." Vega clasped the River Mumma's wrist. "I swear it."

She had nodded. "I know you will."

"I only found him because of you," Kano whispered, clasping the mermaid's other hand.

She smiled sadly. "I could say the same."

They squeezed the hand tighter. "What of Mmoatia?" they asked, the thought suddenly occurring. They had not seen or heard of the faerie queen since their imprisonment.

"Dead, by my hand." The quiet menace in the River Mumma's voice sent chills along their flesh. "Many years ago, her lover tried to take from me, to take what was not his. He did not live to regret his actions. Mmoatia has joined him. What is left of her court has scattered; fled or hiding behind their walls. Where they shall stay." Kano did not doubt it. Without Mmoatia's ancient cunning at their helm and Johnson's armed crew at their backs, the faeries were unlikely to venture away from their placid, indolent existence anytime soon.

Somewhere below, oceans deep and far away, Levi heard this. Even wherever he was, he felt regret, blamed himself for all those weeks spent on the Republic. *Forgive me*, he thought. *I was not quick enough.*

Elsewhere the spiders and the witches pressed herbs and spider silk into hands, swore vows of loyalty and shared embraces. Yvane skimmed a thumb along Vega's cheek. "I did not think I would see these eyes again."

"Well, this is not the last. We will return."

Yvane smiled sadly. "You will. But I shall not be here when you do. Xaymaca has dark times ahead."

Vega cast her eye over where the *something wrong* gathered in the east. "I want to stay. To help."

"You will help. But you will not fight. You will have different battles. You are the fallen star and your brother is the mermaid's son. Do not forget the prophecy, for there is more to come. You will know the future when she has arrived."

Vega nodded.

The River Mumma sent up a mist of her own making, dousing the ship, a thin watery fog of disguise and forgetfulness that would keep them somewhat safe from prying mortal eyes. Levi could not see his mother's face to say goodbye to it but her whispers from their parting floated in and among his dreams, for she was the River Mumma and spoke their language. *Dream well, little one. What will come next, I cannot say. I hope for love and defiance, I hope for courage like yours. When the time is right, you will return and we will be reunited once more. This island is so many things – when the danger is passed I will send for you. You will know the moment when it has come. I will have worlds to show you.*

And so Levi, captain of *The Dragon Queen*, son of a pirate prince and a mermaid, sailed away from magic and adventure, back to mortality. Xaymaca vanished into mist. *We will come back*, he promised. *We are our father's heart and pride. We will beat on, we will not yield.* Sleep tugged at his corners and the fabric between worlds folded around him, an event horizon, a thousand different hues, a thousand different blues.

A Faerie Tale

Darkness in the east was
grasping for glory,
it would spin its own tale,
tell its own story.
It would find each void,
each cold wrathful hollow,
and who could say
what horror might follow?

Fly the Rainbow

Maeve is waiting for you when you arrive. She is standing beside Vega. And beside her, the captain, her brother, the spangled Leviathan, dark skin and thick locs and eyes like the sea after a storm. It is not hard, having seen the way he set the night alight during the show, for you to imagine him transforming. You also recognize the beautiful silver being from the drag show, from Vega's tale. *Kano the nymph*. They have moonstone eyes that miss nothing and hold secrets. *They're weird kids too*, you think.

The anchor is dropped, *The Dragon Queen* steady in the waves. There are people aboard, tens of faces familiar from the party. Big wigs and biker boots and bralets. You watch them throw flowers like confetti, place coins behind masts, old seafaring superstitions, but you know already luck is on your side. Those in search of magic and adventure and community. It warms you. You are not the only one who needs more from your home, who cannot not find peace in the place that your island has become. You see it suddenly, as it was, the Republic of Sheta Island. Bold and lively and free. The sails of *The Dragon Queen* buffet in the wind, raring to go, to show you what else is out there.

"How did you move it?" you marvel. "Without machines? Or magic?"

Levi smiles down at you. "Do you know how the Republic formed?"

You're actually something of an expert in that subject now. "Yes. The witch Nubia sent out a flare of defiance. It made all her allies, all those buccaneers strong enough to defeat the Empire, somehow."

"Exactly. And when you sent out that flare of defiance today, witchling, in defence of our Vega, you did the same. Your rage lifted the winds, filled us with something hot and powerful. And so we moved the ship. My mother told me that she would send for me. She did not say how, but she promised that she would, when it was safe." He touches your head, as though bestowing a blessing. "Nubia united my mother and father. And now here you are, a daughter of Nubia, returning their lost son."

The resentment you had felt earlier, at the idea of a prophecy, at having no choice, morphs into something else. *You did this. You are part of something bigger.*

Levi's eyes leave your face, claim the dark unknowable sea, devour it. "I have travelled many lands, seen so many things – but this life here, this community … this has been my greatest adventure." He sighs. "Ah! I am ready to go home!"

He walks away, up the gangway, to take his place aboard.

You turn to Maeve. "How was it?" you ask her. "Did you see your aunt or your dad?"

She grins. "Nope. Left them a note."

"Maeve!"

"You know I suck at confrontation!"

"No! You've got so much better."

"Yeah, well, baby steps."

"What did your note say?"

"Oh, something about school basically being done for the year and a post-exams research trip. I don't think they'll look too closely into it, to be honest."

"Why?"

"Because I said I'm going with you. And that we're together."

You want to hold her, but your arms are full. Three words dance in the air, just out of reach like the sun lingering behind the eastern horizon, waiting for her cue.

"Are you sure about this?" Vega has changed out of her smoky clothes into those leather pants and flowing white shirt and a doublet of black-and-gold damask. It should be bizarre but it isn't; she looks like herself.

"Yes," you both say in unison.

You pass Kano Bast's box. They don't say anything, perhaps Maeve has already filled them in or, perhaps, after a lifetime (or several), they know what questions needs asking. They cast an eye over the beach, saying a silent farewell. And then walk up the gangway, chest bare and glimmering in the lamp light, a linen skirt about their waist.

Levi is at the helm. He wears a skirt of dark blue, hoisted up to reveal a layered petticoat and pinned with a brooch. His ruffled shirt peeks out of a black-and-gold damask jacket, cut from the same cloth as Vega's. He holds the map in front of him, staring at a spot where you know, unseen by all but him, an X glows green.

You think of Nubia, defiant in her last breath. You thank

her for her eyes, you thank her for Maeve, you thank her for the manchineel tree. You thank her for Vega and *The Dragon Queen*, you even thank her for Five, send well wishes for your father's future out into the lightening sky. You hope she knows you are proud of her, you hope she is proud of you.

You both follow Vega up the gangway, help her to raise it. Captain Levi, the Leviathan, gives an order to *raise the anchor*. There are whoops, whistles, cheers. The sails of *The Dragon Queen* fill with hope and a rare wind. Vega stands beside her brother, the gold in her brown eyes burning determinedly *on*. On his other side is Kano. You stand slightly behind them. You reach for Maeve's hand and you reach for the horizon.

Your heart fills and bursts with crepuscular rays, lighting the way ahead of you, welcoming your dawn. The sun, the closest of Vega's kin, makes her entrance, splitting the sky into marigold and crimson, a thin line of blood over the wide, wide sea.

It's going to be a beautiful day.

Epilogue

*L*et me speak in the language of dreams,
Let me sing your cradle song,
Let me show you what love means,
Let me right what has been wrong.
I know you have been alone,
I know you have had to wait,
I know how to call you home,
I know how to dance with fate.
For all returning, for all who've been lost,
For all who seek, for those who are true,
For all who find self and suffer the cost,
Open your map, Xaymaca is for you…